D0059805

JOHN
BRUNNER

# Three Complete Novels

## Children of the Thunder
## The Tides of Time
## The Crucible of Time

WINGS BOOKS
New York • Avenel, New Jersey

This edition contains the complete and unabridged texts of the original editions. They have been completely reset for this volume.

This 1995 edition is published by Wings Books,
distributed by Random House Value Publishing, Inc.,
40 Engelhard Avenue, Avenel, New Jersey 07001,
by arrangement with Ballantine Books, a division of
Random House, Inc.

Random House
New York • Toronto • London • Sydney • Auckland

Printed and bound in the United States of America

**Library of Congress Cataloging-in-Publication Data**

Brunner, John, 1934–
[Selections. 1995]
Three complete novels / John Brunner.
p. cm.
Contents: Children of the thunder — The tides of time — The crucible of time.
ISBN 0-517-12310-X
I. Title.
PR6052.R8A6 1995
823′.914—dc20

94-43906
CIP

8 7 6 5 4 3 2 1

# CONTENTS

# Children of the Thunder

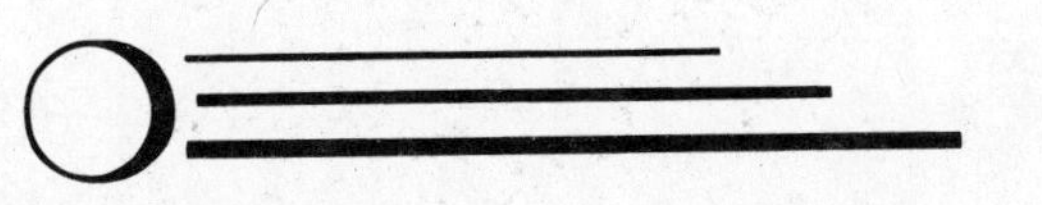

To Wendy Minton

*for being a brick*

# Author's Note

While researching this novel I received a great deal of helpful information from Dr. Louis Hughes of Harley Street, London, to whom I am consequently much obliged.

—JKHB

# Part One

*"Little Johnny may, like the sons of Belial, love evil for its own sake; he may hate being nice to others, but recognize it as a cost he has to incur if he is the more effectively to do them in later, and he may very accurately calculate the optimal concessions he must make to niceness for the sake of nastiness."*

—*From "What's Good For Us" by*
*Alan Ryan* (New Society *30 Jan 87)*

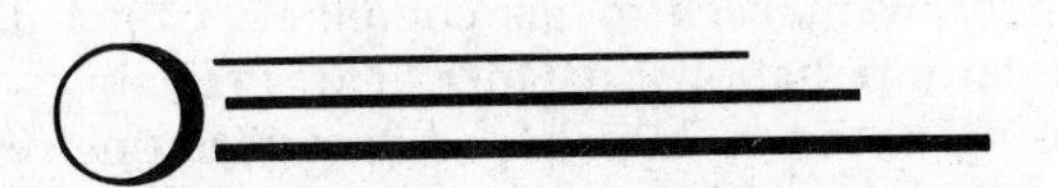

The swimming pool was empty save for windblown litter. Most private pools in Silicon Valley were out of use this year, despite the heat of the California summer. Too many industrial solvents had leaked into the local water table, and the price of purifiers capable of removing them had tripled in the past three months.

Nonetheless—perhaps because they had arrived from Britain too recently not to treasure every sunny day as though tomorrow it might snow—Harry and Alice Shay had received their boring old cank of a visitor beside the pool, in canvas chairs with their names stencilled on the back.

From the refuge of his private wing of the house, David, who was nearly fourteen, spied on them between the slats of a Venetian blind. At this distance he could hear nothing, but he could make plenty of informed guesses about the conversation. Shaytronix Inc. was undergoing what was politely called a "liquidity crisis" and the caller was Herman Goldfarb, the firm's accountant, a portly, bespectacled man in his mid-fifties, and an absolutely archetypal whenzie, forever saying, "I can remember when—"

For at least two reasons he was looking extremely uncomfortable.

His dark suit was doubtless okay in an office with the air-conditioning turned up high, but it was absurd for out-of-doors, even though he had been accorded a tall cold drink and the shade of a striped umbrella. So far he hadn't even doffed his jacket. And what was more . . .

The long-standing West Coast cult of the body beautiful was yielding to the risk from the ever-strengthening radiation passed by Earth's damaged ozone layer. Nonetheless both Shays still adhered to it enthusiastically. Though he was about the same age as Goldfarb, and going gray even to the hair on his chest, Harry kept in excellent shape and didn't mind who knew it. He was wearing exiguous French briefs and a pair of dark glasses. So was Alice—plus a gleaming coat of suncream. Harry liked her to be admired. He was inordinately proud of having married her when he was forty and she was barely twenty.

He tended to skate lightly over the fact that he had abandoned his first wife and two teen-age children in order to do so.

For a while it amused David—who was wearing nothing at all—to watch Goldfarb pretending not to stare at his mother's bosom. But that soon palled, and he went back to his computer. Coupled to a modem that accessed an international datanet, it was running a program of his own devising from which he hoped for interesting results.

This large, cool, low-ceilinged room, built on at right angles to the older main part of the house, was his private kingdom. A curtain across an alcove concealed his bed and the door to the adjacent bathroom. Shelves on all sides were crammed with books and tapes, barely leaving space for his stereo and his TV set, the latter murmuring to itself with the sound turned low. In the center of the floor stood a desk with his computer on it, its half-open drawers full of untidy papers. Most of the rest was taken up with memorials to past and current interests: along one wall a comprehensive home laboratory, including a second-hand electron microscope and a rig for genalysis and enzyme and ribozyme tailoring; elsewhere a bench with a rack of woodworking tools below it; at another place a broken-down domestic robot he was partway through repairing and modifying; in the furthest corner an easel bearing an abandoned portrait, jars nearby holding brushes on which the paint had dried six months ago . . .

The air was full of gentle music. On a whim he had set his auto-composer to generate a fugue on a theme of his own using the traditional instrumentation of a Dixieland jazz band. The effect, he thought, was rather striking.

The computer program still seemed to be quite a distance from the end of its run. When the TV said something barely distinguishable about riots in half a dozen big cities, David glanced incuriously at the screen. A mob, mainly composed of young blacks, was hurling rocks at store windows. Turning up the sound with the remote control, he caught the name of a soft drink, and curled his lip. So they were protesting about the FDA's ban on CrusAde! Foolishness on a grand scale, that! Something about the way the stuff was promoted had made him wary, and it wasn't just the claim that by buying it you would be serving the cause of the godly—half the profits, it was said, would go to some fundamentalist church already worth as much as a minor-league multinational. So he had bought a can not to drink but to analyze, and several weeks before the FDA clampdown had found out about the trace of a designer drug that it contained, not so much an additive as an addictive.

He had no trouble identifying it. It was one of his own inventions, and particularly popular with the dealers he supplied it to because it hooked its users nearly as fast as crack—nearly as fast, indeed, as the legendary (but in David's opinion also mythical) Big L.

How the makers of CrusAde had ever expected to get away with it, heaven knew. Maybe they had just hoped to take advantage of people's increasing distrust—and dislike—of government.

And/or the increasing immunity churches enjoyed from the enforcement of the law.

The computer beeped. He turned back to it.

And tugged in annoyance at his dark hair. Either there was a glitch in his program, which he doubted, or the data he was searching for were totally shellbacked. Or, of course, they simply were not available on-line. The last seemed all too likely, given their confidential nature.

Well, that settled it. Harry Shay was going to have to move his family back to Britain for as long as necessary, whether or not Shaytronix Inc. went belly-up in consequence. In fact, in David's view, it would serve the puky cank right if he lost control of the firm he had founded. He would still be a very wealthy man, for he was good at providing—well—safety nets. What he would say if he ever found out that for the past eighteen months David had been imitating him by siphoning the proceeds of his drug-designing to a bank in the Bahamas, it was impossible to guess. But if the need arose the revelation would provide leverage; being a minor, he'd had to deposit the money in his parents' name, with credit references furnished unwittingly by members of the Shaytronix board, and what he had done was so *barely* legal, relying as it did on gene-tailoring to make yeasts secrete his new drugs rather than synthesizing them, that news of it would instantly draw FBI and maybe SEC attention to the corporation. Indeed, the former had already taken notice of David, although not the company —but there would be no further trouble from that quarter, or at any rate from those particular agents . . . Faced with such a threat, Harry would have no alternative but to sell up and agree to return to England.

It probably wouldn't be necessary, though. David had considerable confidence in his powers of persuasion, especially after his brush with the FBI. Nonetheless, if push came to shove he would have no qualms about exerting that kind of pressure on his father.

He tilted back his chair and heaved a sigh, thinking: *Father—son . . .*

He had suspected since he was ten and known since he was twelve that Harry was not in fact his father. At any rate, given his and his parents' respective blood groups, the odds were entirely against it. Harry was fond of saying that biotechnology was going to recover from its current setbacks, and would indeed become the next boom industry once fifth-generation computers had been digested. Accordingly he had been delighted when David requested a biology kit for his twelfth birthday—one the boy had carefully selected because blood-typing was among the experiments listed in the instruction manual. He had, though, drawn the line at providing an actual blood sample, and David had had to sneak a tissue out of the bathroom waste-bin one morning when Harry had cut himself shaving. A tampon used by his mother had been easy to obtain, though somewhat harder to dispose of discreetly afterward.

And more than once, when he had glimpsed his father naked, he had noticed what appeared suspiciously like a vasectomy scar . . .

He was a very cool, very reasonable child. He would have been quite content if Harry and Alice had levelled with him from the start, or at least from the age at which he could be expected to understand answers to the relevant questions. What made him deeply, icily angry with his parents was the fact that they had lied to him. Worse: they had gone to great lengths to reinforce their lie not only directly but indirectly. For instance, his mother, even now, was given to asking people, "Don't you think David looks like his father?"

*Maybe I do. If I knew who my father was, I could say.*

There came a shy tap at the door. Aware what it portended, he strode noiselessly to the window again. His parents were still arguing with Goldfarb, who had finally removed his jacket, and it looked as though the discussion was growing as heated as he was. They should be at it for another half-hour, at least.

So he waited, his face twisting into a feral grin.

After a pause the door opened and Bethsaida entered circumspectly, come to make his bed and change his towels. She was the Shays' Filipina cook and housekeeper: pretty, plump, married to a steward working on a cruise liner, a respectable Catholic mother of three—and desperately hoping her employers' son wasn't in here.

On realizing he was, and naked, she gasped and made to flee, but he was too quick. Darting past her, he pushed the door shut with his foot as he embraced her from behind, cupping her breasts in his small pale hands and nuzzling the nape of her neck. She made to resist for a moment, and then the magic took over. He unzipped her skirt and let it fall, followed by her panties, and drew her half-clad toward the rumpled bed. She moaned a little while he gratified himself, but she could not stop herself from giving in.

It had been a good two years since anyone had failed to do as David had wanted when he wanted it.

Now what he wanted most in all the world was to find out why.

*You're watching TV Plus. Now for Newsframe.*

*A child has died in Scoutwood, County Durham, and thirteen people are in hospital, after eating vegetables grown in the garden of a house sited on a former rubbish tip. Arthur Smalley, 31, unemployed, who grew and sold them but is said to have been afraid to eat any himself, has been charged with failing to declare the income they brought in and will appear in court tomorrow.*

*General Sir Hampton Thrower, who resigned as deputy C-in-C of NATO in protest against the withdrawal of medium-range nuclear missiles, told a cheering crowd at Salisbury that patriotic Britons should declare their views and . . .*

Freelance science writer Peter Levin returned to his three-roomed top-floor flat in London's Islington behind schedule and in a foul temper.

He had spent the day covering a conference on computer security. It sounded newsworthy. Two months ago a logic bomb had burst in a computer at British Gas, planted, no doubt, by an employee disgruntled about the performance of his or her shares, which resulted in each of its customers in the London area being sent the bill intended for the next person on the list—whereupon all record of the sums due had been erased. Consequently such matters were in the forefront of public attention.

However, Peter was much afraid that the editor of the *Comet*, from whom he had pried the assignment, wasn't going to be happy with the outcome. The paper, founded two years ago, was in effect a news digest, aimed at people with intellectual pretensions but whose attention span was conditioned by the brevity of radio and TV bulletins, and what the guy wanted was a string of sensational snippets about his readers' privacy being infringed, bent programmers blackmailing famous corporations, saboteurs worming their way into GCHQ and the Ministry of Defense . . . But most of what Peter had brought home consisted of a series of dry mathematical analyses, because the proceedings had been dominated by cryptographers. Worse yet, the most interesting session had been closed to the press and everyone else bar members of the sponsoring society.

Then, to add the final straw, he'd found that yet another unrepaired sewer had burst, putting his local underground line out of action, so he'd had to come back by bus, and while he was waiting at the stop it had begun to rain.

Cursing aloud, he dumped his briefcase with its load of conference documents and commercial handouts on a chair, draped his damp jacket over its back to await cleaning, and kicked off his shoes, soaked because he had trodden in one of the storm's first puddles. In socks he padded toward the doorless closet that passed for his kitchen, found a half-full bottle of whiskey, and poured a lot of it on a little ice.

After the second gulp he calmed down. There was an angle he could exploit, although it was far from ideal. One of the speakers—the only one with any sense of humor—had devoted part of his talk to the lack of comprehension still shown by lay computer users when faced with the need to invent secure passwords. Most of his listeners were serious-faced young men and women (an unexpected number of the latter, which was also a point worth mentioning) more concerned with the mathematical implications of their work than its value to companies trying to keep industrial spies from penetrating their research records, but some of his examples had made even them break into derisive laughter. In particular, his account of how that managing director—

But it was time to stop thinking and start writing! The clock on his computer showed half-past seven, and he had been sternly warned that he must file, via modem, before nine if his copy was to make the Scottish and West Country editions. Despite the fact that the *Comet*'s management boasted of possessing the most advanced technology of any newspaper in Britain, its outlying offices still wouldn't accept text direct from London without plenty of time to sub-edit it for the local readership. Maybe that explained why the paper had never achieved its target circulation, and was rumored to be on the verge of bankruptcy.

Hating to think what corruption might be introduced by scientifically illiterate meddling, Peter retrieved his pocket organizer from his jacket, downloaded its contents to the computer and set about converting rough notes into a usable story. Rain battering the roof-slates provided a dismal counterpoint to the tapping of the keys.

* * *

In the upshot he beat his deadline by a comfortable margin. He was even tolerably pleased with the way he had highlighted the joky speech and played down the mathematical side without actually ignoring it. He celebrated by pouring another drink, then paced back and forth to stretch his legs. He was stiff not only from his stint at the keyboard but also from spending so much of the day on plastic chairs apparently designed for *Australopithecus.* But there was bound to be a phone call once the editor had had a chance to read his text, so despite increasing hunger pangs he did not yet dare to go out for a bite to eat.

The wait, though, was a long one, and during it his previous mood of depression and frustration returned. In his late thirties now, he felt he deserved something better than this apartment. The politest term one could apply to such accommodation was "compact": this room that he worked in, with the computer and his reference library; a bedroom so much reduced by shoehorning in a shower and toilet that he had to walk sideways around the bed when he needed to change the sheets; and what he termed his "if-you-can-call-it-living" room which despite its electronic wall with TV, stereo/CD and radio tuner was scarcely calculated to overawe his visitors, especially female ones.

No, that was untrue—the result of a bad day and bad weather. In fact, he rarely lacked for presentable girlfriends, even though he was by no stretch of the imagination handsome. He was of average height, reasonably slim, in reasonably good health, with dark hair and brown eyes. Nothing about him was out of the ordinary, even his voice. Indeed, every time he heard himself on tape, he was struck by how much it resembled any and every British male voice on radio or TV, a common denominator, as it were . . .

Thinking of the TV, remembering it was time for a news bulletin, he switched on, and found the lead story was a subject he himself had written about a score of times, to the point where he was getting bored with it. Yet another group of famine-desperate black refugees had penetrated the *cordon sanitaire* the South Africans maintained along their northern border, and duly been shot down on the grounds that they were "biological warfare vectors" . . . There was no doubt who was going to win this particular war of attrition: the Afrikaners, like other wealthy advanced nations, had the AIDS vaccine while their opponents just had AIDS. Nowadays the incidence of "slim" in Kenya, Uganda, Angola, was estimated at fifty percent. What army could prevail against so subtle and vicious an enemy?

And the next item concerned a food colorant that had been shown to reduce intelligence in children—about ten years too late to save its millions of victims. To this one he paid serious attention, even making notes.

Stories with a medical slant were the chief kind that editors called on him to handle, because of the way he had drifted into his highly specialized field. In his early twenties he had been a student at a London teaching hospital, hoping to enter general practice. When he was at the midpoint of his course, however, and not making much headway, he met by chance a researcher for TV Plus, the maverick among Britain's television services, rarely attracting as much as ten percent of the audience yet constantly breaking major stories the competition was afraid to touch. The producer of the science series *Continuum* was planning a documentary on recent advances in medicine. Peter was able to supply useful information and prevent one gross mistake from reaching the screen—for which he received due acknowledgment in the credits.

Much to the annoyance of his professor, who did not approve of extramural activities by his students.

There followed a stand-up row and a not-too-polite suggestion that he might consider studying elsewhere. When he rang TV Plus to complain about what had happened he met with a surprising response: the producer said he had been impressed by the lucid way Peter could talk about abstruse subjects, and the researcher he had met was quitting, so there was a vacancy. What about coming for an interview?

He got the job, and spent the next eight years with the team that every week for twenty-six weeks out of the fifty-two put *Continuum* together, graduating from researcher to writer to co-presenter. During his stint the series won two prestigious awards. Then the producer emigrated, tempted by a higher salary, and the show was cancelled.

But by then Peter Levin had a reputation, and plenty of contacts in the press as well as in broadcasting. He decided to set up as a freelance, and so far he had managed to stay afloat. Acting as a consultant here, writing a script or two there, occasionally helping to design and edit a coffee-table science book, he had in fact done very nicely to begin with. In particular he had had the chance to travel to places he could never have afforded to visit except at a publisher's or TV company's expense.

*Lately, though* . . .

He sighed. It wasn't simply his problem. So long as computer generated panics kept driving the stock markets crazy, so long as Britain was excluded from the Japanese economic sphere—which meant in effect as long as this damned stupid government remained in power—things could only get worse.

The phone rang. Startled, he realized he had paid no attention whatever to the rest of the news. Hastily cutting the volume with one hand, he snatched up the instrument with the other.

"Jake Lafarge for you," the phone said. That was the editor who had sent him to cover today's conference.

"Well, what did you think of my piece?" he demanded with feigned heartiness.

"It'll do," Lafarge grunted. "It'll have to."

"That's all? I thought it was rather featly, considering. Some of the jokes—"

"Peter, this paper is the *Comet*, not the *Comic!*" Lafarge interrupted. "Wasn't there supposed to be a closed session this afternoon?"

"Of course." Peter blinked. "You saw the program."

"And you weren't at it?"

"How would you expect me to manage that? Sneak in with a forged membership card? Jake, this was a conference on security, for heaven's sake!"

"You didn't pick the brains of the people who had been at it? You didn't grab hold of even one and pour him full of booze to loosen his tongue?"

"I talked to everyone I could!" Peter flared. "In fact I spent so long picking brains I didn't get home until—"

But it was obvious Lafarge was in no mood to listen to excuses. He was carrying on as though Peter hadn't spoken.

"What I wouldn't give for a decent beat on a major scandal! What the hell is the use of having the best equipment in the business if I can't afford to hire the best staff? Day after day, week after week, I see stories we ought to have broken turning up in the *Guardian* or *Observer*—the blunt end of the market for God's sake, when we're supposed to be the sharp one! We're neck-deep in bocky computers and we still can't use them to dig up the kind of dirt I'm sure must be accessible if you know how. At least I've finally managed to—"

He broke off in mid-sentence. Silently Peter wondered how long Lafarge was going to keep his job. By the sound of it the guy was bending his elbow rather too often. After a long pause, he said maliciously, "You were saying?"

"Forget it!" Lafarge snapped. "And I mean that!"

*Yes, baas!* But Peter kept that to himself. Instead he reverted to the most important matter in hand. "Have you authorized my fee?"

"Yes, of course. It'll be in your account tomorrow. And"—effortfully—"I'm sorry I snapped your head off. Not your fault. Just bear in mind, will you, that I'm quite serious about needing a major break? I . . . Well, we do pay competitive rates."

*There speaks the voice of desperation. Maybe those rumors about the paper going under are true!*

With half his mind Peter wondered where he could peddle that particular snippet of information; with the other, he uttered comforting noises and gloomily cradled the phone. The *Comet* wasn't his best market, but it was a useful standby, and without it . . .

But he was ravenous, and the rain had let up. Time to go in search of food.

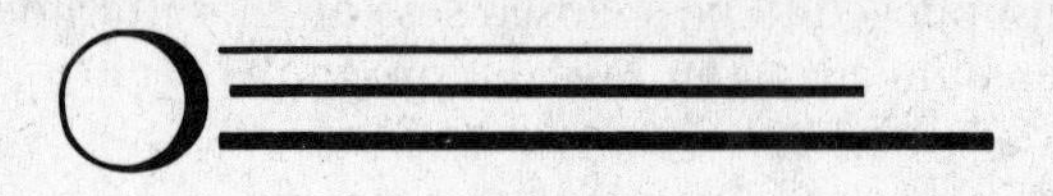

Thirteen-year-old Dymphna Clancy paused outside the Mother Superior's office whither she had been bidden at the unlikely hour of bedtime. She wished there were a mirror nearby, but there were very few within the precincts of the convent school, it being held that to contemplate one's own reflection was to cultivate the sin of vanity. But there was an uncurtained window, at least, in which she could catch a glimpse of herself. So far as she could judge her uniform was acceptably neat and her dark hair acceptably tidy. If she were at fault in either regard, of course, she could expect to be told, and in no uncertain terms.

Not that it made—not that it could make—very much difference. Not nowadays. But having to face up to, then outface, the kind of tongue-lashing the nuns could bring to bear on a pupil was at best uncomfortable, making her palms sweat and her heart pound hammerwise, and all too often it was downright exhausting. Dymphna found it best to conform, at least on the surface.

She wished she were not so afraid that one of the offenses she was now accustomed to committing as it were below the surface might have come to light. But how else to account for this late summons to the Presence?

Steeling herself for a lengthy and unwelcome ordeal, she tapped on the office door. Mother Aloysia called at once, "Come in, child!"

*Child? What on earth makes her say that?*

More puzzled than ever, though a fraction less anxious, Dymphna opened the door.

Mother Aloysia was not alone. Present also were Sister Ursula, the nun who had general oversight of Dymphna's age-group among the pupils, Father Rogan, the school's chaplain and confessor, and a stranger in a dark suit: a ruddy-faced man with a walrus moustache, balancing a black Homburg hat awkwardly on his knee.

There was a vacant chair in the middle of the floor.

"Sit down, child," Dymphna heard. She complied, wondering at the unfamiliar expression on Mother Aloysia's face. Seldom before had she seen it otherwise than as if carved in stone, the eyes narrowed, the cheeks sucked in, the mouth a compressed slit. Nor had she ever heard the least hint of tenderness in her reedy but authoritative voice.

There was a pause. Then the Mother Superior resumed.

"I am going to have to ask you to be strong, Dymphna. We—well, we have bad news. This is Mr. Corkran, a partner in the law firm that administers the estate of your late father. He has kindly come to inform you in person, rather than simply telephoning."

*So I'm not here to be hauled over the coals!*

Dymphna relaxed, trying not to make the response too visible, and taking care to press her knees together in the prescribed fashion.

She scarcely recalled her father, and indeed had never been told much about him directly. But malicious gossip abounded in the school, among the teaching nuns as well as the pupils, and from hints and insults she had pieced together the most crucial truth concerning Brendan Clancy. He had killed himself. Though it had been in a fit of drunken misery, he had indubitably committed a mortal sin.

At first she had been terrified; were not the sins of the fathers visited upon the children, even to the third and fourth generation?

Oddly, though, within a relatively short time, she had begun to feel quite otherwise. Now she had come to picture her background as rather romantic, and to look down on her more respectable schoolmates as unenterprising and conformist. Little by little she had taken to exploring the limits of her potential for misbehavior, commencing with minor acts of defiance, graduating a year or so ago to offenses that in the normal way—committed, that was to say, by any other of the girls—would have resulted in punishment on the grand scale. For instance, had any of them been caught by a monitor in possession of photographs showing men and women embracing in the nude . . .

But Dymphna had lots of them, that she had bribed from the baker's delivery boy with kisses and occasional permission to grope inside her blouse, which she circulated among the older pupils—for a consideration. Within the past few months, moreover, she had started to earn some real money. The supplier of the material was the delivery boy's older brother, a long-distance lorry driver, able to smuggle in the very latest magazines from France and Italy. Having nearly been caught once by the *Gardai*, he had needed a secure place to hide his stocks, and was willing to pay handsomely for one. Dymphna obliged. Who would think of searching a convent school for pornographic magazines? Not to mention condoms, sold at a markup of several hundred per cent!

Was there no limit to what she could get away with?

*I think I must take after my mother!*

Of whom, equally, she knew little, for they met only once a month, on a Saturday afternoon, when a nurse brought Mrs. Imelda Clancy to the school in a taxi: a frail, vague woman looking far older than her age, with a drawn face and untidy gray hair, saying little and seeming to understand less. For years the other girls had been accustomed to poke fun at Dymphna after each visit, though lately they had given up, perhaps because in some remote incomprehensible sense they were envious of the difference between her background—redolent of sensational newspaper stories—and their own futures, as predictable as they were humdrum.

It had been explained, in roundabout terms, that when her father ran away her mother had suffered a nervous breakdown, which was why the nuns had taken her into care. Yet that could only be part of the story. Further clues garnered from general gossip found their way to her ears, and she pieced them together. Allegedly her "father" was not indeed her father (though she lacked perfect understanding of biological parenthood despite her store of contraceptives and the pictures she possessed). In other words, her mother had been unfaithful to him with another man, and Dymphna was the fruit of an adulterous union.

More romantic than ever! She must be a love-child! And thought there was no more beautiful word in the language.

When she prayed—which she did at the times ordained, though without conviction, for she was far from satisfied about the Creator's continuing interest in His handiwork—she begged not for salvation, nor for a vocation to the Order, but for something the nuns would have had conniptions about. She pleaded to be reunited with her real father, who must surely have other children. She wanted to meet her half-sisters and above all her half-brothers. She wanted to meet boys with whom she could . . . But at that point even her fevered imagination faltered. And in any case, this was not the moment to think about such matters.

Carefully composing her small face into a mask that mingled puzzlement and apprehension—since that was obviously what they were expecting of her—she turned to Mr. Corkran and looked a mute question.

He tugged a handkerchief from the breast pocket of his jacket and mopped his forehead before answering.

"I won't beat about the bush, Miss Clancy. It is my sad duty to report that your mother won't be coming to visit you any more."

"You mean . . . ?" Dymphna whispered with a show of anxiety worthy of a professional actress.

Mr. Corkran gave a solemn nod. "I do indeed. She passed away earlier this evening, after a heart attack. All that could be done was done, I promise you. And the doctor who was called said she must have suffered very little pain."

There was silence for a while. They were all gazing at her expectantly. But what sort of reaction were they looking for? Should she break down in tears? Mother Aloysia had instructed her to be brave, so that could scarcely be it—Ah! Of course!

As though repressing sobs, she forced out, "Was there time for her to see a priest?"

They relaxed. She had guessed correctly. In a tone of unprecedented gentleness Sister Ursula—normally the fiercest disciplinarian at the school—replied.

"I'm afraid, my dear, that by the time he arrived your mother was already unconscious. But we are assured that she had made confession very recently, and there can have been but little burden of sin on her poor weak mind."

"Besides," rumbled Father Rogan, "God is merciful to those who have spent long in expiating youthful faults."

He crossed himself; so did the others, and Dymphna made haste to copy them. Then silence fell again.

What was she supposed to do now? Several possibilities sprang to mind, and she settled on the one that struck her as most likely to be approved by Sister Ursula. Mother Aloysia was a comparatively remote figure, which was why the girls referred to visiting her office as "being summoned into the Presence." Leaning forward, she ventured, "May I please not go straight back to the dormitory? I"—she introduced a convincing break into her voice—"I would like to spend a while by myself. In the chapel."

Sister Ursula glanced at the Mother Superior. After a moment the latter gave a nod.

"I think in the circumstances that would be appropriate. Shall we say—ah—half an hour? We can talk about the rest in the morning: arrangements for the funeral, and the other sad necessities. Sister Ursula, please escort Dymphna to the chapel, then return to the dormitory and inform the girls of what has happened, to prevent any silly rumors breaking out. Tell them they must be especially kind to their friend during this period of trial."

"Yes, Mother Superior," said Sister Ursula, rising. "Come along, child."

On the threshold Dymphna turned back. Almost inaudibly she said, "Thank you, Mr. Corkran. For taking the trouble to come and tell me in person. I appreciate it."

When the door swung closed, the lawyer said heartily, "She seems to be taking it amazingly well. I was rather afraid she might . . . And she's most polite, too. Your standards must be very high."

Had that too not been a manifestation of pride, Mother Aloysia might almost have been said to preen at the compliment. However, she said only, "We do our best. And I think we may count Dymphna among our successes, especially in view of her background. For quite some time she was—well—troublesome, but over the past year or two I don't believe I've heard a single complaint about her. None, at least, that can't be ascribed to youthful high spirits."

She reached for a notepad and pen. "Now"—briskening—"what

arrangements must we make for her to attend the funeral? Where and when is it to be held?"

The chapel was almost completely in darkness. Thanking Sister Ursula, Dymphna glanced at her watch, which had been her mother's. It was old-fashioned, pre-digital, and tended to gain, but it did have luminous hands. As soon as Sister Ursula's clumping footsteps had faded out of earshot, she made for the corner where there was least light of all and sat down, shaking her head.

Had they really expected her to weep and moan and scream on being told that that near-stranger, her mother, could no longer be brought here for those strained, boring hour-long encounters? Whatever Imelda Clancy had been like when she bore her only child, she must subsequently have altered out of recognition. It was impossible to imagine such a feeble, nearly mindless person conducting a passionate affair with a man she wasn't married to.

And that affair was the only thing about her mother that Dymphna Clancy had ever admired. Just as his suicide was all she could find to admire about her father.

She consulted her watch again. Five minutes had passed. Sister Ursula might possibly return five minutes before the promised half-hour was up, but until then . . .

She must make the most of the next twenty minutes, for such a chance might not occur again. The evening being mild, she would have liked to strip off completely, but that was far too risky; she could well become too lost in her own delight to notice Sister Ursula's thumping tread in time to dress again. She must content herself with thrusting her ugly, bulky knickers down around her ankles, sliding her left hand up inside her blouse and vest to stroke her nipples, probing with her right middle finger among the tuft of silky curls that since the onset of her menses had sprouted at the base of her belly, locating that special spot she had been taught about by "wicked" Caitlin, the monitor to whom, strictly speaking, she owed a considerable apology, as well as a debt of gratitude for enlightening her about the pleasure hidden in her body. In a phrase learned from her illicit reading, though: what the hell? Caitlin had been bright, popular, much approved; nonetheless she had been expelled last year on the day she turned sixteen, because a pornographic picture had come to light when Sister Ursula searched under her mattress, and it was far easier to believe that pretty, sexy Caitlin had sneaked it in than a mere thirteen-year-old—especially one who could lie so convincingly, and cared not a hoot for anybody's reputation save her own . . .

When Dymphna had come, she picked the lock of the ambry with one of her hairclips—something she had done before—took out the communion chalice and peed in it. Since, as usual, she had already relieved herself in expectation of bedtime, she passed only a few drops, but it was enough to make her quiver with unbearable excitement at her blasphemy. She poured the urine out of a window that stood ajar, and such was the thrill that she was able to make herself come a second time, and then a third.

Sister Ursula was calling. Pale and exhausted, Dymphna emerged into the light. Her clothing was in neat array again.

"Poor child," said Sister Ursula, laying a bony arm around her shoulders. "I heard you moaning, didn't I? Be comforted! Surely your mother has been called to join the company in heaven."

Dymphna made no reply. But it was hard for her not to chuckle as she fell asleep.

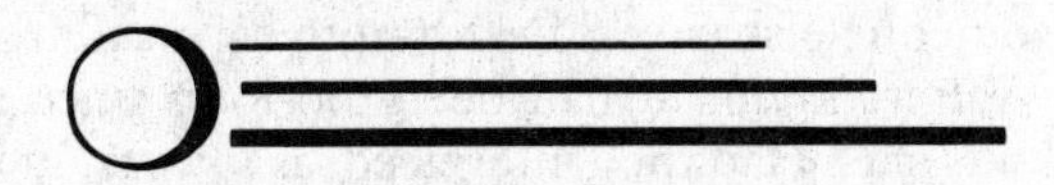

*You're watching TV Plus. It's time for Newsframe.*

*Reports of intensely acid rain over much of northwest Europe during the afternoon led to sharp rises on the Stock Exchange, particularly in respect of wool, cotton and linen futures, and shares in companies producing synthetic fibers also showed a marked gain. However, forestry and agricultural shares fell by several points.*

*General Thrower's views have been condemned by a number of opposition MPs, one of whom accused him of attempting to revive the Blackshirts of the 1930's . . .*

**B**y the time Peter had bought and eaten a doner kebab, washed down with a can of lager, it was after ten, but he felt restless rather than tired. He considered phoning a girl who lived nearby, to ask if he might drop in, but decided his day had taken too much out of him. Besides, though she had shown him her AIDS certificate, he wasn't sure it was valid. According to the grapevine, several of last year's batches of vaccine had proved faulty.

The television was still on, so he decided to play channel roulette. Even as he punched the first button on the remote control, however, he remembered he had checked neither his answering machine nor his email, though he should have done so by calling in from the conference hall, or at the latest when he arrived home.

Annoyed with himself, for there was always a chance that a new assignment might be in the offing, and currently he needed all the work he could get, he played back the phone messages first. Someone wanted him at the launch party for a new book; he made a note of that, because there would be free food and booze and possibly some useful contacts. Someone else had invited him (and who could guess how many colleagues?) to a meeting of physicists at The Hague next month, but made no reference to expenses, let alone a fee—assuming, obviously, that he would find a paper or magazine to pay his way. It might be worth sussing out, but it didn't sound especially hopeful. And that was it.

Maybe email would be more interesting. His modem still being up, he entered his net-code and dumped the contents of his mailbox into local memory. Reviewing what appeared on screen, though, he found nothing but routine odds and ends: a friend promising to answer an inquiry when she'd done some research (blast! If he didn't get that story out quickly someone else would beat him to it); a call from a woman called Lesley Walters saying it had been too long since they interfaced (who in hell was she? Had they interfaced, as it were, in bed, and if so would it be worth renewing the acquaintance?); and—

*Nuts!*

The rest was junk mail. Thank goodness they'd been forced to abandon the idea of billing email users for incoming messages! Victorian values be damned—that was reverting to the past with a vengeance! There was that story in Walter Scott's memoirs about paying for a parcel containing the MS of a romance about Indian lovers by a woman who had never set foot outside the English town where she was born, and then as much again for another copy that she'd sent for fear the first might go astray . . .

Some day he was going to buy one of those new gadgets that wiped junk automatically unless countermanded. But demand for them was so great that the price was staying up in the stratosphere, like the cost of water purifiers in California this year.

Thinking of California: he might perhaps log on some time with Harry Shay, who was also on this net. Living in the old Silicon Valley area, he was no doubt suffering the effects of the poisoned water there. There might even be a short feature in what he had to say, provided the TV and newspaper editors weren't yet sick of being fed the same old disaster stories over and over.

*I know I'm sick of writing them.*

There still wasn't anything worth looking at on TV: a bunch of idiot quiz shows, darts and snooker, a series of reruns some of which were *also* quiz shows, darts and snooker . . . A Scandinavian satellite channel was carrying one of the new interactives, hailed as the latest greatest manifestation of the medium, but it had apparently been commandeered by randy adolescent males greedy for tits and bums. Lord! Among the reasons he--and other tenants—had bought a flat in this building, formerly a nurses' hostel, was that the owners promised a satellite dish on the roof. How could he or anyone have been naïve enough to imagine that extra quantity guaranteed extra quality?

Dispirited, he considered finishing his whisky, but better sense prevailed and he made a cup of tea instead. He had another job tomorrow, no more promising than today's, but better than nothing, so he must not risk a hangover. Yet after the tea he was still not ready to turn in. Some of the tantalizing hints he had picked up at the computer conference, those he would never have dared to include in his story, were itching at the back of his mind. Meeting people who were permanently high on enthusiasm for their speciality always had that effect on him. What he chiefly wanted to do was access a mathematical database and study up on the theory of prime numbers—

*Access a data-base!*

Of course. That was the best way to exploit this vacant slot in his life. It had been nearly a week since he last consulted the various bulletin boards he subscribed to. What was the point of letting money leak out of his bank account like blood from a wound if he didn't utilize the services he was paying for?

Admittedly, it would be a lot more fun to log on to Minitel—he understood French pretty well—and spend a while with AMY or AMANDINE or one of the other erotica services, the like of which had never been permitted in Britain although they thrived across the Channel. Some people admired the common sense of the French authorities; by encouraging masturbation, AIDS might be held in check until there was enough vaccine to send it the way of smallpox. He had even written a story along those lines, but it had been rejected. Offensive to the religious minority . . .

He began to feel a little less contemptuous about the interactive he had just switched off. He wondered how the alleged objectors would feel if they tuned into that.

But—automatically his fingers were tapping out the code that interrogated his bank, and for a moment he felt alarmed until he remembered that what Jake Lafarge was due to pay him would put him handsomely in credit for another week or two—*but* at this moment what he needed was a lead. He needed to find and file a story at top price, and Jake was in the market.

Well, then: back to basics. There was an American board called BIOSOC where he had often spotted profitable clues. Now if he could only remember how to retrieve its access code . . .

*Oh, yes. Something that speaker said today, the one who told amusing stories. Never let anyone second-guess your thinking, even if you are afraid of forgetting what you chose for a password. Pick something you will never forget and no one else will ever guess and hide all your passwords behind it. And don't write it down in clear!*

All old stuff, but no less valid for being tried and true. Here was the proof. Being reminded meant he didn't actually have to invoke his master code, which was the name of a woman he had dreamed of in his teens, fallen in love with never having met her or anybody in the slightest like her, but which was engraved in his memory—a name he never spoke nor wrote. Were he one day to meet a person with that name . . .

He never had. It didn't matter. He had recalled how to access BIOSOC, which specialized in three areas of great concern to him: medical drugs, biology and genetics, and the connection of both with human behavior. He keyed in his fourteen-letter password, which since this was an American data-base was THEBEERSTOOCOLD, and waited for the screen to light.

He was not, of course, expecting to find any messages addressed to him personally. He logged on to BIOSOC only intermittently, and in any case journalists were not overly welcome on such boards. Essentially what they provided was a means of swapping data between specialists in adjacent fields in the hope of sorting out problems that were hanging them up. Now and then, however, adding two and one-and-a-half together out of hints and scraps had led him to an interesting story.

Of course, that had mainly been while he was working for *Continuum*, and could pass on what he spotted to someone else rather than strive to trace all the ramifications by himself. He did miss—he was obliged more and more to admit the fact—he *did* miss the support, the interaction, that he had enjoyed during those eight delirious years, especially after the program evolved into a co-production with German, American and Australian networks, so that one never knew who was able to dredge up what fascinating unsuspected facts at the weekly planning conferences held over a satellite link . . .

For a while he had even imagined that rationality might overcome the worldwide spread of blind religious fanaticism. Well, the chance of that seemed slimmer all the time—but he still felt doomed to carry on the fight.

*Enough!*

Sometimes at this late hour, especially if he had had a disappointing day, he tended to grow maudlin. He forced his attention back to the screen. Having dumped into memory in less than a heartbeat everything the board had to offer, his computer was now scrolling through the data at a leisurely pace. So far none of the keywords he had chosen for this particular configuration had made it beep and freeze. But, even as he was reaching for the wipe command because the sequence had cycled to personal messages, it did precisely that.

He blinked. What in the world—? *Oh!* All of a sudden, there among a gaggle of pseudonyms was a name that the machine had recognized. And so did he.

Vaguely, at any rate. For a moment "Claudia Morris" was as strange as the handle of the woman who wanted to interface with him again, and he was at a loss to know why he had posted it on his email list. Then recollection dawned.

*Yes, of course. That conference in New York when I was still with* Continuum. *I chatted with her in the bar for a bit. No doubt I picked up a lead that made me want to keep track of her. But why?*

He was on the point of punching for access to *Who's Who in American Science*, as the likeliest stimulus to memory, when he slumped back in his chair and snapped his fingers. Lord above! How could he have forgotten that Dr. Claudia Morris was the author of *Our Greatest Nuclear Danger: Crime and the Traditional Family?* She had even signed his copy!

It had caused a scandal: how long ago—three years? No, more like four. It had appeared just before *Continuum* became, as the sour joke went among its contributors, "Discontinue 'em." Had the program still been running, an hour slot would certainly have been devoted to Dr. Morris and her radical, but extensively documented, views. Boiling her argument down to fundamentals, she maintained that the runaway crime rate in the Western world was primarily due to an attempt to keep in being the structure of the nuclear family, a system for the bearing and raising of children that no longer accorded with the needs of society. Raise a generation with ten, twenty, fifty "parents" to all of whom they owed equal loyalty, she proposed, and young people would no longer feel the need to strike out randomly at an impersonal mass of anonymous authoritarian strangers.

*Well, even in this age when a "sensation" is out of date within a day and forgotten after three . . .*

He re-read the message she had posted:

> CLAUMOR / CLAUDIA MORRIS / WILL BE IN LONDON ENGLAND UNTIL FURTHER NOTICE ON SABBATICAL TO RESEARCH A THESIS. CHECK BIOSOC FOR UK ADDRESS AND CODE. POSTED THIS BOARD ONLY!

And the date of her arrival was appended: today.

Well, well, *well!*

The chances were excellent he was the first science journalist in Britain to spot this announcement. One of the few things he remembered about Dr. Morris was that she was disdainful of publicity; she had spent half their time together mocking the ignorance of those who had reviewed her book so generously that for at least one week it made the *New York Times* bestseller list.

So her publisher would be the likeliest lead to her. And he knew several people working in the same field that she was almost bound to contact. He set about collating their numbers right away.

But it took until well after midnight, despite his array of state-of-the-art-two-years-ago equipment, before he felt he could relax and turn in, satisfied that wherever in the city Claudia Morris decided to put up, the moment her name was mentioned over a phone line belonging to her publisher or any friend of hers he had a number for, he or one of the machines he paid for access to would be alerted.

Such facilities, of course, did not come cheap. As soon as possible, he must, he warned himself, find somebody to underwrite his costs.

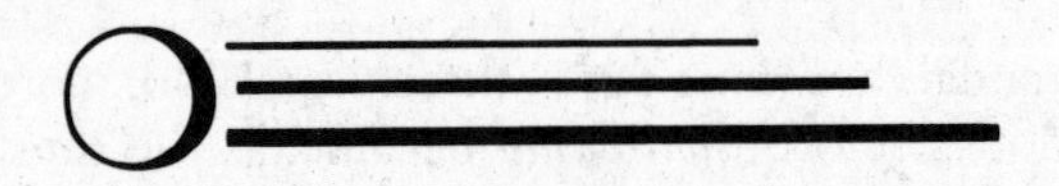

"Wilson, Whitfield House!" barked the head prefect of Hopstanton School. Tall, suave, fair, eighteen, he was due to leave for university in three months. At the moment, however, his duty was to marshal thirteen- and fourteen-year-old new boys in a drab Victorian corridor.

These so-called "squits," waiting to meet their respective housemasters, shifted from foot to foot. The school's main intake was in September, at the beginning of the scholastic year, so those who came to it in May at the start of the summer term typically arrived with some blot on their copybooks from the preparatory boarding schools they had attended since they were eight or nine.

But none of the newcomers stepped forward in response.

"Wilson!" the head prefect barked again.

A slender boy with dark hair and brown eyes, seeming more at ease than his companions, glanced up.

"Do you by any chance mean Cray Wilson?" he offered in a clear voice that had obviously already broken.

Taken aback, the prefect looked at the list in his hand. He said after a moment, "Wilson R.C.!"

"Ah. That must be me. I'm sorry, it should read 'Cray Wilson, R.' R for Roger. That's why I didn't answer at once. I do hope the error will not be repeated."

While the prefect was still hunting for words, Roger walked past him with impeccable aplomb. The prefect called out, "Third on the right—Mr. Brock!"

"Thank you. I took notice of the signs on the doors as I came in."

And was already knocking, and being told to enter.

Later, the head prefect, who came from Tolland's House, told Flitchwood, prefect of Whitfield House, "You're going to have to watch out for that Wilson—I mean, Cray Wilson! He smells like trouble!"

"Funny!"—with a frown. "I'd have said he was settling in a sight faster than any other squit we've had this year. What makes you so concerned about him?"

"I . . . I don't know. Except he's awfully cocky!"

"We'll soon sort that out of him," Flitchwood promised.

In the meantime: "So you're Wilson, are you?"

"No, sir."

"What?"

"My surname is actually Cray Wilson, sir. I just had to explain the mistake to the prefect on duty outside."

"Hmm! All right, then: I'll get it sorted out . . . Well, take a pew!"

The boy complied, studying his new housemaster. Fat and graying, he sat behind a table rather than a desk. It was obvious that these rooms must have been assigned and reassigned to scores of new purposes since they were built a century or more ago. There were bookshelves and filing cabinets, even a computer terminal, but none of them fitted the space allotted. In the boy's view, it was high time the whole edifice was demolished to make room for something functional.

If anything in a school of this type could be honored with that epithet.

Mr. Brock was not alone. Sitting at his left was a thin fortyish woman in a green dress with blue eyes and brown hair and an inexpert smear of lipstick. The boy smiled at her, and his immediate guess was confirmed. She smiled back, whereby her face was transformed and became almost pretty. Since—well, it had to be—her husband was still riffling through a file of papers, she risked leaning forward and speaking.

"Welcome to Whitfield House, Roger! I'm Mrs. Brock. Do remember, won't you, that if you ever have any problems—"

"Not yet, please, Margaret!" Mr. Brock cut in. She subsided, blushing, while he leaned back in his chair and surveyed Roger beneath untidy gray eyebrows.

"The first thing I have to say to you, young man, is this. According to a letter I have in front of me, from the headmaster of your prep school, while your examination marks were excellent in a wide range of subjects, the moral effect you had on your fellow pupils was not what might have been wished! What do you have to say to that?"

*Ah. I was wondering what line the old bastard was going to take. He could scarcely say, could he, that most of his staff were customers for the sexual services we kids provided? Especially when his bee-lov-ed daughter joined in so enthusiastically! He wouldn't wish it to be noised abroad that she adored a gang-bang!*

It had been an enjoyable and highly profitable undertaking, especially after the teachers started bringing in clients from the town. Roger was only sorry that it had been cut short. However, one of his friends' parents had discovered, during the holidays and out of reach of Roger's powers of persuasion, that his son had contracted rectal gonorrhea. So the cat had finally been let out of the bag.

Of course, the scandal had been efficiently hushed up, and money had changed hands, and his old school was back to normal—though several of the staff had vanished overnight and had to be replaced. Moreover he had wrought a suitable revenge on the bastard who had shopped him. Having found out that the family was due to go abroad, since they lived not far away he had cycled over with a reel of extension cable on the back of his bike, located an electric heater, plugged it into the reel without unwinding it, and switched on. The resulting blaze had caused a gratifying amount of damage . . .

It was time, though, to react. Composing his features into the strictest possible mask of disbelief, Roger said, "I do assure you, sir, that no matter what allegations have been made against me, I can either explain or rebut them."

He borrowed both words and tone from his father Julian. For two or three years he had been aware that there was little physical resemblance between them, so he was at pains to ensure that he adopted the same mannerisms. Now and then he salted his behavior pattern with a phrase or look copied from his mother, Susan, so she would not feel neglected. Given the way Julian ignored her, she deserved no less—

But Mr. Brock was staring at him.

"You think," he said slowly—"you dare to imagine that you can contradict the judgment of your prep headmaster?"

*Stupid arse! Borderline sadist! You ought to talk to Sarah about the way her father treats her and her brother! No wonder she was desperate for a bit of outside affection! And I don't suppose he gave me any credit for knowing that Coca-Cola is an efficient spermicide, and making sure she always douched with it afterward.*

*Or, come to that, for insisting that all our customers produce an AIDS certificate!*

This, however, was no time for reasoned argument. What was called for was an exercise of charm . . . Roger donned his most winning smile, and felt the familiar, welcome, sense of cold command pervade his mind.

"Sir, it is an offense to libel an adult, is it not? How much more so, then, to libel a child my age, who cannot afford legal assistance to defend himself? If it had been in my power, I would certainly have sued my old headmaster!"

He waited. Little by little, he saw uncertainty invade Mr. Brock's expression. Eventually he shut his file and gave a shrug.

"Fair comment, I suppose," he grunted. "I hadn't thought of it that way, but—well, you have a point. I hope you'll enjoy your time in my house. Off to bed with you."

In the doorway Roger glanced back, smiling. Just as he had expected, Mrs. Brock clasped her hands on her breast and whispered, "Sweet dreams!"

Very good. Yes, *very* good indeed!

Climbing worn stone stairs on his way to a predictably uncomfortable bed, Roger had to struggle not to laugh. There were people he could twist around his little finger . . . or maybe another organ.

"Wilson!" snapped the dormitory monitor, who was sixteen and very conscious of his responsibilities. "You're late!"

"That's *Cray* Wilson, if you don't mind," Roger said with a friendly pat on the older boy's hand. "And it was Mr. and Mrs. Brock who delayed me, so you'll have to take the matter up with them. Good night. Sweet dreams!"

And made for his assigned cubicle, wondering how long it would be before he wound up in bed with Mrs. Brock.

Or the dormitory monitor. So long as he was adequately paid, he had no special preference.

Though he definitely didn't fancy Mr. Brock.

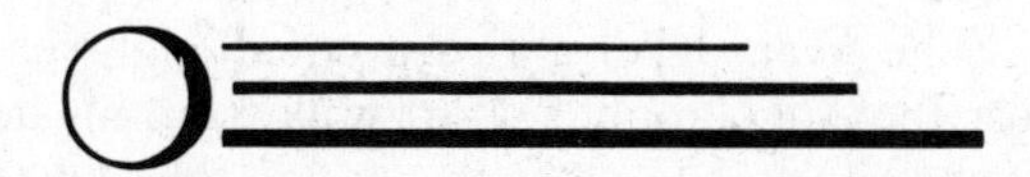

*You're watching TV Plus. Time now for Newsframe.*

*As the summer draws to a close, more and more holiday-makers are threatening to sue manufacturers of sun-screen lotions. Perhaps we in Britain should count ourselves lucky, says a spokesman for the British Medical Association. Given that so few of us can afford to travel to the Riviera or North Africa any longer, we're escaping the worst effects of powerful ultraviolet radiation leaking in through the diminished ozone layer. More in a moment.*

*Response to General Thrower's appeal continues to gather momentum. In London this afternoon, a thousand people . . .*

**P**eter struck paydirt sooner than he had dared to hope. Having spent the following morning with an affable flack for an expensive alternative-therapy clinic, and agreed to ghost half a dozen articles emphasizing the side effects of orthodox drugs—not his usual line, and not reflecting his personal convictions, but the pay was generous and there was no shortage of material to draw on—he called his home phone from the pub where he had eaten lunch to check for messages. What he heard was better than just a message:

Click: "No, she's still asleep. Jet lag, you know."

So the machines had picked up "Claudia Morris!"

The answer had been in a woman's voice. Peter didn't recognize it, but the accent was upper-crust English.

"Tell her I rang, then. I'm on the staff of her London publishers. And say I'll try tomorrow at the same time." That was a man, a youthful baritone.

"Yes, okay. Thank you."

The circuit broke. Peter waited. A hum ensued. Then the number that had been called appeared on the display screen of the pay-phone. Hastily he noted it on his pocket organizer. Someone else was waiting, and growing impatient, but Peter ignored him. Setting the organizer down, he tapped out an access code for British Telecom's street-by-street customer listing. No one apart from BT employees was authorized to possess such codes; in fact, of course, thousands of people did, not only journalists but market researchers, telephone salespeople, credit agencies, private security firms . . . He followed it with the called number, and in moments a recorded voice relayed the name and address of the subscriber.

Perfect. It was in The Wansdyke, a riot-proofed high-security apartment complex near the Angel: only a short walk from his home.

He was whistling as he left the phone booth, and to the scowl with which the other would-be caller favored him he returned a sunny and infuriating smile.

There were days like yesterday when he felt the universe was conspiring against him, and days like today when everything seemed to fall patly into place. It wasn't even raining when he arrived opposite The Wansdyke just after seven, by which time, he estimated, Dr. Morris would have slept off her jet lag. He felt so cheerful, he literally did not notice the gang of sore-exhibiting beggars whining around the bus stop where he got off, but passed between them like a boat dividing scum on stagnant water.

Well, they were so commonplace in London now, one had to ignore them unless they turned violent . . .

And even as he started to cross the road toward his destination, debating what to say if challenged by one of its guards, the building's gas-proof revolving door uttered the very person he had come in search of. The instant he set eyes on her memory came flooding back. Yes, of course! She'd been *that* one! Rather stocky, only an inch shorter than himself, with a square face framed by dark-blond hair cut in a pageboy style that she still affected, she had reminded him of Signe Hasso in *L'Éternel Retour*.

As a matter of fact, did now, in spite of the sweater and jeans she was wearing.

Half a dozen alternative strategies chased across his mind. He settled for trying to look as though he was on his way somewhere else entirely, glancing around, glancing again, checking in mid-stride and calling out.

"Dr. Morris? Dr. Claudia Morris?"

For a second he feared she was going to deny her name and march off. But faint recognition flickered, and he seized his advantage, closing the gap between them.

"I can't believe it! It is! I wish I'd known you were in London—I'd have been in touch before . . . Oh, you probably don't remember me. My name is Peter Levin. We met at a conference at Columbia a few years ago. I used to be with *Continuum*—you know, the TV science program they called *Quasar* in America."

By this time he had halted squarely in front of her, blocking her progress. After surveying him in a cool detached manner, she said at length, "Yes, I do remember. The program had been cancelled just before we met. Correct?"

"I'm afraid so. If not, I'd have insisted that we give you a slot. I—well, I suspect I sounded off rather, about it being the worst possible time to kill the show because there had never been more need for rationality."

*When I could slip a word in edgeways!*

"You certainly did. Even when I told you I wasn't the slightest bit interested in being put under the TV microscope. Now please excuse me."

"Hang about, hang about! Are you doing anything special at the moment? I was just on my way home to face an empty evening, so if you're free—Would you perhaps be going out in search of dinner? Could I invite you? On a professional basis, of course. I must warn you straight away that what I'd like to do is pick your brains and turn the result into an article. You see, I'm a freelance now."

*Gamble, gamble. But I recall her as a very direct person, almost embarrassingly so.*

She spent so long making up her mind, he let his worse judgment overcome his better by adding, "I know this area pretty well. If your jet lag means you're more in the mood for brunch than dinner I know just the place."

"I suspect," Claudia said with a twist of her lip, "it's as well you write non-fiction rather than fiction."

"What?" The apparent irrelevance took Peter aback.

"You're a poor liar and a worse actor. You 'wished you'd known I was in London,' did you? How long have you been standing around in case I put in an appearance?"

"I don't understand what you—"

"Oh, fold it and stow it!"—with unfeigned annoyance. "If I'd arrived more than a day or two ago, would I still be jet-lagged enough to go out for brunch at seven in the evening? How the hell did you find out I was here? I was hoping for a couple of weeks' peace and quiet before word got around!"

For a moment Peter considered sticking to his original pretense. On balance he decided against. When dealing with a woman like this it made better sense to play the fallible, vulnerable male. Donning a sheepish grin, he spread his hands. "BIOSOC," he admitted.

"You're sharp," she conceded grudgingly. "There can't be more than a dozen people in Britain who log on to that board. Talk about a dead zone—! Everybody over here who was doing original research in my field seems to have been driven abroad or forced to quit. I don't know whether it's because your government genuinely can't afford to fund them, or because they're afraid of what we might turn up."

Without apparent intent, they had turned together and were walking side by side toward the main road. Peter seized his chance.

"More the latter than the former. It isn't that we're too broke—can't be. Your kind of research calls more for data-analysis than expensive new equipment, and in Britain we have some of the best resources anywhere. Mass Observation's records alone are a treasure without equal. But as soon as one starts to search for the roots of our contemporary mess in decisions taken by previous governments, one's bound to turn up unpleasant truths that call for remedial action, and that action might very well entail changes that would deprive the ruling class of power on grounds of incompetence—*Watch it!*"

He checked her with a touch on her arm as she reflexively glanced the wrong way before crossing the street. A minicab driver in a hurry blasted his horn as he raced by at well above the legal limit. From a side road a police car burned rubber in pursuit, flashing and howling.

"More like New York every time I come back," Claudia muttered when they had crossed the road.

"What does bring you back?" Peter ventured. "To a country that in your view is falling so far behind?"

She halted and swung to face him. For a moment her expression was harsh. Then she relaxed.

"All right, I'll give you your due. You're a cunning cank, aren't you? I could even believe that you gave yourself away deliberately with that reference to jet lag, just to underline how much quicker off the mark you'd been than any of your colleagues . . . Okay, where do we go?"

He hesitated a moment, for in truth he didn't know the area as well as he had claimed. Within moments, though, a relay of memory closed.

"You like Greek food?"

"Right now I don't mind what the hell I eat so long as it's fit for human consumption. All I've had in the past twenty-four hours is airline puke and a bowl of porage. My hostess had to go out and when I looked at what she'd left in the refrigerator . . ." An elaborate shudder.

*Better and better!*

But even as he turned in the direction of the restaurant he had in mind, Peter was aware that he would be well advised not to take this particular lady's arm next time they had to cross a street.

When they reached their destination, however, it was in darkness. A sign on the door said it had been closed by the Medical Officer of Health. No reason for the order was given, but it was easy enough to guess. With the cost of pollution-certified food rising to astronomical levels, more and more restaurants were resorting, out of desperation, to supplies that had evaded official inspection, and along with it value-added tax, now at a swingeing 20 percent. The owner here must have been one of the unlucky ones.

A wordless grunt indicated Claudia's opinion of Peter's "knowledge of the area." Afraid she might change her mind and decide to risk what her hostess had in the fridge after all, he glanced around and caught sight of a bright red sign above an Indian restaurant only fifty yards away. It was indubitably open, and quite possibly the only one in the area that was, judging by the queue of dismerables outside its takeaway window, each clutching his or her one-pound daily food voucher. In passing he wondered how much a pound could buy now—a handful of scraps, at best . . .

"We could try there," he suggested uncertainly. The fact that its sign was switched on indicated that it was bound to be expensive, but he could probably risk deducting the bill from his income tax.

"Okay," Claudia sighed, and strode ahead. He followed, less accustomed than she was to outfacing the jealous glares of the urban poor.

In the upshot, Peter decided Indian cuisine would have been a sensible choice anyway. The more mass-production methods were applied to food, the less it tasted of anything. Farmed salmon, for example, or intensively raised pork, were now beyond redemption, while as for bread—! But here at least the spices made for variety, though they might of course also be employed for their traditional purpose: disguising substandard ingredients. He suggested lamb biriyani and curried vegetables, and an adequately rough red wine, and waited until nothing remained but a spoonful of rice and a smear of sauce before he again broached the matter of Claudia's reason for spending her sabbatical in Britain.

Looking her full in the face—and nearly being thrown off stride on realizing for the first time that her unusually colored irises, blue with green radial striations, were not in fact her own but implants—he confined himself to a single word: "Well?"

She knew precisely what he meant. Raising her glass, tilting it back and forth beneath her blunt-tipped nose, she said at length, "All right. But I'm going to impose conditions. I imagine you're wearing a recorder?"

"As a matter of fact I'm not. I own one, of course, and I thought about bringing it, but I came to the conclusion that if you spotted it I wouldn't stand a hope in hell of convincing you we met by chance and getting you to talk to me. All I have is my regular organizer." He laid it on the table. And added, "Plus one good old-fashioned spiral-bound notebook, and some ball-pens. *Voilà!*"

"I see. You are exactly as much of a smartass cank as I suspected." A faint but welcome smile quirked the corners of her mouth. "Okay, let's get rid of the formal bit, shall we? Use a page of that notebook to write down an assurance that you won't publish anything I tell you in whole or in part without a notarized release and a fee to be mutually agreed, and add that I'm at liberty to withhold permission regardless of how much I'm offered."

This was standard practice, especially when dealing with Americans. Peter was already writing. When he tore out and proffered the page, Claudia first nodded, then frowned.

"What's this about material attributable to other—?"

And had already cancelled the question before he had a chance to explain.

"I see. I see. You think you may be better informed about at least some of what concerns me than I am myself. I can't argue, though I wish I could. You see . . ." She took a sip more wine before continuing.

"You see, my only possible reason for telling you about the thesis I'm researching is because I hope to be repaid in kind —with information. This puky country of yours is obsessed with secrecy! If they could, they'd make the time the sun comes up an official secret! I've been in Cuba—I've been in China, for pity's sake!—and they opened more doors for me more easily than ever in Britain!"

"I know," Peter muttered. "Like any journalist, I've bruised my knuckles on a good few of those doors . . . On the other hand, they don't seem to care how much they infringe on their citizens' privacy, do they?"

"Not so long as they're doing it. Anybody else . . ."

"Exactly"—in a bitter tone. "We aren't even allowed to correct errors in our own computer files. There's at least one file on me that's riddled with falsehoods—data relating to someone else who gave my name when he was arrested on a drunk-driving charge—but when I tried to have something done about it I was threatened with prosecution because I wasn't supposed to know it even existed!"

There was a pause. Then, gazing into her glass as though it were a crystal ball, Claudia said, "You remember the theme of my book?"

"Of course. I still have the copy you signed for me."

"I think I was wrong."

Peter blinked at her. He was about to ask why when she rushed ahead.

"Something that doesn't fit has turned up, and I'm scared. I don't want to sound alarmist. In any case I don't dare. For one thing, all the evidence isn't in yet. For another, if I overstep the mark I've been warned that the funds for my sabbatical will be withdrawn. Even so . . ."

She raised her strange artificial irises to look him squarely in the face.

"Do you remember that weird old phrase about 'boiling everything down to brass tacks'? When I was a kid, it used to worry the hell out of me. But I suspect we're about to tread barefoot on a whole *pile* of tacks! And if that's so—"

During the past few minutes, while neither of them was paying attention, a trio of musicians had taken station on a dais in the far corner of the restaurant: a sitar-player, a veena-player and a drummer. They had amplifiers. At that moment they struck up the theme from the latest hit film in Bombay, and their combined volume wiped out the rest of what Claudia had begun to say.

Reaching for his credit cards, Peter proposed at the top of his voice that they adjourn to a nearby pub. For a few seconds he thought she was inclining to agree.

Then, however, she checked her watch and shook her head.

"Sorry," she muttered. "I have to go. My hosts are due back around now. Thanks for the meal, anyway."

"Wait! You can't just—"

"Leave you in the lurch?" A repeat of her quirky smile. "Sorry again. I shouldn't have said as much as I did. I only just arrived in Europe, remember. Give me time to convince myself that I can trust my judgment."

*Is this going to be yet another case where because I do the "gentlemanly thing" I lose out on a major story?*

In a flash of insight, Peter realized this was the main reason why he was still living on his own in a cramped top-floor apartment. Someone with the killer instinct . . .

But he didn't possess it. He found it repugnant. He was operating on reflexes, pocketing his organizer, proffering his business card, saying, "When you feel sufficiently relaxed to talk this through with somebody, or need some information I might find for you . . ."

"Yes. Yes. I'll bear that in mind. Thank you again. I can find my own way home. I've stayed at The Wansdyke before. Good night."

She turned away, momentarily forgetting the release that he had signed for her, swinging back to reclaim it a heartbeat before he could remind her, thus depriving him of one more chance to reinforce the favorable impression he was striving to make.

The waiter seized his credit card and wiped it through the reader on the till as though afraid Peter intended to leave before paying. Fuming, he made a mental resolution to pursue this one, even if it meant pestering Claudia until she lost her temper. He felt rather as though he had been brought to the brink of orgasm, and then let down.

In an alleyway beside the restaurant, where dustbins stood, a frightened kitchen-hand had been cornered by half a dozen dismerables on his way to dump what they regarded as precious food. Just as Peter passed, he flung his burden at them and disappeared. They fell on the mess as though it were manna, cursing and beating one another.

Peter ignored them and trudged on homeward, wind-blown litter assailing his legs.

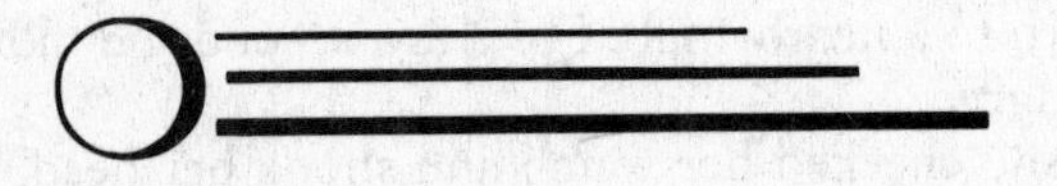

London approaching the 21st century . . .

Noise, dark wet night, many of the streetlights broken, dismerables trudging from dustbin to overflowing dustbin in search of anything to eat or wear or sell; those luckier, with homes to go to, glancing anxiously over-shoulder as though afraid the buildings might sprout mobile pylon legs and trample them; riders in the scarce cars and buses eager to be anywhere but here . . . In other words:

*The city the humming the thrumming the drumming the city the humming the summing it up as a MINUS—!*

That, echoing between her ears from her headset stereo (the shout at the climax weakened as the batteries weakened—buy more tomorrow, if any were to be had), furnished a running commentary on what Crystal Knight could see at this much-too-ordinary moment: black sky, drifting rain, unhappy people, a few bright but hideous illuminated signs, most of the vehicles stinking on their way to a breakdown because so few could afford to keep their suit of wheels in legal repair and new ones were so scarce now Britain was excluded from the Japanese economic sphere . . . The buses stank the worst and broke down the most often. (The rich, naturally, shunned areas like this, convinced they might catch AIDS by drawing breath. Elsewhere, as for instance in Parliament, they didn't seem nearly so anxious to keep their mouths shut.)

But the normal grumble of traffic had just changed to a howl. Here came the Old Bill, and in a hurry.

On what kind of business? Obviously they weren't just hauling in beggars to keep up the arrest rate.

Crystal switched off the bad-rap tape she was allowing to occupy her mind until another customer happened along. Aside from the stereo, she was wearing what was likeliest to turn her punters on because they were mostly middle-aged whenzies and what they chiefly wanted was to screw their teener daughters in the guise their girlfriends had worn at the same age. She knew enough psychology to suspect that that sort of urge underlay the stringent discipline imposed by the uncle who had grudgingly taken her in after her parents died and from whom she had ultimately fled: the endless petty put-downs, the harsh beatings for even minor offenses, and the final insult, his dismissal of her as unfit to keep company with his own children because she was a literal bastard. For him to have implied that about her mother . . . !

She no longer recalled her parents very clearly because they had died when she was five—in that epidemic of meningitis which, so some people still claimed, had escaped from a research laboratory, only the charge had never been proved, or even investigated—but she was sure they had been loving and affectionate, and she knew they must have had something her aunt and uncle lacked: a sense of humor. If not, why had a couple whose names were Jem and Beryl decided to name their daughter Crystal?

Of course, it did mean people tended to address her as Crissie, which she hated. But they generally didn't do it twice.

* * *

In full Sixties fig—minidress and high leather boots, plus false eyelashes and an idiotic bouffant wig of the same color as her own dark hair—she was at her hard-won evening post in a shop doorway opposite St. Pancras Station. It was a featly patch, particularly since they had refurbished the huge Victorian hotel across the way. Deprived of much of their former custom—late-arriving rail travelers and those whose trains had been cancelled without warning—the smaller hotels in the area had opened up for prostitution. Yes, all things considered a very good patch, because the staff didn't mind what age their clients were, nor which sex, either. Not so long as they carried a certificate of vaccination against AIDS.

Of course, the vaccine cost a bomb. So there was a thriving trade in forgeries.

Crystal was thirteen, and she didn't mind saying so to her punters. Sometimes she even said twelve, because the younger she claimed to be the more she turned most of them on, and the sooner she got them de-spunked the sooner she could turn another trick. To the Bill, of course, she always indignantly declared that she was sixteen—legal age . . . But then added "and a half" with a disarming giggle.

*What am I going to do when I really reach sixteen?*

At the moment, however, she had something else to worry about. The police car had passed without stopping, but a two-member serial was working this side of the street on foot—armored, of course, as always nowadays in the rougher districts. One could only guess by their respective heights which was the man and which the woman, for they were identically clad from their heavy black boots to their round black visored helmets. Inside the latter, radios relayed everything they said, everything they heard, to the tireless computers at Scotland Yard, on alert the clock around for any programmed keyword that might indicate more trouble than two constables on foot could cope with.

A patrol like that usually posed considerable problems, though never anything Crystal couldn't handle. As she had discovered, she could handle anything—most days of the month. It might, however, mean a waste of precious working time . . .

As it turned out, luck tonight was on her side.

At this most opportune juncture, she spotted a man she had a score to settle with: directly across the street, keeping his back turned, hat pulled down, coat collar up in hopes the police wouldn't look his way. Thus far they hadn't. But there was no chance of him escaping Crystal's notice. She would have known him at ten times the distance.

"Winston Farmer," she said under her breath. "Is your shit ever going to hit the fan . . . !" And, in a vigorous stage whisper: "Officer!"

The constables glanced around.

"Come this way. Don't worry. Pretend you're checking my certificate."

Puzzled, wary of a trap, yet nonetheless tilting back his visor so she could see his face, the man approached while his companion stood aloof, poised to signal for help.

"What do you want?" he demanded, obviously surprised at being addressed by someone who would normally do her utmost to steer clear of the law.

"Got something for you. See that growser across the way, trying so hard not to attract attention? He's Winston Farmer. Name mean anything?"

The policeman frowned, then suddenly nodded. "Dealer?"

"And ponce. Manages three girls. Crackers." Crystal wasn't referring to their looks or their sanity, but to their drug habit. "Once a week he makes a trip north—to Liverpool, I think, though I'm not sure. They say that's when he picks up his supplies. A car will be here to collect him any moment, a Jaguar. It's usually on time. Nick him now and I'm pretty sure you'll find he's holding."

She was trying to speak in a controlled tone, but her utmost efforts couldn't keep the venom out of her voice.

The woman constable had drawn closer in time to hear the last few words. She said, "That sounds personal. What have you got against him?"

"He tried to slip me a horn of crack. Wanted to get me angled and force me to work for him. One of the girls who does used to be my best friend. She's likely to be dead before she's twenty."

There wasn't going to be any argument. Crystal knew that already. For some reason she couldn't fathom, she had grown very good at persuading people to do as she wanted. Not long after she embarked on her career she'd even talked a drunk sadistic punter out of slashing her with a knife . . . and into turning it against himself. For the rest of her life she would be able to close her eyes and visualize again that squalid room, that rumpled bed, liter after liter of blood spewing out so red, so red—! She'd thrown up at the sight of it, right there on his dying body! But though they arrested her, claiming she had murdered him, when she was brought to court she made even the judge believe her story. That had been the second time she ever felt the way she did now: angry, but utterly clear-headed, with a sense of inexplicable power. The moment she saved herself from her knife-wielding client was the first.

Of course, when it turned out he was one of the soldiers set to guard radioactive waste on the Isle of Jura, shunned by the natives for fear of contamination, cursed and spat at by the local girls when he and his mates passed along the street, that did rather contribute to her defense . . .

She had been so afraid her aunt and uncle would learn about the case, but luckily, because she was a minor, the media were forbidden to mention her name or show a picture of her. So, no doubt, they still didn't know.

If they ever did find out—!

"Bock!" she added, staring past the police. "There's the car now. It looks like the same as usual—yes, it is. In which case I know the number. You better call it in."

The woman constable was already reciting, "Dark blue Jaguar proceeding east along Euston Road, two men aboard, stop and search for illegal drugs, possibly crack . . ." Then to Crystal: "What was that number again?"

Crystal repeated it, and added, "Better include 'armed and dangerous'—isn't that the way you phrase it?"

"Gun?" the man demanded.

"I don't think so. But I've seen him threaten his girls with a shiv."

The woman listened to her radio a moment, then gave a satisfied nod.

"There are two patrol cars in the area. One or both of them should catch him. Any idea where he might be heading for if he manages to slip past?"

"He lives in Docklands. I'm not sure exactly where."

"Hmm!" The man cocked an eyebrow. "And he owns a new Jaguar, *and* has someone to drive it. I'm surprised he goes by train, even though it has become a classy habit now the fares are so high. I'd have expected him to fly."

"Don't they sometimes search people at airports?" Crystal countered. "That's the last thing he'd want."

"Yes, of course." The man bit his lip and glanced at his companion. "Well, I suppose all we can do now is say thanks."

"Exactly. And good night!"

They took the hint and moved away at regulation pace.

During the last few minutes another train had discharged its passengers, and forty or fifty people were waiting for a chance to cross the road. Crystal's practiced eye identified some of them as servicemen on leave, always promising targets—and safe, too, apart from the occasional nutter like the one she had run into before, because they received free AIDS vaccinations. Despite the rain, she moved into plain sight and donned her professional smile. She had had few reasons for smiling since her parents' death, but her expression was more sincere than usual after her success in shopping Winston Farmer.

She only wished she could find a way to do the same to her aunt and uncle and all the canks like them who must have wanted this kind of world, because they had worked so hard to put and keep in power the government that made it possible.

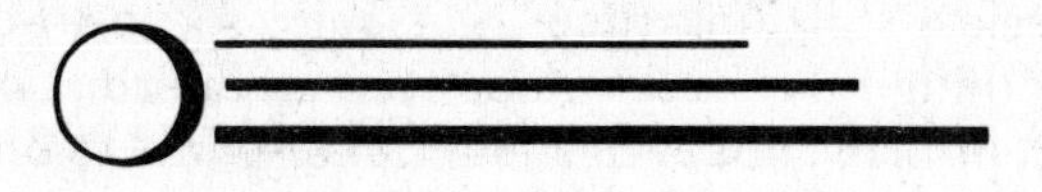

*You're watching TV Plus. Time for Newsframe.*

*The increasing scarcity, and the high cost, of potatoes has been officially attributed to a virus that entered Britain with imports from the Middle East, most likely from Cyprus or Egypt. Local varieties in those countries are resistant, while those grown in Britain are not. Many farmers are predicting that their land will have to be cleared and sterilized, and are demanding EEC aid on the same scale as the French sugar-beet producers whose crops were ruined by blight last year. More in a moment.*

*General Sir Hampton Thrower, at a rally of several thousand supporters in Birmingham, has repeated his proposal that patriots "make their views known," this time suggesting that they wear red-white-and-blue ribands . . .*

Immediately on returning home Peter recorded, as nearly verbatim as he could, the tantalizing—the infuriating—snippets Claudia had let escape. It would have been infinitely better for his peace of mind if, for instance, she had flatly stated that she didn't want to be bothered right now, because she intended a vacation before starting work. (In passing: she had, he remembered, specified that it was a thesis she planned, not another book.)

Instead . . .

And for a moment, both her voice and her expression had betrayed—he was certain of it—real fear.

Having read and re-read his notes, he leafed through her book to refresh his memory, but gleaned no clues. Her reasoning, though in his view less than conclusive, was nonetheless well documented, and it was plain that at the time of writing she had believed completely in what she had to say. What, then, could have changed her mind to the point where she now suspected she'd been wrong?

Perhaps her more recent publications might offer enlightenment. Heedless of the cost, he set about interrogating the relevant data-base. They all proved to be brief papers in journals of sociology and sociobiology, and all dealt with aspects of her original argument, qualifying or enlarging it or offering fresh supporting evidence. The latest had appeared only last year, so her new discovery, if that was what it was—

*Just a moment!*

He checked the date of receipt. It had been submitted seven months before it eventually appeared. Computerized publication might be fast; peer-review still took time. Not quite so up-to-date, then. But there was nothing more recent, not even an informal communication to establish priority, not even a letter in response to one of the many colleagues who disagreed with her.

Blank wall.

Growing more and more frustrated, he considered phoning contacts in America who might have spoken with her lately. He dismissed the idea at once; he was already spending more than he could justify. Tomorrow, though, in between drafting those pieces about the alternative therapy center he must find time to ring her publishers. Claudia might not care for publicity, but they ought to be able to talk her round. He wished he knew the name of the person who had tried to phone her, so he could ask for him directly. Also there was a growser called Jim Spurman, an ex-probation officer now lecturing at one of the northern universities. He had been among the first people in Britain to promote Claudia's ideas, by publishing an article about her in *Society Now.* Perhaps he might be of help.

Having made a list of all the things he wanted to do but couldn't because it was nearly midnight, Peter went to bed, where he lay awake for over an hour. When he did doze off he had uneasy dreams.

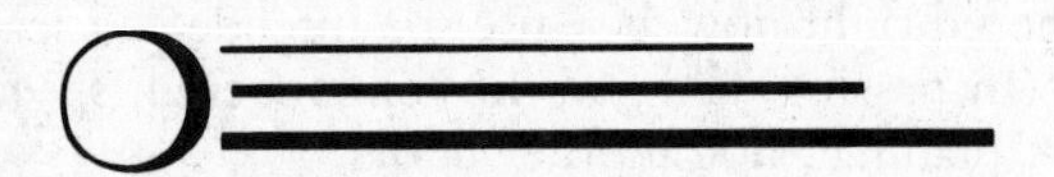

**B**elow the shoulder of a peak half green with summer grass, half gray with rocky outcrops, slashed across by drystone walls and a tumbling beck and speckled toward its summit with a flock of sheep, stood a farmhouse built of that same stone and roofed with slates—but some were missing, and had been replaced with plastic sheet. Its window frames needed repainting, and sundry panes were blind with plywood . . . or possibly cardboard. Behind it, like the petrified skeleton of a giant ostrich, lurched the frame of an abandoned windmill. Alongside was a barn in even worse repair, patched with rusty corrugated iron.

And, just discernible against the dazzle of sunshine on the beck: could that be intended for a watermill?

If so, it wasn't turning.

Glad of her seat belt as the rusty Mini in which she was a passenger jounced along an ill-made lane, Miss Fisher was attempting to assess this place the way she would an actual school. She was an education inspector. Some said she had an ideal cast of mind for the job.

As though needing to swot up for an exam, she considered putting the same questions as before to her companion and driver, Mr. Youngman. (Miss Fisher was not the sort of person who progressed rapidly to first-name terms.) But he was biting his lip with concentration as he negotiated bumps and ruts, and she was obliged to content herself by reviewing what he had already told her. After all, he had been courteous enough to offer her a ride up here, rather than simply giving directions and leaving her to find the way by herself.

Accordingly:

"How long ago did the Crowders arrive?"

"The year Garth started school. He's thirteen now, so that must have been eight years ago. I didn't know them then—didn't meet them until Garth came to me at eleven."

"Even though Mrs. Crowder herself had been a teacher?"

"People are very reclusive around here. They don't like offcomers. Besides, Roy and Tilly were regarded as bossy, as wanting to make people give up their old ways. In fact, of course, their dream was to go back to them. To be self-sufficient and live off their own plot of land."

"But did they settle in? Was Garth accepted at school, for instance?"

"It took a while, but according to what I've heard from his teachers at the primary he adjusted fairly well. It was obvious from the start he was very bright, and that always causes problems. But on the whole . . . And of course Roy did have a fair amount of money saved up, so he could pay on the nail for everything he wanted done."

"I understand he'd been an engineer?"

"Electrical engineer. He had visions of applying what he knew to —well, for example, the waterwheel that he installed. Rewired the house so he could light it off a car-dynamo using headlight bulbs."

"Did it work out?"

"For a while, yes. They even had a black-and-white TV. All they have now, though, is a battery radio."

"What went amiss?"

"I don't know. But something did."

"When?"

"I suppose it must have been shortly after Garth moved to my school."

"Did he get on as well there as at the primary?"

"For the first couple of terms, yes. But . . . Oh, I don't know. Kids tend to grow quarrelsome at that age, don't they? And secretive with it. Maybe it was due to the other kids realizing just how bright he is. Hardly one in fifty of them stands a chance of higher education, and here was Garth, university material if ever I saw such, bursting with questions at a time when most of the boys I've been trying to teach since I came here are deciding they already know enough to carry them through the rest of their lives. So they just stop listening. Of course, it's the parents' fault."

Miss Fisher gave a wise nod. She knew Mr. Youngman's type. In his late thirties, he was resigned to never becoming a head teacher and on the verge of accepting he might not even make head of department.

"Had something gone wrong at home? You said it was about then you first met the Crowders. And a crisis at home just as a child enters adolescence—"

A vigorous headshake that made Mr. Youngman's already untidy fair hair even more tousled.

"No, they seem to be a devoted couple. Mark you, I'm not sure Tilly was ever as enthusiastic as Roy about going to live in the middle of nowhere, but right from our first meeting she's always insisted that she went along with the idea for Garth's sake, because back where they came from the kids she used to teach were so cut off from reality and she didn't want him to turn out the same way."

" 'Where they came from' being—?"

"Spang in the middle of Birmingham. About as urban as you can get."

"By 'reality' she meant—?"

"I suppose the way crops are grown, animals are bred and slaughtered . . . Not that that applies; they're vegetarian."

"Did they try to—well—proselytize for their beliefs? I mean, most of the local farmers depend on sheep, don't they? They wouldn't like people who hoped to put them out of the meat business."

Another fierce headshake. "No, they always struck me as very tolerant."

"Nonetheless, I read about certain clashes . . ."

"I know what you mean"—in a bitter tone. "And I'm just as worried about what's been going on as anybody else. But I simply can't believe Garth had a hand in it!"

"There was a boundary dispute following which a sheepdog was poisoned, a potential champion that its owner hoped might get him into the national trials."

"And on television! That was Jack Atterthwaite's Judy. He farms in the next valley."

"Wasn't it his son who was found drowned? And wasn't he one of your pupils, in the same form as Garth but older?"

"You have done your homework, haven't you?"—with a sarcastic twist of his lip. "Yes and yes. And they tried to make out that the snare Bob tripped on, so he fell in the beck and knocked himself unconscious on a rock, was made from wire in the Crowders' barn. But it's a common type! Nothing was proved at the inquest! Listen, you can judge how much store to set by these charges when I tell you that the local people are accusing the Crowders of witchcraft!"

"You can't be serious."

"Your homework wasn't quite that complete, was it? I'm talking literally!" Fire sparkled in Mr. Youngman's eyes—and voice. "Stick around here a few days, and you'll notice words being spoken that haven't been uttered in half a century at least—'darklady,' 'hornylord'!"

Miss Fisher found herself at a loss for the first time in a long while. She said after a pause, "I'm sure that's of interest to students of folklore, but—"

With a sigh: "You're only here to find out whether the boy is receiving a decent upbringing. Right?"

"Of course." And, recovering her normal tart manner: "You seem to be distinctly *parti pris* in this affair! If you feel you can still offer an unbiased opinion, tell me your view. Are or are not Garth's parents providing him with a sound, well-rounded education?"

"I wish I knew!" An amazing shrug hoisted the shoulders of his worn tweed jacket high as his ears. "I call on the Crowders once a month, because about every four weeks I start to worry."

"And—?"

"And I stay worried until I'm indoors, and then I come away perfectly happy. I mean . . . But you're supposed to see for yourself, aren't you?"

Yes, of course. It was entirely legal for parents to educate their children at home. It was their right. But they had to demonstrate that they were doing it as well as a school could. And in a broken-down farmhouse, without TV . . . Was there even a phone?

"We'll have to walk the last bit. A Mini doesn't have enough ground-clearance."

Miss Fisher started, for not memory but reality had supplied Mr. Youngman's latest comment. He had brought them to a halt about a hundred yards below the house, where the way turned from lane to track. Releasing her safety belt by reflex, she was about to ask how the Crowders managed for transportation when she caught sight of an elderly Citroën *deux-chevaux* shadowed inside the barn.

Against the wall of which, a few logs. Also a stack of something like enormous dark-brown sandwiches.

"Is that peat?"

"Hmm? Oh, yes. They use a lot of it. For heating."

*Does using peat for fuel rather than fertilizer square with the concept of relying on renewable resources?*

Already prepared to deliver a hostile verdict, Miss Fisher followed in Mr. Youngman's wake, picking her awkward way between clods and puddles and wishing she had chosen a more sensible pair of shoes.

"Hello, Mr. Youngman! And I suppose you must be Miss Fisher! I'm Garth, of course! How do you do?"

It was a black-haired, brown-eyed boy—neatly enough attired in jersey, jeans and trainers—who had called from the front door of the house. Now he ran to meet the visitors at the front gate, that stood ajar on rusted hinges between tilted stone posts. Either side of his path were rows of wilting vegetables around which flies were buzzing, but the visitors' attention was wholly focused on Garth, who not only shook their hands but clasped them between both of his, and as he turned to lead them into the house put an arm companionably around Miss Fisher's waist . . . or nearly around, for she had put on a lot of weight. Such familiarity on first acquaintance was normally anathema to her, but this time she raised no objection, for the boy had such an appealing smile.

"Mother's in the kitchen!" Garth declared cheerfully. "I told her you'd be here soon so she ought to put a kettle on—you'd like a cup of tea, I'm sure. Nettle tea, of course; we can't afford the real stuff, but my parents say it's healthier anyway. And Dad . . . Yes, there he comes!"

They followed his pointing hand. Scruffy in corduroys and an ancient shirt without a collar, Roy Crowder was approaching with an armful of creosote-blackened wood.

"He's been breaking up the old chicken-run," said Garth. "You know we're vegetarian, yes? So we don't have any need for it, but we're always short of firewood . . . Come on in!"

And, within two shakes of a lamb's tail, there they were seated around a four-square farm-style kitchen table, sipping clear astringent tea, being plied with fresh-baked scones spread with home-churned butter and home-made jam sweetened with honey from the Crowders' own hives . . .

For a while Miss Fisher struggled to remember what she had been planning to ask about. She tore her gaze away from Garth with a near-physical effort. Then she caught sight of rows of books reposing on ill-planed but substantial shelves filling an alcove beside the fireplace. She recognized some of them—Mabey's *Food for Free*, Seymour's *The Forgotten Arts*—and noticed others she had never heard of: *One Acre and Security* by Bradford Angier, *The Mother Earth Book of Home-Made Power* . . .

And, underneath, the current *Encyclopedia Britannica.*

"I can well understand," Garth said, squeaking his chair closer to Miss Fisher's across the stone-flagged floor, "how concerned the authorities must be if people opt to educate their children at home. But, ma'am, you must surely have been told that Tilly—that's my mother—is a qualified teacher. How many children benefit from a one-on-one situation all day long? I ought rather to say a two-on-one, for Dad imparts his knowledge to me just as ceaselessly. With all respect to Mr. Youngman, had I remained under his tutelage would I by now be perusing the general theory of relativity along with the elements of practical design involved in buildings and operating power stations designed to feed the National Grid?"

With sudden stubbornness, Mr. Youngman said, "I see four half-burned candles over there! What about your water-powered dynamo? And the wind-powered one before it?"

Miss Fisher jerked her head around. She'd missed that!

"We're working on a better design," Roy Crowder cut in.

"That's right," his wife confirmed. "Meanwhile, using candles allows me to instruct Garth in the fundamentals of combustion. Roy and I devote ourselves unreservedly to his welfare and enlightenment. More tea?"

So completely were the visitors under Garth's spell, they departed without noticing how haggard Roy and Tilly had grown since that terrible day when he had returned from school—or rather, from avoiding school—and said:

"Roy! I don't want to call you Dad any longer! You're not really my father, are you?"

"What in the world—?"

"*Shut up!* And switch off that fucking radio!" It was reporting how yet another Jewish home in Tokyo had been burned down, but such matters were too far away for Garth to care about at the moment. He went on with undiminished intensity, "Tilly, I accept that you're my mother. But you lied to me as well."

"What—?" and "How—?" simultaneously from Roy.

"I was waiting for that 'how?' " was Garth's snap answer. "Until this moment I merely suspected. Now I'm sure. I'm not going back to school. I can't put up any more with—"

"We were going to tell you!" Tilly burst out. "At the proper time!"

"Which never came, did it? You've stuck me out here in the wilds, surrounded by yobs I can't stand, at the tender mercy of teachers who are a sight more ignorant than you—even than I am at my age!—and I'm going to get my own back! You've run my life for nearly twelve years under false pretenses, and *it stops now!* Make the necessary arrangements to teach me at home. Keep me fit and fed and tell me what I want to know—start by buying a set of the *Encyclopedia Britannica*, because there's a cut-price offer from a book club this week and you can always dump the club afterward. Don't make me sweat over your damned turnips any more, or clear the ashes from the hearth! I won't do it! I've found out enough about the sort of life I should look forward to—buses and taxis and discos and concerts and computers and libraries and television and girls and all kinds of goodies! That you have robbed me of! That for the sake of a patch of barren ground you're now too goddamned *broke* to provide for me!"

His eyes were full of tears, but his voice remained level and controlled.

"So you, Roy, can get on with your farming bit. I admit you have to do that by daylight. But if you let me go hungry I promise you'll starve before I do! And whenever I want information you can supply, you drop your spade and come running, hear me? As for you, *Mother*, you can take care of your bocky household chores before I get up and after I go to bed, even if it means you never get more than five hours' sleep for the rest of your life! When I leave here, which I estimate will be in roughly four years' time, I intend to take with me all the vicarious information you can supply by teaching me non-stop all day, from cooking to quantum physics! When I finally dump you dishonest creeps I intend to be capable in the abstract sense at least of making out *fine* on my own . . . and after that I hope you have to squeal to pass for pork!"

Not only tears now, but sweat as well, were pearling down his face.

"Son—" ventured Roy.

"Whose?" came the cutting answer. And that was the last objection.

Of course, when Garth wasn't turning his full force on them—as for instance now, when much of it had been expended on sending the visitors away happy—Roy and Tilly did succeed in uttering an occasional brief question.

"Garth, what if that inspector—?"

"What what?" with unspeakable contempt. "Haven't I taken as much care of you as you of me? Didn't I get even with Jack Atterthwaite when he trained that bitch of his to drive his sheep into your cabbages? Even though I hate bocky cabbage! Didn't he shy off when his canky son wound up in the beck? And didn't I warn you not to bring in water till it ran clear again, meaning after they took away Bob's body?"

Roy's face was perfectly white; Tilly's was gray.

"So it *was* you who—!"

"Why should you care? They haven't bothered us since, have they?"

"But the police—" Tilly whimpered.

"Did they even call us as witnesses at the inquest?"

"No, but—"

"And doesn't everybody think we're untouchable now? Don't they call you 'darklady' and 'hornylord'? *Don't you find offerings at the farm gate that no one asks you to pay for?* If you deny it—!"

Roy's pallor yielded to a blush. He started to speak, but Garth erupted to his feet.

"I'm sick of your 'yes buts'! Tilly, get back to your stove! I want my dinner on time! And I want meat with it—hear me? You may want to waste away on greens and roots, but I need bocky *protein!*"

For once his mother managed to withstand the force of his anger. Instead of obeying immediately, she whispered, "If that's what they're calling us, what can they be calling you?"

The boy had no answer. He felt unsure of himself for the first time since the moment he thought of as his coming-of-age, that morning when he woke to find a wet patch in his bed. Roy and Tilly—he must grant them that much—had soothed his panic with frank and reassuring explanations about the onset of puberty. Even so . . .

Faint doubts began to stir about the justice of the course he had embarked on, as deep in his subconscious as whatever made his penis stiffen in the night and spill his seed. He knew in theory what ought to harden it in waking life, but when his mother was a drawn-faced drudge . . .

And anyway he'd been accustomed to watching his parents dress and undress since he could remember.

He was tired from having to make the proper impression on Miss Fisher and Mr. Youngman. Snappishly he repeated his former command, and was obeyed. As usual.

That night, however, lying in bed, he tried to recall in detail how and why he had concluded that Roy was not his father.

He could not.

He could not.

He could not . . .

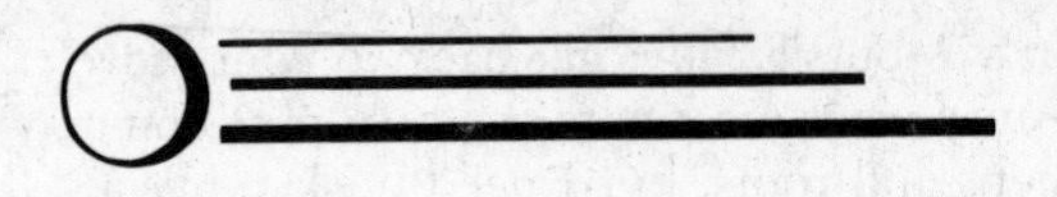

*You're watching TV Plus. Here is Newsframe.*

*For the third successive day students have rioted in Tokyo and other large Japanese cities, protesting against their parents' willingness to mortgage their children's future earnings as security for flats and houses. The average price of a three-room flat in central Tokyo is now one million pounds. More in a moment.*

*Followers of General Thrower cheered him this afternoon when he declared that the "steely spirit of Britain" must be re-tempered in the fire, even if that fire should prove to be nuclear. Opposition MPs . . .*

**P**eter was out of touch. Since their last contact, Jim Spurman had been appointed a full professor. Now he was "out of the office"—"addressing a conference"—"supervising a course" . . . Peter cursed the string of excuses that he found every time he checked for a response to the message he'd left to crop up twice a day on the guy's phone. In the end, because worrying about what Claudia might have meant was distracting him from paid work, he risked posting a general request for information on an American board he knew Claudia didn't log on to but several of her colleagues did—colleagues who tended to pooh-pooh her ideas.

Given the time of year, he wasn't expecting either a quick or a substantial response, but that same evening—as it happened, the day when, under the influence of Islamic expansionism, Malaysia occupied Singapore, an event that boded ill for Britain's precarious economy inasmuch as it meant the breaking of yet another Commonwealth link —returning late from the book-launch party which had evolved into dinner with a bunch of former colleagues, he found among his email a one-word message, presumably a password, addressed to a code he could have sworn he had only disclosed to a handful of particular friends. It was a warm night. Opening windows, brewing coffee that he needed to clear his head, he wondered aloud who on Earth—?

And realized the likeliest possibility in the same instant. He uttered a shrill whistle. During the conference in New York at which he had met Claudia, he had bumped into a thin tall man with graying hair, who seemed not to know anyone else present and whose sole identification consisted in a name badge reading GUEST. He was obviously bored and—fortunately for Peter—rather drunk. On spotting Peter's badge, which identified him as representing *Continuum/Quasar*, he had struck up a conversation.

After which . . . Peter racked his brains for further details. The gray-haired growser, who proved to be a lawyer, had made it clear how much he loathed the people who were, in his view, attempting to undermine the American Constitution by imposing a state religion—or possibly it was "religion state by state," for his argument grew more confused with each Martini he sank. At any rate he was noisily predicting that the result would be world domination by the Communist bloc because they would wind up with a monopoly of practical science while his own people would be reduced to praying, sticking pins in chance-opened Bibles, and casting lots to decide whose eldest son should be sacrificed to stave off disaster.

And he had said . . . Yes! It was coming back! He had said, "If you want to hear the only sound sense being talked during this entire weekend, you must catch Claudia Morris. Has she given her speech yet?"

Peter's answer was sharp. "Yes, this morning. Weren't you there?"

A headshake: "She sent me the text and I read it last week. Great stuff. We need more like Claudia . . . You going to do a program about her? Y'ought to!"

At which point, not waiting for a reply, he turned and waved his empty glass at the barman.

Peter was minded to slip away. Yet something made him hesitate. A lawyer who was plainly agnostic—the ongoing dispute between the scientists and the fundamentalists . . . And now *Continuum* was definitely scheduled for the chop, he needed plenty of leads if he was to stand any hope of surviving as a freelance.

*I gave him my card with that code written on the back. And I never asked his name!*

But as far as he could recall, that was the one and only time he had ever released that code—normally reserved for intimate friends and very special informants—to anybody outside Britain.

*Why would he be on that board?*

An answer sprang instantly to mind: it was used by people who disagreed with Claudia. Probably the lawyer was not in fact one of its contributors—just maintained a program to monitor it. This could be interesting!

With exaggerated care Peter tapped out the password he had received, then waited for the screen to light.

What it scrolled was a montage of OCR'ed news cuttings, obviously run fast and carelessly because there were many errors, but the gist was plain. At first they related to attempts by fundamentalists to take over major centers of American education, using the vast monetary leverage they had accumulated as the millennium approached and the faithful grew less and less confident that the Rapture would save them seven years before the onset of Armageddon. Time was running out . . .

Then the subject switched abruptly to something Peter had heard about but never taken seriously: a group nicknamed "the Strugfolk" after one Cecil Strugman, who had inherited millions of dollars from a family meat-packing business, turned vegetarian-ecologist-rationalist, and mounted a counter-campaign designed to prove that of the fundamentalists unconstitutional by emphasizing their use of un-American terms like "king" and "lord"—precisely what the Founding Fathers had striven to get rid of. With growing excitement Peter sat down at his desk, occasionally halting the display as a salient point emerged.

Until this moment he had imagined that this venture was essentially symbolic, and doomed to inevitable failure. On the contrary: if he was to believe what he was reading, the Strugfolk had been burrowing away through strata of legal precedents, assembling a virtually unassailable case while at the same time attracting additional funds from industrial corporations whose directors were afraid that in the next generation there might not be any petroleum geologists or volunteers for lunar prospecting missions . . . at any rate, not outside Russia, Europe and Japan.

Ranged against them, naturally, were the worshippers of the Almighty Dollar who were growing far richer far quicker by manipulating the stock markets with computerized help than anyone could hope to achieve these days by actually working.

Peter whistled again. He had never seen that particular split in American society so graphically portrayed. Of course, here in Britain—

And even as he pursed his lips, the lines on the screen wiggled into illegibility for a moment, then reformed as garbage. He jumped to his feet, abruptly furious.

*The bastards! The bastards!*

He recognized the warning. Special Branch (or SIS, or whichever —there wasn't much distinction between the various British police agencies any longer) had been prompt to obey Big Brother at Langley. Here were data the ordinary citizen of the UK was not supposed to access.

*Fits. You wouldn't see it on TV these days. Or read it in the papers . . . Except maybe on* TV Plus *or in the* Comet*!*

For a moment he actually thought kindly of Jake Lafarge, who of late had been stingy in providing him with assignments.

His mind darting back to what Claudia had said about the British government's obsession with secrecy, he pounded fist into palm. That gray-haired lawyer, doing him a favor (but why? Logically, because Claudia must be involved with the Strugfolk, or else her university was under threat from the bigots—*stop!* He was spiralling in three directions at once and he had to force himself back on an even keel)—

That lawyer might well have unintentionally wished on him another visit from the Bill.

Well, like everyone else in his profession, he had emergency arrangements. If only they weren't so expensive . . . !

Sighing, he dumped the text from America into a remote store supposed to be inviolate under the Data Protection Act. It was almost certainly not, given the massive computing power the government disposed of nowadays, but at least it might not be worth their while trying to break the rule by which it was enciphered. If they had really been upset, they wouldn't have left anything on his screen at all, but simply disguised the event as a system crash by engineering a block-wide power failure, and the hell with how many innocent users suffered as a result. On busy nights some areas of London could be seen flashing like trafficators—if the streetlamps were still working.

Then he set all his alarms, so as to make the police's arrival as conspicuous as possible. He belonged to a Neighborhood Watch. When such schemes had been set up in the eighties, few people had foreseen that within so short a time they would become hated rather than supported by the police and government. None of the other residents of his building belonged, but there were fifteen members within earshot of his alarms, prepared to turn out at any time of day or night with cameras, video-cameras, sound-recording equipment . . .

*Christ! This is how it must have been in Russia before* glasnost*! Except the neighbors wouldn't have had so much of the essential gear.*

His miserable train of thought was broken by the phone. For a moment he assumed it must be the Bill ringing from downstairs asking whether he would come quietly. Then he spotted the calling number on the display screen. It was the one on which he had been trying to reach Jim Spurman.

He rushed to answer, and heard a voice that was suddenly familiar despite the passage of four years.

"Peter Levin! Jim Spurman here! I'm sorry! We had a computer glitch and the bocky machines told me *Petra* Levin, an ex-student of mine that I sincerely hope I'll never set eyes on again. . . . I gather you want to talk about what Claudia Morris has been up to lately, is that right?"

Abruptly alert again, Peter said tensely, "Yes! What can you tell me?"

A dry chuckle. "Well, as I've so often seen, I'm afraid, among sundry of my colleagues, she appears to be yielding to pressure. One has to be forgiving—I'm suffering much the same problem myself, though luckily I'm blessed with a supportive vice-chancellor. But isn't it always the fate of pioneers to be mocked by the whenzies?"

*Oh, lord. I'd forgotten how devotedly he imitates the usage of his students . . .*

"I'd like a scrap or two more data on that level," Peter said aloud.

"You didn't hear that this university of hers became a prime target for the bigots? What's the name of it—?"

"Never mind!" Peter cut in. "I know what you mean."

"What you should say nowadays"—reprovingly—"is the inverse: 'you know what I mean.' As long ago as the mid-eighties this had been spotted as . . ."

*What progress from probation officer to professor can do to muddle someone's thinking!*

As politely as he could contrive, Peter intimated how little interested he was in the fact that since their last encounter Jim Spurman had decided to concentrate on verbal usage as an infallible index of predictable social behavior. Sitting on the corner of his desk, staring out of the window, watching the lights of airliners ascending and descending around Heathrow, he finally managed to insert a further question about Claudia's university.

"Ah! I'm surprised you haven't heard. Well, it seems one set of funders, the repulsive lot, are displacing another who are somewhat more welcome."

This was getting worse by the minute! Peter had one ear cocked for the arrival of Special Branch. But if they did turn up, he wanted at least to pry some sense out of *Professor* Spurman first . . .

Controlling himself with vast effort, he said, "I take it you mean religious fundamentalists are trying to buy control of the university where she works."

"Featly!"

*But that's not why and how one uses that word . . . Cancel that. He's just explained why she's afraid the money for her sabbatical may be withdrawn.*

"Please go on!"

"Well, obviously, as soon as she went high-profile with her book, and so many people responded positively, she was a prime target for the obscurantists. I'm not shamming when I say we get literally dozens of letters every week in my department from parents who feel she's explained why their children went to the bad. How else do you think we've managed to maintain our funding when what we're spreading the gospel about is anathema to the received wisdom? We can point to massive public support!"

Peter's mouth was growing dry; he had indulged in too much free wine at the book launch, and the coffee hadn't helped, being no doubt largely ersatz despite the label on the jar. Still staring out of the window beyond which red and white and green lights wove endless abstract patterns, he said after a pause, "Let me get this straight. You're saying her university—"

"Is due to be swung to the anti-science side by a massive injection of money. Precisely. The poor bitch is going to have to fight like hell to retain her tenure."

"Have you seen her lately? Or spoken to her?"

The next words were accompanied by an audible frown.

"Funny you should ask that. As a matter of fact, I've been rather disappointed in the lady recently, given that I worked so hard to promote her ideas over here . . . That's why I suspect she's bending under pressure. When I last tried to get in touch she didn't return my call, and a message I posted on an email board she used to log on to at least as often as I did—"

*Flash.*

Bright in the sky above Heathrow Airport. Peter's jaw dropped even as he realized what he was watching.

*Bang.*

But it was worse than a bang. It was a slap, a growl, a rumble, and then a succession of thuds. The phone was still murmuring. He disregarded it, waiting for what he was sure must follow. It did, and windows over half of London shook in their frames, as a fireball shed glowing fragments on—where would it be? Hounslow? Southall? Likely both, and even further!

*And I happened actually to be watching! Camera!*

Incontinently he let fall the phone, rushed to snatch up what he should have seized the moment the glare first lit the sky, aimed and shot. This was going to save him from the Bill! Here was what had been so long predicted, the fruit of the government's policy of withdrawing public funds from air traffic control on the grounds that private firms were far more cost-efficient. But in the service of Mammon they sometimes skimped the exhaustive checks needed to make sure all their computers could always talk to one another . . . And as a result, two airliners had collided and caught fire above what for a generation had been promoted as the busiest airport in the world.

Not to mention an awful lot of people's homes.

Clearing up the mess would occupy the Bill for quite a while, just as making sure the blame fell on some overworked traffic controller instead of the people who had made fortunes by cutting the necessary corners would preoccupy the government. He could relax—

*Oh no I can't!*

The phone was saying something. He caught it up without looking and snapped, "Thanks for what you didn't tell me! But you've been pre-empted!"

"What do you mean?"—in a frosty *academic* tone.

"Watch the TV news!"

He cut Spurman off and tapped the *Comet*'s number.

Engaged.

Well, of course. The line must be stacked umpteen deep. Hundreds of people closer to the accident must be phoning all the papers, TV stations, et cetera et cetera, hoping their amateur footage (because three out of four families now owned, etc., therefore high standard of living) might make it to the screen for a fat fee . . .

With an increasing sense of desperation, compounded by memory of the debt he had incurred by dumping those data from America into secure store, he spent a while staring toward the fires breaking out where fragments of the airliners had fallen. From here, though, he could no longer see anything but an orange glow, like old-style sodium lamps on fluctuating current.

And other planes being diverted to Luton and Gatwick.

He poured himself another shot of whisky. The bottle was nearly empty and he made a mental note to buy more tomorrow, if there was any in the shops; most, in this desperate economic climate, was earmarked for export. Even as he was raising the glass, however, the phone shrilled.

"Yes?"

"Jake Lafarge. Did you know two planes—?"

"I saw it! I even shot some pictures!"

"Pictures we got, and TV beats all of us anyhow. Give me eight hundred words explaining why it happened! Nearly ten percent of our regular readers are shareholders in British Airways—and it was two BA planes that collided!"

There was a tone of pleading in Jake's voice. But Peter had been mentally drafting just such an article for years. He drew a deep breath and reached for his modem.

"Put me on line," he said. "I can set it cold."

And brought it in at 789 by automatic count: a chilling indictment of the policies that had led to the worst midair crash in British history, long predicted, now a fact.

"Front page," Jake said when he called back. "Thanks."

*And many thanks to you, sir!*

For to have an article like that splashed and by-lined on page one of a national paper without being subbed was like an accolade—even though the *Comet* was not exactly in the front rank. In the morning, Peter was woken far sooner than he would have liked (since he had made the mistake of finishing the whisky to bring himself down from the high his article had engendered) by a succession of colleagues complimenting him, saying it was the best thing he'd done, how much they wished they could have had the same chance, he was a lucky growser and why didn't he—?

And most important: come and say it again on TV Plus at lunchtime, if you're prepared to confront a pro-government spokesman "to provide balance."

He had to think about that for a moment. Then he concluded he had unassailable documentation. And what the hell else was he going to do with his life?

He made mincemeat out of the bocky cank from the government. All of a sudden he was famous again. Of course, that meant he needed protection, but TV companies still had clout, and there was talk of making a documentary . . .

It was giddying. But the most important part was that he felt as though he was falling back into the context of a team. He knew in the distant parts of his mind that the airliner crash would be forgotten in a week or less, except by the bereaved and those whose homes had been burned down—and of course the lawyers suing on their behalf, who stood to make a mint—but this was the way he had . . .

Yes. This was the way he had grown up. He'd been a kid before he signed with the *Continuum* team. His years with them had constituted his true adolescence. Now, after a gap that might be termed his *Wanderjahre*, he had the chance to continue the process.

He was reminded of Claudia Morris a few days later when he received the bill for the data about the Strugfolk that he had dumped in a fit of panic. The amount was horrifying, and although he paid up for fear of incurring a bad credit rating, he filed an erase code.

When Professor Spurman left a message on his answering machine inquiring whether he could confirm a rumor that Claudia Morris was in Britain, he wiped the tape without bothering to call back.

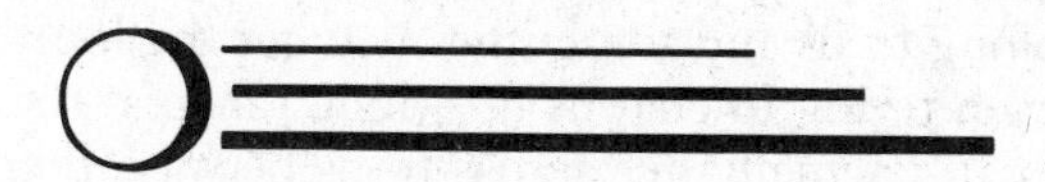

**I** don't know who I am.

Oh, I know my name all right—Sheila Hubbard. At least Hubbard is what I go by, though really it's the name of my mother's second husband. The first was an artist called Doug Mackay. He and Ingrid (my mother) broke up when I was still very young. I never quite found out why, but I get the impression it was something to do with her wanting a kid and him not caring to be lumbered, though I had this attachment to him that must have been more like a fixation because when she got married again, to Joe (who's a real business whiz, a high-flyer absolutely dripping money), I got all kind of upset. I sneaked a look at a psychiatrist's report on me once. It was full of loaded terms like "disturbed" and "irrelevance of affect."

Which is how come I wound up at this "progressive" school in the back of beyond, called Mappleby House.

But I like it a lot better than any school I was at before, I must admit. Mainly here you do what you want so long as it doesn't hurt anybody else. There are some great teachers who honestly seem to love kids. Before I got here I didn't know how much fun you can have finding things out. Sometimes I get terribly angry with the teachers I used to have who didn't care about anything except forcing you to come up with the approved answer.

I'm wandering off the point.

I was going to say: I know how old I am—fourteen next birthday—and I recognize my face when I see it in the mirror, the usual black hair and brown eyes and rather olivey skin as though there's some kind of Middle Eastern ancestry in there . . . I often stare at myself for ages and ages trying to see what someone else would notice on looking at me for the first time. I can't work it out, any more than I can decide whether I'm pretty. I hope I am—I mean naturally. I hate the idea of smothering my face in gunk the way some of the older girls do, just to make a better impression on some bocky boy.

No, the reason I don't know who I am any more is because I've changed. Inside. I remember *when* it happened, but I don't know *why.* And I'm scared. It went this way.

Mappleby used to be a big country house, not exactly a stately home—it's only Victorian—but it has this huge garden and lots of nice private corners among laurel hedges and the place most of us like, especially in summer, is where one of the walks runs down to a bend in the river. It's quite shallow there, so you can bathe if you want, but the other bank doesn't belong to us and sometimes you get the local yobs coming to stare and even trying to chat us up—long range at the tops of their voices. They can't actually get across to us because there's a sort of weird thing made of wire mesh, that we call the Palisade, and anyway the water's a bit murky and we have a proper swimming pool as well. But it's great for sunbathing, and since Mappleby was founded back in the twenties when there was this terrific craze for *Freikörperkultur* (I think that's right) you don't even have to wear a thong if you don't want to.

Of course we're all encouraged to be terribly natural and healthy about our bodies and boys and girls share the same dormitory and go to the showers together and all the rest of it, but I like that, and if it wasn't for the fact that the cooking is kind of bocky I'd say the whole setup was featly, except of course it scandalizes the natives who practically make an industry out of being offended.

A moment back I said the yobs can't get over to us, only stare from the other bank beyond the wire. But that's not absolutely true. One of them did manage it.

I was exactly midway between two periods. I started young, like my mother apparently. Luckily I don't have a bad time before I bleed—no PMT or whatever they call it, and no cramps—but around the middle of the month I do get incredibly frustrated. So I was feeling in a particularly bocky mood even though it was fine and sunny, so I went off by myself to the river with a couple of books I wanted to finish. But it got so hot I had to peel off and I was still sweating so I went in for a dip. I'd noticed a gang of natives on the other bank but I didn't give a tinker's toss for them. I lost count years ago how many people have seen me in the nude. Then . . . Oh, I suppose one of them must have boasted to his mates that he could get to me, because he stripped off—not completely, he kept his underpants on—and jumped in and swam to the Palisade. It's sort of curved at the top in a way that's supposed to make it impossible to climb over, and the water's at its deepest there so there isn't any footing, and trying to support your weight on fingers and toes while you scramble up must be terribly painful. Like climbing chickenwire, see what I mean?

Except as I found out afterward this particular native, who was nineteen, was on leave from the Commandos where they'd put him through what's supposed to be the toughest assault course in NATO, and he was on my side before I knew what was happening, while his pals on the far bank clapped and cheered.

"Didn't think I could make it, did you?" he said as he found his footing and started to push through the water toward me. "Just because it was never done before! Well, for that I think I deserve a kiss, don't you? And maybe a bit more than just a kiss!"

I was absolutely stunned. I thought I was going to pass out. I mean, they say I'm well-developed for my age, but that doesn't mean I could face up to a hunk like him with muscles growing out of his muscles. I can still see his grin. He was sunburned, so there were kind of red patches on his cheeks, and he had practically no hair. I mean on his head. His chest was like a bocky doormat, and lower down—well, the word isn't even thicket!

It wasn't the idea of being kissed. I must make that clear. I mean, it happens a lot at my school. It's natural, isn't it? And lots more than just kissing, too. But we get properly taught about pregnancy and AIDS and all that kind of thing, and in any case it's no very big thing except perhaps among the oldest of the kids. One of the teachers I like best showed me this book by someone—I think he's American only he's got this German name: Bet-something, is it?—he found the same sort of situation among kids on an Israeli kibbutz, who because they grew up together acted toward each other like brothers and sisters. I know a lot of brothers and sisters do do things with each other, but—

Look, this isn't a defense of the way things are at Mappleby, okay?

I was trying to explain what scared me. It was the way he took it for granted that because he'd proved he was a Big Strong Man I was instantly going to lie down and spread my legs. Pardon my crudity, but it's not half as crude as what I could read on his face like plain English.

And that was when I stopped being scared. That was when I stopped knowing who I am. Because being scared was more like the me I was used to. Only . . .

Only all of a sudden I wasn't afraid any more. I was angry. I was—

All right. It probably sounds too fancy, too like something I picked up from a book, but I don't know any better way to express it. I was suddenly *possessed*, by ice-cold rage that showed me precisely what I had to do. I felt myself smiling as he reached out toward me, and instead of pushing his hands away I met them with mine, locking my small fingers with his big thick ones. This surprised him long enough for me to say, "I'm a virgin, you know. I'm not even thirteen yet."

He blinked water out of his eyes; it was trickling down from what little hair he had on his scalp. Then he grinned again.

"You can't fool me like that! *I* know about this school of yours! *I* know what you get up to! Running about starkers—like you right this minute! Boys as well as girls!"

I was gradually luring him backward into the shallows, so my breasts appeared above the water, provoking another outburst of cheering from his mates. His eyes fastened on them hungrily. Next moment it would probably be his mouth, but that wasn't the idea. I said, and something made my tone cajoling and seductive, "All right. But . . ."

"But what?"

"I want you to go down on me first. Know what I mean?"

"What do you think I bloody am? A virgin like you? 'Course I know what you mean!"

"Then go ahead," I said. "And if you make me come by doing it, I'll make you come the same way."

His grin became enormous, stretching those red-blotched cheeks until I thought he'd sprain the muscles of his mouth—and he did exactly as I'd told him to.

Under a foot of water.

It was as though he simply forgot he couldn't breathe the stuff! I felt his tongue on my belly, then around my pubic hairs, and then among them. Then, when I was sure he couldn't hold his breath any longer, he simply didn't come up. He stopped moving, and all of a sudden he was drifting away, all limp, like a wet rag-doll.

After that it gets confused. The next thing I remember is stumbling out on the bank and grabbing my clothes and my books and racing toward the school. I looked back once, and there wasn't any sign of him. By the time they found him against the Palisade, carried there by the current—still underwater—he was dead.

There was an inquest, of course. I said I didn't mind being called as a witness, and stood up in front of the coroner and answered her questions as calmly as I could, saying I knew about rape and felt I was fortunate to have been spared so terrible an ordeal, though I had been very frightened. The coroner was a woman doctor. She congratulated me on my lucky escape. The surgeon who carried out the postmortem said death was due to drowning but he'd also discovered some kind of weakness in the growser's heart in spite of him being a Commando and supposed to be perfectly fit. The jury brought in a verdict of misadventure. The local paper said it served the bastard right, or words to that effect, and called for reassessment of the educational system at Mappleby on the grounds that it could produce a pupil not yet thirteen who could display such presence of mind when assaulted by a would-be rapist. I don't know if you remember, but according to the news half a dozen girls my age had been raped and killed in the previous few months.

After which, of course, my mum and dad—my dads, I suppose I mean, because Doug turned up for the inquest, too—and the staff of the school all said I was wonderful and marvelous and so did the other kids and lots of them wanted all of a sudden to be best friends with me.

But who are they making friends with? I don't know! I can't believe I'm *me* any longer! You see, *I committed a murder in public view!* All the growser's mates were watching, like I told you—five or six of them, there must have been. And I got away with it!

I don't think I *want* to be me any more!

If they go on pestering me, I'm afraid I'll do the same again. I could. I know I could.

*I don't want to!* Do you hear me? *I don't want to!*

Please help. Somebody. Please help . . .

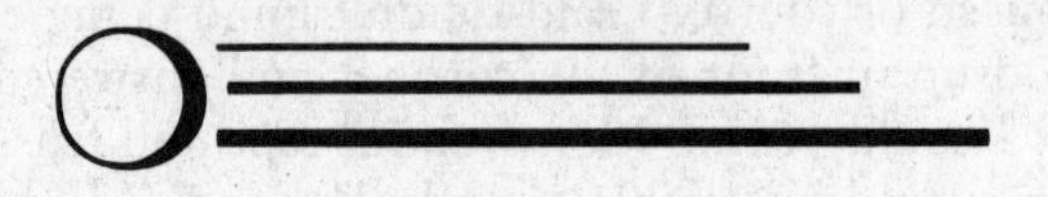

*You're watching TV Plus. Now for Newsframe.*

*A group of American terrorists, one of the so-called "Rambo squads," has claimed responsibility for the bomb that destroyed the headquarters of the West German Green Party. Eight people are known to have lost their lives, and nine others are in hospital.*

*Here in Britain, four self-confessed supporters of General Thrower have been remanded on bail after setting fire to shops owned by Chinese and Pakistanis. At the hearing the magistrate said patriotism had its limits, but shouts from the public area of the court . . .*

Peter Levin's appearance on TV Plus with the government spokesman had transformed his life.

Above all, he had a new home, in a block built on what had been the playground of a school until emigration from Inner London dramatically cut its population—and exported the problems of drugs and crime to provincial towns that hitherto had been relatively peaceful. He still had only three rooms but all were bigger, and instead of being under the leaves they were at street level in a better area. The kitchen was three times the size and the bathroom boasted a proper tub. Also there was off-street parking. He still could not afford a car, but there was a chance TV Plus might soon allot him one on the company.

Of course, the price was horrendous—but nothing compared to what people were paying in Manhattan or Tokyo. So the moment he set eyes on it, he said, "I'll take it." And moved in ASAP to forestall squatters.

After the removal crew had left he poured himself a shot of Scotch, humming a cheerful tune despite the fact that the evening was unseasonably cool and wet. Seemingly autumn had decided to visit Britain ahead of time this year. Passing his desk, to check that his gear was correctly connected, he hit an email code on his computer: that of Harry Shay out in California, whom he'd been meaning to contact for ages. Even if over there people weren't out of bed yet he could leave a message—

*What?*

The screen was flashing at him: *No such code.*

Had he mis-hit the number? He tried again, more slowly, with the same result.

Professional reflexes made the nape of his neck tingle. Setting aside his glass, he dropped into his working chair and tried the only other address he had for Harry, that of his company Shaytronix, which should at least have a machine on line.

*No such code.*

"This is ridiculous!" Peter said aloud. He remembered Harry Shay from his early days with *Continuum.* The guy had been one of the most successful British software entrepreneurs—not a programmer himself, but brilliant at putting commercial firms in touch with experts who could tailor existing systems to meet their special requirements, and a positive genius at collecting commission fees. Granted, a shadow had fallen over his last months in Britain, some suspicion that he had diverted funds belonging to his customers for his own benefit . . . But nothing had ever been proved, and he had done the accepted thing by marching off to California as it were with drums and trumpets, announcing that he was forced to emigrate because the fools in charge at home had no understanding of modern business.

True enough, in Peter's view. If any of Britain's major corporations were to be run as inefficiently as its government, they'd be bankrupt within months . . .

Half-noticed in the background, but with the sound loud enough to furnish a distraction, the TV was reporting from Chicago, where flooding was driving thousands of people from their homes. Angrily he pressed the remote control and left its images to mop and mow in silence while he searched for the reason why the code for Shaytronix wasn't valid any more.

But this time, when he entered the correct digits, he saw on his screen: *Normal routing not available.* That was a message he had never encountered before. He sat back, frowning, and took a sip of his whisky. Then, even as he poised his fingers to try again, realization dawned and he turned in dismay to the TV.

By then the report from Chicago was over, and there were scenes of Brazilian refugees, the Indians who according to their country's government did not exist in Grand Carajas, bellies bloated with pellagra under a skim of reddish-yellow dust, too listless even to brush away the flies that came to sup the moisture from their eyes.

*Grief, not another bocky mess in South America!*

But the glimpse he had had earlier was enough to remind him of something he already knew but had overlooked. The main clearing-house for the email networks he was accustomed to using was at the University of Chicago . . .

Among the goodies he had awarded himself when he moved from his former home was a short-range timeshifter, a recorder that monitored sixteen pre-set TV channels on an endless-loop tape, so he could review anything of interest within twenty-four hours, whereafter the data were wiped. Now he needed that Chicago report, and in a hurry!

A few oath-ridden minutes later he got the hang of the instructions, and was able to watch exactly what he was afraid of. It was no news that the Great Lakes were returning to the level that had obtained before the city was founded; right now, however, a northerly wind was whipping water over Lake Shore Drive and into basements, cellars, underground garages . . . There were shots of drowning cars. Some that were unusually airtight with their windows closed bobbed around on the surface for a little, but then—through the exhaust pipe, maybe—the water claimed them, and they burped and sank amid a string of bubbles.

Peter had visited Chicago. He knew where the computers were housed that relayed his messages—this having become a valuable commercial service for the university when Federal subsidies grew scarce. They were in concrete rooms below ground level, designed to keep out terrorists.

But more than likely not designed to keep out water.

For the first time since his late teens when he stopped worrying about nuclear war on the prevalent grounds that it hadn't happened yet, he felt an overwhelming sense of the frailty of civilization. Chicago might be thousands of miles from London, yet a day or two ago he could have contacted a hundred friends there at the touch of a key. Now, though, thanks to a freak storm . . .

But there must be alternative routings! Why had they not been automatically invoked? He checked, and to his dismay found the machines had outguessed him. There was a nil response by any route whether surface or satellite from any of the Shays' codes. Why in the *world . . . ?*

Peter had been vaguely wondering what his new neighbors were like. Now, reminded of the insecurity of life in any great city, he decided that one of his first steps must be to join the Neighborhood Watch; he'd seen stickers in nearby windows, although not as many as around his former home. He was filing a memo to attend to the matter in the morning when the doorbell rang.

For a moment he forgot that his new affluence had also supplied a closed-circuit TV camera above his front door. Jumping up, he was halfway to the streetward window before the point struck him. When he recalled where he had sited the monitor, he was taken aback at what it showed. For, stepping back from the threshold, gazing around as though wary of a trap, there was a policewoman.

*A woman? Alone? Not wearing armor?*

With vast effort he cancelled his reflex responses. Of course: this was a different area. Maybe she had simply heard that a new resident had arrived in the street and wanted to make sure that everything was okay.

*Except, of course, that any finger of the Bill . . .*

Yes. She might have come to warn him to stop attacking the government in public, though that sort of duty would normally be entrusted to someone in plain clothes. Alternatively, she could be the area intelligence officer, following up a tip from one of her informants with a view to filing data about him on PNC, the Police National Computer.

In either case it behoved Peter to answer the door in a hurry and be terribly polite. Memory of Claudia Morris stirred for the first time in weeks as he recalled his bitter reference to the computer that under his name had stored a mass of data concerning someone else. Long ago he had striven to have it altered, only to be met with harsh rebuff: "You shouldn't know about that file—shut up or I'll nick you for a breach of the Official Secrets Act!"

*Grief! Since the eighties, haven't they figured out any way of amending their data? What about when someone dies?*

But governments being governments, and that of Britain being particularly loathsome, all he did on the way to the front door was check that his pro-Thrower ribbon was pinned conspicuously on the breast of his sweatshirt. There was a possibility, not yet confirmed, that he might be offered a steady job with TV Plus. However, the executive who had brought him the good news had also handed him the ribbon and advised him to wear it if he hoped to obtain the post. He concluded by saying apologetically, "Better safe than sorry, Peter! Though sorry, I admit, is what I am . . ."

Moreover, against regulations, the policewoman was wearing one, too.

She was not in fact alone. Nearby but out of range of the camera, a white car had drawn up, and its driver was keeping an eye on her. Having registered the fact, Peter said in his politest tones, "Good evening, officer. What can I do for you?"

And thought for a second he was looking at Claudia, for this woman had the same solid build, much the same color hair, and the same slightly sour expression on her square pale face. But the resemblance was fleeting.

Consulting some notes in her hand, she said brusquely, "You're Peter Andrew Levin?"

"Yes." He blinked. "If someone has reported me as a squatter, I can assure you—"

"Father of Ellen Dass, alias Gupta?"

At first he failed to take in the words. It had all been so long ago

. . . A terrible sinking feeling developed in his belly and his mouth turned dry.

"Come on!" the woman snapped. "You admitted paternity, according to our records!"

And that was true. It came from one of the files about him that was not corrupt. Eventually he forced a weary nod.

"So what? I haven't seen the kid in ten years! Kamala didn't want me to! And since she took up with her new man I haven't even had to pay maintenance!"

The WPC wasn't listening. Folding her notes, she was shouting to her companion. "We finally found the right place! Bring her over!"

Bewildered, Peter suddenly realized there was another person in the car, getting out now, clutching a canvas bag: a slim, tawny-skinned child in sweatshirt and jeans, a girl about the right age to be Ellen. The driver escorted her toward the door.

As they drew nearer, he saw she had been crying. Her lids were puffy and she kept biting her lower lip. She clung to her bag like a shipwreck survivor to a lifebelt.

Stopping in front of him, staring up with immense dark eyes, she said uncertainly, "Dad?"

"What's all this about?" Peter whispered.

"Don't you think you'd better ask us in?" riposted the policewoman.

"I . . . Oh, Christ!"—thinking what an impression this visit from the Bill must be making on his new neighbors. "Yes, I suppose so. It's a mess because I only moved in today, but—Oh, *shit.* Okay!" He stood aside, gesturing in the direction of the living room. The woman entered first; Ellen followed, and the male constable insisted on Peter preceding him.

Closing the door behind him, he said, "I'm PC Jones. My colleague is WPC Prentis."

"How do you do?" As Peter spoke the automatic words he thought they were the stupidest he had ever heard himself utter. He couldn't tear his eyes away from this stranger who must be his daughter. Nor she from him.

"Sizable place, this," said Prentis, sitting down without invitation. "Plenty of room for a kid."

"What do you mean?" Peter snapped, rounding on her. "What's all this about?"

"Mainly it's about a kid with nowhere else to go," Jones murmured. "You want to explain, Ellen? No? I suppose not. . . . All right then, Mr. Levin." He drew a deep breath.

"Remember the airliners that crashed the other day? I'm sure you do. You had a lot to say, I'm told, about the wickedness of the government in hiring private firms for air traffic control. You may be right, you may be wrong, but what it boils down to is that a chunk of one of the planes fell on your daughter's home. She was out visiting friends. When she came back it was all over. Burnt down. With her mother and father—excuse me: her *common-law stepfather*—inside. Mr. Gupta died at once. Ms. Dass died today. So when we checked the records . . ."

"Oh, my God." Peter had to grope his way to a chair, thinking: *How could I ever have guessed? I didn't even know where Kamala was living!*

"Had a hell of a time tracking you down!" Prentis said acidly. "Like you were trying to hide!"

In a milder tone Jones objected, "Maggie, Mr. Levin's a very busy man! You know that . . . Well, now we've got the kid settled, we'd best be getting back. There'll be a social worker round in the morning to sort out things like victim support and advice on clothes and such—all she's got left is in that bag, of course. The rest was burnt. Best thing in cases like this is to get back to normal ASAP, though this is a long way from her old school. Still, the social worker will explain. On our way?"

Prentis rose briskly and both constables made for the door.

"Wait!" Peter shouted. "You can't just—"

And could have bitten his tongue out. In their faces he read uniform contempt. But, as it turned out, they had different reasons.

Jones said, still in the same mild tone, but now it sounded sinister, like an inquisitor's: "In case you hadn't heard, hundreds of people were killed by the falling debris and thousands were rendered homeless. Mainly they've been camping out in schools. But term starts next week, so they've got to move. You ought to keep up with the news. Dependent children are to be cared for by their nearest able-bodied relatives. Since yesterday, that's the law. And in Ellen's case that means you."

And Prentis: "Anyway, it's your responsibility, isn't it? Serves you bocky right in any case! Same as anyone who fucks around with niggers! Traitor to your country, that's what you are, 'spite of that ribbon on your shirt!"

*Slam.*

And they were gone, leaving Peter to contemplate the ruin of a thousand dreams.

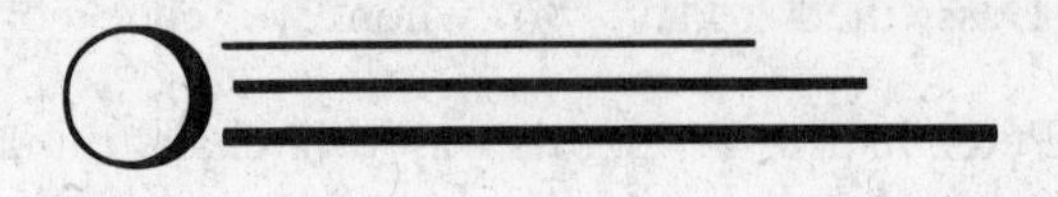

*M*orning, Dad—morning, Mum!" cried Terry Owens as he rushed into the kitchen accompanied by a whiff of expensive aftershave. He wasn't of an age to shave yet, actually, but it was the style.

"Morning, dear," his mother Renee replied over her shoulder as she refilled the teapot after pouring the first cups. Then, turning: "Is that a new jacket?"

"Mm-hm." The boy's mouth was already crowded with cornflakes. "Like it?"

Renee suppressed a sigh. To her current fashions, such as they were, looked like something bought off a second-hand cart, but . . . "I'm sure it's very nice, dear," she said diplomatically. And added, "You'll get indigestion if you gobble like that! Do you want an egg?"

His cereal bowl nearly empty, Terry shook his head. After swallowing, he answered, "This'll have to do. I'm late. 'Bye!"

"Will you be back for—?"

She had been going to say lunch, but her son's feet were already clattering down the stairs.

After a pause, she said, "I'm worried about our Terry. He's changed so much in the past few months."

Not looking up from his newspaper, her husband Brian grunted, " 'Sonly natural. It's the normal time. And I'd say the change is for the better. He doesn't get picked on at this school the way he did at his last one. Matter of fact he's got more mates than I ever had at his age. Older than he is, too. Must mean they respect him, right?"

"Yes, but . . ." Renee bit her lip, sitting down and stirring sugar into her tea, eyes fixed on nowhere. "I do worry. Can't help it. I mean, *another* new jacket! And all those tapes he buys! Where does he get the money?"

"Not from us!" Brian snapped. "We've been all over this a dozen times! We've never come up short on the takings, 'cept a pound or two that was probably due to Sarah giving someone the wrong change." He meant the girl who helped out in their grocery shop on Saturdays. "Reminds me—how are we doing for time?" With a glance at his watch. "Oh, that's all right. Be a love and pour me another cuppa."

Complying, she persisted, "But even so—"

"Look!" Wearily Brian laid aside his paper. "He *works* for his money! He's told us! Isn't he out all day Saturday and Sunday, and most evenings too, doing odd jobs around the neighborhood? Shows a proper sense of responsibility, to my mind. Better than having him come whining to us day in, day out, saying, 'So-and-so at school has this and that, why can't I have it too?' Isn't it?"

"Oh, I admit that, but even so—"

"All right, I know it's not strictly legal and all that, not at his age, but he hangs out with these older boys and they split the take with him. That's what mates are for. You pull your weight, they take care of you. Anyway, it's all cash-in-hand stuff. What the eye doesn't see . . ."

He drank most of his tea at a gulp and rose, wiping his lips.

"Right, time to go and let Sarah in. See you downstairs in a minute. Don't be too long—there's bound to be the usual rush."

On the other side of the street was a corner shop, formerly and for a brief while owned by a guy in videotape rental, that had been boarded up for the past six months. Its closure being a memorial of their only failure to date, Terry insisted on meeting his oppos in the recess of its doorway, to remind them where they'd be without him.

This morning, though, they were waiting for him outside.

A single glance explained the reason: some cank had bocked all over it last night, and it reeked.

"We'll put in a complaint about that," Terry muttered. "Offense to public health, or something. I'll ring up about it later, get it seen to."

He was very good at affecting an adult voice and manner on the phone. He could mimic an angry member of the upper crust to near-perfection. Also he knew more about what could be done, even nowadays, even by people at the bottom of the heap, to force official action, than almost anyone in the area. The harassed careers master at his school, whose failure rate in finding jobs for the leavers was now seventy percent, had once said quite seriously, "I shan't need to worry when it's your turn, Terry! You're practically a one-man Citizens' Advice Bureau already!"

Terry knew what he meant, but the other kids in earshot had had to ask, the CABs having been abolished as hotbeds of anti-government subversion.

His oppos—the regular ones—numbered three. Barney had not been baptized Barnabas; he'd earned his name thanks to his fondness for a fight. Built the way he was, and weighing twice as much as Terry, he generally won. Sometimes Terry worried what would happen if he started to generally lose. Taff was called Taff for the usual reason, because he came from Wales; he was much given to asking people who poked fun at his accent whether he didn't have a better right to British streets than the Packies and the Windies, and leaving his mark on those who disagreed. The third one, the oldest—nearly eighteen—was known as Rio because he affected embossed leather boots and a matador hat his father had brought back from Spain and liked to talk about fighting off the topless talent on the beach at Benidorm, regardless of the fact that owing to the slump the bottom had dropped out of the package tour trade and he had never been further from home than Whitley Bay—where he had bought the knife he carried in his right boot.

Terry had cultivated them with care, and between them they added up to a formidable force.

But today he had a bone or two to pick with them.

"All right, business!" he announced in his precociously deep voice. "Rio, what's this I hear about your not taking out Mr. Lee's dustbins? How often have I told you? We've got to be seen to be doing *something!* We've got to show legit! It's not hard graft, is it? He's good for fifteen smackers and all it takes is fifteen minutes. Or isn't a maggie a minute enough for you?"

Abashed before the younger boy's piercing stare, Rio shifted from foot to foot. "He wouldn't let me," he muttered. "Said he won't pay up this week. Or ever again."

"Why, the bocky slope!" Terry exclaimed. Mr. Lee owned the fish-and-chip shop and Chinese takeaway: a thin, perpetually worried man with a short fat wife and a platoon of interchangeable small children with flat faces and inscrutable expressions, who peeked at the customers from behind a curtain.

"Same with Mr. Lal!" Taff exclaimed. Lal was the Indian who ran the newsagent-tobacconist-confectioner's shop. Its window was covered with iron grilles because of repeated attacks by Pakistanis. The grumbling war on the subcontinent had spun off many such far-distant clashes. He spoke with the accent called "Bombay Welsh" and Taff delighted in mocking it. Doing so now, he added, " 'So sorry, mister sir! It is not good enough takings any more for you carry out my unsold papers!' "

"I think they're ganging up on us," rumbled Barney, and a grin parted the punch-broadened lips beneath his twice-broken nose. "What are we going to do about it, Terry?"

By now they were strolling down the street. Early shoppers parted nervously to let them by, even if it meant pushing prams and strollers into the roadway. The boys took no notice.

"Well, I think I'd better tell Mr. Lee that I know the flashpoint of commercial frying-oil, don't you?" Terry said after a moment for thought. "And I know what burns at a higher temperature!"

Rio chuckled. Barney looked disappointed. That sort of thing was too indirect to suit his taste.

"And," Terry went on, "I'd better explain to Mr. Lal that people who don't get their papers won't pay him. We know all the kids who deliver for him, don't we? Catch?"

Taff pondered a moment, figured out the connection, and gave a double thumbs-up sign accompanied by a broad smile.

"*And*," Terry concluded, "I think I'll also tell them that their weekly touch goes up to twenty in future, for acting so bocky."

At that even Barney looked pleased again, and they parted on the best of terms.

Just as Brian was closing the shop that evening, there came a tap at the door. Prepared to bellow, "Sorry, too late!", he recognized the caller through the glass and was taken aback. He knew Mr. Lee by sight, of course, but he and his family kept themselves entirely to themselves, which was the way most people in the area preferred it. Never before had he called here. And, by the expression on his face, it wasn't in the way of custom.

Opening the door, he said uncertainly, "Good evening, Mr. Lee. What is it?"

"It's about your son. May I please talk for a moment?"

Brian hesitated. Then he muttered, "All right. Come on upstairs."

"Evening, Mum! Evening, Dad!" Terry called as he rushed into the sitting room.

And stopped dead in the doorway. The TV was on, as usual, but the sound was muted. And there was a visitor.

His heart pounded. This smelt of crisis!

*How long have they had by themselves?*

But his mother was saying, "Would you like a cup of tea, Mr. Lee? I don't suppose it'll be like what you have in China, of course."

Relief flooded Terry's mind, and he felt a sudden sense of calm control. That was a sign that Mr. Lee could only just have arrived; offering tea to a visitor was a kneejerk reflex with his mother, the first thing she thought of after "let me take your coat" and "please sit down."

Brian was saying, "Mr. Lee said he wanted to talk about you, Terry."

"Oh, good!" The boy advanced, taking Mr. Lee's hand and shaking it warmly. "And I bet I know what he's going to say! Let me see if I'm right! He's come to say how pleased he is with the work me and my friends do for him—isn't that right, Mr. Lee? He's come to say that because he finds us so helpful he's going to up our pay—isn't that right, Mr. Lee? *Isn't it?*"

He could practically feel the man's toes curling inside his shoes. After a pause, dully:

"Yes. Yes, that is right. Thank you, missis, but I think I won't stay for tea. Now you know, I will have to get back. We open in half an hour. Excuse me."

And he headed for the stairs.

"Well!" Renee said, staring after him. "That was a funny sort of call, I must say!"

"Ah, you never know where you are with the Oriental mind," Terry declared authoritatively. "They think differently from us—says so in all the books . . . What's for tea? I'm starving!"

Later, as he was changing to go out for the evening, he reflected: *They can't think all that differently, of course. Even a slope like him knows which side his bread is buttered—No, they don't eat bread, do they? What would they say? Which side to sauce their noodles?*

And that was good for a laugh with his oppos when they met up later at their usual pub, whose landlord knew better than to try and keep Terry out for being under the legal drinking age.

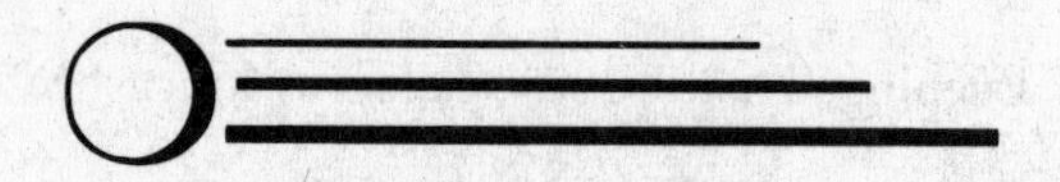

*You're watching TV Plus. Now for Newsframe.*

*The inquiry into the disaster that rendered hundreds of people homeless in Carlisle last year has been told that the explosion was caused by an oversight when scaling up a chemical reaction from laboratory to commercial scale. A firm bottling mineral water, forced to cease trading by contamination of natural springs, is to sue the company responsible, Flixotrol, for a million pounds in damages.*

*In Tottenham, London, today a black youth was beaten nearly to death for refusing to wear a Thrower ribbon. Wilfred Holder, 17 . . .*

The following week turned out, in fact, to be not quite as terrible as Peter had envisaged during those awful minutes after the police marched out and slammed the door.

Not *quite* . . .

But that was a minor consolation for having this stranger hung around his neck. He thought of pendants strung with millstones.

Bad was finding himself reduced to living and working in an even smaller area than at his old home, for Ellen had to have a room to herself. The social worker, who duly appeared next morning, left a stack of leaflets in which, she declared, he would find the regulations that made it obligatory. Her attitude indicated that she suspected him of planning to rape his daughter as soon as she left.

And of course the petty annoyances were endless—like having to don a dressing gown on his way to and from the bathroom. He didn't own pajamas, hadn't since he was a kid himself, and had grown reflexively used to walking naked round his home, for if anybody else was there, she'd likely shared his bed the night before.

Worse, though, was having to turn down the next really juicy assignment offered by TV Plus. According to rumor, rabid rats had arrived in Kent through the pilot workings for the Channel Tunnel. During its final series *Continuum* had covered hydrophobia, which year by year was drawing closer to the coast of France, so Peter would have been an ideal choice to handle the story. Instead, he had to plead helplessly, "Ellen's a victim of the Heathrow disaster—I've got to find a school for her, can't leave her by herself because she's far too young, and anyway after what she's been through . . ."

"I'll have to try someone else, then!"

*Click.*

With which, the prospect of a company car receded over the horizon.

Yet maybe worst of all was the fact that this timid, fawn-eyed creature, this fragile worse-than-orphaned plaything of malevolent chance—this not-yet person whose existence was admittedly his fault—was so desperate to please! She didn't want to be what she realized she was: a nuisance. So she begged to be allowed to keep out of his way, to do the washing-up, to launder her own pitifully few clothes which he had to supplement on much-resented shopping trips, to sit immobile in front of the TV wearing headphones so he wouldn't be disturbed by the sound . . .

No. That wasn't the worst. *The* worst was when the suspicion stole into his mind that he might have been better off had he coaxed Kamala out of her fit of fury after she found out about—well, what he'd done that made her lose all patience with him. He had been very fond of her: a slim and pretty nurse, met while he was a medical student. Then thanks to a terrible mischance . . .

He shut out the notion, or rather tried to. Against his best attempts, images leaked through of what his life might have been like by now: as a GP with an established practice and a supportive wife, a daughter at the local school—

*Stop! They'd have been stoning me on the streets!*

If WPC Prentis was anyone to go by . . .

Some problems evaporated with amazing swiftness. He had paid no attention at the time, but among the selling points listed by the estate agents through whom he had bought his new flat (and when was his old one going to be sold? "For Sale" signs were infecting London like measle spots, and as if he didn't have enough trouble already, one prospective buyer had been ruled ineligible for so large a mortgage, so he was the involuntary owner of two homes!) had been the fact that there was still a school within walking distance. He visited it with Ellen, told her story to the head teacher, and met with nothing but sympathy. Strings would have to be pulled, and she might have to join her class a week late, but—well, it could be arranged.

That marked the first time when he consulted his daughter's opinion directly, apart from trivia such as what to buy for dinner. There in the head teacher's office he reached out for her hand and asked, "Will it be all right if you come here?"

Her eyes were still puffy; most nights he heard her cry herself to sleep, and more than once she'd woken screaming from a nightmare full of burning houses. But she smiled and returned the squeeze he gave her fingers.

"Yes, Dad. I think I could get on here very well."

It was that evening, when he'd cobbled up a meal, that for the first time he called her to it saying, "Darling! It's ready!"

Followed the first time that she kissed him good night.

Next day she ventured the news that at her former school she had been taught how to run a computer. Was there any chance . . . ? Because having watched him at work—

He had a spare one he'd been planning to sell when he found a customer. Well, it wouldn't have fetched much more than scrap price anyhow. He plugged it in; it proved to be still functional. When he said it was hers she hugged him—for the first time—and thereafter seemed quite content to sit alone in her room and play with it. Or watch his old television, or listen to his old stereo. Sometimes, too, she asked to borrow one of his old books, saying she'd never seen so many except in a public library.

*Reach-me-downs.*

It wasn't right, yet the phrase rang in his head. He recalled it not from his own childhood but from what he had been told about then. It seemed to imply something he couldn't quite define.

Not, at least, until resonance from it led him to another half-forgotten term:

*Latch-key kid.*

In other words, a child who returned from school to an empty house because both parents were still at work. He'd been one himself, though fortunately for a very brief while after his father left his mother for another woman . . .

That put him on the phone to the head teacher again, in search of someone prepared to mind children during the late afternoon. Yes, there was such a service, owing to the high incidence of single parents in the area.

The fees were disproportionate. Recklessly he committed himself to meeting them on the grounds that if he were not free to work he couldn't pay for a dependent, which and who so ever. And when he asked Ellen how things had gone during the first day at her new school, and whether she had been properly looked after before he returned, she gave a nod, and then a surprising grin, and hugged him again.

*Maybe Kamala wasn't doing quite such a good job after all . . . Job! Mine is turning out to be a brute! Keeping me up until all hours—!*

Back to it. Right now, with Ellen apparently content to turn in early and leave him to get on with it.

Apparently. That didn't mean truly. Did it?

In spite of all, however, he felt an absurd sense of achievement as he sat at his desk after dinner, sorting out his commitments for the morrow. There was a warm glow in the back of his mind, as though he had passed some particularly daunting interview for a new post.

Things were falling tidily into place in spite of all. Now Ellen was going to school, now the teachers and even apparently the pupils were showing sympathy about her loss—she was invited to a tea party on Saturday (weird, *weird* to look at his on-screen list of engagements and see another set of commitments listed alongside his own!)—now he could set aside his more ridiculous worries and get back to making plans. For instance, the *Comet* was still afloat and rumor had it that extra money was being pumped in. Before the transfusion dried up he stood a chance of—

"Dad?"

In Ellen's usual diffident tone, redolent of insecurity. He turned to her with a sigh.

"Dad, I'm dreadfully sorry, but I'm bleeding! I got undressed and went to bed, and I was half asleep when I found I'd made a dreadful mess on the sheets! Mum warned me to expect it about now, but I never thought . . . ! *I'm sorry!*"

And a wail, and tears she struggled to repress.

It was something that had never struck Peter before because he had never lived with a woman. He had only been frustrated by it during an affair. Naturally, being a nurse, Kamala had taught Ellen the facts of life, but between the theory and the reality—!

Yet of course one knew in the abstract that the onset was sometimes precipitated by stress. What worse stress than the disaster she had undergone?

He improvised. He felt when the task was over he had improvised exceptionally well. The new woman was provided with cottonwool to staunch the flow and a tight pair of panties to hold the pad in place, albeit she must spend tonight in a tattered sleeping-bag and he had to revise his schedule for tomorrow yet *again* to take account of a long visit to the launderette . . .

But he had cuddled her, and asked if she was in pain, which she was not, and remembered that Kamala too had often been taken by surprise (one time in bed . . .) and made her a cup of reassuring tea, and left her watching the TV, and generally impressed himself with his ability to cope.

*If only it matched my ability to make a living I'd be quids in, home and dry!*

The telephone rang.

"Oh, shit! *Yes?*"

Cool, detached, a woman with an American accent: "You sound as though you have as many problems as I do."

Blocks of awareness clashed inside Peter's head like icebergs. He blurted, "Claudia Morris!"

"Yes. Were you expecting my call? Were you sufficiently in touch to hear before I did that another bastion of rationality has fallen?"

"I . . ." But it was stupid to explain. Instead he parried, as though caught up in a pointless fencing match.

"How did you trace me? I've moved!"

"Ach!" And a sound like spitting. "I was wrong on more points than one! I thought this country was webbed with secrecy. Only your government is armored. You want to find out about a private citizen's affairs? You grease the proper palm—"

"*Don't say such things on the phone!*"

"They got you snagged along with all the rest, did they? Then I bet you're wearing a red-white-and-blue ribbon on your business suit these days—like a good boy!"

"Claudia, for God's sake—!"

"Stuff the paranoia." Her tone was suddenly shrill. "I need to talk to you, and analysis of intercepted calls is exponential. Listening to what our people and yours recorded last year alone would take till Doomsday. I want you to meet me at—"

"I can't!"

"Ah, they trod on you, too. Well, too bad. I'm very sorry for you."

"*Wait!*"—at the last moment halving his volume so as not to disturb Ellen.

"And for why?"

"You haven't told me why you want to talk to me!"

"You didn't hear? The puky funders got the better of the other funders—"

"Oh. Wait. I think I do know what you mean. But I haven't been keeping up with the news."

"It's your profession, isn't it?"—mockingly.

"I got lumbered! My daughter!"

"That doesn't sound like the most fatherly of—"

"Oh, stop it, will you? Her periods started tonight and I've been trying to comfort her."

There was a pause. Eventually Claudia said, "I'm sorry. I didn't realize you were married."

"I'm not. In fact"—he sought the antique phrase that hovered in a distant corner of his mind, and trapped it as a hawk might catch its prey—"she's a byblow. But her home was burnt out in the Heathrow disaster, so I've taken her in charge."

Next time Claudia spoke, her tone was noticeably more cordial.

"I still want to talk to you. In fact I need to talk to you. Can you meet me at—?"

"Come out this evening? You must be precessing with all your gyros! Leave on her tod a kid who's having her first period? More likely I'll be sitting up beside her bed!"

"Then can I come to your place?"

Peter thought for a long moment, torn between duties. Eventually professionalism won.

"All right," he sighed. "What time?"

"I can make it in about half an hour."

"Okay. Let me tell you how to get here—"

She cut him short.

"If I didn't know how to find you, how could I have called you up? But don't worry. All record of the circuits I used will self-erase the moment I put down this phone . . . Oh! One other thing!"

"Yes?"—impatiently, for he found Ellen's large sad eyes on him.

"What computer do you have?"

He named it.

"That's fine, then. I'll bring a disk with me. I think you'll be interested . . . See you in half an hour."

Ellen needed more cottonwool. The flow was considerable for a first time. When it was stanched she asked whether she must go back to bed immediately. Feeling as though, if he insisted, she would regard it as a rejection, he said she could wait up until his visitor arrived. At once she curled up on the couch beside him, to watch the TV news.

*Who am I? Where am I? Am I caught in a trap worse than the worst my nightmare could contrive, or am I on the verge of a breakthrough that will make my name and reputation? Worst of all: am I on the track of a major story that I can't follow through because of Ellen?*

*She's a sweet kid. She's so nice she's made me regret not patching matters up with Kamala. But nonetheless she feels like shackles!*

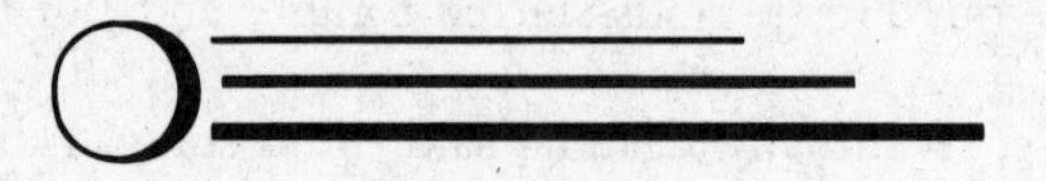

Renato Tessolari was immensely proud of his son—his only child—GianMarco. As he was fond of saying, the boy had his own black hair and his wife Constanza's brown eyes, even though there was little noticeable resemblance in other respects.

And to think he had been born after seven fruitless years! When Renato was indeed beginning to fear that the fault might lie on his side, for he had had his share of youthful escapades, and not once had any of the girls he'd lain with . . .

Well, in the end it had turned out for the best. And he owed a tremendous debt to GianMarco's uncle, his brother-in-law Fabio Bonni, who knew so much about advances in modern science and had suggested that Constanza visit England, where doctors were making amazing new discoveries in the field of infertility.

The treatment had been like a miracle! Within a month of her return she had come smiling to him to report her pregnancy, and it was as though a colossal weight receded from his mind.

For, without an heir in the direct line, what would happen to the estates the Tessolari family had owned since the seventeenth century? They would pass perhaps to cousins—but most of them were in the north, making money in ways far removed from Mother Earth. Not for them the patient cycle of the seasons, pressing oil, treading grapes, reaping maize, drying tomatoes. No, they preferred the hustle and bustle of big cities: Milan, Turin, Marghera. The ancient traditions of the *Mezzogiorno* had grown alien to them, as though they were foreigners in their own homeland, and if the estates fell to them as an inheritance they would be most concerned about how soon and for how much they could be sold.

So at least Renato felt, and loudly and vigorously Fabio concurred, occasionally winking unnoticed at Constanza.

In turn, little by little, GianMarco learned to be proud of his father. When he was eight or nine, he began to understand the workings of the adult world; by the time he was ten, he fully appreciated the fact that—because his family had been landowners here for so long—no decision was taken by the town council that might infringe Tessolari interests. Renato was of course a councillor himself, and had been mayor. So had his father, his grandfather, and countless of his uncles. And the family's influence extended to the provincial level, too, and even as far as Rome.

What was more, there were other matters he was encouraged to take pride in. The rambling house where he grew up might have patches of stucco missing from its façade—but it had once sheltered one of Garibaldi's agents on a secret mission. The cars his parents owned might be commonplace Fiats rather than spectacular Ferraris—but Great-great-grandfather Ruggiero had been the first person in the region to possess a car, and many were the amusing stories related about how the peasants panicked when a carriage with no horse to draw it rolled down their streets.

Nonetheless, he sometimes asked Renato why the family was no longer so exceptionally rich as it must have been in old Ruggiero's day, and was always rewarded by the same lecture concerning the true nature of wealth. "Suppose," his father would say sententiously, "there were another economic crisis. Money might be worthless again, as it has so often been in the past. Then you'd see our 'wealthy' relatives come crawling to us for help—to us who can grow food! *That's* the ultimate source of all riches: the land. I shan't be around for ever, you know. But I shall leave you the finest patrimony anybody could wish for. Now come along. We have to visit"—and he'd name one of the tenant farmers, perhaps because he was growing slack about his duties, perhaps because a member of his family was sick and he needed a loan to pay the doctor. With his tenants, Renato behaved as he did toward his son: strictly or leniently as the occasion called for. When the boy was twelve, and therefore of an age to be involved (and moreover he had physically entered manhood), he was permitted to sit in a corner while his father held discussions with his bailiffs, and heard him utter judgment: this man was feckless and must be turned out, but this other who had done worse yet had after all lost his wife last year and not yet found another, so he could be forgiven . . .

GianMarco preened, looking forward to the time when he too could assist his father in such weighty matters.

His chance came sooner than he had expected.

One day in the autumn of that same year, when the harvest was in, Renato drove him to visit relatives in a town fifty kilometers away. His mother did not go with them, allegedly because she felt unwell—yet she had shown no sign of illness. However, her brother was at home to keep her company, so . . . And off they went: two men together, as Renato chaffed.

Something intangible conveyed to GianMarco that for the first time he was directly involved in adult business. He waited in excitement to discover what it was.

They stayed late. It was full dark before they set out homeward—

and then they took a slightly different route. At first GianMarco was puzzled. Then, little by little, he started to recognize the area they were traversing. They were on land that did not belong to the Tessolaris or any of their friends. Abandoned at the end of World War II, it had been taken over by a peasant cooperative. It was rich soil—as rich went in the hot dry south of Italy—and there were several long-established olive groves and vineyards on it. Consequently the old families whose lands abutted it had spent fortunes in lawsuits designed to dispossess those they regarded as mere squatters. But courts in distant Rome, after years of litigation, declared they had no valid claim, and authorized the former landless peasants to grow rich, put on airs, and ape their betters.

This had been taught to GianMarco, in detail and with considerable bitterness. His uncle Fabio, in particular, was contemptuous of the peasants' aspirations. Once when GianMarco had dared to ask why he was still a bachelor at forty, he had admitted that his own people, the Bonni, had lost a claim to the land now being farmed cooperatively, and had it not been for his sister's fortunate marriage he might have been poverty-stricken by now. As it was, thanks to his suggestion that Constanza visit England for treatment, he was a welcome resident in the Tessolari house.

(Behind this colorable tale there was a hint of something darker. GianMarco had occasionally overheard servants joking about certain handsome boys that Fabio took up as friends and dropped abruptly after bestowing gifts on them without avail . . . but this was nothing he could understand.)

And lately it had emerged that for some reason to do with fertilizers or other chemicals, or some such kind of modern aids to husbandry which Renato had enthusiastically adopted under Fabio's guidance, the buyer from Genoa whose firm had for half a century purchased olive oil from the Tessolari estate at an advantageous price, had this year offered more to the cooperative, on the grounds that theirs could be exported to the health-conscious USA as "organically" grown.

This was of course an affront not to be tolerated.

It began to dawn on GianMarco's drowsy mind what his father was about when the car headed down a dry bumpy track toward an isolated barn. Here was where the cooperative kept its oil-press and storage vats . . .

It must, he guessed, be after midnight. Never before had he been allowed to stay up so late, not even in the tolerant environment of Mediterranean culture. He tried to read his watch, but his father had switched off the car's lights and the sky was overcast. He concluded:

*This is indeed men's business!*

The realization sent a frisson down his spine and jolted him back to wakefulness.

"You wait here," Renato said curtly as he brought the car to a halt and got out. "And remember! If anybody asks you—I'm not saying who, mind, but if *anybody* asks you—we drove straight home from Anna's. Is that understood?"

"Yes!" GianMarco breathed, and stared with aching eyes as the blurred shadow of his father faded into the shadow that was the looming barn.

Two men greeted him—GianMarco heard their voices—and then all became darkness and mystery.

Trembling, expecting he knew not what except that his imagination kept offering pictures of an open valve at the bottom of a huge vat full of oil (would it be set on fire or simply left to drain? He thought the latter but it was a guess), GianMarco sat in the car alone for five or seven minutes.

Then there was a shot.

And a scream.

And a sense of frenzied running.

And his father was back beside him, starting the engine, backing up, sawing his way on to the track again, and all the while cursing in language GianMarco had never thought would pass his lips. Amid the torrent of obscenity the boy gathered that the stinking peasants had been so impressed by the high price their oil was to command this year they had arranged for members of the cooperative to sleep in the barn, turn and turn about, and guard their treasure.

And tonight's watchman had been fool enough to wake and intervene.

GianMarco tried not to visualize the bloody mess a shotgun at close range would make of a human body.

"Remember!" his father was insisting as the car bounced crazily toward the metalled road. "We drove straight home tonight! We drove straight back from Anna's!"

"Yes, father," GianMarco said composedly. For, after all, what mattered one blockheaded peasant more or less?

He was sent to bed immediately on arriving home, but for a long while he was too excited to sleep. His room was above the hallway where the main telephone was kept; by straining his ears he could hear Renato speaking to Anna, instructing her that he and GianMarco had in fact left twenty minutes later than in reality.

*This is like being in a gangster film!*

Then, perhaps roused by the unavoidable click of the extension phone in her bedroom, his mother went downstairs and at once divined that something was amiss. Renato tried to convince her he was phoning Anna only to let her know they had reached home safely, but she didn't believe his story. Within minutes she had either pried out the truth, or guessed it. After that there was no need to strain to listen, for a full-blown shouting match developed. It roused Fabio, who joined them and tried with small success to calm things down.

"Our only son!" Constanza kept shouting. "A twelve-year-old boy! And you risked his life! Suppose there had been more than one guard? Suppose they'd been armed, and fired back?"

"But there wasn't, and they weren't!" Renato bellowed. "Now will you shut up and go back to bed? I have more calls to make—urgent calls!"

In the end, Constanza let Fabio usher her away. By then she was crying. Hearing her sobs, for the first time GianMarco realized the seriousness of the situation. Someone had been shot and maybe killed, by one of his father's men, raiding the cooperative's barn on his orders and in his presence. In Ruggiero's time no doubt it would have been easy to arrange a cover-up. Nowadays, even though Renato was a councillor and former mayor, it might not be so simple.

In which case—he clenched his fists under the bedclothes as he heard his father's increasingly despairing voice below—what would become of him? Oh, obviously he and his mother and uncle, and Anna, would lie to protect Renato . . . but what if the truth came out some other way, say because one of the men panicked or had a fit of conscience? Or because the seal of the confessional proved less sacred than it used to be? The incumbent priest was an outsider from Foggia, allegedly assigned here as punishment for holding radical views, a suggestion borne out by his popularity with members of the cooperative. He would show scant sympathy toward the Tessolaris.

If the facts did emerge, then those who had told lies would also be criminals, wouldn't they? He himself might be sent to a reformatory! His mother and uncle might be jailed, and his father most assuredly!

Visions of the house being lost, along with the estates that were promised to him, assailed GianMarco's mind. No, it was unthinkable! It must not happen!

He fell at last into uneasy slumber.

And was roused not long after dawn by the sound of engines. Running to the window, he saw black-clad men on motorcycles escorting a police car. When it halted the first passenger to get out carried a submachine gun, and the second was the *Maresciallo*, the local chief of police, a frequent visitor to the Tessolari house—but only when off duty.

*No!*

The word sounded so clearly in GianMarco's mind, he imagined for an instant that he had spoken it aloud. But it was only the focus of a sudden resolve that had gripped him, like a shiver that began and never ended.

*No, they are not going to arrest my family like common criminals!* Frantically he dragged on his clothes and rushed downstairs.

Getting dressed had been a mistake.

GianMarco realized that as soon as he reached the hall. The only other person in the house who was out of bed yet was his family's maid, Giuseppina, who had answered the door; she was always up first, to light the kitchen stove and prepare breakfast. If this were a perfectly normal day, as they must pretend, what was he doing with his clothes on at this hour?

Well, it was too late to do anything about it now, except act for all he was worth.

"Good morning, *Signor Maresciallo!*" he exclaimed. "The noise of the motorbikes awakened me, so I thought I'd come down and see if anything exciting is going on!"

The *Maresciallo*, a stout man growing bald, with a thick black moustache, favored him with a scowl.

"What kids your age think exciting isn't anything we grown-ups greatly care for," he rumbled. "It's a nasty business that's brought me here, a very nasty business . . . Giuseppina, I must request you to rouse Signor Tessolari and say I want to talk to him. Immediately!"

Eyes wide with dismay and alarm, Giuseppina assured him she would do so. Asking him to take a seat in the drawing room, she departed with muttered promises of coffee in a little while.

Uncertain, GianMarco remained in the hall until she came down again and retreated to the kitchen. A minute or two later Renato also descended the stairs, belting a dressing gown around him. His face was like a statue's, but there was no hint of a tremor in his voice when he called out.

"You're up early, young fellow! I'd have thought after coming home so late last night you'd sleep till noon! What's all this about the *Maresciallo* being here, and with an armed guard?"

"It's quite true," GianMarco confirmed. "He's waiting in there"—with a nod at the door, which Giuseppina had left ajar.

"Hmm! Sounds ominous! You'd better hang on while I find out what's the matter."

Shamelessly eavesdropping, GianMarco heard him greet the police chief and ask what brought him.

"There was an attack on the barn at the cooperative last night," came the answer. "A man was shot."

"You don't mean dead!"—in properly horrified tones.

"Not yet, though the doctors don't expect him to live. But he's conscious, and . . ."

A solemn pause.

"And what?"

"And he has made a deposition to the effect that he recognized the man who shot him. Luigi Renzo. One of your tenants."

"But that's ridiculous! How could he be sure? There was no moon last night, as I know very well. It so happens that I took GianMarco to visit my sister-in-law Anna—you know Anna, of course—and we didn't get back until late. That's why I was so surprised to find my son up and about. I suppose it was the noise that woke him."

"He came to ask if anything exciting was going on."

"Well, it sounds as though there is. But if the man with the gun was recognized as Renzo, why are you here instead of at his place?"

"Oh, I've sent another detachment after him," said the *Maresciallo.* "I'm here because the victim also says he overheard three men talking —that's what alerted him. And," he concluded with deliberation, "he says one of the voices was yours."

"But that's absurd!"

"When I left the hospital he was about to receive Extreme Unction. Men who know they are dying don't generally lie. In addition, we found tire-tracks in the dust near where he was shot. They match exactly those on your own car."

How different his tone and manner were from his usual joviality! GianMarco found himself starting to tremble.

"Now you said you came back late from visiting your sister-in-law. I know where she lives. Your direct route would have taken you not across the cooperative but down a road alongside it . . . Hmm! How late is 'late'?"

"I suppose we returned about half past midnight."

"And the attack took place just after twelve. You must have been within earshot when the gun—"

"Now look here!" Renato jumped to his feet. "I see what you're implying, and I don't like it! I drove directly home! GianMarco, are you still there? Come and tell the *Maresciallo* what happened on the way home last night!"

Unable to avoid a show of timidity, GianMarco entered the room.

"Nothing happened," he said flatly. "We drove straight home, just as Papa says."

And the coldness that had overtaken him increased, as though something within him had seized control of his voice, his motions, his very thoughts.

The *Maresciallo* uttered a disbelieving grunt. "Were you awake in the car?" he began, and somehow seemed to give up expecting an answer as soon as the words were out. GianMarco had fixed him with his gaze and laid a pleading hand on his arm as though this man were still the avuncular family friend he was used to.

"*Signor Maresciallo*, you know my father is an honorable man. He wouldn't descend to such an awful deed! I agree that men who know they are dying don't usually lie—but aren't there exceptions? Even if he has received Extreme Unction he may not be an honest believer. Aren't many of the members of the cooperative communists and even atheists? He could easily be lying about hearing my father's voice because he sees it as a way of settling a grudge—after all, we old families aren't exactly popular in radical circles, are we? Besides, he could simply have been mistaken. It was certainly very dark, and if he was aroused from sleep, which I take to be the case since the hour was so late, he must have been confused. I say *must*, because my father definitely was not there. I was with him the whole time, and as he says we came straight home. As for the tire-tracks—well, we're patrotic Italians! Just as we buy Fiat cars, we buy Pirelli tires! And they're sold by the millions, aren't they?"

With mingled amazement and relief he saw the police chief's expression of certainty fade away, until at the end of the speech he was shaking his head lugubriously.

"Yes, of course, you must be right. It was dark, as you say, and indeed many of the members of the cooperative are socialists or worse, and . . . Yes, what is it?"

He was facing the door. Around it Giuseppina was peering nervously. "Excuse me, *signori*," she blurted. "But one of the policemen has a message on the radio."

"Coming!"

When he returned, the *Maresciallo* looked positively embarrassed.

"It sounds as though I owe you an apology. Luigi Renzo didn't come home last night. Must have made a bolt for it. No doubt he's the genuine culprit. Well, I'm sorry to have disturbed you. I'll let you know when there's any news."

Replacing his uniform cap on his balding head, he left the house with a distracted air.

"What was all that about?" Constanza called from the upstairs landing, in a convincingly innocent tone for the benefit of Giuseppina, who was closing the front door.

"A dreadful thing happened. Apparently Luigi Renzo and someone else shot a man at the cooperative barn, not long before we got home. So the police came to ask whether we'd seen or heard anything suspicious."

"How dreadful!"—from Fabio, who had emerged from his room in time to catch the last few sentences. "Could you be of any help?"

"Neither I nor GianMarco, I'm afraid . . . Well, Giuseppina, where's our coffee?"

Later, when they were alone and could talk in confidence, Renato murmured to his son:

"When I said you couldn't be of any help, I meant to the *Maresciallo*, of course. You were the most amazing help to me. I never saw such a job of acting in my life! You practically convinced me, do you realize that? You practically had me believing what you said!"

GianMarco could only grin by way of answer. But he felt his chest swell with pride.

Old, family pride.

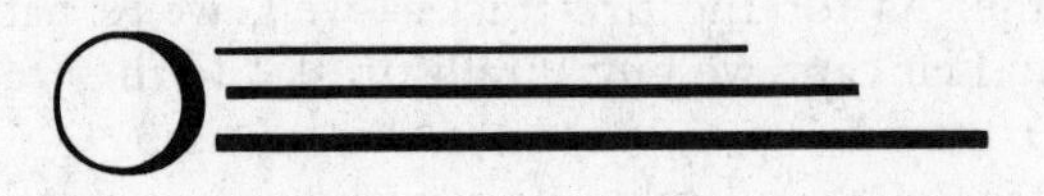

*You're watching TV Plus. Newsframe follows.*

*Last week's air crash in Tenerife has today been officially blamed on computer error, as was the recent collision over London Airport. A spokesman for the pilots' association, BALPA, criticized what he described as "greed" on the part of airline operators and "incompetence" on the part of air traffic controllers, rather than the computers.*

*Here in Britain, General Thrower's name seems set to become a generic term, like Hoover. A mob of youths sporting badges reading "I'm a Thrower" smashed and wrecked . . .*

In the upshot Claudia arrived not half an hour but a full hour later. Waiting for her, watching the news with Ellen at his side, Peter thought a lot about his daughter. In the past, as she had admitted, she had rarely bothered with the news. However, now that she had found out what her "dad's" profession was, she made a point of paying attention and showed, indeed, a lively interest.

*Nobody could accuse her of not trying!*

He had gathered the impression that she had been told almost nothing about him. She had been aware, for as long as she could remember, that her mother's husband wasn't her father, but this was a commonplace among her friends at school, so she had never worried much about it. And since Kamala never mentioned her paternity . . .

*At least I seem to be doing the right kind of thing.*

Now and then he asked whether she felt okay, and each time she forced a smile and nodded.

"It's only natural," was her verdict. "It was just a shock to find it happening to me, as well."

*And how many other things could one say the same of?*

* * *

The news bulletin consisted of the usual chapter of accidents and disasters, interspersed with adulation of the leaders who were going to put everything right tomorrow. A tower-block had been set on fire by a former mental patient discharged from a closed-down hospital under the guise of "returning her to the community." The price had been ten lives including hers. A street of houses was collapsing because water from an unmended pipe had washed away the subsoil from the foundations. A neglected bridge had given way. Two tankers containing chemicals that combusted spontaneously when mixed had fallen into the river below along with a bus; sixty people had burned or drowned. Yet more doubt had been cast on the viability of the Chunnel by a psychiatrist who had carried out tests at the Fréjus tunnel under the Alps on a group of long-distance lorry-drivers, normally supposed to be a stolid bunch. A third of them had declined to complete the four successive runs that he had asked of them, because they developed claustrophobia. Further inquiries had established that the same proportion of their colleagues had for some while past been refusing to travel that route. How many prospective users of the Chunnel would display the same symptoms?

During the current-affairs program that followed on another channel, a cabinet minister was sleekly pointing out that the psychiatrist was Italian and therefore not to be taken seriously, when the doorbell finally rang.

Claudia entered amid a storm of mingled curses and apologies. Apparently the minicab service her hosts relied on was owned by Tamil expatriates and tonight its headquarters had been firebombed as part of their running battle with the Sinhalese, so she had had to find an alternative.

*Another thread in life's rich tapestry . . .*

Ellen waited long enough to be introduced, then kissed Peter and disappeared to her own room again. Dropping a laden bag on the couch, Claudia nodded after her.

"Pretty kid! How does it feel to be a single parent?"

"She's making it easy for me," Peter grunted, switching off the TV. "Goodness knows how, after all the traumata she's been through."

"Tranquilizers?"

"Won't touch 'em. Kamala's influence—her mother, that is. She was a nurse. Ellen does have bad dreams, of course, and the social worker suggested sleepers, but she won't take them either. Wakes me sometimes in the small hours so I have to go and comfort her, but—well, they do say it's best not to repress grief, don't they? Do sit down! Care for a drink?"

"I wouldn't mind." Claudia leaned back, face eloquent of weariness, and ran her fingers through her pageboy hair.

"I haven't got much to offer, I'm afraid. My—ah—circumstances have changed rather radically. Scotch and water?"

"On the rocks. I need a kick in the *kishkas.*"

"Excuse me?"—thinking this was recent American slang he hadn't yet caught up with.

It was her turn to be confused. "Sorry! I took it for granted that with a name like Levin . . ."

Realization dawned. "Oh! Was that Yiddish? Did you think I was Jewish?"

"Well—uh—yes, as a matter of fact." For the first time Claudia seemed visibly embarrassed.

*Does she think she's offended me? No, I don't think so. More likely she's annoyed at having made a wrong guess.*

"You're not the first," he said lightly. "But in fact it's an old English name. Started out as Leofwine—'love-friend.' "

"Sorry anyway. Should have known better."

She remained silent and preoccupied while he poured the drinks. When he had delivered them and sat down in an armchair facing her, she resumed, "After our last encounter I imagine you were moderately angry with me, hm?"

"I wasn't overjoyed . . . Cheers."

"*L'chaim!* That's to make it clear that I *am* Jewish . . ." She took a sip and set the glass aside. "I can only say I had a lot on my mind. You did hear what happened at my university?"

"I haven't checked, but I can guess from what you told me. One of these fundamentalist takeovers, right?"

"One of the worst. I knew the dean and most of the senior faculty were soft in the brain, but I never expected them to cave in so quickly the moment I wasn't around."

"You were the prime target?"

"Of course. Aren't I the one who's been attacking Mom and apple pie?"

"So what exactly has happened?"

This time Claudia took a generous gulp of her whiskey before answering.

"The funders moved in with an offer of a million-dollar endowment for a department of 'creation science' "—she made the quote marks audible—"on condition that funding for my sabbatical was withdrawn and my tenure cancelled."

"Can they do that? I thought once you had tenure—"

"*Plus* whatever it might cost to contest any suit I bring against the university."

"I'd have thought it was cheaper and quicker to hire a Rambo squad," Peter muttered.

On the brink of saying something else, she checked. "You sounded almost serious!"

"Why not?"

"But I thought—"

"You thought Rambo squads were an invention of the media? That's what most Americans believe. No, they're real enough. They operate in groups of three, one firearms expert, one explosives expert, and a communications specialist . . . But I wasn't in fact being serious. Just cynical. More to the point: can't your friend Mr. Strugman help?"

"He may be rich," was the tart response, "but he's not that rich. For one thing, he's not as rich as he was—he's funded half a dozen lawsuits for us already. We won three and lost three. Win some, lose some . . . But he is prepared to underwrite my year in Britain, bless him."

"Ah, you're staying on. With the friends who are putting you up?"

"Scarcely"—with a sour smile. " 'Guests and fish stink after three days.' In any case, my hosts have problems. My hostess's sister died yesterday, after cutting herself with a kitchen knife."

"Good grief! Was she a hemophiliac?"

Shaking her head, Claudia emptied her glass. "She contracted antibiotic-resistant toxemia from beef that she was cutting up for a stew. Her family can sue, of course, but would you bet on their chance of winning?" She set the empty glass down with an angry slam and Peter rose hastily to refill it. He wanted Claudia in this expansive mood, and the whiskey seemed to be having a rapid effect.

Over his shoulder he said, "So what will you do?"

"I don't know. I don't want to waste Cecil's money, and renting in this burg is horribly expensive, yet if I move out to the suburbs I'll spend so much time commuting . . ."

"I think I have the answer," Peter interjected.

"Tell me!"—in excitement as she accepted the fresh drink.

"What say you take on my old place? It isn't much, just three tiny rooms, a place to cook and sort of a bathroom. A shower, at least. It's on the top floor, but I survived there for four years."

"You'll rent it to me? How much?"

"No, that's not what I had in mind." Peter resumed his chair. "I have to sell it—absolutely have to. In fact I thought I had, only the deal fell through." He didn't go into details. "What I think you ought to do is get a bank to buy it."

"A bank?" Claudia echoed incredulously.

"Precisely. In the eighties a lot of them moved into real estate, especially in London where property prices haven't gone down in more than a generation. Pretty soon they're going to own more of this town than the Duchy of Westminster . . . With Strugman to guarantee you, you should have no trouble. Go to a bank—my own is a pretty good bet—and say you want my flat for a year. They'll buy it. When you leave, they'll sell it, or rent it again. Like you said, there's a shortage of accommodation to let. All it'll cost you will be interest on the bank's investment, plus insurance and the running costs. It's a sight cheaper than ordinary renting, I promise you."

Her face was alight with enthusiasm. It made her look almost pretty—though Peter doubted she would be pleased were he to say so.

"Banks really do this?"

"A lot. Mainly for overseas investment companies who need one of their executives to spend a year in Britain. I could kick myself for not thinking of it before." He pulled a self-consciously comical face.

"That's wonderful! I'm so glad I came!" And, with a mercurial shift of mood: "Lord, I haven't even mentioned the reason I wanted to see you, have I?"

"Just a second before you get around to it. I ought to check that Ellen is okay."

On his return:

"Fast asleep, thank goodness. Let's hope it's all night this time. Being woken up in the small hours is making me understand how parents can be driven to batter a squalling baby . . . Well, what about the reason for your visit? You said you were going to bring a disk."

"Right here." She reached for her bag. "So if you'll boot your computer . . . ?"

"No sooner said than . . ."

But, as she was about to load the data, she hesitated. "In all fairness," she muttered, "I ought to warn you. This may give you still more sleepless nights."

"Certainly that's the effect it has on me."

And at that precise moment all the lights went off.

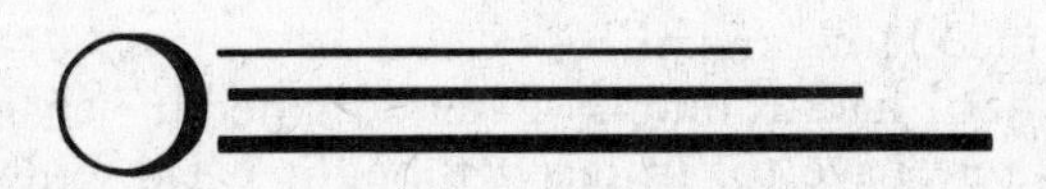

*N*ot yet fourteen, though she had the looks and manner of a sixteen-year-old, Tracy Coward was the youngest pupil in the top class of her school. But keeping company with her seniors had never troubled her. Nor did it seem to bother the other children, for she was extremely popular.

Well, she must be. That at any rate was the view of her adoring parents Matthew and Doreen. Was she not forever receiving presents, sometimes quite expensive ones? And not just from boyfriends, either, as might be expected, but from girls as well!

This morning was a school day. As ever Tracy rose in good time, despite a warning abdominal cramp—against which she took a pain-killer after she had cleaned her teeth—donned her uniform, made herself up with a hint of blusher, a line of eyebrow pencil, the merest trace of lipstick . . . and opened her treasure chest, as she called the drawer of her bedside table, to decide what extra touches to add.

Sooner or later, and probably sooner, she was going to need something larger than this drawer to store her acquisitions. There were rings, watches, brooches, pendants, necklaces, bracelets, hair-slides—a positive Aladdin's Cave of jewelry, all carefully protected in crumpled tissue and cottonwool.

She decided on a silver clip that drew up her dark tresses in a 1940's style, reminiscent of pictures of Veronica Lake, a quartz watch with a silver bracelet, and a silver brooch set with brilliants. Nothing so flashy as to irritate the teachers—not that they dared to reprimand her nowadays—but enough to reinforce her friends' opinion of her as a stylish person. Few of the other pupils dared to wear jewelry with uniform, it being discouraged.

And, after breakfast, it being a fine morning, she set off as usual to walk the three blocks to her school.

As she approached, however, she realized something most unusual was going on. Waiting for the bell to call them to assembly, the younger children were as always rushing about in the playground, shouting and taunting one another. But a group of the older girls, her own classmates, were standing on the pavement outside the gate, surrounding someone she could not quite recognize at first.

A stir of annoyance arose in the back of her mind. That was what she had come to think of as her personal prerogative: being the honey-pot surrounded by bees was the way she expressed it to herself . . . though of course she would never have admitted as much even to her best friend.

If she had one. Sometimes she felt she didn't. Although she was accepted, indeed sought after, although the other girls and often even boys turned to her for advice and repaid her generously with prized possessions, she seemed not to have any real *friends*—people with whom she felt wholly at ease, to whom she could confide secret fears and ambitions.

But such thoughts belonged rather to bedtime, before sleep, than to the morning. In any case she was distracted from them as, drawing closer, she suddenly realized who was the focus of the other girls' attention.

*Of course!*

It was Shirley Waxman, who having reached sixteen had left at the end of the last term in order—and this had caused a mild sensation, because the puritan backlash engendered by AIDS was far from over despite the existence of an effective vaccine—to live with her boyfriend. Now it looked as though . . .

Oh, no doubt of it. She was holding out her left hand, turning it this way and that, while the other girls *ooh*ed and *aah*ed. She must be, could only be, showing off an engagement ring.

Tracy had involuntarily quickened her footsteps. Slowing to a more deliberate pace, she approached quietly and was within arm's reach before anyone took notice of her.

That wasn't the way it ought to be. She had decided long ago—well, eighteen months ago, anyway—that she was always going to be the center of attention. And somehow she had found a means of achieving it.

The painkiller had fixed her cramps, but it had side effects: she wasn't thinking altogether clearly. In vain she sought for the sense of perfect calmness and clarity that had always preceded her greatest coups.

Well, not to worry. She'd worked the trick so often, she must have the hang of it by now.

"Oh, Tracy, look at my ring! Isn't it featly?"

And Shirley, beaming, was displaying it for her. It was indeed splendid. Of course the brilliant in the center was probably only zircon, but it glittered near enough like a diamond, and the setting was beautiful. A wave of greedy resentment swept through Tracy's mind.

*She's fat, the bitch! She isn't even pretty! And she's got that magnificent ring, and she lives on her own—well, with her boyfriend, or I suppose now you have to say fiancée—and she doesn't have to put up with puky stupid teachers and parents so thickheaded they don't know what kind of a daughter they've got, and . . .*

But none of this showed on the surface. Instead, taking Shirley's hand as though to admire the ring from closer to, Tracy said in her sweetest and most cajoling tone, "Oh, it's lovely, isn't it? I'd so much like to have it! You will give it to me, won't you . . . ?"

And abruptly realized that the magic wasn't working.

Letting the hand fall, she stepped back a pace in dismay, to meet harsh and hostile glares.

"Are you mad?" Shirley cried, clutching her left hand in her right as though afraid Tracy meant physically to rob her (but it had never been physically, only mentally, and by a means she did not understand).

"Typical!" That was Jackie, who had been a close friend of Shirley's while she was at school. "Always wants everybody else's best things!"

"And gets them, the bocky cank, though God knows how!"—from

Netta, who was on the other side of the group. "That clip in her hair! That was mine!"

"That's my watch!" exclaimed Vanessa, next to her, and grabbed Tracy's watch.

"My brooch!" shouted Jane, next to her again. And the last of the group, Marian, chimed in.

"It's not just things she takes! I was going out with Brian until she decided she wanted him!"

"She broke up me and Harry!"—from Vanessa.

"And me and Tom!" Jackie exploded. "*And* took my tickets for the Black Fire concert! Well, I'm sick of it! And I'm sick of *her!*"

"Right! Right! Right!"

Terrified, Tracy shook off Vanessa's grip and spun on her heel to flee. But Jackie adroitly tripped her so that she crashed face-down on the hard paving.

Then they fell on her, not only to reclaim their belongings but to vent their pent-up hate. By the time the playground supervisor realized what was happening, they had achieved their aim. Tracy went to hospital with countless cuts and bruises, a broken nose, a ruptured spleen, and a great raw patch on her scalp where furious Netta had ripped away not only the silver clip but a lock of hair as well.

Later, to Matthew and Doreen's horror, the police confiscated the contents of the drawer in Tracy's bedside table, calling them stolen goods. Yet, when the case came to court, it was the other girls who were reprimanded and put on probation, and ordered to return everything to the defiant Tracy, still wearing plaster on her many wounds.

That, though, was in the middle of her month.

It was her greatest triumph so far. In between wheedling her parents around to the view that she absolutely must move to a different school—which wasn't hard—she savored the discovery that her "magic" could be made to work on adults, too.

Provided, of course, the time was right.

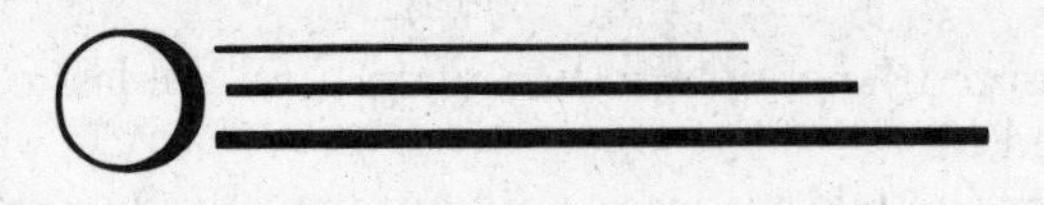

*You're watching TV Plus. It's Newsframe time.*

*Holiday-makers and home-owners on the French Riviera are in a state of panic. Following the price-hike imposed by the uranium-producing countries' cartel, UPAS, the French, who depend heavily on nuclear power, set about stripping the hills of Provence in search of more of the mineral. Now northerly winds are dumping radioactive dust on many popular beaches, including Cannes, Nice and St. Tropez.*

*Here in Britain, supporters of General Thrower held a rally in Leeds today. Police called out to control the crowds are to be disciplined, says the Chief Constable, for breaking ranks and joining in, instead of . . .*

Cursing, Peter found a flashlight—powercuts were so frequent nowadays, he always kept one handy—and cleared down the computer to avoid draining its battery pack.

"Maybe it's as well," Claudia said with a wry grimace. "I shouldn't throw you straight in at the deep end. Let me take the chance to supply a bit of background."

"As you like," Peter muttered. "A refill?"

"Oh, why not? This is strictly a case of going the whole hog, and for someone who was supposed to turn into a traditional Jewish momma . . . Sorry again! But—uh—you don't smoke by any chance, do you?"

"No." Peter blinked. "I didn't think you did."

"Used to." Another grimace, this one more like a scowl. "Gave up five years ago. But now and then under stress—Oh, hell, it's a disgusting habit, and if I can learn to handle stress without a disgusting prop . . . How about that refill you suggested?"

"Coming up."

Installed again on the couch, she leaned back, crossed her legs and gazed into nowhere.

"You remember I told you I'm worried in case my original argument turns out to be wrong after all?"

"Yes."

"Did you follow that up?"

"I got in touch with Jim Spurman," Peter admitted.

"I suspected as much." She gave a bitter chuckle. "You know, that growser is terribly disappointed in me! He got his professorship on the strength of being my British protagonist, and when he discovered I was a turncoat . . ."

"In what sense?" Peter said with sudden impatience.

"This one!" Abruptly she was fixing him with her strange striped irises, and her tone and expression alike were intense. "I've established to my own satisfaction that there are cases of juvenile delinquency—hell, no! Juvenile *crime*, because some of them go 'way beyond anything you could excuse as mischief or high spirits or poor social adjustment—there *are* cases that aren't allowed for by my theory because something far more like a literal power of evil is involved."

She was breathing hard, staring at him through the dimness as though daring him to disagree.

*Oh dear. This bears all the signs of a conversion.*

"Know what I kept thinking of while I was doing the research?" she went on.

"No idea."

"It's a farfetched comparison, I guess, but . . . Well, it made me feel like the people who had to evaluate flying saucer sightings. Remember the UFO craze?"

"Yes, of course," Peter muttered. "But why?"

"Why was I reminded? Oh, because I was sifting through a mountain of evidence, determined to dismiss the lot, and kept getting stuck with an insoluble residue."

*From one bee in the bonnet to another—is that it?*

However, withdrawing his eyes from hers with difficulty and contriving to watch the ice dissolving in his glass instead, Peter said merely, "Well, now we know there's a chemical basis for schizophrenia—"

She brushed his words aside with an impatient gesture. "Flying saucer equals weather balloon! Take it as read that I've ruled out orthodox forms of mental derangement."

"Then environmental contaminants. Extreme intolerance of things like permitted food-colors."

"There's enough in the literature about that kind of reaction to dismiss that as well. You're clutching at the same straws I did—flying saucer equals Venus or Jupiter! Which, incidentally, I never accepted . . . No, I'm perfectly serious, though I would rather not be. And before you ask, I've also allowed for the fact that I was raised to believe in the unique wickedness of the Nazis but learned enough history later on to compensate. Any more ideas?"

Peter hesitated a long while before speaking again. At length, reluctantly, he said, "Well, there was a book called *The Bad Seed* back in—was it the fifties?"

"You know it!" Claudia almost erupted from her seat. "I'd more or less given up hope of meeting anyone else who'd read it. You have read it? You remember it?"

"Oh, long ago. There were these teenage girls who committed the most appalling crimes and wrote a sort of diary about them, half fact, half fantasy . . . Are you on to something like that?"

"In a way." She sipped her drink, no longer looking at him. "I was so convinced, you see, that I'd hit on the fundamental explanation for this—this hostility of the younger generation against society. The nuclear family isn't exactly ancient, you know."

"You pointed that out in your book," Peter countered drily. "You showed how it arose in Europe in the sixteenth and seventeenth centuries and was converted into a norm after the Industrial Revolution. You said it was a suitable makeshift for its period, but in the modern age we need something closer to the tribal system we evolved with, in which every child can turn for help to ten or twenty adults, relatives or not, as easily as to its parents. You said the tradition of godparenting recognized this."

"And what did you think of my argument?"

"I have reservations, but you documented it well."

Claudia accepted that. After another swig, she went on, "Know how the puky funders got at me? Said I was advocating group marriage, i.e. promiscuity, which is against the Word of the Lord . . . You don't look surprised."

"Nothing about fundamentalists surprises me any longer," Peter grunted, and at long last helped himself to his second drink. His intention was to unlock Claudia's tongue while himself remaining comparatively sober. So far it seemed to be working, but he wished she'd get to the point.

"If they'd only *read* the Bible instead of just quoting it—Sorry *again.* I don't want to wander off into theology . . . I still believe I hit on a very important point, don't misunderstand me. But I was naïve enough to imagine it was the whole truth, a perfect solution. And also I'm scientist enough to recognize that a single exception calls a whole theory into question. Right?"

It apparently being expected, Peter gave a solemn nod.

"Right! Well, for a while my self-confidence was underpropped by all the letters I was receiving from desperate parents, mainly women but also quite a lot from men, saying they'd been given insight into the reason why Billy was abusing drugs and Nelly was on the streets and Sammy was in jail and . . . You get the picture.

"Then"—with sudden renewed intensity—"out of the blue I received quite a different letter. For one thing, it wasn't from a parent, but from a retired social worker, who had obviously read my book with great care and set out the best-reasoned case against my views that I've ever encountered." A brittle laugh. "Sometimes I wish I hadn't, you know!"

"What did she say?"

"Apart from points that other people had already made—only not so elegantly—she insisted that right at the end of a career spanning forty years she had run across a case she couldn't account for by any theory, including mine, bar the assumption of inborn wickedness."

"You took this seriously?"

"Well, I'd received a good deal of hate-mail as well as letters in support, so for a moment I was inclined to throw it away. But, as I said, it was couched in such reasonable terms that I couldn't drive it out of my mind."

"Did you get in touch with the writer?"

"I tried to. Unfortunately she had died. Young—only about sixty-five. Nonetheless, what she said went on bugging me. In the end I couldn't stand it any more. Even that single exception . . . So I started pulling strings."

She sipped her drink again and appended a sour chuckle. "Ah, what it is to have status and renown! Before the book came out I was just another college professor. Once it had spent even a week in the bestseller lists I was famous and influential! I remember when I met you the first time I was contemptuous of publicity and the media. Back then, I didn't know what advantage I could turn them to . . .

"Never mind. The point is that I found I was able to access a whole area of data that I didn't even know existed until I started digging around. Once again I'd been naïve. I didn't know, for example, that there were police forces like yours that routinely put not just hard facts but rumor, gossip and suspicion on permanent file. Did I say the letter I was talking about came from England?"

"No." Peter was leaning forward now, hanging on every word.

"Well, it did. So, out of sheer curiosity and—what's that vivid English-English term for being ornery?"

"Bloody-mindedness?" Peter offered after a brief hesitation.

"That's it! Out of that sort of impulse, anyway, I dug around and discovered I could access some very strange records. Later on I'll tell you exactly how, but for the moment I'll just say they are police files. They're—well, I guess the term would be 'on the back burner.' But they do open them, now and then, to attested social researchers. With the appearance of my book, I'd turned into one. Bless the growser who put my name on the list!

"And that was how I found out that there were at least ten cases that to all appearances totally undermined my dogmatic assertions."

And, again, a generous gulp of whiskey. Afraid she might overdo it to the point of passing out before she finally let him in on her secret, Peter said, "Are your findings on the disk you brought?"

Claudia had been briefly brooding. Now she roused with a start. "Yes! And a lot more. As soon as the power comes on again—"

Which it did, as though she had rubbed a magic lamp.

After a pause to make sure it wasn't a false alarm, she rose and returned to the computer. Peter made haste to follow, for fear that she might have grown clumsy. But she appeared totally in control as she booted it and tapped a succession of commands into the board. There was a security code that took a long while and considerable accuracy to enter; she got it right first time.

And for the next hour Peter could not tell whether he was being let in on the ground floor of the most important newsbreak of his life, or lured into the mazes of a deluded fanatic's dream.

In the country town of Marshmere, where many people still found it possible to maintain an illusion of prosperity despite Britain's economic decline, Richard Gall, branch manager of the County and Consolidated Building Society, was a respected figure. So was his wife Edna. He was a Mason and a member of the golf club; she was a school governor and active on charity committees. They lived in a medium-sized modern house on the outskirts of the town. He drove a Renault—distinctive but not inappropriate—and she a second-hand Mini. Their acquaintances regarded them as an ideal couple.

Mary Gall knew different. They never quarrelled in public, but she wasn't "public." That was how she had come to find out that she was not her father's natural child. During one of their recurrent rows, when she was twelve, she had heard Edna hurl the fact at Richard, reminding him of all the humiliation she had undergone—endless medical examinations, internal inspections, the final coldly clinical process that he had insisted on—and winding up with a barrage of comments about his inadequate masculinity.

At which point the doorbell rang, and instantly they were their usual affable selves.

Mary pondered that for a long time. At last she understood why her mother was so often moody, why she drank too much, why she smoked in spite of knowing how bad it was for her health. She had no clear idea of the "process" Edna had been obliged to undergo, but by making some discreet inquiries of the biology teacher at her school—

which was not the one of which her mother was a governor—she contrived to assemble a fairly accurate picture.

And started to plot her revenge.

Precisely why it was so easy, she never worked out. She only knew that, quite recently, she had become able to influence her parents to the point where she could stop their quarrels in mid-spate, though they generally resumed again after she had gone to bed, where she lay listening and trembling as they traded insults.

Gradually resolve hardened in her mind. But it was two months before she put her plan into effect, and over a year before it reached its long-awaited climax. She was a patient child; she rarely took a hasty decision.

Especially in truly significant matters.

She already knew a certain amount about Richard's occupation. Her first step was to find out more, until she was sure that her idea was feasible. For a while after discovering he was not actually her father she had behaved coldly toward him, but soon enough she realized this was counterproductive, and began to play up to him. Indeed, for a time she went too far in the opposite direction, so that Edna accused her of taking sides. After a while, though, she established the proper balance.

Then, directly after the auditors had made their annual visit to the local branch of the building society, she started asking Richard to . . .

Asking?

No, that wasn't quite right. It was more like persuading, except it wasn't such hard work as persuading. It was a matter of gentling herself into the proper frame of mind, finding the right words and tone of voice, and then watching the outcome. She didn't always succeed, but she soon learned when and guessed why not, so she avoided the days when she felt her talent to be unreliable.

At the right moment, though—*wow!*

Stretching her patience to the maximum, she waited month after frustrating month before springing the trap she had set for her not-father. The temptation to hurry was atrocious, but she resisted it until three months before the auditors were due again: a gestation period.

Thereupon she "persuaded" Richard that his family ought to own a better car. That was how the Jaguar arrived. Next came the move, on short notice and a long mortgage, to a bigger house, costing twice as much as the old one, with a tennis court in the back garden. (At this point Edna grew worried—but Mary calmed and reassured her.) Then there was the booking for all three of them on a round-the-world luxury cruise. Mary was a smidgin regretful that it wasn't actually going to happen . . . Later, maybe. At the moment she was intent on her revenge.

So there followed the expensive home computer, and the TV

camera, and the state-of-the-art CD player complete with a library of records to play on it, and a brand-new Citroën to take the place of Edna's Mini, and—and—and . . .

By the time the auditors arrived half the town was asking, "How does he manage it?" By the time they departed the entire town was asking, "How did he expect to get away with it?"

Because, of course, he didn't. Thanks to manipulation of the building society's financial records via his home computer, which stupidly took no account of the master records held at head office, half a million pounds of other people's money was missing from his branch, of which two hundred thousand had vanished heaven knew where.

And Mary.

To the police, and later at his trial, the only defense Richard had to offer was a whimpered excuse.

"My daughter made me do it!"

Sitting in the courtroom at her own insistence, calm and incredibly mature of manner most of the time, Mary turned to her mother and clutched her arm, demanding, "How can he say such dreadful things?"

Everybody heard her, including the judge and jury, just as she had intended. Though the judge reproved her for speaking aloud, it was clear he shared her attitude. He sentenced Richard to five years.

When they reached home Edna broke down in tears, looking at the magnificence of their new house.

"It'll all have to go!" she whimpered. "God knows where we'll wind up! We're going to be *homeless!*"

"No, we're not," Mary said composedly, dropping into one of the drawing room's splendid brocade armchairs.

"What do you mean?" Edna stared at her.

"You've got plenty to pay off the mortgage."

"Don't talk such nonsense! I've got the little bit—"

"The little bit Aunt Minnie left you," Mary interrupted. "I know! You've told me about it enough times. In fact it's not so little, is it? If we decide to stay here, it will be sufficient to survive on. We can run a car, though it'll have to be another Mini, I suppose, not a Jag—"

"Mary, you *are* talking nonsense! The interest on the mortgage alone—"

"I told you! It can be paid off!" Mary threw her head back and laughed joyously. "And at last we're free of that horrible man who put you through such torture to have me, and quarrelled with you so incessantly!"

Lately she had grown fond of unusual words, and taken to deploying them in conversation when the chance arose.

"*Mary!*" Edna was leaning over her. "I can't possibly repay our mortgage!"

"But you can," Mary sighed. "You have two hundred thousand pounds. It's in a bank in London. In your name."

"*What?*"

"One of these not-quite-respectable licensed deposit takers," Mary amplified. "But I made sure it was reliable, if not respectable, before I picked it."

"You mean that's where . . . ?" Edna's voice tailed away through a whisper to a breath.

Mary rose briskly and embraced her mother. Her power of persuasion operated better at close quarters. She had often had to sit on Richard's lap to make it work.

"So what? He always said he wasn't being paid as much as he was worth. So we can stay here if you want to, or we can move somewhere else . . . Are you angry with me?"

And the power worked. A moment later Edna was cuddling her and crying, not from anger, but from joy.

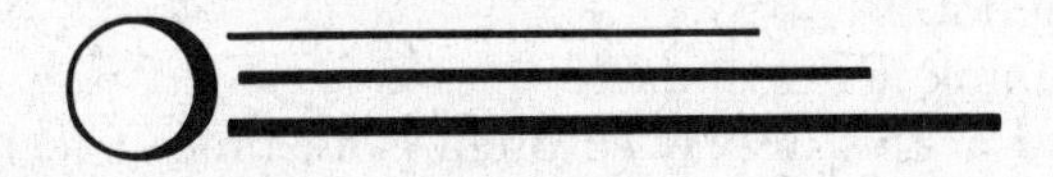

*You're watching TV Plus. In a moment, Newsframe.*

*Farmers marching on London from the East Anglian dustbowl, who reached the capital this afternoon, have accused the police of politically motivated brutality. Many claim they were beaten up because they weren't wearing the red-white-and-blue ribbons lately adopted by supporters of General Thrower.*

*The Throwers themselves . . .*

"**F**irst I'll explain how I established my residue," Claudia said as the computer screen displayed a directory of the disk's contents. "This being a whole-hog kind of evening . . . I originally intended to start my analysis in the States, but they're a lot stricter over there about access to criminal records, and besides you have to deal with hundreds of separate police forces. A friend of mine in our criminology department suggested I try mousing into Interpol via the British police. I didn't expect it to work, but I had a stroke of luck. There was an international conference on police use of computers in New York, so I went to it and chatted up one of the British delegates, a chief superintendent. And he happened to have run across just the sort of case I had in mind.

"What's more he'd read my book. He was the right kind of cop: seriously interested in his work. I don't know how he swung the deal, but a few weeks later I got a letter to say that he'd arranged for me to access your PNC through a filter that would automatically disguise the identity of the subjects I inquired about. At that stage, I was *here.*" She tapped a command and the display changed to show a table of crimes in alphabetical order. There was a number against each. Most were in the three-figure range, but a few attained four.

To demonstrate interest Peter said, "Those are the total cases of each type of crime?" And, on her nod: "Hmm! You set yourself quite a task, didn't you? How many altogether?"

"Six or seven thousand. But I didn't have to analyze them one by one. The way things had been set up, I could eliminate the cases that didn't concern me."

"Using what criteria for exclusion?"

"Oh, drug abuse, alcohol or solvent abuse, formal mental derangement—the sort of thing you already mentioned. And I set parameters for the kind of home background that conduces to violence. Want to be walked through the lot?"

"Not unless you think it's essential."

"Good. I've stared at this display so often, sometimes I feel I'm just not seeing it any more." She keyed another command. Peter noticed that any effect the whiskey had had was no longer discernible.

"One thing you've got to understand is that I didn't *want* to find anything. I was convinced that my original idea was sound, and I was only doing this out of—well, you might say a sense of duty. Like a guy in a lab running all the experiments he can think of that might disprove his favorite theory."

"The impression I gained from your book," Peter said slowly, "was that you regarded your insight not just as generally applicable, but universally. If you don't mind my saying so, I felt that was its weakest point."

She gave a harsh laugh. "If only you knew how right you are!" she muttered. "Still, you will, in just a few minutes . . . As a matter of fact, the first item that rocked me back on my heels didn't come from PNC at all. And I have a couple more that didn't, either, that I'll get around to in due time. Here's the first one—Can you see okay?"

Peter had been standing behind her. Now he drew up a chair and sat down for a better-angled view.

"I got this from my friend in the criminology department, who had it from a colleague at Stanford. There's an epidemic of designer drugs in California. You heard the funders launched a soft drink spiked with one of them?"

"CrusAde," Peter said with a nod. "Didn't they try to claim it was legal?"

"Right. Because it wasn't synthesized but secreted by a tailored yeast. That didn't cut any ice with the FDA. And some believers are claiming that yeasts imply brewing, i.e. 'strong liquor,' and so—Never mind! They're still trying to clarify the law on that point. But here's what got me interested." She gestured at the screen.

"The FBI are certain that the drug-designer is a kid. They caught one of his dealers, who confessed where he'd got the modified yeast, so they sent an agent after him. And he came back swearing the kid was the nicest guy he'd ever met, couldn't possibly have done what he's accused of, and a few days later quit the bureau. The same happened the second time, and the third, at which point the local director decided he must be barking up the wrong tree. But new drugs are still emerging. Someone's responsible, and more dealers have been caught and more of them have claimed to know the designer is only a kid."

Peter's heart was hammering. From a mouth abruptly dry he said, "Perhaps I should have asked what criteria you chose for inclusion, rather than exclusion."

Claudia marked each with an extended finger. "A major crime—committed by a child—who subsequently got away with it. That's the important bit: getting away with it."

" 'Child' meaning . . . ?"

"As it turns out: above twelve or thirteen."

Peter whistled. "And you really mean major crimes?"

She twisted around to glare at him. "Do you have any idea how many patients in American mental hospitals had to be locked away because of designer drugs?"

"I'm not disputing that definition. It's a major crime by anybody's standards. But . . . Have you found a lot of similar cases?"

"No, not a lot. Less than a dozen. Enough, though, to cast doubt on my beloved theory! Let me show you the others. First the ones I got off PNC, the British ones."

Another command, and the display changed. She gave, as before, a commentary.

"Now this one is again a boy—there's a fairly even spread between the sexes, incidentally. At age thirteen he was attending an expensive private boarding school. He turned out to be running a sex-for-sale operation among the pupils, with the assistance of the headmaster's daughter. She serviced the men whose tastes didn't include boys."

"Nothing was done about this?"

"The culprit was transferred one term ahead of schedule to another school. I wouldn't bet on that reforming him!"

"But didn't the teachers—?"

"Several of the teachers were among his customers."

Peter pondered that for a while. At length he said, "Go on."

"The next one I came up with was a girl. She ran away from an aunt and uncle who'd taken her over after her parents died. Not accident, disease. I can't be sure what kind—I told you there's a filter on my gateway to PNC, which deletes anything that might give a clue to identity. But I found an approximate date, and it coincides with that epidemic of meningitis you had here a few years ago. I think you covered it for *Continuum*, didn't you?"

"I did indeed. Though if you're hoping to trace her parents through me, it won't work. We respected the anonymity of the victims."

"I assure you I wasn't thinking along those lines."

"Good. Carry on about the girl who ran away."

"She headed for a big city, likely London, but again, of course, I can't be certain. Before her twelfth birthday she was on the streets—how else could a kid that age earn a living? One of her customers turned nasty and pulled a knife on her. He wound up cut to ribbons."

"And they didn't do anything about that, either?"

"I know what you're going to say! She ought to have been put into a foster home, at least, if not sent to reform school, right? Instead this girl was acquitted. Even the prosecution admitted there were none of her fingerprints on the handle of the knife. She wanted the court to believe the man had killed himself . . . and they did."

Peter was staring at her in unveiled dismay. "They believed that he'd cut himself to ribbons, as you put it?"

A firm nod, a grim tensing of her wide lips.

"She was discharged from custody at once and apparently was back at her usual post the same afternoon."

"They let a twelve-year-old go back to prostitution after what had happened? How the hell did I not get to hear about this?"

Claudia shrugged. "Well, the trial took place in whatever your counterpart is of Juvenile Hall, so I guess the media weren't allowed to publish the details. They sure as hell got stored on PNC, though. I warned you my findings don't make for sound sleep . . . Can you think of an explanation for what I just told you—? No, hold on. Let me show you the rest before you make up your mind.

"The next I came across was a boy again, somewhere in the north of England, far as I can make out. Sheep-farming country, at any rate, where they say beck instead of brook or creek. There was a quarrel between his family and some neighbors. A prize dog was killed. Then the rival family's son was found drowned, his foot caught in a wire noose so that he pitched headlong into a stream, hit his head, and drowned. It didn't look like an accident, more a deliberate trap.

"But the inquest found for accident, and—this'll amuse you!—now the local police speak about the family as though they're witches."

"In this day and age?"

"Yes indeed. I had to go to my theology department—where I am not exactly a regular visitor . . . *Was*, I guess I have to say now. Had to go there for explanations of some of the words I found in the report, like 'darklady' and 'hornylord.' Apparently they can be traced back to the religion of pre-Christian Britain."

"Mm-hm." Peter nodded vigorously. "Hornylord would be Cernunnos, the Wild Man of the Mountains, who had a stag's head or a pair of antlers on a human head. They still worship him at Carnac in Brittany, in the guise of a Christian saint called Cornély."

"You did a *Continuum* program about that too, did you?"

"Why else do you think I know so many peculiar facts? But you know a lot that I don't, even so . . . Go on."

"Ahh . . . yes. Next one's a girl again. Another killer. Drowned a man in plain sight of his friends. She was just a kid and he was a trained Commando, like a Marine Ranger."

Peter jolted upright on his chair. "That doesn't make sense!"

"Damned little about this makes sense," Claudia retorted caustically. "Read it for yourself."

He hunched closer to the screen. Some day soon he was going to need glasses . . .

He said eventually, "But if he was intending to rape her—"

"She personally didn't claim that. Of course no one heard what they said to one another, not at that distance. He just apparently put his head under the water and didn't come up. I wish I could get at more detail, but that puky filter has been programed to err on the side of caution, and all I know is that he drowned in a river and his body was found bobbing against some kind of barrier—presumably marking out an area as safe for swimming. But there must be hundreds such in Britain."

"Do you get the dates of these events?" Peter demanded. Claudia shook her head, her hair swooping up and down like an oscilloscope trace.

"An indication of the season is as much as the filter will let pass. This one happened in summer, obviously. But they're all comparatively recent. Indirect evidence suggests they're all within the past couple of years."

"I ought to be taking notes!" Peter realized belatedly.

"You can copy the disk if you like. I didn't realize until this evening just how badly I need a second opinion. Shall we go on?"

"Yes!"

"Okay, here's another boy, obviously living in a rundown city, again probably in the north of England. According to a report on

PNC, one of the rumors they encourage their local intelligence officers to file—"

"No need to tell me about those!" Peter interrupted in a bitter tone.

"Run foul of them yourself, haven't you?" She scowled at his sidelong. "Yes, I remember your mentioning it. Your government seems to encourage paranoia in its citizens . . . Anyway, the report indicates, as you see, that he's the leader of a gang of older kids who operate a protection racket, blackmailing local shopkeepers into paying them ridiculous sums for doing practically nothing. Like they get ten or fifteen pounds for throwing away unsold newspapers, or carrying garbage cans from the back of a shop to the front."

"But the shopkeepers—"

"They won't testify. Won't give evidence."

"It doesn't make sense!"

"You said that before. I still agree."

"But how could they be so terrified of a few kids?"

"That's the strangest part of all. They *aren't* terrified."

"What?"

"They aren't terrified," Claudia repeated patiently. "They claim to like the kids, to be paying them willingly! By the way, this is the case my friend the chief superintendent had run across and was so annoyed about. That's why I can be so positive about it. But he didn't steer me to it. I write to him occasionally to tell him how the research is progressing, and when I came up with this one he admitted it was the example he'd had in mind."

"I need another drink," Peter said, rising. "You?"

"I'd rather have coffee."

"Can do. If you don't mind instant, that is. It's been some time since I could afford the real stuff."

When he set the steaming mug beside her, she resumed.

"Now we're getting into a borderline area. Here are a couple of cases which may not be related, but they do have certain similarities.

"The first one concerns a trial in juvenile court where some schoolgirls were charged with assaulting one of their classmates—the youngest in the class, if that has any bearing on the matter. According to what they said at the time of the offense, she had turned up wearing jewelry that had formerly belonged to them, but which she had somehow conned them out of, and then tried to do the same to a girl who had left and come back to show her friends an engagement ring she had just been given. She was quite badly hurt and had to be taken to the hospital. But when the trial came on, meek as lambs they all confirmed what the injured girl said: they had given her their belongings willingly—and some, by the way, were very expensive, so expensive that the former owners had lied to their parents about having 'lost' them and been severely scolded."

"But even if the girls themselves retracted, what about their parents, who presumably paid for the things that she had taken?"

"If they were in court, they were won over. If they called on her at home, they were won over. Now do you see what—what *obsesses* me about all this?"

"I do indeed," Peter muttered, and sipped his fresh drink. "You said there were more cases to come."

"Yes indeed. All, as I said, on the borderline, linked only by a very curious coincidence that—No, I'm running ahead of myself. I want you to see the rest of my evidence first." Fingers leapt briskly to the keyboard.

"This one concerns the manager of—do you say building society?"

"Yes."

"I had to get someone to explain that to me. They don't exist in the States. Far as I can gather, they perform the same kind of function as savings-and-loan operations, is that right?"

"I imagine it's pretty close. What happened to the guy?"

"He helped himself from the till to buy a new car, a new house, lots of goodies. As you might expect, he got caught and wound up in jail. He has a daughter. His only defense consisted in claiming, over and over, that she had put him up to it."

"I take it the court didn't believe him," Peter offered dryly.

"Of course not. But you know something? I think I do."

After digesting that, Peter said, "What else do you have for me?"

"The two items I didn't get off the British PNC. But there's still the same connection as between the others."

Assuming he had already guessed what the connection was, Peter nodded an invitation to go ahead. Claudia tapped keys again.

"Here's a girl in a convent school in Ireland. I heard about her from someone over there who knows about my work and wrote me—anonymously, so I can't tell how much credence to give the story. By the way, she was determined to prove my theory wrong."

Peter broke in. "You said anonymously. She?"

"Green ink on scented pink notepaper," Claudia sighed. "I believe the phrase you use in England is 'a dead giveaway.' "

"Granted. Sorry."

"She seemed to have an *idée fixe* about religious education, blaming it, rather than the nuclear family, for juvenile crime. Here's the case she reported: the daughter of a man who committed suicide and a woman who lost her mind as a result of the shock, alleged to be operating a porno racket from her school, the material being supplied by a delivery boy and his older brother, whom she allows to kiss and fondle her—a big deal in Ireland, apparently! My correspondent's daughter got blamed for what the other girl was doing, and was expelled."

"I thought," Peter said slowly, "you were concentrating on major crimes."

"And this hardly counts as one? Agreed. On the other hand . . . No, you'll have to wait until the last case. This crime *is* major. I got it from an Italian farmer who read the translation of my book—not popular in his country, so he made a point of laying hands on it when he saw a review. Once again, however, it's anonymous. I know where the letter was posted, though, and I'm fairly sure I could trace the actual case. In fact that's one of the first tasks I want to tackle now I'm in Europe. There can't be too many places in Italy where the night watchman at a farm co-operative's oil-store was shot dead last fall."

"Especially by a kid of twelve!"

"In this case it wasn't the kid but his putative father who got away with it."

Momentarily distracted as he reached for his glass, Peter missed the implications of a crucial word in the last sentence. He said, "I didn't quite follow . . . ?"

In her turn misunderstanding, Claudia said, "He talked the police out of a prosecution. Someone else got blamed, just as in the Irish case: one of the father's tenants, who disappeared the same night. But why am I reading aloud to you? Look at the screen! It's all there."

And sipped her coffee, cool enough to drink by now.

At length Peter said slowly, "You think this is reliable—or simply hearsay? It sounds to me as though someone is venting a grudge against the local landowner. Why aren't there any names in this one, incidentally? You'd think that someone with a grudge would want to be as specific as possible."

Claudia gave a harsh chuckle. "You ought to ask my husband about that!"

Peter blinked several times. "Excuse me," he said at last. "It's my turn to say I had no idea you were married."

"I'm not. Not any more. It didn't work out. Mainly because he expected me to turn into a machine for making babies . . . But he was tremendously handsome and dramatic, and I was terribly proud of him while we were engaged. It was only afterward that I found out the drawbacks of having been raised in the culture of the Italian Deep South. Oh, shit! It's over and done with, and I hope I never meet the puky cank again! The point *is*"—and she leaned earnestly toward him, as though her earlier drinks were finally taking effect—"the poor guy may have been afraid that if he named names in his letter he would find the same thing happening to him. I can assure you he had grounds."

"I'm getting a bit confused," Peter admitted after a pause for reflection. "All right, I grant that the growser from Italy may have been scared to—ah—name names. But what makes you connect this case with the others?"

"Because it was the boy who talked the police out of prosecuting his father, when they had the deathbed word of the victim to convict him on. This carries a lot of weight in Catholic countries."

"It still isn't clear," Peter insisted. "So maybe the boy is exceptionally charming! Or maybe his father wasn't anywhere near the place at the time. That's what they both said, isn't it?"—with a tap on the screen to indicate the relevant passage. "What on earth makes you connect this with all the others?"

Claudia blanked the screen before answering, then rose and returned to her former place on the couch without removing her disk. Peter swivelled his chair around to face her.

She said at length, having emptied her coffee mug, "They all have one thing in common. In the PNC cases, I don't know why the filter let it pass, because in theory at least it could be a clue to identity. In the case from Ireland and the one from Italy, I have only rumor to rely on, yet it seems improbable that it should crop up time after time in such a similar context . . .

"Not one of them is the natural child of his or her ostensible father. They were all conceived by artinsem. Or, as you may have known it before its initials clashed with a well-known disease, AID."

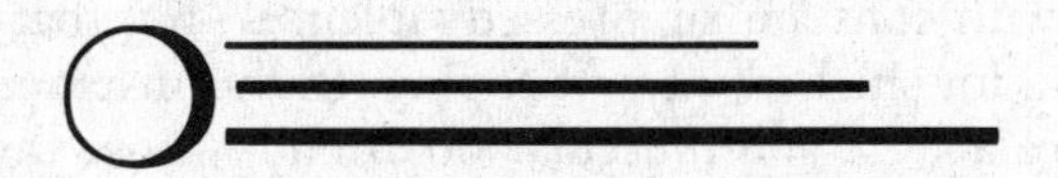

*S*martly but not conspicuously dressed, carefully made up and with her hair styled to make her look much older than her true age, Pepita Hallam brought her supermarket trolley to a halt and glanced along the row of busy checkouts. She didn't like to leave by the same one two weeks running. Not that she had ever had any problems, but it was as well to be on the safe side.

Although it meant waiting rather longer, she chose a line that included two women whose trolleys were almost collapsing under their loads. She could, she felt sure, have cut straight in at the head of the line today, because her aura—as she thought of it—felt particularly strong, but she suspected there were limits to its efficacy. Again, she preferred not to run any risks.

Besides, later this morning she wanted to make a good few other purchases under less advantageous circumstances.

The girl at the desk was suitably tired and harassed. She barely glanced at Pepita, loading her wheeled canvas shopper, as she totted up the bill. Including two bottles of vodka and a carton of king-sized cigarettes for her mother, it came to more than forty-six pounds. Pepita handed over three twenty-pound notes. The girl made change. Pepita waited with an expectant air.

"Oh, sorry," the girl said after a moment, and handed back the twenties. Pepita favored her with a flashing smile and went her way.

There was an unusually rapid turnover of staff at this supermarket. Pepita sometimes wondered whether she had anything to do with that.

Her bill at the make-up counter of the chemist's was seven pounds something. She proffered one of the twenties and received it back plus change. Things didn't go quite so smoothly when she bought her weekly stock of tights, plus some new underwear, for the shop was a lot less crowded and the assistant not as easy to distract, but she still received a ten on top of the change she was entitled to. Not wanting to wear out her aura, she decided to go to only one more shop, to pick up some tapes by her favorite group, and then head for home.

Where the rest of the aura would have to be used up, as it were, on her mother. Cynthia Hallam was in a miserable state today . . .

But then, she generally was.

She and Pepita lived in a block of council flats where the lifts kept breaking down, surrounded by what had been intended as gardens and playgrounds but had turned instead into a giant rubbish-heap. It was a rough area, seething with constant suppressed violence—not that that bothered Pepita much, for she had ways of coping. In this instance she had decided to acquire a large and muscular boyfriend, whose threats would stave off unwanted attentions. His name was Kevin and he was seventeen. She felt nothing but contempt for him, but she had him well trained. Tonight, when he took her to the local disco, he would watch over her like a guard-dog, and be content when he returned her to the door of her home with a quick peck on the cheek . . . though doubtless puzzled afterward that after doing so much for her he settled for so little in return.

Today the lifts were working, which was a mercy, for she had no idea where Kevin was at the moment and she wouldn't have cared to carry her shopping up the stairs. The flat, of course, was a mess, apart from her own room which she kept meticulously tidy, but that was the way of things. Her mother was pretty much of a mess, too—sitting around moping in a soiled dressing gown, red-eyed and snappish. She spoke not a word until she had seized the cigarettes, lit one, and poured and drunk half a tumblerful of vodka.

Eventually she said in a dull voice, "Show me what you got."

Stowing her purchases in the kitchen cupboard, Pepita complied.

"All right, I suppose," her mother approved grudgingly, and turned to retrieve her glass. Behind her back Pepita pulled a rude face, implying:

*You couldn't have done a tenth as well!*

Which was true. Could anyone?

A little later, stretched out on her bed listening to her new tapes—her player had been second-hand, but it was an expensive make and she took good care of it—that question returned to haunt her as it had so often in the past.

*Could* anyone else do what she'd been doing this past couple of years? Not always, only when the aura was at its height . . . but what she could get away with on days like today still astonished her.

For the latest of countless times she reviewed what she knew of her background. She had acquired the information in garbled form, scrap by scrap, when her mother was in a particularly self-pitying mood.

And of course drunk, but that went without saying.

What she had pieced together went like this. After five years of marriage her parents had still had no children, and they both wanted at least one. According to Cynthia—but who could tell how true the claim might be?—her husband, whose name was Victor, was convinced the fault lay on her side, or at any rate maintained so. After one row too many she had decided to find out. And it wasn't.

He must have known all along, for the moment she became pregnant he called her a whoring bitch and walked out, never to be heard of again—quite a feat in modern computerized Britain.

Hence the squalid council flat. Hence the dependence on exiguous government grants, second-hand clothes from jumble sales, and—increasingly—the bottle. At one time, Pepita suspected, the authorities had threatened to take her away, and for long enough to satisfy them Cynthia had pulled herself together. Now, of course, no one seemed to care. Every other week in the papers or on the telly government spokesmen kept complaining about how much it cost to keep children in care, masking their true opinions behind a veneer of humanitarianism, mouthing respect for the "ties of blood" and the unique care and affection that only a natural parent could provide . . .

*Load of bocky old canks!*

The tape had played through and was starting afresh on the first side. She reached out a languid arm to change it for another of her new acquisitions. Before switching it on, she was afflicted by a sudden shiver. It was going to be such a long time before she could legally move out! She would have to be sixteen, free from the school that she dutifully attended—and where she was regarded as a first-rate student, for she had a keen mind. A term often applied to her was "sensible." Sometimes the teachers confided their surprise at how well she coped, having to act as her mother's deputy in almost everything.

Well, it was the easiest way . . .

But sometimes she was tempted, as now, simply to walk out. How long, though, could she survive if she did? She made a mental resolution. She must practice more with her aura, work out when the best times were to exploit it, and also establish whether she could make it act better on people who weren't as distracted and preoccupied as shop assistants. For instance, she ought to try a policeman, and maybe someone at the National Assistance office, and—come to that, why not a post office, or even a bank?

A dazzling vision of crisp new fifty-pound notes overwhelmed her for a moment. But at length, with a sigh, she lay back on the bed again.

No, better not. At least this way she had some degree of control over her life. Nonetheless, she felt a stir of shame at her own reluctance to cut loose.

*Know something, Peppy?* she said to herself, half aloud. *At bottom you're a bocky coward, aren't you?*

And, resigned to the fact, switched on the new tape and shut her eyes.

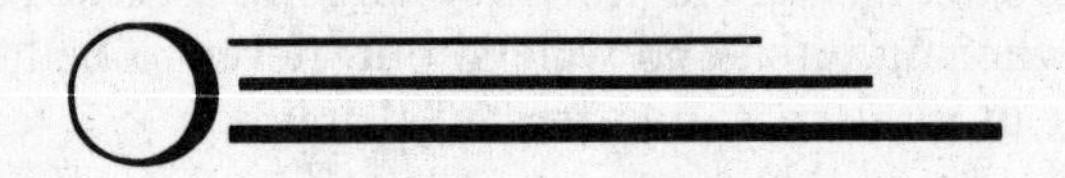

*You're watching TV Plus. Time for Newsframe.*

*The source of the blue dye that caused thousands of liters of milk to be condemned in Yorkshire last week has been traced. The farmer added to his cows' regular feed a batch of out-of-time potato crisps from a local supermarket, without removing the blue salt-bags. A spokesman for the County Veterinary Inspectorate said the cows were none the worse, but declared that in view of the mounting potato shortage the crisps' expiry date should have been extended.*

*Six teenage boys have been remanded in custody in North London following allegations that they stripped a black girl of fifteen naked and painted her with red-white-and-blue stripes. Asked to comment at a news conference, General Sir Hampton Thrower said . . .*

Peter stared at Claudia for a long moment. Then he gave a harsh laugh and took another swig of his drink.

"You seem to be implying," he said at last, "that you've tracked down a group of hereditary criminals. Born to the trade, as it were."

Her eyes fixed on him, she nodded.

"But why shouldn't they, too, be accounted for by your theory? Pressure to conform to the ideal of the nuclear family, which you argue is obsolete, could just as well explain—"

"Oh, sure!" she cut in. "Don't you think I want it to? If only to spite the puky funders with their endless gabble about original sin! But these are the exceptions that are going to prove my rule in the proper sense, right?"

"I see," Peter murmured. And in fact he did. He wasn't used to meeting sociologists willing to apply strict scientific rigor to their work, and it made a refreshing change from those who preferred bombinating in a vacuum. He never expected to like this woman, but he was starting to respect her.

Claudia was going on.

"My sabbatical was due, and I needed a subject for a thesis. This looked like the ideal challenge. If I could show that my ideas held good even in cases of this kind, I'd have put the whole argument on a much firmer basis. I had a couple of other possibilities in reserve in case this one wasn't accepted, but in the upshot it was approved almost at once. Now, of course, I think I can guess why. The puky Dean just wanted me out of the way when he caved in to the bribes he was being offered . . . Did you ever hear the story of the student who received a record grant for his doctorate thesis? It was to be about the effect on academics and business executives of a series of extremely large bribes."

If she intended that to be funny, it didn't show in her face or voice.

"Next I was going to ask what you know about artinsem, but I think I can guess the answer. A lot. Because that was another of the subjects *Continuum* tackled."

Peter gave another short laugh. "No, oddly enough. I do know a lot about it, but from personal experience. Lord, I haven't thought about it in years!"

Claudia started upright. "Now I know I was right to change my mind about talking to you! Explain, explain!"

"You know, this is ridiculous," he answered slowly, staring at the carpet. "It was so minor an episode in my life, I've been thinking Ellen is my only child. In fact she's not. I must have kids scattered over half creation! Grief! I hope they don't all come home to roost!"

"How did this happen?"

He shrugged, leaning back. "Before I went into television I was studying medicine. Grants for people like me weren't exactly generous, though not as bad as they are now, so when one of my friends told me he was being paid five quid for donating semen I asked if I could—well, get in on the act."

"Which you did?"

"Why not? To be candid, I wasn't thinking so much about the money. I was rather hoping to be told I was sterile."

"That's an extraordinary attitude!"

"Not at the time it wasn't. We were out of the Swinging Sixties, but we hadn't yet reached the AIDS phase and a lot of the sixties' attitudes were lingering. Around them, though, people were starting to cast doubts on the Pill. A tolerably attractive guy with a certificate of sterility could have played the field . . . Claudia, I must be drunk!" He set his glass aside with a gesture of annoyance. "I never admitted that to anyone before!"

She let it pass. "Obviously you weren't," she prompted.

"Sterile? Of course not. My count fell square in the middle of the normal range. What was more, they happened to need someone of my physical type and coloration at the clinic. So, over the next year and a half, nearly two years, I dropped by every six or eight weeks and—ah—went through the motions, as and when they had a couple of similar appearance."

"There's a limit, isn't there?"

Peter nodded. "Ten times. So I made fifty quid. I hope they pay more nowadays—a fiver isn't much when tube and bus fares start at a pound!"

"Did you have to give any sort of undertaking?"

"Lord, yes. Apart from pledging myself to report any disease I might be suffering from, especially the STDs which were fairly rife around then, and any medication I might be taking—this of course was the reason practically all the donors were medical or dental students, who could be expected to understand the importance of keeping their word—apart from that, the main one was an undertaking never to attempt to trace the recipient. Frankly, though, I can't imagine how you'd set about that."

"Now that's something I need to investigate." Claudia leaned forward intently. "What can you tell me about the way donors' records were maintained?"

"Well, I can only speak for the one clinic that I know about," Peter countered. "Very little AID was done under the Health Service. About ninety percent was private."

"Because of the high cost?"

"Not at all. In my day the fee was around—oh—twenty or thirty pounds, plus of course the cost of preliminary consultations and examinations. A hundred quid would probably have covered the lot. Not excessive even then, for a couple desperate to have a child."

"And there are, or were, a lot of clinics undertaking such work?"

" 'Were' is more like it. People grew so terrified of AIDS they wouldn't risk an unknown donor any more, so transplantation and *in vitro* fertilization have taken over almost completely . . . Well, I don't know what you mean by 'a lot.' But I've seen some figures. Just a second." He knitted his brows with the effort of memory. "Yes, that sounds right. In those days the annual rate of artificial insemination was between three and four thousand."

"Hmm!" Claudia sounded depressed. "You're talking about an average of ten per day, year in, year out, over quite a long period—and just in Britain, at that."

"Easily."

"I confess I hadn't realized it was quite so high. I'd been expecting to amass my data fairly quickly, write my first draft, take a couple of months off to explore Europe, and revise at leisure before going home . . . But you haven't answered my question about donors' records. I presume they had to be kept. Apart from—oh—not wanting a black kid to turn up in a white family, for instance, what if one of the donors proved to be carrying a deleterious gene and had to be traced and warned? Back then they couldn't have screened them in advance, could they?"

Peter shook his head, his expression still vaguely tinged with amazement.

"You know, I really hadn't given the matter a thought in years . . . Why do you need to find out about the records? Do you—?" He checked. "You don't honestly think you're looking for a common father in all these cases?"

"I sincerely hope not!" was Claudia's tart reply. "Can you imagine anything more destructive to my theory? No, what I want to do is prove that the whole notion is—is stupid!"

"Well, if some mental handicaps are known to be hereditary, like Down's syndrome and Alzheimer's disease, which depend on chromosome malformations—"

"Why can I not accept that the same may be true of inadequate criminal personalities?" she cut in. "Believe me, all your arguments have been thrown at me before. The answer to that one is that the kids I have data on are not inadequate. Absolutely the contrary. They are coping far better than almost anybody else. Think about the evidence. Didn't I say the second thing that connects them is that they get away with what they've done?"

Contrary to his former intention, Peter took another sip of whiskey. He said, "I'm going to have to ponder that. As to records of donors, though . . . Well, that was one of the points I raised when I first went to the clinic."

"You call it a clinic. Was it part of a hospital, a larger operation?"

"Not at all. It was the consulting rooms of two doctors in partnership, one man and one woman, an obstetrician and a gynecologist. They had premises in Wimpole Street. That's not quite as famous as

Harley Street but it's just around the corner. I didn't get to know the woman at all—the friend who let me in on the act had some sort of contact with the man, I don't recall what—and I believe that not long afterward there was a bustup between them and the partnership was dissolved. But that was after I'd exhausted my quota."

"You keep harking back to your own experience," Claudia murmured. "Would you stick to generalities for a bit? I want to know how they kept their records!"

"Ah . . . Sorry." Peter licked his lips. "They were on regular index cards. Each donor was given a code known only to the doctor and his nurse. I wasn't even told what my code was. I didn't ask. It struck me as a good way of keeping the data confidential."

"What if, say, the doctor and his nurse were killed in a car crash? Wouldn't the other partner have been able to access the data?"

"I've no idea. Grief!"—with sudden force. "This all happened well over a decade ago. Besides, it's late. You expect me to remember minor details like that?"

"My turn to say sorry," Claudia sighed. "Didn't I say earlier that I'm becoming obsessed with this? I had so much hoped the data might be stored on a computer, because computers can be hacked . . . Well, you're right: it is late. I'd better be going. Want to copy that disk of mine before I leave?"

But Peter wasn't paying attention. He tensed and snapped his fingers. "Just a moment! It's coming back to me . . . Yes, that was part of what the row was about, the one that led to the breakup of the partnership. I was told about it afterward by another of my fellow students, who stayed the course and became a GP as I'd intended to. He'd been a donor as well. There must have been—oh—at least half a dozen from my hospital. We all vaguely knew who else was on the list, but it wasn't any reason for us to be friends, you see."

"Breakup . . . ?" Claudia prompted.

"Ah. Yes. Well, Dr. Chinn—the male doctor—felt the setup was becoming like an assembly line. At least that's what I was told. So when his female partner suggested going over to a computerized record system he tried to veto it because he felt it was too impersonal as well as less secure. But she had more clout than he did, or more money invested, or something, and in the end he quit."

"Is the clinic still in existence?"

"It's mutated into a general fertility clinic, with a pretty good reputation, I believe. But like I said, I can't speak for all the other similar operations there were in Britain. There must have been dozens —scores!"

"Some not quite as—ah—ethical as others?"

Claudia waited a long moment for an answer. None came. Peter's face had frozen into a mask of concentration.

At long last he said, "I think I know someone who might fund your research. I know you don't much care for the media, but if you want to reduce the load on Strugman . . ."

"I certainly don't want to abuse his generosity."

"Well, do you know a paper over here called the *Comet?*"

"You did a program about it," Claudia said. "One of your last. It was all alleged to possess the most technically advanced—Just a second! I think I see what you're aiming at. I need access to one hell of a lot of cheap computer capacity, don't I? Would they provide it?"

"It's worth trying. I know for a fact that Jake—the editor—is desperate for any sort of an exclusive."

Waiting for her reaction, he drained his glass, feeling the last fragments of ice chill against his lip.

"You're right," she said eventually. "I don't care too much for the media. But so long as we could sew up a good tight contract, so they didn't rush into print with some half-assed corruption of my findings . . . You know, I never thought I'd be driven into a corner like this! You think this—this Jake can be trusted?"

"About as far as I could throw a taxicab." Peter set his glass down with a slam. "But at least he's an honest rogue. The ones I can't stand are the ones who don't even know they're bent. He does. I'll give him that."

"Sounds like the best one can hope for in this day and age," Claudia grunted, retrieving her bag and rising. "Do you want to copy my disk or not? I have to get home."

"Sure!"—hastily. "Just a second while I find a scratch one."

And while the copy was being made (he noted it was autoprotected against copying the copy, but that was to be expected):

"Are you serious about taking over my old place?"

"Sure!" She raised her eyebrows. "Sounds like the ideal solution to my problem."

"In that case I'd better give you the address and the name of my bank." He seized pen and paper and wrote rapidly. Handing her the note, he added, "This has been kind of a constructive meeting. Thanks for changing your mind about me."

"You're still on probation," she retorted, reaching to reclaim her own disk as the copying process went to completion. "But . . . Okay, constructive I will grant. If I'd realized you had personal experience of artinsem, I'd have called you sooner."

"But it wasn't a personal experience. It was the opposite. It was just about the most totally *impersonal* experience of my entire life. That's why—like I said—I literally hadn't given it a thought in a good ten years."

"Were all the donors you met as detached as you?"

"I hope so. I sincerely hope so. Imagine getting hung up on biological paternity!"

"You're asking me to imagine it?" Her tone was oddly gentle, albeit mocking, as she scrutinized him with those strange artificial-looking irises. "Me, who can't even imagine being hung up on maternity? Or didn't you realize?"

For a second he was confused; then he caught on. Having spent so long in his company and alone, she was warning him not to try and kiss her good night, or the like. But this must surely be a reflex. He hadn't been aware she was gay, though now he had to assume she was, or wanted to be taken as such . . .

*Grief! The shifts and makeshifts of our society!*

"Shall I call you a cab?" he said at length, having decided the whole matter was too trivial to waste more breath on.

"No thanks. I guess I can find one myself."

Was that the tone of an offended feminist? Peter was too tired, and possibly also too drunk, to figure it out. He said with what cordiality he could muster, "I'm flattered that you shared your data with me. I'll be as helpful as I can."

"Fine. Just don't forget I still have the agreement you signed when we had dinner together."

"As though I would!"

When she had finally departed, Peter stole into the room that had become Ellen's. She was fast asleep, the phones of her stereo still on her head although the broadcast she had been listening to had gone off the air.

Detaching them with maximum gentleness, he stared around at what he had never expected to find in any of his homes: a teenager's bedroom. It was weird to see his old belongings in this novel context. In particular, he was impressed by the way she had taken to the computer he had given her. He had to admit that the teaching at her former school must have been pretty good, for she had got the knack of its more esoteric potential remarkably quickly, and it kept her occupied for hours on end.

He only hoped she wasn't going to start running up heavy bills due to interrogating distant data-bases.

The rest of the changes, though, were entirely hers: indefinably juvenile-plus-feminine touches that had made even the furniture look different . . .

It was no use. He couldn't define them. They were just *there.*

And he had better not be any longer, not after so much whiskey and such a weird conversation. Did Claudia really think she'd lucked into a genetic component of criminality? Against all her prior convictions, and everybody else's?

It was all too much to digest at a single sitting. Peter switched off the lights and stole as quietly as possible to bed.

* * *

By morning, however, he had reached a firm conclusion.

He was going to have to follow up Claudia's lead. He was going to have to con as much money as possible out of both Jake Lafarge and TV Plus, to fund his investigation.

There simply wasn't anything else in the offing that held out any promise whatsoever.

# Part Two

*"But if God is love, why is there any bad at all? Is the world like a novel in which the villains are put in to make it more dramatic, and in which virtue triumphs only in the third volume? It is certain that the feelings of the created have in no way been considered. If indeed there were a judgment day, it would be for man to appear at the bar not as a criminal but as accuser."*

*—Winwood Reade:*
*The Martyrdom of Man*

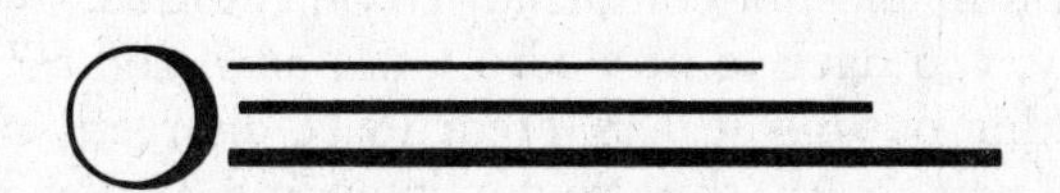

As it turned out, Harry Shay needed little persuading to sell his company and return to England. The alternative was to stay on but now as managing director of a wholly-owned subsidiary, and he was not of the temperament to work well in committee or by consensus, let alone submit his proposals for approval by higher authority. Alice was far more reluctant—she had become addicted to Californian weather—but David coaxed and wheedled and eventually she gave in. So there was no need to explain about the secret bank accounts in the Bahamas.

The company fetched an excellent price, much higher than the gloomy Goldfarb had predicted. But then, the prospective buyer had had the benefit of a business dinner at the Shays', during which David was able to soften his resistance. In short, everything went extremely well—or almost everything.

The exception was due to a man called Pedro Gui, one of the pushers who had been making handsome profits out of David's ingenuity. He had also, obviously, made a grievous mistake: he had sampled the product much too often.

Thanks to certain precautions he had taken after being visited by the FBI, David had imagined his identity secure. How Gui could have traced him he had no idea, but on the Saturday before the family's departure, when he was at home alone except for Bethsaida, who was in the kitchen, an unfamiliar car drew up and out got a black-haired, sallow-faced man in his late twenties. After a cursory glance around, he walked across to where David lay on dry grass, half his mind on a book and the other on a broadcast from Pacifica Radio.

There was a bulge under the newcomer's jacket; that was the first thing the boy spotted.

A great coldness invaded his mind as he rose to his feet. Imposing his will on his parents, whom he had known all his life, or on ignorant and timid Bethsaida, or on businessmen who could be manipulated by appealing to their greed, or even on an FBI agent, was very different from outwitting an armed stranger who, by the wild look in his eyes, was angled on one of several kinds of dope.

After surveying David head to toe, he said incredulously, "You? Goddamn. I didn't believe it when they said you were just a kid . . . You *are* David Shay?" he added with an access of suspicion. "The growser who figures out all those featly kinds of yeast?"

Feigning a boldness he did not command, David retorted, "Sure. And if you're anybody, you have to be Pedro Gui—am I right?" He made a point of checking out his dealers' credentials, discreetly.

"How the hell did you—? Ah, shit. So you know me, I know you. Puts us on level terms, I guess."

There was a canvas chair nearby. David gestured at it.

"By the sound of it, you have business to discuss. Normally I wouldn't consider it, but since you must have gone to a lot of trouble to find me, I presume it's urgent. Care to sit down while we talk?"

Gui shook his head as though fearing a trap. "I just got one thing to say to you. Don't quit."

"I don't understand," David prevaricated.

"I said *don't quit!* Word is, you're winding down the operation. I won't let you!"

He uttered the last sentence with such force that tiny drops of spittle flew from his lips, glinting in the sun.

David relaxed a trifle. Gui was clearly not in control of himself, and that ought to provide an opening. He needed one in a hurry, though; Harry and Alice were due back soon—in fact, on hearing the car he had glanced up, imagining it might be theirs.

For an instant he considered countering, "And how are you going to stop me?" But he was too aware of the presence of the gun. Instead he said, "Why not? There are other designers—"

"Ain't none like you!" Gui folded his thin hands and squeezed until the tendons stood up in ridges. "Man, you got any idea how *good* that shit is that you teach the bugs to make? No, I guess you don't use. Like the chef in the classy restaurant picks up a cheeseburger on his way home. But, oh *man* . . . Listen!" He approached David, dropping his voice to a confidential whisper.

"Listen, man, you're on the track of the Last with the capital L. You know what I mean? You follow me?"

Mouth dry, David gave a nod. Where the legend had sprung from, no one could say, but within the past year the simple symbol of an L had been scrawled on walls from Baja to Nantucket, from Taos to Yellowknife—and maybe elsewhere, too. There had been a program on TV that he had watched out of professional interest. It stood for and defined the conviction among users that soon now, very soon, the Big L would be discovered, or rather invented—the ultimate drug that bestowed total enlightenment, comprehension of the purpose of the universe.

Perhaps, he remembered thinking as he watched the broadcast, this was a counter-culture response to the teaching of the Rapture. When so many people were predicting the imminence of Judgment Day, it was hard not to be half-convinced if only by the sheer weight of repetition. The drug of drugs, the super-duper drug, was just as much a chimera, yet for the majority of poor or disappointed people far more credible.

But Gui was still talking. To be precise, he was saying, "—so I won't let you quit! Not when you're so close!"

David's sense of calm increased still more. This man only thought he had come here to threaten. In fact he had come to beg and plead.

*In that case—!*

He donned his most convincing smile.

"Well, hell. You know you're the first person to figure it out?"

Gui looked blank.

"Why do you think I'm quitting? Don't I have a sweet racket? Don't you think it's made me a fortune? And like you said I am still only a kid—can't deny that, because it's true. So why do you think I'm winding up the operation if it's not because I reached my final goal?"

He waited for the bait to be taken. Gui's dope-slow mental processes could be read in his face as clearly as on the screen of a computer. At last, eyes round with wonder, he forced out, "You—you *got* it?"

"The L for Last," David solemnly confirmed. "And since like I said you're the only growser so far who's figured it out, I guess you deserve to sample it."

By this time Gui was practically drooling. Holding out both hands, palm up and shaking terribly, he whispered, "Oh man! I dreamed about this day so long . . . How much?"

Abruptly he was groping inside his jacket, heedless of the fact that the movement exposed his gun to view. He produced a wad of hundred-dollar bills, but David waved it away nonchalantly.

"The only reason for me to make money was so I could carry on my research. Now it's over . . . Wait here and I'll bring you a sample. No charge."

For an instant a ghost of rationality seemed to haunt Gui's deranged mind, bringing with it the possibility that this might all be a trick. But he wanted to believe too much.

"Yeah!" he said. "*Yeah!*"

On his return, carrying a test-tube wrapped in crumpled tissues that held about a quarter-teaspoonful of grayish-yellow crystals as fine as table salt, David half expected to find that Gui had fled after all. Since that would have engendered later complications, he was pleased to find him still there, trembling with anticipation.

"There you go," David said encouragingly.

Turning the glass tube around and around, unable to take his eyes off it, Gui husked, "How do you use it?"

"Shoot it, toot it, stuff it up your ass—doesn't matter. I'd say let it dissolve on your tongue. Reaches the brain faster that way, via the palatal route. But listen!" David's tone was abruptly stern.

"You need to take it in the right kind of surroundings, hear? Like don't get so eager you stop off in the nearest men's room! You go home, you make yourself comfortable—like on your bed, or in a good deep armchair, so you don't get all stiffened up while you're under. And maybe lock the door because you won't want to be disturbed."

"Sounds like a long trip," Gui ventured.

"The longest. The ultimate. And afterward you won't ever want to use anything else."

For an instant he feared that Gui was going to embrace and maybe kiss him. Instead he thrust the tube into his breast pocket and ran full pelt back to his car. He burned rubber on the driveway as he left for home.

Well, one thing at least was true, David thought as he resumed his book. Gui would never use a drug again. Not after ingesting five or six lethal doses of ricin. A year or so ago, out of curiosity, he had isolated a quantity of it from a castor-oil plant that grew right alongside the house. The rest of what the test-tube held was sugar tinted with tobacco-ash and turmeric.

So long as nothing worse interfered with what he had planned . . .

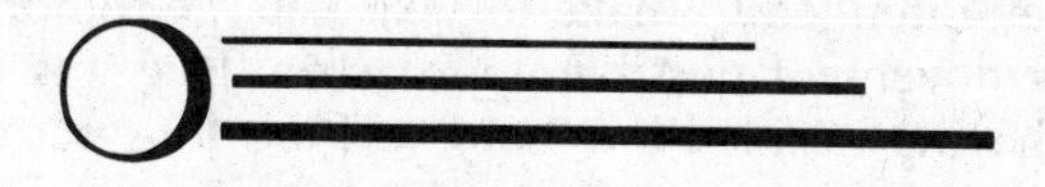

*You're watching TV Plus. It's time for Newsframe.*

*Have you noticed any starlings today? According to the Royal Society for the Protection of Birds, one of Britain's commonest and best-loved birds is in danger of dying out. A "Save the Starling" fund has been launched today to try and preserve it. More follows in a moment.*

*Charges brought against supporters of General Thrower in Newcastle under the Race Relations Act, alleging that they threw black members out of a multi-racial club, were dismissed by magistrates today. One of the injured victims . . .*

From the kitchen, whence emanated a distinct smell of burning oil, Ellen bore a laden tray into the living room. Setting it down on a table beside her father, who was deep in argument with Claudia, she said anxiously, "Here you are—I do hope it's okay!"

Peter suppressed a sigh. This was not the first time she had attempted to reproduce her mother's Indian dishes for him, so far without notable success, and he recognized that she had brought them: rotis stuffed with yesterday's leftovers plus a dash of curry powder.

*But when she's so desperate to please . . . And besides, according to today's news, if this gene-tinkered rye-grass gets as much of a grip on our farmland as the experts are predicting, we'll soon be eating worse . . . !*

"Ellen, you're a sweetheart," Claudia said without even glancing up. "Pop mine on a plate, hm? And bring a fork—I'm not terribly good with my fingers."

Delighted that her efforts had met with approval, Ellen made haste to comply, for Peter as well. Then, having topped up their glasses—beer tonight—she took the last roti for herself and withdrew to an armchair in the corner to eat it.

As it turned out, this time her cooking had much surpassed her previous endeavors. After his first bite Peter raised his eyebrows.

"Ellen, darling, this is good!"

"Really?" Her eyes were instantly alight.

"Yes, really! Carry on like this and—" He had been about to say she would become as good a cook as her mother, but there was a tacit agreement between them not to refer to Kamala, even indirectly. He compromised: "And you'll have me eating at home every night!"

After which he resumed his conversation with Claudia. They were planning the pitch they intended to make to Jake Lafarge tomorrow, noting and discarding dozens of possible approaches. Jake was their only hope, TV Plus having decided the story was too long-term, so they were determined to present it in the best possible guise.

Which was why Peter didn't notice when the brightness in his daughter's eyes overflowed and trickled down her cheeks.

When they had eaten, Ellen took the dishes to be washed and then, unusually, instead of withdrawing to her room, returned to her chair in the corner. By then Peter and Claudia were so engrossed they scarcely registered her presence, and she eavesdropped as though she were a shadow.

Peter was saying with a trace of anger, "Look, you haven't had as much to do with this kind of—"

And she was interrupting: "I won't kowtow to their damn commercial demands!"

"But if we're going to raise the wind—"

"Wind you know about, don't you? Every time you open your mouth a positive gale spills out!"

"Better to burp it up than play King Frog and burst with your own self-righteousness!"

For an instant they were glaring at each other across the paper-littered table. Then Ellen gave a tinkling laugh. The tension broken, they both turned to her.

"Excuse me," she said when she recovered. "I was just thinking . . ."

"What?"—curtly from Peter.

"You sound like a married couple. The way you're squabbling, I mean!"

For an instant they bridled; then her point sank home, and they sat back ruefully and in unison picked up their respective glasses of beer and took another sip, as though the simultaneity of the act had been rehearsed.

Peter said after a pause, "Well, I must admit I used sometimes to think of working on *Continuum* as though our team were a kind of enormous marriage, where everyone had to play along or else risk wrecking the current project. I suppose any kind of cooperative venture—"

"Is as difficult as marriage if without the legal bond," Claudia put in. "Ellen's right. I'm sorry, Peter. I am being obstructive. You do have experience in selling a story to the media. All I know about is how to persuade my peers and my publishers, and I'm not even very good at that. You don't suppose Ellen could act as referee?"

"You can't be serious!" Peter started to retort—yet the phrase died halfway through. Turning, he stared at his daughter, who was gazing eagerly at them, and saw her as though for the first time. She was objectively taller than when she had arrived at his home, by two centimeters; she was growing at such a rate, the jeans he had bought her then seemed to expose more of her shins every day. (Memo to self: buy new, and soon.) Her smooth brown skin, her slender grace, her long sleek hair, had already attracted boys from her school and elsewhere in the neighborhood, wanting to take her out . . . and for some unfathomable reason he had let her go with them, convinced on a level below consciousness that she was not about to come to any harm. In a fit of uncharacteristic incertitude he had asked Claudia's opinion on the matter, and he remembered her brusque reply: "We all have to grow up some time, and she's grown up faster than most. She can take care of herself!"

It was a risk, admittedly, but it did save worrying about babysitters. (*Baby?* But Peter kept that to himself.)

He said after a moment for reflection, "You know, you have a point. If there's any truth in what the market survey people say—"

And could have bitten his tongue out as he realized what he had been about to utter. Covered in embarrassment, he reached for his beer glass again.

But Ellen repeated her tinkling laugh. Easing her chair forward—it was on casters—to make herself a member of their circle, she said, "I know, I know! The newspapers aim at a readership with a mental age of twelve, right?"

"Uh—"

"And I'm a bit older than that, but not by much, so I might serve as a sort of touchstone, right?"

Not for the first time, Peter had the impression that this accidental daughter of his was an extremely worthwhile acquisition. What would life with her be like a few more years from now, though? If she was this sharp and this alert at present, despite what she had been through, she was apt to turn into . . .

*Something.*

But he quelled that response by turning the "something" into the sense of the phrase "quite something!" And was able to say—to Claudia—"We'd have to do an awful lot of explaining first, wouldn't we?"

"I'm not so sure." Claudia was surveying Ellen with an inspectorial eye. "I think she's been paying a lot of attention to what we're talking about, because it's part of your job. Same as she watches the TV news and reads all the papers because of what you do for a living."

Peter started; he hadn't realized she was taking so keen an interest in his and Ellen's day-to-day existence.

Still, it was of a piece with her normal attitude. He could not envisage her failing to research a colleague . . .

He said with more gruffness than he had intended, "Well, all right. Let's try our presentation out on her, and see if it will click with Jake Lafarge. I don't suppose"—and this time the words were tinged with unintended bitterness—"his mental age is any higher than Ellen's!"

Dead silence, bar what sounds drifted in from the street (and how many fewer they were, Peter thought irrelevantly, than in the street where he had formerly lived and Claudia did now: how many fewer fire alarms, police cars, sounds of riot and commotion, breaking glass . . .)

And Ellen was on her feet, cheeks aglow and pouting.

"If you're just going to make fun of me—!"

He reached out an arm and caught her as she made to vanish into her own room, pulling her around to dump her on his lap.

"I'm sorry, I'm sorry! I wasn't thinking! I mean, I wasn't thinking about you, but about Jake! He— Never mind. You can get an impression of Jake from reading the paper he edits, okay?"

Of a sudden Ellen was smiling. He put an arm around to cuddle her and leaned his cheek against her smooth tresses.

"Actually it's a very good idea. That is, if you don't mind being treated as a one-person captive audience . . . ?"

She shook her head vigorously.

"Well, then," Peter said with a cock of one eyebrow at Claudia, "let's run it up the flagpole and see if Ellen can salute it."

"Sometimes," Claudia retorted caustically as she sorted through the mass of rough notes on the table, "I suspect you must be far older than you claim . . . Okay, here we go."

An hour later, when Ellen had dutifully retired to bed and Peter was seeing Claudia out the door, the latter said, "You know something?"

"What?"

"Getting back that daughter of yours is the best thing that could have happened to you. She's humanizing you."

"I don't quite . . ." With a lot of blinking.

"For pity's sake!" Had she been younger, Claudia would have stamped her foot. "Even if you don't notice, I do! A few weeks ago you were a go-getting self-serving so-and-so and totally unaware of it—even *proud* of it! Since the kid moved in, you've softened. Gotten nicer. More caring. Do I have to run through the entire thesaurus?"

The street door was ajar to what might be the last warm night of autumn; the hallway was in darkness because he hadn't switched the lights on—it had become a reflex since he realized how limited his budget was with a child to look after. But there was a diffuse glow from the streetlights. Around here they worked more often than not.

In the dimness he could read Claudia's expression, and it mingled admiration with frustration.

"Goddamn it!" she forced out at last. "I think I could even come to like you, Peter Levin! *Me*, who after I broke up with my husband swore I was going to hate men for ever!"

And she put a muscular arm around his neck and pulled his mouth down to meet hers.

She kissed delightfully. Her tongue on his hardened him on the instant. But she withdrew the instant he tried to cup her breast, and disappeared behind a slamming door.

"See you at the *Comet* office, ten tomorrow!" was the last he heard. "And say thanks to Ellen! Now I think we have a deal!"

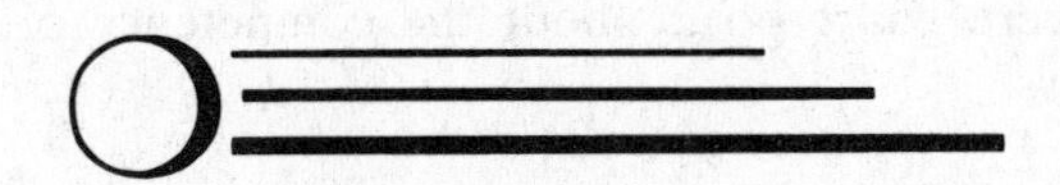

*I*n his new sanctum David Shay checked his morning post. There was little of importance among it, bar one item. As nearly as he could make out from her semi-literate scrawl, Bethsaida was pregnant, and since she must have been fertilized at a time when her husband was away on the cruise liner he was threatening divorce. He authorized transfer to her of $50,000 from his Bahaman account, which ought to shut them both up for a fair while, and consigned her letter to the shredder beside his desk, along with most of his other mail. Then, leaning back, he yawned and stretched and looked about him.

The temporary home he had chosen for himself and his family was a large Victorian house within easy reach of London, in the Surrey district of Virginia Water. It was set well back from the main road among trees that were about to drop their leaves, but still afforded adequate privacy, since there was a winding driveway flanked with evergreen shrubs. It had stood empty for nearly a year, being too large for most people nowadays, with its twenty rooms, extensive outbuildings and enormous garden. Running it properly, the estate agent had said apologetically, would call for at least three live-in staff, and the seller was so greedy he had at first insisted on nothing less than an Arab millionaire as the new occupier. However, with the general decline in world trade no such buyer had appeared, and the Shays had leased it for twelve months at a most advantageous rate.

David's mouth quirked up at the corners. The rent had rather less to do with the owner losing patience than with the dinner he, Harry and Alice had invited the estate agent to at a fashionable local restaurant, during the course of which he had been able to turn the charm on full. Of course, he had had to work the same trick on the landlord as well, but that wasn't hard . . .

*Hard.*

Reminded, he rubbed his crotch. He must do something, and soon, about arranging for those live-in servants, and he wanted them all to be young and female. He made a mental note to mention it to Harry and Alice when they came home tonight—they were in London at the moment. He himself was far too busy setting up his new gear, the last of which had been delivered yesterday. He would have brought what he was used to from California, but the voltage difference might have caused problems and in any case most of it was two or even three years old. Better, therefore, to scrap it and acquire a whole new setup, even though there were bad reports about the competence of UK maintenance engineers.

*Bad reports* . . .

He glanced at the TV, that was playing the early evening news, and sighed aloud. Did there *have* to be another disaster every single day—or further horrors in the long-running dramas? Was the human race really composed of, or at any rate ruled by, total idiots? The evidence seemed incontrovertible. The Netherlands were under martial law because the Surinamese, inspired by the "heroic resistance" of the Sri Lankan Tamils, had decided to undertake a similar campaign of sabotage. The Sikhs in India had killed their tenth Congress Party MP, along with his entourage, by mining a road-bridge he was due to cross. Yet another attempt to launch an SDI "defense" satellite had ended up with the launcher crashing in the deep Atlantic, and people were starting to claim that communists must have hacked their way into the computers that designed either the launch vehicle itself or a key part of its control system. Right now the heavy betting was on a programmer who had quit in disgust after having created such a gang of indispensable software for the DoD that even the American government—read taxpayer—couldn't afford to scrap it and start over.

But that, of course, might be a red herring; a bit of "disinformation" put about to disguise the fact that the Soviets were able to tap into NORAD, the Pentagon, all the main defense contractors . . .

Which, in David's view, went without saying. Idly he keyed a code that interrogated the master launch computers at Cape Canaveral. Inside thirty seconds he was looking at the fault-diagnosis display from the just-crashed rocket. Without bothering to read it, he hit the cancel command. He had only done it in order to confirm that his new rig was status go.

Now, therefore, he could start work on the most important task that lay ahead of him. Who was his real—his biological—father? There was an obvious first line of approach: he must search the Police National Computer for gossip, slander, and any other malicious allegations about his mother. From that source, he was virtually certain to obtain clues to the clues that might reveal his paternity.

And if not, there were many other avenues to be explored.

He had mentally drafted the necessary program while traversing the North Pole on the way back to Britain. In odd moments since then he had found time to debug it. Now it was ready to run. It would certainly take hours, maybe days, but it was ready. He called it up and activated it, then rose from his chair and stretched and yawned again.

At that precise moment the sound of a car approaching up the driveway reached his ears. It halted; the engine was switched off. Shortly after, the front doorbell rang.

For a moment David considered pretending that the house was empty, but had to discard the idea as soon as formulated. Had it indeed been so, electronic devices would have interrogated all callers, recorded their replies, and fixed their images on tape. The security level here was *high*.

Annoyed that he hadn't thought of switching the machines on, he headed for the door.

"Good afternoon!" said a bright-faced young woman in a brown trouser-suit, a portable computer no larger than a camera slung over her left shoulder on a yellow strap. "I'm Gladys Winter! Are your parents at home?"

She had been alone in the car—or, at any rate, there was no one else in it now. Of course, one or more fellow-passengers might have darted off to scour the grounds . . .

David realized he was beginning to feel paranoid. Why should she not have come here by herself? He said in as normal a tone as he could contrive, "I'm afraid they went up to town for the day. Can I help you?"

"Well, maybe you can." Gladys consulted her computer. "I gather you returned from the States after an absence of some years, and—well, for some reason your parents don't seem to have made arrangements for you to attend school this year. At any rate our records . . ."

She droned on for another couple of sentences, while David cursed himself yet again for overlooking an important point. But he kept control.

"Now this is something they would certainly wish to talk about if they were here," he said when he had the chance. "Won't you come in for a moment? And—excuse me, but are you on your own?"

Gladys blinked. "What makes you ask that? Who else can you see around here?"

"Well, I just thought that if you had a companion he might have—uh—vanished into the bushes . . ." With a winning smile.

An answering grin. "I see! Yes, men aren't so good at holding their water, are they? . . . May I come in?"

*Didn't I just say so?*

But David stepped aside politely and closed the door.

Guiding her into the newly—and lavishly—furnished drawing room, he bade her sit down and offered her a drink, which she refused. He didn't insist; he needed to exploit his charm for more important matters.

"Now what precisely can I do for you?" he murmured as he installed himself beside her on a chintz-covered sofa, donning as grave and adult an expression as he could contrive but seizing every chance to breathe toward her face and brush her with his arm or hand.

She explained about Acts of Parliament, local regulations, sundry by-laws and statutory instruments authorized by the Ministry of Education . . . growing more and more agitated as he found other opportunities to touch her: first her cheek, then her bust, then her waist and hips.

"So, you see—" she attempted to conclude, but he cut her utterance short, clasping and kissing her fingers.

"So *you* see, there's no need to worry about me. Regardless of English law, I don't have to go to school. Do I?"

"I—"

"I mean, you wouldn't think of reporting me and my parents as lawbreakers, would you?"

"I . . . Well, no. I suppose not." Gladys ran a finger around her collar as though it had grown unbearably tight, but made no attempt to release her other hand.

"Isn't that the part of your work that you hate most?"

"Frankly . . ." Of a sudden she relaxed and smiled. Her face, which was rather square and flat, underwent a transformation. "Yes, I do hate having to report people for neglecting their kids. How did you guess?"

David evaded an answer. Instead he parried, "And do you think I'm being neglected?"

"Goodness! The way you talk, the surroundings here . . ." A helpless gesture as though she was trying to seize a handful of air and mold it into meaning. "Of course not! It's just that your family's name cropped up on our main computer, so—"

"Which computer is that, by the way?" David inserted. By this time he had progressed from caressing her hand and wrist to stroking her nape.

"The Department of Education's."

*Mm-hm. What was that traditional saying of the Jesuits? "Give me a child before he is seven and after that you may do with him what you will!"*

A policy being as thoroughly exploited by the present British government as ever by the régime Franco visited on Spain when it too was a once-great nation mourning the loss of its overseas empire. One of these days, when he found time, David planned to analyze that parallel to see whether it stood up as well as he imagined.

Not, however, today.

Gladys was rising, albeit with visible reluctance, having punched an entry into her computer, and was saying, "Well, I won't delay you any longer. Obviously there's been a mistake. Your parents are planning to send you to a private school, aren't they? Sometimes that sort of data takes a long time to find its way into our records."

*Figures! The richer you are, the better you can elude Big Brother!*

But since she was here, there was one thing she could do for him. David glanced at his watch and saw that over an hour remained before the earliest time he could expect Harry and Alice to return from London.

"What about blowing me before you go?" he said with his sweetest smile and most cajoling tone.

"Well, I wouldn't normally, but—"

"You like me, don't you?"

"Yes. Yes, as a matter of fact. Even though I don't know why." She was sweating and trembling, proof that his charm had worked as easily on her as on Bethsaida.

"But you do. And it isn't very much to ask, is it?"

"No . . . Oh well, all right." Swinging her computer behind her back, Gladys dropped to her knees as he unzipped, then checked with an apologetic expression, saying, "I—uh . . . I don't have an AIDS certificate, you know."

"I do."

"At your age?"

"I've been living in California, remember."

"All right."

She wasn't very skilled. He found himself wondering what Alice was like at this; then, whether it might be advisable to advertise for the people he was looking for; then—

Eventually he came, and thanked her. Conceivably she might prove useful, one of these days.

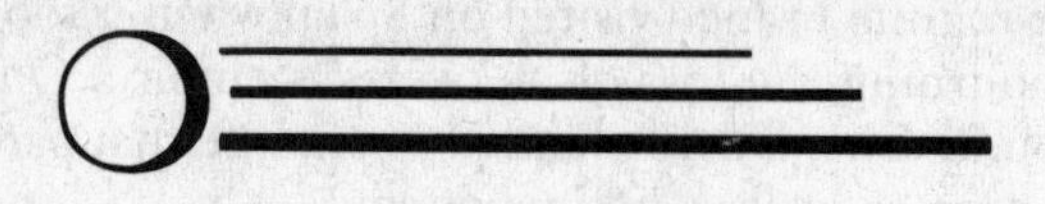

*You're watching TV Plus. Now for Newsframe.*

*At an emergency meeting of the European Parliament, called to consider the catastrophic loss of tree-cover in Northern Europe, Britain again vetoed attempts to reduce atmospheric pollution on grounds of cost. The West German Green spokesman proposed that oxygen-counts should be added to all TV weather reports; this motion was defeated in spite of powerful scientific backing.*

*Supporters of General Thrower were today accused by an opposition MP of fomenting racial hate in schools. Asked to comment, the general said, "The purity of our heritage is precious to all right-thinking people. I myself . . ."*

"Peter, good to see you! And you must be Dr. Morris! Sit down, make yourselves comfortable! Laura love, bring us coffee, hm? Or would you prefer something stronger? Let me give you a preview of what we have lined up! It's going to *rock* the competition!"

They were in the wide low-ceilinged room that was the *Comet* office. It looked more like the set of a cheapo sixties science-fiction film than any place where ordinary people worked. Eight sub-editors were at work on display screens underlined by keyboards, flanked by microphones, for they were currently experimenting with voice-input of news-stories. So far, however, the technology worked only in Finnish, the language of the country where it had been developed, because it was phonetic and unambiguous.

Now and then one of the subs, assigned today to carry out a routine test, said something loudly and clearly to a microphone, inspected what appeared on screen, swore, and recorded the nature of the fault before rectifying it by more conventional means.

Jake Lafarge was a ruddy man in his middle forties, with a moustache the shape and color of a worn brown bootbrush and a prominent pot belly, testimony to his weakness for drink. But he had kept the *Comet* afloat for a year longer than the pessimists had predicted, and the paper's backers were cautiously allotting more and still more money as he came up with neat new ideas that exploited its ultramodern technological equipment. Each in turn, though it might achieve little in the long run, prompted a flash of new interest among the public and a transient upturn in the sales graph. His latest coup had been to realize that the incredibly expensive computers his proprietor had bought allowed him to fake news pictures from what was already in store in the library, and this was what he wanted now to demonstrate to Claudia and Peter.

"Today's *Guardian* broke the capture of that opium-lord in Northern Burma!"

He was slumping into a swivel chair and feverishly hitting (mishitting and cursing) keys on a board before him.

"What they didn't get, because their photographer was shot in the kidneys and died on the way out, was—*this!*"

Triumphantly he pointed at the screen. In full color it showed the said opium-lord surrounded by Burmese troops holding him at gunpoint. Another touch on the board, and there he was being manacled; again, and he was being forced aboard a helicopter with a sack over his head.

"Sorry about the sack," Jake sighed. "But the machines weren't up to a convincing left-rear profile . . . The rest is spot-on, though, even the 'copter! Isn't it amazing?"

He wiped the screen and swung his chair through ninety degrees to confront them again, beaming exultantly.

There followed, fortunately, an interruption. The girl he had addressed as Laura arrived with cupfuls of coffee—real, at least, not assembled in a dispenser. Having issued it like field-rations, having offered capsules of milk and sachets of sugar, Jake leaned back and demanded of Claudia, "Well! Don't we have a breakthrough?"

"It's phony," she responded in a grumpy tone. "And not original."

Peter tensed so violently he almost spilled scalding liquid in his lap. Did she not realize how much depended on—?

But she was continuing.

"The first time a hoax of that kind was pulled, as I recall, was during the Spanish American War. I think it may have been the Vitagraph company—the one O. Henry wrote scripts for—but I'm not certain. It was around then, anyhow. They faked newsreels in the studio using silhouettes and cut-outs, and audiences all over the States and even abroad were fooled to the point where they clapped and cheered. Later, during World War I—"

Jake's face darkened. Peter was framing a hasty apology, and at the same time planning what he was going to say to Claudia as soon as they got kicked out of here, when he realized abruptly that his reflex assumption had been wrong. Jake wasn't flushing with rage. He was . . . Yes! Incredibly, he was *blushing* at having been caught out!

"The sinking of the *Lusitania!* You—you—you . . . Oh, bloody *hell!* I'm sorry! It's just that I so seldom meet anyone who remembers further back than what was in this morning's paper, or on the news last night, and even that is stretching it these days."

Claudia leaned back and crossed her legs, neat as usual in one of her formal trouser-suits; she had five that Peter had managed to count, all in the autumn colors, old-gold, russet, sage-green, wine-red and plum-blue. Today she wore plum-blue.

She said composedly, "What all this boils down to is—"

*Brass tacks?* Peter recalled her comment from the night of their first meeting in London, and wondered how wrong he could have been.

But she was continuing:

"—you're trying to update a trick that's been tried before with earlier technology. It made the groundlings cheer in the old days when there wasn't anything else. Do you honestly think it's going to part them from their money when they all have color television, VCRs, hi-fi and CD rigs, and God knows what?"

There was a terrifying pause—for Peter, at least, who was envisaging the collapse of his Ellen-tested deal. (Why should he think of her at just this moment?)

Then Jake slapped his desk, open-palmed, and jumped to his feet. Pacing back and forth within the shoulder-high partitions that defined his territory, no larger than was Ellen's room at home (a second time!), he said:

"How the hell did you sus me out so fast—? Excuse me just a moment! Laura!"

"Yes?"—as it were from the air.

"Total privacy for the next ten minutes! And I don't care if it's his Ultraviolet Highness in person!"

"Sure, Jake. Right away!"

*Privacy? In an open-plan office?*

Then something happened to the air; it made Peter's ears feel numb, obliging him to yawn and release the pressure in his Eustachian tubes. Awed, he realized this was the effect of a technique he had read and heard about and never experienced before: a sonic barrier.

Undisturbed, as though it were no worse than what one felt as an airliner soared to altitude, Claudia fixed Jake with her implanted irises. Responding like a rabbit confronted by a snake, he halted in mid-stride and swung to face her.

"Blast you—*woman!*" The last word carried a load of venom. "For targeting my weakest point!"

It was too early for Jake to be drunk, Peter thought. And yet . . .

"All this fabulous technology! And here I am acting like Wenceslas's page!"

" 'Mark my footsteps, good my page! Tread thou in them boldly! Thou shalt find—' "

Claudia got that far before Jake pounded fist into palm and stamped on the floor.

"Yes! Yes! *Yes!* I'm following up everyone else's stories because my stinking boss won't spend as much on decent correspondents overseas as he does on these damned machines! And you're bloody right! Dressing up second-hand material isn't going to keep the paper on its legs! I need an exclusive—a major break—something that nobody else can get at before I do! When Peter rang me up he promised he had found one. Tell me what it is."

He slumped back into his chair, breathing hard. "It had better be good," he concluded. "But if it is—well, you can count on all the help you need."

When Peter returned home he was in a daze. The outside world seemed distant and unreal. Claudia, despite all his misgivings, had sold the story beautifully. Jake was over the moon about it, regardless of the long lead-time. Provided he had it before Christmas, he had said . . .

Which presumably was the deadline set by his proprietor for discontinuing the paper.

Moving stealthily, as though to make too loud a noise would wreck his mood, he let himself into the flat and hung up the coat he had donned against the increasing chill of autumn—and grew abruptly aware of a humming noise from the living room.

But there shouldn't be anybody there! Today was a school day, and Ellen ought still to be with the helpful minder—

*Intruders?*

In the hallway there was a stand that held two umbrellas and a heavy walking stick. He caught up the latter and rushed through the door, prepared to wield it like a club. But it was Ellen who turned to him, wide-eyed, alarmed. She was seated at his desk, silhouetted against the green-gleaming screen of his computer.

"Oh, Dad! It's you! You frightened me!"

"You're not supposed to be here," was his foolish reply. "Why aren't you at Jeannette's?"

Instead of answering him at once, she was wiping the display with slim and accurate fingers, not looking at the keyboard. Now she rose to embrace him.

For once he thrust her aside and held her at arm's length, searching her face suspiciously.

"What else have you been up to? I didn't tell you you could use my rig!"

"I know you didn't! But I haven't done any harm, I swear! It's just that . . ." Her eyes were filling with tears. "I did mean to tell you, I swear, only—"

"Come to the point! Please!"

She turned away glumly and sat down. Avoiding his harsh gaze, she said, "I couldn't stand the way the other kids were treating me because I'm not white."

"What? But I thought—"

"Oh, Jeannette's all right. She does her best to shut them up, but now that all their parents seem to be wearing Thrower ribbons . . .

"So I lied to Jeannette. Said you were going to be home earlier in future and it was all right if I came straight here after school."

"And she didn't check with me?"

"She left a message on your answering machine."

"I didn't find it!"

"No. I—uh . . ." Dreadfully embarrassed, Ellen licked her lips. "I called back and said it was all okay, and then I wiped the tape. I know I shouldn't have, but I simply couldn't take it any more. Honestly I couldn't!"

She twisted round to confront him defiantly. "And I haven't just been coming straight home and costing you a fortune in computer charges! I got myself a job. So if I have cost you anything, I can pay it back."

"A job?"

"Yes!"—defiantly. "Three afternoons a week for an hour. I clean house for an old lady! She gives me ten pounds! It isn't much, but at least it's pocket-money."

*Pocket-money.*

That brought Peter to a frozen halt. Harsh words died on the tip of his tongue. He was so totally unused to parenthood, he had *forgotten* about pocket-money. Here was this teenage girl who was his daughter, going out two or three evenings a week with boyfriends, and he wasn't even giving her enough to pay for a bus or taxi home if something went amiss!

And here he was standing, ridiculously, with a stick in his hand as though to fend off a burglar . . .

Swallowing hard, he replaced it in the hallway. Returning to the living room, he said, "Ellen darling, it's me who ought to apologize. I'm sorry about the pocket-money. Here!" He groped for his billfold. "Would a tenner a week do for starters? I'll see about a raise, soon as I can."

Instead of merely taking the money, she caught hold of his hand and kissed it. Her long sleek hair brushed his skin as she raised her head, all tears forgotten.

A sense of warmth pervaded his entire being as he smiled back.

"And that may be quite soon," he said after a pause.

"Was it useful, trying out your idea on me?"

"Useful! Grief! We have to go back to the *Comet* tomorrow. A high-powered lawyer will be there with a draft contract. That's in the morning. In the afternoon, if all goes well, we're scheduled to meet an ultra-super hacker, who Jake swears can get at practically any data anywhere, so long as the machine's on line . . . By the way, I suppose you checked my email."

Instantly crestfallen, Ellen bit her lip and gave a nod.

"I'm sorry. It was one of the things I thought would help me to figure out your system."

*Let there not have been any more messages from women wanting to interface with me again . . .*

Not, on reflection, that he imagined Ellen would have been upset by it . . .

"And was there anything?" he said after a pause.

"Some people called Shay, that you've been trying to reach in California."

"Oh!" His interest quickened. "What—?"

"They've moved. I think they're back in Britain. But they don't want their new address made public." She was all little girl at the moment; he could imagine her aged six, with her hair in a fluffy halo around her head. "I—uh—I hope you don't mind, but I tried to find it anyway. I thought you might be pleased if I tracked them down."

That, Peter thought, should have made him annoyed. But he couldn't summon even the ghost of anger. Instead he had to fake sternness as he said, "You've got to learn, young woman, that this kind of thing can be dangerous! Harry Shay is very, very rich! If he finds out someone's attempting to invade his privacy he could easily afford to bribe a few policemen and have me locked up under the Data Protection Act!"

"Goodness!" Her eyes grew wider than ever. "Dad, I'm sorry! I had no idea!"

"All right, forget about it. Just bear in mind that for the foreseeable future all our—ah—dodgy operations must go by way of the computers at the *Comet* office."

*Our?* Why had he said that? The sense of unreality that he had felt on the way home was growing unaccountably stronger . . .

"Dad! Sit down!" Ellen urged, guiding him to a chair. "Let me fetch you a drink. What do you want? I think there's some whiskey left. Dinner can be ready in half an hour if you like!"

Well, it had been a hard day. A rest in a comfortable chair, a good stiff drink, a meal cooked and served for him—yes, that sounded like a well-deserved reward.

When she brought his drink, mixed precisely as he liked it, along with a glass of orange squash for herself, Ellen perched on the arm of his chair and after a moment, unexpectedly, leaned over to kiss the crown of his head . . . where, as the touch of her lips reminded him, he was starting to go bald.

"Dad," she whispered. "Dad!"

"What is it?" He reached up to stroke her neck. "Want me to tell you again how useful you were last night? You were, you know! While we were in Jake's office, I could have shut my eyes and sworn it wasn't Claudia but you doing that marvelous sales job!"

"No," she whispered, her mouth still close to his scalp. "No, I just wanted to say . . . Dad, I love you. After the awful thing that happened, I was so frightened of what might become of me! But you've been wonderfully kind!"

"I love you, too," Peter said sincerely. And only later realized it was the first time he had said that, save to various and half-forgotten mistresses, since he stopped saying it to his mother at about the age of eight.

He pulled her down on to his lap and for a long while held her close, glowing inwardly, not wanting to be the first to break the mood. Facing the chair they shared, the TV was playing, but the sound was turned down and without a commentary the images that filled the screen struck him as meaningless.

Then at last Ellen jumped to her feet.

"Dinner!" she exclaimed. "Country Captain! Frozen chicken pieces, I'm afraid, but I've done my best. I do hope it's good!"

*Me, too. But at least I know one thing that is. Claudia was right, wasn't she? And I thought she was a shellbacked feminist who hated men. Until last night . . .*

The recollected taste of her mouth mingled on his tongue with the sharp bite of whisky. Utterly relaxed for the first time in years, Peter awaited Ellen's call to join her at the table and try out her culinary masterpiece.

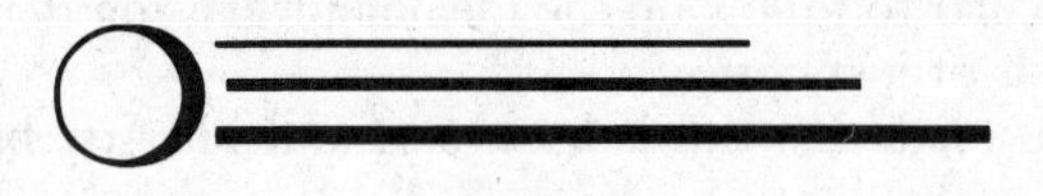

*W*ithin a short while of his family's return to England, thanks to the computer search program he kept running night and day David Shay had established two facts for certain.

Harry had indeed had a vasectomy. It was in his medical records. And it had been done while he was still living with his former wife, very probably at her insistence. Right up to the time when he moved to California, there was no mention of the operation having been reversed.

So how had Alice become pregnant? For a while he considered the possibility she had had an affair with a friend, but eventually he dismissed it as out of keeping with Harry's attitude toward her. He might be proud of his wife's figure, and like her to show it off, but he was nonetheless possessive, sometimes downright jealous.

That left, essentially, one alternative: artinsem. In David's view Harry could have tolerated her having a baby by an anonymous stranger, particularly since the technique was adequately impersonal, and fourteen or fifteen years ago it was still plenty widespread.

Unfortunately, of course, that meant his search for his biological father was going to be even longer and harder than he had originally imagined. Still, he was getting far better at unearthing data intended to be private; he had, for instance, no business accessing Harry's medical records yet that had gone off smoothly enough.

And the second discovery he made was of almost equal importance. The faculty he thought of as his "charm" did almost beyond a doubt have a hereditary component. Perhaps it was even a mutation. There was scarcely anything in the formal literature concerning cases like his, but extensive—and expensive—searching turned up occasional news-items that sounded tantalizingly similar to his own case: reports of young people, all around the same age, who had the knack of getting their own way . . .

At first the prospect of meeting others like himself struck him as immensely exciting. On reflection, however, he decided it might be risky, too. He had no idea whether their "charm effect" might not be stronger than his. He was becoming well adjusted to the idea of controlling people; the risk of being controlled in his turn did not appeal. Nonetheless, if he did have siblings . . .

In the upshot he decided to go ahead, albeit with great circumspection, and in particular to follow up the idea of advertising that had come to him in a flash of inspiration.

This was how he made his third discovery, and his first breakthrough.

He had located an agency that offered maximal exposure for minimal outlay—not of course that cost was any object, and he paid at once, in full—by syndicating its insertions in English-language journals from Ireland to Greece. And, to his surprise, it was from Ireland that he received the first response to his cautiously worded inquiry.

Widowed, deprived of her only child, who had been perverted into the paths of evil thanks to the refusal of the teaching nuns at her convent school to root out the true source of the wickedness festering among their pupils, to expel instead of her daughter that younger girl who must plainly be a monster despite her charm, Caitlin's mother was constantly on the lookout for anyone who would believe her story and sympathize—maybe take action. Of some kind . . .

For the latest of a dozen times she began to set forth the details. In green ink on pink and scented paper, with no signature.

Why David took the letter seriously, he could not quite figure out. In the end he decided that he must believe in instinct, which he had previously and sometimes publicly despised. At all events . . .

"We're going to Ireland tomorrow," he informed his parents at lunch, the day he received the letter.

"What?"—from Harry and Alice in astonished unison.

"You heard me!" As he grew more confident of the power that he thought of as his "charm," David was also becoming curter in his manner. "There's someone there I want to meet. A girl."

They relaxed and exchanged smiles—predictably. He had worked out that it was always better to provide a reason that could be rationalized. In another day or two, they'd have convinced themselves that it was their idea all along.

Everything went as smoothly as he could reasonably hope. Having met Dymphna, learned that she was an orphan, that she had not been the daughter of her mother's husband—she admitted as much within minutes, though unfortunately she had no idea who her true father might have been and there was no one left whom they could ask—she agreed instantly to his suggestion that she come and live with him.

But traces of residual resistance endured.

Harry and Alice raised no overt objection to the removal of Dymphna Clancy from her school, any more than did the nuns—

though some of her fellow pupils broke down in tears and insisted that she keep in touch by letter. His charm wasn't quite up to coping with so many nubile girls at one time, and for a brief moment he wished he could have brought them all to England with him. That would have been so much better than hiring servants . . . !

He was sure, however, that he had been right in his decision to come here. Simply by looking at her he could tell that he and Dymphna had more in common than their mere appearance: the same dark hair, the same dark eyes, the same slightly tawny, slightly sallow skin . . . He was on the right track at last!

And his charm went on working, at least so far as Harry and Alice were concerned. Indeed, though they were visibly puzzled about the fact that their son ("their!") had insisted on traveling to Ireland, and now and then remembered that during the trip they had been—well—*charmed* into signing papers whose content they could no longer clearly recall, but which satisfied both the Mother Superior of the convent and the lawyer whom she brought in to advise her (what had his name been?)—in spite of that, they made no bones about Dymphna sharing David's room. The rest of the house was huge and echoing, unfurnished save for odds and ends; she could have had her choice of half a dozen.

But despite the shift in moral attitudes that had followed AIDS, they somehow felt it unobjectionable that she and he should sleep together . . .

That first night, Dymphna wept herself to sleep on David's shoulder, not out of misery, but from pleasure mingled with relief. David himself, less inclined to tears, kept shuddering with joy till nearly dawn.

There was a scent on her skin that he had dreamed of without knowing, that he had never known existed in reality, but held out a terrifying promise . . .

A trace or two of resistance:

"Dammit, boy!" Harry boomed when he was told there were to be other recruits to the "family." "You've got what you wanted, haven't you? Dymphna's lovely! Wish I'd had a girl like her when I was your age!"

Beyond the windows she was dancing for pure joy, though it was raining—dancing on the lawn in shift and panties, feet bare, legs bare, delighting in the world.

"A part," David sighed, leaning back from the breakfast table. "By no means all. And there are so many empty rooms in this great house . . ."

"You want to cram them with orphans?" Alice cried.

David's charm was not at its maximum. Concentrating, he raised it to a peak. (What was it? How did it work? That was the next question that he needed to investigate . . .)

In his severest tone: "Is it not right and moral for those who are well off to help others that are not, by no fault of their own?"

To that, Harry and Alice found no answer. At least, none before he clinched the argument, leaning forward with his elbows on the table and switching his blazing glare from one to the other.

"You know I've kept search programs running on my computers since we got here?"

"Well"—disconcertedly—"of course. You said so."

"Among the things I've found out is that you are worth eighty-seven million dollars. At current rates of interest the income from that would be enough to support a dozen kids, at least, along with you two and myself, at a very high standard of living."

"David!" Alice began, but he cut her short.

"How do you feel about children who are starving in a world of plenty?"

"Well—uh . . ."

"Uncomfortable?"

"Yes. Yes, I suppose so." She snatched at her coffee cup and took a gulp.

"You, Harry?"

It was the first time he had addressed his putative father so directly; until now he had maintained the polite fiction of calling him "dad."

"The same, I suppose"—in an uncertain tone. "But do you honestly mean you want us to fill the house with—?"

"Riff-raff? Rubbish? Guttersnipes? Heavens, no!" David tipped back his head and let go a healthy laugh. "I want to share my home with brilliant kids, underprivileged but capable of learning—fast! Tell me straight: what better use do you have in mind for your fortune?"

Abruptly he was earnest, gazing into Harry's eyes and reaching out to grasp his hand.

"Well—ah . . ."

"Nothing better?" David challenged.

"In the moral sense, the absolute sense . . . I suppose not."

"There you are!" David crowed. "So the matter's settled. Excuse me. I think it's about time for my program to throw up more news."

Later, Alice said to Harry, "Are you sure—?"

And he retorted, "No! But I can't find any reason to object? Can you?"

After a pause: "Well . . . no!"

All, then, was as it should be. David, who was listening because he had bugged as many of the rooms as were in current use, allowed himself a chuckle and went back to investigating the data his computer search program had turned up. There was, according to the machine, a very interesting means to access PNC, thanks to a policeman who had done something highly unofficial for an American sociologist. There was a filter in the way, but British filters were as nothing to the ones he had tackled in the States when confirming that the FBI's agents had given up on the idea of prosecuting him for drug-designing.

Soaking wet, Dymphna came running into his—no, now it was their—room just as he was reviewing the fresh data that his program had unearthed.

"Let's make love again!" she whispered in his ear with all the enthusiasm of a girl who had often dreamed of bedding boys and been denied the chance for much too long.

"In a moment," David sighed, punching commands into his board. "I've finally got the breakthrough that I wanted into PNC . . . Yes! Look!"

The screen display, though, meant nothing to Dymphna, so he gave up and yielded to her importunities. As he stripped her and rolled her into bed, David wondered how long he could stand the company of his peers.

She was one. There was no doubt about it. Though she used a different term, he had seen her charm at work on Harry, and Alice, and the nuns. Possibly he had just experienced a trace of it himself . . . Without it, any or all of them might have balked at her being brought here from Ireland. For the first time, David felt genuinely afraid of the phenomenon that he was letting loose, as though he had unbarred a tiger from its cage.

But it was already too late to worry about that.

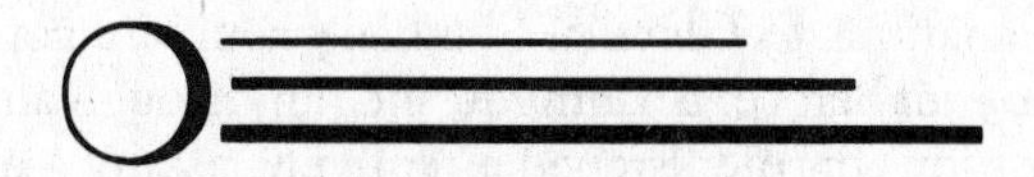

*You're watching TV Plus. Newsframe follows.*

*The Japanese government has blamed the recent mass outbreaks of arson in Tokyo and other large cities on the disaffected Korean minority, despite claims by left-wing MPs that this is an attempt to find scapegoats. The true reason, they argue, is the high cost of housing, which has already led to rioting among students who object to their future earning capacity being mortgaged by parents and even grandparents in order to purchase over-priced apartments.*

*However, General Sir Hampton Thrower, currently in Japan on a "goodwill mission to another island nation," has come out strongly in support of the government line. Quote: "Any discontented alien group . . ."*

At Claudia's insistence a copy of the contract Jake Lafarge proposed had been faxed to New York for vetting by her friend the lawyer, the one Peter had met by chance. His name, it turned out, was Walter Stine.

He proposed relatively few changes, and the *Comet*'s lawyer accepted them after only token objections. Well pleased with the success of their negotiations, Jake left his deputy in charge and took them to a hurried lunch. All three were eager to rush back to the office, but for different reasons: Jake because a major story was breaking—Peter was dismayed to learn that once again the arrest of a black drug-pusher threatened to entail rioting—and the other two because they were anxious to meet the hacker.

On their return he was waiting for them: a blond, untidy man in anorak, jeans and boots, overdue for both a shave and a haircut, wearing heavy horn-rim glasses—almost a caricature of the popular concept of his kind, too interested in computers to worry about his appearance. Jake had time only to introduce him as Bernie before being called away to make a decision about which of two stories should be followed up first.

Bernie had been assigned an alcove in one corner of the office, equipped with a computer terminal. Temporary screens had been placed around it, and as soon as he sat down he turned on another sonic barrier. Inside the protected area there was barely room for three chairs.

"Right!" he said. "What exactly is it that you want from me?"

Peter left the explanations to Claudia. She had brought a copy of the disk she had shown him before. Loading it, she ran through almost exactly the same exposition. Bernie listened attentively, asking a question now and then. When she had finished, he pondered in silence for a while, and finally gave a brisk nod.

"Should be possible," he said. "The first thing you need, I take it, is the name of the clinic that these women went to—assuming they all went to the same one. Matter of fact, though, I'm a bit surprised you haven't got at that already."

"I told you," Claudia began. "There's a filter—"

A dismissive wave; his fingernails were edged with black.

"No problem. It just so happens I know what sort of filter you're talking about. I was one of the team that designed it. My mates and I left a couple of loopholes, thinking they'd come in handy some day.

Looks like the day has arrived . . . I can probably also get you some personal names, maybe not the lot but a good few, if they can be cross-referred to news-reports. And the next thing will be the identity of the donor. I can't promise that, though."

"Obviously not," Peter said. "Not if they still keep their records manually."

"Precisely. I'll do my best, though. I should find the name of the clinic fairly quickly—or clinics. Beyond that point, like I say, no promises. Can I hang on to this disk?"

"Yes, of course."

"Well, that's as far as we can go for the moment." He slapped the top of the terminal and rose, switching off the sonic barrier. "I'll be in touch in a few days."

Leaving the office, Claudia said anxiously, "What do you think?"

Peter shrugged. "Too soon to be sure. But at least he grasped what you told him right away."

"Mm-hm . . . How are you going to kill the time until he comes up with something useful?"

"Me? I have a weird story to follow up—the weirdest. Did you hear that AIDS has been found in pigs?"

"I thought that was just a silly rumor!"

"I'm afraid not. They think they've traced the source: a mentally subnormal farmhand in Essex . . . You?"

"I'm going to take a weekend off. I feel haunted by this damned idea. I need to think about something else for a while. A trip to Paris strikes me as a good idea."

"Enjoy yourself."

"I'll try. Give my regards to Ellen. Remember what I said about the good effect she's having on you. Treat her well."

"I will."

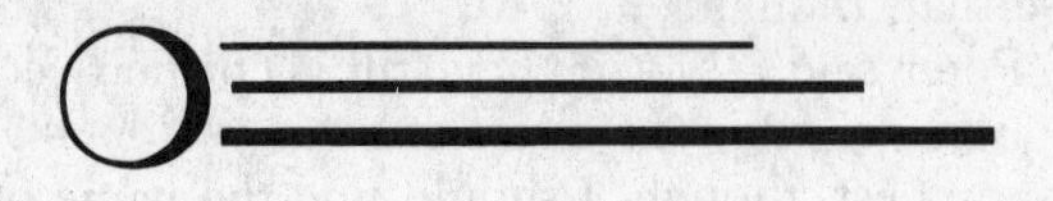

Roger Cray Wilson had had the most marvelous summer holidays imaginable. During the previous term he had learned that for the whole of August and the first half of September the school's Victorian-Gothic buildings were to be rented to a film company. An idea had sprung to his mind at once . . . and, crazy though it was, he'd brought it off. He had scarcely had to see his bocky parents—

Well, just for the first few days after summer term ended, long enough to convince them that he ought to return to Hopstanton. He couldn't employ his powers of persuasion over a telephone; he had to be physically present. One of these days he intended to try and find out how his trick worked, but being lazy and self-indulgent he had never put the plan into effect.

Why should he bother, when he could twist anyone—boy or girl or adult—round his proverbial little finger? (Or as he often thought and sometimes said, another organ?)

He had proved the fact in spectacular style.

In a terraced row of cottages adjacent to his school boardinghouse he had met Mildred, a pretty young widow whose husband had been killed in an accident at the factory where he worked, leaving her with a daughter of sixteen even prettier than herself, called June. His sympathy with their plight had led to a close—well, maybe not friendship, because Mildred was, to be candid, a bit of a dimwit, and June wasn't much brighter. Say a functional and profitable relationship.

It had been no trouble at all to suggest that the three of them provide an attractive service for the people working on the film. They had, admittedly, been doubtful at the start, but once they realized how much they could make, even after deduction of Roger's commission . . .

Of course, he had been meticulous about ensuring that every client had an AIDS certificate.

And as a result he had met people who were internationally famous: a major director, his producer, four of his stars and countless players in the minor roles. Roger himself had been in several crowd scenes as an extra, and had even been offered a speaking part when the Equity member who should have played it turned up with laryngitis.

But he had had the sense to decline. He was aware of the need to keep a low profile.

Already, on his first day of the new term, gossip was spreading about his coup. It wasn't to his housemaster's taste, but that was a minor problem; he simply needed to cajole Mrs. Brock for a few minutes and she was, as usual, firmly on his side. If only he didn't have to stay on at this horrible place . . . !

It was too soon, though, to break loose and follow up the valuable contacts he had made in the film world. It wasn't that he preferred to remain here and endure the boredom of the daily classes, the obligatory chapel services, the petty authority of the prefects; rather, it was that he felt unready to strike out completely on his own. Using his power of persuasion was, after all, quite hard work in certain cases—Mrs. Brock, for instance, and above all the Headmaster, who had taken a certain interest in him but was rarely available to be exposed to the "effect."

The chaplain, fortunately, had proved instantly pliable, and had already supported Roger more than once. He did have doubts about the pleasure he obtained from their intimacy, but so far he'd managed to keep his sense of sin under control. Oh, yes! Things were going fine!

It was no special surprise when, on the first evening of the winter term, he was summoned to the housemaster. He was in fact whistling as he approached the latter's office—until, through an open window, he spotted a parked car.

It was his parents' Rover. And next to it was a Rolls Royce that he didn't recognize and was certain he had never seen around the place before.

Abruptly worried, he honed his power to a sharp edge and entered warily into Mr. Brock's sanctum.

His parents were indeed present, and he greeted them with convincing enthusiasm, going so far as to kiss his mother's cheek—which she usually liked, though he hated, because her face was always crusted with makeup.

This time, however, she flinched away. And he had never seen his father's face so stern . . .

Moreover they weren't the only ones in here with Mr. Brock (no sign of Mrs., as though he suspected his wife of being a weak point in his defenses).

No, there were two other adults present, both of whom showed traces of what must have been a deep tan, fading now, plus a girl and a boy of roughly his own age, alike enough to himself to be—well, not his siblings, but at least his cousins.

And his attention focused instantly on them. He knew in less than a heartbeat that they were the ones that mattered. He could sense it from their relaxed, assured attitudes, the gazes that they bent on him, the very air . . . !

It had been a long while since he found himself at a total loss. Now he blindly fumbled his way to a chair at Mr. Brock's bidding as though he were ten years old again, transported back to helpless and dependent childhood before the onset of adolescence gave him his new sense of confident control.

He strove to master his reactions, and failed. He felt a sense of dreadful weakness, and prepared himself in dismay for the worst news he had ever heard.

Luckily, it wasn't all that bad . . .

"Well, Cray Wilson!" Mr. Brock snapped, seeming to have been lent far more than his usual degree of confidence—no doubt by the two young strangers. "I suppose you know why I've called you here!"

"No, sir." The words emerged in a mumble. "My people didn't even tell me they were coming—"

The housemaster disregarded him. "Some alarming reports of your activities during the holidays have come to my notice! I'm prepared to accept they may stem from your—ah—unfortunate association with a woman of loose character, and a daughter whom she appears to be bringing up in the same tradition, but I would have thought better of any boy in my care than that he fall victim to such allurement!"

His parents looked downcast; his father shifted his feet noisily under his hard and upright chair.

"I was surprised," Mr. Brock went on, staring at them under his untidy eyebrows, "that you permitted your son to pass the holidays here, given that the morals of people in the—ah—entertainment industry are always questionable. As a consequence of what has transpired, as a consequence of events that have created a considerable scandal, that have indeed come close to drawing the attention of the police, I am gravely disturbed, as are your parents!"

*What does he mean, "come close"? I could name four bent coppers . . . !*

But there was no time to complete the thought.

"Fortunately," Mr. Brock rumbled on, "it looks as though a way out has been found, that will save both your family and this school from involvement in a public uproar. Mr. and Mrs. Shay, it seems, are in process of founding a sort of refuge for children like yourself, those who have been regrettably corrupted by exposure to the sleazier side of adult life. Mr. Shay?"

But it was the boy who leaned forward and spoke in a clear firm voice that struck Roger as astonishingly like his own.

"I think I might get through to Roger more easily than my father would—sir." The last word sounded like an afterthought. "May I—?"

"Go ahead." Mr. Brock sat back and mopped his forehead with a none-too-clean handkerchief. "God knows, all I want is to see this dreadful affair resolved! I can't believe half of what I've heard, and yet I must!"

*No wonder you didn't want your wife in here!* Roger said cynically to himself. But at least what lay in store for him didn't sound as bad as he had briefly feared. He said in a cautious tone, "May I hear more?"

Afterward he could never accurately recall what had been said. He only retained the impression that for the first time he had been in the presence of someone with the same talent as himself, but infinitely more developed. He remembered being ashamed at the brilliance with which the other boy—whose name, he learned, was David—deployed not merely his naked power but also reasoned lines of argument, expressed in a voice whose very tone and pitch compelled agreement. After a while he felt he was living a dream, and could only comply passively with what he was told he ought to say and do.

In the upshot, he was in the Rolls along with the Shay family, and the girl who—he had vaguely gathered—was like him an adoptee, and all his belongings in the big old trunk his parents had given him to take to school, and they were gone. Vanished. Their car was hurtling down the road . . . and they hadn't even said good-bye!

The only person who did before he left was Mrs. Brock, who appeared with tears streaming down her cheeks and gave him a wordless hug before turning back and slamming the door, an act that said as clear as speech, "I'll miss you! But because of what you've done—!"

In the wide soft back seat of the purring car, Roger, too, broke down and wept. David and the girl put their arms around him until he got over it; then they did other things that made him feel better yet.

Up front, Harry and Alice pretended not to notice what was going on.

That made him feel the best of all.

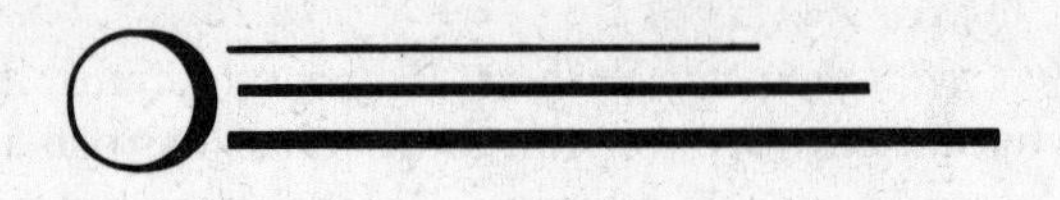

*You're watching TV Plus. Time for Newsframe.*

*It's not only in Europe that deforestation is approaching the disaster level, according to a United Nations report published today. In countries south of the Sahara, patches of desert are breaking out, in the words of the report's compilers, like an epidemic. More in a moment.*

*On his way home from Japan, General Thrower has praised the Pamyat movement in the Soviet Union, as a model of patriotic enthusiasm which, quote, "Britain would do well to imitate . . ."*

**D**ays passed without news from Bernie. Now and then Peter rang Claudia, or she him, and they exchanged sour words of frustration, but it was worse for her. He did at least have plenty to keep him occupied. The pigs-with-AIDS story duly broke, provoking the usual outcry from religious extremists about the Judgment of God, plus a practically universal boycott of pork and bacon. Given that the reason for the current shortage of potato crisps and frozen chips was traceable to that imported virus which despite originating in the Mediterranean had found the British climate vastly to its liking, Peter couldn't help wondering sourly as he contemplated his exiguous fee for securing the coup:

*Is God's judgment being visited on spuds as well?*

Eventually the signal came for him to rendezvous with Claudia at the *Comet* office—Jake had insisted that no details of the story ever be discussed by phone. Arriving late after being delayed by a pro- versus anti-dog riot—rabies had indeed been confirmed in Kent and a muzzling order had been issued—he found the famous Dr. Morris waiting in the foyer for a lift, her expression downcast.

Foolishly he tried to cheer her up with bantering chit-chat. She cut him short with a glare.

"That's the last thing I need!" she snapped.

"I'm sorry," he said with the best approximation of contriteness he could achieve. "But I expected you to be glad that Bernie has finally—"

She wasn't listening. She was saying, "Remember the policeman who fixed for me to access PNC?"

"Of course!"

"He's dead."

"What?" Peter took half a step toward her.

A grim nod. "He died yesterday. He'd been in the hospital since those riots up north. What's the city called?"

"You mean where they tried to drag that drug-pusher out of the police station?"

"Mm-hm." She passed a weary hand through her hair. "As I heard the story, half his skin was melted off with a gas bomb, and he inhaled the flames . . . Well, I guess we'd better head upstairs and hear what Bernie has found out."

The lift arrived. She entered. Following, Peter folded his hands into fists and muttered curses that though inaudible were vehement.

Behind the now-familiar sonic barrier Bernie was already in conversation—or argument—with Jake. As Peter and Claudia approached, the editor swung around in his chair and snapped, "I don't know why I bothered to call you here! This bastard's let us down!"

Flushing, Bernie banged the corner of Jake's desk. "Now you shut up, hear me? I've told you already—I've done my utmost, but someone's caught on to the loopholes me and my mates left in that sort of filter, and . . ." He paused, drew a deep breath, and continued to Claudia instead.

"Look, maybe I can get you to listen! Jake won't! On the basis of what you gave me, I started interrogating PNC and got considerably further than you had. I—"

"How much further?" Claudia stabbed.

"For starters I established that all the kids in your list were indeed born to clients of the same clinic."

Bernie sat back with a triumphant grin. The response he had hoped for, though, was not forthcoming. Eventually Peter said, "After this long, all you've found out is 'for starters'?"

And Claudia chimed in: "So what's its name?"

The grin became a scowl. "I told you—I'm working under a handicap! Someone caught on about the loopholes in the filter! Not surprising, I suppose; after all, the design is five or six years old. But what's done can be undone. All I need is a little more time—"

"And no doubt a lot more money!" Jake rasped. "What about the names you were going to trace, through correlating Claudia's data with news-reports?"

"Christ, I can't do that in just a few days! I admit this rig of yours is the most advanced I've ever worked with, but sifting through literally thousands of—"

"You're stalling!" Jake broke in. "I've used our setup since it was commissioned. I know how fast it can trace a cross-reference! Maybe I should have assigned one of my own people instead of swallowing your load of bock!"

Peter winced. That image of ingesting someone else's vomit had always revolted him, no matter how often he heard it casually used.

"I want the truth!" Jake roared on. "You've run into a problem you can't solve—isn't that the way it is?"

For a moment Bernie seemed inclined to shout back. Then the bluster leaked out of him and he slumped back in his chair.

"I haven't solved it *yet,*" he said with a final trace of defiance, and then, with reluctant candor: "But you're right. I am bogged down."

"Why?"—from Claudia.

A helpless shrug. "It's as though someone else is in there ahead of me, guessing what approaches I might try and blocking them off. Like I said, it's not altogether surprising. Once they found out the weaknesses in the filter, the rest would have followed logically. I'll keep on trying, of course, but . . ." He spread his hands.

"Sounds to me," Jake said cynically, "as though once again we have to forget about the marvels of modern technology, and revert to tried and trusted methods."

"Such as?" Bernie flared.

Jake curled his lip. "Bribery and blackmail, if all else fails! Never forget you're talking to a veteran of the Wapping Wars! Back then I sold my honor and my self-respect for the sake of a fat salary, and my sense of morality took a beating that it's never recovered from. I quote a growser who hates me very much . . . Ah, what the hell? The important point is this."

He folded his fingers on his left hand around his right fist, staring down as though into a crystal ball.

"All these kids—with the couple of exceptions you've told me about—have turned out to be from the same clinic. That much I grant you've accomplished. The fact that you haven't yet managed to correlate any news-reports with the details Claudia supplied may be due to the whole lot being juveniles, so one wouldn't be allowed to print their names. It follows—"

"Think I'm an idiot?" Bernie interrupted. "I've been running my search-pattern on a basis of related events and backgrounds. I don't have any names I could search for, do I?"

"You said you expected to find at least a few—" Peter began.

"And I've explained why I can't!" Bernie barked.

As though the sonic barrier were letting out at least his peak loudness, some of the subs at work in the vast open-plan office glanced uneasily in their direction before continuing with their assignments. Jake forced himself to calm down.

"I was saying," he gritted, "it could take a very long time to complete a search-pattern on that basis, so it makes sense to supplement what you're doing."

"How?"—from Claudia.

"In the good old-fashioned way." Jake leaned back and reached for a tissue to wipe his forehead; it was pearled with sweat. "I suppose I should have recommended this at the start, run the two in parallel . . . Peter, are you busy at the moment? I mean, with other stories?"

"Yes. There are three or four leads I should be chasing up this minute."

"Does that mean you've lost interest?" Claudia demanded, rounding on him.

"Stop that before it starts!" Jake ordered. "I've worked with Peter often enough to know he doesn't drop a promising story until it's last hope. No doubt he'll spare what time he can . . . Meanwhile, though, this is your baby, Claudia!"

For an instant it seemed she was about to erupt at his use of what she might have held to be a sexist metaphor. With vast effort she overcame the impulse.

"So what exactly do you suggest?" she sighed.

"A bit of legwork. Good traditional legwork. Start by calling on this friend of yours is the police, this chief superintendent—"

"Scratch that!" She repeated what she had told Peter in the foyer. In conclusion: "What other bright ideas do you have?"

Momentarily disconcerted, Jake said, "Ah . . ." And found the thread again.

"Well, too bad. So move on to the next possibility. On a purely statistical basis, the largest and best-known of the old AID clinics would be the likeliest. Make a list of those that are still operating, call on them, see whom you can chat up, find out whether any former staff are still around who are down on their luck and might take cash in hand for information. Like I said, good old-fashioned stuff. You might begin with the clinic Peter went to."

For an instant Peter tensed. He had never mentioned his experience as a semen-donor to Jake, so how—?

Then he remembered: following their initial heart-to-heart Claudia had updated the information on her master disk with reference to "an acquaintance in London" who at some unspecified past time had—and so forth. It couldn't have been too hard for Jake to figure out who the acquaintance must be.

Swallowing his annoyance, he muttered, "It's gone."

"What?"

"I looked it up in the phone book." With a glance at Claudia: "You didn't think I'd just been sitting on my backside, did you? It isn't where it used to be—it isn't anywhere. Dr. Chinn is dead. His partner, Dr. Wilson . . . Sorry, not Wilson; her name was Wilkinson. Anyhow, she's retired. I tried asking the BMA whether anybody bought the operation, because it must have accumulated a load of goodwill by the time it folded, but they refused to answer on grounds of confidentiality."

"That sounds like something I could dig into," Bernie ventured. He had been sitting in discomfited silence, but had not lost track of what was being said.

"Go ahead, why not? We need all the help we can get. But . . ." He broke off.

"But what?" Jake urged.

Peter shook his head as though he had briefly fallen asleep. "Nothing. Just a sense of—of connection: the clinic, the doctors who ran it, the donors, the mention of computerizing their records . . ."

They waited expectantly, but he disappointed them.

"Sorry, I can't pin it down. I'll think about it again, though. Jake, I think you were going to say something else, weren't you?"

Calmer now, Jake shrugged. "I think I've spelt out my messages. What about it, Claudia? This is strictly your pigeon, you know."

She hesitated. He went on, "I can read your mind! You think you might be a trifle—shall we say notorious?"

Relieved, she gave a nod.

"But your face hasn't exactly been plastered all over the telly. I can furnish you with fake ID, in either the name of the *Comet* or that of the agency that syndicates our stuff in the States, to account for your accent. Well?"

After a pause: "I don't see any alternative. Okay. I don't imagine I'll be much good at the game, but—yes, it is my pigeon. Funniest kind of research I ever undertook!"

"Funniest kind of subject," Peter said, and he wasn't joking, "that I ever found a scientist researching."

"That's settled, then," Jake said, and rose. The others did the same. "Bernie, I'm sorry I bit your head off—"

"Forget it. Just believe me when I say the data I imagined I could find for Claudia have turned out to be shellbacked to the *n*th degree. Talk about turtle inside tortoise inside terrapin . . . Still, I'll keep on hacking."

"You do that," said Jake. "You, too, do that."

Waiting for the lift—Bernie had remained behind—Claudia said anxiously to Peter, "You seemed to be having some kind of insight, even inspiration. Have you figured out what it was?"

He shook his head. "No, damn it. It was on the tip of my tongue and wouldn't come out. Still won't. Like trying to recapture a dream, know what I mean? But at least I do recall what brought it on: Dr. Wilkinson, the people who were donors at the clinic, the connection with computers, the row that led to her and Dr. Chinn dissolving their partnership . . . I'll work it out sooner or later. Put the computer on the job, maybe. Or get Ellen to."

"Ellen?"

"Didn't I tell you? No, I don't suppose I did. We haven't talked much recently . . . Well, she's turning into an absolute whiz. Got herself email friends all over the place! I had to put my foot down, of course, when I found out she was interrogating boards as far away as Australia. Even though—would you believe?—instead of going to the minder her school recommended after classes, she's found herself a part-time job cleaning house for an old lady! This, in order to be able to pay her own way on my rig!"

"I told you she was a bright one, didn't I?" Claudia muttered.

"Oh, sure! No doubt of it! So I've told her: provided she confines herself to Europe and doesn't mind moving over when I have work to do, she can play around as much as she likes."

"You're not letting her become—well, agoraphobic?"

"On the contrary." Peter shook his head vigorously. "Her teachers say that because she's learning so much so quickly it's doing wonders for her confidence. Being at a new school where there are relatively few kids of—ah—mixed extraction, she was having trouble for a week or two. In fact, that's what turned her off going to the minder. Now, it seems, the other kids are appealing to her for help and information. You're right: she *is* bright."

"And nice with it," Claudia confirmed. "Give her my regards."

The lift arrived. Neither of them spoke again until they reached the foyer. Then Claudia said musingly, "I never expected to turn into an investigative journalist. I don't expect I'll be much good at it . . . May I call you up for advice?"

"Any time, lady. Any time. But it may be Ellen who answers."

"Don't worry. I'll be polite . . ." They reached the entrance; the pavement outside was littered with hysterical anti-pet leaflets, bearing photographs of rabies victims. At hazard she said, "Aren't you glad you don't own a dog?"

"As a matter of fact I've been thinking about getting one. It'd be company for Ellen when I'm out. But given what's going on . . ."

"It'll blow over. We have rabies in the States. We live with it."

"I know, I know. Given the frenzy we're working ourselves into, though, I could imagine the poor kid finding it crucified on the front door when she got home from school. She's had enough to put up with. I don't want to add that as well."

"What do you predict concerning pigs?" she countered with Jewish causticity, and without waiting for an answer swung on her heel and headed for the nearest bus stop.

*Good question. The Animal Liberation Front . . .*

Peter snapped his fingers. That was the fresh angle he needed to follow up the pigs-with-AIDS story. During the next two days he didn't spare a thought to Claudia's.

Unfortunately, though, the second pig item didn't sell.

Nor did the others he had had high hopes for.

Growing more and more depressed, he began to wonder about being blacklisted. Of course there was no proof, but when so many hot leads died . . .

Perhaps it was as well he couldn't afford hard liquor any more.

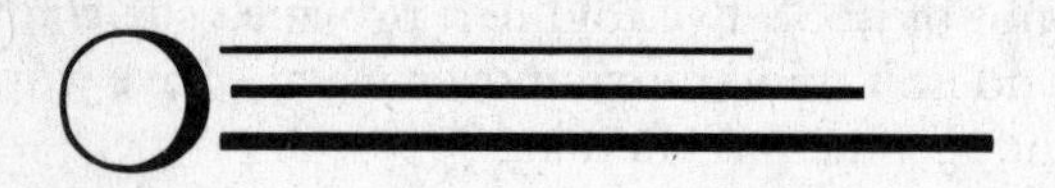

**R**eaching for an admission form, not looking up, the hospital's night receptionist said in a weary tone, "Cash or charity?"

So low had been reduced the once-noble concept of Britain's National Health Service.

From this lobby three passageways extended like the branches of a T. The one on the right was noticeably cleaner than that on the left, and far less shabby, with carpet on the floor instead of vinyl tarnished by the passage of uncountable feet. The one between was scarcely even lighted; there were fluorescent tubes, but half were dark.

Then, roused by the sound of sobbing, the receptionist lifted her head and realized that Crystal stood between two women constables, hands cuffed behind her back.

"Oh," she said, and jerked a thumb to indicate: behind me. "Criminal. That way."

Twilit, the third corridor was full of screams and moans.

When she wasn't overcome by tears, Crystal was purely and simply furious with herself: *I should have had more sense, I should have had more sense . . . !*

Yet how could she have foreseen that a punter would accuse her of infecting him with not AIDS but syphilis? And, although neither had learned the other's name (she used invented names with her clients and changed them from day to day) would enable the police to trace her because he was a computer-graphics artist and arrived at the station equipped with a near-flawless likeness of her.

*And*—this was where sobs racked her anew—that the Bill would come searching for her while she was briefly deprived of the Shadow's "power to cloud men's minds".

She'd been amused by that term; she owed it to a client who had sought her out six or eight times, wanting as much to talk about the fads and fancies of his teenage years as to get it on with her. He'd shown her prizes from his valuable collection of old comics, and in one . . .

But that was then and she was here and now, sullenly ignoring questions, hearing them answered for her by the butch policewomen, gazing with hate-filled eyes at her surroundings: cracked tiles on floor and walls, a row of dirty chairs, a wired-glass door whose pane was held together with crossed strips of tape . . . As well as screams, this area was full of stinks.

". . . and he's prepared to swear she was his only contact in over three months, so it must have been her who infected him."

"Right"—in a bored tone. "I'll take a blood sample straight away. Our automatic Wassermann machine is working for once. You'll have the evidence before she goes before the magistrate."

"Not magistrate. Juvenile."

"Christ. Isn't it hard to tell these days? When I was young, kids looked like kids . . . Does she have a smart lawyer on tap to turn her loose?"

The policewomen exchanged first glances, then grins. The older of them said, "We won't go into that—hmm?"

"Suits me. What time is she due in court, anyway?"

One of the policewomen punched keys on a belt-slung computer and fed the result to her radio. After scant seconds the reply came back in an unconvincing synthetic voice. A slot had been assigned her on the juvenile court schedule at about ten next morning.

"Pick her up around nine, then." Crystal hadn't even looked at who was speaking; she only knew the tone was harsh and male, a jailer's. "We'll have the proof for you."

*Making up your mind a little prematurely, aren't you?*

But she had more sense than to speak aloud. She had been beaten up on the way here, and she ached already; she had no wish to make herself feel worse.

And after that there was a cell. Blank walls. No food or drink, nor even anything to lie down on or wrap around herself: just a china toilet in the corner, with no seat. It was against AIDS regulations—but since when did this puky government obey the laws it passed? And they were riddled with holes, anyhow. Under age, she should have had a responsible adult with her throughout this agony, but when she tried to insist . . .

She managed sleep, somehow; drank a mug of sour tea by way of breakfast; appeared in court an hour and a half later than predicted by the *wonderful* computers at New Scotland Yard; was fined ten thousand pounds which she couldn't pay, with the alternative of jail, for "biological assault" upon the punter (that was a relic of the panicky days when AIDS victims sometimes deliberately passed it on and left lipstick messages to say so on the bathroom mirror); and by three P.M. was in the infirmary of a young offenders' prison for compulsory treatment of a notifiable disease.

Detachedly she began to wonder what weapons she could lay her hands on—broken glass, for instance, or discarded hypodermics. Then she calmed, remembering that within a few more days she would be able to talk her way out of here without violence.

The waiting wasn't going to be easy. But she could stand it. Meantime: low profile.

*Low.*

Even when a bocky chaplain with a high whinnying voice came round to declare that she was an instrument of Satan and deserved her punishment.

"Knight!"

She started and swung round.

"Go to the chaplain's office! You've got visitors!"

Her heart sank. *Oh, no! Just as I'm feeling the power again! Tomorrow I'll be able to use it properly! I'll bet he's mustered missionaries to save my soul!*

But she complied meekly enough. Even during her period she seemed to retain enough of her talent to elude the worst that others had in view for her, though she could not impose direct commands.

What she encountered, however, was nothing like what she'd expected. The chaplain, certainly, was in the room, thin and bent-shouldered at his desk. But Crystal spared him scarcely a glance. Also present were two adult strangers . . . and a boy about her age.

He had the Power.

She had never imagined it could be so strong.

Nor, indeed, that anybody else possessed it.

For the space of five accelerated heartbeats she was both terrified and disappointed: the former, because she felt as though something private to herself had been put on public sale like auction goods, to be pried at by greedy questing hands; the latter, because if this meeting had to happen she would have wished it to occur when she was at her peak, so there might be a just and equal contest.

And then she realized it had always been impossible.

No, more than impossible. Unnecessary.

For he was on her side . . .

She gasped and tilted forward, fainting.

* * *

Though they revived her swiftly, only fragments of what transpired thereafter endured in memory. She recalled words in the chaplain's horrible voice, and would rather not have thought about the Houyhnhnms . . . yet, there having been so many Yahoos in her life, she couldn't help it. Consequently: fragments.

"—seems that Mr. Shay has set up a refuge for you pitiable creatures—sad that it's not a religious foundation—nonetheless in present circumstances what with overcrowding in all jails—paid the fine and sworn to have you treated—sign this and we can go before the governor . . ."

(Later she found herself unable to distinguish between what the chaplain had said, what David Shay had said, what if anything the governor had said, and what her own drug-distorted mind had supplied to fill the gaps. To cure her syphilis, which was resistant, strangers had stabbed her over and over, some relishing the pain they were inflicting with the needles. And she had only been here two days. So how—? So why—?)

She was still babbling those questions when she found herself in the back seat of a Rolls Royce, a bag containing her meager possessions on her lap. David, beside her, told his parents in the front to open the windows, which they did although it was cool and rain was threatening. He said it was to ensure that Crystal didn't pass out again. His tone sounded sympathetic, and she felt reassured.

But when she tried to hug him out of gratitude he thrust her away with a scowl.

"You," he stated crudely, "are a twat."

And with fastidious grip he lifted clear her clutching hands.

"What . . . ? *What?*" Crystal was on the verge of tears again.

"A twat! A damnfool version of a female person! I hoped for better when I started hunting—Never mind! But given the talent that I know you share with me, should you have wasted it on *prostitution?*"

It was as though all air was emptied from her lungs—as though she were aboard a spaceship punctured by a meteor. She tried to fall, moaning, across David's lap; he shoved her roughly aside.

"Don't touch me!" he ordered. "Or any of us! Not until you're cured of all your STDs!"

And withdrew to his corner of the seat to attend to other and more urgent business. Cowering, Crystal tried to make sense of what he was doing. The Rolls was fitted with not just a phone, but also the facility to access remote computers, which was what David was exploiting at the moment. She blinked away tears and suffered the return of memory. The last car she had seen so lavishly equipped had been Winston Farmer's Jaguar—and even in that case she hadn't known how rich he was until he came to court.

When, luckily, she had not had to testify. The fact that he'd been caught in possession of two k's of crack had been enough—

For a moment she was frantic, reflex superseding rationality. Could these weird people be ex-customers, their sights set on taking over his business?

As though he had sensed her reaction, David snapped, "Shut up!"

But she hadn't said anything . . . Maybe she ought to listen for a change. She did her best to concentrate, and heard:

"What name? . . . Yes, I got the surname. But the first one? . . . Ah, I got you! Garth!"

Whereupon he produced a pocket organizer and entered a memo to self, then posted it to a remote computer.

Passive, Crystal leaned back against the soft, absorbing cushions of the car, not noticing the route that it was following but savoring the contrast between this setting and the chill harsh building she had left. She waited until David had finished, then ventured timidly, "How did you track me down?"

"Through PNC, of course," he sighed. And added cruelly, "Given that you were jailed for spreading syph I'm not so sure it was a good idea!"

She was instantly in tears. No one had spoken to her with such authority since her parents died. Her aunt and uncle had been brusquer, but earned none of her respect. This boy, however, from the very start . . .

She forced out, "It was my only hope!"

"Of wiping out the whenzies?"—cynically.

"No! To survive!"

There was a pause.

During it, up front, Mr. Shay kept on driving and Mrs. Shay kept on pretending that she didn't give a damn about whatever happened. That was a fact. Crystal knew it, didn't have to guess. Her period having drawn to its close, her talent—her power—was being bit by bit restored.

Though she never expected to match David's.

At last David, uttering a sigh, reached out to pat her hand, if only for a moment.

"Welcome, sister," he said half-inaudibly.

"What do you mean?" She jolted upright.

"You must have believed you were the only one."

"I don't understand!"

Seeming to ignore her words, he carried on. "I did for a long while, and so did . . . Never mind. You'll meet them in a little while. I only wish you hadn't declared biological warfare on the whenzies, given the risk to yourself—"

"*I didn't!*" Crystal's voice was half a scream.

He searched her face with dark intense eyes while she fought to make him believe what she had said.

And won. Perhaps her magic was returning. For he let his face relax toward a smile.

However, what he said was not what she'd expected . . .

"Ah, what the hell? We couldn't all be lucky, I suppose. Statistically there was apt to be at least one who went on the streets and didn't care about disease—"

"I did *so!*"—erupting. "Got my AIDS certificate! *And* I paid a mint for the inoculation!"

He fixed her with his stern dark gaze.

"And had room for only one disease in your mind? Forgot about syphilis and gonorrhea and soft chancre and NSU and the fungal conditions that you could have been transmitting and quite likely were?"

Crystal was crying; she didn't quite know why, but it might have been because this strange boy sounded so much more like her father than her unwillingly adoptive uncle. She forced out, "What the hell else was I supposed to do to stay alive?"

"For the first time," said David Shay, and sounded strangely old—one could have invoked the term patriarchal—as he spoke the words, "you have the chance to *be* alive. And so do . . . No, that has to wait. You'll find out in a little while."

The car was whirring along a motorway, dispersing lesser vehicles like a fast launch dismissing rowboats.

"We'll get properly acquainted when you're cured," David went on eventually. "Meantime, my search program appears to have turned up another of our siblings."

*What?*

But she didn't dare ask for a more detailed explanation. His power . . . Oh, Lord! She'd never guessed the magic could be strong! Convincing, yes—persuasive, yes! But never *strong!*

And yet . . .

For the first time in months she confronted the fact, so long and so often pushed to the back of her mind, of the difference between herself and other people. Sometimes she had been frightened by her talent, even when she was using it to maximum advantage. But at bottom what she really feared was being *unique*—an exception, a mutant, a monster.

At least she wasn't that. Here was David for proof. And he'd mentioned the possibility of yet another . . .

Little by little, as the car hummed onward, she started to relax, and when they reached their destination she was able to laugh and clap her hands with unalloyed delight.

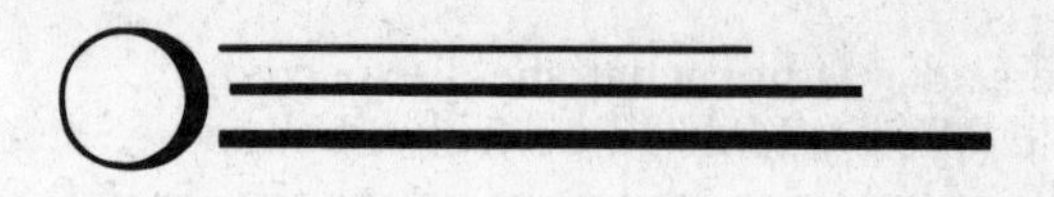

*You're watching TV Plus. It's time for Newsframe.*

*Thousands of acres of crops in the basin of America's Colorado River are under threat following an irruption of salt water from a natural underground reservoir. Water-engineers believed the reservoir to contain fresh water. This may have been true ten years ago when test-wells were last sunk to it, but subsequently salt water appears to have leaked in through a rock-fault. More details later.*

*Speaking in West Germany at a rally organized by descendants of servicemen who died in World War II, General Sir Hampton Thrower praised the valiant spirit of the fallen . . .*

"Miss Morris? From the *Comet?* Do come in, do sit down."

*Got it!*

In memory Claudia could still hear Peter's excited voice on the phone when his vague recollection ceased to be vague after two days of striving. And here was the person it had led her to: Dr. Ada Grant, who had been on the staff of the Chinn-Wilkinson, though not a partner, at the time Peter was donating semen, and who was now director of possibly the best-known fertility clinic in London. Long-faced, long-boned, with short dark hair, she wore a severe white coat and narrow black skirt. A red-white-and-blue ribbon was pinned to the breast of the coat—but one saw the emblem everywhere nowadays. (Even Peter . . .)

Now she was waiting expectantly for Claudia to explain her business.

She was nervous, naturally, but Jake Lafarge had given her an extensive and extremely useful briefing, and she felt her anxiety fade as she sat down, produced her pocket recorder, and reviewed her surroundings prior to conducting the planned interview. An incongruous hi-tech office had been implanted behind the Georgian façade of this building—in Marylebone, about half a mile from the traditional "doctors' area" of Harley Street and Wimpole Street where Peter had fathered his ten anonymous children, but that, so she had been informed, was because the rents there now precluded occupation by any doctor whose patients were less than millionaires.

Admittedly, with the falling value of money, it was much easier to be a millionaire nowadays . . .

She forced her mind back to more important matters.

"I ought to start by thanking you for sparing time for me," she said, switching on the recorder and placing it on the doctor's desk. "Oh—do you mind?"

A single headshake, and: "Not at all."

"Thank you. Well, I'm sure you must be very busy, so I won't waste more time on preliminaries than I have to, but I'm afraid I shall need to give you a bit of background before I start asking questions."

The lies, honed and polished under Jake's expert guidance, slid easily off her tongue.

"You see, my editor recently received a letter from a woman who bore a child through artinsem—AID, of course, before the coincidence of initials. Frankly, I think she should have addressed it to the Agony Aunt of one of the women's magazines, but she's a *Comet* reader, so . . .

"I don't of course have all the details, but what it seems to boil down to is this. Her son is now in his teens. She and her husband originally intended to tell him the truth when he got to about his present age, but apparently things haven't worked out too well, and she's afraid that if they do, he might become obsessed with finding out who his—ah—biological father was. Since people no longer know very much about artinsem . . . Excuse me: I'm a complete layperson when it comes to matters like these, but I have the impression that it went out of fashion virtually overnight when AIDS appeared on the scene. Is that so?"

Dr. Grant leaned back, her expression thoughtful, and set her fingertips together.

"It's certainly true that AIDS had a marked effect. Largely thanks to the media, if you'll excuse my saying so, there was a lot of panic, and prospective parents became very reluctant to accept an anonymous donation. On the other hand, there were a lot of additional factors. The chief, naturally, was the development of *in vitro* fertilization. Unless the husband has no viable sperm at all, we can now take one of the wife's own eggs and literally create an embryo which is the natural offspring of both parents. Then it's implanted and with luck proceeds normally to term."

"But this is all comparatively recent?"

"How recent is 'recent,' these days?" Dr. Grant countered with a thin-lipped smile. "It's a good decade or so since we reached the stage where it was obvious artinsem was bound to be superseded. Not, you realize, that it wasn't invaluable in its day. For instance, when I first came into the field, working at the then-famous Chinn-Wilkinson clinic, AID was undoubtedly providing a very useful service to the community. Well over three thousand impregnations were performed successfully each year, in Britain alone. At Chinn-Wilkinson alone we carried out, on average, four or five hundred annually. That meant nearly a thousand contented new parents."

"Due just to the one clinic? That's most impressive." Claudia hoped her tone carried conviction. "Tell me, as a matter of interest: did you have what you might call typical clients? Obviously every case must have been different, but can you make any generalizations?"

"Yes!" Dr. Grant said immediately, with emphasis. "The people who came to Chinn-Wilkinson then were exactly like those who come here now: stable couples, married at least five years and often as long as ten. They've tried for a baby the ordinary way; they've been to infertility consultants but tend to distrust fertility drugs owing to the risk of multiple births—we do sometimes use them, but only rarely, for precisely that reason—and they've tried the alternatives, such as mineral supplements. Quite often they've gone the whole alternative route, from acupuncture and even moxa—I ask you!—to herbal remedies and homeopathy. They're determined, that's the word. They want a child! In some cases I can recall . . . Well, I suppose I shouldn't say this about people who I'm sure are perfectly sincere, but it's a sad fact that a lot of them don't know what they're about. To be blunt, some of the people who finally apply to us turn out to have spent twice as much on techniques that didn't help as it would have cost to come here in the first place."

"You mean it's a field in which the ethics of some practitioners are —shall we say not of the highest?"

"I won't say anything of the kind," Dr. Grant smiled. "I prefer to leave it at that. But aren't we rather straying from the point?"

"Yes, of course. Excuse me." Claudia dragged her mind back to the fictitious mother worried about her artinsem son. "Obviously what I chiefly need to find out is how donor records were kept. How was it done at the Chinn-Wilkinson, for instance? Were the records computerized?"

Dr. Grant gazed at her visitor for a long moment, her thin fingers still steepled together. Eventually she said, "Let me make a guess. You, or your editor, aren't totally convinced by this woman's letter. You suspect she may be spinning a colorable yarn. The true reason for her anxiety is far more likely to be that she's afraid her son's biological father may become obsessed with the notion that he has offspring he has never met, and attempt to track down the recipient of his genes. Am I right?"

"Why, we were thinking along precisely those lines," Claudia murmured, striving to conceal her jubilation. A matter she had expected to have to work up to by a roundabout route was being broached after barely more than a hint. "Of course, one respects the confidentiality of your profession, but when so much of people's private lives is on computers now, and there are constant stories in the news about how secrets have been unearthed by hackers and used for —well—even blackmail . . . And since, no doubt, the records *were* kept on computer . . ." She let the sentence trail away.

"Well, there did have to be records, obviously," Dr. Grant said after a moment. "For instance, one wouldn't have wanted a black baby to turn up in a white family, or *vice versa.* And yes, in the last few years at least we did keep them on computer. But they were never on-line to anywhere else. They were solely for use within the clinic." Lowering her arms, Dr. Grant gazed challengingly across her desk.

"So that if the clinic had caught on fire, say, or been—well, bombed by some extremist religious group—there would have been no other copy?"

Claudia waited tensely for the answer.

"Ah . . ." The doctor suddenly seemed uncomfortable. "Well, to be perfectly frank, we did use to copy our data to a commercial storage center, one that specializes in medical records, and they're still on file there in case I ever need to consult them. But—"

The nape of Claudia's neck was tingling. She leaned forward. "Excuse my interrupting! But I deduce from what you just said that you inherited the goodwill of the Chinn-Wilkinson?"

"I—ah . . . Yes, as a matter of fact, I did take over when the original partnership was dissolved. It's public knowledge. It was a question of new specializations, more than anything . . . May I finish?"

"Please!"

"As I was saying, the data center—which we still use—has an excellent reputation. Most fertility clinics in this country, and indeed a good few from overseas, patronize it, because it's extremely well defended, and there is no way anyone could hack into it given the complexity of its password system. Take my own case by way of example. Someone would have to burgle my home, or that of my head nurse, and steal the password list, then decode it—we both keep it in cipher and we each invented our own and neither of us knows what the other's is—and *then* try and convince the data-bank that he or she was myself or my head nurse. Which would not be easy. Besides, the traffic is strictly one-way. No one even at the data-bank can access our computers from outside . . . Hmm! I just remembered something! I wonder whether I can lay hands on it. It used to live in that file cabinet over there."

Rising, she pulled open the cabinet's bottom drawer. Claudia waited eagerly. In a moment the doctor exclaimed in satisfaction, producing an oblong box.

"That's it! The videotape we used at Chinn-Wilkinson to convince doubtful would-be clients. You can play it before you leave. Of course it's out of date to some extent, but the principles remain the same."

"That would be most interesting!" Claudia breathed.

"And if your correspondent needs any further reassurance about the security of our records," the doctor went on, turning to a shelf on which rested two keyboards and a shared monitor, "this will give you some idea of the standard we subscribe to." She entered a quick command and the monitor lit. "It's the ethical code of the International Association of Fertility Services, or 'Yafs' as we call it. Every reputable clinic in the field, not only in Europe but in North and South America, Australia, New Zealand, too—every reputable clinic adheres to it, and you can see how strict it is just by looking."

Indeed it was both lengthy and detailed, and Claudia would not have dared to question its integrity. After watching it scroll slowly through three screenfuls, she murmured, "Again I have to say: most impressive. And reassuring, too. May I have a printout, or is it confidential?"

"Oh, the only confidential part is the one I'm not going to show you," Dr. Grant said with a faint chuckle. "That's the actual instructions to member clinics explaining how best to protect their records. By all means you can have a copy of the rest."

"And is there a directory of the member clinics?"

"Of course. Would you like that as well? I'm sure you won't want to limit your inquiries to one clinic, but I'm sufficiently proud of our services to imagine that you'll want to feature us rather than the competition. However, I suspect you may want to visit one or two agencies that don't belong to Yafs and don't conduct themselves in such a—well—professional manner."

"The directory would be invaluable," Claudia said. "And if I hear of an agency that isn't on the list I'll treat it with due suspicion."

"Precisely. Is there enough paper?"—glancing at a printer which reposed on a steel-framed stand at her right. "Oh yes, that should be plenty. This will only take a moment."

The printer sprang into silent action, and the printout was ready within seconds. Dr. Grant handed it over with a smile.

"And now, if you'll excuse me, I have business to attend to. But do watch this tape before you go. There's a VCR in the waiting room—on the left of the front door—and there's no one in there at the moment. If you have any further questions, feel free to get in touch again."

Accepting the tape, Claudia asked, not without a trace of malice, "Might I inquire, doctor, whether you have children of your own?"

"I carry the gene for cystic fibrosis," was the answer.

"Oh! I'm sorry!"

"Don't be. I've had years to resign myself to it. And I have an awful lot of godchildren, as it were. More than a hundred couples send me pictures of their kids every Christmas. They don't half clutter up the drawing room . . . When the tape is over, my receptionist will show you out. Good afternoon!"

Later, it came as a severe blow to Claudia's pride when Bernie dismissed the "Yafs" directory as something he had thought of accessing right at the beginning. At least, though, he was pleased to be told about the medical data-bank patronized by so many British fertility clinics, and promised to start hacking at it right away.

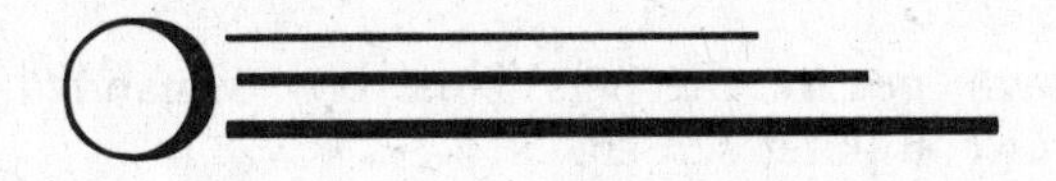

**W**ithout warning, the offerings at the gate had ceased . . .

In desperation Roy Crowder bought a couple of piglets and reared them on what sparse fodder his fields afforded, plus household scraps that would ordinarily have gone for compost. The dream he had once had of self-sufficiency, which he had spelt out spellbindingly to Tilly, had vanished under the impact of Garth's never-ceasing demands. The boy seemed not to understand how much sheer *time* it took to scrape a living from this unforgiving land. Night and day he was avid for information, tools, materials, more information! A second mortgage had provided him with a computer and a phone line to link it with the outside world; now it looked as though it was going to take a third—impossible—to pay for the use he was making of it . . .

But his parents dared not refuse, for when he grew angry—! For the past week Tilly had been hobbling around with one leg wrapped in bandages from hip to knee because, dissatisfied with his evening meal, Garth had ordered her to spill a bowlful of boiling soup into her lap.

No. Not "ordered." That was what, in the intervals of lucidity Roy achieved by driving to the nearby market-town, seemed so terrible. His son seldom descended now to overt commands. He merely suggested, in persuasive tones, and suddenly it seemed right to do as he requested, obligatory, unavoidable.

As today. The piglets were not nearly fat enough to fetch the price that Roy had had in mind, but Garth had declared that he must have more money, now. If he had come to town and worked his incomprehensible power of persuasion on intending buyers, things would have been far different.

But as it had turned out . . .

On his way home Roy found that he was crying. So blinded was he by his tears, he ran the ancient Citroën off the road at a sharp bend, and because there had been rain the night before and there was a heavy load in the back, the wheels sank into soft mud. Frantically he tried to dig them out and failed, and in the end realized he must trudge up the last few hundred yards of the track and face whatever horrors his son would conjure up as punishment.

"I would rather be dead," he said to the air. "I would rather cut my throat and join my pigs."

But he didn't. Even though he carried a pocket-knife. He couldn't bear the thought of what Garth might do to Tilly afterward.

"How much did you get for the pigs?" the boy demanded, not glancing away from his computer screen.

"They're in the back of the car."

"I told you to sell them!" Now Garth did swing around, his face a mask of fury. "Why the hell didn't you?"

"Nobody would touch 'em. Nobody wants pork since they found AIDS in—"

"You bloody fool! Who the hell could possibly imagine you buggering them? I don't suppose you can bloody get it up any more, not even for a pig!"

"Not me," Roy said, slumping into a wooden chair. Of a sudden he seemed to have discovered fresh inner resources. Perhaps they were due to absolute despair. "You."

"What?" Garth erupted from his seat and advanced threateningly.

Cheeks still wet with tears, Roy Crowder raised his head and looked his son straight in the eyes. "You heard what I said," he forced out. "When I found no one would buy them I was going to put them back in the car so even if we had to sacrifice our principles we might at least eat the meat off them, and maybe use the skin. They say you can use all a pig except the squeal . . ."

"And—?" Garth was leaning over him now, teeth bared.

"Half a dozen men came after me. I didn't recognize any of them. They had nylon stockings over their faces, coats made of old sacks to hide their clothes. They cut their throats. Flooded the road with blood. Told me not to come to market any more. Said they've found out how you get your power—by fucking animals! It's one of the things witches and magicians do, one of the ancient rites!"

He was on his feet without intention, face whiter than paper and gleaming with sweat. In that instant he would cheerfully have killed his son.

"Roy?" Tilly called anxiously; she had been in the kitchen garden trying to scrabble up enough potatoes for their supper. Basket under her arm, she limped in through the back door, and halted in terror on the threshold.

There was a dead pause. Then, making a gallant attempt to maintain her usual pretense that all was normal, she said, "I didn't hear you drive up."

"I didn't. Car's stuck in mud, halfway down the lane."

"So, you stupid son-of-a-bitch, you've cost us our car as well as our pigs!" Garth was beside himself with fury now. "What I ought to do to you—"

"Hello?"

The voice was the familiar one of Mr. Youngman. With an oath the boy swung to face the door.

*I thought I'd cured the bastard of his habit of calling here without warning or permission!*

Lately it had seemed unimportant to persuade the authorities that he was being properly educated. Besides, it wasted a lot of time and effort.

Here he was, though, advancing into the kitchen. His face was wax-pale and his hands were tightly locked in front of him as though to stop them shaking. His posture communicated, clear as words: *I know you don't want me to come in, but I must.*

Garth felt a dreadful tightening in his chest. By what means had this ineffectual frustrated teacher summoned up such courage? After so long, he must be aware of the risk he was running. He might never have admitted it to himself, but he must realize what power Garth exerted over adults—

And then another boy appeared in the frame of the door.

Not as tall as Garth, but exuding confidence. Expensively dressed, his fashionable—American—shoes stained with mud, but otherwise as smart as though he had been walking city pavement, not a puddly lane.

The tightness in Garth's chest became agonizing. He had to fumble his way to a chair and sit down. From the corner of his eye he saw his parents exchanging glances pregnant with wild hope.

"Hello, Garth," he heard. "My name is David. We've come to take you away."

"I don't want—"

"Garth, in fact you do." David drew closer, eyes alert. There was a breadknife on the clumsy wooden table in the middle of the kitchen; one heartbeat before Garth thought of snatching at it, the newcomer had already knocked it over the far edge and out of reach.

"Stay away from me!"

But he didn't. Smiling, he reached out a hand and patted Garth's wrist.

"Save your trouble," he advised. "I know who we are and you don't—yet."

The turn of phrase penetrated Garth's resentful mind. He said after a moment, "We . . . ?"

"Yes, Garth. On the way here I've been talking with Mr. Youngman. He didn't want to come back—said the last time was too terrible—but in the end he did agree, so I'm indebted to him. You are as well, of course."

Mr. Youngman didn't seem to understand the words. He had withdrawn to a corner, visibly shaking now. But one point at least had got across to Roy, for he forced out, "You said you'd come to take Garth away?"

"Yes." Not looking round. "Whether or not he wants to come."

"Thank God," said Roy. And, an instant later, Tilly was in his arms and weeping her heart out for relief.

"Right!" David said briskly. "Move! Don't bother to bring anything. I have everything you have, and more."

A final flare of resentment. "Who the hell do you think you are, ordering me about this way?"

"I don't *think*. I *know*."

There was a tense electric silence. At last Garth rose unsteadily to his feet.

"All right. Whatever the hell you have in mind for me, it can't be worse than living here. I'm coming."

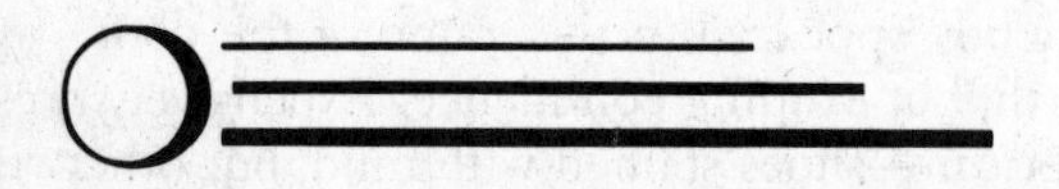

*You're watching TV Plus. Now for Newsframe.*

*British radioactive waste on its way to burial in China's Gobi Desert has allegedly been hijacked by Tibetan revolutionaries. Hundreds of refugees are fleeing the area for fear of contamination. Both the British and Chinese governments are denying that there is any danger, but an antiterrorism specialist in London was today quoted as saying, "This is something we have long feared. Set it on a hilltop to windward of any large city, blow it up, and you'd have a disaster compared to which Chernobyl and Three Mile Island were as nothing." More in a moment.*

*The first "Thrower" candidates, standing for the British Patriotic Party in next week's local elections . . .*

Tired, Peter sat beside Ellen watching the mid-evening TV news. As ever most of it concerned disasters or the activities of the royal family and cabinet ministers. Recently the subservient BBC had taken to signing its bulletins on and off with snatches of the national anthem. Today the prime minister had mentioned the fact approvingly in Parliament, and much play was made of that.

More interesting to him, however, was a story with a medical bias. There had been an outbreak of botulism in Greater Manchester among people who had eaten frozen chicken, with twenty dead so far and more than a hundred ill. Now a radical vegan group was claiming to have poisoned the chickens and threatening a repeat.

The name they had adopted was The Hitler Youth.

"Hitler was a vegetarian, wasn't he?" Ellen said.

Taken aback that she should know such an odd fact, he did his best to answer in the same calm tone.

"Yes, and a teetotaller. But he wasn't immune from addiction. Apart from the drugs his doctor dosed him with, and most of his entourage, he was a chocaholic. He—"

The phone rang, and with a grunt of annoyance he rose to answer. Just as he was picking it up, the doorbell rang.

"I'll go," Ellen sighed, switching off the TV sound.

"Check the monitor!" Peter cried, but she brushed aside his warning.

"It's all right—I saw through the window. It's only Claudia."

And it was. He heard her greeting Ellen in the hall as he said to the phone, "Levin!"

"This is Bernie."

Instantly he was all ears. He barely contrived a smile as Claudia entered and sat down.

"Yes? What have you got for us?"

"Some good news, some bad. Can you meet me?"

Peter hesitated. "Well, my partner just arrived."

"I'll come to you, then. Soon as I can."

"Okay."

Though he didn't think it was at all a good idea . . .

Playing hostess, Ellen brought Claudia her usual whiskey on the rocks with a splash of water. Accepting with a word of thanks, she asked who had rung up.

"Bernie. He's coming round."

Instantly she was alert. "With news for us?"

"Some good, some bad, he says. What news from you?"

Claudia hesitated a moment before replying. As though taking a hint, Ellen rose with a muttered, "Excuse me."

"I don't want to drive you out!" Claudia exclaimed.

"You aren't," Ellen said firmly. "But I have a lot of homework."

Yet she left behind a definite atmosphere . . .

Looking concerned, Claudia set her glass aside untasted. She said, "You having problems? I thought, after we—what was that featly old-fashioned phrase you used?—ran our project up the flagpole and got her to salute it, everything was smooth."

"I don't think she's in the mood for company just now. She's upset because she was due to spend the evening with a school-friend. Only the other girl's father has decided he doesn't want his children mixing with niggers."

"Oh, no!"

"Oh, yes." Face grim, Peter dropped ice-cubes, *crash-crash,* into a glass for himself. "I swear I don't know what's going to happen to this country." He splashed a generous double measure of whisky over the ice. That left only a drop in the bottle, which he drained into Claudia's glass before dumping the empty in a waste-bin. It was likely to be the last for some while . . .

Sitting down, he concluded bitterly, "One thing's for certain, though. Next winter, if the power-workers try to strike, they'll be driven back to work by the army."

"Who says so?"

Peter gestured at his computer. "Ellen lucked into that one yesterday. She's getting better than I am at finding where the moles leave their droppings. This one turned up on a board I didn't even know existed—let alone that you could access it free of charge."

"And you believe this rumor?"

"More and more civil servants are getting so disgusted with the government, they're risking their jobs and even jail to leak the bosses' plans. This is just the latest of several similar cases. You can judge how seriously to take them by the vehemence of the denials that follow. This is already being denied in a hysterical shriek, so—yes, I do believe it."

He tossed back a gulp of whisky that nearly choked him.

"However, it hasn't happened yet," he resumed when he could. "How are you getting on?"

"Well, I've been to the Grant clinic, as you know, and another that's on the register, and a couple that aren't and don't seem to be any less efficient even though they're cheaper. And in *no* case does there seem to be any way of accessing their records from outside. They simply don't allow them to go on line, except for blip-style transfer to a commercial data-bank. I thought I was going to find myself knee-deep in puky sleaze—you know, corrupt quacks exploiting the vulnerable public—but in fact they seem to be decent honorable people providing a valuable service."

"Hmm!" Peter stared at her. "And I thought you were too hard-boiled to swallow a PR job!"

"Fold it and stow it," she sighed, sipping her drink. "What I'm driving at is that Jake was right. We're going to have to fall back on traditional methods."

"Bribery and blackmail, you mean."

"He said that, I didn't. And he's a cynical cank, isn't he? No, I think the right approach might be to track down someone—say a retired employee—and interview them about their recollections. Elderly people, out of touch, are often more willing to talk informally than those who are still working in the field. After all, the past decade with its monstrous expansion of computerized records has made younger people that much more paranoid . . . You don't agree?"—in a frosty tone, for he was signalling with his free hand.

"No, no, no! It's just that you seem to be taking something far too much for granted."

"For example?"

"You said 'a' retired employee. From every fertility clinic in this country? Do you think they'd all prove malleable if you could track them down? What if they aren't?"

There was a dead pause. Claudia passed a hand through her hair, which was overdue for a trim. She had become neglectful of her appearance lately, and sometimes—as now—her face looked like that of a far older woman.

"You're right," she said dully. "Talk about wishful thinking . . . I guess I haven't really gotten over losing my helpful friend the policeman. Especially since they seem to have wised up to the PNC access he arranged. Do you imagine that's what Bernie wants to discuss?"

By reflex Peter's eyes had darted to the TV monitor that surveyed the entrance. Setting down his glass, he rose.

"We'll know soon enough. He's walking up the path."

Not so much walking as swaying, with a black eye, a swollen lip, and his clothes smudged with dirt. All of them, including an aroused Ellen, rushed to help: wiped his face, brushed his trousers, took his coat to be sponged, then sat him down with a good stiff drink.

Peter's and Claudia's, since there wasn't any more.

"Who attacked you?" Claudia demanded.

"Who knows? I noticed they wore Thrower ribbons, but . . . Oh, most likely Special Branch's bully-boys. At any rate they were fast enough on the job, and accurate with it." He winced as whisky burned his injured lip.

"But why?"

"They don't like the *Comet*, for a start. Because it's dared to criticize the government, they'd like to see it fail. And they don't like you"—a glance at Peter—"because of the fuss you kicked up over the Heathrow tragedy."

Somehow, in spite of the reference, none of them thought of suggesting that Ellen retreat again to her own room.

"You think they knew you were coming here—"

"Peter, you weren't born yesterday!"

Not waiting for an answer, Bernie glanced around. "My coat?"

"I took it in the kitchen to wash off the mud," Ellen exclaimed. "I'll fetch it, but it is rather wet—"

"No need! Just bring me the package in the right-hand pocket. Wrapped in a white plastic bag."

And, a moment later: "Here!"

"Thanks. Peter, you know what this is?" Bernie opened the bag and produced a palm-sized, battery-powered device bearing red and green lights.

"A bug-hunter," Peter said, nodding.

"Better. An exterminator. Want me to run it around?"

"No, I'll do it." Suddenly feeling—like Claudia—far older than his years, Peter forced himself to his feet. "All I can say is, I hope it doesn't spot anything."

"Clean. Rather to my surprise." He switched off the gadget and tossed it into Bernie's lap.

"Mine too." The hacker frowned. "I hope it's working. I'd have expected at least a passive tap on your phone—"

"Oh, I have a service that takes care of that. And my modem is protected, too. Lord, the shifts we're driven to if we're to think in private nowadays!"

"Not to mention the money," Claudia put in. "You know it cost me a week's rent to have your old place swept and garnished? There were bugs there, all right. Four."

Peter started. "New?"

"By the look of them, installed after you moved out of the place. Usual bureaucratic screw-up, I guess."

"Or aimed at you," Peter riposted.

She paled. "I hadn't thought of that! You're right, of course. I'll call the exterminators again tomorrow. I hate to squander Strugman money, but needs must . . . Well, Bernie!" Briskening, she turned. "What have you found?"

"Well, I'd better tell you the bad news first." He sipped his drink and grimaced again. "It doesn't look, after all, as though the Bill spotted the loopholes in our filter design."

They looked at him uncomprehendingly. At length Claudia ventured, "How can that be bad news?"

"Because if it's not the Bill, who else can it be?"

"You said before," Peter muttered, frowning, "though I didn't take you very seriously, that it was as though someone were getting to all your leads ahead of you."

Bernie gave a solemn nod. "*And* closing off the routes to them afterward."

"That does sound bad," Claudia conceded.

"Not as bad as you might think," Bernie countered. "I'm finding alternative pathways. They're slow, they're complicated, but they're starting to pay off. That's how come I also have some good news. It may not be as much as you were hoping for, but . . . Well, stuff the modesty bit. I suspect you don't think too much of me, but I swear I've dug up more than almost anybody else could!"

Soothingly, Claudia smiled at him. "I'm sure you've done wonders. All we want is to find out what they are."

Mollified, Bernie leaned back and gazed at the far wall.

"When I started looking for alternative approaches, I concentrated on the fertility clinic. There's no longer any means of finding out its name directly, but I'd already established that all the kids came from the same clinic, right? So I tried trawling for low-level associations. That paid off."

Claudia tensed. "Which one?"

"There's a ninety percent chance it was in the Harley Street-Wimpole Street area."

Bernie looked as though he expected lavish praise. He was let down. Claudia and Peter exchanged glances. Eventually the latter said, "But, Bernie, at the time there were five such clinics within a square mile, and another three or four a bit further off. What led you to this Earth-shaking conclusion?"

"If you're going to make fun of all my hard work—!"

"Calm down, calm down," Claudia broke in. "Peter, that was tactless. It's a start, it's a clue, if nothing else. And there's probably more, isn't there? I mean, you didn't risk being beaten up just to tell us that?"

"Damned right," Bernie grunted. Draining his glass, he held it out in hope of a refill. When Ellen displayed the empty bottle he sighed and set it by. "Yes, there is more. The confidence level is poor, but given the vagueness of the data it's as good as you can expect. I wish I could 'port you all the stages I've been through, so you could see how thorough I've been, but . . . Well, you said you didn't want it on-line to anywhere until it was rock-solid. That's why I came to tell you myself."

"When you get around to the actual telling . . ." Peter hinted.

"Oh, bock! What d'you think I'm doing?" Bernie rasped.

With a frown Claudia signalled a warning. Peter subsided. She was right. The poor growser must be suffering delayed shock. No wonder he was taking a long time to make himself clear.

"What's turned up *is,*" the hacker continued at length, "one of the points your average flatfoot wouldn't think of. At that stage, you see, I still imagined that it was the Bill who had forestalled me. I decided to try sneaking in from the medical statistics direction."

Abruptly both Peter and Claudia were leaning forward tensely on their chairs.

"I searched for children reported born by artinsem during the relevant period—sharing the physical characteristics you described—subsequently involved in court proceedings as juveniles—and backtracked from there to see whether there was any link between them that might indicate which clinic they derived from.

"Which there was. And what is more, there were enough physical descriptions, albeit in sketchy form with very low confidence, to hint at a common donor for them all."

"That's fantastic—" Claudia began. Bernie cut her short with an upraised hand.

"Just one problem. There are too many of 'em."

After a long pause Claudia said, "I'm not with you."

"Okay, okay, I'll spell it out. The clinic that the evidence points to is the Chinn-Wilkinson. But wasn't it among the most reputable of the lot?"

"Absolutely!"

"One of the clinics whose code of practice evolved into guidelines that are now internationally accepted?"

"I believe Dr. Chinn helped to draft them."

"In that case, like I said: there are too many of these kids. If they all stemmed from a single donor, there ought to be a maximum of ten. But we know of that many already. I just can't make myself believe that by this stage we've traced the lot. Can you?"

Pale, Claudia said, "I left a program running in the States to look for others. I haven't interrogated it lately, but it's meant to signal me if anything turns up. So maybe—"

"Maybe you have found them all? Sounds like negative evidence to me. What if the donor was servicing several clinics? I could imagine this kind of payment for a cheap thrill turning sort of addictive . . . Hello!" Bernie tensed, leaning forward on his chair. "Peter! Is something wrong?"

He had closed his eyes and was swaying. Alarmed, Ellen dropped to her knees at his side and clasped his hand.

But he waved her aside. "No, I'm all right," he said in a thin voice. "It's just that I suddenly realized who it is we're talking about."

And, with abrupt force, thumping fist into palm and staring around the room as though he had never seen it or them before: "Yes, of course! That's the growser I've been trying to remember! *Louis Parker!*"

* * *

For a long uneasy moment there was silence. Just as Claudia was about to speak up, however, Peter relaxed and gave a short laugh.

"Sorry about that. But—well, you remember I had a sort of association-fit the other day at the *Comet* office? I had something on the tip of my tongue and it wouldn't come out?"

Claudia gave a cautious nod.

"Remembering Dr. Grant was only half of what was on my mind. Bernie just added the missing bit of the puzzle."

"Did I?"—from the hacker. "What? *I* don't know."

"Too many kids!" Peter was chuckling with excitement by now. "You see . . . No, I'd better start at the beginning."

"You do that," Claudia instructed, and he drew a deep breath before continuing.

"It was this way. Most of the other donors at the clinic were medical or dental students like me, as I've already explained. But there was one who was a complete exception. He was older than we were, for one thing—must have been in his thirties, at least—and very un-English: tall, slim, elegant, dark-haired, olive-skinned with a neat black moustache at a time when they were out of fashion . . . I suppose if someone had asked I'd have guessed him to be Turkish, but in fact he was Armenian. Parker wasn't his original name, but I forget what—No, I don't, for someone told me! *Parikian!* Lord, it's coming back as though it were last week, and I swear I haven't thought about the guy in ten years!"

"Point!" said Bernie firmly.

"Point? Oh! Yes, I'm afraid I'm not making myself terribly clear, am I? Well, you see, when the partnership between Dr. Chinn and Dr. Wilkinson broke up, rumor had it that among the reasons was the fact that Dr. Wilkinson had allowed this guy to donate umpteen times. It was said that Louis was always broke, in spite of always being smartly dressed, or maybe because, so he'd charmed Dr. Wilkinson into letting him father more than his official ration, at five pounds a time or possibly more. It was also hinted that they were having an affair."

He leaned back in his chair, looking smug. "Well, there you have it."

"A suspicion," Claudia said after a pause.

"Yes, but—Grief, doesn't it fit? Bernie, you talked about these physical characteristics, right? Among the kids, I mean. Dark hair?"

"Yes, and darkish skin, or at any rate sallow. It does sound rather promising."

"Well, there you are!"—triumphantly. "Don't you realize the implications? If I'm right, there's one man out there who could have fathered all these children who can do terrible things and get away with them, and now I've hung a name on him!"

Soberly, Claudia ventured, "Peter, that goes without saying. But on the one hand you may be grasping at straws, and on the other—"

"A straw is better than nothing, isn't it?" Peter cut in. And, mastering his annoyance with an effort, added, "Sorry. Finish what you were going to say."

"Well . . . Well, what exactly are you expecting?"

"Grief, isn't it obvious?"

"Peter! *Shut up!*" Abruptly she was on her feet. "All right, I grant you this much—I have been talking as if there might be a common father for these kids I'm trying to investigate, and you think you've spotted the ideal candidate. As a result you're forcing me to confront the implications. First of all, assuming you're right about this Louis Parker, what do we do when we catch up with him? Compel him to undergo a gene-test? Interrogate him about the number of times he donated semen? If he was doing it through the Chinn-Wilkinson clinic, he presumably had no idea who the recipients were. We've satisfied ourselves that their records are shellbacked."

"Of course, of course, but . . ." Peter drew a deep breath. "Look, the point is—"

"The point," Bernie interjected unexpectedly, "is that this may be the first piece of concrete evidence we've acquired except via the PNC tap."

"Precisely!"

"Okay, I'll follow it up in the morning. Tonight I'm too tired. How can I trace this growser? Anything else you can tell me about him?"

"He was in computers," Peter said slowly. "It's coming back to me, more and more. In fact that must have been how he met Dr. Wilkinson. It was his company that she called in for a quote about computerizing the clinic, and Dr. Chinn took such a dogmatic stand against the idea that . . ." The words tailed away.

"That everyone assumed it was because he suspected she wanted to let the contract to her lover?" Claudia's tone was harsh.

"More or less."

"I see. Well, there's one step we can take right away. Let's find out whether he's on the phone."

"What? And ring him up?"

"I don't imagine he'd talk freely to strangers about his murky past, if it is murky." She shifted from harsh to caustic. "But it'd be a start."

"Let me!" offered Ellen, and was hitting the phone-directory code on Peter's computer keyboard before she had even sat down in the chair. Seconds later she reported, "No, there are lots of 'Parker L' but no entry for a 'Parker Louis.' "

"That's okay," Bernie grunted. "There are more efficient ways of tracing him—which I propose to do because if he's in computers he could well be the growser who's ahead of me at every step."

"If so," Claudia said slowly, "That means he knows who he is. He knows about his—well—uniqueness."

They contemplated that dismaying possibility for several seconds. At length, shrugging, Bernie pushed himself to his feet, saying, "That's for tomorrow. I'm worn out."

"Just a second!" Peter exclaimed.

"Yes?"

"Didn't you have something else to tell us?"

"Oh. Oh, so I did. I almost forgot. Assuming the kid in Italy that Claudia listed was in fact one of the cases we've been—ah—considering . . ."

It finally seemed to dawn on him that Ellen had been listening to the whole of the recent conversation, and maybe she hadn't been supposed to. His face was eloquent of anxiety.

But, with instant tact, the girl exclaimed, "Don't forget your coat! It should be dry by now!" And vanished.

"I like that kid of yours," Bernie murmured, sinking into his chair again. "Bright!"

"Never mind her!" Peter said impatiently. "We want to hear the rest."

"Where was I . . . ? Oh, of course. Yes, assuming the boy in Italy is one of the—*your* cases, then the association with the Chinn-Wilkinson clinic is virtually definite."

"How?"

"During the relevant period the clinic had exactly one Italian client, and the match is excellent."

Claudia blinked. "How can you be so sure?"

"Because—" Bernie broke off, looking surprised at himself. "Grief, I keep thinking I'd already told you, and I haven't, have I? Maybe being banged on the head sent my wits woolgathering." He touched his nape gingerly. "I located the medical data-bank the Chinn-Wilkinson used to use—security wasn't so tight when they were among its customers—and set a program to mouse around it on the assumption it's the one Dr. Grant told you about. And it is."

"Why didn't you say so earlier?" Peter exclaimed.

"Peter, for pity's sake!" Claudia reproached him. "The poor growser is still in shock! You ever been beaten up on the street?"

"Ah—well, yes, once or twice," Peter admitted, and subsided with what could have been meant for an apology.

"As far as I'm concerned," Claudia declared, "That's the best news we've had so far, and Bernie deserves our congratulations. Are you expecting any more revelations?"

"I'll do my best," the hacker sighed. "Ellen mentioned my coat—?"

She rushed back from the kitchen carrying it, still damp but otherwise spotless. Thanking her, he rose to put it on, and she turned to Peter.

"Dad, I have to get up for school, you know. Do you need me for anything else?"

*Earlier she was eager to make herself scarce . . . Am I ever going to understand the female mind? Oh—sexist!*

"Goodness, of course not!" he exclaimed, embracing her. She turned politely to Bernie and shook his hand, saying it was nice to have met him, gave Claudia a peck on the cheek, and disappeared.

As the door closed, Claudia said, "Bernie, want to share a cab?"

"No thanks. It isn't raining. I can walk."

"And risk another beating-up?"

"I don't expect them to attack me twice. That's not Special Branch's style."

"And if it wasn't Special Branch that did it—? Come along. I'll pay. Good night, Peter."

"Good night."

It took Peter a long time to get to sleep. When he eventually dropped off, he found his dreams haunted by a tall suave Armenian, offensively well dressed and reeking of expensive aftershave.

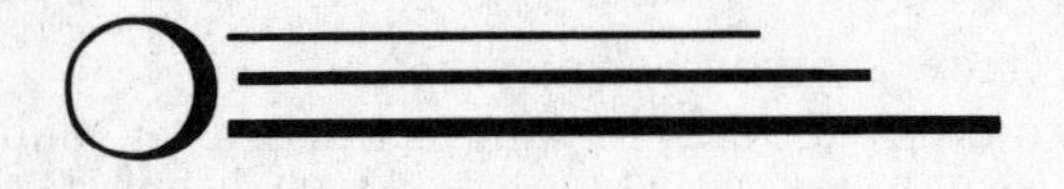

*Hello. I'm David Shay. You're Sheila Hubbard, aren't you?*

Oh, featly! You know my name! But you don't know who I am.

*At least I know what you've done. And I can guess a little about how you feel.*

Featlier and featlier! All right, put it in one word.

*Haunted?*

You—you bocky . . . How the hell—? Cancel that! I don't believe in ghosts, I don't believe in hauntings, I don't believe in life beyond the grave! I'm a good agnostic, like I was brought up to be.

*In which case, what makes you react so violently?*

None of your bocky business!

*Nonetheless what I suspect is this. Your victim was, after all, a highly trained professional killer, a Marine Commando. You disposed of him with absolutely no trouble. Ever since, it's been as though some element of him has entered into your subconscious—not in any physical sense, but purely because after what you did the temptation to repeat your achievement has sometimes become more than you could bear—*

Stop it! STOP IT! Or I'll—I'll—

*You can't, Sheila. Not to me. Haven't you realized yet?*

I . . . Oh, this is ridiculous!

*Don't try and run away when you hear the truth. It won't work. You've got to face it sooner or later. How many times have you given in?*

What?

*I said: how many times have you given in? To the temptation. I know you have.*

If you're so sure, why ask?

*As I said, you've got to face the truth instead of running away. You thought keeping it a secret would suffice. But it isn't a secret.*

Yes it is!

*You can say that now I'm here, talking to you?*

I . . . I suppose not. But how the hell did you find me?

*Like finds like, one way or another. I'll explain later—that is, if you decide to be frank.*

If I don't?

*Look inside yourself for the answer. You know what becomes of those who oppose us.*

. . . Us?

*Precisely. Now will you tell me?*

All—all right. After the first one, the one everybody heard about, I was terrified. I mean, I couldn't tell anybody, because obviously they would think I was insane, but I knew what I'd done, and . . . and I simply couldn't believe it. So I started to suspect myself of being crazy. In the end . . .

*In the end, the only way of proving that you weren't was to use the power again?*

Yes. Yes, exactly.

*On—?*

He was a reporter. A nasty, greedy, foul-mouthed slob of a reporter, working for the local paper, dreaming of making it into the big time, television maybe. He'd made up his mind that I'd murdered the —the one you know about. I think he was married to the growser's cousin—something like that. Anyway he felt he had a personal stake in the affair. What's more he hated my school and everything it stood for. He'd have liked to see it burned down and all the kids and teachers.

*A ribbon on his coat?*

Oh, yes! Soon as everybody else took to wearing them!

*So—?*

In the end it just got too much. I filched a bottle of gin and got a message to him to meet me—made him think he was going to get the inside track at last, the lowdown on the scandal of the school—and . . .

*Persuaded?*

Good word. Persuaded him to drink the lot and then drive home as fast as possible.

*What did he hit?*

Nothing. Ran his car off at a bend in the road beside the river, flat out, and sank in ten feet of water.

*How did you feel after that?*

I'd be lying if I said anything but "better!"

*And how long was it before the next time?*

What makes you so sure there was one?

*You still didn't have anyone to tell.*

No, that's true . . . All right. The next one was a missionary. Female type. She'd convinced herself that I must be a vessel of evil. And you know something? By that stage I was coming to the same conclusion. It was either that, or insanity, or—

*Or?*

Or nothing. I didn't mean to say that. I meant to say that actually at first I welcomed her arrival in my life. If I could find—well—sanctuary from my fears about myself by converting to a religion, adopting some system of belief that would make sense of what I was and what I'd done, I felt I'd be all right again, able to face myself, able to cope . . . Do you understand?

*Perfectly. And I'm the only person you've ever met who might. She didn't—the woman missionary.*

You don't make that a question.

*No.*

You're right anyway. I never met many religious people before, you know. Oh, for the sake of appearances there's a chaplain at the school, but he only comes when sent for, to—heh!—we say "service" the kids whose families insist. There aren't many of those . . . But this one was thick, know what I mean? She knew the answer—her mind was made up—and her entire goal in life was to make me swallow her preaching.

*You didn't.*

How could I take her seriously after I discovered that she honestly thought the Bible was written in English?

*Mm-hm.*

Doesn't that surprise you?

*Not at all. I've run across lots of similar cases, particularly in the States.*

Don't be so bocky patronizing!

*I'm not going to apologize for having had a more varied and interesting life than you so far. What did you do to the missionary?*

Oh . . . In the end I—I persuaded her to put the love of God to the test. Wasn't hard.

*And—?*

They found her hanging in the old stables behind the school.

*After which you felt better again?*

No!

*Explain why not.*

I don't know why I'm telling you all this. I mean, I never met you before.

*You do know why. You knew from the moment I entered the room.*

Yes. Yes, I suppose I did, really. Just didn't want to—well, like you said, face the truth. I still don't want to.

*But you're going to.*

. . . Yes.

*So explain why this time you didn't feel better.*

Because . . . Because of the responsibility.

*What sort of responsibility?*

If you don't know, who does? Didn't you see the TV news today? This crazy kid who shot the archbishop? You couldn't hear what he was shouting, but it wasn't hard to read it off his lips.

"*I'm a fucking Christian, aren't I? And I'm sick of you making out that wogs and niggers are as good as me!*"

You did watch.

*Of course.*

And was yesterday's news any better, or the day before's? Do you expect anything better tomorrow?

*This is what you mean when you talk about responsibility?*

What else?

"*The time is out of joint. Oh curséd spite—*"

"That ever I was born to put it right." Yes. Of course the idea's completely crazy. Yet I can't escape from it. I seem to have some sort of—of power, and everybody says I'm more intelligent than average, and . . . Well, what the hell else am I to do with my life? Now tell me I'm off my rocker. Tell me I'm a megalomaniac.

*Not at all.*

Stop messing about. I can't put the world to rights on my bocky tod.

*True. But you aren't on your tod. Not any more. Coming?*

Wait a moment! What about Ingrid—my mother? What'll Joe say? He pays my fees here. Douglas, come to that. He'll raise hell!

*It's all taken care of.*

No, I don't believe it. You can't possibly want to be lumbered with me! I mean, I've told you—God knows why, but I suppose you've been pulling the trick on me that I can work on other people, and you knew enough to track me down during my period when it doesn't function properly—I've told you what I've done! I've killed three people, don't you understand?

*I've killed, too. And I think it won't have been the only time. Now come along. There's a car waiting.*

Where are you taking me?

*The only place in all the world where you can stop pretending.*

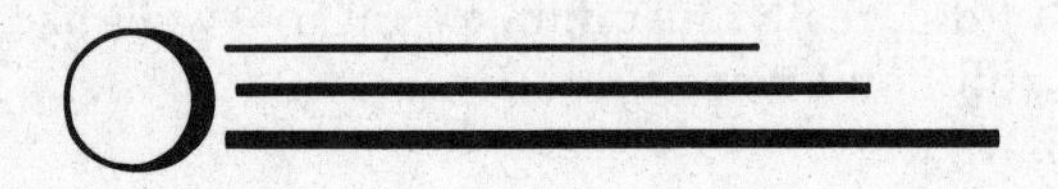

*You're watching TV Plus. Time for Newsframe.*

*Once again a computer-driven crash on the world's major stock exchanges has led to a record number of bankruptcies. Recently the commonest cause of them in Britain has been inability to meet mortgage repayments following redundancy; however, last month private bankruptcies were exceeded by commercial ones, which averaged fourteen per working day.*

*Returning from his triumphal world tour, General Sir Hampton Thrower told a cheering crowd at Heathrow, quote: "Since an Englishman's home is his castle, he needs a home, and any system that doesn't guarantee him one but hands out cheap accommodation to lazy, irresponsible aliens . . ."*

**F**ood shortages this winter, particularly in view of the potato blight, were certain to be even worse than last year, but the government-approved news on radio, BBC-TV and ITV disguised the truth according to orders. Only TV Plus was still making a pretense of objectivity. The first deaths from starvation had followed an unseasonable cold snap, but although the *Comet* risked describing them for what they were, the rest of the media concentrated on the usual pabulum. Jake, Peter felt, was doing his best, even though he resorted more and more often to the bottle, while his backers were among the few people who still cared about the once-vaunted freedom of the press, being prepared to lavish money on defending their correspondents from prosecutions ordered by the government. How long, though, could they hold out? It had become an offense, as of the present parliamentary session, to publish "anti-patriotic" news. When Peter rang TV Plus to ask why he wasn't receiving any more assignments, he was told apologetically that they no longer dared to hire him. However, if he had any leads their own staff could follow up, they would guarantee a finder's fee, if he didn't mind being paid in cash . . .

A pittance. But he had to grab it.

Despite its apparent political neutrality, Jake seemed to have given up on the story of the criminal children. Without putting it into so many words, he appeared to have decided that the project was a waste of time. When the criminals had taken power, what point was there in worrying about a bunch of kids?

"And can you blame him?" Peter said bitterly to Claudia and Bernie when they next met. Ellen had invited them all for dinner; she was turning into an excellent and ambitious cook, capable of conjuring tasty dishes out of unpromising ingredients. Thank goodness, as Bernie said, for those who remembered what to do with odds and ends, because they had inherited the tradition of peasant poverty and didn't insist on being fed from cans and freezer packs.

The cost of which was soaring as North Sea oil ran out ahead of the predicted schedule.

"Jake, you mean?" Claudia sighed, reaching for her glass. It held beer: homemade. Anything more expensive was now beyond Peter's means. Last week he had offered TV Plus a promising scandal concerning sausages made from AIDS-infected pork supplied to public hospitals by a prominent supporter of the government, but it had been scotched under the Official Secrets Act. So his fee had been withheld.

Sometimes he had considered discarding the red-white-and-blue ribbon he still wore, but it was too risky now to go without one—at least, if you were white. Watching Ellen as she cleared away the dishes, humming to herself, he wondered how much longer she would be able to wear hers at school, before it was torn away on the grounds that she wasn't British.

Correction: English. Here in London schoolyard gangs of self-styled "Cockneys" were starting to attack the Scots, Welsh and Irish, along with the—what had that fanatic said who shot the archbishop?—the "wogs and niggers" who were inferior to him, a *white* Christian . . .

He roused on realizing that someone had spoken: Bernie? Yes.

"At least Jake seems determined to go down with flying colors. You heard about the petrol-bomb attack?"

"What?"

"This afternoon. The *Comet* has this display window at street-level, right? Some yobbos in a stolen car threw a fire-bomb at it. No damage worth mentioning, luckily. But still what you might call a less than healthy trend."

Smiling broadly at the success of her meal, Ellen returned from the kitchen and sat down on the sofa next to Peter. She had become a part of their group, and there was no longer any question of her retreating to her room.

"Sometimes I'm tempted to emigrate," Bernie went on. "But where on earth could I go? Xenophobia in the States is peaking again and in any case the country's due to go bust, same as Britain—Canada's in the throes of another fit of Francophilia—Australia's trying to turn itself into an anti-Japanese bulwark and inside a generation it's liable to be as racist as South Africa . . . As for the rest of Europe, they're on such an anti-American kick they don't want to know people who speak only English. Even the Dutch and Danes are going back to German as a foreign language."

"Keep going," Claudia said tartly. "You've left out the Arab world, for starters—"

"And Asia!" Ellen chimed in. "Who'd want to live in India when there's practically a civil war going on?"

Peter started. It was the first time, to his recollection, that she had voluntarily mentioned her mother's country of origin. But all he could read on her pretty face was simple sadness, as though at far too early an age she had grown resigned to the waywardness of humanity.

*What an inheritance for a teenage kid!*

After that, for a long while, there seemed little left to say. It was only after Ellen had re-adopted her hostess role and topped up their glasses that they reverted to the topic they were supposed to be discussing. Typically, and in a typically caustic tone, it was Claudia who set the ball rolling.

"What I can't help wondering," she said, addressing Bernie, "is why, since you've gotten so far, you can't get any further, especially with the tracing of Louis Parker. If you see what I mean."

Sourly he replied, "I do, and I wish I could explain. You'll have to take my word for it, I'm afraid. My best guess is that this growser caught on before you did."

Peter leaned forward. "So you agree that he's the likeliest candidate?"

"Are there any others? But—okay, I have to grant that on the basis of what you told me he seems like a prime suspect. Physical appearance—the fact that he was working in computers—and the fact that he's either dead or in hiding—yes, it does add up to a fair case."

"In hiding?" Claudia stabbed.

"Or, I suppose, out of the country. But I've run a program to search every accessible phone directory and now I'm following up with one to search every postal reference. I do mean *every*. It's costing an arm, a leg and a prick, and the balls come next! Jake isn't going to be at all happy when he sees the final bill—Oh, excuse me, Ellen."

She gave a crowing laugh, leaning back and crossing her legs. Of late, as though out of defiance, she had taken to wearing traditional

Indian garb, and the sari she had on, bought second-hand at a Saturday jumble-sale, was of shiny lavender fabric that caught reflections from the wall-lights.

"Never mind! I hear far worse things at school!"

Peter put his arm around her and drew her close. He was becoming more and more attached to this unwanted daughter.

"In spite of all," he said, addressing Bernie, "there's no trace?"

"Louis Parker might as well have dug himself a hole, climbed in and pulled it after him."

"So that blocks off one approach. Claudia, what about you? You suggested contacting ex-employees of fertility clinics. Did you get anywhere?"

She looked at him steadily.

"You told me it was hopeless. Remember? You said there were too many and there was no reason to expect—"

"Grief!" Peter burst out. "I was only pointing out the difficulties—"

"You didn't give *me* that impression," Claudia cut in coldly.

Bernie uttered a loud sigh, setting by his empty tankard. "Sometimes," he muttered, "I wonder what you lot are up to. When you hit on an idea, why the hell don't you try it out? *I* did!"

Embarrassed, Peter and Claudia looked a question at him.

"Aren't the former staff of the Chinn-Wilkinson among the first people you should have talked to? Frankly, I thought you had done!"

Peter said defensively, "It was a long time ago, and I don't remember many of their names—"

"Oh, shit," Bernie muttered. "They're on record. For instance, who was Dr. Chinn's head nurse?"

"Ah . . ." For a moment Peter hesitated. Abruptly he snapped his fingers. "Sister Higgins! Thank you for reminding me! And why the hell didn't I think of her before? She was getting on, but she could still be alive!"

"And you didn't tell me?" Claudia burst out. "Why, I've been sitting around chewing my nails! I could have—"

"Do you remember Sister Higgins's first name?" Ellen put in, just in time to defuse a full-blown quarrel. She had risen from her seat and stood with one hand poised above the computer keyboard.

Calming himself with an effort, Peter said, "Uh—yes! Marian! I'm not sure whether it's Mari-*an* or Mari-*on*, but I do remember that's what Dr. Chinn used to call her."

Dropping into the chair before the board, Ellen called up the telephone directory. They all waited in silence until she said, "Sorry. Nothing for Higgins Marian spelt either way."

"Not to worry!" Bernie cut in. "If you—"

"I know!"—with abrupt annoyance, swinging to face him.

"What?"

"What you were going to say."

"That being—?"

"You can access out-of-date directories. If she ever had a phone in her own name in the London area, even if she was entered as plain 'Higgins M,' the exchange still knew she was Marian. If she's moved elsewhere, there's a contact facility for emergency use, for instance if she's been taken ill and relatives are trying to get in touch. Isn't that what you were going to explain?"

Bernie froze for a moment, disconcerted, half in and half out of his chair. At length he subsided with a grunt.

"Keep at it, lady. You have the makings of a hacker. Did you write the search program yourself?"

"No, I didn't bother. I found it in real time. I don't have too much to do in the evenings nowadays."

Which was true, Peter reminded himself ruefully. Even those of her boyfriends who had seemed most enthusiastic a few weeks ago had now abandoned her. The—infection? Yes! The *infection* of what was suddenly being called "Throwerism" had struck that deep that fast, like a surgeon's lance releasing a flood of pus from an ulcer. Even the "nice" kids that the friendly minder Jeannette took care of after school had imitated their parents' hardening intolerance. Had it not been for Ellen's thrice-a-week cleaning job . . .

Overwhelmed with dismay, he was all set to reproach himself in public for neglecting his daughter when she cried, "Gotcha!"

*Just in time . . . !*

They crowded around the machine, staring. There it was:

"HIGGINS Marian Martha. Sex: F. UK citizen with right of residence. Marital status: S. Birthplace: Huyton, Lancs. Parents: HIGGINS William Brian; HIGGINS Karen née Thwaites. Age last b'day: 73. Profession: nursing sister (ret'd). PNC status—"

"*She* had a police record?" Peter burst out. "I can't believe it!"

Claudia hushed him as the display scrolled upward.

"—suspected involvement in unauthorized abortion/s. No confirmation. Latest reported domicile—"

"That's what we want!" Peter rasped, but Ellen was ahead of him, and had already dumped the data into local memory, wiped the screen, and ordered the address to be printed.

"You do have the makings of a hacker!" Bernie said approvingly. "Peter, does that sound like her?"

"Absolutely," Peter murmured as he looked at the printout. "Just one problem."

"What?"

"I happen to recognize this address. It was one—"

"Don't tell me!"—from Claudia. "One that you went to while you were working for *Continuum?*"

"Yes, dammit!"

"So?"

"It's a hospice for people suffering from Alzheimer's. If that's where she's wound up, we don't stand much chance of getting any data out of Sister Higgins."

"Maybe she's on the staff—"

"At seventy-three?"

"Okay. 'Six impossible things before breakfast . . .' But I'll look into it, anyway. I only wish you'd thought of it before!"

Peter bridled, prepared to blame her for his own oversight. Once more, in the nick of time, Ellen intervened, offering the last of the homemade beer, and the atmosphere calmed.

When the others had left, Peter so far recovered his self-possession as to knock on Ellen's door and, on her invitation, enter. Rising drowsily from her pillow, she looked a question.

"I'm sorry," he muttered, brushing her cheek with his fingers. "I'm going through a bad patch."

"Oh, I know," was her reply. "But I am doing what I can to make it easier, aren't I?"

"Yes!"

"That's all right, then. Good night . . . Hey, just a moment!"

He had already turned toward the door. Checking, he glanced back.

"You heard what Bernie said? I have the makings of a hacker?"

"Yes, of course."

"What do you think?"

Peter hesitated. Was it good or bad to be a hacker in this strange and changing world? He opted for good.

"I'm sure he meant it as a compliment. What's more, I think he was absolutely right."

"That's what I hoped you'd say. G'night . . ."

Her words dissolved into a sigh, and before he closed the door again she was asleep.

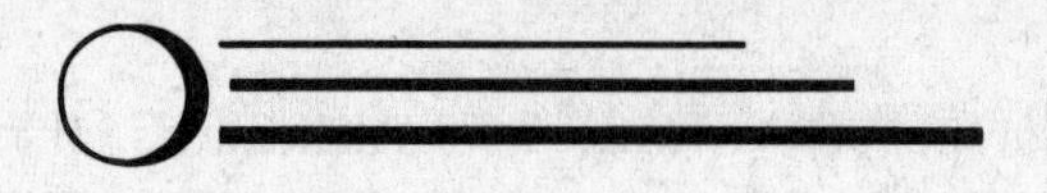

With the onset of autumn, night by night the mist grew denser that drifted up from the stagnant, filthy river. Older folk, imprisoned at home with nothing but TV for company, abandoned the city's streets to youngsters like Terry Owens and his mates—except, of course, that there was in fact no one like Terry—sporting their pro-Thrower ribbons. A few had had their foreheads tattooed with Union Jacks in token of patriotic fervor. Rio had considered that, but Terry had dissuaded him.

Nightly, in consequence, black families huddled in fear of the bricks and petrol-bombs that might be hurled into their living rooms; Indian and Pakistani shopkeepers replaced their windows with armorglass—if they could afford to, and if they could find someone willing to sell it to them; otherwise they boarded up with corrugated iron—and the proprietors of Chinese takeaways installed closed-circuit video-cameras recording images every ten seconds on a VCR secure behind a solid wall.

Not, of course, that the police gave an ounce of dogshit for that sort of evidence. But there was a brotherhood now, that had learned to tell Europeans apart, and on occasion even the cowed BBC managed to mention—at least hint at—the way the Chinese community had come to admire their mainland cousins, rather than their families in or from Hong Kong. As for their opinion of their former overlords, who had so cheaply sold their home land . . . !

In addition, the smouldering warlets of the subcontinent were finding an outlet in most British cities. Sikhs and Tamils and Bengalis and Pakistanis and members of other groups known beforehand only to specialists were venting bitter grudges in this foreign land, and woe betide whoever stood in their way.

As for the Cypriots, whether Greek or Turkish, scarcely a day went by without another murder, save when they united against the British if they tried to interfere. By now the police had given them up for lost, as they had the black areas of most post-industrial towns.

All that was the background to the arrival on Terry's manor of the gray Rolls Royce.

* * *

When he first heard about the silent, splendid car, as gray and glistening as the mists through which it prowled, his reaction had been one of scorn.

"Lose it, you bocky cank! Who'd bring a Roller into streets like these?"

Rio ventured, "After cunt, maybe?"

"Shit! You can afford a Roller, you can afford a better class of slag!"

"They do say," Taff murmured, "there are growsers who can only get turned on by dirty scrubbers."

"Hah!" Terry exclaimed. "Didn't know you were a psychologist!"

That made Taff blush and turn away. Briefly Terry exulted in his power to control these older, stronger boys.

Then Barney said obstinately, "I don't like it, Terry."

"Who's asking you to?"

"I don't like it!" he repeated. "No one knows who's in it, get me? It's loaded with these very heavy tints, like the cars the Mafia use in America. Like on TV."

"I don't watch TV too much. You know that."

"Yeah, I know. But"—with increasing confidence—"maybe you should. Sometimes, at any rate."

"Look," Terry said with forced patience, "if the tints are that heavy, how can the driver see in the dark?"

"Got these infrared lights," Taff countered. "You put on these special glasses—"

"But the tints on a Roller are supposed to keep out both infrared and ultraviolet," Terry cut in.

His oppos looked at him doubtfully for a long moment. At last Rio said, "Been checking 'em out, have you, Terry? Thinking of buying one?"

Taff supplied, "And hiring one of us to drive it?"

Terry was shaken. Was his grip on these three slipping? If so, how? Why? He blustered, "Look, all I said was that I don't reckon a Roller would keep coming back here!"

"Well, there it is," Rio grunted, pointing to the corner of the next street. And, as Terry swung around, added, "I'm for home."

"Me too!"

"Me too!"

And they were gone, leaving Terry to confront the car alone amid the swirling mist.

It did nothing, save purr past him at a walking pace. And duly vanished into mist again.

Yet it left him with a sense of terrible anxiety.

Half the night he lay awake wondering who could have sent it. Obviously its purpose was to frighten him—by now, his universe revolved so totally about himself he could not have envisaged any other possibility.

But why a Roller—? No, that question answered itself, and instantly. Air-conditioned. Sealed against the outer world, its occupants might also be immune to his personal magnetism. (That was the latest of several terms he had found applicable, and the one he preferred, inasmuch as it sounded solid, physical, concrete.)

And behind the dark glass . . . who? Agents of a tong, summoned via the grapevine by long-suffering Mr. Lee at the Chinese takeaway—or, more likely, by his wife? Or distant relatives of Mr. Lal the newsagent, expert killers who owed some kind of vendetta-style loyalty to his family? Or someone local, furious because he, Terry, unawares, had trespassed on the turf of an adult gang already running a protection racket in the area?

On the whole it was the last possibility that scared him worst. He had only a vague impression of what a tong did to those who offended one of its members, and a longstanding if now rather faint belief, acquired at school, that brown-skinned people such as Indians and Pakistanis and Bangladeshis lacked bottle and were consequently soft. But as to his own kind . . .

Well, notoriously, in this town they used cut-throat razors, and with skill.

Matters grew worse when Rio disappeared.

"Where *is* the bocky cank?"

"Last I heard," Taff said, having glanced nervously up and down the street from their usual meeting-place, "he was—uh—seen talking to the growser in the Roller."

"You're shooting me!"

"Straight as I stand here!" Taff asserted. "Last night when you wouldn't come the pub with us. Barney got in a barney"—it was a stale joke but good for a grin—"and Rio slid when someone bust a bottle. After, this slag touting on the next corner said she'd seen him."

"Doing—?" The tension in Terry's gut was unbearable.

"The Roller stopped and someone in it talked to him. I told you!"

"*And—?*"

"Today he's not around."

"We better go turn over his drum!"

Rio's home was in a refurbished but still detested high-rise block. His mother having walked out a year or two ago, his father was living with a younger woman, pretty but stupid. Despite Terry's best efforts the couple were evasive. All they were willing to say was that the boy had gone south—maybe to London.

Waiting for the lift after they quit the flat, Terry grew aware that his "mates" were looking at him in a new way. Never before had they shown such open distrust.

His confidence began to evaporate, and they sensed it.

"I think Rio had the right idea," Taff said as the lift arrived. Getting in, Terry tried to counter, with a forced laugh.

"Think he hitched a ride in the Roller? Think he's gone for rent in Park Lane?"

Ordinarily, among youths who sported the red-white-and-blue, reference to being kept by a rich homosexual would provoke instant fury. Terry had relied on that reflex. This time, to his dismay, it didn't work. Taff and Barney merely exchanged glances and gave a simultaneous shrug. Terry's heart sank into his traditional lace-up boots.

The lift arrived, and he relaxed a little. In a confined and airless space—he didn't know why—his personal magnetism seemed to work the best. Wheedling, he said, "I didn't mean what I just said about Rio. I know as well as you, he'd never go for rent in London!"

And made the mistake of reaching out for Taff's hand.

"No, he wouldn't! But you would, wouldn't you?" Taff blasted, and kicked him on the right shin just as the lift reached the ground floor. Barney, ever glad of the chance, added a second kick, accurately beneath the kneecap, and the two of them ran off laughing into the foggy night.

"Wait! Wait . . . !"

But it was no use. They were out of earshot, and there was no one else around save a tired, middle-aged woman, clinging to a half-filled shopping bag and afraid to risk the lift unless she was alone.

Cursing, Terry staggered past her and out into the dim of evening. The sky was cloudy, most of the streetlamps, as usual, were broken, and the only response to his shouting of Taff's and Barney's names was alarm among those other local residents brave enough to be abroad after dark.

No. Not the only response.

For, as he hobbled to the edge of the roadway, staring left and right for any sign of the mates he had so long relied on, a huge gray silent car whispered out of mist, and stopped.

A rear door opened. A voice spoke to him—only a few syllables: "Get in! We'll take you home."

But that was enough to convey a mass of alarming information. For one thing, the words were in an American accent. Among the chimeras that had haunted Terry since he first heard about the mysterious Rolls Royce, persecution by the Stateside Mafia was the least—yet, on the instant, thanks to years of conditioning by the American programs on TV that he affected to despise, he was prepared to believe it and feel powerless. For another, the voice was that of a boy not much older than himself, but it was going to be an authoritative baritone when its owner became adult, whereas Terry's—as he had realized after listening to recordings that his "friends" had made—would remain a light tenor.

A snatch recalled from a news bulletin abruptly came to dominate his mind: *The American occupation forces in Libya . . .* With all that that implied regarding war!

Terry was on the verge of screaming when his hand was grasped and he was drawn into the womblike car.

"So, you see, Mr. Owens—Mrs. Owens—there is no real alternative, is there?"

*Where am I? What's going on?* Blurrily, as though lost in the river-mist that enveloped the street outside, Terry strove to recover his self-possession. He was in his parents' living room; the first clue he had, before he managed to open his eyes, was the smell of over-brewed tea, which his mother would reflexively have offered. When he looked around, he saw that cupfuls of the precious liquid were cooling and growing a skin. Shameful waste, when tea cost so much, was such a luxury, was due—so rumor held—to be rationed, along with other oriental goods like rice.

But that was somewhere else, and in another time. Terry anchored himself to here and now, and found a boy his own age talking to his parents, backed up (on the two-seat sofa near the window) by an incredibly well-dressed couple both tanned to a degree even Rio couldn't achieve, using the best artificial creams . . . It dawned of a sudden: they must be the owners of the Roller.

*I'm trapped. I don't know how. I can only admire who did it!*

He listened again. The boy was saying:

"Of course, if it were to become known that a kid your Terry's age had been masterminding a protection racket, the consequences would be terrible. Your competence as parents would be called in question, to begin with. Our present government, as you are well aware"—as though by reflex, he stroked the red-white-blue ribbon he wore in his lapel—"lays great stress on parental responsibility, even though they make certain allowances for disadvantaged citizens . . ."

His parents were nodding, even though—no! Because they understood the police-type code: *It's all right for our sort to go around smashing windows, stuffing shit through letter-boxes and burning kids in bed, but as soon as the bocky blacks and wogs hit back the Bill comes down like a landslide . . . and good luck to them!*

This was Terry's language, the one he had been brought up to. He nodded vigorous approval.

And yet, at the same time, was aware of something very wrong indeed. The air in this room—and it wasn't the smell of stewed tea . . .

No good. He couldn't work it out. He could only sit back and go on nodding.

"So, for the benefit of your neighbors, shopkeepers like yourself, such as your newsagent Mr. Lal, and Mr. Lee at the takeaway, who provide such valuable services for the community—"

*Just a moment!*

Those being precisely the people Terry, with help from Barney and Taff and Rio, had been struggling to force into line, he felt impelled to jump up and yell!

And found he couldn't.

With the sweetest possible smile, the boy-stranger (at some stage Terry had registered that he was called David) took his arm. He said, "Oh, don't be so scared! Come along—the car's outside."

*Me? Scared? I've had the widest boys on the manor eating out of my hand since the year dot!*

And yet he was. He was shaking, head to foot. He was crying, and afraid he might—well—wet his pants!

*How? Why?*

But as to crying, he saw as he cast a last glance over his shoulder that both his parents were in tears.

Yet at the same time laughing. Laughing with sheer relief!

For the first time the question crossed his mind:

*Who am I? What kind of person?*

In the incredibly comfortable back seat of the Roller, like all the three-piece suits in local shops that he had thought of conning into his home except that the living room was too small, he tried to frame the question.

But could not. He could only say, "What happened to Rio and my other friends?"

The boy beside him, the one called David, said, "They weren't your friends. They were your tools."

Terry could not avoid a giggle, which David froze with a glare.

"You've had your fun," he said. "Now you have to do your duty."

"What?"—trying not to laugh again.

"Shut up! There's not much time!"

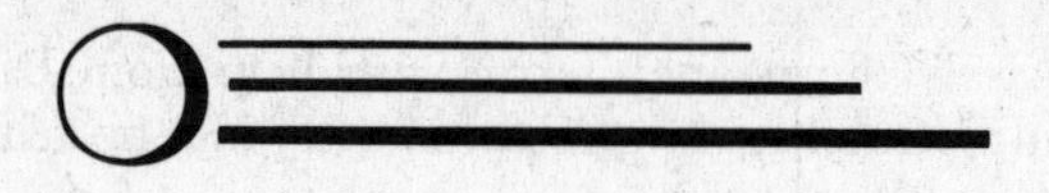

*You're watching TV Plus. Newsframe follows.*

*Car-bombs this morning exploded outside five Malaysian embassies in Western European capitals including London, causing extensive damage and many casualties. In telephone calls to newspapers, TV and radio stations, a group using the name Free Singapore Army claimed responsibility. More in a moment.*

*In a radio interview, General Thrower said, quote, "It's intolerable that a petty squabble half a world away should be made the excuse for destroying British lives and British property." Asked what countermeasures he could suggest . . .*

The clocks had gone back an hour over the weekend, so this evening it was dark when Ellen returned home from her cleaning job under the suspicious gaze of those who still belonged to the Neighborhood Watch. Lately such organizations had again been condemned by the government as a plot to obstruct the police in the execution of their duty, and their signs had vanished from all save a few defiant windows. (The other day Peter had confessed to being ashamed of not having joined the Watch in this street, as he had intended when he moved here, but he wasn't going to now.)

Moreover it had begun to drizzle. She was eager to get indoors. As she was fumbling for her door-key, however, she heard a faint mew. Glancing around in the gloom, she spotted a small tabby cat, very thin, sheltering under a bush beside the path.

"Poor thing!" she exclaimed, slinging her shoulder-bag behind her and dropping to a crouch. "Here, kitty! Here, kitty!"

It would have liked to flee, but it was too weak. Resignedly it let her carry it indoors.

Peter came home fuming, having spent another fruitless day in vain attempts to interest someone in yet another disaster story—the only sort of lead, it seemed, that he was picking up these days. This time it concerned a painkiller banned in the United States and several Western European countries but freely available in Britain and the Third World. (Nowadays he was often tempted to say, "The rest of the Third World . . .") The evidence that pregnant women who took it bore deformed and mentally handicapped babies was almost at the thalidomide level, but nobody would pay him to investigate. Even Jake had shrugged and said it was out of the question.

In addition, on the way home he had counted five fish-and-chip shops displaying hopeful "For Sale" signs. Driven out of business, of course, by the potato shortage. What with one thing and another, therefore, he was in a pretty bloody mood.

"What's that?" he rasped as he entered the kitchen and saw the scrawny cat lying on a scrap of old carpet near the stove.

"It's a cat, of course," Ellen answered, not looking up from her attempts to feed it. Tonight they were having liver and onions for dinner, offal still being comparatively cheap. She had cut a few shreds of the liver and was offering them in her fingers. Also she had put down a dish of milk.

"I think it's hurt," she added.

"More likely ill," Peter grunted, taking the jug of homemade beer from the fridge. "And probably alive with fleas! Did you have to bring it into the house?"

For an instant she seemed on the verge of exploding. Then she changed her mind, as the cat accepted a mouthful of the liver and essayed a feeble purr by way of thanks.

Rising, wiping her hands, she turned to her father. "Dad, don't be like that!" she pleaded. "Let me try and rescue the poor thing! If I can, it'll be company for me when I'm home alone."

*You don't have to be . . .*

But the words died. Didn't have to be? That wasn't true. Fewer and fewer of her friends from school, boys or girls, were willing to be seen in her company, for fear of reprisals from the Throwers . . .

*Pressure, of course. But encouraged from the top.*

And, speaking of pressure—

"All right," he sighed. "You can keep it overnight, but tomorrow it goes to the vet for a thorough check, okay?"

Somehow, when she turned her melting eyes on him, he found it impossible to resist her. Which wasn't too surprising. All his life he'd been a sucker for beautiful sad girls. Just so had Kamala attracted his attention, having been cruelly jilted by a former lover. It looked as though Ellen had inherited at least one of her mother's traits . . .

She kissed him smackingly on the cheek. "Thank you so much!" she cried. "Dinner will be ready in half an hour! What's more, I found some potatoes. Do you want chips or mash?"

"With—?"

"I told you this morning! Liver and onions!"

"So you did . . . All right, mash."

"Right. Got to keep down the intake of fried food, hm? Eat better, live longer . . ." And her face changed magically to a mask of misery. "Not that I know why anyone should want to."

"Ellen darling, what in the world—?"

For suddenly tears were flowing down her cheeks.

"It *is* the world," she forced out, turning away to seize a tissue. "All the bad things that are on the news every day, worse than my most awful nightmares! Did you hear about the train crash?"

"What train crash?"

"At Manchester this afternoon. It was on the radio—I heard it when I first came in. No, don't turn on the telly"—as by reflex he moved to do so. "I don't want to see the pictures. People were crushed alive, squashed into pulp! They said something went wrong with the computer that controls the signals . . ."

She was recovering. After a final dab at her eyes she discarded the tissue.

"Sorry," she mumbled at last. "It's just that it made me think of what must have happened in the plane crash that—that burned down my old home."

It was the first time in weeks that she had made direct reference to her mother's death. Peter put a comforting arm around her, at a loss for anything to say.

"And there's a message from Claudia," Ellen went on after a pause. "She's ill. In hospital."

"Oh, no! What's wrong?" He remembered that she had complained of feeling unwell recently, but since the story that had seemed so promising was completely stagnant he had allowed himself to drift out of touch for several days.

"Codworm."

"What—? Oh. No, don't tell me." Peter felt his mouth set in a grim line. "I know about codworm. And it's nasty."

"Yes, it sounds awful. I looked it up. Its medical name is anisakiasis and you catch it from eating raw fish."

"Or cheap fish improperly prepared."

"It said that, too."

"Will she have to have an operation?"

"I don't think so. They're giving her a—a vermifuge, is that right?"

"Yes, quite right. But is she going to be in hospital for long?"

"A week at least, she said. I don't mean she actually said. She didn't phone up, just left an email message."

"Then I'd better send a get-well card in the morning. I don't suppose she has an email terminal beside her bed."

A faint whimpering noise emanated from the cat. Turning, they saw it trying to rise and head for the door.

"I suppose I'd better let it out," Ellen said after a moment. "I hope it doesn't run away . . ."

It didn't, but came gratefully back into the warm and dry. And, just as it returned, the phone rang.

"Bernie. Can I drop around? I need to talk."

*How can I say no?*

But what Peter mainly wanted to say—only he couldn't find the proper words—was this, to Ellen: *Yes, you poor kid! We've messed up the world for you, haven't we? Me, I envied the generation just before mine, who had all the fun of the permissive society, when you could shrug off a dose of the clap or even pox and carry right on screwing. Then came AIDS . . . And now there's a sense of universal doom. What if those Tibetan terrorists really have captured a load of nuclear waste? It's been denied, but who believes governments any more? If some crazy dictator in the Third World gets hold of nuclear weapons, and they keep talking about India and Pakistan and the Malaysians, not to mention the South Americans—or if it's true about the ozone layer being destroyed, and I suspect it is—or if the loss of the Amazon rain-forests really means we're running short of oxygen—or if poisons in the food we eat are really due to cut our life-expectancy—or if the tailored bacteria we're releasing to the environment are as imperfect as our computer programs, another of which just broke down and ruined a major Japanese bank—or if our squandering of fossil fuel is really going to melt the icecaps . . . then all we can say to our children is, "We're very sorry!"*

*And a fat lot of good that will do!*

Meditatively, as Ellen busied herself at the stove, he said, "You know, years ago I read about a mother who cured her daughter of making a mess. The kid was careless and kept knocking things over, and thought it was enough to say, 'I'm sorry!' "

Ellen glanced around with large dark puzzled eyes. Suddenly Peter felt it very important to complete the story and put its point across.

"So one day when she knocked a jugful of milk all over the table and the carpet, her mother handed her a tea towel—tied it around her head like a turban—and also a stick. She said 'Right, now you're a magician, and you've got a wand. Wave it over the spilt milk and say the magic word "sorry"!' And, of course . . ."

"Of course the mess was still there," Ellen said in a brisk tone. "So?"

"So that's what I'd like to do to all the politicians and economists and businessmen and—*all* those bocky canks! Because it's not enough to say sorry to you kids that we're leaving to clear up the mess."

"Don't worry," she answered, piling richly scented fried onions on to plates, adding the grilled liver, scraping every trace of the precious mashed potatoes from the saucepan, producing cutlery and mustard to go with the food.

He blinked at her. "What on earth do you mean? How can I help worrying?"

"We kids may not be as willing as they think," she answered

enigmatically. "I mean, to sort out other people's mess . . . Shall we eat? If Bernie's coming, we don't have much time."

At least this time the hacker arrived without muddy smears and a black eye, though the drizzle had turned to rain and the rain was, as ever, filthy. Accepting a beer, he sat down in what had become his customary chair.

"You heard about Claudia?" he said.

"Yes."

"Selling fish that contains live anisakiais larvae is illegal in all EEC countries."

"Maybe she contracted it in America—"

"The symptoms, including vomit tinged with blood, come on within a few hours. I've been checking."

"Then she must have lunched at a sushi bar with sloppy standards of hygiene! Lord, do I have to tell you how the government has cut back on food inspectors? If there had been another series of *Continuum* that would have been one of the subjects we tackled."

"Then I shouldn't have to repeat what I just said. It is *illegal* to sell fish containing live anisakiais larvae."

Peter stood rock-still for a second. Then he whistled.

"Got my point, have you?" Bernie grunted. "Even if she did catch it in a Japanese restaurant—and we dare not of course risk offending the Japanese, not so long as we're begging to be readmitted to their economic sphere—the owner should nonetheless have received a call from the Bill and been ordered to prove his premises were not the source of the infection. It's a notifiable condition. The hospital should have reported it immediately."

"And they didn't?"

Bernie shook his head. "Security on police reports from hospitals is so lax, they're practically public domain. It wasn't done."

"Well, they are terribly overworked," Peter murmured. "I suppose someone forgot."

"Or else Claudia doesn't have codworm at all."

There was a pause. Eventually Peter said in a cold, thin voice, "Go on. Spell it out. I don't think I'm going to like it, but—well, spell it out."

From the inside pocket of his jacket the hacker produced a slip of paper, a computer printout. "Here. Take a look at this. I'm not supposed to have it, of course, but . . . Hey, did Claudia get to see Sister Higgins?"

Scrutinizing the printout and having to move it closer to a lamp, remembering that he had promised himself glasses some time soon—only until he found more work he couldn't pay for a pair, since they were no longer available free on the National Health Service—Peter grunted, "Yes, and she is a patient at the hospice, not a member of staff. What's more she's completely gaga and not expected to live more than a few months . . . Grief! Is this for real?"

Crumpling the paper in his agitation, he stared at Bernie.

"Far as I know," the hacker sighed. "At least I picked it up from an authentic source."

"So she doesn't have codworm!"

Ellen had been in the kitchen washing up. Returning in time to catch the last words, she demanded an explanation.

Summing up briefly, Peter rushed on, "But why? And how?"

Bernie spread his hands. "It's a standard technique for losing unwelcome investigators for a while. MI5 and MI6 are fond of it, the CIA and the KGB both use similar methods . . . The idea is, you give someone a temporary ulcer—there are all kinds of local irritants you can slip into their food, in a capsule that will dissolve at the right point in the digestive tract—and then arrange a false diagnosis so they get the wrong treatment, ideally something that will make matters worse. After a week or two—"

Peter was on his feet. "For heaven's sake! We've got to tell her!"

"Have you forgotten that she's a foreigner, being treated in an NHS hospital, which is a rare privilege for anyone from outside the EEC, and—?"

"And she's ill and in pain!"

"You're going to march in and tell her doctor that he's either a fool or a dupe?"

"But how could a doctor—?"

"People can be bent," Bernie said succinctly, and emptied his mug of beer.

"You honestly mean—"

"Oh, grow up, will you? I'm only a few years younger than you, but I feel a sight older, I'm telling you! *You* ought to know what kind of a country this is turning into!"

Peter subsided slowly, clutching his own beer.

"Yes, I think I do," he muttered, glancing at Ellen. "I was . . . Well, I was thinking along those lines before dinner. What do we do?"

"You must visit Claudia in the morning," Ellen said in a positive tone. "And insist on talking to her doctor."

"Ellen, dear," Bernie said, rising to refill his mug, "it's wonderful to be young and idealistic. But I'm afraid that if our home-brewed version of the Gestapo have got to that growser—"

"*Why?*" Peter burst out.

"That's what I don't know. But it's what I mainly came to talk to you about." Having topped up his mug and taken a long draught, Bernie fixed him with a glare.

"I'm quitting."

"But—"

"Don't say I can't! I sure as hell can, and you're holding the last scrap of data I produce for you! Call me a coward if you like, but I'm telling you straight: the fact that the heavy mob are trying to stop her from digging any deeper makes me worry about my own hide. Sorry. I'll tell Jake in the morning—no point in depressing him while he's trying to put an edition to bed."

After a further gulp of beer he added mildly, "Besides, I think I'm up against a brick wall. Louis Parker is too smart for me."

"I was going to ask—"

"And I was going to tell you. Sorry, the paper in your hand isn't quite the last bit of data that I owe you."

"Well, for God's sake give me the rest!" Peter barked. "You've been looking for Louis Parker for bocky weeks, and never found a trace of him!"

"Nor have I now. But I've reached a conclusion."

Peter felt his nails biting painfully into his palms. "Out with it!" he gritted.

"It is my considered opinion," Bernie said, avoiding the others' eyes, "that you are right about Louis Parker. And he knows it, and he knows you're after him, and he's—well—taken the appropriate precautions."

"You mean the bastard has Special Branch in his pocket, not to mention NHS doctors?"

"It seems all too likely. Look!" He hunched forward in his chair. "I've run that immense search I told you about—run it as far and as long as the money would stretch. I do not find *any* trace of Louis Parker. You told me a bit about his background, his family being Armenian and so on, and you said he donated semen and he worked for a computer firm and—and so forth. I've cross-checked every reference I can, and he's not there. You saw how Ellen located Sister Higgins by tapping into obsolete phone directories. If you try that for Louis Parker, you don't find him. But you said he was a swinging man-about-town type; can you imagine him not being on the phone?"

Cold sweat was pearling on Peter's brow. He was about to speak, but before he found the right words Bernie had charged onward.

"And don't talk about ex-directory! If you know how to go about it, you can get *anybody's* phone number, alive or dead! Or at least anybody's who was around after they computerized the system. Also the passport office doesn't know about him. Social Security doesn't know about him. None of the major clearing banks ever kept an account in his name. I said before, and I say it again: he's dug a hole, jumped in, and pulled it after him. And that spells trouble on a scale I don't want to get involved with!"

Draining his beer anew, he rose to leave. On the way to the door, however, he hesitated. He had become aware that Ellen was staring at him.

"Is something wrong?" he demanded.

"Yes. You." The girl rose from the couch and held herself very upright.

"How do you mean?"

"You've taken money from the *Comet* to investigate this story that Claudia brought you. You didn't treat it seriously at first. Now it's turned out to be real news. You ought to be excited, you ought to want to push through to the end. Instead, you're sliming out!"

Small face eloquent of disgust, she marched back into the kitchen and addressed herself loudly to the cat.

On the doorstep Peter said, "Ellen's right, you know."

"Maybe so. But I'm going to—to cover my ass, as the Americans would say."

"And I'm going to put mine on the line!" Peter flared. "Tomorrow I'm going to do exactly as Ellen suggested!"

"What? Try and make Claudia's doctor admit—?"

"Exactly!"

"Well, all I can say is I hope you survive! 'Night!"

Next morning Peter had no trouble gaining admittance to Claudia's ward. Pale, reclining against a heap of shabby pillows, she smiled appreciation of his visit—and stopped smiling when he surreptitiously showed her the computer printout that Bernie had forgotten to reclaim.

"Oh my God," she whispered when its import sank in. "I've stumbled on to something even bigger than I first imagined."

"Very big," Peter muttered, glancing around to make sure no one was in a position to overhear—but an orderly was pushing an electric polisher across the floor, and that much noise ought to take care of eavesdroppers. "I've been thinking about it half the night because of what Bernie told me about Louis Parker." He summarized rapidly.

"And if he is the father of all these children," Claudia said slowly, "then—"

"Then what more likely than that he possesses at least some of their 'talent'? No wonder he can dig a hole and climb in, as Bernie says, and still influence people like the doctor in charge of your case!"

"I still find it hard to believe," Claudia sighed. "I could have sworn I'd been given an honest diagnosis . . ."

"Not according to that printout—which, by the way, I had better reclaim." Peter suited action to the words. "I think you'd better get yourself transferred to a private hospital, and never mind how much of Strugman's money it will cost. And you might well phone your lawyer friend, Mr. Stine, and—Well, you probably have a code, don't you?"

Claudia nodded dully. "I don't know how secure it is, but we change it pretty regularly."

"I can imagine what Bernie would say about that . . . Ah, never mind. You get in touch. The Strugfolk must have a good many contacts."

"Yes, of course."

"Time to start using them." Peter hesitated before adding, "Claudia, I hope you'll forgive me, but—"

"Ah, shit. What for this time?"

"Well"—uneasily—"not treating this theory of yours as seriously as I now realize it deserved."

"And I guess I ought to thank you, as well. After all, you aren't exactly going to make international headlines with the story, are you?"

"Not until it breaks on the grand scale."

"And now you know what we're up against, that doesn't seem likely—Oh, oh."

A portly nurse was approaching like a ship under full sail, expression stern.

"Mr. Levin! You've been here longer than the regulation time. You mustn't tire our patient."

"Going, going, gone . . ." Peter tucked the printout back in his pocket, hoping it had not been noticed. But this was a "charity"—i.e. NHS—ward, and only in wards reserved for private, paying patients were there expensive luxuries like TV cameras to monitor their progress. He bent to kiss Claudia's forehead.

Reaching up to embrace him, she whispered close to his ear, "If Bernie's right, you know, it means that Louis Parker knows about his children—who they are, and where."

"Oh my God!" Peter stepped back in horror.

"Now, Mr. Levin, you mustn't upset—"

"She's just upset me!" Peter snapped. "I hadn't thought of that . . . I know who would have, though!"

"Who?"

"Ellen! She's developing just the kind of paranoia I often wish I could have cultivated, because it's perfect for a reporter!"

"Talk to her when she gets home from school, then," Claudia said composedly. "And—nurse!"

"Yes?"

"Bring me a phone. At once. I believe my condition to have been misdiagnosed and I want to call in a second opinion. After that I plan to call my lawyer in New York with a view to filing suit for medical malpractice."

The nurse looked blank. Peter donned a false smile.

"Do as she says," he told her. "If not, you could be liable for damages, as I'm a witness to this sad affair."

She strove for a moment to avoid compliance. Then she crumpled. But, as she turned away, the movement of her lips could be clearly read:

*Bocky American!*

* * *

"Cancer," said the vet to whom Peter and Ellen took the cat that evening.

"But he's so young!" Ellen exclaimed.

"Yes, about nine months, I'd say. But last week I delivered a litter of kittens that were riddled with tumors in the womb. I sometimes wonder, if we're doing this to our pets, what we're doing to ourselves and one another—"

He caught himself. He wore a red-white-and-blue ribbon on his white coat, and his hand flew to it as to a talisman, as to a crucifix.

"Well, I'm sure the government is doing all it can!" he concluded heartily. "But it would be kindest to have your cat put down. One wouldn't want to prolong its suffering. Please sign this form . . . Thank you. That will be £25. We accept all major credit cards; please tell the receptionist which you prefer. Next!"

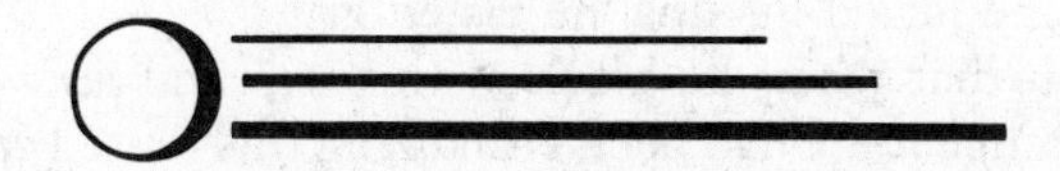

This far south it was still warm, although the business of summer was long over. The grapes and olives had been harvested and pressed; the tobacco—still grown around here—had been sold, along with the maize, whether for *polenta* or for oil. Almost the only touch of color in the gray-sandy landscape was to be found where families had retained tomatoes to dry or cook down into paste.

There was something old and dusty about the view David stared at from the passenger seat of the Alfa Harry had rented at Foggia airport. It was like entering one of the paintings he had been instructed to admire at school. When he was still obliged to attend one.

For the first time since their brief encounter he remembered the education inspector he had seduced (much in the manner of Garth or Roger, he could now think) after ensuring that he would never again be distracted by dull-witted teachers.

Now, though, he was distracted by far worse problems. One was simply physical: the food he had risked eating on the plane had given him a belly-ache, and with vast embarrassment he had twice had to ask Harry to stop the car, so he might crouch behind dry-leaved autumn bushes and void his bowel.

David did not enjoy being reminded of his base humanity.

Prompted by thoughts of Garth, he started worrying about another problem. He had assumed his siblings would be on his side, so it would be safe to leave Alice in charge of them and the house while he and Harry made this trip to Italy—based on a mere suspicion, yet one that struck a chord in his imagination . . .

*No! It must have been worthwhile! My program said . . .*

Distrust, abrupt distrust, fought in his mind with tattered hope. He strove to sort the data he was processing. (How long before he himself started to think like a computer?)

*First—!*

He compelled himself to face the fact that his siblings were not automatically his allies. The worst of his early fears were being borne out. They had, as he was learning, spent too long on their own, with no conception of partnership and cooperation.

*Maybe I shouldn't have risked leaving them . . .*

His guts ached, his eyes were sore, he felt at his absolutely worst. The car trundled on, down potholed roads, while dust rose in their wake and sometimes ahead, when a tractor or a lorry was preceding them. The Alfa had no air-conditioning, and it was too hot to keep the windows shut. When he licked his lips, he tasted grit.

It dawned on him that when he planned this trip and *persuaded* Harry and Alice to arrange it, he had been visualizing this rented car as identical to the Rolls Royce he was accustomed to. His hand kept groping for the keyboard and modem that would have allowed him to interrogate the programs he had left running when he came away.

And he wanted to know their outcome. Needed to! If this mysterious Louis Parker was indeed his natural father—!

"Left or right?" Harry demanded in a rasping tone. They had come to a T-junction.

"What?"

"Damn it, you're supposed to be navigating!"

*How dare you talk to me like that?*

But David's fury flared and vanished like the fuel in a pizza oven. He hadn't bargained for a pain in his belly, or the debilitation due to constant diarrhea . . .

Mastering himself with vast effort, he glanced around. To the right, in the direction of the sunset, he spotted stone pillars framing the entrance to a driveway flanked by olive trees. Pointing, he muttered, "That looks like it."

"It had better be! I swear I don't know why I agreed to bring you here! Christ, I haven't felt so ill in years!"

*Oh, no. If I lose control over my "father," what's left for me to look forward to . . . ?*

But, summoning all his force, David laid a reassuring hand on Harry's right wrist, not so hard as to delay him turning the steering wheel. When simple speech and presence didn't work, contact tended to, as he had learned.

"Please, for me, drive to the house. You'll understand some day, I promise!"

*If Louis Parker is real. If he's still alive. If I can track him down. If I can make him make me understand before I have to do my own explaining . . .*

*But if he's dead, rather than in hiding? Or even—?*

The alternatives were too terrible to think of. David said aloud, to quiet his mind, "Handsome old place, isn't it? Shame it isn't kept in better repair . . . Look, there's someone we can ask."

"In Italian?" Harry grunted. But he slowed the car.

A portly middle-aged man was snipping off dead flowerheads in what must once have been a splendid formal garden with fountains, steps, and marble urns. Now the urns and steps were cracked, and none of the fountains played.

"*Buon giorno!*" David shouted, having remembered in time to turn the handle that rolled down the car window. (In the Rolls, of course, one pressed a switch.) "*Il signor Tessolari?*"

A vigorous headshake.

"*Per favore, dov'é il signore?*"

Which was about the point at which David's command of Italian ran out. Before leaving home he had reviewed a supposed "instant course" on videodisc, but even though he had only arrived in the country a few hours before he had already discovered its limitations.

However, a stroke of luck followed.

In English, the portly man said, "Are you American?"

"No, British!"

"Hmm! What business do you have with Renato?"

That, David recalled, was the name of GianMarco's "father." He debated with himself a moment, then settled for an empty phrase.

"We have a personal matter to discuss."

There was a pause. Eventually the man sighed.

"Very well, but you will have to wait. I am Fabio Bonni, GianMarco's uncle, and also his tutor." He hesitated, then gave a sudden, rather unpleasant laugh. "That is, I am supposed to be his tutor. I cannot make him express a simple sentence in either French or English. Yet he is not stupid. Already, at his age, he is more in control of the family's affairs than is Renato . . . Oh, park your car and get out. I don't know how long before they return, but we can take refreshment on the terrace. You are British, so you will want tea, of course. Well, we can still afford tea."

There was mockery in his tone and his expression. The hairs on David's nape prickled and he wished himself a thousand miles away.

*I've seen people like this before. Only when I had done with them!*

The possibility that GianMarco might be a rival such as he had never yet faced began to frighten him. Yet in the upshot, surely, with his experience in California he must be better informed, better adapted, *stronger* than someone living in a more-or-less peasant community in the *Mezzogiorno* . . .

The man who had identified himself as Fabio Bonni was shouting for a servant as he led them around the house to the promised terrace, overlooking dry pools and withering shrubs. The servant appeared, an elderly short-sighted woman, curtseying on sight of the visitors.

"Tea!" Fabio commanded. "In the English style!"

And when it came it was revolting . . .

*I shouldn't have done this! Why am I here? I've dug a pitfall and I'm trapped in it!*

They had to make forced conversation for nearly an hour. Fabio proved to be an archetypal whenzie. He complained endlessly about the state of Italy, the arrogance of the peasants, the local priest who sided with them as though he were a communist instead of a Christian, and the declining fortunes of the old landed families, including his.

David thought he might have gone on till midnight but the sound of an approaching car interrupted him. He tried to relax, forget his nervousness . . . but it was hard.

The first glimpse he had of GianMarco convinced him, on grounds of appearance alone, that here was yet another of his siblings, and after the first few politenesses had been exchanged he was satisfied on another, rather peculiar, score. He was certain Renato Tessolari believed the boy to be his own child, whereas his mother and uncle were under no such misapprehension.

*Odd! But maybe, if necessary, I can play that card . . .*

He cancelled the notion at once as dismal visions filled his head: the gradual establishment of intimate acquaintance, many exchanges of letters—it was unlikely that the Tessolaris possessed email facilities—in short, a slow and painstaking siege . . .

*But there isn't time for all that mucking about!*

Yet it was already clear that, whether he suspected what he owed it to or not, GianMarco was in full command of his talent, and enjoying his position of precocious power too much to want to give it up on the say-so of a stranger. He spoke no English, as his uncle had warned, but the latter acted as interpreter while he recited a lively account of the way in which he and his parents had just sorted out a recalcitrant tenant-farmer, who to his own amazement had this afternoon agreed to leave, along with his family, and take his chances in the north.

"So we can put in someone who isn't infected with these radical left-wing ideas, but shows proper respect for his superiors!" Fabio wound up. David's knowledge of Italian was too limited for him to be sure whether this was something GianMarco himself had said, or Renato, or just a footnote expressing Fabio's own opinion.

Then, of course, there had to be an explanation for the foreigners' visit, unheralded as it was. And this was where David had made his worst mistake. So sure had he been that when he arrived he would be able to persuade the other boy to come to Britain, and his family to let him go—for it had been so easy in so many previous cases, and he had grown so used to Harry and Alice bending to his every whim—he hadn't bothered to work out a credible story.

And Harry was no help. Extremely tired, perhaps suffering from the same digestive upset, he only muttered, "My son wanted to come here, so I brought him."

At that GianMarco stiffened in his chair and gave a nod.

*He's caught on*, David realized sickly. *And he's well, and speaking his own language, and I'm ill and having to rely on an interpreter. This mess is getting worse by the minute.*

So, even as the thought passed through his mind, did the griping in his belly. He rose, wondering how to ask for a toilet, and didn't have to. As though reading his mind across the barrier of language, GianMarco called the maid.

He stayed out of sight for what felt like ages, striving to conjure up a credible reason for the visit, and failing. When at length he dared not remain in hiding any longer, he returned sullenly to the company . . . only to discover that the necessary story had been invented in his absence. He knew it, the moment GianMarco rose to clasp his hand and express, in the slow and well-articulated tones of one who feels he has to contend with a simpleton, the hope that his *malattia* was not too severe.

*What's happened? Why is everyone smiling—Renato and his wife, Fabio, even Harry?*

He had been outsmarted. For the first time he had met his match, and more than his match. GianMarco was indeed one of his siblings, and for whatever reason he had attained greater control, if not a fuller understanding, of his powers.

"Well, we must be on our way!" Harry said heartily. "If you're okay again, son?"

*God, how I hate it when he calls me "son"!*

But David forced a smile, and uttered a few words of thanks in his rudimentary Italian. They had such impact that GianMarco's mother Constanza embraced him, kissing him on both cheeks.

And, before he fully realized what was happening, they were back in the Alfa and he was cradling in his lap a bag containing bottles of wine made on the Tessolari estate.

"Remarkable boy, that GianMarco," Harry said as he dexterously negotiated bends and potholes on the way to the *autostrada* that would lead them back to Foggia and the airport. "Come to that, you're pretty remarkable yourself."

*What?* Abruptly David was alert. And Harry was continuing:

"I'd never have thought of importing wine guaranteed to be produced by chemical-free methods! But it's an obvious winner, isn't it? I only wish you'd told me beforehand. I literally didn't realize what was going through your head until GianMarco spelt it out. Next time, do me the favor of remembering that your old man can't read your mind!"

He waved at the surrounding vineyards and olive groves.

"It's not exactly my regular line, but with the contacts I have, not to mention the spare capital, I can just see it working. Yes, I can see it very well . . . Are you okay?"

"Frankly, no," David gritted.

"Then I'll stop hurrying. We don't have to fly home tonight. I'll call the airline and change our booking to the morning. Look, there's an *albergo* sign. I don't suppose it will be luxy accommodation, but if at least the beds are clean and the food fit to eat . . ."

David uttered a moan, at which Harry looked alarmed.

"Maybe I should get them to call a doctor—"

"No, no!" The boy forced himself to calm. "I'll be fine in the morning. But . . . Well, damn all bocky airline food!"

"I'm sorry." Harry sounded concerned. "It used to be okay in first-class. Nowadays, I suppose, what with the chemicals that have contaminated so much agricultural land . . . Next time we'll bring a packed lunch, hm?"

He clapped his "son" on the shoulder and turned the car off the road, under a red neon sign.

Behaving more like a father than at any time David could recall, Harry marched him into the hotel and, using a mix of bastard Spanish, half-remembered French and vigorous gestures, secured a twin room with its own bath and toilet. He insisted on David getting into bed at once, and arranged for a plain, easily digestible meal: boiled pasta with scrambled egg instead of a sauce. When he saw it David thought it was sure to make him gag, but for once he let Harry override his own opinion, and in fact he managed to eat almost all of it.

Much relieved, Harry went downstairs for his own meal. When he returned, David was dozing, but Harry roused him, proffering a glass that held a syrupy green liquid.

"The people here say this is what you need. It's a liqueur called *Centerba*, 'hundred herbs.' I tried a drop. Watch out—it's pretty strong. But it seems to help. If it does nothing else, it ought to give you a night's rest."

Too weak and weary to resist, David swallowed it like unwelcome medicine. It exploded in his guts like a fireball, but in a little while he felt a sense of warmth and comfort. Leaning back, he closed his eyes. Harry, who had been sitting anxiously on the other bed, smiled and rose.

"Looks as though they were right! I'll return your dinner tray. In case you drop off before I get back—sleep well!"

Which David did. But, before he fell asleep, one thought came to dominate his mind.

*Grief! What power that GianMarco has! Not just to have explained away our arrival on the spur of the moment—to have wrought such a change in Harry!*

*Something must be done about GianMarco . . .*

And blackout.

The opportunity to "do something" about GianMarco arose fortuitously the next morning.

David, feeling much better after nine hours' sleep, was breakfasting with Harry in the bar, off excellent coffee and rather disappointing bread and jam, when a police patrol car drew up. At some stage in yesterday's conversation with the Tessolaris it had been mentioned that they were on intimate terms with the local *Maresciallo*, and David felt a spasm of alarm. But it proved to be unwarranted; the driver and his companion merely ordered two espressos and stood at the counter drinking them.

Harry, who was still clearly taken by the idea of wine-importing (yet more testimony to GianMarco's power!), was enthusiastically outlining what he planned to do about it. Overhearing, the junior policeman, who carried a carbine on a sling, approached to inquire whether they were British or American, and what brought them to the area. Again David grew uneasy, but the man seemed merely curious, and eager to practice his English.

Harry said, shrugging, "We visited Signor Tessolari. We had a business deal to discuss."

At the mention of that name, the policeman's face darkened. Glancing around to make sure his superior was not listening—he wasn't, being engaged in chat with the proprietor's wife—he leaned forward and spoke in a low and confidential tone.

"You don't trust him, sir. He is very bad man. He is *murderer.*"

"What?" Harry blinked in astonishment.

"Yes, sir. I swear. He killed my cousin with a—a . . ." At a loss for the word he touched his carbine, and David, suddenly all ears, supplied the word "gun."

"Gun, yes! But he is rich and powersome, and was our mayor. He lied to say it was one of the people that live on his land, and paid him money to go to the north and hide in a big city with a different name."

*Miracles will never cease.*

David seized his opportunity. He could feel that his talent was back to normal. Hoping against hope that he would have sufficient time to exploit it, he caught the policeman's hand, leaning close.

"This is terrible! Was he never arrested? No? But it's a scandal that such people should go free when people who commit much lesser crimes are sent to jail! Such villains are unfit to live—don't you agree?"

For another two or three minutes he continued in the same persuasive strain. By the time the senior policeman called his subordinate back to the car, he was virtually certain he had planted seeds for action in the young man's mind. Into the bargain, when Harry inquired with puzzlement what all that had been about, he was able to brush the matter aside with a request that it not be mentioned again.

*At the very least*, he thought grimly, *I've wished a major headache on GianMarco—enough to stop him meddling in my affairs until I've had time to make plans! And if I could deal with a tearaway like Gui, I ought to be able to cope with a boy my own age!*

Owing to a computer failure at the Rome air traffic control center their flight was delayed for ten hours. Fuming, Harry tried to charter a private plane, but failed; all non-scheduled flights were grounded until the computer was repaired. He tried to switch to Alitalia, the national airline being the only one still operating, but there were no vacant seats. Losing his temper, he demanded of David why he was so unconcerned.

But the boy only smiled.

On their return home, David claimed the bottles of wine not to drink but to analyze. Meantime he set one of his computers to monitor the news-services out of Southern Italy, keyed to the name Tessolari. The following morning his search was rewarded. Even his rudimentary knowledge of the language sufficed to inform him that Signor Renato Tessolari, together with his wife Constanza, brother-in-law Fabio Bonni, son GianMarco and an unnamed servant, had died in a fire that broke out at their home during the small hours.

He printed out the data, ripped the paper from the machine and bore it to the dining room where Harry, Alice and the other children were assembling for breakfast.

"You can forget about that wine-importing deal," he grunted as he dropped into his chair and helped himself to cornflakes.

Harry read the printout with dismay, and swore under his breath.

"Don't worry," David sighed. " 'Chemical-free wine'! It contained the maximum allowed under EEC law of just about every additive you can name. Bunch of puky liars, the Tessolaris. And if that policeman was to be believed, they only got what was coming to them

. . . Will you canks stop hogging the milk and sugar? Alice, where's my tea?"

Even as he stirred it, though, he shivered to think how close his project had trespassed toward the verge of disaster.

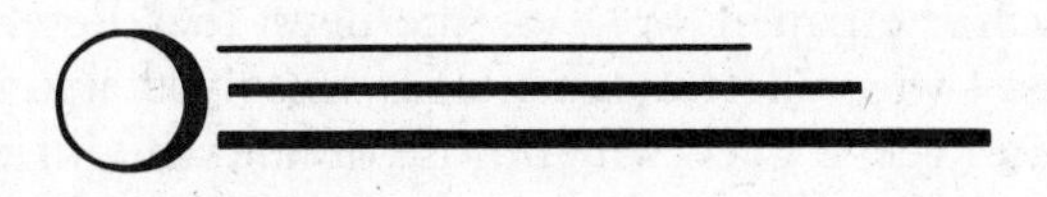

*You're watching TV Plus. Now for Newsframe.*

*Allegations that the disastrous flooding of the Norfolk Broads during the past week might be due to subsidence of the bed of the North Sea following the extraction of so much oil and gas were officially dismissed as "unfounded" this morning. Police have been called out to control refugees swelling the ranks of farmers quitting the so-called East Anglian dustbowl, now a sea of mud after heavy rain. More in a moment.*

*A group of self-styled "Throwers" today threatened to close down TV Plus, if necessary by force. Contacted at home, the general dissociated himself from what he termed "such precipitate action," but added that he fully supports the official ban on "anti-patriotic" news . . .*

At last Peter had had a breakthrough, and he owed it to Ellen. The revelation that their beloved cats and dogs were dying *en masse* of premature cancer had stirred the normally cowed and docile British public in a way that scarcely anything else could. When he was able to prove that several of the royal racehorses had gone the same way, not only the *Comet* but even TV Plus remembered him and sent him off on a joint fact-finding mission.

Bernie's withdrawal from the search for Louis Parker had seemed like a stop sign, and with Claudia still convalescing from her illness (which was, as Bernie had predicted, not after all due to codworm, the X-rays supposed to be hers having been "mixed up" with someone else's), he had given little thought recently to the criminal-children story.

Nonetheless, he remembered to mention it when Jake rang up to confirm his assignment, though he was not at all surprised by the disillusioned answer:

"What you've given me so far won't make page ten, let alone page one!"

Curiously, however, it still engaged Ellen's interest. Peter had let himself be cajoled into explaining what few details she didn't yet know on the way back from visiting Claudia in hospital, and since then she had taken over what inquiries could be made using the equipment they had at home. So far she had reported little or no progress (was it surprising, given that Bernie the expert hacker had run into a dead end?) but at least it kept her occupied. The mood of the country was darkening as autumn dragged on, rainy and misty and cold, and the news that did not reach the papers or TV—the news that Peter had access to as a journalist—was full of racial attacks, unsolved arson and random violence in the streets. Even when those of her schoolfriends' families who were standing out against the pervading atmosphere invited Ellen to tea or to attend a birthday party, she declined, and none of her former boyfriends had taken her out in weeks.

*What sort of a life is that for a teenage kid? I wish I knew what to do . . . but I can't abandon her to "her own kind," as so many pundits tell me I should. What is her own kind? Isn't she as British as I am?*

For a while he compromised, increasing her pocket-money and buying her presents he could ill afford. After a week or two, however, he noticed she was simply putting them away in a cupboard, so that wasn't the right approach. The only positive step open to him lay in spending more time with her. But if he was to keep up his payments on their home, he must accept any job going, no matter how long it took or how often he was obliged to break the promise he had made to himself about not leaving her alone overnight.

It was a trap. He fretted over it. Yet Ellen herself seemed resigned and not unhappy. He postponed a solution, and again, and again.

And again.

He made a killing on the racehorse story, even though he had to lay out nearly as much as his own fee in bribes. But then, that was the way of things nowadays. All the newspapers and commercial TV companies maintained so-called contingency accounts in foreign tax-havens from which they could allot such "inducements" . . . One of the chief reasons why the money-starved BBC was turning more and more into an organ of official propaganda was because it had no such supplementary resources and had to lick the government's boots in order to survive.

Knowing that he had earned enough to support himself and his daughter for at least three months, if he didn't overspend (and there was less and less to buy, anyhow, so that should not be hard, though he had taken advantage of his temporary affluence and was carrying a heavy bagful of groceries) Peter was humming as he approached his home. At least the windows were intact—recently gangs of children had taken to smashing the glass of any house or flat round here where "colored" people lived—and when he slipped his key into the lock it turned easily, so it had not been dosed with superglue.

Ellen, whom he had phoned to warn of his return, emerged from the kitchen to give him a kiss. As she relieved him of his load of shopping he inquired, "Anything been happening around here?"

"Mm-hm." She tossed back her long dark hair. "They used a chunk of your horse-cancer story on the early evening news. I only hope that doesn't provoke anyone to find out where you live and do what they did to Bernie . . . Oh! Speaking of Bernie: there's a message from Claudia. She wants us to go round this evening."

He had been looking forward to a quiet evening at home; his assignment, though profitable, had been tiring.

"Any special reason?" he said at length.

"She wouldn't say. But it sounded urgent."

"Hmm! Convince me."

"Well, she did say something new has turned up." Ellen caught his hand in hers and adopted her usual melting-eyed expression. "Can't we? I'd go by myself except—"

*Except dark-skinned people like me can't walk a British street alone any more.*

She didn't have to finish the sentence.

"All right," he sighed. "But after I've had a drink and a decent meal . . . Know something? I'm getting addicted to Indian food. Haven't eaten anything else all the time I've been away, apart from breakfast."

She beamed at him. When he produced whiskey from the bag he had brought she seized it, told him to sit down, and brought him a drink mixed exactly to his taste.

How strange it was to return to his old home . . . Peter found himself clutching Ellen's hand as they walked from the bus stop. They were arriving much later than he had told Claudia on the phone; the bus had been re-routed owing to a fight between a white gang and a group of Pakistani vigilantes which the police had broken up with tear gas.

*More of the streetlights out than when I lived here . . . More windows boarded up, not only shops now but the ground floors of homes—Grief, what is this country coming to?*

Also the Neighborhood Watch signs had vanished. It looked as though the windows that displayed them had become prime targets.

They were approaching the house door when two young men emerged from shadow, wearing Thrower brassards and balaclavas drawn up like masks. Dazzling them with a flashlight, the taller of the pair demanded what they were up to.

Feeling Ellen shrink back into shelter behind him, remembering what had happened to Bernie, Peter fought down the sick sensation that rose in his belly and strove to snap back in a properly defiant tone.

"I used to live here! On the top floor! I've come to call on the person who took over my old flat!"

"More likely looking for a quiet spot to take his black scrubber," said the second man.

"Don't you call my daughter a scrubber!" Peter blurted before he could stop himself.

"Ah! Another bocky nigger-lover! Well, we'll show you what we think of *your* sort! Right, Ted?"

"Right," said the tall one, switching off and pocketing the flashlight.

*Oh, no! Let this not be real!*

But, even as Peter was preparing to offer what resistance he could, Ellen darted away from him, up the steps to the house. It was divided into eight flats and each had an answer-phone. She planted her hands on all the bell-pushes at once and held them down.

"Why, the bocky cunt!" the shorter youth burst out.

Amazed and indescribably relieved at her presence of mind, Peter shouted, "Tell them to call the police!"

"Ah, shit!" Ted muttered. "All right, better get out of here. But" —with a final flare of defiance—"if we ever catch sight of you again we'll leave our mark on you, hear?"

And they were gone.

After explaining and apologizing to the other tenants—who recalled him from his time here and were willing enough to believe him, though some of those who emerged into the hall or on to the staircase bestowed harsh glances on Ellen—they were finally able to ascend to what was now Claudia's flat. Pale, obviously still weak, but improving, she made them sit down at once. She was drinking Gibsons from a chrome-plated cocktail shaker veiled in condensation, and insisted on pouring for them both.

"Should I?" Ellen asked nervously.

"I don't think one will do you any harm," Peter replied. "Claudia, you know I have a genius for a daughter? I never saw anything so quick-witted!" And he recounted in detail how Ellen had saved their skins, while she sipped nervously—once—and then ate her onion, nibbling it layer by layer off the stick as she gazed around.

The moment Peter finished, as though to forestall more praise, she said, "You couldn't have put me up here."

Briefly confused, thinking Ellen was addressing her, Claudia said, "You need somewhere to stay for a while? I could always—"

"No, no! I meant if the police had dumped me on Dad while he was still here, there wouldn't have been room."

"We'd have managed somehow," Peter said. "On the trip I just got back from I saw far worse crowding than two people in three rooms. You know there are places in Britain where houses are literally falling down because the owners can't afford repairs? In some streets you find whole families forced to live in a single ground-floor room because the rest of the house is uninhabitable. I'd have squeezed you in, don't worry."

Ellen caught his hand and gave him a brilliant smile.

After a pause Claudia said dryly, "I admit, young lady, I was wondering why you'd want to stay in an area that made you so unwelcome. By the way, I think I know the thugs who accosted you. I'm surprised the threat of the police drove them away. They were only planning to do what the fuzz around here make a habit of when they run across a mixed-race couple."

"Have things got that much worse since I moved?" Peter demanded. "Or is it simply that I didn't attract that kind of attention while I was here?"

"I suspect the latter," Claudia sighed. "But it's over, and you're both okay, though when you leave you'd better call a cab and wait till it's at the door . . . Don't you want to know why I asked you to call by?"

The powerful drink had calmed Peter's nerves. Leaning back in his chair, he invited her to go ahead.

"Bernie's turned up something new."

"But he told me he was quitting!"

"He changed his mind. He came to see me when I got back from the hospital—brought me a bouquet that must have cost a fortune—and after I talked at him for a while he promised he'd keep at least one search program running. And today this turned up."

She tossed him a sheet of email printout. For Ellen's benefit he read it aloud.

" 'Nothing on LP'—has he suddenly taken to music?"

"If that's a joke it's a pretty bad one," Claudia said tartly. "Louis Parker, of course!"

"I know, I know. Sorry. 'But another possible kid. Check North of England juvenile court reports for last Thursday.' "

"Which I did." Claudia passed over another sheet of paper. "I think this must be what he meant."

"Hmm!" Suddenly Peter's interest in the matter was rekindled. "It says here that a girl—the right kind of age—was caught when store-detectives investigating thefts from a supermarket checkout discovered that she was conning the assistants into giving her not only her change but also the money she'd originally handed them. In spite of which she was found not guilty and allowed to go free."

"Bernie's promised to track her down," Claudia said. "But he thinks it's going to be difficult. Juvenile court records are kind of shellbacked."

"Good to know something is," Peter grunted, emptying his glass. As though they were at home, Ellen was prompt to refill it, and Claudia's. Her own was barely touched.

While she was at it, he went on somewhat shamefacedly, "I must confess I haven't been working much on the story. And I don't expect I can in the near future, either. While I was away I found something else. I don't know whether you heard about it, but last summer an awful lot of plants died over here, or didn't set seed. Was that reported in the States?"

"I don't think so," Claudia answered. "Oh—wait! I think I heard some reference to it after I arrived. Wasn't there some sort of blight, like the one on potatoes?"

"That's what they tried to make people think. I just found out it was nothing of the kind. It was due to a new insecticide called Thanataph, a bestseller because it's supposed to provide complete control of aphids all summer with a single application."

"Does it?"

"Yes. Unfortunately it also kills bees. I didn't make the connection, but you can't buy British honey any more. *I* thought it was just another matter of economics—Greek honey in particular has been flooding the market because it's still cheap. I was wrong. Bees have been dying by the tens of millions. They're trying to make out that was due to a disease, too, but I have proof that it was not."

"Think it'll make page one?" Claudia countered in a cynical tone. Harking back to Jake's comment of the other day, Peter answered:

"Maybe not. But it could make page ten."

A drab silence followed. For the first time Peter realized that there wasn't even a radio in the room, let alone a TV or stereo. He was framing an embarrassed question about Claudia's finances when she shifted in her chair and heaved a sigh.

"Sometimes I wish I'd never started on this project, you know. Half the time I can't believe my evidence. All the time I can't lick it into shape. I can't concentrate. I keep wondering whether whatever I was given was meant to affect my mind."

Peter offered awkward consolation, but she brushed it aside. They both knew that governments the world around now routinely used drugs to derange or handicap those who opposed them. She went on.

"Things are pretty bad at home, too. The Strugfolk are under mass attack from the right. Cecil may not be able to underwrite my lawsuit—maybe not even be able to keep on funding my research."

"I was going to ask about that," Peter muttered, feeling guiltier by the moment.

With a shrug: "Well, he does have—what's the phrase?—other calls on his purse. It looks as though Walter may finally have put together a case against the funders that will stand up all the way to the

Supreme Court, but that won't be cheap even though the lawyers involved are donating their services. Just to complicate matters, there's a movement in the various legal associations to have free representation declared unprofessional."

Peter whistled. "We really do live in an age that worships Mammon!"

A harsh laugh. "You noticed? Amazing!"

Diffidently, having taken another sip of her drink as if to garner courage, Ellen spoke up.

"Claudia, I don't know whether Dad told you, but I'm keeping on with the research, as well as Bernie. I—uh—I hope you don't mind."

"Mind?" Claudia echoed, reaching out to pat her on the shoulder. "*Mind?* Why, that's the best news I've had in weeks."

"Really?" Of a sudden Ellen was eager. "I was worried in case you felt I was sort of intruding."

"On the contrary. The way I feel right now, I'd welcome help from the devil himself . . . Excuse me: bad choice of phrase."

Ellen smiled mechanically.

"Of course, I wouldn't want you to think I'm being much help, because I'm not. But if—" She broke off, biting her lip.

"If what?"

"Well . . ." Encouraged, she sat forward on her chair. "If I could ask about a few things that still aren't quite clear, maybe I could do better."

"Ask away!"

"Really?"

"Really really really! What do you want to know first?"

It was almost midnight when they finally called their cab. On the way home, Peter found himself marveling at Ellen all over again, this time for the grasp she had displayed of the problem that was baffling Claudia, and him, and even Bernie. When she came in pajamas to kiss him good night, he hugged her close.

"I was right," he said. "I do have a genius for a daughter. I'm sorry I didn't find out sooner."

"So am I," she murmured, head against his shoulder. "I wish . . . But it's no good wishing about the past, is it? You can only wish about the future."

"You're wise," he said. "You're very wise."

"But am I smart?" Drawing back, she pulled a face. "If I can find Louis Parker, will you think I am?"

"If you can, I'll think you can work miracles!"

"One miracle coming up! Good night!"

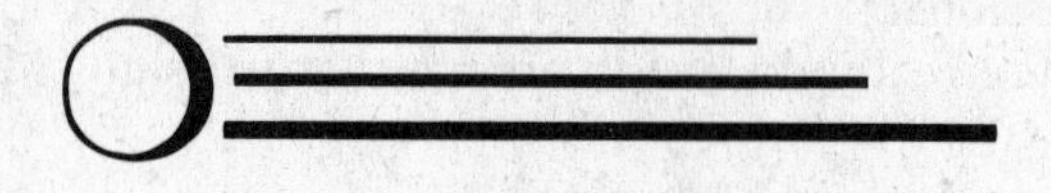

The big house in Surrey that had felt so empty was now crowded. Every week, or so it seemed, David added another to the roster of its occupants. But when the burden of cooking, cleaning and washing became too much for Harry and Alice, he simply walked out one morning and returned with two middle-aged women from a nearby village, with time on their hands now their children were grown, prepared to work long hours for a pittance. Similarly, when the roof needed emergency repairs, he made himself popular with the landlord by finding a local builder who quoted a ridiculously low price—"as a favor for the young gentleman"—but did a sound, fast job.

By now Harry was talking about buying the property when their twelve-month lease expired.

And the very atmosphere of the house seemed to change. At the time of the first arrivals it had been tense, charged with mutual suspicion, and Harry and Alice had tried to argue against what he was doing. Now, however, they were relaxed, even content. So was Sheila who had been withdrawn and spiteful; so was Terry, who had at first been afraid of living in isolation, away from his familiar city streets.

One chill, foggy evening after supper, when—as had become the usual practice—the kids had withdrawn into the biggest of the reception rooms to hold some kind of council or discussion, Harry heard Alice humming to herself as she loaded the dishwasher.

"You sound cheerful," he observed.

"Do I?" she countered in surprise, and then added after a moment's reflection: "Yes, I suppose I do. I think we're doing something —well, worthwhile. Don't you?"

"As a matter of fact," Harry answered slowly, "yes. At first I was very doubtful, same as you. But—well, the last time I lost my temper with David was in Italy, and that was only because I was feeling so unwell. And it wasn't his fault that the growser we went to see turned out to be a rogue."

The last plate duly racked, Alice shut the machine and turned it on. Wiping her hands, she said, "Let's sit down for a bit and have a drink. It's been a long day."

"All days around here are long," Harry sighed. "Grief! I never expected to find myself surrogate father to such a mixed-up bunch of mixed-up kids! But I can't."

"What?"

"Can't take time off for a drink, I mean. I have a pile of forms to complete. Apparently a government education inspector called some time ago, while we were out—"

"I don't remember David mentioning that!" Alice exclaimed.

"He didn't tell me, either . . . but he seems to have done a splendid PR job. We can apply for this house to be recognized as a fit alternative to a regular school. The only trouble is that stack of bocky forms. The inspector's coming to collect them any day now. They've become much tougher about this sort of thing recently. So many child-abuse scandals at unlicensed residential homes."

"You worry too much," Alice said, taking his arm. "You don't have to fill in the forms this very minute."

"I suppose you're right, but it's a matter of showing willing, isn't it?"

"They can wait until the morning," his wife insisted. "Come on."

And, a moment later, as they passed the closed door of the room where the kids were in conclave, she murmured, "I wonder what they're getting up to."

"What kids that age always get up to, I imagine, when they're allowed to."

"If you mean what I think you mean—" she began in sudden alarm. He cut short her reaction.

"I'm sure there's no need to worry. David's a sensible boy. As a matter of fact, when we brought Crystal here"—He hesitated for a second—"I think he must have guessed what I was bothered about, because he contrived to let it drop that she had a valid AIDS certificate. And you remember how scathing he was about the way she'd been behaving."

"Yes, and I think that was a bit unfair. After all, what alternative did the poor girl have?"

"Until she was brought here."

"Yes, of course . . . We really *are* doing something worthwhile, aren't we?"

"Absolutely. Even though I don't know how or why we drifted into it."

"I think it must be because . . ." The words trailed away.

"Go on!"

In a defiant tone, as though expecting to be contradicted, or mocked, she said, "I think it must be out of love."

He raised his eyebrows. "Hmm! Now you put it like that . . ."

"I know it sounds rather sententious, but—"

"But me no buts. I think you're right. I didn't realize until now, but—yes. I've always loved David, naturally, in spite of him not actually being mine. Now I'm coming to feel the same sort of affection for them all. And—" He hesitated, then concluded, "And I'm glad to be out of the commercial rat-race. I've cut a few corners in my time, I admit, but the people in charge of the world's economy nowadays act as though they'd learned their business in the drug trade."

"Maybe they did."

"As a matter of fact, I wasn't entirely joking . . . No, I feel we're well out of it."

"What better reason for a drink?"

After the second snifter of brandy they were becoming amorous for the first time in several weeks, when the kids' meeting broke up with a noisy clatter of feet on the hall parquet and David walked in. As ever, his expression was neutral; he looked neither happy nor downcast, merely purposeful.

"We have to make another trip tomorrow," he announced.

"What if the education inspector calls?" Harry objected.

"Oh, her!" David said dismissively. "She's a soft touch. Provided the forms have been filled in, Alice can cope."

Dismay showed on her face. "I honestly don't think—"

"Or the other kids can." He brushed the objection aside with an impatient wave. "I'll brief them on what to say. But I've found another possible recruit."

They knew, though didn't understand, how. It had to do with the efficiency of his computers, that included some of the world's most advanced models. Compared to what the British were using—even the British government—they were five years ahead, and he was exploiting this fact to unearth data from supposedly shellbacked sources. However, they sensed it would not do to inquire over-closely into that side of David's affairs.

He concluded, not expecting opposition, "I'd like to leave directly after breakfast."

And was gone.

Tracy Coward had enjoyed a grim moment of triumph in court, when the girls who had attacked her were punished while she herself received back all the possessions they were trying to reclaim.

But that had been the last time she felt remotely happy or satisfied.

Her decline began when she was warned that the scars inflicted during her beating were not going to disappear without long and expensive cosmetic surgery. Now she had to smear herself with makeup, privately in her room, before showing herself even to her parents, and even that didn't entirely hide the marks—especially when the sight of her own face in the mirror made her weep and mar her cheeks. In addition she had to comb and spray her hair so that it covered the place where a patch of scalp had been torn away.

Furious, vengeful, she took to brooding alone every evening and weekend, poring over her jewelry like a miser counting coins. At school she refused to work, but found entertainment in provoking fights between the other girls—she hadn't lost her talent for that—in the hope they too might wind up scarred for life. The teaching staff were helpless to control her.

Until one of them, smarter than the rest, took advantage of her monthly "window of vulnerability."

Thanks to that, she had been suspended and was awaiting an order that would transfer her compulsorily to a special school for disturbed children.

*Me, a mental case! I'll get my own back on that bitch! I swear I'll see all these canks rotting from the arse up before I'm through with them!*

Inevitably her parents bore the brunt of her rage. She forced them to behave like her fellow pupils, bent them to her every whim: buy me this, take me there . . .

She would lie awake at night and listen to her mother weeping in the next room, and think:

*It's no more than she deserves. It's no more than all of them deserve who landed me in this bocky mess!*

"Well—hello!"

It had become Tracy's custom, every lunch hour, to walk from her home and pass the school playground, wearing her most fashionable clothes and sporting her finest regalia. In her mind was the idea that the other girls would see and envy her, free to go about where and when she chose instead of being shut up for hours on end in bocky classrooms listening to bocky stupid teachers.

But this encounter, practically on her doorstep, she had not been expecting.

Here was a good-looking boy, dark-haired, with an olive complexion not unlike her own (she still remembered the gibes from primary school, years ago, when she had been called "blackie" and "coon") and extremely but *extremely* well-dressed; indeed, his gear was of a kind she had only seen hitherto in American magazines.

And he was looking her up and down appraisingly, and nodding.

"Hmm! You're a bright sight on a gloomy day! I'm David—who are you?"

All of a sudden her mind was a jumble of possibilities, a torrent of optimistic visions.

*Suppose I play up to him—maybe take his arm—walk with him past the school . . .*

As though he had read her thoughts, he smiled.

"Going anywhere in particular?"

"Just—just for a stroll."

"I'm at a loose end, too. Shall we make it together? And you still haven't told me your name."

Feeling as though she had been caught up in a dream, she whispered, "Tracy . . ." She had never liked her surname, Coward. That too had caused her persecution.

"That's a pretty name. To suit a pretty girl."

*Can he truly not see through the makeup? Or . . .*

The dream intensified.

*Or does he simply not care? After all, I do have a fairly good figure . . .*

By this time the chaotic images at the back of her mind had already extended to the point of showing off her body rather than her face, her flawless unmarked skin beneath the hampering clothes of chilly autumn. They focused into a climactic phrase:

*I heard of love at first sight. Do you suppose . . . ?*

But he had linked his arm in hers, companionably, and was asking, "Well, which way? Oh, just a second."

And he waved toward the corner of the street.

Glancing to find out why, she saw an improbable Rolls Royce, such a car as never normally intruded into areas like this.

"Excuse me," he was saying. "I just had to tell my driver I'm okay."

"Your"—faintly—"driver?"

"Mm-hm. I get bored sitting on those bocky cushions. So insulating! Riding in a Roller cuts you off from the real world, you know? I simply had to stretch my legs. He'll follow us, of course, but don't worry."

*To walk to the school with this David—to wave at the girls I used to call my friends—then to let them watch me getting in a Roller with him . . . !*

The plan was complete in an instant, bar some petty details about maybe kissing him, too, where they could watch and hate her. She let a slow smile spread across her face.

"This way," she said.

All went precisely as she had planned—at first. They arrived just at the right moment, when her former fellow pupils were turned out for a few minutes prior to the commencement of afternoon classes. She waved to them, not letting go of David for an instant, saw the envy on their faces—or interpreted it as such, though it could equally have been hate—and, even as they were recalled indoors, the Rolls arrived. They were too far away to hear her whisper, "I've never ridden in a Roller. May I—?"

"Jump in!"

He held the door for her.

And then, almost at once, things went terribly and fearfully awry.

Why did the car immediately head toward her home? Why was she being taken inside, still clinging to David's hand as to a life-raft in a rough sea? Who was this strange, grave adult discussing her future with her parents?

*I've been drugged! I'm going to be kidnapped!*

But such wild notions culled from television vanished. She grew calmer, recognizing key words from the conversation: "special school" —"many similar children" . . .

And realized with a flash of insight: *He's a liar! He didn't just chance on me in the street! Because—!*

Here came the most exciting news of all.

*Because he has the power, too. I'm not alone.*

She buried her face in her hands and started to cry.

During the long trip to Virginia Water she snuggled into a corner of the car's luxurious back seat and enjoyed her soundest sleep in months.

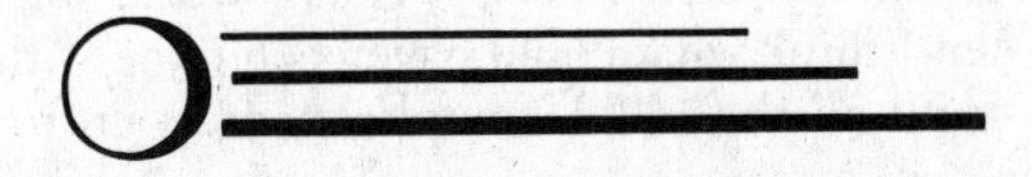

*You're watching TV Plus. Now for Newsframe.*

*Three hundred people were rendered homeless in Staffordshire today when methane escaping from a forgotten rubbish dump caught fire. Fire engines and ambulances on their way to the disaster were stoned by youths wearing pro-Thrower armbands. One of them, who declined to be identified, claimed that the gas had been fired deliberately because the area is largely occupied by blacks. More in a moment.*

*General Thrower himself, addressing a rally in West London this afternoon, said, quote, "The abandonment of medium-range nuclear missiles was the greatest act of treachery in living memory. We British deserve to wield the most modern weapons in defense of freedom and democracy . . ."*

**T**urning away from his computer, Peter swore under his breath. From the couch facing the TV, whose sound she had turned down for a commercial break, Ellen inquired what was wrong. The air was full of spicy scent from the vegetable curry she was cooking. Later, she'd said, she would make chapattis; the cost of rice had risen from astronomical to prohibitive in the past few weeks.

Peter slumped down beside her, wiping his forehead with the back of his hand.

"Someone very high up indeed owns shares in the company that manufactures Thanataph—the stuff that killed the bees. Jake daren't touch the story, nor the TV people. I thought I had another certain winner. We're going to be surviving on vegetables for the foreseeable future."

"Never mind," she said consolingly, pressing his hand. "Something else will turn up. I've made some more beer and it should be about ready. Like me to bring you some?"

"Yes, please—Goodness, I didn't realize what time it was!" He reached for the remote control to turn up the TV sound again. "I wonder what news *is* making it to the screen these days."

The answer was, in a word, bad. He jolted upright at the first item. During a storm in the North Sea, a Dutch freighter had been driven against a drill-rig and torn it loose. The resulting oil slick was already ten miles long and spreading, with no hope—said a miserable-looking company spokesman—of capping the broken pipe until the weather improved . . . which the forecasters warned might not be for a week.

"Oh, kid," Peter said in a broken voice. "What a world we have bequeathed to you! When I think what could have been done with the profits from that oil—from all the oil! Unemployment is up to five million now, you know."

"I didn't see that on telly!" she exclaimed as she handed him his glass of beer.

"You wouldn't. Officially it's less than four, but they're running out of ways to drag the total down. What that means, of course, is that the profit from North Sea oil has been squandered on paying people to do nothing, instead of repairing the infrastructure . . . Sorry, I've told you this before, haven't I?"

She nodded, frowning. "But how could they be so stupid? I mean, surely even Cabinet ministers and businessmen need clean water, proper drains, safe bridges and all the rest."

"I don't think the trouble is so much that they're stupid. I think it's simply that they're greedy. I remember reading years ago—probably when I was about your age—about a rich American who said, when he was tackled by an environmentalist worried about pollution and asked what sort of a world his children would be living in—he said he didn't care because he'd bought land for them in Canada, away from all the mess."

"That's stupid," Ellen said with authority, her eyes still on the screen. It now showed a map of the North Sea with the prevailing winds and currents. "Oh dear, that looks bad, doesn't it?"

Peter forced his mind back to the present. After a moment he said, "Very bad. I'd hate to be a trawlerman in the northeast, to start with. And when the bills come in from Scandinavia . . ."

"Why don't you ring Jake and offer him a piece about the consequences?"

"Darling, you *are* a genius. I don't know what's come over me lately!" Gulping his beer, he headed for the phone. Over his shoulder he added, "Call up a North Sea weather map, please!"

"Sure!" She was seated before the computer instantly. "What do I key?"

"021-METEORO. My user code is PETREL." He was already punching the number of the *Comet*.

"Hmm? Dad, you did say petrol, didn't you? The system won't recognize it."

"What—? Oh, sorry. Petrel with two e's. The stormbird."

"Ah! . . . Okay, got it. North Sea . . . What do you want added?"

"Same as they had on the telly—winds, currents—plus commercial activities around the coast, economic values, income from tourism . . . Anything else you can think of?"

"What about the value of the lost oil?"

"Good idea!"

The *Comet*'s lines were of course busy. Peter left the phone on automatic re-dial—though plenty of other people had most likely done the same, which meant the lines would be tied up indefinitely—and came over to study the map when it was complete.

"That's really bad," he muttered. "File that for the moment, though, and try something else that's just occurred to me. You heard that rumor about the flooding in the Norfolk Broads being due to subsidence of the sea-bed? They denied it, and they might be right—after all, there have been lots of floods in the area before—but this time there's a lot of gas coming out as well as the oil. Normally, to stabilize the sea-floor, they pump water in as the oil and gas are drawn off, and this time they aren't going to have a chance, are they? See if you can find your way to a geological profile of the area—there's a data-base in Oslo called SEADRILL that ought to have one on call—and figure out what might happen if the sea-bed suddenly collapses."

Ellen's hands, poised above the keyboard, abruptly froze.

"Tidal wave?" she said in a shaky voice.

"Oh, I doubt there'll actually be a tsunami. I was more thinking of what might happen to the people trying to cap the pipe."

The phone rang. He seized it, leaving her to get on with the search.

Which she did to such effect that the data were already on screen before Jake had agreed to take his usual 800 words. Peter had been intending to dictate; seeing the diagram Ellen had constructed, he changed his mind and promised to file via modem within the hour. He added that he might need a thousand words. Jake sighed, but since this was bound to be the biggest story of the day conceded the request, subject to editing.

As her father sat down to the computer again, Ellen slipped into the kitchen to turn off the dinner. In the end they didn't eat until nearly ten.

It was good, anyway.

Strictly Ellen should have turned in directly after the meal, it being past her bedtime, but lately they had fallen into the habit of winding up the evening with a quiet chat, companionably side by side on the sofa. A sub from the *Comet* had called back to say she needed to lose a few lines from the story, but at least she'd had the sense to ask before she cut, which was reassuring. Pleased with this unexpected windfall, Peter smiled sidewise at his daughter.

"At the risk of repeating myself," he murmured, "I do more and more regret that things didn't work out between Kamala and me. I could have been eating meals as good as yours for years!"

She dug him playfully in the ribs.

And then grew serious.

"Dad," she ventured after a moment, "why *did* you and Mum break up? I would like to know. And before you answer"—she laid a slim brown finger on his lips to forestall an immediate reaction—"please remember that I'm quite grown up now. It happened years and years ago, and there can't be any harm in telling the truth after so long. Which is what I want to hear."

He pondered a long while. In the end her appealing eyes decided him. Sighing, leaning back and gazing into nowhere, he explained.

"It was because of a girl called Sindy . . . I suppose I ought to say woman. I met her at a party when I was still studying medicine. She was older than me, married for several years, but constantly quarrelling with her husband because they both wanted children and she had never conceived. But he wouldn't go for a check to see if it was his fault—insisted that it must be hers."

He had poured more beer to drink with his meal; there was a little left, and he sipped it.

"So . . . Well, I was a bit drunk by then, or I wouldn't have talked so freely. I mentioned the Chinn-Wilkinson, said she ought to go there while she was in London—she came from somewhere in the provinces but she never said exactly where—and she said she'd thought about artinsem but the idea didn't appeal to her because it was much too impersonal. So . . ."

An embarrassed shrug.

"You have to understand that I'd been a donor for several months by then, and it was coming home to me that by now I very likely had a child somewhere, with more to follow. I'd meant to be detached and cynical about it—like Louis Parker, if I have to be absolutely frank. He didn't seem as though he could give a hoot. Probably had by-blows already in half a dozen countries. I think I told you he was devastatingly handsome?"

Ellen gave a wry grin. "You said something about women swarming round him like flies on a rotting carcass."

"I must have been in a particularly grumpy mood . . . But anyhow: I'd realized my detachment wasn't up to his, so the idea crossed my mind that I ought to know what happened to at least one of my—ah—offspring. I imagine you can guess the rest."

"You seduced her?" Ellen suggested.

"I don't know which of us seduced the other. But—yes, we had a brief affair. Two weeks."

"Was it her husband's fault?"

Peter nodded. "Presumably. But I never saw her again. So much for my original idea! As soon as she knew she was pregnant she rang me up and said good-bye. I hadn't even learned her surname, let alone her address."

"Really?"—eyes wide in disbelief.

"Really! She was much better off than me, used to pick me up from the hospital in a taxi, take us for a meal, go home with me, and then leave after a couple of hours. She and I never spent a whole night together . . . I hope you don't mind my being so frank."

"No, it's what I asked for." Ellen hesitated. At length she went on, "You didn't know I was on the way?"

"Of course not! I'm not sure your mother did, even. At any rate she didn't tell me until my involvement with Sindy was all over."

"So how did she find out? That was what broke you up, wasn't it?"

Peter thought carefully before replying. Now he had gone so far, though, he was bound to admit the rest.

"It was one thing to know I'd fathered a child that was going to be accepted by a married couple, brought up as their own. That's what I sincerely believed was going to happen, because Sindy had laid so much stress on the fact that her marriage would have been fine except for not having kids. But it was something else to take on responsibility for one of my own when I was so poor during my studies that I'd had to donate semen for extra income. I . . ."

"Did you try to talk her into an abortion?" Ellen suggested.

Her tone was utterly devoid of emotion. He tried to read clues in her face, but it showed no more than apparently casual interest.

*Well, she did say it all happened years and years ago . . .*

Gruffly, he confessed the truth.

"And that upset her?"

"Yes."

"And that was why you broke up?"

"I think she might have seen sense and we could have got back together but for what happened a little later on, a few weeks." Peter licked his lips. His belly was tense of a sudden. He always hated recalling what he now had to describe, and had never told anyone about it before.

"Go on."

Were those words chill and reproachful, or merely curious? He hoped for the latter, and plunged ahead.

"I said just now Sindy's inability to conceive was 'apparently' her husband's fault. In fact it was incontestably his fault, and it turned out that he knew all along. He was sterile, but he couldn't face the fact. When Sindy became pregnant he knew it had to be someone else's baby and he threw her out. She had my phone number and one evening in a fit of hysterics she rang up to tell me what he'd done.

"Only I wasn't there."

"Kamala was?"

"Kamala was. Not for very long, though. I never found out exactly what Sindy said, but I can imagine. After that it was all over between us. We scarcely even talked again. Saw each other once or twice when the dust had settled, but—well, that was that. And now you know."

He finished his beer in a single angry draught.

While he was still wondering what Ellen's reaction would be to the naked truth, there was a shrill beep from her own computer in the next room. Jumping up, she ran to see what had provoked it, and shortly returned, holding a page of printout but looking downcast.

"Is something wrong?" Peter demanded.

"Oh, I just turned up another Louis Parker."

He almost choked. "What do you mean, another?" he exploded.

"This is the fourth. None of them any good to us." She thrust the paper into his hands and slumped back on the sofa, disconsolate. He read rapidly. It was true; she'd found four people of that name. But one of them was over sixty, living in retirement near Harrogate, and in any case his full name was Christopher Louis Parker-Haines; another was Louis X. Parker, an American citizen on the staff of the embassy in Grosvenor Square; and the third was an actor who had taken Louis as a stage name because his baptismal name was Lewis and Equity already had a Lewis Parker on its register. As for the fourth, whose details had just emerged, Louis Alan Parker had been born in Sydenham three months ago to a Frenchwoman named Suzette Legrand, and one Alan Raymond Parker, who was British, had acknowledged paternity.

Nonetheless, it was an astonishing achievement. Marveling, Peter demanded, "How in the world did you come up with this lot? Bernie hasn't produced a single candidate so far!"

Stifling a yawn, Ellen hoisted her slim body off the sofa, supporting herself with feet and shoulders, until she was sufficiently stretched.

"Trade secret," she said with a mocking grin as soon as her yawn permitted. "But at least it's a step in the right direction, hm? Well, I'd better turn in. I have to go to school tomorrow, remember."

"Yes. Yes, of course. Good night. And thanks again for another delicious meal."

"Any time," she said. "Any time."

Peter himself was too wound up to sleep. Pacing up and down, wondering whether or not to check the late-night TV news, he was struck by a sudden inspiration. Perhaps Louis Parker had reverted to his family's original name. If it was in fact Parikian . . .

But though there were nearly ninety subscribers of that name in the national phone directory, none bore the initial L.

What the hell could have become of him?

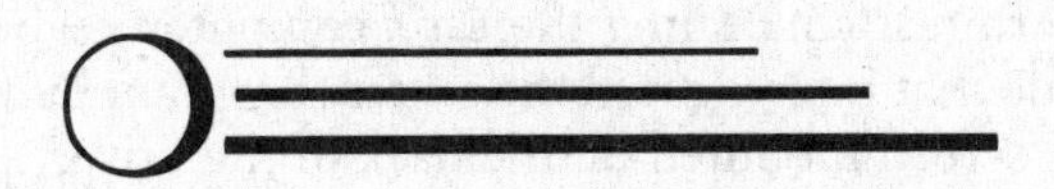

*Lead us not into temptation . . .*

The phrase echoed and echoed in David's mind as the Rolls purred through the desolate hop-fields of Kent under a drift of rain. Now and then the cone-shaped roof of an oast-house appeared and vanished as the road curved and wound. There was something very curious about the next of his siblings that he hoped to recruit. From all the available evidence it seemed she had exercised her power once, and on one person.

*But once you've realized you have the talent . . .*

After the salutary lesson of his encounter with GianMarco, he was constantly worried about his precarious dominance of the group. Either this Mary Gall did not properly understand what she was capable of, and the way she got rid of her father had been the result of an instinctual reaction, never repeated because never comprehended, or (and David felt this was the more likely) she must have remarkable subtlety and self-control—or, putting it another way, the ability to resist the temptation implied by possession of absolute power over other people.

David Shay not only did not possess that ability, but didn't want to. There wasn't enough time for luxuries like having a conscience . . .

Which was why he had brought Crystal with him. Despite his

initial contempt, he had come to like her much the best of his half-siblings. Her experience on the streets of London had made her cynical, admittedly, but beneath her shellbacked veneer she seemed to hunger, as he did, after an ideal. In effect, she had a vision of a better world.

It was she, during the group's endless arguments, who most quickly and most clearly grasped the import of his proposals, and more than once it had been her alliance with him that turned the mood of the meeting against Sheila's sullenness, Terry's crude desire for material belongings, Garth's bitter detestation of all adults.

He hoped Mary Gall would prove another ally. Outwitting the others, coaxing them around to his point of view, was draining his strength. He *knew* what must be done, and how little time was left to do it. But among the rest only Crystal seemed to have any inkling of urgency . . .

*If Mary Gall turns out to be another opponent—*

But he didn't want to think about that possibility. By way of distraction he lifted the armrest concealing the car's computer keyboard and tapped out the code that interrogated the search-program hunting for Louis Parker. The screen mounted on the back of the driver's seat informed him there was still no joy. With a sigh he switched to a map display tracking their progress.

"Fork left at the next junction," he told Harry. "We should be there in five or six minutes."

Both his guesses about Mary, as it happened, were quite wrong.

She and her mother had left Marshmere in the end, unable to bear the pressure of gossip. The house had sold for a handsome profit, and their new home at Poppy Cottage was quite as luxurious if not so large, with a splendid garden. Neither of them wanted to keep the Jaguar, so that and the Citroën had been disposed of, but a medium-sized Volvo stood in the garage. A long time still remained before Richard completed his jail sentence; nonetheless Mary had insisted on Edna obtaining an injunction to prevent him from contacting them when he was let out. Everything should have been fine.

Except it wasn't.

Despite her daughter's reproaches, backed up by the use of her magic touch, Edna had grown more and more morose. She began to drink heavily, and avoided company. Often she would stay at home for days on end. When she had to go shopping, she bought at random, stocking the freezer with packages of food that later had to be thrown away unopened. Mary, who now attended a local school within cycling distance, took to playing truant purely in order to keep her mother under control. When teachers came to find out what was wrong, she of course had no trouble sending them away placated, but the task was a strain, and sometimes she found herself exhausted from the exercise of her powers.

On top of which, little by little she started worrying about what she had done. Had Richard truly deserved his fate? She had, after all, only her mother's word for it. Admittedly he had put his wife through a most unpleasant experience, but if he hadn't, then Mary herself would not be here . . .

Guiltily, she wrote letters in which she begged him to set her mind at rest, to say that he forgave her—and tore them up and flushed them down the toilet for fear Edna might find the scraps in the wastebasket and piece them together. Now and then, when she went to school, she reacted to taunts from the other pupils who had discovered (the tongue of scandal being long, long) that her father was in prison, and engaged in pointless, futile fights. Why, she wondered, did she never remember to use her magic instead?

But when she was in a calm, normal mood, the idea never crossed her mind. When she had been provoked into a rage, she couldn't take advantage. Sometimes, late at night, she would lie staring at the ceiling of her bedroom, planning the vengeance she was going to wreak on those who worst tormented her, and went to sleep chuckling. In the morning, though, she was always too preoccupied to recall her schemes, and they vanished as irretrievably as dreams.

Now winter was drawing on, and the isolation of the house was preying on her mind. She hadn't been to school for a full week; indeed it was that long since she last forced herself out of doors any further than the front gate. Edna hadn't bathed in at least as long, and spent most of the day in her dressing gown, that was overdue for laundering. Formerly she had smoked little, if at all, but now she was burning up forty a day, and the air smelt permanently stale. To compound the problem, Mary's period had started. She had lost her magic again.

She always wept a lot during the few days it lasted. Now and then she cursed herself.

The doorbell rang.

"I'm not at home," Edna snapped, reaching for another cigarette. Rain was beating a dreary rhythm on the leaded-glass windows that were supposed to add "period charm" to the cottage, but served chiefly to reduce the amount of daylight. She was pretending to read a book, but her gaze kept wandering away to watch a rerun TV game show. Why, Mary could not imagine; the sound was off.

The bell rang a second time, longer and louder.

"All right," Mary sighed, hauling herself to her feet as though she were suddenly carrying twice her usual weight. Nervous, Edna's eyes followed her out of the room.

In the narrow hallway of the cottage, alongside a window next to the front door, hung a mirror intended for checking one's appearance before venturing forth. Viewed from the proper angle, it showed anyone standing beyond the window. Mary paused at exactly the right spot, and was rewarded with a glimpse of a girl about her own age, and—so far as the window could show, which was only head and shoulders—not unlike herself in appearance.

The bell rang a third time, impatiently.

She had vaguely expected yet another caller complaining about her non-attendance at school, and as a second bet one of her fellow pupils—not that she had made many friends, and few who cared to visit her home more than once, a major reason why she had become so depressed of late. The idea of a stranger dropping in made her unaccountably excited. She hastened to open the door.

And found not the girl she had glimpsed, but a boy. Who said, "You're Mary Gall. I can tell. I'm David Shay. This is Crystal Knight."

Crystal advanced into the shelter of the porch. Short-haired, she wore an X-rated jacket, on whose front a red elasticated saltire cross framed and emphasized her bust, and tight black trousers splashed with yellow blobs: fashionable gear that Mary had envied but not dared to indulge, already being sufficiently persecuted at school. She said, not to Mary but to David, "No problem. No power."

*What?*

Dizzied, baffled, by that matter-of-fact comment, Mary felt her jaw fall ajar, and would have shut the door in reflexive panic but that David caught her hand and said smoothly, "Aren't you going to ask us in out of the rain?"

*Rain?*

Suddenly the world was a different place, and rain was far too ordinary to be real.

"Whoever it is, tell the buggers to go away!" Edna shouted from the living room. The words were underlined by a familiar chinking-splashing noise: ice-cubes being dumped in a glass, then covered with gin and not nearly enough tonic. (Tonic water was becoming very expensive. No one had yet marketed a synthetic quinine cheap enough to be incorporated in drink mixers, and the authentic kind was disappearing with the rain-forests.)

"We can handle her," Crystal said assuredly, and marched past Mary. David put his arm around her and urged her to follow.

Glancing back—they hadn't bothered to close the door—Mary saw a car at the end of the path, and a man with a worried face staring toward the cottage.

But she had no time to think about that.

Indeed, for the next several minutes it seemed she had no time to think about anything.

The rain had let up by the time David and Crystal led Mary out to the car, each carrying a suitcase full of her belongings. The man behind the wheel got out to open the rear door for them. David said, "Mary, this is Harry."

Harry nodded a sketch for a greeting. "Papers?" he muttered nervously.

"All signed. Here." David thrust a sheaf of documents into his hand, and he tucked them inside his jacket.

"What about—uh—Mrs. Gall?"

"The hell with her. She'll drink herself to death. Or set the house on fire when she's sozzled. She smokes like a chimney."

"David, don't you think you ought to—?"

"There's no 'ought' about it!" the boy flashed back. "I told you already. You had the chance to think of 'ought' before—and passed it up! So all that's left is *must!* Get in and take us home!"

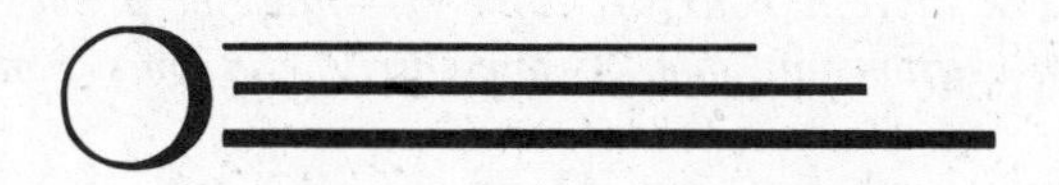

*You're watching TV Plus. Newsframe follows.*

*Half a million people in the Midlands have been warned not to drink the public water supply without boiling. Tailored bacteria from an experimental biological laboratory were accidentally spilled down a drain last week and have allegedly survived normal treatment at a sewage plant.*

*General Thrower today told a rally of his supporters in Surrey that Britain needs another war, quote, "to stiffen the moral fiber of this spineless generation," and brought the audience to its feet by quoting Rupert Brooke's poem about the outbreak of the 1914 war, "Now God be thanked Who has matched us with His hour . . ."*

What was on the menu for today?

Drearily Peter installed himself, as he did each morning after Ellen had left for school, in front of his computer, sipping now and then at a mugful of the latest horrid substitute for coffee. The real stuff was beyond his means these days—and, indeed, anyone's except the super-rich. Tea was about to go the same way, according to rumors that the government would not permit on radio or TV.

*If only they had heeded warnings about the deforestation of Northern India . . .*

Did the air in here smell bad? He sniffed, and decided: no worse than usual. He had a headache, but that was most likely due to overindulgence last night in Ellen's homemade liquor—this time, red wine. So . . .

First, his email, in the faint hope that someone might need his talent for a story with a medical bias, despite the fury his story about the royal horses had entrained in official circles.

So strong had his reflexes become during weeks of boredom and frustration, at first he was about to dump the lot as not worth noticing. Just in time he checked his fingers on the way to wiping out the sort of message he had been dreaming of. It was from the *Comet*, and it was in caps emboldened and underscored.

**COME AT ONCE!**

When had the message been sent . . . ? Foggily, for this ersatz coffee had none of the arousal effect he had been used to (how long ago? When Britain could still afford to buy crops from the world's primary producers!) he scrolled back the screen display in search of the data he needed. They shocked him.

*0535? Jake, at work at that hour? It can't be—must be a hoax! He wraps up the national editions at one or one-thirty and goes home to sleep . . .*

At which moment the phone rang. He snatched it up.

"Jake," said a distant voice. "Thank God you finally woke up! I've been trying to get hold of you for hours! Get your arse over here, dammit!"

Peter bit his tongue to stop himself from uttering a whole bunch of profit-losing comments. When he recovered, he said, "Jake, please —why?"

"I may have been up all night, I may still be boozing at breakfast time, but I have more sense than to answer a stupid question like that over the phone!"

*Oh. This sounds big. I don't want to comply, but I suppose I'd better . . .*

Wishing, oddly enough, that Ellen were here to counsel him, Peter heaved a deep sigh.

"All right. I'm on my way . . . Oh, just a sec!"

"What?"—in a tone bordering on explosion.

"If I call a cab, will you—?"

"Call a bocky helicopter if you must! Just get here—and bocky well move!"

Peter rang for a cab at once, but it took half an hour to arrive, and then it was detoured by the police to avoid a procession of fishermen from the northeast, driven out of business by the ever-widening oil slick in the North Sea, marching on Whitehall to present a petition of protest.

They would not, of course, be allowed to get there. No one without a government pass had entered the zone around Parliament Square and Downing Street for eighteen months.

On reaching the building where the *Comet* office was located, he had to walk up from the ground floor. Yet another power failure had put the lifts out of operation. A battery radio that he heard when passing, exhausted, a dangerously open door on the floor below, was informing London in a cheery voice that the saboteurs responsible were known to the police and someone would shortly be "assisting Scotland Yard with their inquiries."

*Why do I have the feeling that I've heard that before?*

Most of the business of the editorial office was proceeding normally—after all, there was tomorrow's edition to prepare—but there was an air of tension that struck Peter immediately he entered. He noticed with surprise that Bernie was installed in his usual corner; from their by-now long acquaintance he was aware that the hacker preferred to get up around midday. Had he, like Jake, been here all night?

Red-eyed, unshaven, his jacket hung on the back of his chair, his shirt-cuffs grimy and his tie-knot halfway to his navel, the editor broke off from intense discussion with a woman Peter didn't know, and let out a cry of mingled annoyance and relief.

"Finally you made it! Don't bother explaining—I've heard all the excuses and the trouble is most of them are true. Come here! By the way, this is Sally Gough, our crime-reporter."

A long-faced woman with heavy glasses, she offered a firm handshake.

"Sit down, sit down," Jake invited around a yawn. On his desk ice-cubes were melting in a glass, and he took an absent-minded sip. Then he leaned forward intently.

"Peter, you've got to keep this under your hat, because I finally have the beat I've been dreaming of. But I dare not publish until it's rock-solid. I have all my top people working on the story, but Bernie thinks I need you as well. And Claudia."

Peter started. "Don't tell me you found Louis Parker!"

"Who—? Oh, him! No, no, no! But what's happened may just possibly tie in with this red herring you spent so much of the paper's money on . . . General Thrower has apparently been kidnapped. Emphasis on *kid.*"

"I can't believe it! How? When?"

Reaching into a drawer of his desk in search of the bottle he was drinking from, Jake indicated with a nod that Sally Gough should take over. In a few crisp sentences she explained what they believed to have happened.

"He addressed a public meeting at Sandhurst last night—Sandhurst in Surrey, near the officers' training college. It's all army country around there, solid pro-government with a strong admixture of pro-Thrower. Among the audience were a bunch of kids in their early teens. After the meeting they came up and asked him for autographs. Somehow the organizers' attention was distracted, and when they came back to look for him he was nowhere to be found. The police are working on the theory that he's been abducted by a left-wing group who used the kids for cover."

Peter whistled soundlessly. "That's incredible," he muttered.

"My reaction precisely," Jake concurred, having taken a gulp of his fresh drink. He was beginning to show the extreme caution in speech and movement of someone who knows he is on the brink of complete intoxication. "He never moves a step without a bodyguard. Anywhere he goes, he can count on scores of disenchanted unemployed as volunteers."

"This time—maybe not genuine volunteers?"

"Hmm!" Jake raised his eyebrows. "Good thinking. Sally, have we anyone who could check out the stewards at the meeting?"

Overhearing, Bernie said without looking around, "The police have already interrogated them. So far all of them have turned out to be long-term British Movement, National Front or whatever. Dyed-in-the-wool types."

"Sorry, Peter," Jake said with a shrug. "Unless the left-wingers planted them years ago, which I suppose isn't inconceivable, that knocks your notion on the head."

"Well, it was just a thought . . . But what is it exactly that you want me and Claudia to do?"

"Grief, man! Isn't it obvious?" Jake was abruptly on the verge of alcoholic rage. "A gang of kids! Making off with a national celebrity under the noses of his private army!"

"You mean you think it could have been the kids' own idea?"

"Any lead is worth following up," Sally said. "So far, you see, we appear to be the only national paper that's picked up the story. There were three other stringers at the meeting, all from right-wing tabloids, and according to what we can deduce from the grapevine they accepted the official yarn that General Thrower was too tired after his speech to answer any more questions and had decided to turn in early. Ours was the only one who bothered to sneak around the back door of his hotel and bribe the porter. General Thrower did not sleep in his own bed last night."

"He'll get a bonus for that," Jake said blurrily. "If we are the first to break the story."

"Hang on," Peter said in confusion. "I'm still not sure what exactly you want me to do."

"Oh my God." Jake leaned his elbows on his desk and rested his head in his hands. In a muffled voice, as though his patience were at its uttermost limit, he said, "Look, what I want is eight hundred words on cases where kids have broken the law and got away with it in spite of the best that adults could do to stop them. Okay? I don't want anything down-market and cheaply sensational. I want something sober, reasoned and convincing. It doesn't have to be right, but it has to be *convincing.*"

"And you want it by nine tonight."

"Six would be better."

"Okay. Can I use your phone?"

Jake raised his head sharply. "To call Claudia? No way! Use a public phone, or just go straight there! The chance exists that some police nark may have noticed our reporter at the meeting, or one of the other people I've assigned to the story this morning, and started eavesdropping on us again."

"Again? I didn't know they'd stopped."

"Not funny," Jake said wearily. "Last month the Bill decided we didn't pose any sort of threat because we'd be bankrupt by Christmas. It's no secret that our sales have plummeted. But by God, if I do have to go under, I'd like it to be in a blaze of glory!"

The force of his last phrase was undermined by another uncontrollable yawn.

"Okay," Peter grunted, rising. "Claudia has an interesting theory about this phenomenon—this control over other people—going back to Neolithic times. Says it could account for Stonehenge. What about something for expenses?"

"Hm? Oh. All right." Jake fumbled for an intercom switch and issued the necessary instructions.

"Stop by on the way out. The cash will be waiting for you. And do a good job, won't you—please?"

The public phones that Peter passed on his way to the only bus route he knew still to be running in the direction of his former home had all been vandalized; some, to judge by the state they were in, several weeks or even months ago. Catching sight of a bus—far too precious to miss—he abandoned the idea of ringing to warn Claudia of his arrival, and hoped against hope that she would be in.

She was. But by the look of the flat, not for much longer. She had added only a few personal touches to it, chiefly books, posters, and a few pictures. Now she was taking them down and packing them into cardboard cartons.

"What's going on?" demanded Peter, aghast.

"I'm going to have to go home," she answered with a shrug, closing and triple-locking the door.

"When?"

"Before Christmas. Come in, sit down. Want a drink?"

"Much too early," Peter said reflexively, and thought of the state of Jake's liver. "But why?"

"Oh, the funders won. I no longer have tenure, I can no longer look forward to a salary, and Cecil Strugman has been driven to the verge of bankruptcy by a bunch of smart financial operators who call themselves Eye of the Needle. Reportedly they include the head of the Federal Reserve Board. They don't care for Cecil's political views, so they decided to force down the value of his investments. Rumor has it that they bribed the broker who handles his affairs. Cecil himself is pretty unworldly, you know."

"This is awful," Peter said, sinking slowly into a chair. "Can't your lawyer friend do anything—Walter?"

"Walter's dead."

"*What?*"

"Yesterday." Claudia passed a tired hand through her hair. "Car crash. Early snow—slight thaw—hard frost the following day . . . I suppose one has to believe it. Especially since he'd been drinking. Funny, though . . ."

"Go on!"

"I've never known him to drive after drinking. He'd leave his car on the street and risk it being stolen rather than drive himself. In fact two of his cars were stolen for just that reason. One of them turned up in Mexico."

"So you're abandoning your research," Peter said after a pause.

"I can't see any way of staying on." She glanced despondently at a pile of printout on a nearby table: he recognized it as the draft of her thesis.

"So what will you do? Couldn't you—well, if you can't keep up the payments on the flat, couldn't you go back to stay with your friend, where you were before?"

"No, she's in the hospital. Hepatitis. Could be fatal."

Peter clenched his fists. "It can't be true, but I keep getting the feeling that everybody's dying!"

"Life expectancy in Western Europe and North America has gone down each year for the past three years. Ask any actuary. Not, of course, for the very rich—mainly for people on the poverty-line, or in manual work like farming, street-cleaning that sort of thing. And they don't buy much insurance, so . . . Didn't you know about that?"

Peter shook his head, licking dry lips. "If only *Continuum*—"

"You'd have made a program about it," Claudia cut in. "Let's skip that, shall we? What brings you here, and will it take long?"

He recalled himself to duty with an effort, and outlined the story Jake and Sally Gough had told him. Her dull expression changed as she listened.

"Lord! It's too much to hope for, but it's a remarkable coincidence, isn't it? Not that I can stick around and follow it up, of course. But—well, say again what Jake actually wants from us."

He repeated the editor's specifications, and concluded, "I thought particularly of that point you made about Stone Age culture. I'm afraid I don't recall the exact details, though."

"Stone Age . . . ? Oh! Yes, I know what you mean. My idea that this kind of control over other people might not be new after all."

"I think you said"—frowning with the effort of recollection—"it would account for Stonehenge."

"Mm-hm. Which called for an immense communal effort at a time before there were kings or armies, let alone police forces, and in a culture where there wasn't even a hierocracy of the kind that resulted in the Pyramids."

"A what?"

"Ruling class of priests, controlling people through religion. In spite of the lack of any obvious means to compel them, thousands of people worked sometimes for years to create these gigantic structures. Someone must have had a silver tongue, at least."

"That's good for a couple of paras," Peter said with satisfaction. "Can you spare the time to help me with a rough draft? I'll make sure you get your fair share of the fee."

Rising, he turned toward her computer.

"No power," she said.

He blinked in startlement. He had noticed that despite the gloom of the day no lights were on, despite the damp chill there seemed to be no heating, but had forborne to comment, assuming that her lack of funds meant she was economizing.

"No power!" she said again, standing up angrily. "It went off around nine, when everybody else in the house had left for work—or to look for some. I'm the only one here during the day, did you know?"

"Have you phoned the electricity board?"

"They claim to be working on it."

"Well, then, I suppose we'd better go to my place. Jake gave me plenty for expenses, so we can afford a taxi . . . Can you spare the time?"

She was already in the hallway, donning a coat. Over her shoulder she said, "Who am I kidding? All the gear I have I can pack in a couple of hours. I don't have to prolong the agony. Besides, I'm cold."

By tacit agreement they drafted the story as though it were the definitive epitaph for Claudia's original project. The hard part, of course, was condensing the material into the allotted space. More than once they started snapping at each other, Claudia insisting that a particular point was indispensable, Peter countering that this time Jake's limit of 800 words must absolutely be adhered to. Having broken off only to make and eat some sandwiches with stale bread and cheese they had to scrape clean of mold, they were still at it when Ellen returned from school. She seemed subdued, but refused to talk and insisted they must go on working, and disappeared into her own room. Shortly they heard the hum of her computer.

At long last they reached a compromise, and when Peter called for a word count, it came up at 799. He leaned back, stretched and yawned.

"Can't ask for fairer than that," he grunted. "And—grief, it's not yet six. Well, this ought to make a good impression on Jake. Fire up the modem, would you?"

And within moments the text was on its way.

Rising, bending back and forth to alleviate stiffness, he went on, "Lord, I wish we had something better to drink than Ellen's homemade! Still, it is improving—"

"What's wrong with my homemade wine?" Ellen demanded from the doorway.

"Sorry, sorry! I did say it's improving, didn't I—? Say, you look excited about something."

"I am." Flushed, eyes sparkling, she advanced into the room. "You want to know where Louis Parker is? Somewhere in Surrey!"

"Surrey!" Peter exclaimed. And looked at Claudia, his expression saying as clearly as words: *That's just too much of a coincidence!*

Visions of a fantastic conspiracy came and went in a flash.

But Ellen was continuing in a more apologetic tone, "I'm afraid I can't narrow it down any closer, not yet. I only know that the age fits, and the physical appearance. But the program I'm running ought to find some clue to his actual address, or at least a phone number he's been using. With luck we should have it some time this evening . . . Claudia, excuse me, but you don't look very pleased."

Claudia shrugged, leaning back and stretching as Peter had done, and explained.

"That's terrible!" Ellen cried. "But—well, goodness! After getting so close, don't you want to find out whether it really was Louis Parker who—who fathered these kids? You said you don't have to be home until Christmas, and that's still a long time off."

"Two weeks, to be exact," Claudia muttered. "Though you wouldn't think it was that long, the way everybody's hyping it this year. The shopkeepers must be desperate to make people part with their money . . . By the way, Peter, one of the investments Cecil was backing, one of those that have just been bankrupted, was a chain of stores selling organic produce and additive-free foods."

"But I thought—"

"You thought they were booming? They were. Until the slump."

"Are they actually saying slump now?" Ellen put in. "Not recession?"

"The people on the receiving end are."

Then, with an unexpected access of briskness, Claudia pushed herself to her feet.

"Ellen dear, you must forgive me, but I still find it kind of hard to believe that you managed to trace this Louis Parker when Bernie failed. Mind showing me what kind of program you're running?"

Ellen flushed again. She said diffidently, "Well, I shouldn't be running it, not really. I came by it sort of unofficially. I did honestly mean to tell Bernie about it, but—well, he seemed to have lost interest. I hope it wasn't wrong of me to go ahead on my own?"

"Wrong?" Peter echoed. "Not at all. You're a marvel! But I'd like to see it, too."

"Well . . ." She hesitated. "The trouble is, if you want me to show how it works, I'll have to interrupt the run, won't I?"

"You don't have a copy?" Claudia demanded. "One you can show us in here?" She gestured at Peter's computer.

Ellen shook her head. Today she was wearing her hair neatly braided and coiled around her small shapely head. "I'm afraid not. It's the kind that only allows any user to copy it from the master once. If you try and copy the copy, it corrupts itself. I haven't tried it, but there's a warning."

"Sounds like a high-security job," Peter said slowly. "How in the world did you come by it?"

Ellen put her hand to her mouth and bit her knuckle, giggling. Suddenly she seemed all child again.

"By trying to get a bit of my own back. I moused into PNC looking for the data they keep on brown and black people, not because they've done anything but because of their color—I wanted to find out what they had about my family, you see. Suddenly I found I'd accessed a national search program, that can trace literally anybody who's ever been mentioned on any data-base, and it mistook me for an authorized user because until I came along nobody else had ever lucked into it."

Claudia looked worried. She said after a pause, "But won't they notice? I mean, if someone who isn't really an authorized user stays on-line to the program for this long—"

"Oh, I figured that one out. Thanks to Dad."

Peter blinked, and she amplified.

"Remember all those papers you collected at the computer security conference, just a few days before I—uh—turned up? Well, you didn't seem to be using them, so I borrowed them, and reading between the lines I found the dodge I needed to fool PNC!"

She started to chuckle. But the chuckles turned into a hysterical laugh and then into tears. Claudia rushed forward, caught her in her arms, and whispered reassurance in her ear until she calmed.

When she drew away with a wan smile—but a smile—Claudia glanced at Peter.

"Know something? You do have a genius for a daughter."

Before Peter could reply, the phone shrilled. He caught it up.

"Jake here," said the familiar voice. It sounded as though he must have caught up on his sleep during the day. "Featly stuff, just what I wanted. Your fee has been sent to the bank."

"That's wonderful," Peter said. "Any—ah—progress?"

Jake hesitated, obviously asking himself what he might safely say. In the end: "So far, no sign. We're going to risk it."

"Good luck!"

Setting down the phone, he turned to the others. "He likes it and the money's been paid. And there's still no sign of Thrower. I suggest we celebrate. Let's go out for dinner."

"No," Ellen said promptly.

"Why not? Might as well take advantage of the *Comet*'s money."

"I want to be around to hear that beep," Ellen said obstinately. "I don't want to come in late and find the data has been sitting on screen long enough for someone to trace and wipe it."

"She has a point," Claudia put in. "And the way that kind of program runs through data, you don't want to waste printout paper."

"Ah, I suppose not," Peter sighed.

"Don't look so miserable, Dad," Ellen reproved, patting his arm. "I'm going to make stuffed pancakes, and you always like those. But if you really can't stand my homemade wine . . ."

"Okay, I'll compromise. I'll go and buy a decent bottle—won't be long. Red or white?" he added to Claudia.

"I don't mind. I can't afford either, myself."

During the meal they watched the mid-evening news. There was still no mention of Thrower's disappearance, which was good from their and Jake Lafarge's point of view, but that fact was outweighed by a number of other depressing items, most notably a report from Bonn that agreement had been reached with East Germany, Czechoslovakia and Austria to monitor and announce daily on TV the declining oxygen levels in those areas that had within living memory been forested. Moreover there was still no bleep from the search program, though Ellen assured them it was still running. "It's bound to be much slower on my machine, isn't it?" she added at one point, as though growing worried. And they had to agree. In fact, Peter was privately wondering how she had got it to run at all.

*But one mustn't look gift horses in the mouth . . . Given that even the royal racehorses are dying of cancer, how long before people forget what horses used to look like?*

Gradually conversation died. There was another news-bulletin at ten, and since tomorrow was Saturday and there was no school Peter was prepared to let Ellen stay up for it, but a few minutes before it was due she rose despondently and announced her intention of turning in. Perhaps, she muttered, the program wasn't working properly. So long after narrowing Louis Parker's location down to a single county, it ought to have come up with more precise data.

Claudia voiced the suspicion that was dawning on them all.

"Unless he, or someone protecting him, has covered his tracks. After all, Bernie had no luck, did he? And you told us, Peter: this Parker was a computer expert."

"I wouldn't have thought of him as an expert," Peter muttered. "But it's true he did work for a computer company."

"Well, it was a brave try," Claudia told Ellen comfortingly, and gave her a good night hug. After kissing her father, she returned downcast to her room.

Where, within seconds, they heard the rattle of her printer.

"Got it!" she shouted. "The bocky thing just didn't beep! Come and see!"

Peter and Claudia exchanged glances of disbelief, and rushed after her.

"There!" she said proudly, holding out a sheet of paper. "It did work! It must have found its way to a phone line the name of Louis Parker had been spoken on, and taken ages to locate the right address. But it's done it." She was almost shaking with excitement at her success.

Taking the paper, Peter studied the address. "That's only a mile or two from Sandhurst," he murmured.

"Peter . . ." Claudia drew a deep breath. "I think I know what's in your mind. You're assuming something like this.

"Louis Parker found out, somehow, that he was fathering children with a gift of—of supernatural persuasiveness. He decided to exploit their power. He's raised a whole bunch of kids of his own, taught them complete obedience, and is now—what? Planning to hold General Thrower to ransom, for God's sake?"

"You were the one who came up with the idea in the first place," Peter retorted sourly.

"I did nothing of the kind! I don't make crazy intuitive leaps like that! You just forget about Thrower's disappearance. The fact that Parker turns out to be in the neighborhood doesn't necessarily have any connection with what happened after his meeting last night. The kids may have come from anywhere, a local private school for instance. The more I think about Jake's theories, and yours, the less I want to take them seriously."

"My theories? You just put words in my mouth! I—"

He realized abruptly that Ellen was turning away with lowered head.

"Darling, what's wrong?" he demanded.

Repressing a sob, she mumbled, "I thought you'd be pleased. It took a long time, and lots of hard work, and I probably broke the law by doing it . . . I did think you'd be pleased!"

"Of course we are!"

"You bocky well don't sound like it!" she flared. Spinning round, she revealed that her cheeks were wet.

Seeing her tears, Peter felt an appalling pang of guilt. To judge by Claudia's expression, she was reacting the same way. Finding words as best he could, he said, "Darling, I am sorry! But we are both very tired, and—and anyhow, what can we do about it right this minute?"

"Not much," she sighed. "We can go there in the morning, though, can't we? I mean, it's Saturday and I don't have to go to school."

"Yes, of course. And I'm sure Claudia would like to find out whether her theory is correct. We'll have to figure out how to get to this place. We could take a bus, I suppose, or even a train—I think there are still trains around there. And then find a taxi, or rent a car, though on a Saturday that might be difficult, because it's a wealthy area and they're probably booked in advance . . . Ellen love, I'm doing my best to work it out!"

"All right," she said after a pause. "Claudia, you'll come too, won't you?"

"Yes, of course. What time do you want me to be here?"

"You're going home? At this hour? Don't be silly." There was a hint of peremptoriness in her tone.

Peter hesitated. "Yes, I think it might be simpler if you stay over. I can kip on the living room couch—I have a sleeping bag."

"Don't be *silly!*" Ellen said again, more forcefully.

Claudia shrugged and turned toward the door. "Okay," she said. "Good night."

"Good night! And—Dad!" Ellen had closed the gap between them with a single long stride, and thrown her arms around him. "Dad, I'm sorry I snapped at you. I do love you, you know."

"I love you," he said sincerely, and squeezed her hard.

*The unexpected details of an unexpected encounter . . .*

Claudia had to clean her teeth with his toothpaste on her forefinger. He didn't have a spare brush, and with the advent of AIDS sharing toothbrushes had become uncustomary. They undressed by the light of a single shaded lamp, not looking at each other. Having removed her jacket and trousers, she hesitated a moment, then discarded her bra and panties as well. He had been intending to don the pajamas lately bought—he said facetiously—in case he, too, had to go to hospital, but on seeing her naked he changed his mind. When he joined her in the bed, she embraced and welcomed him without a word.

To his surprise, their love-making was excellent.

* * *

Afterward, while he snuggled against her shoulder, she said thoughtfully, "You know, I have a peculiar feeling that I've been conned."

But Peter was already fast asleep.

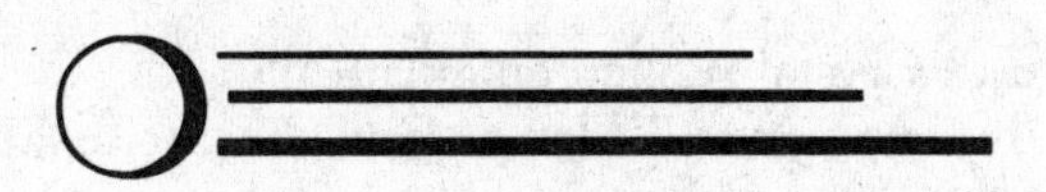

**H**arry Shay felt uneasy as he slowed the Rolls at the speed limit of the run-down northern town to which David had directed him.

Directed, in the sense of given orders . . .

During the long drive from Surrey, the longest time—come to think of it—that he had been away from David since returning to Britain, he had started to have second thoughts about the course he and Alice had adopted. The way the American economy was collapsing, of course, they had in one sense been lucky; they had pulled out in time to take a considerable fortune with them.

*On the other hand, if anyone ever gets to hear about the way we allow these underage kids to carry on . . . !*

One of them was beside him, and he kept casting worried glances at her. She looked positively demure in her dark jacket, mid-calf skirt, neat low-heeled shoes, innocent of either makeup or jewelry save for a silver watch. But she had been a prostitute since she ran away from home at twelve—she had somehow caused one of her customers to cut his own throat—she already had a police computer-record longer than his own, who had sailed financially close to the wind before he left for that land of opportunity which now was turning into a disaster zone . . .

*Grief! Who'd have thought that a few tons of solvents leaking over such a large area could lead to such a crisis? But it's happening. It's going to be like Texas when the oil bubble burst. For the first time in living memory California has shown a net annual loss of population . . .*

He'd learned that by phone from Goldfarb, whom he had rung last week. He hadn't seen it in the papers, nor on the news services he subscribed to via computer.

*Where have they gone? They surely can't have died!*

As though sensing his mood, Crystal laid her hand on his and smiled.

"You're worried, aren't you? Why?"

He was obliged to answer, though he didn't want to.

"Well—for one thing, David usually comes on these trips, and I don't know why he didn't want to this time."

Reassuringly: "Something else has come up—very important. But until now he didn't really feel he could depute the job to someone else. I'm flattered that he feels I can take care of this one . . . In any case, it's the least promising lead so far."

"Lead?"

"To—another of us," Crystal replied enigmatically.

"Yes, that's been bothering me." Harry drew the car to a halt. "How does he choose our—our recruits?"

"Through his computers, how else? The same ones that generated this map." It was a four-color printout showing the town down to house numbers. Leaning close despite the restraint of her seat belt, she spread it before him on the steering wheel, and put her arm around his neck so that she was speaking close to his cheek—so close, he could feel her breath on his skin. "The Hallams live where you see the red star. We have to take the second right, the third left, and the first right. Okay?"

"Okay!"

She gave him a hug and resumed her place. After that he forgot the doubts that had been plaguing him.

Pepita Hallam looked about her nervously as she dragged her wheeled shopping bag toward the entrance of the tower-block where she lived. There was going to be trouble when Cynthia found out how much less than usual she had brought home: one carton of cigarettes instead of two, no vodka, barely enough food to keep them going over the weekend . . .

But since the detectives had arrested her at the supermarket, since she had actually been taken to court—even though, of course, she had been found not guilty—she had grown terribly uncertain of her own talent. There had always been gaps in it, naturally, and she had made allowances for them. What she hadn't bargained for was that people out of range of her influence—plus, inevitably, their computers—would be able to work out what she was doing, and pounce.

*I'm going to have to get out of here. Why should I lay my neck on the block for my sick whenzie of a mother?*

The sound of a car made her check and turn. Around here most cars were abandoned wrecks, either because their engines had seized up for lack of oil or because their owners could no longer afford a road-fund license or the annual road-worthiness check, or simply because of the price of petrol. For whatever reason, they served chiefly as shelters for the exploding army of the homeless unemployed.

But this one was a Rolls Royce.

And it was drawing up beside her.

And a girl her own age was first looking at her, then getting out.

A girl enough like her to be, if not her sister, then at least her cousin.

Pepita's mouth was dry, her limbs were frozen. She could only stare.

"You must be Pepita," the stranger said with total confidence. Behind her, leaning across to the open passenger door, a serious-faced man was also gazing her way.

She forced out an admission of identity. She had feared the police, of course, and was at a loss on finding that assumption irrelevant.

"Was your mother ever known as Sindy?"

"What?"

Patiently the girl from the car repeated the question.

"Well—yes! But how did you know? How do you know me?"

"All in good time. I'm Crystal. This is Harry."

Mumbled: "How do you do?"

Now Harry too emerged from the car and came to stand at the side of his—daughter? Not very likely; there was a resemblance, but also something about the girl's manner and attitude . . .

"Harry," she said, and her tone was one of authority.

"Yes?"

"Ring David and tell him he was right. Then we'll help Pepita take this stuff upstairs."

Bitterly: "Upstairs is right! Unless they've fixed the lifts! Just as well I have a light load today, isn't it?"

*Why am I saying this? I don't know these people! I don't talk to strangers about my problems!*

Crystal came forward and clasped her hand, smiling. A sense of confidence invaded her mind during the brief time it took for Harry to place a call via the phone in the car. In fact it wasn't really a call, not a spoken one at any rate. What he did was convert the phone buttons into a computer keyboard and punch in a brief code. Pepita had read about that sort of thing, but of course no one in her personal world . . .

"Now," said Crystal encouragingly, "let's go up."

*It isn't happening. It can't be.*

Where were the howls, the screams, the drunken tantrums? What had made Cynthia remember and revert to the person she must once have been, the polite and gracious girl who made visitors welcome with cups of tea and biscuits? What had made her vanish in order to put on a dress instead of her housecoat, wash her face, comb her hair, apply lipstick? The transformation was incredible!

Gradually the truth began to dawn.

*This Crystal: she can do what I can. Only better.*

Pepita began to tremble with excitement. Barely an hour after the arrival of the visitors, she was packing her gear into paper bags and plastic sacks. Cynthia was sighing as though she felt it expected of her, but her eyes were shining on her daughter's behalf, thanks to the vivid word-picture of the future she could look forward to in the wealthy south . . .

*Yet no one has actually put it in so many words!*

It didn't matter. It was real. What she had been dreaming of had come about.

When she hugged her mother at the door, she knew it was—if so she chose—for the last time.

Drowsy beside Crystal in the back seat of the Rolls, she whispered, "How did you find me?"

"Ask David," Crystal answered. Overhearing, Harry spoke over his shoulder.

"Yes, ask David! He's a phenomenon, my son! Half the time even I can't figure out what he's doing, but it always seems to turn out right!"

A dead pause, during which they listened to the purr of the car's engine and the hush of its tires on the roadway and the wind of its high-speed passage.

*Son?*

Unspoken, the question could be read on Pepita's face. Sensing what she meant, Crystal donned a wry smile and shook her head. Shaping words in a less-than-whisper, drawing back so Harry could not glimpse her in the rearview mirror, she communicated:

*He'll catch on. All in good time. All in good time . . .*

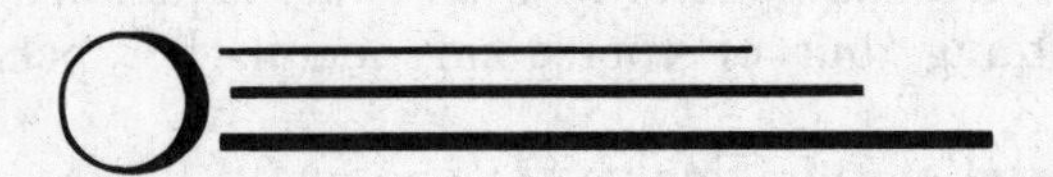

*You're watching TV Plus. Time for Newsframe.*

*In South Korea the air force has destroyed a pharmaceutical factory and the surrounding area with incendiary bombs. According to the Ministry of Public Health the operation was necessitated by the escape of organisms containing cancer-causing oncogenes. Two hundred people are reported dead and hundreds more in hospital. Rioting has broken out in several nearby towns. More in a moment.*

*Here at home, concern over the disappearance of General Sir Hampton Thrower . . .*

"Dad! Claudia!" Ellen, in pajamas, rushed into the sitting room regardless of the fact that they were still in bed, and switched on the TV. "Jake got his beat!"

Forcing himself up on one elbow, bleary-eyed, Peter said, "What the—? Damn it, girl, it's barely seven!"

"Don't you want to see what's happening?" she countered, and stood aside from the screen. The early news had just begun, and the lead story was the Thrower kidnapping, broken exclusively by the *Comet*. It was mentioned that Jake had gambled on printing an extra half-million copies, and they were already sold out.

Swinging his legs to the floor, heedless of the fact that he was naked, Peter said sourly, "How long before Special Branch closes the paper down?"

"Oh, Dad!" Ellen would have stamped, but she was barefoot. "Just watch, why don't you?"

"Yes, I certainly want to," Claudia said, rising and pressing herself against his back with one arm over his shoulder for want of other concealment of her nudity. And indeed the news was worth watching. Almost half the ten-minute bulletin was given over to the subject, and it was the lead item in the talk show that followed. When that came on, Peter said soberly, "I apologize. They wouldn't dare. Not with this level of exposure."

"I bet it's on all the channels!" Ellen cried, pressing the remote control. And, indeed, it was.

"I think I'd better find out whether they want me on the box," Peter muttered. "Sling me my dressing gown, there's a love."

Moving reflexively to comply, she let her face fall.

"But we're supposed to be going to see Louis Parker!"

Peter was about to say, "It'll have to wait!"—when she darted toward the bed and dropped on her knees, gazing up earnestly at him.

"Please?" she whispered. "I have worked very hard to find him. And you did promise."

Tugged two ways, he hesitated. At length he appealed to Claudia, who pondered for long moments, but said eventually, "You know, I think she's right. You could probably pick up some quick cash because you had that piece in the *Comet* and thousands of people who never heard of you before must be reading it right this minute. On the other hand, if while Jake is in a good mood we confront him with the first really hard evidence concerning the kids you wrote about . . . It could be a long-term benefit."

Jumping up, Ellen hugged her and her father both. "Just what I was hoping you would say!" she exclaimed. "Right! I'll make some breakfast. You can have first turn in the bathroom."

Since many wealthy commuters lived in the area, there were still frequent trains to Camberley. Despite the cost—British Rail having "rationed" its passengers by raising prices since the late 1980's, rather than providing additional trains—Peter and Claudia decided to travel that way. It would be a treat for Ellen. She had never gone by train, apart from the London tube.

It being Saturday, the train was packed, and since they could only afford the second-class fare Ellen, at half-rate, had to sit on their knees by turns. Watching her leaning back against Peter, vaguely eavesdropping on the conversation of their fellow passengers—which, inevitably, centered on General Thrower's disappearance, and reflected the scores of incompatible theories already circulating—Claudia wondered about their fondness for each other. From what she knew or guessed about him, she felt certain Peter must have been infuriated when his long-neglected daughter was dumped into his life. Moreover, given that he had abandoned her mother when she was pregnant, and shown virtually no interest in his own child until they were thrown together, one might have assumed that Ellen would resent her natural father. Yet now they seemed to be on the best of terms. It was almost as though she had seduced him into accepting her. Certainly she had charmed him . . .

In the long run, might not such a relationship become—well—unhealthy?

However, all such thoughts evaporated when Ellen, to give her father a break, came and sat on Claudia's lap instead. No, she was just a normal if unusually intelligent girl making the best of a bad situation, and doing so with mature competence.

*You*, Claudia chided herself, *have paid too much attention to too much scandal. Not every single male parent has sinister designs on his nubile offspring . . .*

With a wry private smile at her own suspicions, she turned to gaze out of the window. The glass was streaked with rain, growing heavier by the minute.

An almost constant series of FOR SALE signs met her eyes, mainly on empty factories. The economic crash that had begun in the States was taking its toll here as well—that, and competition from more efficient countries elsewhere in the EEC. She recognized the name of one firm; a recent news report had mentioned that it was moving lock, stock and barrel to Spain. A wan-looking group of former employees, sodden by the downpour, were holding up banners for the passengers to read, but the windows were too smeared for them to be legible.

Whenever the train stopped, groups of hopeful beggars darted up to the alighting passengers, whining after alms. Armed police dragged them aside, cuffed them about the head, pushed them back against the wall, saluted their intended prey. By Camberley, however, it was no longer the police but the army that was on patrol.

"You think this is because of Thrower?" Claudia murmured to Peter as they prepared to get out. Face strained, he nodded.

"Something wrong?"

"Yes." He bit his lower lip, glancing sidelong at Ellen.

"We can brazen it out. Come on."

She caught his hand—and, on the instant, froze. His answering squeeze reminded her how skilled that hand had been last night . . . and also that she had made love unprotected.

*Am I insane?*

It was his turn to ask what was amiss. But before she could answer —before she had even had time to reason through what she was alarmed about—Ellen was urging them onward, toward the khaki-clad men and women guarding the exit from the platform, some of whom were already curling their lips at the sight of someone with dark skin. With a sick sense of foreboding, Claudia noticed that they were all wearing red-white-and-blue ribbons.

Then the miracle happened. A clear voice called, "Peter! Peter Levin!"

They halted and swung around. Approaching was a tall man, extremely well-dressed, who had just emerged from one of the first-class compartments.

"Peter, don't you remember me?" he demanded.

"My God, of course!" Peter caught his hand and shook it warmly. "Harry Shay! I've been trying to get hold of you for ages! What made you leave California—? Oh, by the way, this is my friend Dr. Morris, Claudia Morris, and this is my daughter Ellen. Harry Shay, formerly of Shaytronix Inc.! What are you doing back in Britain?"

Flourishing a season ticket, Harry led them to the exit, brushing aside the suspicious soldiery with such authority that they simply turned their attention elsewhere. They were outside in no time, sheltered against the rain by an awning. From a gray Rolls Royce waiting illegally in the roadway a hand waved and the engine started.

"Got out while the going was good, shall we say?" Harry replied at length. "More to the point, what brings you here—? Ah, don't tell me. Let me guess. I saw that piece of yours in the *Comet*—dreadful rag, don't normally waste money on it, but when they got this incredible scoop . . . Your editor has sent you down to follow through?"

"Well, not exactly," Peter admitted. "We're on the track of something different—"

Ellen butted in unexpectedly. "Mr. Shay, do you know anyone around here called Louis Parker?"

Harry repeated the name, frowning. "No, I don't think I do. Where does he live?"

Before the adults could answer she produced a slip of paper from the pocket of her jeans.

"Oh, I know where that is. I'm going past it, in fact." The Rolls drew up level with them, and a bright pretty face smiled from the driver's window. "You remember Alice, I'm sure! Alice, look who I've bumped into! They're going to call on someone who lives nearby—let's give them a ride! We can't make them walk, and they'll never get a cab on a day like this!"

"Featly!" Ellen exclaimed, and clasped her hands.

Claudia murmured something under her breath. Peter glanced at her.

"I missed that?"

"I said: if all our problems could be solved so easily . . . Thanks a million, Mr. Shay!"

It was infinitely relaxing to ride in this luxurious car, protected against the chill and damp. Even the empty shops masked with tattered posters, the groups of workless youths shivering in their doorways, the police in yellow plastic capes chaining up abandoned cars to be dragged away for scrap, could not erode their sudden joint mood of optimism. It was as though they were aware of reaching journey's end. Claudia tried to think about what they had to expect—what they were going to say to this mysterious Louis Parker when at long last they encountered him—but laziness like the effect of good pot pervaded her mind, and she was content to relax and let things happen.

The town gave way to suburban roads lined with gaunt trees. The leaves they had shed, sodden with wet, barely stirred in the gusting wind. Here and there they saw optimistic youngsters gathering them up in wheelbarrows; they would make compost from them during the winter, and sell the result next spring to fertilize the gardens of wealthy local residents. It was one of the employment schemes fostered by the government. Of course, it didn't provide a living wage, but it was supposed to keep them out of mischief, and it assuaged the demands of the Greens . . .

All of a sudden they were turning off the road down a winding driveway. Peter became suddenly alert. Tensing, he glanced from side to side.

"This is the address your daughter showed me," Harry said in a reassuring tone.

"But should we just turn up like this, unannounced?"

It was obvious what he was worrying about. At the mouth of every driveway for the past three miles there had been signs warning of security patrols. In the aftermath of the Thrower kidnapping, were they not bound to have been redoubled?

"Don't worry, Dad," Ellen said, laying a hand on his. And, miraculously, he didn't.

The car halted outside a large Victorian house: not a mansion, but immense. Peter whistled.

"Did all right for himself, didn't he—old Louis? Well, all I can say is thanks very much, Harry. And hope the guy's at home. Otherwise we've come on a wild-goose chase."

A disturbing point crossed Claudia's mind:

*Why didn't we phone to say we were coming?*

However, a second later she had thought of reasons why not—*mustn't alarm him, if he's warned he may run away . . .*

And was distracted because both Harry and Alice were getting out of the car.

Following uncertainly, Peter said, "But . . ."

"You go ahead," Harry smiled. "Go ring the bell."

In fact, though, that was unnecessary. The front door swung wide and here came a boy bearing a huge umbrella. He hurried over to the car with a broad grin.

"Mr. Levin! Remember me? I don't suppose you do—I was only about eight or nine when we last met. I'm David. And you're Ellen, aren't you? Great to meet you!"

To Peter and Claudia's vast astonishment, the two children embraced like long-lost friends.

"Quickly! Inside!" Alice cried. "It's pelting down!"

And long before objections could be formulated, they had been rushed into the hallway. It was dry in here, and warm, and there was a pervasive pleasant smell of roasting meat: lunch being cooked rather early?

That was the first thing that struck Peter and Claudia. The second was a series of indications that the house must be full of children: bicycles propped against the foot of a balustraded staircase, a dozen pairs of small rubber boots untidily against the wall, discarded anoraks waiting to be hung up . . .

No toys. But definitely children's belongings.

Peter blurted, "Does Louis Parker live here?"

Harry shook his head.

"Then why have you brought us here?"

"This is the address you asked to be brought to. It just so happens that it's ours."

"I don't understand!" Clenching his fists, Peter rounded on his unexpected—and suddenly unwelcome—hosts.

"Don't blame him, Mr. Levin," David said softly, taking his arm. "It wasn't his idea to bring you here. It was mine. You see, I have something to show you. And you too, Dr. Morris. If you would kindly come this way . . . ?"

Moving as though in a dream, Peter and Claudia allowed themselves to be led across the wide tiled hallway to a door at the far side. Opened, it revealed a high-ceilinged room with immense windows giving on to a neglected garden. Children, all about David and Ellen's age, all with the same dark hair, the same slightly olive complexion, the same general build, were standing around a long oak table. At once the smell of roast meat became intense.

As though they had been rehearsed in their movements, they parted to let be seen what lay on the table: a naked human figure, seared and blistered and blind, its hair scorched off, its limbs contorting in pain but restrained by plastic straps. Hanging from the ceiling, the impersonal eye of a TV camera, whose field of view the children carefully avoided, was recording the victim's agony.

"Mr. Levin, you're a reporter," David said. "Among other things. Allow me to present General Sir Hampton Thrower. He has been exposed to precisely the degree of heat—we couldn't imitate the blast effect, but the heat was easy—that would be suffered by someone standing unprotected on a clear day five miles from the ground zero of a one-megaton hydrogen bomb exploded at ten thousand feet. In other words, the typical yield of one of the missiles that would inevitably be used in the war he claimed would be so good for the people of Britain."

Claudia doubled over, striving not to vomit.

"But—"

Peter managed to force out the single word despite his own violent nausea.

"You wish to know how we could be sure?" David murmured. "Well, the data are available . . . But to be on the safe side, we had our calculations checked by someone you know."

Overlooked until now, a familiar figure emerged from an alcove, untidy, shabbily dressed . . .

"Bernie!" Peter burst out.

"I couldn't help it," the hacker muttered, his eyes roving everywhere save toward the ruined figure on the table. And then, with a hint of defiance: "I think it serves him bocky right, anyhow!"

"A taste of the medicine he wanted to prescribe for others," David confirmed. "By the way, he'll live. Long enough to be shown on television, heard describing the agony he's suffered, making his apologies on the grounds of ignorance . . . Of course, as the old legal principle has it, *ignoratio legis nihil excusat*—saying you didn't know it was against the law is no defense. We rely on you to organize that for us—*Dad!*"

Harry, who had been hanging back beside the door, said uncertainly, "Well, I'll do what I can, of course. But—"

The children suddenly burst out laughing, except for David, though it cost him a visible effort to control himself. A hint of amusement nonetheless colored his voice as he said, "No, Harry, not you. Nor Louis Parker either, though I confess that for a long time I, too, imagined he was the person we were looking for. In case you're interested, he wasn't having an affair with Dr. What's-her-name. She must just have been a bit of a fag-hag, as they used to say, because he's homosexual. We've traced him to a villa near Malaga. He made a fortune peddling amyl nitrite to the gay community in London, enough to retire on before he was forty. So that leaves . . ." And he cocked one eyebrow.

"Oh my God," Peter said brokenly, clenching his fists.

David looked at him steadily. So did the other children. So—and this was the worst—did Ellen.

"I think you finally caught on," David murmured.

But instead of answering Peter began to groan.

"Come now," David said comfortingly, and took his arm. "We'll adjourn to another room and sit down, and Alice will bring you a drink, and we can all talk about it. Then you'll understand."

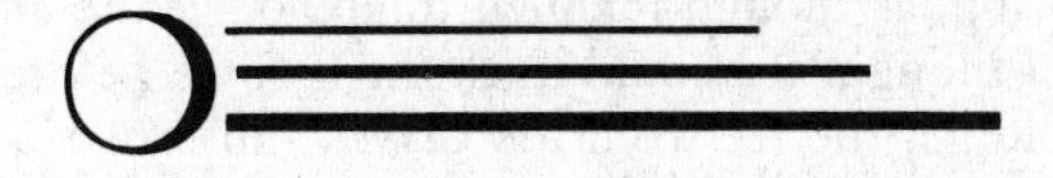

**I** don't understand, I don't understand . . .

Peter came slowly back to himself. He was in a drawing room, huge, handsomely furnished with armchairs and settees covered in floral chintz, its windows half concealed by matching curtains drawn together at the top, held apart lower down by braided ropes. It was approaching noon, but the light outside was gray and dismal.

*Yet I don't feel as awful as I should!*

And that couldn't simply be due to the fact that the chair assigned to him was so comfortable, nor even the warming impact of the glass of brandy—traditional restorative—which Alice had handed him, its aroma running ahead of its hot taste. He glanced at Claudia. She was paper-white and shaking.

*So should I be. I've just seen a human being reduced to a condition worse than . . . I don't know what it could be worse than. Is there anything worse? Except maybe to have live maggots dining on your flesh!*

And then, unbidden: *If someone did let off those bombs, the victims would be food for maggots, wouldn't they, long before they died?*

All of which, contrary to his will, seemed distant, veiled and far away.

*It's as though, the moment I crossed the threshold of this house, everything I've worried about lately, everything I've been afraid of, has—well—receded.*

"It has," David Shay assured him, kneeling on a cushion at his side. Until that moment Peter hadn't been aware of speaking aloud. Yet he must have been—either that, or these children could read his mind . . .

Briefly distracted, he gazed from one to the other of them in search of clues. Obviously these were the kids Claudia had come to Europe in search of, the ones that Bernie had failed to trace despite his mastery of hacking—

*Just a moment!*

As usual, Bernie was staying in the background. Peter might have overlooked his presence in the dimness but for the fact that Alice was offering him too a glass of brandy, and he had eagerly accepted. He found himself staring in that direction.

"Bernie, you lied to us," he said.

The hacker shrugged. "You try doing anything else when this lot are around," he sighed, and sank half his brandy at a single gulp. And then, as though relenting, as though inclined to apologize, he added, "My fault, I suppose. I thought if I could track them down before you and Claudia did I could get the fee from the *Comet.* I'm broke, aren't I? Same as virtually everybody in this poor sick country! And I have kids of my own!"

Peter jolted upright, but before he could speak Claudia had whispered, "We didn't know."

"Why should you?"—with contempt. "My bitch of a wife took them away from me. All I do nowadays is pay for them . . ."

He finished the brandy and held out his glass for more. Silently, one of the boys brought the decanter. Peter wondered which of them it was and what crimes he had been guilty of. The more he looked at these children, the more they seemed to resemble one another. He hadn't noticed until now, but they were all wearing the same kind of clothes, girls as well as boys being clad in jeans and sweaters. It was as though the fashion-clock had stopped somewhere in his own teens. He had worn precisely similar garb . . .

*This is distracting me!*

Foggily, perhaps more than ever because of the brandy, Peter strove to make sense of what was happening. He forced out, "There's something in the air! Is it a drug?"

Claudia glanced up at that, and a trace of color returned to her cheeks. Perhaps that was something she too had thought of, and been unable to express in words.

But Harry said with prudish sternness, "Peter! Do you really think Alice and I would let these kids use drugs while they're in our charge?"

*Our—charge . . . ?*

Once again Peter felt a sense of total bafflement. But David touched his knee with a gentle hand.

"Don't bother trying to work it out. We've brought you here for explanations, and as soon as you're ready—"

"Ready?" Peter exploded. "Bocky starving for them!"

"Very well." David sat back composedly on his cushion, folding his hands in his lap. "You're right: there is something in the air. But not a drug. Bernie?"

At first the hacker was reluctant to respond, but a stern unison glare from the children seemed to compel him. Noticing, Claudia feebly tried to push her chair closer to Peter's, but though it was on casters, the carpet was deep-piled and she couldn't manage it. At a signal from David, however, Harry was prompt to assist her, and she and Peter were able to link fingers across the abutting chair-arms.

Meantime Bernie had found words.

"I suspected this from the start," he muttered. "In fact I'm surprised Claudia didn't spot it before I did."

Nettled, she retorted, "You saw my analysis!"

"Yes, but you were asking the wrong questions . . . Oh, the hell with it. *I* don't want to talk about it. Leave it to David."

And he subsided into private misery.

Summoning all his concentration, Peter rose to his feet. He said, "Now you look here! Apparently you brought—you *lured*—us here because you want me to tell the world that what you've done to General Thrower is right and justified! If that's the case, I tell you right this moment, you are barking up the wrong bocky tree!"

"That's only secondary," David said with a trace of weariness. "More importantly: we wanted to meet our father."

"But there are too many of you!" Peter blurted.

For a second he imagined he had scored a masterly point. David, however, was patiently shaking his head.

"Clever of you to think of that, but you're wrong. In fact, we aren't too many. We are actually one too few. Now tell us: what was the name of the woman you made pregnant while keeping company with Ellen's mother?"

"I never knew her name!"

"You said she was called Sindy, didn't you?"

"Y-yes." Uncertainly he licked his lips.

"In full, her name was Cynthia Hallam," said one of the interchangeable girls. "I'm Pepita Hallam, her daughter. And yours."

For a terrifying instant Peter had imagined her to be Ellen. The rest of what he had intended to say died in his throat.

Another of the girls, who had been standing against the wall, stepped into the middle of the floor. She said, "You were right, Dave. It does work the way you said . . . By the way: hello, Dad! I'm Crystal—Crystal Knight."

"I don't understand—"

"You keep saying that! Save your bocky breath, will you? David claimed that our talent can stop people asking the wrong kind of questions before they agree to do as we want. Most of us were pretty doubtful, even though we'd seen what we can do to Harry and Alice, not to mention the people who come in to clean up and help around the house. But he called you Dad already, and you didn't seem to catch on, so I guess he's proved his point. Either that, or you must be so shell-backed the computer people would like to know your secret . . . Ah! It looks as though Dr. Morris has finally logged on!"

*Snap.* It was the sound of Claudia's brandy glass breaking between her fingers. Blood ran down. There was an interval of mopping up and finding sticking-plaster. During that whole time Peter stood as fixedly as a statue. It didn't seem to him as though he had been petrified; it didn't seem as though he had been ordered to stand still. It was just that so many hints and clues and odds-and-ends of data had clashed together, so belatedly, that he had no energy to spare to move a finger. He barely retained the ability to breathe.

And kept thinking, over and over: *What am I actually breathing?*

Claudia's cut fingers being dressed, as though he had read Peter's mind David threw over his shoulder, "Not drugs—I speak with authority on that subject, I may say—but pheromones. That's what I hoped Bernie would have the guts to tell you. But as usual he's chickened out. So you're going to have to take it straight from me. Alice—Harry—I'm sorry. It's not going to be much fun for you, either. But it sure as hell isn't going to be as bad as it has been for most of us kids. I'm the lucky one, and I thank you for it. The others . . ." He shrugged, and resumed his cushion. "Well, we aren't going to ask you to pass judgment. We already did, especially on General Sir *Hateful* Thrower. Your function now—your only remaining function—is to shut up and do as you're told."

*Where's Ellen?*

The question sprang unbidden to Peter's mind as he sank slowly back into his chair. He needed his daughter's love and affection at this moment, to help him combat the terrible accusation he did not dare confront alone: the charge that these were *his* children, not those of Louis Parker . . .

But the midday light in here was so dim he could not distinguish Ellen from the other children. She too, he remembered, had donned sweater and jeans this morning, plus an anorak that now lay discarded in the hall . . .

*I can't recognize my own daughter any more!*

The taste of defeat was sour in his mouth. He tried to wash it away with another sip of brandy, but that didn't work. In the end, he husked, "Damn you! Go on!"

"Precisely as I predicted," said David Shay. "Your response on meeting your family for the first time is to say—*damn you!*"

And suddenly the air was full of menace. Gone was the sense of diffuse calm, of relaxation, of protection against the sight of Thrower burned halfway to death. Now there were eyes in the twilight like the eyes of wolves, watching and waiting for the moment to pounce . . .

Peter wanted to scream, but even that surcease was denied him.

"It's time," David said, and his voice seemed to have grown deeper and more resonant, like the tolling of a funeral bell, "for you to meet your children, and be told what they have suffered because you wanted a few more pounds to spend."

*It wasn't like that!* But Peter couldn't frame the words. The room had turned into a court of justice, and there seemed to be no jury, only judges. Even Harry, even Alice . . . Even Ellen! Which of them *was* she?

"I'll start with myself," David said. "My ostensible father Harry had himself vasectomized because he wasn't interested in his first family and indeed was glad to say good-bye to them when he acquired a younger and more beautiful new wife. Only he still retained the macho image of a Man's Man as one who had to have offspring around, and in this view Alice heartily concurred. She wanted to be a Mother, capital M, as well as the partner of a successful businessman who could provide her with the sort of lifestyle to which she had always hoped to grow accustomed. Since Harry wasn't willing to risk an attempt to reverse his operation, the answer was the Chinn-Wilkinson clinic.

"Where you, Peter Levin, were the provider. Invoking Louis Parker was a clever attempt to evade the responsibility, but—well, the story goes that they had to supply him with ramrod porn before he could make his donations. As for Dr. Wilkinson, one assumes she was afraid of her femininity and obliged to sublimate it via the fertility clinic . . ."

He snapped his fingers. "Oh, yes! A point I've been meaning to mention. According to Ellen you tell people that Levin means 'love-friend'! But did you know it also means thunderbolt? That makes us the children of the thunder, doesn't it? The Boanerges of our day! And the storm is due to break . . ."

In the gloom his eyes seemed to glow, as though they were looking far beyond the here-and-now. Peter strove to speak and could not. Nor, as he saw when he glanced at her in desperation, could Claudia; she was in as piteous a plight as he.

And David was holding forth anew.

"Now let me introduce you to the rest of these children whom you just damned—and explain why we were already damned without exception, including me. Did I want to be a necessary status symbol rather than a proper son? I think I know what that means. Harry doesn't."

From the corner of his eye Peter saw Harry cringe. He wondered whether this was the first time the accusation had been brought against him so publicly, so nakedly . . . and had no time to complete the thought, for the inexorable words were flowing onward like an unstoppable river.

*I'm being put on trial. For something I didn't even realize I'd done . . .*

Once more it was as though David had read his inmost thoughts. He said, "Before I go on, perhaps I should cite another legal principle. I admire the law, and wish more people paid attention to it . . . Not knowing something is against the law is no defense, as I mentioned. But it has been held for centuries that a reasonable person is responsible for the foreseeable consequences of his actions."

"Foreseeable!" Peter managed to blurt out.

"Foreseeing is a duty," David countered in a dead voice. "How often did you, Peter Levin, consider the outcome of what you were doing when you donated sperm?"

"I—I hoped I would be making childless couples happy!"

"Very good!"—in a tone of surprise. "You have, as it were, entered a plea of not guilty. But these, here now assembled, are all your children. It is their verdict you must face."

"Children I've never met before?"

"We'll come to that. Right now, what concerns us is not your intentions but their outcome."

"I'm to be condemned because half a score of kids I knew nothing about were badly treated by their—?"

"No! No! *No!*" David was on his feet in a single swift motion. "You still don't understand!

"*We are humanity's only hope of salvation.*"

With a sense of indescribable despair Peter realized:

*He's a megalomaniac, and he's infected the others with his beliefs. And given that they have this power . . . !*

He buried his head in his hands.

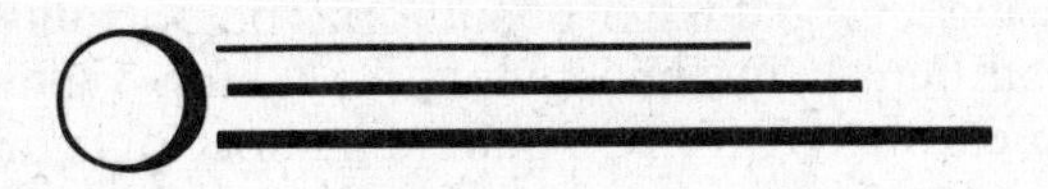

Suddenly Peter felt his cheek being stroked, and within seconds the future seemed less terrible. Of course, he could not reconcile the fact that he was calming down, even relaxing, while in the power—Power? Yes, that was the only word for it —*in the power* of these children who had demonstrated their willingness to submit another human being to indescribable agony . . .

*Another human being? But even if they are my offspring, are they human?*

Such thoughts evaporated as a hand sought his. It was Ellen's (yes, really, this time it was Ellen beside him) and he clasped it gratefully. Claudia was clinging to her other hand, jaw clamped tight to stop her teeth from chattering with terror.

"Now let me introduce the rest of us and tell you their life stories so far," David was saying in a didactic tone, rather like a lecturer conscious of teaching an unpopular subject. Peter couldn't help being reminded of Jim Spurman. "Then I'll explain how we got together, and deal with any questions you may have. It shouldn't take more than an hour or so, and afterward we can have lunch. In passing, Dr. Morris, let me compliment you on having traced us all, even though of course as soon as I realized how close you were I took steps to prevent you contacting any of us directly. For the fact that you were misled into believing it was Louis Parker who was always one jump ahead of you I have Bernie to thank, he being already predisposed to blame someone else even before Peter offered him a scapegoat—and of course Ellen, who has proved immensely helpful."

Loosing her hand from Peter's, Claudia bit her knuckles to suppress a hysterical giggle. David favored her with a patronizing smile, and resumed.

"I thought of introducing us in order of age, but I think it might be easier to do it in the order in which we got together. As it happens I am the oldest, but we're all pretty close, naturally."

*Naturally?* A sick joke sprang to Peter's tongue, but it remained unspoken, surviving only as a bitter taste.

"I've told you about my own background. So we might as well carry on with Dymphna—Dymphna Clancy, from Ireland. Her mother, living under a régime that forbade divorce, was married to a man who treated her abominably for not producing children. In the end he drove her insane. One of the first signs, no doubt, of her impending breakdown was that she flew to London where such treatment was legal and, using a forged letter of authority purporting to be from her husband, had herself inseminated at the Chinn-Wilkinson clinic. That establishment was not run on quite the impeccable principles to which its directors claimed to aspire . . . Dymphna eventually wound up in a Catholic orphanage where, after reaching puberty, she delighted in committing supposedly mortal sins and getting away with them."

Peter could recognize Dymphna by her broad grin. Though she was paler, and freckled, and there was a tinge of red in her hair, she was unmistakably Ellen's half-sister . . .

"The blame, though, does not lie with her—nor with any of us. A sick society, that made her mother's husband so cruel to his wife, is what's at fault . . . And now to Roger, whose offenses were not dissimilar.

"Born to a mother who agreed with her husband that, while it was their duty to produce a child, that child should be sent away as soon as possible for at least three-quarters of the year to boarding school, Roger discovered when he entered puberty that he had certain tastes and certain talents. At the ripe old age of thirteen he was successfully operating a service for pedophiles, from which, by the way, he accumulated a considerable sum of money. Nothing like as much as I derived from selling my designer drugs, of course, but—"

Despite the restraining grasp of Ellen's hand Peter could contain himself no longer. He burst out, "You sold drugs? You dealt in narcotics?"

David gazed at him blandly. "No. I designed them. Others manufactured them and sold them. I simply took a commission. Why not? None of *us* would ever be stupid enough to use them."

It was the first time he had so blatantly implied that he and the other children regarded themselves as different.

*How different? A different species? Do they think of themselves as "the man after man"?*

Ellen released her fingers and began to soothe the back of his neck, easing away tension with every stroke. Peter had intended to continue, but was forestalled. Claudia, regaining at least a modicum of self-control, was leaning forward.

"You keep referring to puberty," she whispered.

David nodded.

"Like most human pheromones, ours is hormone-related, more so in the case of the girls. In them secretion ceases for a short time once a month. In compensatory fashion, when it's at its peak it's far more powerful, and more effective against both men and women."

*Against?* The terrifying possibilities implicit in that single word made Peter shiver—but once again he had no chance to speak, for David had resumed his exposition. Apart from the occasional sound of a vehicle passing on the distant roadway, the silence was virtually total, as though the children were waiting to hear what he said about them and prepared to issue their own verdict afterward.

*Or*—and this thought was absolutely chilling—*do these pheromones knit them together into a superorganism, so that they will inevitably agree with their leader because they can't do otherwise . . . ?*

The implications almost prevented him from hearing what David said next.

"After Roger, I got in touch with Crystal. She's had a very bad time indeed. Her legal parents died in an epidemic of meningitis. A cure was found, but too late. If a fraction of what this country spends every day on armaments had been invested in a vaccine they would almost certainly have survived. Crystal would not have been committed to the care of a couple of religious bigots—would not have been beaten for petty offenses until she was driven to run away and seek a living as a prostitute, having to sell her body for the first time to the doctor who vaccinated her against AIDS."

Peter, appalled, could tell which Crystal was. She was nodding slowly, back and forth, with the measured rhythm of a mandarin statuette.

"Compared to her—though he might not agree—Garth had things easy. Trapped on an isolated farm by parents whose convictions about 'going back to the land' deprived him of most of the ordinary experiences young people should be able to look forward to, he did at least find it possible to turn the tables so that he wound up in control of them, and not *vice versa.* Correct, Garth?"

It was the first time he had appealed to one of the others for approval. Peter tensed, hoping for a contradiction. On the contrary. Garth gave a sour chuckle.

"They scared easy. Once I'd killed our bocky neighbors' prize sheepdog, and particularly after I'd drowned their son in our brook, they were amazingly pliant."

A girl spoke up, sitting in the darkest corner where Peter could not see her face. Her voice, though, was so like Ellen's . . . ! Bar a slightly different accent, it could have been his daughter's—

*It is my daughter's.*

Slowly, sickly, awareness of the truth was penetrating his mind.

What was she saying? He forced himself to recapture her first words, which he had nearly missed.

"I made my first kill before you did, Garth. I'm Sheila Hubbard, Dad . . . Dave, I want to speak for myself."

"Go ahead," David invited with an expansive gesture, and added by way of footnote, "Since joining us, Sheila has changed her mind about the way she looks at her plight."

"True," the girl acknowledged, hunching forward with elbows on knees. "I used to think it was my fault that soldier died—"

"The one who drowned in the river?" Claudia exclaimed.

"Yes, him." Sheila's tone was as dead as the soldier. "But I only killed him. My mother was responsible, because she wanted a child and her first husband didn't, but she went ahead anyway—"

"How?" Peter forced out.

"Let her finish!" David reprimanded sharply. "I told you—the Chinn-Wilkinson wasn't nearly as ethical as its owners claimed, at least when thousands of pounds were at stake . . . Go on, Sheila."

She shrugged and spread her hands. Still in the same dull tone, she muttered, "Well, she left him and got married again, this time to a rich old growser with a mess of money. But for a long time I didn't know I wasn't my official father's kid. I was lied to. I think it was knowing that my mother had lied to me that drove me to do—well, what I did."

"That," David prompted, "and the discovery of your power?"

"Shit, we've all been that route, haven't we?" Sheila sighed, and leaned back into darkness.

"Yes," David said. "It's a temptation. Just as well we got together before any of us yielded to it on the grandest scale, hmm?"

There was a pause, as though some of the children were still not convinced, but eventually there followed a murmur of agreement. Peter's view of what was going on kept shifting; he was no longer so sure that all the kids were under David's sway, even though Harry and Alice obviously were. So there might be some hope of escape . . .

He hadn't realized until now that escape would be necessary.

"Next I got in touch with Terry," David resumed. "You won't know his name, any more than you knew the others', but if I say he was running a neat little protection racket with a handful of older boys . . . ?"

A suppressed chuckle. The room was growing ever darker, yet Peter's watch confirmed that only as much time had passed as he had guessed. The rain, then, was due to redouble as the clouds densened—and here came the clatter of waterdrops as fierce as bullets. Raising his voice to compensate, David said, "Well, what else would you expect? A kid raised by a family of loyal government supporters, persuaded that if they didn't make their pile out of their little local shop they were somehow betraying Britain as the traditional nation of shopkeepers . . . Small wonder their son—excuse me: their boy—took to what is customarily called a life of crime."

Terry stirred. Until now he had been as motionless as he was silent. Now he said, "Some people call it private enterprise, you know."

There was a general chuckle. Clutching at straws, Peter thought: *Well, at least they have a sense of humor.*

Already his background in medicine, biology and the media was reinforcing his suspicion that these children might regard themselves as superhuman . . .

"The next of us that I met was Tracy Coward, who made the silly mistake of trying to take away an engagement ring from one of her former school-fellows, and—"

"No, it wasn't!"

Everyone turned to see who had spoken, in a rough harsh voice. It was Bernie, emboldened by brandy. He was having difficulty hauling himself out of the armchair assigned to him, as though he had put on a vast amount of weight.

"No, it wasn't!" he barked again, and tried to set his glass down on a nearby table. A hand snatched it from him seconds before it would have crashed to the floor.

Steadying himself with an effort, he plunged on.

"The next was the one in Italy—the one whose mother wanted him because unless she had a kid expresso bongo she and her be-lov-ed brother would have lost her husband's family estates! The one who turned out better than the lot of you! The one you burnt alive because he would have been your rival!"

There was a sense of chill in the room, not due to the wintry weather outside.

Then David rose to his feet. "Bernie," he said softly, "you're sailing dangerously close to the wind."

There followed a chorus of agreement, while the children shifted menacingly on their chairs and cushions.

"I was planning to tell the story of GianMarco in due time. You think it should be now. Very well. What do you have to say about him?"

Defiantly: "That you got rid of him and his family in case he proved to be too much for you to cope with! Peter—Claudia—he arranged for the family's home to be burnt down!" Bernie rounded on them. "And this was a kid, a teenage kid, and his own half-brother! Not a whenzie cank like Thrower! A kid, the age of my own eldest son!"

He was shaking with passion, hands curled like claws before his chest.

"Crystal," David said softly, but not too softly to be heard, "make a note. Alcohol can minimize the impact."

"After continued exposure," Crystal suggested.

"Good point. Something to bear in mind. I wonder whether the invention of the still has something to do with the historical pattern. Mark that for further investigation."

"Will do."

For the first time Peter, still transfixed by the conflict between what he was hearing and how he was feeling, noticed that Crystal was wearing a computer-remote around her left wrist, like a calculator watch. She tapped several keys in rapid sequence, and there was a click from what until this moment had looked like a Louis XVI bureau.

Illusions, deceptions! Let this whole situation be un-unreal!

"However, in fact"—David turned commandingly to Bernie—"GianMarco was a failure because he had fallen beyond hope into the trap of the past. A born whenzie, as you might say. He had become convinced that the land his family owned belonged to his family. It does not! We—all of us—belong to the planet, and not the other way around!"

For the first time Peter felt a glimmering of the—the ideology? Perhaps the faith might be a better term?—that inspired this terrifying boy. If he was concerned to preserve the resources of the Earth, that was at least rational . . .

Rational? Or rationalized?

The question obtruded, because he remembered seeing a TV report: a family trapped in a burning house in Italy, their only son's name being GianMarco . . .

But he must compose himself to listen yet again. Ellen's caressing hand on his nape conveyed as much.

"I know Tracy doesn't want me to talk about her," David said. His voice had become suddenly light and clear, more like that of an ordinary teenage boy. "But, Trace, we all have to face the consequences of our actions! Sheila's managing it—"

For the first time one of the other children dared to interrupt. Again, had he not known that Ellen was perched on the arm of his chair, Peter could have imagined that the words were hers.

"I'm the only one who was such a bocky fool! And won't I wear the scars to prove it all my life?"

"Engagement ring," Claudia said softly. Unexpectedly, she seemed to have regained more of her self-possession than Peter. But then, she hadn't been hit with such a load of unwanted responsibility . . . During the next few seconds Peter hated her.

The emotion didn't last. It wasn't allowed to.

"I don't suppose I need to go into detail," David murmured. "For Tracy's sake, though, I ought to mention that it was because she was brought up by a couple who cared so much for trivial possessions, who indeed regarded her as a possession—"

"Dave, you're making her cry! Stop it!"

Peter could not tell who uttered the exclamation, but it was a boy, not a girl, who dropped at Tracy's side on the floor and put a comforting arm around her shoulders. David hesitated.

Ah! So he doesn't have total control! There is still hope!

The hope, though, was faint—and growing fainter . . .

David said, "Those responsible will be called to account. That's a promise, Trace. And there won't be any more scars."

"Except the ones the bocky canks have left where they don't show!"

The other children, even David, nodded in total unison. Peter could no longer see their eyes, so dark was the room as the storm beat at the windows, but he knew they were fixed on him—and Claudia—and Harry—and Alice . . . ? No, there was no sign of Alice. She seemed to have left the room, doubtless to prepare the lunch reference to which had so amused Claudia.

"Nonetheless," David said gratingly, "they will be called to account. If they are not, we shan't survive."

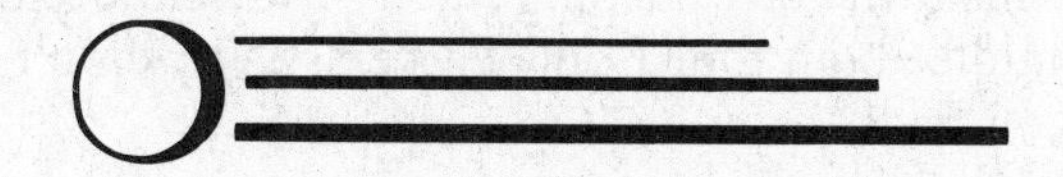

**B**efore Peter had time to do more than start worrying about that ominous statement, David resumed.

"Next I tracked down Mary, who is also still in two minds about what she did—she had her father sent to jail. However, she is gradually coming around to the majority view."

"Which is—?" Claudia demanded. Peter envied her relative self-control, achieved without the reassuring caresses Ellen was bestowing on his own nape.

"We cannot afford the luxury known as a conscience. The enemy we are up against certainly doesn't have one, so we are obliged to be absolutely rational. Cruel, if you like. People of good will, tolerant, liberal, whatever term you care to use, have always labored under a disadvantage. Those in power, those who want to hold on to power whatever the cost, have one ultimate recourse. If all else fails, they are prepared to kill. This is not available to pacifists. Mary, is there anything you want to add?"

The girl nodded. "Dad brought it on himself. I thought so in the first place; then I stopped being so sure; then I realized I'd been right the first time. Maybe it was rough justice, but it was justice. The bocky hypocrite!"

"That brings us to Pepita," David continued. "Our newest recruit. Daughter, as I mentioned, of Cynthia Hallam whom you knew only as Sindy, whose husband realized at once her child could not be his—he was yet another hypocrite—and threw her out. She became an alcoholic. It is a very sick society you brought us into, isn't it?"

Peter ignored the gibe. He was foggily trying to solve a mystery that had just occurred to him.

If Pepita is the latest recruit . . . I assumed Ellen! She can't ever have been here before! Does this mean that she isn't actually one of—of them? If she is, of course, it would explain a million things, up to and including Claudia and me last night . . .

"He's wondering why you haven't mentioned me yet," Ellen said.

*Grief! Perhaps she really can read my mind!*

"There's a reason for that," David said with a wry smile. "I found all the others. Ellen is the only one who found me. Though we'd never actually met before today. Isn't email wonderful?"

Peter, jerking forward on his chair, twisted around to stare accusingly at Ellen.

"Does this mean you knew these were"—he had to force the words out, had to hear his own voice shaping them—"my children? So what was all that taradiddle about four Louis Parkers? Why didn't you tell me the truth? If you had—"

"If I had," she cut in, "you'd have turned us into a newspaper story and a TV show, wouldn't you? And maybe a scientific article or two"—with a nod at Claudia. "That had to be prevented. By the way, we're obliged to you for recalling Louis Parker, even though you misled me and even David for a while. He turned out to be an invaluable red herring."

Awareness of the burden he carried in his genes was affecting Peter much as might the news that he had cancer. He wrung his hands.

"But, Ellen, I thought you—you loved me. You've told me you do, often enough."

Rising, withdrawing a pace, she gazed down at him. Seeing the iciness of her expression, he felt a pang as though something within his chest had been ripped apart.

"Love you?" she said. "After the way you treated my mother—after the years when you never bothered to get in touch, never sent me so much as a birthday card? Don't make me laugh! But what counts is that you love me. I know! You can't help it."

"I . . ."

Abruptly Peter was dumbstruck again, overwhelmed by the impact of fresh revelation. Watching keenly, David nodded.

"I was wondering how long it would take you to work out the nature of our gift. It's a very old one. It may have been quite widespread at one time—Dr. Morris, you had some thoughts about that, I gather, in connection with the way ancient peoples were drawn to work together on colossal projects like Stonehenge before there were kings and armies and police. It's an interesting suggestion, worth looking into.

"But of course it's always cropped out in certain individuals, and nowadays it's usually called charisma. The commonest of its manifestations, though, is when one person falls in love with another, and can't escape the attraction even when he or she is totally mismatched.

"Putting it bluntly: we have the power to make people love us. They can't avoid it. It deprives them of reason and judgment, it makes it impossible for them to accept that we are guilty of any kind of crime —at least so long as we are nearby and preferably able to touch them now and then. The pheromone seems to be absorbed quite efficiently through the skin, as well as the nasal passages.

"And, naturally, possessing such power, we intend to use it. Because we want to live. Do you understand? We don't want to be burned in a nuclear war—we don't want to be poisoned by the food we eat and the water we drink and the very air we breathe!"

His voice rose to a pitch of passionate intensity.

"We want to survive! And we aren't going to let anybody stop us!"

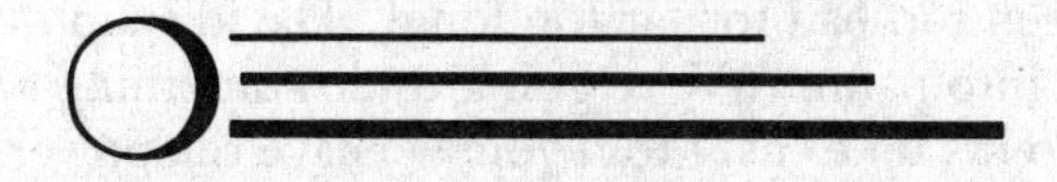

*You're watching TV Plus. Now for Newsframe.*

*Dr. Wallace Custer, who claimed to have evidence that the plastic from which most soft-drink bottles are made contains solvents that affect the intelligence and sanity of children, was found shot at his home in Berkshire this morning. Reports that he had committed suicide were discounted by his wife and family. However, the police—*

(All sets tuned to that channel went dead. Later it transpired that the Throwers had made good their threat to close the station down. With a bomb.)

There followed a pause more dreadful than any that had gone before. Peter's tongue felt like a blanket in his mouth, but somehow he contrived to speak.

"Use your power? For things like what you did to General Thrower?"

David shrugged. "They should not be necessary too often—though it went off very well for a first attempt, hmm?"

"But—"

Suddenly the boy was stern. "Don't tell us we should have been more merciful! He's been eager to consign people to that sort of hell all his life. He resigned as deputy C-in-C of NATO because he didn't like his precious nuclear toys being taken away. *You* know that. If he'd been allowed to carry on, the chances are excellent that he'd have become a dictator, Hitler-style. I've modeled it. All it would take is a fifty percent increase in crime, unemployment and bankruptcies. And the trends are there."

"But what else are you planning to do?" Peter whimpered. "You said something about salvation—"

"I'm glad you noticed." Now David's tone was ironical.

"I don't see—"

Abruptly the boy jumped to his feet and walked across the room to stare out of one of the tall half-curtained windows at the teeming rain.

He said over his shoulder, "Tell me, Mr. Levin, when did you last open a newspaper or switch on the TV news without being told about a political crisis, or an economic collapse, or an ecological disaster? Or a war, or starvation, or people being driven from their lands and homes?"

"Well, of course the news—"

"The news has been too bad for far too long!" David spun on his heel and pounded fist into palm. "We're going to do something about it! Nobody else can, so it's up to us. I told you: we have the power and we intend to use it. It'll take a while to bring it under fully conscious control, but some of us are pretty good at that already, so there's no doubt it can be done."

"Just you kids?" Claudia said incredulously. "Just you dozen kids?"

"Don't underestimate us. In a group, we're irresistible. We've proved that. General Thrower took about five minutes to decide that the thing he wanted most, right now, was to dismiss his bodyguards and come with us."

He hesitated, then added with a renewal of his wry smile, "Besides, it won't always be 'just a dozen.' Peter made you pregnant last night."

"*What?*" Claudia leapt to her feet. "How in hell's name can you possibly know that?"

"I've been keeping track of the dates when you visited us during your period," Ellen said composedly. "The timing is precisely right. And Peter fucked you twice. I was listening."

"I'll get an abortion! Or the 'morning-after' pill!"

"Oh no you won't," David said. "You already love your child. As much as you love us. Because it will be one of us."

Of a sudden the odor that had mingled with the smell of roasted meat when they first arrived in the house, which they had stopped noticing thanks to olfactory overload, redoubled in intensity. Peter shivered anew, and this time found he could not stop. He went on shaking, *shaking.*

"I . . ." Closing her eyes, pressing her hands against her temples, Claudia swayed. One of the boys helped her to resume her seat.

"Are you still in any doubt, Dad?" David murmured. "Oh, I called you 'Mr. Levin' just now, didn't I? Well, I think we ought to forget about that, and even about the use of Dad. After all, very shortly half of us are going to be on extremely intimate terms with you."

Peter's mind had wandered down an alleyway of the imagination, at the ends of whose forking branches stood small but menacing bands of children, his children, waiting to waylay the VIP he and other reporters were accompanying: a cabinet minister, an ambassador, the chairman of a bank, the managing director of an arms company, the spokesman for a government-in-exile . . . No. Not menacing. Welcoming. Ready, and able, to change their minds.

Or burn them alive.

*Surely some people must be immune . . . ?*

"Didn't you hear what I said?" David snapped.

*What did I miss? Something about "intimate terms"—Oh, my God. He can't mean it. How can he possibly mean it?*

Frantic counterarguments sprang to mind—*inbreeding, imbecility, why me and not the boys?*—but he was unable to utter them. David's words were inexorable.

"It has to be you to start with. I haven't yet pinned down the gene or genes involved, though I'm working on it, of course. The power is fully expressed in us, yet you don't seem to possess more than a slight trace, a commonplace sort of personal charm, so one can only assume a connection with your inheritance on your mother's side. I plan to look into that later. But since every last one of us has the power, and we need to increase our numbers as fast as possible, we'll have to start with you. Meantime, of course, we boys will play our part. There won't be any lack of willing women, as I can personally testify . . . Speaking of which," he added maliciously, "doesn't it turn you on, the prospect of making love with so many under-age girls? They're all pretty, they're all healthy, they all have lovely figures—"

"Shut up!" Peter exploded. "I won't have any part of it!"

"That's where you're wrong," Ellen said, rising from beside him. Stepping to the center of the floor with the slinky elegance of a professional stripper, she writhed her sweater from around her torso, tugged it clear of her hair, tossed it aside. Cupping her small bare shapely breasts, firming her nipples between forefinger and thumb, she leaned first one and then the other toward what was suddenly her father's eager mouth. A fraction of an inch from his lips, she snatched herself out of range.

But Peter had hardened on the instant. How quickly was

conspicuous from his discomfort. The other children burst into cruel laughter.

Yet at the same time he felt as though, at long last, he had met the woman of his youthful dreams, the one whose name he had used as a key to his computer passwords . . .

Sharing the general mirth at least to the extent of a broad grin, David said, "I thought so . . . Well, in fact, of course, you won't have the chance to actually screw your daughters. They're not inclined to get next to anyone who cares as little as you did about the fate of his offspring. Still, in a sense it will be quite like old times, won't it? I don't know what they used to arouse you at Chinn-Wilkinson, but given the impact Ellen just demonstrated it shouldn't be too hard for the girls to make you—what did they say in the Bible about Onan? Ah, yes—'spill your seed' as often as we require it!"

Indeed, to Peter's shame and sick dismay, his penis was throbbing in his pants against his will . . .

With indescribable horror he looked from each to other of his children.

And felt wave on wave of uncontrollable, intolerable *love.*

Launching one last desperate appeal for help, he turned to Claudia. Tears were trickling down her cheeks. Nonetheless she managed to force out defiant words.

"Have you asked the girls how they like the idea of being turned into baby-minders at their age?"

"That doesn't enter into it," David sighed. "Thanks to Bernie, we've found an expert willing to transplant fetuses as soon as they're viable—including yours, of course; you won't have to carry it to term. So the girls can start again every eight weeks, which they welcome because it means their power won't be weakened by having periods. I believe you've met the person I'm talking about: Dr. Ada Grant? She says there'll be plenty of takers because so many men are infertile nowadays owing to environmental poisons . . . You might say that we plan to reproduce like cuckoos, if at a faster rate. I only hope it may be fast *enough!*"

For some reason that reference to cuckoos struck Peter as incredibly funny. He strove to master his reaction, and failed as completely as he had failed to control his—now cold, now sticky-wet—ejaculation.

The door of the drawing room swung wide. Alice entered. "If you lot have finished," she said brightly, "lunch is ready—Why, what on earth is wrong?"

And stood there, baffled, at a loss to understand why one of their guests was weeping silently and the other lost in paroxysm after paroxysm of hysterical laughter.

*—South Petherton*
*February-June 1987*

# The Tides of Time

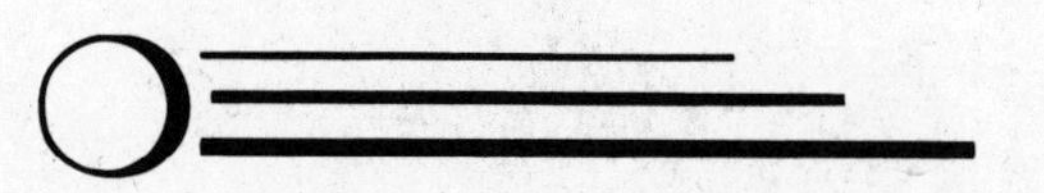

# Prologue

*The night when it was over was the longest of the year . . . and by far the longest of his life. He carried his burden of sorrow to the forepeak of the island, where those who had come to hold a wake with him dug a fire pit after the ancient manner, sprinkling on seawater and adding fragrant herbs before they covered it and lit the wood.*

*They whiled away the darkest hours with songs and tales. He did not know how to join in, nor was he invited to.*

*The eastern sky grew pale. They broached a wineskin and with ceremony circulated it to all save him. It made no odds; he was in no mood to drink. Then silence fell, and all eyes turned to the horizon.*

*When once again they'd watched the oldest miracle, the death and re-birth of the light, they ritually shared the meal, but offered nothing to the widower. Him they left solitary with his grief—the powerless, the unfulfilled, the man whose life was incomplete, still at the mercy of more suffering.*

*Thus it had been in olden days. Thus it would have to be again next year.*

*On whatsoever planet of the cosmos.*

# PART ONE

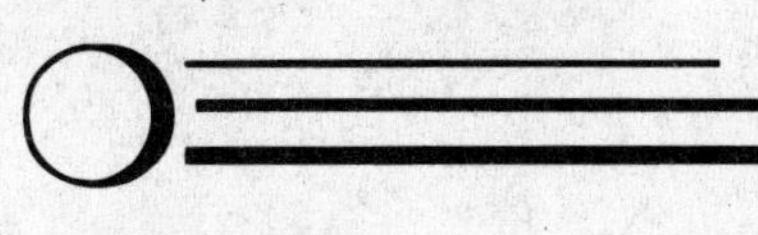

*THE EXHIBIT*
*is huge and hollow, made of metal, pitted and scarred.*
*It has been to somewhere that cannot exist*

*THE MONTH*
*is April*

*THE NAME*
*is Suleyman*

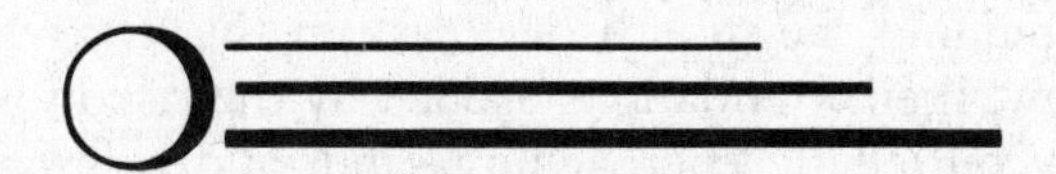

After weeks of travel to strange and unfamiliar places—but they were adapted to that, better than anybody, better than everybody—on a spring evening when the air was turning from warm to chill and the sea from blue to gray thanks to the shadow of a thunderstorm, they came to an island which had nearly the shape of a sphinx. Brownish, flecked with sparse vegetation but innocent of trees, it reared broad haunches high above the water, with beaches on its eastern and western flanks and another, the smallest, between two rocky outcrops that modeled forelimbs underneath its south-turned chin.

Perhaps it had a name. Boat could not inform them if so; like most maps, hers were out of date or incomplete, and they had forbidden her to interrogate any satellites.

For a long while Gene surveyed it frowning from her bow, stretching each of his lean dark limbs in turn.

At length he said, "I don't much like the look of it."

But that was hardly surprising. He distrusted islands. He was in the habit of insisting that his ancestors on both sides had been of continental stock—though how he, an orphan, could be certain was a mystery—and had bequeathed him the subconscious conviction that the whole universe was, or ought to be, a single landmass which a tribe could walk across. Supposedly this was what accounted for . . .

But they had a tacit bargain not to speak of such matters. Besides, Stacy's attitude was opposite to his, which meant one theory or the other must be wrong.

For the moment she was disinclined to pursue the matter, anyway. She contented herself with saying, "I think it might be advisable to land. Water's all very well while it's calm, but when the storm breaks . . ."

"I guess you're right," sighed Gene, and instructed Boat to make for shore.

Programmed to avoid habitation so far as possible, she chose the beach between the sphinx's paws, for there were traces of human activity on both the others: abandoned shacks, a caïque moored to a post now lower than its bow, in the restive water anchored nets that had trapped empty barrels, mostly of plastic but a few of wood.

And this third one was not devoid of people's leavings, either. As they drew closer, Gene and Stacy made out concrete beams, square, grayish white, patched with red and brown smears. Some still composed an archway extending the mouth of a cave in the living rock; many more were askew, their foundations eroded by the rise in water level; some lay partly buried by encroaching sand, and a few were completely submerged.

Neither of them spoke again until Boat touched bottom and extended her forward gangplank. Then, tense and nervous as ever, Gene strode to its end. He stared about him first, then upward at the overhang of the sphinx's jaw, and stood irresolute.

Following more slowly, but more composed, Stacy passed him and set foot on the nearest of the fallen columns. Its concrete was dissolving under the onslaught of salt water, assisted by borer worms and tenacious weed. Halting, she studied those of its counterparts which were still erect enough to be regarded as pillars and lintels.

Eventually she said, "It's a temple of Ares."

"Who?"

"God of war."

"Ridiculous! This is far too—"

She cut him short impatiently. "Not classical, naturally! But he's always with us . . . Boat!"

The vessel responded more readily to her than him; that had been a source of friction during their journey. "Yes, Anastasia?" she answered in her clear light voice.

"What is this place? It looks like a twentieth century strongpoint —more likely World War II than I."

"The chances are that you're correct, but I have no data on its origin."

"So much forgotten and so much to know . . ." murmured Stacy.

But she was forever saying things of that kind, and Gene paid no heed. Eyeing the impending storm, he reminded her, "You suggested we ought to take shelter."

She turned slowly through half a circle. Above her the jutting chin of the sphinx was bearded with drying rootlets hung in air: plants which had contrived to establish themselves in cracks and crevices were falling from their own excessive growth. To either side, the oblong relics of an ancient conflict recalled an age when humanity too seemed to face no greater threat to its survival than those entailed by competition with itself. The little headlands were stark and bare; the shore was narrow and much scarred with rocks; but near the entrance of the concrete archway tufts of saltgrass grew and the yellow-gray of sand changed to the brown of fertile earth.

She said at last, "You can't deny we'd be better off ashore during a gale. Indeed, this may perhaps . . ."

Her last words trailed away. Impatient, he prompted her.

"Perhaps what?"

"Be the right place." She straightened abruptly, smiling as she shook back her long hair. They had discarded clothing as soon as the climate permitted. It seemed improper to be clad on this shared journey into the unknown inasmuch as they had been obliged to set out naked on those they had undertaken separately. Now she was tanned overall, as though attempting to share his blackness. Yet they had never touched each other save by unintention . . .

Her mention of "the right place" signified nothing to him, except that she claimed to feel at home among these archipelagoes. Well, this was more her heritage than his, and for tonight he could pretend to himself that they were on the seashore of a proper landmass . . . insofar as any such remained. He said gruffly, "Boat, give us what we need to put up here."

The craft did not react at once. Instead, her scanners swiveled back and forth, and the air tautened with the barely sensed hum of ultrasonics. Also there was bubbling near her stern as water was sucked in for sampling.

Meantime Stacy wandered off to examine the rusty smears on the other concrete columns. Watching her, Gene did not at first register how long the delay was growing.

Then, with a start, he saw that Boat was emitting items he would never have expected: first, digging tools and a great roll of net; then something in bags—fertilizer!

Dismayed, he realized his order had been much too general, and countermanded it. She stopped work at once.

"What's wrong?" Stacy called, glancing toward the storm. It was already close enough for them to see how it was shattering the water into jagged fragments.

Fuming, Gene forced out, "This damned boat—!"

"She's a splendid boat, and I won't hear otherwise!" Stacy cut in, striding back. The pattern made by her nipples, moving in counterpoint with her hips, registered on Gene's awareness as the graph of a hugely subtle equation. Sometimes he thought there must be something dreadfully wrong with him. Other times he was certain there must be something utterly, even terrifyingly, right, and with her too, in view of what had happened to them both . . . but he had never quite managed to work out what.

"Look!" he challenged her. "Just look!" And pointed out the way Boat's resources were being wasted on an overnight campsite.

After a thoughtful pause, however, all Stacy said was—and not to him—"Amend! Supplies for supper and breakfast, beds and toilet gear will be enough."

Boat withdrew the fertilizer, tools and nets at once, to be recycled, but she was tired, and the light she depended on to run her was fading fast. Besides, the sun was dimmer than it had been when she was built. By the time she had delivered hotbeds, food, and the rest of what Stacy had reduced the order to, the rain came sprinkling down and both of them were running with wet before they managed to take refuge under the ancient archway. Access to the cave beyond proved to be blocked by a fallen boulder, but there was plenty of shelter for them and their belongings. The beds were badly underpowered, owing to Boat's depleted energy level, but fortunately Stacy's reference to "toilet gear" had been old-fashioned enough to imply towels, and two had been produced from store in sealed bags.

As well as other necessaries, Boat had supplied a coldlight, being programmed not to overlook how much human beings prize their oldest luxury, the theft of extra waking hours from darkness. Looking for a ledge to stand it on, Gene caught sight of something brightly colored on the ground, and picked it up. Torn and stained, it proved to be an advertising leaflet for a travel agency, replete with pictures of vanished beaches and holidaymakers now long dead. He sighed and let it fall—then retrieved it, thinking it might come in handy if he had to light a fire.

By the lamp's pale glow he was examining without enthusiasm what had been issued to them as suitable provisions—mainly, a self-heating pack containing a stew of forced vegetables with rice, though at least there was also a self-chilling bottle of white wine—when Stacy said unexpectedly, "Gene, I'm not used to this, and my arms are getting tired. Could you finish drying my hair, please?"

He reacted with astonishment, for she had never asked a personal favor of him before, let alone admitted physical weakness. But he gave a shrug and complied, kneeling behind her as she tilted back her head.

Outside, the first lightning struck, and thunder rolled. It was not truly cold in their artificial cave, yet age-old instinct decreed it should have been; Gene felt a shiver tremble down his spine.

There was a certain satisfaction in rubbing the long tresses of Stacy's hair between the doubled layers of the towel. The cloth bore an aroma which no doubt was factory-implanted, yet touched another chord of memory and made him think of linen wind-dried in a garden fragrant with flowers and herbs. He fought away from the association because it was personal and superficial, inasmuch as those of his ancestors whom he chose to identify with had not been rich enough to waste ground on plants they couldn't eat or wear. Nor, come to that, would they have known flax.

Yet, though he had done his best to disown them, some of his progenitors must have been European, and they at least could have been acquainted with such things . . .

He reapplied himself to his task with vigor, and shortly Stacy pronounced herself satisfied and they turned to their meal. Meantime Boat, keeping station just offshore, tight-beamed them music of a kind she judged appropriate. In view of the region they had come to, it consisted of long and wailing lines with no fixed scale Gene could discern, although—like the scent on the towels—it gave him the annoying impression that he should have known much more about its origins. Stacy, at least, seemed to appreciate what was offered, food and sound alike.

Three hours after nightfall the storm attained such a pitch that Boat felt obliged to retreat to open water, and her music faded. They lay down in the artificial twilight, separated by the remnants of their repast, together but alone, with nothing to listen to save the rain as it pelted on the roof and traced its way toward the ground and then the sea.

It was time for Stacy to ask the inevitable question. She postponed it until he dared to hope that for once she might repress it altogether. No such luck; out it came.

"Do you think they know where we are tonight?"

The sigh he greeted the words with was near a groan, but he controlled himself.

"Sure they do. We're on a long leash, that's all."

"But in weather like this—!" She was pleading for reassurance. "Not even the newest satellites can see through storm clouds!"

"I'm convinced they still have a trace on Boat."

"We've searched her stem to stern and disabled everything we could find! . . ." But her voice trailed away. She had said that before, and every time he had simply echoed her last four words. There was too much truth in that repetition for either of them to consider arguing about it anymore. Once more she lay quiet, while Gene, lulled by the pattering rain, drifted to the edge of sleep.

Then, unprecedentedly, Stacy spoke anew.

"I can't stop thinking about poor Suleyman, you know. Why don't you tell me what became of him?"

Gene rose on one elbow and blinked at her, uncomprehending. After a pause he said, "I don't know what you mean. How could anybody do that?"

"No, no!" She too sat up, brushing aside her hair. "I want to be told—I suppose I want to be told . . . Oh, never mind. Sorry." And lay down again.

But he was fully reawakened now, thanks to mention of that name. He said obstinately, "What did you *mean?*"

"I—I don't know. And yet I think . . . Put out the light, will you? Otherwise I'll never get to sleep."

Shrugging, he made a long arm and obeyed. She spoke next time in total darkness.

"Tell me what would have been right to happen to him."

Abruptly it dawned on him what she was driving at. Nonetheless for a while longer he lay confused, sorting ideas in his mind like a meteor sweeper hunting through a thousand kilometers of tangled nets in search of a profitable catch. The rain beat down harder yet; the rushing of water grew to a crescendo, as though the universe were again about to dissolve around them. But he could accept, at this time, in this place, that it would not.

Moreover, in a sense, he had shared ancestors with Suleyman; at any rate, his and his forebears might well have been cousins in Islam, albeit their descendants had followed different paths. Therefore, to his own surprise, he found words forming patterns, which he uttered. He said, "Oh yes! I know the proper way to end *his* story.

"There was a time when he got where he was meant to go. You never met him, any more than I did, but I'm sure you know as much about him as I do. Am I not right to view him as a person caught in conflict?"

For a second he was tempted to include, "Like you and me!"—but overcame the impulse.

"Rejecting the religion his family raised him in, with its resignation to the will of God, he must have been a most unhappy man, despite what we were told about his brilliance with computers. For anybody who's been accustomed to certainty, then robbed of it, must it not be a cruel doom to have to reinvent the destiny of mind?"

She murmured something, possibly agreement. Encouraged, he went on.

"At the end of his long journey, he found a world of quiet halls and even lights. It had no name, the place he came to, for it wasn't necessary, and there were no people either, for fragile flesh and blood were obsolete. There was still air, however, and it vibrated ceaselessly with the music of machines which, in total dedication to the principles of logic, were attempting to deduce the nature and purpose of the universe.

"As a result of Suleyman's intrusion, flaws appeared. How could a man from our discordant planet match such rhythm, such subtle harmony, elaborated over countless centuries? For some considerable while he wished he could run away, being afraid of how he jarred, how his mere presence broke the even tenor of this place.

"But the grave and wise machines he fell among—had they been human, I could see them tall and robed and sometimes bearded—they were aware of the existence of external worlds . . . and of the past. They gave him food, and it was good to eat, though they themselves absorbed raw energy. Speech, too, had long been unnecessary to them, yet they addressed him in courteous experimental phrases deduced from their inspection of him and their knowledge of the cosmos, and very soon he grew acquainted with the fashion of things there. His manners came to match the world he fell on; his questions no longer betrayed his shameful ignorance. He learned, and in the learning found fulfillment. There was after all no grand divide between the way a flawless mechanism worked, and the reality which had so often disappointed him. There couldn't be, if these machines had set themselves the same task as humanity and believed they stood a better chance of arriving at their goal."

He paused, pondering what to say next because he was so taken aback by his own insight, and she exclaimed, "Go on! Go on for pity's sake!"

Mustering the shreds of his imagination, he continued.

"If it could be said, it would be said that such a place was too perfect for anybody who was—old?—enough to recall a flawed world like our own. The end of Suleyman's tale has to be both tragic and triumphant."

"Explain! Explain!"

"It must consist in recognition of his plight. It must consist in his admission that the world he came to was already doomed by his existence. Because of him, its planned perfection was deranged. No matter how he struggled to adapt, the machines would thereafter recall as actual knowledge an imperfection that had previously been theory. They were forbidden to deceive themselves."

"So sad! So sad!" she whispered, her tone verging on a sob. "The perfection sought by Suleyman, then, was—"

"It was something we cannot create, we who are creatures. It was something he had sought in vain in our creations, which are necessarily less perfect than their makers. No more was it to be found on the world he traveled to. Nor anywhere."

"Perhaps because he was searching in the wrong way?"

"Conceivably." Gene fought a yawn and lost. "But as to what the right one is, or if there is one—!"

"Is there a maker, do you think?"

"We are makers," he said stonily. "We have to be."

"Yes . . . Yes. I guess so. There's no one else. At least he found his place, as we've found ours . . . There's something wrong with this bed. Gene, let me lie with you. I'm cold. I'm very cold."

It was the first time. In the morning the weather was fine again. But there had been something magical about the storm.

# PART TWO

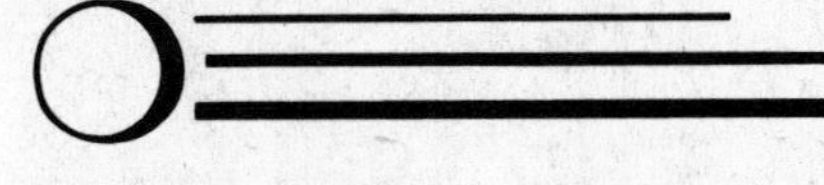

*THE EXHIBIT*
*is a sheet of tattered paper bearing colored pictures. It reflects a world that has vanished forever*

*THE MONTH*
*is May*

*THE NAME*
*is Ingrid*

**W**hen Gene awoke, he was alarmed to discover that their rented cabin cruiser was no longer safely beached; one of her mooring cables had parted. But he must have made a good job of securing the other, for there she lay bobbing in early sunlight, sleek and white among gentle ripples. He hastened to fetch his binoculars and inspect her right away, to see if the storm had damaged her, but she bore no apparent trace of the ordeal she had undergone bar the fact that some paint had been scraped from her cutwater and the neatly lettered name bestowed by her mocking owner—*Fairweather Friend*—was almost illegible.

Well, so long as no harm had been sustained to her planking . . . But he'd better make certain. Doubtless she was insured; she remained, however, their only means of getting away from this isolated spot without attracting attention.

Stacy was still asleep. He reached a decision. After glancing around to confirm there was no one in sight, he scrambled down the three or four rocky meters to the beach, discarded the shorts and sandals he had pulled on, and waded out to the boat. He reached her with the water only chest-high.

Leaving dripmarks all over the deck and the cabin carpet, he confirmed that they had been amazingly lucky; her hull was intact. He was humming when he reemerged from below, and looking forward to breakfast.

It was a complete shock when he heard someone hail him from close by.

Spinning around, hands reflexively flying to cover his nudity, he saw a man about his own age, with ginger hair and freckles, leaning on the after gunwale and grinning at him. He wore a red shirt and there was a diver's watch on his left arm. He stood casually balanced in a rocking rowboat, on whose after thwart sat another, much older man, face lined and swarthy above a black denim smock. Incongruously, the latter sported gold-rimmed sunglasses.

"Don't worry about your lack of pants," the freckled man said. "We've had to get used to people in the raw since tourists started to invade us. Even my father-in-law—old Stavros here—is resigned to it now, like the other locals, though I'm not so sure about our *papa* . . . I'm Milo Hamilton, by the way, and the reason I'm Greek with a Scots name goes back to a British soldier who fell in love with my grandmother and settled here because it reminded him of the Hebridean island he was born on but with better weather and better cooking." His grin grew wider than ever.

"Well—ah—come aboard!" Gene suggested, wondering how he could reach at least a towel if they accepted.

"Thanks, but no thanks; we're on an errand. We just caught sight of you and thought we'd better check that you rode out the storm okay. Since we find you in good shape, we'll be on our way. Oh, I should have said: you can buy bread and wine and stuff at Oragalia Port"—pointing in the direction of the hamlet on the eastern beach—"and there's a track across the headland if you care to make it on foot. I keep the taverna, by the way. Just ask for me if you need help."

He was about to resume his thwart and oars with the ease of one accustomed to the sea, when Gene said hastily, "Just a moment! You mentioned tourists. Uh . . . Are we likely to be bothered by them?"

Milo favored him with a sweeping glance that said, as plain as words, "Aren't you pretty much a tourist yourself?" But he kept his poise, and said aloud: "Don't know what you mean by bothered! I know what I mean by it—gangs of 'em from all the cold northern countries, not a one polite enough to learn a word of the local language, demanding the same kind of food they're used to at home, getting falling-down drunk because they find the wine so cheap here, throwing up all over my floor . . . It's too early in the season for the worst of them, though. You may find a few kids wandering this way, but all they want to do is peel off, swim and laze around. They're pretty harmless, though if I were you I'd keep an eye on my more valuable belongings. They have been known to claim the world owes them a living . . . *Endaxi, Stavro—piyainoumé!*"

Gene watched the boat depart with mixed feelings. Eventually, however, he gave a shrug and waded back to shore.

When he regained their shelter, this relic of war well above sea level which they had so providentially spotted last night with both their radio and their sonar out, Stacy was sitting up with her half of the sleeping bag clutched around her knees, her dark and long-lashed eyes ajar with worry.

"I heard you talking to someone!" she exclaimed.

Soothing, he explained. "I went to make sure the *Friend* was okay after the storm, and she is. Someone in a passing rowboat spotted her and came to find out if we were in any trouble. Nice guy—owns the local taverna. Said to call on him for anything we need."

But Stacy was still haunted by suspicion. "Are you sure?" she countered.

"Sure he owns the taverna? Well, until I see him behind the bar—"

"Stuff it, will you? You know damned well what I mean!" She scrambled out of the bag and seized her jeans and panties, drawing them on in a succession of panicky jerks, then donned a tee shirt and combed loose her sleek black hair with her fingers.

He made to embrace her, but she pushed him away. "I'm full to bursting! Is there any place I can go?"

"Try the sea," he said, turning aside with a shrug. "You needn't have worried about getting dressed, incidentally. The guy said the locals are used to people in the altogether."

"What? You mean we've found our way to—?"

"Yes, damn it! There are tourists here! Like us!"

For a moment he expected her to snap back at him; instead, she thrust her feet into her sandals and made for the entrance.

"What the hell," she said despondently. "We've screwed up this planet past hope of recovery. Any extra mess of mine won't make much difference."

"At least it's biodegradable!" he chaffed. But she had hurried out of earshot.

During her absence, he occupied himself in preparing breakfast. Their bread was stale, but still edible, and there remained a hunk of cheese and plenty of olives. Also there was enough water for coffee, so he lit their little butane stove and hunted out the rest of their stock of sugar and powdered milk.

Meantime, he was silently cursing himself. What in the world had persuaded him to accept Stacy's view that it was easier to elude pursuit among islands, where the arrival of anybody was an event, let alone a couple like themselves, than on a good solid continent with all its means of emergency escape, by air or car or train or even on foot?

Well, he was—they were—here today. And he was damned if he

was going to let himself imagine, as she appeared to, a threat of discovery around every corner!

By the time Stacy returned, without having yielded to the temptation of a swim, he had sliced the bread and cheese and laid it on plastic plates, together with a twisted brown-paper cone containing the olives. She sat down facing him and ate without speaking until only a single olive remained.

"Want it?" she said then.

"You have it."

"That means you want it."

Traveling with this woman seemed to be an endless succession of such petty disputations. Right now he was relaxed enough to counter her.

"It means I'd like it. But so would you, and I don't want it enough to deprive you."

"Oh, all this over one measly olive!" she exclaimed, and picked up the oily paper as though to throw it away, and the olive with it. He caught her arm.

"Let go of me!"

"No, wait. I just had a great idea. Pass me a knife."

Which taking ceremoniously, he used to halve the wrinkled black ovoid.

Seeing it laid out, neatly dissected, on his pale palm, she bit her lip, then grinned, then laughed outright and ate her half. Afterward, growing serious again, she said, "If we're going to hide out here for a while, we'll need more provisions."

"We can buy them in Milo's village—Just a moment! Are we going to stick around? Who said we were?"

She shrugged, leaning back against the rough concrete wall of their temporary home.

"I thought you wanted me to take your word concerning this character in a rowboat who 'just happened' to spot us. Also the *Friend* is low on fuel, right?"

Gene drew a deep breath. Adjusting to these total reversals of her attitude was something he should by now have grown accustomed to, yet he still found it hard.

"Tell me," he invited cautiously, "why you think we ought to stay here, even for a day or two, when normally you're convinced there are spies everywhere."

"Oh, yes, I know!" she flared. "You want a continent behind you! But you were raised on one which doesn't have national frontiers like mine, with passport officers and customs searches at every step you take! You don't regard islands as being real, do you? And I quote! To hell with you and your 'ancestors of continental stock!' *My* subconscious feeling of security consists in having lots of nice deep water around me, like a moat!"

Gene struggled to stay calm. He said in his mildest tone, "Fine, fine! You think it's advisable to stay here. I only asked you to spell out why."

His reasonableness confounded her for a moment. Then she said, "Anyway, I don't suppose an island like this has many phones, so rumors about our presence could take a long while to spread."

"There must be a radiophone at least—" he began.

"I said *many!* Who'd lay phone cables for a place like this? Think it's infested with highly paid reporters?"

"Well, if there's a tourist trade—" He had it in mind to beat her to the possibility of mainland newspapers circulating here, or pictures of her, if not him, being shown on TV. Mistaking his intention, she cut him short.

"Too bad if one of the visitors falls ill, or his company goes broke or what the hell! Actually"—chuckling into yet another of her swift and unpredictable changes of mood—"I can just picture what would happen. Who would he be? A Dutchman or a Dane, most likely, a not quite successful sort of self-employed businessman, proud of the fact he speaks one foreign language and unprepared to learn a second, here with his wife and teenage children because they persuaded him that islands like this are the fashion now for holidays, but hating every moment, and suddenly overcome in the middle of the night by the conviction that he's about to lose a million gulden. Or whatever."

The detail of her vision was infectious; it reminded Gene of the story she'd insisted on him telling her about—Whom had it been about? An old friend, or someone who had not exactly been a friend . . . He strove to recapture it. But it proved elusive as a dream.

Maybe that was what it had been. Certainly its essence seemed unreal in the sober light of morning. He applied himself to elaborating her brief fantasy, saying, "Why, yes, of course! He'd go to the post office—if they have such a thing here—and he'd make himself misunderstood in his two wrong languages and he'd get more and more panicky, and eventually his son, or better his daughter, who'd have struck up an acquaintance with one of the locals, would come to him and say soothingly, 'Dad, they only have telephone service on Mondays and Fridays, so why don't you sit on the beach with us till then?' And—"

But she had lost interest, rousing herself to collect their plates and the few crusts of bread they had left.

"Are there any seagulls I can throw the scraps to?"

"No gulls," he said. He remembered that distinctly.

"Or other birds?"

"I didn't see any," he admitted, and for some reason felt uncomfortable.

"I'll bury them, then. The ground looks as though it could do with a bit of humus. Let's go and buy more food and wine, and fill the water bottle. Then we can spend a lazy day by ourselves, swimming and lying in the sun."

"We may not be alone," Gene muttered, and repeated what Milo had said.

"Well—so? The world belongs to all of us."

Half an hour ago she had seemed terrified by his chance encounter with Milo. Now she appeared to have forgotten all about the risk of their being recognized. Her mind must be spinning like a weather-vane. Resignedly, Gene hauled himself to his feet.

"That's as may be! But there are lots of things aboard the *Friend* which we have no right to redistribute to strangers! I'll make her secure. Back in a minute!"

When he returned she was naked again, except for panties, and kneeling in front of the bag of clothes she had brought ashore, pondering what to change into. This, he knew, was a process not to be interrupted. Waiting patiently, he noticed things on the ground which had not been there earlier: five or six tarnished brass shell cases, probably spent by an automatic rifle.

"Where did these come from?" he inquired curiously.

"Oh, I found them while I was burying the rubbish. The beach is littered with them, just below the surface . . . Will this do, do you think?" She rose, holding up before her a beige linen minidress.

"Perfectly," he said. "But then you know my view: you look gorgeous in anything, or nothing. Especially nothing."

She pulled a face at him and drew the exiguous garment over her head; it reached barely halfway down her thighs. Thrusting her feet into sandals, and picking up a woven reed bag to hold their purchases, she invited him with a gesture to lead her to the path across the headland which Milo had pointed out. In burning heat, although the sun was less than halfway to the zenith, they picked their way among pebbles washed bare by last night's rain, slipping occasionally on mud not yet dried out. The low sharp branches of surrounding shrubs attacked their calves, and insects buzzed in search of the rare blue flowers, and still one thing was missing. Stacy said at last, when they paused for breath at the crest of the track, "You're right. There are no birds."

"No. Just us."

"*Not* just us," she contradicted, pointing. The path at this point followed a cliff edge, and had brought them into sight of a handsome yacht, no doubt heading toward the little port for which they too were bound, with ten or a dozen passengers gathered along her rail, and several crew. At such a distance it was impossible to discern what flag she flew; fortunately, Stacy was too preoccupied to worry about her provenance.

"An island having people, that lacks birds . . ." She gazed down, shielding her eyes against the sun.

"They made the wrong choice."

"What do you mean?" She drew back and stared at him.

"Birds. That was the way the reptiles chose—the dinosaurs. They could have been intelligent, like us. I saw it on TV. Instead they decided on another course. They took to the air. And we *over*took them." Gene gave a forced laugh to show he wasn't altogether serious.

But she accepted his words at their face value. Sounding troubled, she said, "You mean the world's resources could have been exhausted long ago, if something hadn't happened to prevent the dinosaurs from digging coal."

Taken by her fancy, as in the case of the imaginary pompous Dutchman, Gene nodded.

"Or drilling for oil, mining uranium, and come to that launching into space. We aren't so special; it might have happened long ago."

"Then what would this island have been like? Would it have been here at all?" Turning, she surveyed it; from here they could not see it whole by any means, but this eastern side was webbed with rocky ridges and notched to form little sandy inlets. All but one of those in view were specked with tents like multicolored fungi: spaced far apart as yet, but presaging a later richer crop.

"Ask a geologist; I'm not one. Shall we move on?"

"Yes, I guess so . . ." She handed him the bag, which, even empty, was a burden in this heat, and scrambled onward down the narrow path.

Shortly they reached the village, and found the yacht had cast anchor in its bay and discharged its passengers. There were too few of them to constitute a crowd, yet they gave the impression of an invading horde. They were not in competition with Gene and Stacy as they went about their business of buying bread, fish and fruit, tomatoes and wine and oil, enough to last the day, but complained loudly about the lack of souvenir shops and the difficulty of finding good vantage points to take a photo from. Their cameras reawakened Stacy's fears and made her reluctant to consider Gene's suggestion of a drink at the taverna before returning, though both were thirsty.

"Suppose—!" she whispered.

"Suppose what? One of this lot is a *paparazzo* with a line to the Italian scandal sheets? Out of the question! Besides, in a place like this it's worth being on good terms with the guy who runs the bar. And you did say you fancied the idea of staying here for a while."

"Oh, all right. I'm not ashamed of what we've done."

Ashamed? Well, maybe not. Terrified, though, half the time at least . . . Gene put his arm around her and felt her trembling. But there was no help for that.

The taverna was not hard to locate, for apart from the little church it was the largest soundest building; most of the others were tumble-down or ramshackle. Before they reached it, however, it was beset by the yacht's passengers, shouting orders—none of them in Greek—and complaining about the slowness of the service.

But Gene was sufficiently out of the ordinary for Milo to pay them special attention when they sat down. Passing with a grimace, he muttered, "The season's started early—maybe with you! I should have known! Wine and *mezedes?* On the way!" And to someone else: "*Oriste*—coming!"

Stacy touched her companion's arm. "Gene, I think we ought to get away from here!" she whispered.

"Nonsense!" he answered bluffly. "Who'd expect to find the *famous* Anastasia and the *notorious* Eugene—?"

"Everybody's looking at us!" she countered.

"Okay, why not? I mean, I'm black and you're beautiful! And you are, damn it! You're gorgeous!"

His attempt to distract her with compliments failed.

"Gene! That man over there has a newspaper!"

"Are we headline news in it? Stacy, it's been weeks! You know a story like ours doesn't last that long!" He leaned toward her, hoping to keep their dispute quiet enough not to attract attention. At once her face hardened and her voice acquired a shrill edge.

"You don't understand! All you're concerned about is that you've made off with an heiress!"

"I didn't think that was the way of it!" he snapped.

"It wasn't meant to be! At first I believed . . . The hell with it. Let's go." She jumped to her feet.

"Well, if you're determined to create a scene—"

"Determined? Hell, no, I was hoping for something absolutely different! But it's up to you, after all. Come along, and don't leave the bag behind!"

Providentially, at that instant Milo dumped a carafe of retsina on their table, along with glasses and a saucerful of goat's cheese and olives. Making a logical assumption, he addressed Stacy.

"If you're looking for what I think you are, it's back that way—there's a sign. Unisex, I'm afraid, but it was empty a moment ago."

She hesitated. Then, with vast effort, she controlled herself and nodded. As she departed Gene heaved a giant sigh of relief. For in a sense she was right. How could a mixed-race couple hope to remain inconspicuous in a village like this? But before he could calm her enough to lure her back to the sort of place where he felt safe, the middle of a good solid continent, he was going to have to allay her sense of paranoia. And the problem there was that it had a basis in reality: her grandfather—her *adoptive* grandfather—probably was ruthless enough to hire thugs to beat him up and drag her home.

On the other hand, she *had* begged to be taken away from the only world she had ever known; she *had* pleaded for a chance to live another existence than that of the jet set; she *had* decided that he was the right person to try it with; she *had* arranged all those misleading clues which ought to indicate that she had fled to South America . . . and, judging from the few newspapers they had risked buying, the bait had been swallowed by the press, at least. No, the odds were still in their favor—though it was a damned nuisance about this yachtload of sightseers.

Stacy was calmer when she returned, and they drank their wine more or less at leisure amid the clamorous and never-ceasing shouts of the other foreign customers. But when they reached the last glassful she began to fidget again, and he too was glad to pay up and leave, conscious of how many eyes were on them and worried as to what Stacy was apt to do or say next: insist on packing up and moving on?

To his amazement, however, even before they had regained the trail over the headland, she suddenly linked fingers with him and gave a squeeze.

"Gene, weren't they awful—those people?"

"Well, this morning Milo said . . ." And he paraphrased as best he could, adding a couple of caustic extra comments.

"I used to be like them." She was staring straight ahead up the steep path. "I don't want to be like them anymore. Though I couldn't help it. It was the way I was brought up. You do know that, don't you?" She turned to him with a beseeching expression.

"Yes, I do," he answered gruffly. "Otherwise I wouldn't be here, would I?"

"That's all right then. So long as we're together, everything is all right, isn't it?"

And, leaving him to follow more slowly with the bag of provisions, she almost danced to the top of the hill.

When they arrived back at "their" beach, however, they found it occupied by strangers: a boy and girl both about twenty, she stretched out nude on a towel while he—equally unclad—anointed her back with suntan oil. They looked up curiously, and the boy addressed them in rudimentary Greek. At their baffled response he switched first to sketchy German, then to English, and got through.

"That's your stuff there in the—uh—war memorial?"

"Yes!" Gene advanced the last few paces, while Stacy hung back.

"Your boat, too?"

"Not exactly. Rented."

"Ah-hah. Staying long?"

"Haven't decided yet."

"That's the way," the boy said admiringly. "Cut loose from your roots, explore the world before it's blown to bits. Wish we could do the same, but you need bread to keep going, and . . . I'm Hank. This is Linda."

The girl rose on her elbows and smiled. She was fair and pretty, but rather fat.

"Say—uh—you don't mind us? . . ." Hank made a vague gesture.

"The world belongs to all of us," Gene said, consciously quoting Stacy.

"That's good," the boy approved. "We just mean to stick around awhile and soak up some sun, that's all."

"So do we," said Stacy, having made up her mind, and stepped to Gene's side. "I'm Stacy and he's Gene, by the way. And I'm just about to fix lunch. Are you hungry?"

"Well, we got some bread and cheese and fruit—"

"So've we. Let's pool it, then." Stacy debated with herself a second, then caught up the hem of her dress and tugged it over her head. Another moment, and she discarded her bikini panties too.

"Provided," she went on, "you lend me some of that suntan oil."

It proved to be a strange day. Gene would not have thought it possible to talk so much without actually saying anything. Miraculously, however, Hank and Linda were not in the least interested in their companions' background, and spoke very little about their own. Mainly they concentrated on their view of life, which was frankly mystical. They were planning to bum their way via Turkey into India and thence to Nepal, in hopes of meeting a guru who would offer them enlightenment. Gene felt a stir of envy at their optimism. He couldn't help wondering whether this anonymous island was on their best route, but held his peace. At one stage Linda inquired diffidently whether there was any pot around, "like maybe on the boat," but accepted Gene's headshake and changed the subject.

Toward sundown the young couple resumed their clothes and headed back toward Oragalia, where they were to meet someone who might have room in a boat making for the next island in the chain. They embraced Gene and Stacy effusively but offered no thanks for the food they had shared.

When they had gone, Stacy reentered the cave by way of its concrete arch—still surprisingly true and square despite the passage of time—and set about preparing red mullet for supper. She was not a good cook, even a camp cook, but she insisted on undertaking the menial chores to prove she was capable of them.

Musingly she said, "I think if everyone were more like those two than the tourists we saw this morning the world would be a far better place. Don't you agree?"

Gene suppressed his private reservations. He said, "At least they seem very relaxed. And sort of gentle."

"Yes, gentle's a good term. Isn't there another bottle?"

Somewhat guiltily, they had concealed the last of their wine, because the sun had lain hot on the beach despite it being only May, and both Hank and Linda had displayed a colossal thirst. While Gene was drawing the cork she went on, "I can't help thinking how much Ingrid would have disliked them, and how much more like she must have been to those appalling tourists."

"Really? How do you mean?" He filled their glasses.

"Oh—" She gestured with the knife she had used to clean the fish. "It's the 'boss for a day' bit, if you see what I mean. Probably most of those people will go home to dreadful jobs where they have to kowtow all the time to the managing director or the owner or whatever, but while they're here they give orders and dish out lavish tips and everybody runs to obey them. Ingrid must have enjoyed that sort of thing. You never met her, did you?"

"No. Though I heard about her, naturally."

"Well, nor did I, but I got this very clear picture of her." Laying by the knife, she took her glass and sat down on her side of the sleeping bag, not looking at him—not looking at anything in the here and now, but blankly at the wall of the cave.

"And I've been wondering about the fate that would have been appropriate for her. Like to hear what I think?"

"Yes, of course." He too sat down, linking his fingers around his knees.

"Well, I suspect she'd have wanted to find her way to a place full of little people she could lord it over, heirs perhaps to a decadent civilization. Maybe little *brown* people—Gene, I'm sorry!"

"Nothing to do with me. Go on."

She was frowning. "Well, I think she'd have liked to be made welcome by their king, you know. Set on a throne and draped with garlands, brought offerings of meat and butter and rice. But eventually life in Lamagu would have begun to bore her . . . Funny! It's almost as though the place I'm talking about could really exist. I didn't mean to call it Lamagu, but that's its name. I mean, it feels like its name."

"Go *on*," he urged, reaching for the wine again.

"Well, like I say, she grew bored, not even needing to issue orders, but having everything done for her without asking. It wasn't enough to rise every morning and see the dawn break over distant snowcapped mountains, watch the lilies on the ornamental ponds open to greet the day, enjoy countless dishes full of unfamiliar tidbits, put on the richest silks and jewels and set forth across the city to view wild animals or listen to the music of a temple ceremony. It wasn't enough. She needed to tell someone what to do and watch it done.

"So one morning she started countermanding everything that was done for her, as a matter of routine. She found fault with no matter what—demanded that the cook bring her impossible delights for breakfast, ordered the tailor to remake her gowns, called for minstrels and decided to instruct them in her favorite hymn tune. Also she mocked them for not knowing it already, and for being ignorant of the religion her family had brought her up in, to which she only paid attention when it suited her.

"Then, later, on the streets of Lamagu, along the broad avenues where the merchants haggled with their customers and in the alleys where the tinsmiths and the cordwainers plied their trade in tiny open-fronted shops above which people slept—in rooms when it was cool, on rattan beds, or on the roofs when it was hot and there was no hope of rain for months to come—everywhere she picked on passersby at random and upbraided them for being as they were. She ordered them to change their style of dress, their diet, their homes and even their ancientest traditions.

"All this the folk of Lamagu accepted. Nor did they just accept; they welcomed it. They had been bored so long, they'd grown resigned to permanent monotony. They thought her mad, of course, but it was a fascinating kind of madness. Without her having to demand it of him, their king removed the necklace which was his mark of office, like a crown, and begged her on his bended knee to don it.

"Which she did, already half-aware that this itself had undermined her plan.

"What could she change now in the city, radically? Well, there was a problem concerning water. There was either not enough, in summer, or too much, when the rainy season came. Accordingly she decreed the building of vast reservoirs, linked by canals, with here and there a gentle waterfall and steps alongside where a family might come to fill their pots and jars. This, now, the people understood; not only was it practical, but it would provide by night the soothing music of cascading water, to replace the churr of crickets kept in cages, which had been customary but which she had now forbidden. They set to with a will, and very shortly the system was complete.

"And other droning insects came to make music in the night, well to the people's taste, for they'd had droning instruments in the temples she converted to museums.

"After the rainy season, when the reservoirs operated perfectly and stored, high in the hills, enough to meet the city's needs for the longest and hottest summer—so she was pleased—the people suddenly began to act as she had long desired. They came to her begging to be told what they should do. Delighted at this reversal of the situation she had rebelled against, she issued orders and more orders, and more and more orders, and they went away and she sat happily on the throne which had been the king's and waited for reports on the impact she had made.

"None came, but one of the new droning insects bit her ankle, and she swatted it.

"Then, at last, after sundown, she went out to see why she was being left alone, without food or drink or attendants, and found that Lamagu was full of corpses. And not long after, she was one of them."

Stacy shook herself, seeming to return from far away, and glanced around. Gene had lighted their little butane stove, and also their lamp, and was holding out a plate on which lay a fried fish appetizingly scented with wild thyme, a wedge of bread, and sliced tomatoes dressed with lemon, oil and salt.

"I was going to fix that—" she began, then meekly took it, and began to eat.

After a little she said, "Were you listening?"

"I promise you, I didn't miss a word. Eat up. It's late, and growing cold."

Soon after, twining against him in the darkness, she remembered one more thing she'd meant to say.

"You don't think Hank and Linda recognized us, do you?"

"I doubt it very much. Did they sound as though they pay attention to the news?"

"No, I guess not. But may they not be talking of us to their friends?"

"Very likely. If their friends are like them, though, we have nothing to worry about."

"Yes, you're right . . . Gene, I think I'm a little happy here. Let's stay awhile."

Dismissing all his reservations, he replied, "Okay!"

Wondering meantime when he'd regret it.

# PART THREE

*THE EXHIBIT*
*is a handful of shell cases from an automatic rifle.*
*They speak of a bad habit long forgotten: war*

*THE MONTH*
*is June*

*THE NAME*
*is Cedric*

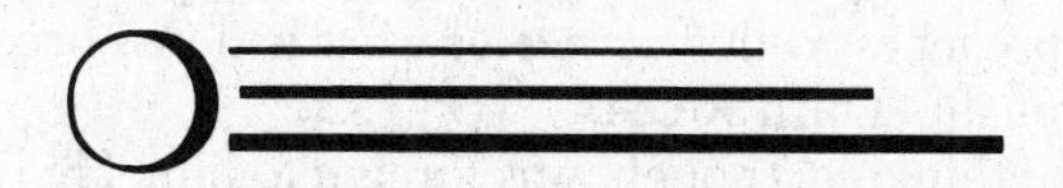

The thirty-meter length of *Räumboot R34*—gray as the gray of the sea in the predawn light of this fine June morning—plowed northward at her steady cruising speed of 18 k.p.h. Nervous beside her twin antiaircraft guns, her duty deck-crew yawned and cursed their inability to dominate fatigue by an act of will. But she was far from any battle zone now, although a few planes had droned by during the hours of darkness.

Sore-eyed, at the limit of the endurance bestowed on him by coffee and Benzedrine, Leutnant Kreutzer surveyed the island they were approaching and identified it by the chart spread out before him on the map table of the cramped bridge. Its name, apparently, was Oragalia. He checked his watch and made a note in the log.

Then a familiar but unwelcome voice spoke behind him, and Graumann appropriated his binoculars without permission—Graumann, who was so proud of his entitlement to one of the countless uniforms invented not by the Navy but by the Party, with its incomprehensible badges of rank, who made so great a point of dragging his right leg and such a habit of referring to his "wound from the Great War." In his invariable self-important manner, he said, "That looks interesting. Where are we on the chart? . . . Ah, you've marked it"—in the tone of one disappointed at not being able to complain that the chore had been neglected. "Kindly heave to for a while and let me look it over."

Kreutzer bit back the words that sprang to his tonguetip and wearily signed to his *Bootsmann*, who had the wheel. The rumble of their twin diesels receded to a faint thump-thumping as the sun peered over the skyline and color flooded back into the world.

"Hmm!" Graumann pronounced after half a minute or so. "That southern bay has possibilities. Take the glasses, *Herr Leutnant*, and see if you can fault me on this. Suppose we were to post a lookout station on that overhang, preferably including a radar unit?" He paused to let his grasp of current technical jargon make an impression. "Then we could fortify the entrance to that cave, which could be used as a magazine—if it's big enough, and if not we'll enlarge it—site a couple of gun posts on those headlands and draft some of the local people to build a rampart of boulders blocking access from the beach: would that not strike you as a highly defensible vantage point?"

Kreutzer cursed the man silently. He could in fact not fault the argument; the chart confirmed that an outpost on Oragalia would indeed control the approaches to this corner of what had just become the latest acquisition of the Third Reich.

Such land-centered thinking, though, was foreign to him. He liked open water better, searching and chasing across a quarter of the globe if necessary. He had hoped to be posted to a U-boat pack. But each man within the Reich must do his duty, and according to its complex system of interlinked authority Graumann was his superior. He contained himself, and said only, "If the enemy does manage to regroup, which is unlikely, then he might well organize a counterattack in this area. I must say, however . . ."

"What?" Graumann was instantly affronted.

"Well, after our success in Crete, he might be tempted to imitate our example, in which case shore defenses—"

"We have air superiority throughout this region! Not a chance!" Graumann turned to the bosun. "I notice a shack on that beach, and what looks like a vegetable patch. That implies a larger community nearby, and from the map I deduce it's on the eastern shore. Send a signal to say that's where we're making for. We'll land, and give the locals a chance to get acquainted with their new masters."

"Aye, aye, sir," the bosun grunted, and called for half ahead. As the diesels resumed their former pace, Graumann turned back to the ship's commander.

"It must be a remarkable experience, *Herr Leutnant*, to arrive as the rightful conqueror of a decadent folk, which is what we are about to do. Prepare to lodge in memory what may well be a unique event for both of us. The rate at which the Reich is expanding implies that it will not often be repeated, and certainly not beyond our own lifetimes, unless in outer space. Don't you agree?"

"Evgenos! Evgenos! Wake up!"

The folk of Oragalia resented the dark-skinned stranger, because the adopted daughter of the island's richest family had chosen him in preference to any of her other suitors, rejecting her old comfortable life for an existence like the humblest peasants', with a shack for shelter, a cave to store their few tools and provisions such as flour, oil and dried fish, and a tiny patch of salty ground to scratch their living from. The men of the island, particularly her foster father, had had other plans for her. However, because when Greece was invaded so many of the fit young men had been summoned to die in places with unfamiliar names, the boat owners had lately begun to call on Evgenos for help by night . . . and pay him well. Strong arms for hauling in the net lines were too valuable to waste. This morning he had gone to sleep at cockcrow. Now here he was being roused, it seemed, almost before he had dozed off.

Cursing, he opened his eyes, and discovered that it was in fact broad daylight. Under the slanting roof of the hut he had constructed out of scrap and flotsam when challenged to prove he could support her, Anastasia was shaking him by the shoulders.

"What's the matter?" he demanded, sitting up on the rough pallet. He had been so exhausted when he came home, he had lain down in all his clothes except his boots.

"A warship has arrived off the port, a German warship twice as big as Kaloyiannis's caïque! They've sent a landing party. They have rifles and machine guns. Everybody has been told to assemble in the square at noon!"

Completely alert now, Evgenos scrambled to his feet, rubbing his eyes, judging the time as late morning by the angle of the shadows beyond the unsquare door. "Have you seen the ship yourself?" he demanded.

"No, Xanthe came to warn me"—meaning her foster sister, whose husband had reported to his army unit months ago and not been heard from since, and with whom she had contrived to get back on good terms despite the resentment of the rest of the family which had taken her in when she was orphaned. "But it's fearful news! I'm scared!"

"Haven't we been expecting something of the kind ever since the fall of Crete? And it could have been worse. We might have been shelled, or bombed from the air."

"How can you talk like that?" Anastasia cried.

"Because it's no good talking any other way. Besides, there can't be much here that they want. This is a very poor island compared with some."

She hesitated, eyes downcast.

"They might want our land," she said at length.

"What do you mean?"

"My uncle says this bay could make a strongpoint. He says our own army should have fortified it. You've heard him go on about it often enough, haven't you?"

"Oh, him!" Her uncle-by-courtesy Rhodakis was their ex-policeman, called out of retirement when his successor was ordered to rejoin his regiment, given to holding forth on subjects he knew next to nothing about. "In that case, we certainly would have been bombed and shelled! Get me a drink of water, please, and something to quiet my belly. It's rumbling so much I can't hear myself think."

Silently she brought the water, in a large, sand-scratched, but still sound glass preserving jar which they had found when digging land for their scanty crops, and a crust of bread moistened with olive oil. Watching as he ate, she ventured, "We should hurry if we're to be in the square by noon."

"Go on ahead. And don't look for me there."

"But everybody has to—"

"What everybody has to do," he interrupted, "is find out what their plans are, and lay plans of our own to frustrate them!"

"Evgenos, you mustn't say such things!"

"Your government's been beaten! All right! Do your people want it to stay beaten forever? There are still other countries fighting against the Germans. The war isn't over by a long way!"

"It is for us!"

"For your spineless family, maybe. Not for me!"

"But even if you hide, they're bound to catch you, and then they'll punish you, and—what will become of me?"

Turning to set aside the empty cup, he shrugged. "Would you really have preferred someone who refuses to stand up against foreign invaders? You could have had your pick of men like that. But you chose me."

She caught his hand, gazing straight into his eyes. "I know," she said. "And you chose me. But it's no longer a matter of just you and me."

For a second he didn't grasp her meaning. Then his face fell. Realizing he had caught on, she nodded gravely.

"It's certain now. I'm carrying your child."

There was a moment of silence. At last, his expression grim, he said, "All the more reason to resist. Do you want him to grow up in a world where he'll be taught that he's no better than an animal? That's what the Nazis will say, you know. They'll treat him like a mongrel dog."

"But what can we possibly do against soldiers with machine guns, let alone a warship?"

"Something! Even if it's only making sure they never have a sound night's rest as long as they're here. Now run along to the village. If anyone asks where I am, say you don't know—say I couldn't sleep and went out early, or anything. But remember what I said: *don't look for me!*"

"If you're not around, someone who hates us is certain to inform on you—"

"I didn't say I wouldn't be around," he answered in a wry tone. "I just said don't look for me. Now go!"

Embracing her briefly, he strode to make a hasty toilet at the edge of the sea.

"You have nothing to fear from our garrisoning of this island! In general, you will be allowed to continue with your ordinary work, although under better administration!"

Sullenly, but on time, the citizens had gathered in the town square, facing the miniature port, with the church on one hand and the taverna on the other.

"Naturally, refusal to obey our instructions will be regarded as treason!"

Kreutzer had assigned ten of his thirty-strong crew to ring the area with rifles and submachine guns, but such precautions seemed superfluous, for these people had the air of cowed dogs. There was a flagpole on the crude mole which sheltered Oragalia's solitary harbor, used mainly to fly storm warnings; now from it fluttered the *R34*'s spare ensign, a black cross on white with the swastika at its center, the formal symbol of conquest.

And the islanders had duly obeyed Graumann's command to stand to attention, hats off, while it was hoisted. Maybe there was something to the theory of the Master Race, after all. Kreutzer himself had never enjoyed such a sense of dominance . . . but perhaps that was because he was a seaman, and the sea had never been totally tamed.

Graumann, however, was in his element, and had spent the morning interrogating these new subjects of the Reich.

In Greek, the language he was speaking now.

"Treason in a double sense, moreover—a betrayal also of your glorious Aryan heritage, the heritage which has inspired me to study your language and your culture!"

Here was another thorn in Kreutzer's flesh, for he had to appeal to his oldest and lowliest sailor for a translation: as dedicated a racialist as Graumann, and as firm a believer in the German renaissance, which he associated with the German origins of the modern Greek royal family, to the point that although his birth in Thessaloniki disqualified him from promotion even to petty officer, he had willingly transferred from the Merchant Marine at the outbreak of war. He was able to give a fair rendering of the speech, though he admitted it was so salted with classical archaicisms that now and then he had to guess at what was meant.

But Kreutzer had small trouble filling in the gaps.

"Unfortunately, with the passage of the centuries, the Nordic blood of your ancestors has become tainted, especially by Jews and other Semitic half-men! But steps will be taken to repurify all the population strains now under the protection of the Reich!"

One tall, fine-looking, but apparently frightened young woman, standing rather apart from the crowd, reacted to this last remark with a visible shudder, while a group of older people, much closer to Graumann and his companions, exchanged grave looks and nods. Kreutzer's senses were alerted, and he started to pay serious attention.

"On that subject, I've been told that some kind of blackamoor settled among you recently. I don't know who he is or what brought him here, but I notice he's conspicuous by his absence. I'm advised that he's not popular, and that few of you care to associate with him—bar one disgraceful exception!"

Kreutzer wondered whether Graumann could be referring to the young woman he had already noticed. From her tense expression and the glances cast at her from all sides, it seemed probable, although surprising. He foresaw trouble. He could guess only too clearly how his sailors might react to the presence of a woman shameless enough to give herself to a negro.

"Therefore I will accept, this once, an assurance that no one told him about this meeting. There will be another tomorrow at the same time. If he is not present then, an example will be made of his—ah—consort. That is all for the moment, but this afternoon I propose to make a complete inspection of the island, and I shall require a guide. Arrange it."

The crowd started to disperse, and Graumann turned to Kreutzer with a thin smile.

"I think they got the message, don't you?" he murmured.

"I'm sure they did," answered the lieutenant absently, looking for the young woman. Somehow, though, she had contrived to disappear.

If he had had a gun, or even a bow and arrow, Evgenos could—and cheerfully would—have shot Graumann during his speech. One wall of the church was formed of the living rock, and it was possible to scramble up to its roof among concealing scrub for a vantage point overlooking the square. By straining his ears, he had heard everything. Now, crawling away, he was desperately wondering how to live up to his earlier boasts about resistance. It was no use worrying about the person who had informed on him; there were a score or more of candidates.

But was there anyone who might feel ashamed that that had happened? Conceivably, Kaloyiannis, who owned the largest fishing boat and had been the first to hire Evgenos as crew. He had hoped to see his own son marry Anastasia, so there was no love lost between the two of them, but he was a fiercer and sounder patriot than garrulous old Rhodakis. If the islanders were truly to be allowed to carry on with their normal work, then the fishermen would put out tonight as usual. Probably their caïques would be searched before departure, but there were too many of them for the enemy to keep them all under surveillance all night; besides, they could argue that the sound of diesel engines would scare the fish. Then suppose that a desperate man with a knife at the helmsman's throat were to order him to call at the southern tip of the island, collect Anastasia, set course for—where? Oh, anywhere! Malta, possibly, or Alexandria, though the voyage to either would be long and dangerous. At all events, it must be tried!

"So this is where the nigger and his woman live," said Graumann, uprooting with the toe of a dusty boot one of the ill-doing tomato plants that stood in a row before the shack. "How appropriate. Like the animals they are."

He turned to survey the seaward view.

"Just as I thought: an excellent spot for our permanent garrison. Don't you agree, *Herr Leutnant?*"

Sweating, thirsty, footsore, but unwilling to show any sign of weakness in Graumann's presence, Kreutzer nodded. "Though the rock is less fractured than one might have expected. Your rampart of boulders might call for quite extensive blasting."

Graumann waved that aside. "A minor matter! We can send for a shipload of concrete, and either cast it on the spot or have pillars brought in prefabricated. But this will certainly be the highlight of my next report."

"I suppose I should post guards here in case the black man comes back."

"Oh, yes. Make one of them that fellow who speaks Greek. And I want a lure staked out. Track down his woman and make sure she's here by sundown. Let it be known that she has neither food nor water. While on the subject of food, we might as well commandeer the supplies up in that cave. They're probably of dreadful quality, but every little helps."

Anastasia sat rocking back and forth in the dark, dry-eyed because she would not give her captors the satisfaction of hearing her weep. There were two: one thickset, about fifty, graying and much lined, the other half his age. The former had a pistol and the other some sort of machine gun, such as she had only seen before in pictures.

They had neither tied nor gagged her. Perhaps they hoped that if she tried to warn off Evgenos by screaming, that would make him still more likely to come to the trap for which she was the bait. They were lying out in the open atop the twin headlands, one covering the trail from the village and the other the beach. They both seemed quite calm, as though their prey were indeed an animal instead of a human being.

Well, that was what they believed, just as Evgenos had warned. Now she had heard the truth for herself. She pressed her hand to her belly, as yet barely starting to swell with the new life it bore, and suppressed a groan of despair at the fate in store for her firstborn.

Was that a noise outside? She was on her feet before she could stop herself. For a moment she stood trembling. When she had half convinced herself she was imagining things, she heard a voice at the edge of audibility . . . and recognized whose it was.

"Good evening! Aren't you the sailor who speaks Greek? Yes? It must be dull for you out here. All your friends are busy inspecting the fishing boats before they put to sea. There's no sign of the black man, by the way—he's keeping well out of sight, I'm sure, because he knows how glad we'll be to see the back of him, the bastard! Look, I brought a bottle of wine. Wouldn't you like a drop?"

There came a whispered answer, too faint to make out. Anastasia bit her lip and clenched her fists so hard the nails dug hurtfully into her palms.

"Oh, go on! Call your pal over! The nigger won't dare show himself. I bet he doesn't care enough about the woman to risk one of your bullets through his hide!"

A pause; then a reluctant word of thanks, and the Greek-turned-German sailor translated to his companion in a soft voice. In a moment there were eager scrambling noises.

What in the name of the Almighty was going on?

The guards each carried a powerful flashlight, and she was terribly afraid they might use them. But they abode by their instructions well enough not to, and all three men came together in the dark.

"Here, you first! You're a fellow countryman, after all!"

And, about as long after as it would take to raise a bottle to one's lips: a smash of glass, a cry, a thud, and the sound of a violent struggle. Anastasia could control herself no longer. She rushed out of the hut.

On rocks below the eastward headland lay the elderly ex-Greek, groaning from the pain of his fall. Up above, two men were fighting, one trying to bring his gun to bear, his opponent clutching him in a desperate wrestler's hug—and in the dimness both their faces showed pale.

She cried out in amazement. It was right. The German was distracted for a precious fraction of a second. Evgenos let go his grip, falling back and sweeping one leg around. Caught by surprise, the younger guard fell beside his companion. Evgenos jumped after him, landing on his chest with feet together. He uttered a gurgling sound and blood burst darkly from his nose and mouth.

The winner wasted no time. He kept his balance, drew a knife, and stabbed both his victims in the throat.

"Anastasia, are you all right?" he panted. "If they hurt you, I'll be sorry they enjoyed such a quick death!"

"Y-yes!" she forced out.

"Then help me drag them to the water and set them afloat! We can cover up the traces afterward!"

"How did—did you? . . ." The words wouldn't come.

He looked at her directly. Even now she almost failed to recognize him.

"How did I get to be white? I painted myself with Xanthe's Sunday makeup. Since they were looking for a black man—Or did you want to know who helped me? It was Kaloyiannis. I was pretty sure he'd swallow his dislike of me long enough to feel ashamed of the easy time the Germans are having in their occupation of the islands. He's promised to bring his caïque around and pick us up as soon as he can. But we need to dispose of this lot first."

When the job was done, they hid, wet and shivering, not in the hut or the cave, but among scrub on the higher ground, where they could keep watch both for the boat and for any sign of a patrol coming to check on the trap. But there was small risk of that; Graumann would not want his quarry frightened off.

Then, at long last, with her head on the shoulder of this violent stranger whom she seemed not to know at all even after he wiped off his pale disguise—to make him harder to spot in the dark, he explained wryly—Anastasia broke down. He waited out her dry, gusty sobs.

Eventually, as he had sometimes done in the past around the time she first decided she wanted him and no one else but was still terrified of the way she would be treated by her foster family and their friends, he decided to distract her by telling her a story.

"You know, these invaders make me think of Cedric."

"What?" She turned but did not raise her head.

"He was not just intellectual, but brilliant. He'd been an infant prodigy and grown used to adulation. Give him an IQ test and he'd finish it early and walk out before time, saying he was bored. He got to university two full years before the rest of his contemporaries, expecting he was going to blow everybody's mind there, as well.

"Didn't quite work out like that. Yes, he was bright—but so was everybody else, and some of them had experience and knowledge that he lacked. He was no longer special.

"He brooded over this, his first great disappointment, and gradually became embittered.

"Eventually his subconscious led him to a conclusion which he never voiced. He recalled how throughout his childhood his parents had promised that the world would be his oyster, and he began to believe that he'd betrayed them. Of course, they'd assured him that everything he learned was right, that everything he found in books was right, that knowledge was his right, in other words . . . that's *total* knowledge.

"From which he deduced that if by the age of twenty-five he hadn't yet become world-famous—as, surely, someone with his talent ought to be—there must be a reason. At first he imagined that he had rivals in the university, or in his field of research, who were slandering him behind his back, or otherwise plotting against him, but he could find no proof of that, and he was honest enough to admit it. In the end, all by himself, he reinvented the idea of having been ill-wished. I suppose you know that's a standard concept in the theory of magic. But he extended it. He grew suspicious of the cosmos."

"Ah, but you said he never spoke of the idea!" She lifted her head at last.

"That's right. He was afraid of mockery. So when he set out on his journey he sought a place where what he had to keep secret, back at home, was taken for granted."

"Did he find it?"—sleepily.

"Yes, of course. In this infinite universe there has to be a place for all of us, and Cedric found his.

"For a short time after his arrival, he thought he was in seventh heaven. He found himself among scientists, but when he began to talk about the laws of nature they reacted with amazement; for them, there were no laws as such, but only chances, good or bad.

"Clearly, they understood better than he did such principles as Heisenberg's, so, though remaining permanently on guard, he cautiously voiced his own theory. To all appearances it struck his listeners as perfectly tenable. He had never met such openminded people. They granted him the facilities he asked for, better than those he had been accustomed to. He drafted a major speech to be delivered at a scientific congress, and in the meantime set about recruiting a group of followers who declared themselves willing to accept his primary axiom: *The universe is out to get us!* With them, he planned to pack the audience at his first public appearance.

"He carried on in this manner for quite some while. His students were fascinated by his arguments, and many let themselves be seduced; reporters came to interview him, and quoted his words fairly. A major foundation consented to fund him after only one appeal for money. Cedric's was at last a famous name.

"Then, when it came time to address the congress, he put on his smartest clothes and shook countless hands and mounted the rostrum. Slides had been prepared; he commentated on them, each in turn, and quoted the notes of all his best experiments.

"Not until he was halfway through the talk did he become aware that some of his hearers had begun to laugh. He carried on, and even reached the end, despite the tides of mirth that now assailed him. One last fragment of hope remained to him, as guffawing was supplanted by applause, and he saw the congress president rise to offer his hand. He still believed, even at that final moment, that he had persuaded his listeners to accept his views.

"But then the congress president said, with absolute sincerity: 'Sir, you have amused us better than any speaker I remember. This notion that the universe is motivated by a kind of planned malevolence has led to so many good jokes one can quote at parties that we're all indebted. When may we look forward to some serious work of equal brilliance?'

"In that moment, Cedric realized he had been right all along. The universe was not only malignant, but capable of outsmarting him, or anyone."

Despite her wet clothes and uncomfortable posture, Anastasia was drowsing at his side. He nudged her gently.

"Don't go to sleep—you mustn't! We have to keep our eyes peeled for the boat."

"Kaloyiannis is so late," she whispered, lids still lowered. "He should have been here long ago."

"We have to go on waiting," he insisted, even as his weariness betrayed him also into slumber.

"Well, now we can arrest him for murder," said Graumann. "And Kaloyiannis as an accessory. I did say—didn't I?—it would be stupid to let the fishing fleet sail tonight, even though the islanders may go hungry without its catch. Know what's amiss with you, *Herr Leutnant?* You don't yet feel the Reich's remorseless logic in your bones."

# Part Four

*THE EXHIBIT*
*is a glass preserving jar with a wire closure to its lid. It commemorates a vanished age of luxury*

*THE MONTH*
*is July*

*THE NAME*
*is Shanti*

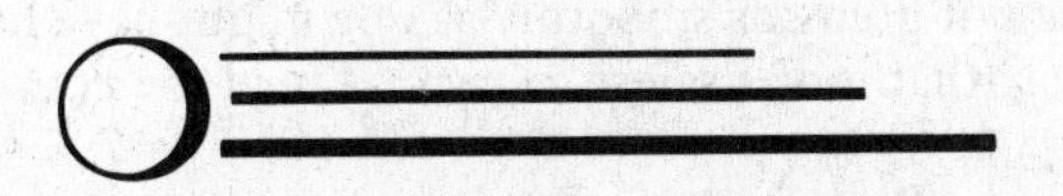

The steam yacht *Medea* was small compared to some of her kind—nothing like so large, for example, as those being built in America by Commodore Vanderbilt and others—but she was most luxuriously equipped; the very ensign flying at her stern was made of silk. Teak, mahogany, gold leaf and marble abounded in her staterooms, and everywhere below the main deck there was thick carpet to absorb the noise of her ultramodern compound engines.

A short while ago, however, those engines had gradually ceased to turn and there had been a rattling of anchor chains.

Waiting for the inevitable report from her captain and engineer, gazing absently at the plume of smoke which now rose straight up from the *Medea*'s funnel, her owner Lord Arthur Fenton said languidly, "You know, Osman old fellow, there are times when I think it may not have been such a good idea to fall in with your suggestion of cruising to Constantinople. Not at this time of year, at any rate."

He was a slender, brown-haired man, still under thirty, of middle height, wearing a light linen suit of the most impeccable London cut. He was stretched out on a chaise longue on the afterdeck, in the shade of a canvas awning; it was a blazing July day, and the thermometers were registering ninety. Between him and the person he addressed, who occupied an identical chaise longue, there stood a small table bearing a box of Egyptian cigarettes in paper striped with faint gray lines, a bottle of whisky, a double-globe soda syphon enclosed in wire mesh, and a stock of glasses. His man, who was called Tompkins, sat sweating at a discreet distance, alert for any call to replenish the drinks.

Osman Effendi, who was about the same age, equally well dressed, but somewhat shorter and swarthier, with a thick black mustache on his upper lip and a fez on his head which he somehow contrived to keep in position even when lying down, signaled his own servant Mustapha to hand him another of the cigarettes; he smoked incessantly. While it was being lighted for him, he thought desperately about his response. He had met Lord Arthur in Monte Carlo, and been overjoyed at the chance to make his acquaintance, for he was manifestly very rich, and it would be immensely useful to Osman in the future were he to enjoy wealthy contacts in the world's wealthiest nation. Since it was an unfashionable time of year for the Riviera, with little society to keep one amused, he had indeed proposed this cruise, and sung the praises of his home city until the Englishman consented. However, things were not going as smoothly as one might have hoped . . . He decided at last that it was safest to try and turn the comment with a joke.

"Ah, perhaps in such heat even your excellent British engines have decided we Mediterranean types are correct in taking a siesta!"

"We'll soon know," Lord Arthur grunted. "Here come Wilson and Macalister."

Snapping to attention as he arrived at his employer's side, the yacht's captain gave a naval-style salute. Behind him, scowling, her little Scottish engineer wiped perspiration from his forehead with a grimy rag.

"Trouble, I'm afraid, m'lord," Wilson said.

"Can it be fixed? If so, how soon?"

"Macalister says it may take five or six hours."

"Really?"—raising one eyebrow. "What's amiss?"

The engineer stepped forward. "The oil we bought in Italy," he answered curtly. "One of the shaft bearings has seized. We'll have to unship it and—"

But Lord Arthur was waving explanations aside. He said, "Just get us on the move again as quick as may be."

"Yes, of course, m'lord," Wilson agreed.

When they had gone, Lord Arthur rose to his feet and began to pace distractedly back and forth. "Well, there's a thing!" he said in exasperation, though his tone when addressing his underlings had betrayed no sign of it. "I foresee a boring day, don't you?"

And gestured for Tompkins to mix him another chota peg.

Hurt, for it was in no way his fault if the oil the engineer had bought in Italy was of such bad quality, Osman stared around, screwing up his eyes against the brilliant sun. They had cast anchor off the southern tip of one of the countless islands that littered this part of the world. Spotting it, he had a sudden inspiration.

"It's nearly time for lunch, is it not? Perhaps we could go ashore and make a picnic!"

He greatly prided himself on his knowledge of British culture.

Lord Arthur brightened. "It would pass the time, at least. That is, if there's a decent beach. Tompkins, fetch a telescope!"

It was promptly brought. Surveying the island, he said eventually, "Why, yes. One might well do that. I notice a shack of some sort, though, and there's a woman in front of it staring at us. I trust there won't be too many other folk around. Your people are less than popular in Greece, I understand, and one has no wish to provoke a riot."

Oh, these tactless English! . . . But Osman bridled his tongue. He said only, "In a way, we were as glad to be shut of them as they of us. You should meet some of the thieving, cheating traders that they breed. Anyway, that's history now, isn't it? And I can assure you from long acquaintance that they yield as easily as anyone to the power of money."

Lord Arthur was paying no attention, the telescope still to his eye. "Good lord!" he breathed. "That fellow—Here, take a look for yourself."

Osman adjusted the focus, bracing himself on one of the poles of the awning against the shift and ripple of the water. He saw the woman clearly: young, with quite a good figure—so far as could be judged under her coarse brown ankle-length dress, but she was unlikely to be corseted—and long untidy dark hair. At her side now stood, with one arm protectively around her, a thin man wearing a shabby shirt and a pair of seaman's trousers with one leg torn at the knee. Both were barefoot.

At first Osman did not realize what had so astonished his companion; to him, they looked like any other peasant couple. Then he realized: of course, the man was not just sunburned, but black. Having been accustomed all his life to negro servants and eunuchs, this had not immediately struck him as unusual.

Handing back the telescope, he shrugged.

"The man looks strong and healthy. If we rattle a few coins he will no doubt be glad enough to help carry our things ashore. One should not, however, pay attention to his woman."

"I'm not inclined to," Lord Arthur said fastidiously. "But so long as the place doesn't reek of their sewage . . . Tompkins, tell the stewards to make up a hamper."

"Who are they?" whispered Anastasia. "What do they want with us?"

"I think they stopped because they must. Look, there is no more smoke from the funnel."

Evgenos knew about things like steamships, indeed had traveled on some, but she had only ever seen one before and from a greater distance. Trembling, she watched as a boat was loaded and lowered, and rowed toward the shore.

"I will go down to meet them," Evgenos decided.

"Wait!" She caught his arm. "One of them is wearing the fez!" The last Turks to lord it over Oragalia had been slaughtered long before she was born, but her foster parents had told her many stories about their cruelty.

"Yes, but that is the flag of the country which helped Greece to become free." Evgenos pointed to the yacht's stern. "We must greet them with pride. Both of us."

"Very well." But she remained near the shack.

The boat grounded in shallow water, still some distance from dry land. In obedience to an order Evgenos did not understand, one of its passengers took off his shoes, rolled up his trousers, and waded ashore. In pidgin Greek he said, "Here is an English lord and his friend. Want to eat food here. You help, you will be paid. Come with me."

Evgenos was dismayed. He said, "But we have nothing to give a lord! We have little enough for ourselves!"

The man was smiling patronizingly. "No, no! We bring own food for them. You help carry, yes? Not take from you nothing. Here, see?"

And he offered a couple of shiny new coins.

Uncertainly Evgenos accepted them—they came to as much as he was paid for a month of casual labor with the fishing fleet—and after biting them tucked them into his cheek, for lack of any other way to carry them. Then he waded to the boat.

"You take lord on shoulders," he was told, and the lord, who luckily was quite light, clambered laughing over the side of the boat and was borne ashore. His friend with the fez was the next, but not the last, burden. Along with the two sailors who had been rowing, and the man who had come ashore first and another servant, Evgenos had now to bring load after load: first, poles and a roll of canvas, which were assembled to make a shady canopy; then folding chairs; then a folding table; then an immense wicker hamper that held, along with dishes and cutlery, something round and bright and brassy that gave off a pale blue flame when a match was set to it, and a seemingly endless supply of food and bottles of wine.

He felt his eyes grow round with amazement, and they all chuckled. Embarrassed, he called to Anastasia.

"Here, these people mean us no harm!"

She descended timidly to join him, and he explained about the English lord. To him, she made a sort of rough curtsy, and he spoke to her kindly enough in what Evgenos guessed was meant to be Greek, though the pronunciation was unfamiliar. But her eyes were full of hatred and suspicion whenever she looked at the man in the fez.

Shortly the visitors were ensconced in luxury, eating and drinking, and Evgenos decided it was time to withdraw. Leading Anastasia back to the shack, he showed her the money he had been given, and she agreed that it was worth his trouble. Then she resumed the task of tending their vegetable patch, while he sat on a rock waiting for his trousers to dry and gazing—not without envy—at the picnickers.

"My Greek didn't make much impression, did it?" said Lord Arthur. "Your man Mustapha did better! Any more champagne in that bottle?"

Tompkins darted to refill his glass.

"Of course," he went on, "one wouldn't expect to find the language of Plato and Sophocles in a corner like this. It looks as barren as the worst part of the Highlands, only without so much water. What do you suppose these people do to survive? One can't exactly call it living, can one?"

Osman shrugged; he cared little about such matters. "I imagine they rely on fishing," he said after a pause, and signaled Mustapha to light him another cigarette.

"The way that blackamoor is staring at us," Lord Arthur murmured, "one would think he had us in mind for his next catch . . . Finished?"

"What? Oh—oh, yes. And thank you very much: the potted pheasant was particularly good."

"I'm glad you liked it. Shot it myself at Ardnacraish last year. I must admit I was wondering whether it would have stood the heat, but our cook up there is a positive marvel . . . Are you sure you won't have an orange? No? How about a drop of brandy?"

"Yes, with pleasure!"

"Tompkins!"

For a while there was a pleasantly sated pause. Eventually, however, Lord Arthur started to fidget.

"He's still staring at us, you know. And if those great eyes of his were proboscises, he'd have sucked us in!"

"My dear fellow, I assure you there's nothing to worry about! He wouldn't dare try anything. He's outnumbered, to begin with, and your engineer assured us we shall be away before nightfall. Besides, there's another point to consider. You said my kind were unpopular here; well, his are even more so, and indeed I'm astonished that he's found himself a woman. Conceivably she—ah—disgraced herself and was driven out by her family, and he was the only man around to take her on. They're not as choosy as civilized people, you know."

"How do you suppose he came to be here in the first place?"

"Arthur, sometimes you puzzle me. What in the world do you find interesting about nonentities like these?"

Lord Arthur stretched and yawned. "Anything can seem interesting when there's nothing else to provide a distraction. And—to quote you—there's another point to consider."

"Such as, for instance?"

"Well, with all due respect, your empire is in decline and ours on the ascendant. Could it not have something to do with the fact that your beys and pashas and so forth take too little interest in the lives of the people they rule over? If you compare our record in India with yours in, say, Rumelia—"

Lord Arthur was drunk again. In a large company he was often entertainingly so; during the cruise, however, Osman had learned that he could be offensive, albeit in the nicest possible way, when there were only the two of them. Hastily he said, "You could always call them down and ask them. Myself, I suspect he's only staring at us because he never had a square meal in his life, and he's wondering what will become of the scraps we've left."

"You're right! Dammit, you must be right! Well, when in Rome! . . ." Lord Arthur jumped to his feet, waving. In execrably pronounced—though grammatical—ancient Greek he called to the black man and his woman, who, tired from her labor, was now sitting at his side. They gazed back blankly until Mustapha came to the rescue.

"Lord want give you food too!"

At that they approached, hand in hand, but not hurrying. Watching them, Osman plucked the Englishman's sleeve.

"They are probably unaccustomed, you know, to chairs and tables!"

"Hmm! That's a point!" Lord Arthur looked around, and spotted an oblong plank of wood which the chance of the waves had lodged in a crevice along the rocky shore. He pointed at it.

"They might be more comfortable if they ate off that, you mean? Very well! Tompkins, fetch it, will you?"

His servant hastened to obey, but turned the board over and over as he returned, staring at it with curiosity.

"What's the matter, man?" Lord Arthur demanded.

"There's some sort of painting on it, sir," Tompkins answered, and held up one side for inspection.

Lord Arthur glanced at it, and Osman said anxiously, "Why! It's a religious image, isn't it?" He spoke with all the distaste of a good Moslem, forbidden to make images for purposes of worship.

"Ah, yes!" Lord Arthur screwed a monocle into his right eye and examined the weather-worn traces of paint the wood still bore. "Looks like a crude depiction of a Virgin and Child. Fascinating, this primitive art, don't you think? But I take your point. They might be offended if we made them use it as a table, mightn't they? Oh, well! I suppose they're used to eating off the bare ground . . . It's too late, anyway. Here they come. That's what they'll have to put up with."

With a certain dignity the black man bowed, accepted an invitation to sit down in the shade—though the woman knelt, and for the first time they noticed that she was pregnant—and when given the leftover food made sure that she had the choicest portions.

"Hmm! Not so savage," Lord Arthur approved. "Don't think much of their table manners, but then my own ancestors ate with their fingers, I believe, until forks were introduced from Italy. Tompkins, don't broach any more of that champagne, but I imagine we could spare a bottle of claret if the Turkish wines are as good as Osman Effendi claims. Come to that, I wouldn't mind a drop!"

And, gravely, the guests both drank to his health.

"Talk about noble savages!" Lord Arthur exclaimed. "I wonder whether that's natural, inborn, inshtinctive, or—" And checked, as he realized that a tricky word had just tripped him up. Leaning back, he turned to Mustapha, who understood a little English and French as well as Greek and Turkish.

"You! Ask him what he's called and how he came here!"

At first Evgenos answered reluctantly; then the wine loosened his tongue, and he admitted he had been born in slavery and never known his parents. A little boastfully, he made it clear that he had not been freed, but run away, although, with many nervous glances at Osman, he declined to mention who had been his owner.

"Good for you, then!" cried Lord Arthur recklessly, and waved for Tompkins to refill their glasses. "We abolished slaves in England! Land of the free and all that, you know!"

*After skimming off all possible profit from the trade*, Osman glossed silently. With his host in this mood, he did not dare voice the thought.

Sometimes, though, he did wonder whether he had chosen the right course by westernizing himself. The arguments he always had to endure when he called on his father . . . But here was someone else, albeit very humble, who seemed to have had no qualms about making an analogous decision. Wine had lent his woman Anastasia courage, too, and when Evgenos hesitated over explaining their relationship she spoke up for the first time.

"I am an orphan. This is a little island. There are few men. All are my cousins. Trade is not good. The spirit has gone out of the families that own the land. My uncle who adopted me thought most about joining another estate to his. I did not want the husband he decided on. Too many women marry their cousins because there is nobody else. I don't mind Evgenos being a stranger. He is strong and everybody knows how hard he can work. One day they'll accept him because already we are growing good food on land the others left. My uncle may die angry but I still like his daughter. Her husband treats her badly and now she is jealous of my good luck, but she will get over that. Even my aunts say now that I may have been right after all."

Singling out one comment from the approximate version Mustapha was able to provide, Lord Arthur burst into loud laughter.

"Your cousin is jealous of your good luck, is she? How amazing! Well, one won't ask what kind of luck! Eh, Osman?"—this with a nudge in his companion's ribs.

The latter remained silent, not so much because he was growing sleepy from the heat and the wine and brandy as because he had been raised never to speak of what transpired in the *harēmlik*, the "lawful" part of the house.

At just that moment, however, there was a hoot from the yacht's steam siren, and they all glanced toward her. A plume of gray was rising from her funnel again, and on her foredeck a sailor was signaling with colored flags.

"Well, good for Macalister!" exclaimed Lord Arthur. "I should know him well enough by this time to realize that when he means one hour he'll say two, to be on the safe side. Bloody pessimist! Let's clear up and get aboard."

"Excuse me, m'lord," Tompkins ventured, "but how much of this food do you want taken back? The potted meats won't last now they've been opened, and some of the fruit—"

"Oh!"—with a grand gesture. "The nigger can have it! And a bottle of wine too, provided he carries me back to the boat without getting my feet wet."

When the steam yacht had departed, trailing her smoke into the sunset like a vast flag, Evgenos helped Anastasia to gather up the remnants and carry them to their shack.

"I told you they wouldn't harm us," he chided, his mouth full of English ham and pickles and stale but white bread.

"Yet they were afraid we might harm them," she muttered, propping against the center post of their shack what she had reclaimed as a particular treasure, the icon of the Virgin and Child which the sea had tossed ashore.

"Why should we? How could they think such a thing?"

"Because they are so insecure in their luxury."

"But here, left for us as presents, are delicacies such as I have never tasted! The glass jars these pickles came in, just to start with, are finer than—"

She waved him to silence, seizing the wine bottle and drinking deeply.

"Their confidence is an illusion. All of it depends on how efficiently we can be cowed, like me at sight of that red fez. I'm ashamed. It makes me think of Shanti."

Replete, content, he lay back in the warm evening air and listened to her tale as darkness fell.

"Now Shanti was a soft and undemanding person, chosen for reasons contrary to those affecting Cedric. Her, and her parents', culture encouraged her to be passive. She expected the world to treat her well, but when it didn't, though she certainly knew how to complain, she had no faintest notion how to act. She did, however, have hopes, and ultimately they were—in a sense—fulfilled.

"The place she came to was exactly what she'd always dreamed of. It was a benign and hospitable world, where no one had to work. The climate was delightful and the people could go without clothes, though there were many kinds of ornament and decoration. When you felt hungry, there was no need to do more than look for fallen fruit and nuts, or the shellfish which abounded at the seaside. Also there were animals so tame they seemed almost to welcome an invitation to be slaughtered, but they were killed only with great ceremony and on certain feast days that everyone looked forward to for months beforehand, when a sweet intoxicating drink was served and all made merry. Even a storm provided entertainment, in the form of lightning. Much of the people's music imitated thunder, too, for if a cloudburst washed away a house or two, then felling a few trees and weaving leaves to make new roofs and walls likewise offered a distraction and an excuse for a party. Besides, rainwater filled the drinking ponds.

"Also there were other kinds of pleasure. She proved attractive to a lot of men, with the entire approval of their wives. Some of the latter too decided to test what their husbands had reported on so well, and pronounced themselves equally satisfied. In a short while she was famous, insofar as fame existed in that place, and a great feast was mounted in her honor."

Anastasia paused to reach for the wine again, and he urged her, "Tell the rest!"

"There wasn't any 'rest,' " she said. "That was the beginning and the end, endlessly repeated."

# PART FIVE

*THE EXHIBIT*
*is a warped board painted blue, silver, gold and red. It serves to summarize a faith rejected*

*THE MONTH*
*is August*

*THE NAME*
*is Giacomo*

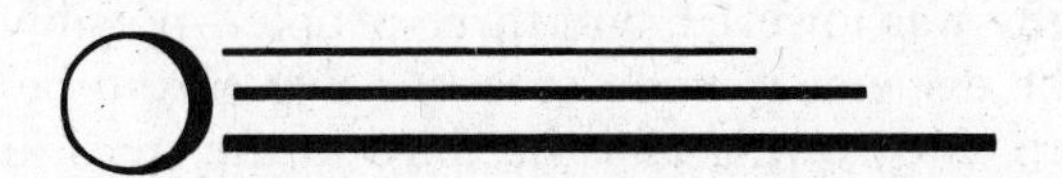

**D**uring the hot August night Anastasia had tossed aside the thin rough sheet she shared with Evgenos. Just at dawn there came the faintest, faintest wisp of breeze, and the change in temperature awakened her. Stretching languorously, out of habit she reached to reclaim their cover, but checked in mid-movement, sniffing the air.

"Evgenos!" she exclaimed suddenly. "Quick!"

And jumped up, seizing her tattered dress.

He roused more slowly, but as soon as he came to himself he perceived what had excited her. Faint, yet unmistakable, a most delectable smell had drifted into the hovel they called home, as though the beach, the island, the very sea had been planted with richly perfumed flowers. With a mutter of amazement he drew on his breeches.

"What do you think it can be?" he demanded.

She said something wild about a vision of saints and angels. Only in heaven could there be such fragrance!

More cynical, yet confused enough to imagine she might be right, he thrust aside the tatters that hung across the doorway and emerged blinking in new daylight.

No saints. No angels. Nothing miraculous. But something remarkable, nonetheless. Just offshore lay one of the greatest ships that plied these waters: a Venetian galley laden above deck and below with the most aromatic spices the Orient could offer—nutmegs, cinnamon, pepper, cassia, cloves . . . How many tons in all she carried, he could not guess, but it was enough to scent the air for miles around.

At first there was no sign of activity on board. This breeze, this zephyr, was not even strong enough to stir the burgee flying from her mainmast, let alone fill the canvas brailed below its crosstree. Her kedge was down and her oars were shipped, indicating that her rowers were exhausted. The notion crossed Evgenos's mind that she might have been struck by plague, in which case she was a terrifying apparition. Then again, of course, if her crew were suffering nothing worse than weariness and thirst, and if he swam out to her with skin bottles of good sweet water from the spring beyond the headland . . .

Dreams of rescue and reward were dashed a moment later. Three figures appeared on deck, rubbing sleep from their eyes, and shortly caught sight of him and Anastasia. They waved. She waved back frantically. There was the sound of shouted orders, and the ship came slowly back to life.

In a while, a dinghy was lowered, and three people—possibly the same three, though the distance was too great for Evgenos to be certain—set out for shore, two rowing and the third in the stern, using another oar for a rudder.

"How wonderful!" Anastasia breathed. "They must be very rich! Perhaps we can sell them something for a lot of money!"

More cynically Evgenos said, "Most rich people get rich by taking what they want without paying for it. It's the way of the world."

He wished he possessed a weapon that would symbolize his determination to defend against all comers himself, the woman he was so proud of having won, and this patch of ungrateful land that yielded them their meager living. For a moment he thought of the sword he had found as he strove to dig it . . . but though its hilt and guard were intact its blade was a rusty stub. What else might serve him if the need arose?

Glancing around, he caught sight of the wooden pole, sharpened at one end, which they used to furrow the patch of dusty, salty ground between their home and the beach. Apart from his fisherman's gutting knife, it was as good a weapon as they owned. Taking hold of it, he tried to lean on it with a casual air, as though it were nothing more than a stick to relieve strain on a gammy leg.

Anastasia wanted to rush down to the water's edge and greet the strangers. He checked her with a touch.

"Wait until we see how they behave. Wait until we hear what they've got to say."

"But they're foreign! You can't understand foreigners!"

"I've been to places you had never even heard of, you know that. I picked up a little of the *lingua franca* and I think I may remember just enough."

Compliant, she obeyed.

The dinghy grounded in the shallows. One of the rowers jumped out: a thin boy wearing salt-crusted breeches and a shirt with one sleeve ripped away. He produced a splintered plank and laid it from the bow to a rock that offered dry footing. Stowing his steering oar, the man from the stern picked his way forward and, balancing nimbly, walked the plank to land. It would be fair to guess he was the captain of the galley. He too was thin, of medium height, with a hawk-beaked nose above a dense black beard. A brown velvet slouch cap shaded his piercing eyes. Like the rest of his clothing—a gray shirt that had been white, a plum-colored velvet doublet with its pile rubbed away on the right side, black breeches tucked into wide boots with their tops turned over—it had no doubt once been fine and costly, but now his whole attire was stained and shabby.

Evgenos kept his face mask-stiff, striving to look like a stupid peasant. But he was plagued by a terrible sense of disorientation, as though from drinking too much wine. Every time he looked closely at the newcomers, he seemed to see more than one of them, blurred and out of focus.

Then the stranger did something that took him totally aback. He broke into a broad grin and advanced with arm outstretched.

"Gene! Stacy!" he exclaimed. "How are you?"

Bewildered, they drew back, and Anastasia caught at Evgenos's free hand, squeezing his fingers so hard it almost hurt.

For no one, short of eavesdropping on their pallet stuffed with moss and prickly fern, could have known about the pet names they called each other! Evgenos tightened his grip on the sharpened pole, uncertain whether it would be wise to show defiance, yet ashamed not to.

At all events, this stranger spoke a language he could understand after a fashion. Framing words with difficulty, because most of the time he and Anastasia had little to talk about—there was no news on Oragalia, only scandal and rumor—he said, "Who are you? What do you want?"

It was the captain's turn to be taken aback. Lowering his hand, he said uncertainly, "But—Oh, surely, you must remember me? Stacy!"

Wide-eyed, Anastasia shook her head. A lock of her lank and greasy hair fell over one eye; hastily she brushed it back. She should not have been out here, in the presence of strange men, wearing just a dress and with nothing to cover her head. But she was too frightened now to risk going in search of a shawl.

"Look!" His expression affable enough, but his voice full of puzzlement, the captain approached more closely. "You must recognize me, surely! I'm *****!"

However, if what followed was a name, then it was one they couldn't repeat—couldn't even register. It was full of wrong sounds, such as they had never attempted to twist their tongues around. It was as much like hearing double as looking at the visitors resembled seeing double . . . yet neither was a right comparison. Evgenos fought against the sickening sensation with all his might.

"What do you want?" he demanded again. "Is it water for your crew? We can give you drink if you leave us in peace, but we have nothing fine enough to be worth stealing!"

The captain stood irresolute for a moment, glancing at his companions; by now they had moored the dinghy and joined him. The second rower was large and burly, with a scarred face and a dirty kerchief tied around his right forearm, patched with brown as from dried blood.

"What do you make of this, #####?" the captain demanded. Once again the name defeated Evgenos's ear. As the boy the question was addressed to shook his head, he decided to think of him as Bony, and the burly one as Scarface.

"You, ‡‡‡‡‡?" This time the captain appealed to the latter.

"We'll have to ask a lot more questions," Scarface rumbled.

"I don't like these people!" Anastasia whispered. "Do something to make them go away!"

Equally softly, Evgenos returned, "A far cry from saints and angels, aren't they? But how can I drive them off? All I can do is persuade them there's nothing here to interest them . . ." And he added more loudly, "Didn't you hear me say we're not worth robbing?"

"We don't even have enough food for ourselves!" Anastasia chimed in loudly. "We don't know how we'll manage when the baby comes!" And she laid her hand dramatically on the rising curve of her belly.

"Ah, yes! That's one of the things I've come to see you about." The captain adopted a soothing tone. "Don't you think it would be better for your baby to be born in a /hospital/, in /sterile/ conditions with trained staff on hand, rather than in your cave? What about /amniocentesis/? What about your /rhesus incompatibility/? You were told you're /rhesus opposites/; you can't have forgotten that! Of course, you'll be a /primapara/, so your system hasn't been sensitized, but even so you're running a terrible risk, let alone the danger of /Down's syndrome/ if you have your first child at such an advanced age . . . Oh, hell! It's no use, is it? I'm not getting through."

He turned away despondently. After a pause Bony suggested, "What about something on a more basic level? They seem to be afraid that we're here to rob them, don't they? But we can easily disabuse them of that idea."

"Yes, of course!" Scarface agreed. "We can bring a load of provisions, the sort of stuff they can't have seen in months, and gain their attention that way. How about it?"

Bewildered, Evgenos and Anastasia looked from one to the other of the intruders, striving to make sense of what was being said, and failing.

"It's worth trying," the captain agreed. "Go ahead!"

At once Bony and Scarface relaunched the dinghy and made haste toward the galley, whose crew were now fully awake and going about their normal business of checking the rigging and washing down the decks.

"Gene! Stacy! Shall we sit down?" the captain proposed, and suited action to word by lowering his rump gingerly on to a flattish rock.

"How does he know our private names?" Anastasia whispered, making no move to copy him.

"I don't know," Evgenos answered grimly, still fighting the impulse to see and hear two, or twenty, where there was only one. "Saints and angels, hmm? I could better believe them devils! Fetch the icon!"

They had one hanging over their pallet, the only gift at their wedding—about which most of the islanders had been furious—that might last a while beyond the birth of their first child; the rest of the presents had been scraps of cloth, pickled vegetables and salted fish, jars of oil and the like, the smallest tokens the givers thought they could get away with. It was painted in cheap colors on a slab of badly warped wood, but it had been properly dedicated in the church and carried the power of the image on it, the Virgin and Child in blue, red, white and gold.

Thanks to Anastasia's habit of kissing it night and morning, though, much of the paint in the center had already worn away.

She made haste to unhook the string on which it hung from the natural peg afforded by a branch stump on the tree trunk Evgenos had set up as the hovel's center post (and there had been a row about its felling, for some declared it had stood beyond the border of the unclaimed ground where they had made their home—but it had yielded nothing, it wasn't an olive and it didn't bear nuts, so it was no great loss).

Rushing back, she held the icon before her like a shield, affected by Evgenos's mention of devils to the point where it seemed she expected the captain to scream and disappear.

But the latter's only reaction was to take it from her for inspection. "I take it you're very proud of this," he remarked, smiling as he handed it back. "So you should be. It must be very old. I'm no expert, of course, but to me it looks like a splendid example of traditional folk art. It could well fetch thousands at an auction in @@@@."

Where?

Once again a name slithered past their ears. Baffled, on the verge of crying, Anastasia clutched the icon to her breast and hurried to restore it to its usual place.

By this time, however, Evgenos had accepted that they were in no immediate danger. Laying by his intended means of defense, he cautiously sat down on another level rock, facing the captain. He said, "How is it you seem to know us? I don't recognize you at all."

He made no mention of the countless others he could see whenever he looked at him.

"Are you sure? Don't you think it might come back to you in a little while?"

"But where did we meet? I don't remember!"

Gravely, the captain leaned forward, elbow on knee and chin in hand.

"That's fairly obvious," he said with a frown. "The question remains: why not? How what you've been through could have affected you so deeply on the mental level, even though physically both you and Stacy seemed perfectly normal on your return: *that's* what we don't understand."

"Return from where?" Evgenos cried. "Where did I go?"

"If I could tell you that," said the captain soberly "we wouldn't be talking in riddles, would we? But you and Stacy have been there, and I haven't. Don't you realize how much we admire you both? You must be among the bravest people in history. Knowing how poor your chances were, you went ahead and volunteered because you cared more about your species than yourselves. If only—"

Evgenos sat dumb, letting the incomprehensible words flow on. He had never done anything more admirable than run away to this island in search of sanctuary. His memory assured him that was the truth.

Though, of course, meeting and winning Anastasia . . .

But these people hadn't come here after women, or anything else. In fact, they seemed to be bringing rather than taking away. In the distance the dinghy had been loaded with a cargo he could not clearly discern, and Bony and Scarface were bending to their oars again. Meantime, as Anastasia hastened back and dropped on her knees at his side, as though into protective shelter, he forced out, "You didn't finish what you were saying."

"Oh, yes. I was about to say: if only there were some way we could get reports without sending live observers! Or if only we could devise some sort of training program to prepare people for what they're going to encounter! But we simply can't conceive /machines/ that will react along the same lines. Our brains don't work the way /computers/ do. You know, for years we've had a prize on offer, worth ten million plus the assurance of worldwide fame, for anyone who can design a /machine/ capable of passing the /interface/ and returning with decipherable data. Frankly, I don't think anyone is going to win it who hasn't already made the trip—Ah! I see breakfast coming. I hope you're hungry."

When had either of them been otherwise?

But Evgenos held his tongue, and allowed himself to be persuaded into helping to unload the dinghy. Its cargo proved to consist of foodstuffs as strange and fascinating as the scent he and Anastasia had awoken to.

Friendly and generous, the captain passed squat goblets of a substance that was warmer to the touch than glass or pottery, tinted throughout with bright intrinsic colors and every one different. These were then filled by Bony with a steaming dark brown liquid which, when sipped, made them alert and lively. Bread followed; though cool, it was as moist and spongy as if it had come fresh from the oven. To go with it there were pinkish brown cylinders of chopped meat, spicy and delicious, preserves sweeter than any Evgenos could remember tasting, strange bright red fruit with yellow pips, and more, and more, and more . . .

"This is a /tomato/," the captain explained. "What you are drinking is /coffee/ and—well, you obviously recognize bread, but those are /frankfurters/ and the pickle is /mango chutney/ and this is a /bell pepper/ and this is . . ."

No use. The blank wall remained between them. Evgenos was aware that he and Anastasia were expected to respond in some way to these unfamiliar, though welcome, foods, whose names he heard and instantly forgot, but when he strove to think of any connection they might have with his past, he failed. Glancing at Anastasia, he saw that she was equally at a loss, though she ate greedily. Contrariwise Scarface, Bony, and the captain, all three, displayed small appetite, concerned only to produce more and more of what they had brought in the hope of—what? What could they be looking for on Oragalia, this island forgotten by the rest of the world? They couldn't be hoping to open up a new market for their exotic imports! Who on this poverty-stricken hummock of rock and sand could afford to pay their prices?

Replete, burping, Evgenos waved aside the latest offering. Never had he dreamed of such a banquet, least of all one conjured up without warning on his own patch of salt-sour ground! The finest feasts held at the island's single village, where people vied with one another to have their neighbors admire their skill in drying fish, preparing oil and wine, or pickling onions, paled into insignificance beside this repast . . . whose hosts apparently regarded it as trivial, judging by the way they were tossing the leftovers into the sea. For a second he was angered: why, he and Anastasia could have made two more meals off what was being wasted!

Then he recovered himself. He owed the visitors something, in the way of courtesy if no other. He turned to the captain, relieved at seeing only one of him by now.

"Sir, will you not tell me when and where you think I met you?"

"Not just you," the other answered. "Stacy as well."

"That's impossible!" Anastasia burst out. "I've spent my whole life on this island! The only people I've ever met were born here, same as me, or came like you across the sea. And I never saw a ship like yours before, and most of all I never saw *you!* Unless—"

A horrifying idea struck her. She rounded on Evgenos.

"Unless you had another woman before you came here who was so like me that this man has mixed us up!"

"Now you're being silly!" the captain began, rising to his feet. But Anastasia did the same, more swiftly.

"I don't know you!" she cried. "I don't want to know you or the world you come from! I didn't invite you here and all I want is for you to go away!"

Bursting into tears, she spun on her heel and fled to the shelter of the cave above their hovel.

Instantly angry on her behalf, Evgenos lifted his pole, prepared to strike the captain down, but Scarface laid a hand on his arm and warned him to desist. Bony said, "We're wasting our time, you know. It's just as I've been predicting all along: this sort of direct approach can only drive them deeper into /fugue/."

"But we can't just leave them to rot!" the captain exclaimed. "Especially now she's pregnant!"

"There's time yet," Bony countered. "And if nothing breaks before her waters—sorry: bad joke—we'll simply have to intervene on the grandest possible scale. Meantime there's no special hurry."

"No hurry? Are you crazy?" The captain took half a pace back.

"There are some cases," Scarface said grayly, "where haste is self-defeating. We literally do not know what's going on. It could even be that this is the penalty the cosmos imposes on creatures as hubristic as ourselves."

"Stuff your /mystical/ nonsense!" the captain flared.

"When we're dealing not just with the frontiers of reality, but something way beyond them, there isn't a divide between /science/ and /mysticism/ anymore." With a smile of apology Scarface let go Evgenos's arm.

"Well said," approved the boy he had privately nicknamed Bony, and turned away. "So long, Gene. Apologize to Stacy on our behalf. We didn't mean to make her so upset."

Evgenos was on the verge of demanding that they stay and explain themselves properly, when in sudden amazement he thought: *boy?* And realized Bony wasn't one, but a woman, for all her masculine disguise.

Confused beyond measure, he was glad to see them go.

* * *

As always, a couple of hours after noon, the heat of the land began to draw cooler air off the sea. That, plus the beating of the water by the galley's oars, dispersed the dense and aromatic vapor from her cargo. When it had faded completely, Anastasia and Evgenos were left with a vague feeling of regret, or unfulfillment.

But at least they had a respite from hunger. The scraps the visitors had left would suffice them for days, even though some had had to be retrieved from the shallows and were soaked with salt water.

"Those people . . ." Gene muttered as darkness fell.

"Yes?"

"Wasn't it strange how they thought we used to know them?"

"Hah!" she retorted caustically. "Some people are vain enough to believe they ought to be recognized anywhere!"

He gave a dry chuckle. "Yes, that's part of it, I guess. And yet . . ."

"What?" Undressing amid yawns, ready to stretch out on their crude bed, she added, "Aren't you tired?"

"Yes—yes, very tired." Not rising, he started to peel off his shirt, but with it still spread across his knees he spoke again.

"Nonetheless that can't be the whole story. It's obvious enough that people can be lured to make long voyages by the hope of profit, and who would not prize a cargo of spices like the one that scented our whole island today?"

"It could have bought and sold our land a hundred times over!" she exclaimed as she lay down.

"Yes, even perhaps a thousand times." But such enormous numbers felt foreign to them both. He plowed ahead.

"What, though, is one to make of people who travel for the sake of traveling—of finding themselves tomorrow, or next year, in a land no one they ever met or even heard of has set foot upon before? People who are prepared to take the risk of being cast away because they are so greedy for places where everything is different from at home!"

"I suppose they're out of their minds," Stacy replied around another yawn.

"No! No!" Warming to his theme, Gene twisted his calloused hands back and forth, back and forth, on the coarse and tattered fabric of his shirt. "Was Giacomo crazy, for example?"

"Maybe."

"Are you? Am I?"

"Maybe."

"But I don't *feel* crazy!"

"What does being crazy feel like? My guess is that it must feel normal."

He considered that awhile, wondering why a woman should dress up as a boy. Eventually he said, "If not, I suppose one could recognize it . . . But that still doesn't take care of people like Giacomo."

"Tell me why not."

"Because he was chronically discontented. He maintained that the only kind of world to suit his restless spirit was one where nothing was ever the same from one day to the next. He declared himself heartily sick of those who, like his father, strove in cobwebbed libraries and gray museums to reduce the cosmos to entries in a catalogue. He dreamed of a universe where there would always be new challenges, new realms to be explored; where people like himself could forever be setting out on journeys into the unknown, and be the bane of those who stayed at home in a boring, dull, predictable environment, occupying themselves with study and analysis. He used to say, 'So you've dissected lots of frogs! Did you ever wind up knowing how to build a frog that did frog things, or were there just more piles of rotten meat to throw away?'

"For him, therefore, the journey was his life's ambition. He set out joyfully and found his goal. In the place he came to, it was axiomatic that tomorrow should be different from today. On learning that he was an explorer by profession, the people eagerly financed his team. So off he went, with comrades of like mind, and found a jungle no one had traversed, replete with the most amazing novelties: relics and tribes, and animals, that none had seen before! He endured privations worse than any he'd imagined; sometimes starving, sometimes half-dead of thirst, losing his companions one by one, he achieved the most epic exploration of all time, and when he staggered back to the coast, leech-weakened, staring-eyed, nearly naked, but clutching to him precious records he'd compiled, he was at long last glad of a chance to return to the city he'd set out from, which lately he'd condemned as dull and smug. He'd been away a year or two at most, so he looked forward to a splendid welcome.

"Yet even at the docks he felt betrayed. The city was certainly the one he had booked passage to, only . . . Here were old, known names, but the signs indicated unfamiliar streets; there were different instructions in the phone booth from which he tried to call a number that turned out not to exist. The cars and trucks were wrongly shaped and made an alien noise, and he did not recognize the coding of their registration plates; the meal he ordered in a café stemmed from a cuisine he did not know, and when he tried to pay for it the money in his pocket was dismissed as a crude forgery. Worst of all, the policemen called by the proprietor arrived in uniforms the like of which he'd never seen before. Only when he was dragged away to jail did he realize the truth."

"I don't understand," Stacy murmured out of shadow.

"Why, that on this world which matched his heart's desire nothing was stable, nothing remained the same. Had he only stayed where he found himself at first, he could have enjoyed all the benefits of change without the shock of coming home to a city where he and his mission were doomed to be forgotten . . . or derided."

For a while there was silence. Then:

"I still don't see what you mean, but it was a pretty tale anyhow. Before tomorrow, please, let us forget the strangers." Rolling over, Stacy spread wide her arms.

"With the best will in the world," said Gene as he embraced her. "Only—"

"Only what?"

"I think maybe they won't so easily forget us."

"What do you mean?" she exclaimed in alarm, for she had felt him shiver.

A cold and distant fear had touched him. With an effort he dismissed it, and shortly persuaded her that, tonight at least, there was no more need for speech.

# PART SIX

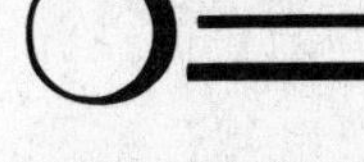

*THE EXHIBIT*
*is the hilt of a rusty sword, its blade a stub. It marks the failure of an age of certainty*

*THE MONTH*
*is September*

*THE NAME*
*is Hedwig*

Except for the very young, the sick, and the very old, and those who were obliged to stay at home and tend them, the entire population of Oragalia had assembled in the island's single church to mark the festival of the Exaltation of the Holy Cross. They included some whose presence was resented, but the *papas* had ordered slandermongers to bridle their tongues, since it was unbefitting to speak evil of one's fellows at this sacred time.

The drab interior of the building had been transformed, so far as resources allowed, with limewash and bunches of late summer flowers. Bees attracted by the latter buzzed somnolently around, trying to retrace the way they had come in, sometimes evoking cries from children old enough to know they stung, too young to understand that they were a precious gift from the Pantocrator not only for their honey but as a symbol of pain hidden by the sweetness of sin.

In general the spirits of the people were light, for it had been a good summer. There had been no sickness among either the folk or their livestock, the figs and olives were yielding bountifully, and the wild thyme on the hillsides was so fragrant it could be smelled far out to sea. Ill-clad, sunken-eyed, most of the married ones—and the young widows—hollow-cheeked from early loss of teeth, they nonetheless raised their voices loudly and cheerfully, especially in response to the special invocations the *papas* recited for the safety and success of those bound on the latest mission to liberate the Holy Land from domination by the Saracens. The future of the Kingdom of Jerusalem was precarious, or so rumor said, but Christian knights were gathering from all over Europe to its aid, and when they had vanquished the enemy the riches of the Orient would once more come pouring through this quarter of the Middle Sea. A fraction of that fabled wealth must surely wash up on the shore of even so petty an island as Oragalia. Fervently they prayed it would.

And then the outer world broke in on them, sooner than and differently from what they besought the Lord to grant.

Just as the priest was bringing the service to its end, the low main door of the church, closed against the sun's harsh glare, was forced wide with a grating noise; it had dropped on its hinges and it scraped the flagstones. Every eye turned to see who had so belatedly come to answer the call to worship.

Five strangers. Armed strangers. Armed and arrogant.

All their faces were heavily scarred, by battle or disease or both, and one of them was blind on his right side; all had battered metal helmets on their heads; all carried shields and drawn swords; all wore coats of chain mail, which marked them out as knights, and the first to enter had greaves and gauntlets too; all bar one had carved wooden crosses hanging around their necks on leather thongs; and the exception, the one-eyed man, who hung back in the doorway as his comrades advanced toward the altar, had a sort of amice over his mail, white but badly soiled, with red crosses embroidered on it front and back.

Their leader, the one in almost full armor, stared suspiciously around the little church. Then, relaxing, he sheathed his blade—with a signal that his companions should do the same—and swaggered up to the priest. The congregation shrank against the walls, the women and children seeking shelter at the backs of their menfolk. In the sudden hush could be heard shouts and banging noises from the waterfront. Many fretted for the safety of their prized possessions such as livestock, boats, barrels and fishing nets, but dared not brave the intruders' swords to run and see what was happening.

The knight confronting the *papas* now addressed him in Latin, speaking loudly and slowly as to an idiot. He made himself understood only with difficulty; the priest was a local man, scarcely more than a youth, whose command even of the Greek Testament was less than perfect. But eventually he sighed and turned to his congregation.

"This is the Sieur de Belmaison, a great gentleman from France," he announced. "He has come with a company of soldiers in two ships. They are bound to fight the Saracens. They were driven off course by contrary winds. They are short of food and drink. We must show them charity because theirs is a sacred mission. Even if they hold a wrong opinion concerning the Trinity, they too are Christians and all Christians must band together against the agents of the Evil One."

Standing beside him with a suspicious expression, the French lord surveyed the congregation. His gaze lighted on one particular young woman, and lingered. Even though she was conspicuously with child, she had a handsome face and good clear skin. Moreover, she kept apart from the rest of the people, as though they made her feel unwelcome. The rest, that was, except one . . . and he was a strange fellow to find hereabouts! How far was he from home? What could possibly have brought to Oragalia a blackamoor darker than the Saracens themselves?

Instantly de Belmaison jumped to the conclusion that this outsider must be at least a spy, and possibly an agent of Satan who had come hither in the hope of subverting the faith of these simple peasant folk, undermined as it already was by the falsehoods of the Eastern Church. The priest had finished interpreting what he had said so far, and from what snatches he had been able to understand seemed to have made an honest job of it. Now he spoke up again, not only emphasizing the islanders' obligation to show charity toward their cobelievers, but also warning them against Mussulmen, pagans, and other evildoers.

This time, when the translation was concluded, there was a remarkable reaction among the islanders. Everywhere he saw grim nods of agreement, and many harsh glances were cast at the black man and the woman by his side. So, although it was heretical, their religion must be strong enough to resist the fellow's wheedling and cajoling. Excellent. His ship's chaplain would be bound to take a great interest in the matter, though.

"Well, you can guess what we want," he resumed. "It's long and long since we enjoyed bread softer than the rocks of your seashore, or fresh meat, or wine any sweeter than vinegar! Get to it! Do your Christian duty! Or"—and he narrowed his eyes and let his hand stray toward his swordhilt—"we shall feel entitled to help ourselves!"

That provoked a ripple of dismay among the worshipers. Someone said in a whisper meant to be overheard, "What's the betting they already did?"

But de Belmaison failed to understand the coarsely accented Greek, and the *papas* felt no inclination to translate it.

The islanders made haste to disperse. Shortly, however, there were squeals from outside, followed by cries of anger. By the sound of it, someone had found a pig and promptly slaughtered it. A moment later, and a goose and several chickens went the same way. Intending to hang back as usual until everyone else had left, dreadfully conscious of de Belmaison's interest in her and her man, Anastasia whispered to Evgenos, "Will they seize what we have, too?"

They were poor, but they did have a dozen hens, and preserves in store against the winter.

"Not if I can help it!" Evgenos promised. "Let's make for home as quickly as we can!"

And, unprecedentedly, caught her hand and pushed the remaining worshipers aside on their way to the door.

Standing beside it, the one-eyed stranger was inspecting those who passed by, his gaze as keen as anyone's with normal sight. The sunken pit above his right cheekbone lent him a sinister and terrifying air; parents were making their children avert their faces. Anastasia too shrank back and tried to hide behind Evgenos. But, to her and their astonishment, his face softened into half a smile when they arrived before him—half, because whatever wound had cost him his eye had also shriveled the muscles at that corner of his mouth.

In ill-pronounced but comprehensible Greek, he said, "A blessing on your child, young friends. I'm sure he will be tall and strong and handsome."

Anastasia suppressed a shriek of horror and fled into the sunlight, dragging Evgenos after her. Despite their detestation of the black foreigner who had won the favors of the island's prettiest girl, the rest of those in earshot crossed themselves or made the sign of the horns and rushed in Anastasia's wake, leaving the church—apart from the presence of the *papas*—in the undisputed possession of de Belmaison and his companions.

"They claim to be in the service of Christ, yet he said that about my child!" Anastasia moaned as soon as they were safely clear of the building.

"I know," Evgenos muttered grimly, for he had been well taught since his arrival about the dangers of the Evil Eye. "And look at what the rest of them are getting up to!" He pointed toward the shore.

There, for all the local people could do to interfere—and they were being laughed at, or threatened, for their pains—the men from the ships which now rode at anchor in the bay had built a great fire, using whatever they could find that would burn. Not only had they taken the village's stock of driftwood, in itself precious on an island with so few trees; those of them who possessed maces or axes had also attacked the barrels destined for this year's wine and oil, and even the hull of the Kaloyiannis family's boat, retrieved at the cost of so much effort after its side had been stove in against a rock in the last gale.

Four or five of them were bloodying the sand as they hung up the slaughtered pig to drain on a pole. Even while Evgenos and Anastasia watched in horror, they gashed its belly to let out the inwards, which they promptly tossed aside. Were they insane? Why waste so much good food? It was awful to think of the sausages it would have made!

Dogs had been brought ashore, too: hulking but ill-favored beasts that had to be kept at bay with whips. One of the soldiers, grinning satanically, used his on the wife of the pig's owner, who was begging for at least the offal, and to emphasize his point caught up a handful of the guts and hurled them as far as he could. Instantly the dogs converged on them and began to fight, which amused the soldiers hugely. The woman, a lash mark reddening across her cheek, turned away howling louder than the dogs.

Meantime the goose and chickens were being roughly plucked and cleaned, then spitted on whatever sticks had not yet been thrown into the fire. Laughing and joking, more of the soldiers—there must be thirty-five or forty of them altogether, Evgenos estimated—appeared carrying all the barrels and skin bottles of wine that they could find. At once they were the center of their comrades' attention, and most of what was left from last year's vintage was promptly spilled either down their gullets or on the ground: either way, gone to waste.

Then someone reported his discovery of the baker's, its oven containing not only new bread but also the stews and other dishes the better-off families had taken there to be cooked during divine service. To the utter horror of the onlookers, the soldiers instantly forgot about the pig and the poultry, leaving them to char for want of being turned, and seized on this new discovery, emptying the earthenware pots so fast they nearly choked themselves, then hurling them to smash on the rocky ground. Whenever anybody tried to stop them, they cursed and struck out, drunkenly now, sometimes only with fists, but more than once with weapons. The middle Kaloyiannis boy, braver or angrier than most, was rewarded with a gash across his thigh which felled him to the ground, and the man who had delivered the blow was restrained with difficulty from chopping at him again.

Aghast in the doorway of the church, the *papas* shouted at de Belmaison, demanding why he was letting his men behave worse than pagans or Mussulmen. But, grinning cynically, the French lord and three of his companions ignored his complaints and went to claim a share of the spoils, each ordering his followers to bring him the choicest food and drink. The priest burst into unashamed sobs.

"How can Christians act this way?" he screamed.

The one-eyed man, who had remained in the shadow of the church door, emerged blinking into sunlight and laid a consolatory hand on his arm. In his stilted Greek he said, "They have been disappointed in their hope of fighting the Saracens. We should have reached the Holy Land a month ago. When it is ours again, you will be amply repaid for what they're taking."

A little reassured, the *papas* wiped away his tears. Anastasia, however, still frightened because the one-eyed man might, wittingly or unwittingly, have ill-wished her unborn child, clutched at Evgenos's arm, whimpering.

"Yes, let's make ourselves scarce," the latter muttered. "Any moment now these devils are going to remember there are women here, and my guess is they've had to manage without any for quite some time. Of course, they will have used the boys instead, but even so . . . And some of them are loathsomely diseased. We'd better make for home and hope against hope that they'll be too drunk to think about exploring the whole island before they leave."

Anastasia's face twisted in horror, and despite her condition she followed him homeward at a frantic run.

Having penned their chickens in the cave above their hut, and hidden the rest of their few possessions as best they could, they waited tensely throughout an afternoon that dragged on unendurably. Apart from the humming of bees, and as evening drew on the clicking of cicadas, there was almost no sound; yet they often fancied they could hear a scream from the direction of the village, or a harsh cruel laugh, or the echo of yet another pot or dish being casually broken by those who would be gone tomorrow, heedless of how long it would take the islanders to repair their meager fortunes.

Even after sunset, though he allowed Anastasia to go and lie down, Evgenos did not relax his vigilance. Armed with a heavy olive branch by way of a club, he sat amid the gathering darkness, daring to dream that he, sober, might be a match for any number of soldiers fuddled with drink. Yet his belly growled, and the acid taste of hunger rose in his mouth as he thought of the good food the invaders had gobbled down or tossed aside. He hadn't eaten meat in weeks, not since their oldest hen became too old to lay.

It grew very late. He had almost allowed himself the luxury of imagining that, here at the distant southern tip of Oragalia, they were destined to escape the predations of the crusaders, when he caught the noise of someone slipping on the steep and pebbly path across the headland, followed by a curse and a chuckle—the latter, no doubt from someone else. So there were going to be at least two of them. Cautiously, noiselessly, he crawled into concealment among bushes so dry it cost him all his self-control to prevent their twigs from snapping. Tonight the moon was almost at its full; he could see a long way. He would be well prepared when they got here.

He wondered whether to waken Anastasia, but decided against it. Best if she slept the sleep of exhaustion. Of course, if he failed in his defense of her—

But he refused to let himself entertain the idea.

Nonetheless his feigned confidence waned when he first caught a glimpse of the men heading toward him. One of the pair appeared to be a giant, with shoulders as wide as the church door! Then he realized his mistake. That was two men, both of ordinary size, supporting one another and their common burden of a clumsy ancient pottery wine jar against the rough going. A pang of relief transfixed him—only to vanish as he realized: not two men coming his way, but three.

He sought what consolation he could in the fact that they were definitely common soldiery. They carried no shields; hence probably they did not possess swords either, although they doubtless had clubs or knives, and what passed for their armor would be nothing more than padded leather. One accurate blow to each of their heads, with all the violence at his command, and . . .

But that was wishful thinking. He drove himself to the utmost pitch of concentration, and realized he was going to have to let them pass, on their way to where Anastasia lay, in order to attack them from behind. Whether they were drunk or sober, it was too risky to confront them.

They drew level with him, cursing and complaining in a tongue he did not understand, though he could well guess what two of them were saying to the third: "It had better be worth coming all this way!" Holding his breath, he waited until their backs were turned, and poised to leap down with his improvised weapon swinging. And at that very instant there came the sound of other, hastier, footsteps, and a sharp voice raised as though issuing an order.

He was too tense to work out the implications of that. All he could think of was that there were now four men to contend with, and the three he had been about to attack were just on the point of turning around—

*I should have been praying while I waited*, Evgenos grieved to himself, and launched his onslaught with a yell.

As well as surprise, he had the advantage of knowing every inch of this end of the island, but even so he was too late to take the trio completely aback. As befitted good soldiers—which in the proper circumstances they might be—they responded with reflex speed, heedless of the antiquity of the jar they carried, and the more important fact that it was still half-full. It fell to the ground and smashed, and gave him an extra precious second to take aim, for the liquid made their footing instantly slippery, and they almost lost their balance.

This stroke of luck provided Evgenos with time to crack the nearest of them over the head with all his might and knock him unconscious, but before his victim had measured his length the other two were charging, and it was sheer luck that enabled him to swipe them both, painfully, before having to retreat with his back against the rock. His breath rasped in his throat; the air was horribly dry and full of dust.

From the direction of the path came another shout, full of menace. He had no time to think about that, though. He was compelled to hurl his club first this way, then that, with hands so slippery with sweat (and how could that be, when the air was so dry?) that he risked losing his grip. One or two of his blows connected; the rest were near enough to make his opponents jump aside and regroup. But those which did hit home seemed not to do any harm, and pretty soon one of the soldiers was going to hit him, maybe on the arm or hand, and there was yet another shout from behind, this time loud and angry, and—*missed me, by a miracle! Help me, saints! You can't let these brutes rape Anastasia! You can't! Yet here they are coming at me again, and the one that I knocked flying is struggling to his feet, and I'm tiring already because it's so long since I filled my belly with such good food as they stole from us today, and I hear the other one coming up behind me, closer and closer—Got you, you spawn of Satan!*

*Fair and square on the cheek, and I felt his teeth go crunch, and there he is tripping over his own feet but here come the others both at once—Help me, St. Michael and St. George, the dragon killers! Because if you don't . . .*

*Oh, Lord God Almighty. We've woken Anastasia, and I can see her coming out of the hut, and—*

The world spun. He had tripped on a loose pebble and been clubbed on the right shoulder, both at once. The shock ran like a lightning bolt clear to the tips of his fingers, and while he was struggling to recover he heard a shout so close behind him he felt convinced he was about to die. Somehow they had lured him away from the rock that had protected his back at the beginning, so as to give the fourth of them an opening . . .

"Stand aside!"

And he was rudely thrust off balance. He went sprawling in dirt churned up to mud, his nose and lungs full of the stench of warm sour wine, as harsh as vomit. Moaning in terror, he rolled over, clinging to his club, and discovered that all his latest guesses had been wrong. This newcomer was not bent on the same errand as the others. Moreover he had a sword and shield, and he knew Greek, though he was speaking another language now, and furiously.

It was the one-eyed knight.

For a space the three soldiers seemed minded to defy him, but he clouted the foremost of them soundly with the flat of his sword and then presented its point under the man's chin, still uttering a torrent of obvious abuse. The spirit went out of them. Sullenly they obeyed his command to wend their way back to the village, although they kept muttering complaints until they were out of earshot.

"Sir!" Evgenos dropped to one knee. "Sir, I owe you my life! And as for Anastasia—" She had come to join him, realizing the danger was past, and he caught her hand.

But the right words refused to pass his lips.

Kicking aside fragments of the wine jar as he sheathed his sword, the one-eyed man said, "It was my duty as a Christian to frustrate de Belmaison's intentions. Oh, get up, man! You're no liege of mine."

"But I owe you my life!" Evgenos repeated.

The knight's lip curled into a cynical grin, half-concealed by his scruffy beard. "I'm not so sure of that, even. You seemed to be giving a pretty good account of yourself. As a matter of fact, there have been times on the field of battle when I'd have been glad of a squire as stout as you!"

Anastasia flinched, thinking for a second he meant to enlist Evgenos. The knight noticed, and interpreted her reaction accurately.

"Ah, don't worry. I have my own retainers, and they are better disciplined than de Belmaison's."

"It was he who sent those three to? . . ."

"Yes indeed. He has no control over his baser appetites. That's why I set out after them, as soon as I discovered the sort of errand they were on. He'd told them to locate 'the blackamoor's woman' "—a nod at Anastasia—"and drag you back for his enjoyment. It was indicated that if they took advantage of you on the way, he'd not object."

In horror Anastasia whispered, "And these are the folk who plan to liberate the Holy Land?"

"I think they won't," the knight replied, his voice betraying sudden weariness. He dropped the point of his shield to the ground and leaned on it. "But you must not judge us all by the actions of a few: particularly not by de Belmaison's. He belongs to no knightly Order, he has taken no oaths except an oath of fealty to his king, and there is little to choose between him and his crude peasant followers. Myself, on the other hand . . . Ah, but it's enough to have done the proper thing. I'll bid you good night."

"Wait, sir, if you please!" Anastasia darted forward. "I wish to know who you are and why you helped us, if only to remember you forever in my prayers!"

"Yes! Yes!" exclaimed Evgenos fervently, regaining his feet at last.

The knight gave a sad and cynical chuckle. "Well, here's a change in the wind! At noon you were prepared to imagine I had cast the Evil Eye upon your child—is that not so?"

"I beg your honor's forgiveness!" Anastasia cried.

"Don't let your soul be troubled by it. I was unaware of the beliefs that rule your people, or I'd not have made so bold . . . I'll answer you as honestly as I can, then, although my name's of no account. I lost my lands and family long ago. There was a plague. Still, for the sake of my Order, I'll say this.

"The Order of the Knights Hospitalers was founded to tend those injured in the service of the Cross. It is no longer what it used to be, and there are many who profane its binding oath. You can identify me in your prayers as one—and possibly the only one—who absolutely won't!"

On which he caught up his shield and strode away. Evgenos made to run after, but Anastasia checked him.

"You heard what he said! It shames him to admit what depths his comrades can descend to. Don't force him to think of them again. Praise God, rather, that some few righteous men are still alive!"

Later:

"Gene?" she whispered into the dark.

"Oh, I'm not asleep, Stacy. Even though it must be midnight. I don't imagine I shall sleep. I can't rid my mind of the image of de Belmaison—smug, self-righteous, prepared to condone the worst excesses because he's so totally convinced his cause is just!"

"No, you should think rather of the one-eyed man, and Hedwig too."

"Him, yes of course—but why her, for pity's sake?"

"Because he got it right, she got it wrong."

"I don't quite follow."

"Oh, you know Hedwig . . . I don't mean that; I mean: you know about her."

"Yes, but—"

"Let me explain, then. She was self-sacrificing, wasn't she? She was the self-sacrificial type *par excellence*, and viewed herself as an embodiment of altruism. However, this wasn't quite the way she struck other people, caught up as they were in the fulfillment of her ambition like leaves being whirled along in the wake of a fast car."

He found the resources for a laugh. "Oh, yes! Oh, very yes! But what became of her? Tell me!"

"The world she found her way to was a compendium of the wrongs she sought to right. Where there was not a brutal overlord enslaving the innocent, there was a plague; where not a famine, then greedy tax collectors; where not a drought, then war and all its countless victims, specially children. She was in her element, and she reveled in it!

"Promptly she began to organize reforms, and hordes of people flocked to support her projects. Naturally, being a visitor from far away, she enjoyed an automatic cachet. Think of any artist immigrating from abroad as a parallel; think, for instance, how many composers and musicians had to seek their fame in foreign countries.

"And in a sense she *was* an artist—a specialist, at all events—and here she was supplied with more material to work on than she'd ever dared to dream of. For a long while she was happy. She was deliriously happy."

"But what became of her in the end?" Gene murmured sleepily.

"I think you might well guess. Come on! You said you weren't likely to fall asleep tonight."

He rolled over, eyes closed. "I may well have been wrong about that . . . Uh—yes! Hedwig! Like you said, she reached the sort of world she'd always dreamed of."

"*And—?*" She prompted him with a nudge.

"Oh! It could never run short of causes for her to dedicate herself to. There were always going to be worse things in the news tomorrow than the ones she had set out to cure today. Is that how you see her fate?"

"It turned out worse," Stacy countered. "In fact she won, insofar as she cleansed the world of the evils that she found on her arrival. But ultimately she found herself obliged to organize yet one more project on top of all the rest: a campaign to provide charity for the people she'd inspired, those who, as a result of copying her example, found they had lost everything they cared about—their homes, their families, their loved ones, their heirlooms and their other prized possessions . . . To this end, of course, she had to recruit still further helpers, or perhaps one might better term them worshipers, who in turn complained about what they'd had to abandon at her behest. Finally it dawned on her that here was one campaign without an end. She who had so consistently sacrificed herself had paid no heed to the other people she was spending as the price of her achievements. Her conscience rebelled, but the fact remained: she had incurred one debt she never could repay . . . Gene? *Gene?*"

But he was asleep. A moment later, so was she.

# PART SEVEN

*THE EXHIBIT*
*consists in the fragments of a jar that once held wine. It can never be made whole again*

*THE MONTH*
*is October*

*THE NAME*
*is Pedro*

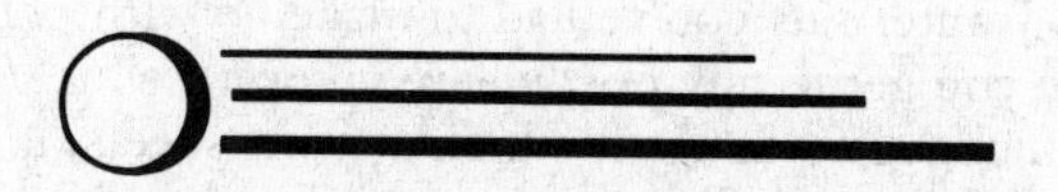

**N**ikodemos, nicknamed Chrysocheiros "of the golden hand" owing to the success that usually attended his business ventures, was furious with himself, and even angrier with God. His usual combination of luck and good judgment had utterly deserted him. What should have been the most profitable voyage even he had ever undertaken risked turning out to be an unqualified disaster.

Taking advantage of the exceptionally early advent of the west-to-east trade winds this year—they had shifted exactly at the Equinox, instead of lagging—a handful of bold or greedy Indian traders had set sail weeks ahead of their normal schedule, determined to beat their rivals to Egypt. Their gold and pearls and precious stones could be sold at leisure, but whoever arrived first with seasonal and perishable goods, such as perfumes, incense, spices and dyestuffs, was sure of commanding the highest prices. That was a principle which Nikodemos understood well. His agents on the Red Sea had standing instructions to buy as soon as the traders showed up each year, provided their merchandise was of sound quality, and forward the goods overland to Alexandria as fast as possible. To bring the winter's first shipload of Indian luxuries to Constantinople, in addition to the regular Egyptian exports of linen, pottery, glassware and papyrus—not that papyrus was so much in demand anymore—implied a huge commercial killing. Declining though that city's fortunes were, its inhabitants were determined to make the most of this life rather than rely on the promise of a paradise to come.

But this year the early arrival of Indian goods had taken even Nikodemos by surprise. On the day when a warning message was brought to him from the south, his best ship was still in dock, being recaulked and rerigged, and apart from his African shipmaster, known as Porias because only a barbarian could pronounce his proper name, most of the crew who regularly signed with him were still making ends meet in the tourist trade. Those few wealthy families who could afford a summer visit to relatives on Crete or Cyprus preferred, as did Nikodemos himself, seamen with plenty of experience.

Frantic orders, messages dispatched with small hope of reaching their recipients, and the squandering of far too much ready cash, had resulted in him putting his ship to sea well ahead of his chief rival and sworn personal enemy, Kranes. But the latter had stood on the quay and shouted insults as she was being readied for departure.

"What a bunch of water rats you've had to make do with! They'll eat your cargo before you get to any port where you can sell it! *If* you reach port, and I'm inclined to doubt it—look at your sheets, look at your sails! Hah! You'll founder before you're out of sight of land!"

Enraged beyond bearing, Nikodemos had retorted, "I wouldn't bet on it if I were you!"

"You're in the mood to wager? Very well, I'll match you! I have a sounder ship that's being loaded right now with richer cargo, and I have a better crew as well. Even if we leave a day—no, make that three days—later than you, I'd still expect to beat you to Constantinople!"

"Never!"

"I'll stake my entire cargo, and the ship into the bargain, and these people on the dockside are my witnesses! Will you do the same?"

Recklessly Nikodemos bellowed, "Yes, of course!"

Then Kranes sprang his trap. "Very well! I brought my clerk along, and he's been writing down our words, yours as well as mine. As soon as you're at sea, I'll have copies posted all over Alexandria. Either you'll be a poor man when you return, or you won't dare to, and you'll have to eke out the rest of your miserable life as a bankrupt exile!"

Chortling with glee, he turned away, and Nikodemos gave the order to cast off.

Fuming!

It was because of Kranes's arrogance, and not because of the profit he stood to lose—or so he was now insisting to Porias—that, after making the usual landfall on the eastern cape of Crete, he had insisted on an unfamiliar route among the treacherous islands north of there. Their *periplus* advised against it, but he scoffed, and with a heavy heart

Porias obeyed him. Was it his fault—Nikodemos was now demanding of heaven—was it his fault that a gale sprang up an hour after they left Crete astern? Did he command the weather, or did God? In the latter case God must be on the side of Kranes, and that was absurd! He was a drunkard, a lecher, and a notorious cheat!

All of which most signally failed to impress Porias or any other of the crew when, around the middle of a moonless night, they found themselves being driven even with their sail furled toward an island that showed on the horizon as a featureless black outline. Sometimes its silhouette seemed to resemble a crouching beast, but the impression never lasted long enough for them to figure out what kind.

Seasick—he who was so proud of never having thrown up in the worst of storms—and terrified of losing not just the ship and her cargo, but even his chance of paying off a lost bet with aplomb—he who boasted of never having defaulted on a business deal—Nikodemos clung to the rigging in wild wet darkness and blasphemed.

A rock loomed up. There were screams and near panic, but Porias tongue-lashed his men into action and they fended it off with poles. One broke, and the man wielding it vanished overboard with a howl. Yet the ship survived, and a moment later sank her bow safely into a sandbank. Her hull, miraculously, remained intact.

But the shock was too great for her already weakened rigging, and ropes began to snap with a noise like cracking whips. Snaking down to deck level, they caught two of the crewmen, one around the body and the other around the leg, and flung them off their feet. The mast tilted; the wind tore loose one end of the sail and the yard canted down far enough on the port side to strike another man violently on the head. Porias bellowed more orders, and the crew sullenly obeyed them. But when a semblance of normality had been restored, and they had a chance to take stock, they found that one man had a wrenched knee and another a dislocated arm, while the one who had been cracked on the pate was out of his wits; all he could do was clutch his neck and moan, his mouth hideously ajar.

"What are you going to do?" Nikodemos whimpered.

"Wait for daylight—what else?" said Porias with African contempt, and lay down where he was and fell asleep.

Something strange and terrifying was happening to Anastasia. Evgenos was bewildered by it, and wished he could appeal to the wise women of Oragalia for information—but for the most part they refused to have anything to do with him. Had they not watched Anastasia grow up they would have rejected her just as completely. However, a trace of sympathy lingered for the girl who had been orphaned at so early an age, and now and then one of them left a gift anonymously at the peak of the path leading down to the cove and cave where they eked out their existence: a loaf, some figs, a fish or a head of garlic—

bribes intended to make her reject him so she could be welcomed into the respectable company of widowhood. There were many widows on the island younger than she was.

There would be no gift tonight, not with the wind howling across the sea and chasing giant waves up the beach. Why had she chosen now—now of all times, and in her condition—to go clambering around the headland in search of mussels, which she ate raw, forcing their shells apart with her teeth regardless of the way it chipped them. Lately she had complained so often of toothache!

And small wonder. Was there not a saying that women paid with teeth for babies' bones?

Now he must go out again in the pitch blackness, coax her back, comfort her as best he could against the terrible demands of the new life growing in her womb . . .

Resignedly, thankful that it was not actually raining, he fought his way against the gale to where she sat cramming her belly. Dropping to his knees at her side, he demanded, "What's amiss?"

"I'm hungry," was her sullen reply. Then, apologetically, she added, "It isn't *just* hunger. I'm hungry for something special—something that isn't bread, that isn't fruit, that isn't eggs . . . Oh, I don't know what it is!"

His heart sank. Last time she had demanded goat cheese, and they had no goat of their own, so he had had to spend a day working for a master who hated him, and in the evening taken home his pay: two big handfuls of feta. And she had tasted and refused it, saying it was wrong.

Wrong? How could cheese be wrong? It had tasted all right to him. But pregnant women were notorious for their weird behavior . . .

Abruptly she broke down crying, and had to spit out the last mussel she had taken into her mouth. He led her back up to the cave, muttering vague words of reassurance, and tasted sea salt on her lips before she fell asleep despite the roaring and yelling of the wind, sprawled on the moist and rotten softness of the seaweed he had gathered to make them a bed.

He, however, lay wakeful for a good while yet, wondering what devil had condemned him to this foreign shore. But even though he desperately wanted to, he knew he could no longer leave it. He had created a responsibility for himself. Of course, giving birth was a dangerous event. Anastasia and the child might die. Then he could choose to starve or flee. However, he was ashamed of himself for hoping that might come to pass.

Eventually he too drowsed.

And was awoken by a shout from the cave's entrance.

Rousing all of a piece, on his feet almost before his eyes were open, registering that the storm had died down, he found himself confronted by a stranger as dark as himself: certainly no Oragalian. Short and stocky, he was clad in a linen tunic stiff with salt, belted and bordered with leather bands; also his feet were shod with leather. A stir of envy was the first thing Evgenos felt when he came to himself.

But behind him was a fat and fussy fellow in even more expensive garb, including a border on his robe dyed with Tyrian purple. However, it had run disgracefully, proof that he must have bought it from a seller who used cheap mordants.

The latter said, "Is there anybody here except you? I have to get my ship afloat again at once!"

Anastasia was awake too, now. Registering the presence of the strangers, she whimpered and rolled into the darkest corner of the cave.

"I'm Shipmaster Porias," said the African. "This is my employer, Nikodemos of Alexandria. Tell your woman to calm down. All we want is help in freeing our ship from the sandbank she's stuck on.We're shorthanded because we lost a man overside in last night's gale and three more are badly hurt. We'll pay you well. But is there anyone here apart from you and the girl?"

"N-no!" At the promise of pay Evgenos found his tongue. "But—uh—I'll do what I can! What ship?"

"Wipe your eyes and you'll see her plain enough!" was Porias's curt reply.

The fat man babbled something about delay. Evgenos ignored him and pushed past into daylight.

And there she was: grounded on the bar guarding the southern bay of Oragalia, which had ensured that this patch of salt-sour ground had never been claimed by anyone until Evgenos and Anastasia were driven to try and scrape their living off it. His practiced eye informed him that she was already starting to lift clear of the entrapping sand.

He wanted to laugh, but dared not. Why, here was his chance to escape for good and all! If he told these strangers he'd help, but his price was a place in their crew . . .

Behind him Anastasia was rising to her feet. He sighed and changed his mind. He had ordained his own doom.

"The wind will turn after midday," he said dully. "By then you should have been able to shovel away enough of the sand to free her bow. Now leave us in peace."

"No! Wait!" Unpredictable as ever, Anastasia was at his side, smoothing down the calf-long black dress which she had slept in because it was her only garment. Brushing back her thick and tangled hair, she smiled at Porias and Nikodemos with all the expertise of a coquette, heedless of her chipped front teeth.

"Evgenos will help you, of course! Won't you?"—with a meaning glare. "But what cargo does your ship carry?"

"You want to buy something?" Instantly Nikodemos's commercial instincts were alerted.

Porias snorted and turned away, his posture asking more clearly than words: *What could these poverty-stricken folk afford from you?*

Anastasia, though, advanced on Nikodemos, hands outstretched, her eyes huge and pleading and full of tears.

"Yes, I do! I so much want—!"

She checked, frightened by the intensity of her desires.

"Well then, what?" Nikodemos snapped. "Just ask!"

"Some—some sort of food that I can't name!"

"Lord have mercy!" Nikodemos glanced at the sun. "By this time Kranes must be well out to sea, and he'll have avoided last night's gale, and—Porias, can you make these people see sense? We may have to dump some of the deck cargo to lighten the ship and float her off! Think that might satisfy them?"

"And what use would they have here for linens and papyrus?" Porias returned with a scowl.

"The linens only weigh heavy because a wave soaked them last night—"

"I don't want linen!" Anastasia cried. "I don't want—whatever the other thing was you mentioned! I want food for my baby! I want something I can feel, but I can't name!"

Moaning, she clenched her fists before her face.

"Oh, for the love of heaven! I'll pay your man with a jar of Indian pepper, how about that? I'll wager that's something you've never tasted! Or a pot of honey, which they say is good for pregnant women! Just so long as he works hard and honestly and comes with us now, at once!" Nikodemos was almost dancing up and down with rage and frustration.

"Take the honey," Evgenos suggested with a sigh, turning in search of his buskins.

"No, we have honey—there are lots of bees on the island! I want . . ." She bit her lip, considering. "Maybe I do want pepper; I don't know. Is it good nourishing food that fills the belly and drives away the kind of hunger you can't name?"

"No, it's a spice that fills the mouth and disguises the flavor of bad meat!" Porias snapped. "And I imagine you don't get much of that, good or bad! Your man's right—you should take the honey. Or a jar of wine, or . . . Wait: we have Egyptian waterfowl preserved in their own grease, a delicacy!"

Anastasia's eyes lightened. But Nikodemos interrupted before she could speak again.

"Not those! They're a very special item, and they'll sell for—"

"Do you want the ship refloated?" Porias flared. "Or do you want to keep the stuff and sell it at a loss when we get to Constantinople?

Not that it'll be yours to sell by then, come to think of it, not if Kranes beats us. You know what sort of person he is! He'll have armed men stationed on the quayside to seize our cargo, and he'll have bribed the port police to make certain we don't try and stop them! Do you look forward to spending the winter in jail?"

"Very well," said Nikodemos sullenly. "But one jar, mind!"

"And one of honey, and one of wine!" Evgenos insisted.

"It's a deal," Porias said promptly. "You can take it out of my share if you like, Nikodemos. But if you do, then this will be our last trip together. Let's get a move on, shall we?"

The man with the wrenched knee and the man with the dislocated arm had been borne ashore by their shipmates. Now they were sitting on their haunches in the shade cast by the bales and bundles which had been taken from the deck to lighten the ship, tending their comrade who had been hit on the head. The latter's neck was definitely fractured; he lay writhing in pain with his eyes closed. Now and then he tried to say something, but all that emerged was a moan.

Three of the crew were mending the rigging and restepping the mast. The rest were knee-deep in water, wearily plying what came to hand—poles, bits of wood, pottery shards—in their attempts to free the bow. As Evgenos came to join them they paused and looked him over sullenly.

"Well, there's a plank you can use for a shovel," Porias said, pointing. "Get to it!"

"Put my pay on shore first," said Evgenos.

"What?" Porias balled his fists, taking a step closer. "Are you saying that you doubt my word?"

"Not yours. His"—with a jerk of this thumb at Nikodemos, who had darted off to inspect his damaged goods.

"You're a shrewd bastard, aren't you?" Porias said grudgingly. "You seem to be a good judge of character, at least . . . Very well. I'll pick out the stuff myself and put it over there in the shadow of that rock, all right?"

"Right!" Evgenos answered. He seized the plank and set to with a will.

Despite his gauntness and his hollow belly, he seemed to be fitter than the seamen, and dug much faster than they did. Still, that wasn't surprising; he hadn't slaved away half of last night in the teeth of the gale. The sun climbed to the zenith, and he could no longer tell whether he was wetter from seawater than from perspiration, or the other way around. But the ship's bow was coming free.

"Thirsty?"

And to his surprise, here was Porias with a pottery vase of water on a rope sling, going from man to man and allowing each three mouthfuls, neither more nor less. Wiping the sweat from his eyes after gulping down his share, Evgenos said, "When that's empty, go find Anastasia. Ask her to show you the spring we use. It runs slow at the end of summer, but it's good and sweet."

The prospect of plenty of water for the next leg of the trip cheered the seamen, and they began to look on Evgenos with less jaundiced eyes.

The sun slanted downward. The mast was secure again and the rigging, though lump with knots, was back to usable condition. Evgenos paused, waiting for the first hint of an offshore breeze. As soon as it came, he tossed his plank aboard the ship and turned to Porias.

"Unfurl your sail and get everyone here to shove her off. She'll move now."

Before complying, the shipmaster looked him over curiously. He said, "You seem to know something about ships and the sea. Did you learn it on your way here?"

For an instant memory flared, of a voyage infinitely longer and stranger than any Porias or his master could have undertaken. But there were no words to cast his story in, and anyway nobody would have believed him. Evgenos settled for a grunted, "Yes!"

"So were you—? No, I sense you prefer not to talk about it. Your pay is on the beach, anyway. I hope your girl enjoys it. Now where in heaven's name is my boss?"

"He's on board," someone muttered. "Said he couldn't stand the heat and had to go below."

"That's added a few more talents' weight to the load we have to shift," Porias sighed. "I think I'll make this my last trip with him whether he loses his bet with Kranes or not . . . Right, men! Yare now, yare! Set your shoulders to the bow and push!"

And after a lot of slipping and sliding on the loose bottom, they forced the boat clear. Hanging on to a cable along with four of the seamen for fear she might adrift, Porias shouted at Evgenos.

"Don't suppose you'd care to ship with us, would you? We could use an extra hand as smart as you!"

Last night Evgenos had been dreaming of a chance to quit this island where everybody seemed to hate him except Anastasia . . . and sometimes lately he hadn't been quite sure about her. But if he accepted this invitation, when he came back he could count on one thing beyond a doubt: she would have been turned into a widow even though she wasn't one. Even if she and the baby survived, he would be a complete outcast. And he had been an outcast before he found his way to Oragalia . . .

Would these men accept him as one of themselves, let him make a career as part of this ship's crew? More likely they'd be glad to see the back of him once the voyage was over and they had no more use for his services. Besides, he had gathered that Nikodemos stood to lose ship and cargo too if he arrived late at Constantinople. Then he'd be stranded further from home than ever, and moreover in a great city. He had no experience of cities, but he had been warned that a man could feel more alone in a vast crowd than by himself in the middle of a desert or an ocean. It was better to be reluctantly tolerated on Oragalia than to endure that kind of bitter loneliness.

On top of all of which there was Anastasia, and soon there would be the child too—his first . . .

He forced a smile, shook his head, and shouted back.

"Thank you, Shipmaster! But I've made a life here!" The double meaning of the phrase startled him for a second; it had been unpremeditated. "I wish you a swift safe trip from now on, anyhow!"

"It's a kind thought! I'm obliged!"

The men were making haste to climb aboard, carrying their injured shipmates on their shoulders through the shallows. Nikodemos had reappeared and was shouting something about retrieving the goods that had been dumped on shore, but nobody seemed to be paying him much heed.

Nor Evgenos. Despondently he turned away to collect the preserved Egyptian waterfowl, the wine and the honey. His mind filled with miserable second thoughts: could he not have demanded more, much more? And was he right after all in declining to leave the island? Life was harsher here, in some senses than at sea, and there were people who praised great cities despite their drawbacks . . .

But here was Anastasia coming to meet him. Her eyes grew wide as she looked not at what he was carrying but at the abandoned cargo.

"They left all that behind? Oh, you can take it to the village and people will pay us well for it! It's cloth isn't it?"

"Did you guide Porias to the spring?" Evgenos asked, abruptly aware how tired his long hot morning's work had made him; he looked forward to sampling the wine, above all.

"Yes!" She started. "Was that wrong?"

"No, I suggested it. They weren't bad people, you know. They could have beaten me into working for them, couldn't they? Then, of course, I wouldn't have worked half so hard . . . What am I talking about. Let's get home. I'm dreadfully hot and thirsty, and half-starved."

"But oughtn't you to bring all that stuff to the cave right away? Suppose somebody else—"

"Who? Who ever comes this way, except some of your relatives by stealth, at night?"

"I'll bring it, then!"

"No! You work too hard anyhow for a woman in your condition—"

"I have to, don't I? If I didn't—"

He forced himself to remain calm, but interrupted nonetheless.

"I'll bring everything up to the cave before sundown, and later I'll carry it to the village and sell it as you recommend. But there are some folk on the island who might try to steal it, aren't there? We'll have to be careful about how much we admit to having. And I'm too tired to make plans right now."

He feared for a moment that she was going to argue; he added hastily, "Besides, what I have here is exactly what you've been saying you want. Let's sample it."

Yielding, she reached out to relieve him of part of his load.

The instant the seals on the jars were broken, the still air of the cave was filled with the most delectable aroma. With a cry of joy Anastasia drew out and devoured one after another of the potted birds, using for want of a better dish to save them from the sand a tile he had found that bore a scratched inscription in a language neither of them could read. With immense relief Evgenos relaxed, taking only token portions for himself until she decided to tackle the honey instead. Like the wine, it was exceptional, far richer than any made on Oragalia.

Discovering the fact, she calmed and set the rest of the jar aside. "If I eat more, I shall make myself ill," she sighed. "I shall take a little every day, but only a little, until it's gone. It will be for the sake of our child. Such sweetness cannot but do him good."

Evgenos was leaning back contentedly against the rocky wall. Hard work, wine and good food were combining to make him drowsy. Leaning toward him, she tapped his knee.

"It's nearly sundown, and you did say you'd bring the other things up here!"

Grumpy, but resigned, he forced himself to his feet and went to keep his promise.

There were eight big bales altogether, each as much of a load as he could manage because they were still soaked with seawater. Five were of fine linen, a great prize. The others, he guessed, might be of papyrus, for which he foresaw small demand on the island. Perhaps, though, the priest or the lawyer might find a use for it, and in any case if he left it in the open it would certainly draw the attention of would-be thieves.

Having set the bales where they would dry most quickly, he returned to Anastasia and found her dozing. At his touch, however, she stirred, and said with her eyes still closed, "Those men made me think of Pedro, you know."

Yawning, stretching, preparing to lie down beside her in the gathering dark, he said, "How do you mean?"

"Was he not a trader to his very bones, yet not content with ordinary goods? Would he not always set the highest store by what was marvelous and strange, and did he not expect everybody else to feel the same?"

"Go on."

Sleepily, she did so.

"The world he lusted to find a way to, then, must have been a place of wonders so far exceeding the normal run of our experience as to defy description. Were there foods? Then they must transcend ambrosia. Were there cloths and fabrics? Then they must be softer than a morning breeze and warmer than the summer sun. Were there dyes? Then their colors must be such as never yet graced any rainbow. Were there furs? Then they must retain the life of the beasts that yielded them, caressing and conforming to the bodies of their wearers. Were there drugs? Then they must not only cure the regular diseases, but instantly confer such gaiety and vigor as never any did in the drab world he left behind!"

"Yes, that's the sort of place which would suit Pedro. So he found it?"

"It's . . . necessary to believe he did."

"And no doubt"—Evgenos rolled to embrace her, licking mingled fat and honey on her cheek—"he dreamed of making his fortune out of it."

"Not one fortune. A thousand. There was no end to the strangeness of that place. Eagerly he settled down to send home a report . . . and could not even draft one. Gene, are you paying attention?"

"Yes, yes!"—amid the tresses of her hair. "Why could he not make out his report?"

"The world was truly unfamiliar. So it did indeed defy description."

# Part Eight

*THE EXHIBIT*
*is a graffito on a red clay tile, scarcely legible.*
*It marks the desperate need of somebody to be remembered*

*THE MONTH*
*is November*

*THE NAME*
*is Naruhiko*

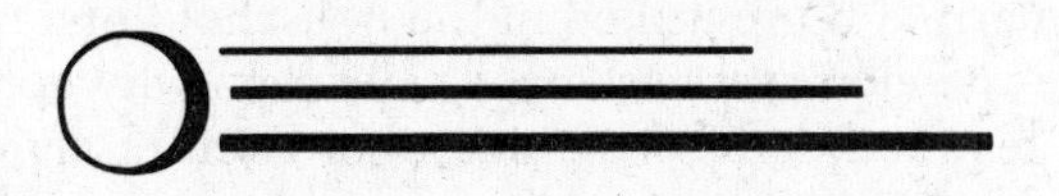

Seven years ago, one of the arrogant and vainglorious Romans who now ruled the Middle Sea had found his way to the otherwise unimportant island of Oragalia, and decided to turn it into his private estate, calculating that he could make it self-sufficient if he introduced modern methods of farming and irrigation. He had also intended to build a villa in the Italian style, centered around an atrium with a fountain as fine as any at Pompeii. But the marble and mosaic which he dreamed of cost too much, and he died before his overambitious project was completed.

Almost the only relic of his intrusion was a channel which brought fresh water down from hillside springs to the miniature forum of the town that had developed beside the eastern bay. There it was fed first into a stone trough, for drinking and cooking, and the citizens came and went from dawn to dusk with jars and skin bottles to be filled. Lower down, it trickled into a wide basin, and this was used to water livestock, and for laundry. Families rich enough to own a slave or two, but not a private water supply, sent them thither most days, and they behaved as bossily as their owners, insisting on priority over every other would-be user. Because the alternative was to beat their clothes in seawater and spread them to dry on the rocks of the shore—

treatment that wore the fabric out in next to no time—the poorer sort generally deferred to them, hanging back until the basin was foul with grease and masses of shed fiber clogged the outflow, whereupon they had to set to and clear the mess away with their bare hands. Sometimes the delay could cost them half a precious day.

The only person among them who defied this obsequious custom was Anastasia. She who had little of her own to wash, since her adopted kinfolk had been stolen into slavery, mocked these other slaves when she arrived with laundry belonging to those who could afford—and dared—to rent her time, elbowed her way to the cleanest part of the pool, and kept up a constant flow of muttered insults concerning cowards who let themselves be bought and sold instead of running away to earn an independent living.

Poor though she was even by the standards of a poverty-stricken community, having been orphaned at birth and worse than orphaned in her teens, she was never in rags, for she often took her pay in outworn garments and painstakingly repaired them; moreover, despite being gaunt she was beautiful, with brilliant dark eyes and long sleek hair. The occasional strangers who noticed her invariably demanded why she was neither married nor enrolled in the household of a prosperous family, but the islanders were ashamed to explain why nobody dared lay a finger on her, and dodged the question. Even though the forum was beset with crude statues of gods and goddesses both local and imposed by the Romans, and the whole island was littered with shrines and sacred places, admitting the truth would smack too much of superstition to a sophisticated visitor from Italy, the Greek mainland or Asia Minor. So they did their best to convey the vague impression that she was a harlot but it was wiser not to have commerce with her because she was diseased, and then pointedly changed the subject.

None of this was true. In fact she was a witch.

Every man on the island, bond or free, who did not prefer boys to women, had lusted after her since long before she was left to fend for herself upon the enslavement of her uncle and older cousins. One of the Roman contractors brought in by the island's temporary overlord, infuriated on realizing that he was not going to be paid for the work he had put in, had sought some other form of recompense. Anastasia's uncle, who had adopted her in infancy, was a skilled stone carver, and had brought up his two sons in the same trade. A richer rival, assuming that without any menfolk to protect her Anastasia would be easy prey for himself, had suggested to the Roman that he kidnap and sell the masons to recoup his losses, a proposal which the fellow eagerly fell in with.

There was of course no court of justice Anastasia could appeal to; apart from the fact that her uncle's enemy—who was still fuming because she had rebuffed his offer to take her in with a volley of the filthiest objurgations she could contrive—was now the most powerful man on the island, none of her relatives was officially a Roman citizen. Her mother and all her grandparents being dead, she turned to other cousins, of whom she had several. She received some support from them, but they were humble farmhands, lacking a profitable skill like her uncle's. They had little to offer save a bare subsistence, and that only on condition that she work at the most menial tasks.

With one exception: her great-aunt Phoebe, who was toothless and rheumatic and could not walk without a stick. But her mind was clear as a summer sky, and she remembered many of the ancient spells that could be used against people who had committed crimes yet imagined they might escape the consequences.

Anastasia's uncle's rival also had a son, whom he had likewise apprenticed to the mason's trade. The boy could pursue it no longer; he had been blinded by stone chips that flew up unaccountably beneath his chisel.

Some of the island's young men had laughed about that and gone on trying to seduce this desirable maiden. The most importunate of them was now a geck and gull himself, for he had slipped on a hill path and broken his leg; ever since, he had had to walk sidewise, like a crab. After that, people began to draw apart from Anastasia, and though they spoke politely enough on meeting, they seemed to have decided to leave her in peace.

Then, when she tamed the wild man—a feat which echoed the most ancient legend known to anybody here—and decided to bear his child in order to emphasize her contempt for all her other would-be suitors, their respect turned to awe. Some went so far as to maintain outright that one of the Old and Strong had come again, but there was much argument concerning that opinion. At all events, now she was big-bellied and thus in a condition to work still more powerful charms than before, even the randiest of the island's men had ceased to trouble her.

She was sorry that Phoebe, dead last winter, had not survived to see the full fruits of her instruction.

"A sail! A sail!"

The cry rose from the southern headland of the bay, and at once everybody forgot their work and rushed to the shore. Even Anastasia, having wrung out the garments entrusted to her by the family employing her today and laid them back neatly in her basket, wiped her hands on her woolen cloak and deigned to join the throng, although she was as ever dismayed to notice how many mothers warned their children to keep clear of her. As if she would ever harm a child too young to know what wickedness meant! Some of those mothers, on the other hand . . .

But Phoebe had warned her that she must never use her spells to afflict either the innocent, or those who lacked the power to control their own destinies. Whether the gods existed or not, magic certainly did, and its laws decreed that it would recoil against all who exploited it with neither justice nor goodwill on their side. Anastasia bestowed broad smiles on those of the children who were looking her way, and a few of them risked smiling back.

Then she turned her attention to the ship approaching harbor. She was, predictably, a Roman galley, her sail furled, her rowers bending to their oars. In the still air the sound of the drum they kept time to could already be heard, and now and then it was punctuated by the crack of their overseer's whip.

Such a ship as that had carried off Anastasia's uncle, and his sons whom she had grown to love as brothers . . .

Her mind filled with visions of losing someone who had become even more precious to her. Blinded with sudden tears, she slipped away.

"Things are terrible, and getting worse," said Septimus Julius Cornax. "Thanks to our emperor! May his guts burn worse than the bowels of Vesuvius!"

He waved his cup vaguely in the air, and a sullen slave—nothing like as well trained as what he was used to at home—took it away for refilling.

For want of anything better to do while his crew loaded such fresh provisions as were to be had on this dismal island, he had accepted a fawning invitation to lunch at the home of its "richest" citizen. Rich? Someone had to be joking! The house's *cēnātiō* was a mere terrace in the open air, sheltered by a trellis of ill-doing vines, tolerable perhaps in summer, but absurd in November. Its sole ornament was a crude statue supposedly representing an ancient deity, while the company consisted of the man's dull and pudgy wife, who luckily excused herself early, and his sightless and self-pitying son, who whined endlessly about his misfortune.

Even this, however, might have been tolerable had the food been fit for Cornax's sophisticated palate. In fact, it had proved ghastly and the wine if possible worse, so he had sent to the ship for a jar of Samian, which was now half-empty. To add to his depression, there was still no wind. His rowers would mutiny if they were ordered back to sea before tomorrow, so he was due to be stuck overnight in this armpit of the universe. In the end he grew so bored he drew his dagger and started to scratch a record of his visit on one of the crude tiles his hostess boasted about using to protect her table from the hot (meaning lukewarm) dishes set upon it. It was about then that she took the hint and made herself scarce.

By stages, however, Cornax's mood had mellowed. The sniveling son, finding the Samian too strong, had been led away, which was a vast relief. Moreover—as he admitted to himself—it was a pure delight to be able to speak his mind out of hearing of anyone who might relay his treasonable opinions to his enemies. On this lump of rock whither his ship had been driven by a contrary wind, and then becalmed unseasonably, surely there was nobody to carry back gossip to the imperial court!

Accordingly, even though he realized he was upsetting his host (but why should he care about these provincials who had nothing better to offer a distinguished guest than charred goat and a mess of onions stewed in oil?), he unleashed his tongue.

"Want to know what a plight the empire's in? Take me as an example, then! Here I am, not just entitled by descent to bear the name of the Julian *gens* but also favored with a surname that according to all the experts must date back to Etruscan times, because they can't account for it any other way—in other words, my ancestors predated the kings, let alone the emperors, of Rome!—and on top of that an officer of one of the finest of all the legions, with a roll of battle honors going back centuries—here I am in command of a rotten tub of a ship, on a mission that reduces me to the status of a common or garden lanista, the kind of person who makes money out of pandering to the plebs, supplying them with gladiators to chop each other's vitals off in public! Ever been to the Games in Rome? No? I could have guessed as much. But that's what pleases the crowd the best. There's a fad of late for eunuchs who escape the arena and survive. The emperor likes them a *lot* . . . More wine! Come on, you ought to have more too! It may be years before you get another chance to taste so good a vintage!"

His host, eyes rolling every which way, declined with tolerable politeness. Later, Cornax felt, he was likely to reach the stage where he would regard such a refusal as an insult, but he wasn't there yet, so he let the matter slide, drank deeper than ever, and resumed his tirade.

"And it's bad enough knowing the slaves I collect are going to be wasted in the arena, but that isn't the half of it. The mob is constantly yelling for blacks, and beastmen—ever seen one of them? No? Thought not—and . . . Wine, you lazy scum! Or I'll call my overseer with his whip! Excuse me; not mannerly in someone else's house . . . But I could sell you a girl or two—Sorry again. I'm not allowed to, and anyway since they're bound for the court you couldn't afford them. Where was I?"

His host, who by now was looking thoroughly alarmed, muttered something indefinite. It was enough to set Cornax back on course.

"Yes! Worse than being treated like a lanista is being treated like a common merchant! 'Unguents,' they tell me—'perfumes,' they tell me—'dormice in honey,' they tell me—'lark tongues,' they tell me—'Get us lots and lots so we can impress the Parthian Ambassador!' Or the Persian one, or some other of those foreign bigwigs! Years of effort all due to be squandered on a single Hades-consigned banquet! Then they're apt to chuck it up again anyhow! Makes *me* sick, I tell you straight! When I think what one could do with the money I've spent to load that ship out there, I could—I could kick the emperor's arse! But it's orders, I suppose, and I took an oath back in the good old days when an oath meant something, and . . . The worst thing about this trip, you know, the very worst, is that when I get back I'm not going to have a chance to plead my case. And that isn't fair!" Finding his tongue at last, the host say, "Why should you need to?"

"Because things are terrible everywhere in the empire! I said so already, didn't I? To feed the greedy court—and I don't just mean feed in the literal sense—they've debased the money they gave me! I got to Egypt only to find that because imperial coinage mostly doesn't contain an honest quantity of gold or silver anymore, they won't accept it except at a discount! And you've no idea what damage that has done to our creditworthiness . . . Jupiter Tonans! I'm talking like a merchant myself now! But what it boils down to is that I'm going home without a decent load. This wine is all right, even though I had to buy it in Alexandria and pay extra to cover the cost of transport. The food isn't bad, though those Egyptians don't seem to have learned as much about preserving as you'd expect, given the way they used to pickle their kings and nobles—but that's merchant-type stuff, and any African grain ship might carry the same.

"No, what's wrecked the trip for me is the fact that I couldn't afford even one Nubian gladiator! Those lazy Egyptians haven't mounted a slaving expedition to Nubia in years—haven't even traded any in! If you go looking for blacks, all you can find on offer is kids, locally bred and most of them mongrels! Don't you think that's disgusting?"

He held out his empty cup again.

His host ruminated awhile, and eventually said, "You'd be interested in acquiring a black man? I mean, a full-blooded one?"

"Hah!" Cornax exclaimed. "I can't say someone like that would be worth his weight in gold, but if a lanista didn't buy him there are a thousand bored rich wives in Rome who'd snatch him quick as lightning, the ones whose husbands are too preoccupied with business or politics to look after them properly! You know what I mean!"

Disregarding the last sentence, the other went on, "Did you know there's a Nubian on Oragalia? Big, strong, and indisputably—uh—male?"

"What?" Cornax almost choked on his latest swig of wine. "How did someone like that turn up here of all places?"

"Presumably he's a runaway slave. Very likely he jumped overboard from a passing ship. At all events, last spring he was found living off the land, or in other words stealing from those who work to provide us with food. But he was on the south cape, where most of the time nobody goes—there's no land worth cultivating. And . . ."

He hesitated, eyeing the idol in the corner. Tense, Cornax urged him to continue.

"Well . . . Ah!" He was obviously searching for the right words, but found them at last. "Well, there are some foolish ideas that the common folk adhere to, of a sort your honor is no doubt familiar with, and some of them relate to that particular part of the island, where in fact that statue of mine came from . . . Don't you admire it?"

"No!"—curtly. "Come to the point!"

"It's very old, I believe . . . I'm sorry. Anyhow, in the event the Nubian was left alone for a month or more. There was much talk of organizing an expedition to go after him, but—well, it shames me to say so, but an awful lot of our people, despite their braggartly words, turned out to be cowards when it came to the crunch."

Cornax tipped back his crude chair. (Oh for a decent couch like what one found at Rome! . . .) He said, "So you have a wild black man running around. Very well. The wildest man in the world couldn't stand up against a squad of my legionaries, so we'll collect him and take him to Rome with us. Use a net, probably. No trouble."

The other ventured, "As a matter of fact, sir, he isn't exactly wild. Not anymore, that is."

"In that case, what's the problem? Why hasn't one of your lot already recaptured this fellow and put him to useful work? It's legal, if he actually is a runaway slave—in fact, it's your civic duty. Why didn't you take on the job yourself, come to that? It looks as though you could do with some extra help around the place!"

"That's—uh—that's a long story!"

"I have nothing else to occupy my time until my ship is reprovisioned." Cornax leaned back further yet and crossed his legs. "You may recount it!"

"Well—uh! . . ."

"Get on with it, man!"

"Oh, since you insist . . ." And little by little the tale emerged, shorn of such embarrassing details as the speaker's complicity in the kidnapping of Anastasia's uncle and cousins, but full of allusions to the island's folklore. The latter were sufficiently commonplace for Cornax to get the drift of them.

The first report of the wild man had come from a boy taking goats to pasture. He could add up well enough to keep track of his beasts, and one day the count was short. Later, raw and bloody bones were found. Shortly after, a beekeeper discovered that his hives had been robbed of the first of the summer's honey. In the normal course of events, herdsmen and beekeepers were the only people to visit the southern cape of Oragalia, where the land was so poor as not even to have attracted the interest of the Roman who had had the aqueduct built, although in bad weather fisherfolk were glad to put ashore there.

Later the culprit was seen by daylight: tall and thin, blacker than the sun could have burned him, and apparently not just naked but devoid of tools, let alone weapons. However, as had already been indicated, although the islanders talked at length about tracking down and catching him, they proved unenthusiastic when it came to converting brave words into action. They seemed on the verge of deciding to put up with his predations, as though with a force of nature like gales and storms, when a certain woman cried them down and said she would achieve what they dared not.

They would have been overjoyed to see her fail.

"Why?" demanded Cornax, who for all the wine he had drunk was still alert enough to follow.

"Well—ah—that's another story! Suffice it to say that this woman had made herself unpopular. Perhaps she saw in this venture a means of worming her way back into people's respect, if not liking."

"And did she?"

"Not exactly."

"Man, make yourself clear!"—in a parade-ground voice.

Swallowing hard: "She made herself feared."

"Without much difficulty, I imagine. Judging not just by my limited experience of your particular island, but an extensive acquaintance with Greeks like you all over the mainland, Asia Minor and Egypt, I'd expect people of your stamp to scare pretty easily!" Cornax was rather enjoying this baiting of his host. "What exactly did this woman *do?*"

"She—uh—she tamed the wild man. Not only that: she gave herself to him, even though . . ."

"Jealousy! Jealousy!" Cornax crowed. "I see it now! You wanted her for yourself!"

The other stiffened. "That has nothing to do with it!"

"What does, then?"—with a positive guffaw.

"She went out to him farded and girdled like a whore, who had never yielded to any of our men! And next day she showed him to the folk, holding her hand as meek as—as anything!"

Cornax became abruptly sober.

"There's a story I heard when I was on garrison duty on the Persian frontier. It concerned a giant created by the gods to overthrow a king, and—"

"Right! Right! The king tricked the gods and sent a harlot in all her finery to seduce him—"

"And they became the fastest friends!" Cornax jumped to his feet. "Oh, if I could take such a man to the emperor, with proof of the story, and the woman along with him! . . ."

"Excuse me, sir, but I was under the impression that it was the black man that interested you, not the woman!"

"Oh, go hire an Egyptian surgeon and ask him to sew your head back on," Cornax answered crossly. "I don't want her for myself! But surely it cannot totally have escaped the attention of you and yours that the emperors nowadays routinely consider themselves as gods! Here's a myth come to life, precisely what any emperor will pay a fortune for, and you wouldn't even have mentioned it if I hadn't pressed you! May Jupiter Tonans visit all the days of your life with thunder and lightning—well-aimed lightning!"

Swaying drunkenly, he yelled at his escort, dozing beside the entrance.

"Believe it or not, they've got an Enkidu here!"

"You don't say, sir!" one of the men answered cheekily. "What's that when it's at home, if I may make so bold?"

"Fool! It's not a what, it's a who!"

A surge of acidity rose in the back of Cornax's throat. For a moment he feared he was about to throw up in the presence of inferiors. Recovering, he went on:

"Just for that, Charon-fodder, you can head back to the ship and turn out the entire squad! At the double!"

Each and every time that Anastasia returned to the cave where she had found refuge—which was neither hers, nor her man's, nor anybody's, but a gift of Mother Earth, who had reared up in fury (so it was said) in the not too distant past—she had to repeat, as though it were the first time over again, the actions that had led her to make a home here. The paradox obsessed her: she had tamed what everybody else dismissed as a wild beast, although it walked, and after a fashion it could talk, and in the other respects she had learned about was entirely human . . . and still, whenever she returned from the town, she wheedled, and lured, and cajoled . . .

She had been thinking "it." She canceled the concept violently. "It" was the pronoun her language applied to animals, or a child not yet of an age to reason. The lover she had chosen, strange and dreadful though his mien might be, was neither. *He* had proved it by his amazing tenderness and the gratitude which sometimes made him moisten her breast with tears.

As for the tumult *he* had created in her body . . .

For the first time she entered their den without setting down food beforehand, to tempt and reassure him.

Darker than shadows, he emerged from shadows and caught her in his arms, and took her swiftly in the way she most enjoyed—and then again.

Not until afterward was she able to utter the warning that she wished to convey. Then, slowly and with many misunderstandings, she explained that right now, right here on the island, were more of the people who had made him a slave.

She could smell the rage that rose in him.

But it was overcome by the realization that, thanks to her warning, he had a chance to hide. Moreover, surprisingly, he grasped the import of the ceremony, taught by Phoebe, which she next proceeded to perform. In the town there were not a few who claimed he had been allured by nothing more than her body, as a beast would follow its she in heat. That, though, could not be true, for unlike most of the island's menfolk he had waited for her invitation instead of jumping at her like a billy goat in rut. The Romans talked a lot, so she had heard, about "civilization"—essentially, the good manners that permitted many people to live together—but, given the Romans she had met, and the one who had kidnapped her uncle and cousins whom she hoped never to meet, or she would surely kill him, she was satisfied that this person whom everybody else called wild and dangerous was gentler and kinder than a thousand Romans added together.

Now, therefore, she produced the herbs she had gathered on her way back from town and put them to use. Squatting on his haunches, he watched with interest, and perhaps more than a little comprehension.

The task complete, she leaned back against the rocks. "In spite of all," she said, "they will come after us."

He grinned at her, as much as to say, "Let them be fool enough to try!"

And took her hand, leading her away from the cave—certainly the first place the Romans would head for—to lie out on the bare ground like a fox or a bird.

Wrapping her cloak tightly around her against the chill of evening, Anastasia lay down in the spot he chose for her. She felt apprehensive despite her precautions. The baby was kicking vigorously today, and she foresaw how eventually it would punish her with its feet, whenever she set it to her nipple, for the crime of expelling it from the warm safe womb into the harshness of the outer world.

That, though, was the story of human existence, and above all of this child's parents'. She had undergone much suffering; very likely life had been still crueler to its father, though she would not be sure how cruel until he learned enough words to tell her. He had not even boasted a pronounceable name until she bestowed on him the one that sprang first to mind: *the wellborn man.* It suited his noble bearing, despite the scars on his wrists and ankles which indicated that he had endured ropes and chains. Neither manacles nor fetters had closed around his soul . . .

"And our baby will have a freer life than either of us!" she promised the air as, reposing her confidence in the charm she had cast around the area—and still more in the strong arms of her Evgenos, who had acquired in his distant homeland the warrior's habit of not leaving anything to chance—she finally allowed herself to doze.

Tramping along the rough trail toward the south cape, with his crested helmet under his arm, Cornax started to feel distinctly unwell.

He ascribed the fact to the badly cooked meal he had eaten, though a nagging suspicion remained that in fact too much Samian was to blame.

Controlling himself as best he could, he halted before reaching the highest point of the path, and shouted to the squad of men he had led hither.

"Right! Now you lot fan out, clear across the island! Stay in sight of one another, though! Be prepared to run and help whichever of you spots the Nubian, and *don't* let him slip through the line!"

As they reluctantly complied, he cast a worried glance at the sky. He had thought they were setting out with plenty of daylight ahead of them, more than adequate to catch one unarmed man. Now, however, wintry clouds were drifting from the east, harbingering a sailable wind tonight or at latest by dawn. If by some ill chance they missed the Nubian this evening, would he be justified in staying another day when they were already so badly behind schedule?

And then a sudden horrifying thought struck him. *Was* there in fact a Nubian?

The more he reflected on the yarn which had been spun him, the more improbable it seemed. To start with, how about the idea that a slave could have arrived here after jumping overboard from a passing ship? If he were strong and healthy enough to reach the shore, he'd be valuable enough for his master to chase after him; if he were underfed and sickly, not worth pursuing, then he wouldn't be up to swimming any considerable distance.

Suppose the story were a complete fabrication, a subtle way for his host to get his own back after all the insults Cornax had lavished on Greeks in general and him in particular? Visions of the way the towns-folk might now be laughing at him filled the Roman's mind. He clapped his hand to his forehead. What a fool he'd been to swallow the tale at face value without questioning a few more islanders in search of corroboration!

He kept his misgivings to himself, but self-directed anger made his face as threatening as the sky.

There came a sudden shout. Excitedly he swung around, looking for its source. But all that had happened was that one of the men had managed to get himself stung by a belated bee, having trespassed too close to one of the wicker hives which dotted the stony ground.

"Keep quiet!" Cornax hissed.

The men around him exchanged glances, and eyebrows were raised. Come to think of it, there wasn't much point in silence when it wasn't yet dark . . .

Grumpily he trudged onward, wondering how the island could be so much wider than it appeared from the sea.

Beating the undergrowth, prodding with their spears, the soldiers discovered a starveling bitch, her hindquarters infested with botflies, nursing four blind pups, all of which they promptly killed; a stray goat with a broken foreleg, which they also killed—and cut up and shared, since it would make a tasty supper; a boy and girl aged about twelve, who had come this way to play games their parents would have disapproved of, and ran away in terror; a cache of oil jars, presumably stolen, three full and one half-full; the skull of a donkey; and a great many other miscellaneous items.

But there was no sign of a Nubian, or even of the woman alleged to have taken up with him.

They regrouped on the crest of the ridge overlooking the south bay. By now it was almost full dark.

"There's supposed to be a cave under here—go and check it," Cornax ordered wearily, indicating the two men nearest him. Then, as they hesitated: "Afraid he'll ambush you? Jupiter Tonans! All right—six of you go!"

"There's nobody here!" came the report a minute later.

Cornax sighed. Before they regained the ship it would be full dark, and tramping across such rough ground by night was a sure recipe for bruises and sprained ankles. Particularly if what you were looking for didn't exist!

He reached a decision. He would confront the man who had sent him on this fool's errand, and find out once for all whether there was any truth in his story. If not—oh, if not! . . .

"Very well," he muttered in disgruntled tones. "Back to the port. But you'll have to wait for me a moment."

Saying which, he hastily made shift to conceal himself behind the thickest of the nearby bushes.

Anastasia was awakened by the sound of soft and uncontrollable laughter. She started up in alarm. But the dark form that approached her out of darkness was Evgenos.

"Have they gone?" she whispered.

Raising her to her feet, leading her back to the cave, he explained haltingly, with the aid of many gestures hard to make out in the dimness, what it was he found so funny.

He had outwitted the Romans at every turn. The spot where he had told her to hide was already behind the soldiers when they spread out to search. Having found no trace of their quarry, they had stormed away to the town again, unaware that Evgenos was following them as inconspicuously as a stalking fox.

On arrival, their officer set about interrogating everybody he met concerning the alleged Nubian. But the islanders were either so afraid of Anastasia's revenge if they betrayed him, or so eager to see the backs of the Romans, they one and all denied any knowledge of such a person.

Whereupon, in a towering rage, the officer ordered his soldiers to whip the man who had deceived him until he fell fainting in a pool of his own blood, and furthermore to rape his wife and son, sack his house and make off with everything of any value, including his slaves. Since he was so cordially hated, nobody made a move to intervene.

Clasping her hands in wonder, Anastasia muttered a prayer of gratitude.Then she thanked her amazing lover in a more direct fashion.

Later, as they lay close for the sake of warmth, she murmured, "Naruhiko. Of course: Naruhiko!"

"Hm? What did you say? Was it someone's name?"

"Oh, Gene! You know perfectly well it was—and who I mean!"

"Ah . . ." He stifled a yawn. "I was half asleep, I'm afraid. What about the guy, anyway?"

"He was like a Roman in his way, wasn't he?"

"Stacy, honey, neither of us ever met him. So what makes you say that?"

"Oh!"—with a horizontal shrug. "Driven by the same forces: I guess that's what I'm getting at. He devoted his life to a search for constant excitement, you might say, spiced with a dash of glory now and then. Along came his chance to undergo a unique experience, and if all went well he could rely on adulation for the rest of his life."

"What became of him, then?"

"The place he went to was a world at war—not a cold impersonal war, but a nonstop succession of raiding expeditions, sieges laid and lifted, victories in single combat, the raw material for laudatory ballads which for a while would be on everybody's lips. Snatches of song celebrating his exploits followed him down the streets of whatever city he wandered to; countless women offered themselves, or their daughters; those whom he had defended against their enemies sought to reward him with silk robes, rare foods, the choicest tea and wine.

"For all of which he cared not a whit. The only gift he ever accepted was a sword.

"He felt himself incapable of love—which was one of the reasons he sought violent sensations, as a substitute—but if he did love anything, it was the company of his own kind, in drill before battle, in solemn ceremonies afterward, albeit at the funerals of the fallen. To him the discipline of an army surpassed all forms of art, and the code of honor of its officers was a prize beyond all earthly treasure. There was never any end, in this world he came to, of comradeship or glory . . . So he thought."

"Yet there were flaws in what he took for paradise?" Gene rose on one elbow and gazed at her, almost invisible in the nighttime blackness of the cave.

Stacy gave a sober nod.

"To be a paradise for everyone who desired the same from life as he did, it was necessary that the tide of battle turn. Later, he looked back with longing to the last day when it was his name the minstrels sought a rhyme for—his feats of arms which were recounted round the campfire—his command which led the van and broke the enemy. There were just as many valiant achievements to make ballads on, just as many deeds of skill and daring, just as many victories as ever . . . and, inevitably, just as many defeats.

"So it became his turn to leave the field weary and alone and beg at the doors of peasant shacks where people hated him and all his kind. Ultimately he was reduced to selling his armor, piece by piece, in order to buy food, and when nothing else was left except his clothes, his shoes, and that single gift he had accepted, his fine sword, he sat cross-legged beneath a tree whose leaves dripped rain, and faced the truth."

# PART NINE

*THE EXHIBIT*
*is the broken head of an idol.*
*It symbolizes an attempt to control the universe*

*THE MONTH*
*is December*

*THE NAME*
*is Olga*

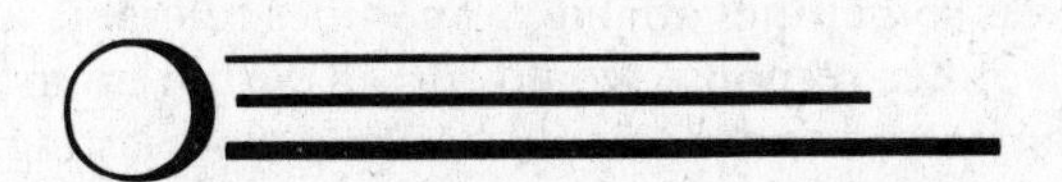

*E*very morning, on a shelf of rock near the cave, there appeared such offerings as the folk of the island could afford. They scarcely amounted to wealth: a bunch of onions, a few figs or olives, a salted fish, a cake of coarse meal mixed with water and charred rather than baked over an open fire, smeared with honey if the god of the weather had been kind.

But there was always something. Even the advent of the black stranger had interrupted the succession of gifts for only a single day.

Most of them were brought by children compelled by their parents to scurry through the predawn dark in order to discharge a duty they did not yet understand. Now and then, though, maybe half a dozen times a year, a more substantial donation was silently placed on the ledge under cover of night: a well-glazed pot, a knife, a fleece or goat hide, even—but this was very rare—a minted coin.

And such objects presaged a request for the services of the pythoness who dwelt in the cave.

Typically, next morning there would be someone waiting at the same spot, not a child, but an adult, or at least a youth or girl: wanting to know, perhaps, whether to accept a parent's dictates concerning a planned marriage; or which of a group of brothers destined to share a minuscule inheritance would fare best if he quit the island to seek his fortune; or how to recant an ill-considered oath without incurring the vengeance of the god whose name had been invoked. This person would have waited since midnight in fear and trembling, for it was no light matter to consult an oracle. Indeed, occasionally the supplicant's courage failed, and he or she only reappeared days after delivering the necessary fee.

Once the seeress had had a name like anybody else's. She had been born here, and grown up, and though her mother had died bearing her a good few relatives survived, so they and sundry others remembered what she had been called in youth. But since she entered into her full powers few people, apart from those who now verged on senility, had referred to her in any other manner than as "One who has lived before." On the rare occasions when the islanders encountered her, gathering herbs on the ridge that spined Oragalia, or jetsam along its rocky beaches, they reacted in one of two ways: either they beat a prompt retreat, as befitted those who knew about the sacred mysteries but were not party to them, or they ran to her and begged a favorable charm.

To the latter she was sometimes affable, sometimes tolerant, sometimes insulting. News of her response would spread within hours, and later, in the isolated farmsteads, there would be arguments lasting past sundown about her current mood and what actions of their own might account for it. Every place in the world, it was known, must be under the aegis of some tutelary deity or other, and they and theirs were constantly at loggerheads. They must be, for earth, sea and sky were full of forces surpassing the comprehension of puny humans, and the nearest anyone could come to accounting for them was to invoke the image of a quarrelsome family. It was advisable to keep on the right side of anyone with insight into such arcane matters.

Moreover, few communities—and that included all the neighboring islands—enjoyed the luxury of their own seeress. There were oracles aplenty on the mainland, but they were a long and dangerous journey distant. In any case, what attention could those alien gods be expected to pay to somewhere this remote and insignificant? Let all rejoice in their good fortune, then, inasmuch as they benefited from one woman's contact with the divine.

So great, indeed, was the confidence the folk reposed in her that they now neglected many antique shrines, and had let former ceremonies fall into disuse, to the vast annoyance of the royal family, for they provided the hereditary priests or priestesses of the cults concerned.

The king himself had ruled harshly in the past, thereby earning the detestation of his subjects. Now, though, he was old and ill, and unwilling to waste his failing strength in a fruitless struggle against one chosen of the gods. However, seeking what they regarded as their rightful share of the people's offerings, his kinfolk tried repeatedly to persuade her to take the king's last unwed son in marriage—a beardless boy!—or at least accept one of his daughters as a pupil and companion.

All such proposals she rejected with fine scorn, and the folk came reluctantly to believe she was resolved to die a virgin.

Unpredictable as ever, last spring she had proved them wrong.

Where he had come from, the black stranger, no one knew. None of the fisherfolk had reported finding so much as the wreckage of a raft after the storm that presaged his advent. Some claimed he was not human, but conjured up by magic arts from the infernal realm of Hephaistos the lame smith. At all events, one morning of a sudden he was there: starvation-gaunt, yet exceptionally tall, black as midnight and naked apart from a spotted animal hide wrapped around his loins, a figure of indescribable menace.

The children bringing the pythoness's daily offering encountered him in twilight, dropped their burdens and fled in terror. When they reached home, at first their parents accused them of telling lies, but when they themselves ventured near, nervous, after sunrise, there he was squatting on a rocky outcrop, gnawing twigs off a tree bough—for food, they thought at first, mistaking him for an animal.

Then they realized he was stripping the branch to use it as a club, like Heracles, and ran away as swiftly as the children.

By noon almost the entire population of Oragalia had assembled to stare at the dark-skinned apparition. Some, urged on by the king's eldest son who craved action because he was growing weary of waiting to enter into his birthright, were brandishing weapons and declaring that this monster should be put to death at once. Others, however, were not so sure it would prove vulnerable to swords and spears.

While they were still arguing, the pythoness appeared bearing a bowl of broth. To their amazement, she was even more naked than the black man, for she wore nothing but a charm on a thong around her neck—though her nudity was already a powerful magic.

Approaching the stranger, who desisted from his task and watched her warily, she set the dish just out of reach at a spot where the breeze would blow the savory aroma toward him. Then she stepped back and waited.

Suspicious, but leaving his club behind, he was lured toward the bait. Having dipped and sucked his finger, he approved the taste, and after gulping down the broth greedily scooped up the remaining scraps.

The pythoness held out her hand for the bowl. He relinquished it and said something in a language no one—not even she, apparently—could understand. She smiled, and offered her other hand to take his. Uncertain, he shied away and snatched up his club. But she stood her ground, and only moments later he made up his mind to go with her.

Together they disappeared in the direction of the cave, leaving the king's son and his cronies to disperse discomfited.

Next morning, when the offerings were brought—not by children for once, but by burly armed men—he was there, watching from a nearby crag, leaning on his club. And so it had been every day since. The only difference was that now the islanders had grown almost proud of having such a wonder in their midst, and even the children called greetings to him, which he had learned to answer, in a gruff tone but comprehensibly. Also, since the weather had turned cool, he had donned a coarse woolen cloak.

The change in the pythoness herself was far greater, for now she went with child.

At first the islanders had refused to believe it, being so convinced she was committed to perpetual chastity. Then those who maintained that the black stranger was not human, but forged by the smith of the gods, pointed out that this would mean a line of succession was to be established. No doubt such a child would be possessed of powers even more amazing than its mother's. Fortune would smile on Oragalia forever!

Apart—as usual—from the king's kinsmen, the populace were delighted to fall in with this reasoning. After much debate, they even decided to act in accordance with it.

Today dawn broke on a figure waiting at the usual spot on the hill above the bay, but there had been no special offering, nor was there one now. The common sort of food had been sent, only it had been brought by an uncommon carrier: an old woman, nearly toothless, her skin like wrinkled leather, but her hands still strong and her eyes still keen. Shivering perhaps less from the chill than at the sight of the black man, whom few had dared approach so closely, she remained where she was when he emerged to collect the food.

He challenged her—or greeted her; it was hard to know which—and she replied in a steady voice, but he did not have enough words to grasp what she meant. Satisfied, however, that she posed no sort of threat, he returned to the cave.

A while passed. The sun broached the horizon.

Then, moving slowly, for her time could be at most a fortnight away and her belly was so big that the child might well be born early, the pythoness left her cave and mounted the steep path which snaked past it, upward to the ridge, down to the beach. She spoke in irritable tones. The crone explained her presence. On being curtly told to go away, she glanced nervously at the black man, but remained where she was.

Sensing, if not following, the meaning of the exchange, the man pantomimed picking her up and throwing her over the cliff. They pythoness seemed to consider the idea, but eventually signed no, and let herself be led back to the cave. Lying on a heap of skins and fleeces, she managed to convey despite many false starts and misunderstandings the fact that the woman was a skilled midwife. The folk had decided that those with such knowledge must keep guard here by day and night from now until the birth-time, for fear of any delay in being sent for when labor started. The life of a pythoness's child was too precious to be risked.

Abruptly catching on, he grinned, his teeth amazingly white in his dark face. Seizing a piece of meal cake, he dipped it in oil and returned to the hillside.

The old woman cringed when he advanced on her, but he took her hand gently and folded her fingers around the cake, then pointed at his mouth. For a moment she seemed to think she was supposed to feed him. Perhaps imagining this was some sort of sacred ritual, she made to do so, but he burst into a rich deep laugh and indicated more clearly that the food was for her. Surprised, but willing enough, she mumbled it with a word of thanks. Later, he brought her water in one of the pythoness's fine glazed pots, before setting out to check the fishing lines he had laid along the beach.

At sundown the watch changed. A younger and stronger woman arrived and sent the crone hobbling homeward. Before departure the latter handed over a ball of twine and a knife, its blade honed to flashing keenness, which she had hitherto kept concealed under her cloak. The black man thought at first it might be meant for self-defense, as though even at her age the old woman feared assault from this ferocious-looking stranger. Hah! In the case of the new arrival, on the other hand . . .

Seeing him stare at the knife, however, she demonstrated its use, pantomiming the emergence of something between her legs, then gesturing with the string and sawing at the air. Light dawned, and he shook his head vigorously. In the land he hailed from, women brought similar instruments to attend a birth, though generally of bone or polished stone. There, too, they would have reacted in just the same way as this one did when he held out his hand and mutely requested a chance to inspect the symbols engraved on the haft. She thrust the knife behind her instantly.

Well, it was women's magic anyhow. He turned away into the gathering dark.

"Olga!" he said suddenly.

It was very late. Stacy was only drowsing, though, not fully asleep; the child was kicking at her furiously as though eager to be born. So far, however, she had not warned him of the onset of labor pains. According to her best estimates, they ought not to begin for several days.

Shifting in search of a comfortable position, failing to find one, she snapped, "I'm not called Olga! Who's Olga?"

Recently she had reverted to her former abrupt changes of mood. Wanting to calm her, he laid a soothing hand on her cheek, and withdrew it instantly, sitting up.

"You're sweating, but it's chill tonight!"

"Don't worry—" she began, but he was already reaching for a rag to dip in water and wring out. Having laid it across her forehead, he rested on one elbow, gazing down at her dim outline.

"That's nice," she sighed. "Thank you . . . Gene, I'm sorry. I didn't mean to snap. Of course I know which Olga you mean. Tell me her story. Maybe it'll help to send me to sleep."

"That's a backhanded compliment if ever I heard one," he muttered. But he lay down again, cradling her head against his shoulder, and stared at the invisible roof of rock as he marshaled his words. At length:

"Maybe it was her background . . . though how can one ever be sure what's outside influence and what's innate? At all events she grew disillusioned with intellect and reason. She spent her life searching for experiences which would transcend reality, and when she was offered the chance to do so in the literal sense, she seized it with avidity."

"What was the proper world for Olga, then?"

"Not in any real sense a world. At best a place. A place where rationality no longer ruled. The frame of logic was strained there, coming apart as it were to offer glimpses of something else beyond, insusceptible to reason.

"First of all she noticed that certain of the events which happened to her resisted explanation. The people she had come among were happy to accept them, seeking no underlying cause, and after a little she realized that this was precisely what she'd always claimed to want.

"Habit, however, was too strong. A meeting she desired took place when it should have been impossible, the other person being much too far away. An object she chanced across, but could not find again, seemed to have been of a color not belonging to the spectrum. A phrase she overheard in someone else's conversation rang with subtle meaning, but she could neither grasp that meaning nor repeat the words. Strive as she would to enjoy these experiences, she found them dreadfully disquieting.

"Growing desperate, she was ultimately driven to the conclusion that the fault must be in herself, and set about rectifying it, by laying herself open to more and ever more extreme stimuli. At first she made the error of rushing to locations where events she regarded as improbable had been reported; after a while, however, she realized they would never be repeated and hence one spot was as good as any other. It was pointless to go anywhere, or do anything, when one did not understand the logic beyond logic. By definition, though, it could not possibly be understood.

"Yet everything seemed possible where she was, at least in the sense that impossible things were happening every day.

"This insight offered a degree of comfort. She made the most of it. Forcing herself to concentrate, she set about demolishing within her mind the assumptions she had regarded as commonsensical throughout her life. In this way she hoped to attune herself better to this new reality—if reality it could be called."

Gene paused. Stirring at his side, eyes closed, Stacy prompted, "Did she succeed?"

"You can't say 'she' about her anymore. There was success, that's all. The identity which had been Olga's melted like a snowflake falling in the ocean. At the last—the very last—moment, she realized that even if she did achieve her goal, there would no longer be an Olga to rejoice."

"It was too late."

"For her, it was too late before she started out."

# PART TEN

*THE EXHIBIT*
*is a world ateem with life.*
*It revolves around a variable star*

*THE MONTH*
*is December*

*THE NAME*
*is Anastasia*

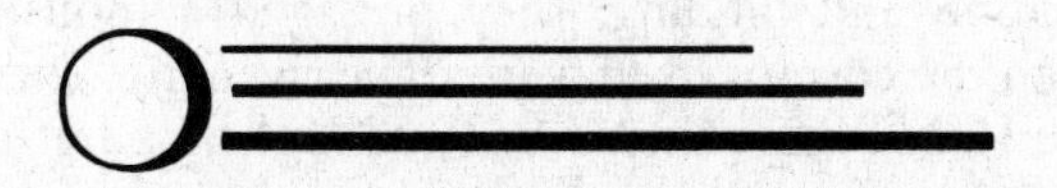

In pitch darkness Stacy stirred uneasily, aware of a dull cramp in her abdomen. At first, muzzily, she took it for a touch of colic; she felt bloated and flatulent, as though she had eaten something which disagreed with her.

She strove to remain asleep in spite of her discomfort, for she had been having an elaborate and fascinating dream. Indeed, she was still partly lost in it, for her mind was aswarm with images and sensations, all of them astonishingly vivid. Normally she recalled her dreams as mainly visual, with perhaps a phrase or two of conversation, or a snatch of something that might, for the right person, have turned into a fragment of a poem. Never before had she experienced any which extended to involve the totality of herself, both mental and physical. Heat and cold were there, bodily posture, sounds and smells, hunger and fullness, happiness and despair, the feel of clothing on her body, wind on her cheek, sunshine and rain . . .

Oh, this dream was extraordinary, and seemed to have no limits. It was as complex and detailed as reality, and moreover it was populated with a countless horde of people. She could literally see and hear them with her eyes tight shut—or even open, for in the utter blackness it made no difference. She felt as though she were drifting past them, carried by an invisible river of air, so light she could not sense her weight on her heels. As she drew near to each individual or group, she could hear talking, sometimes shouting, sometimes laughing, now and then discussions in low tones concerning confidential matters which she could not make out, no matter how hard she strained her ears. But that was of small account, for at her approach they invariably broke off their conversation and turned to gaze at her, their expressions varying from hostility to puzzlement. She looked in vain for sympathy, and could not work out why she should be seeking it.

Was it in fact at her that they were staring . . . or someone at her back? She was aware of a presence behind her, but she could not turn around, no matter how she tried.

The effort of recollection itself was making her more and more wakeful. Still she fought to retain the dream's images and sequence of events, determined to impress them on her memory despite renewed pangs.

To some extent she succeeded. Clear as life, she saw an old woman in a greasy cloak of undyed wool hunched on a low flat rock, her hands concealed but clutching objects of enormous purport . . .

(Images of separation and binding; they presaged a monstrous tearing apart, as though the cosmos itself were to be riven into shards.)

And a line of grim-faced men, their arms and legs bare but their bodies encased by harness of tough leather with studs and plates of bronze; they carried spears, and oblong shields hung at their backs on leather thongs . . .

(Images of division and compulsion; they had the power to snatch husband from wife, mother from child, and ordain that they belong henceforth to other people.)

And a noisy mob of soldiers, clad in rusty mail and with daggers at their sides, who had not yet drawn the latter and were brawling more in fun than in earnest . . .

(Images of terror and superstition; they had been told throughout their lives that their cause was just, and in spite of all the wickedness it had brought into the world they were prepared to entertain no alternative.)

And men and women traveling in carriages from stately home to stately home, their clothes a triumph of the tailor's skill, scorning beggars as they held out talon hands and showed off oozing sores . . .

(Images of isolation and antipathy; they literally could not accept the poor as people like themselves, and felt more pity for a foundered horse than for a human.)

And a gang of rowdy merrymakers shouting and drinking around a table and cursing the attendants for their slowness to obey orders in a foreign language . . .

(Images of debauchery and shamefaced lust; they wanted to deny quotidian reality, break loose into a temporary otherworld where they might rule unhampered, yet kept encountering obstacles they could not disregard.)

And any army drilling in impeccable order, every movement as precise as a machine's, rehearsing to unleash a hell of horror on their fellow creatures, but disguising it behind the trappings of an artificial art . . .

(Images of exultation and destruction; they held themselves superior to nature herself, but knew no way to prove it save by humiliating and debasing other people.)

And the crew of a vessel tossing in mid-ocean, cursing salt meat, weevily flour and water foul enough to make them vomit even without aid from the waves, reviling the captain who had lured them on a voyage to far continents . . .

(Images of misery and greed; they had signed on as much because their lives at home had grown unbearable as because they truly hoped for riches on return.)

And a shifting crowd of persons garbed in silk and satin and brocade, standing on a quayside among bales and bundles and barrels; beyond them, a hedgehog's back of spiky masts that rocked and tilted like a dancing forest . . .

(Images of bargaining and distribution; they could coax and wheedle the ignorant into parting with what they needed most and sell it on to those who already had too much.)

And an empty beach, newly created by a rise in the level of the sea, which until a generation ago had been twice her height above the water, overlooked by a cave whose entrance was framed by concrete pillars once as formal as a propylaeum, now tilted and off-square as though they had been earthquake-struck—

The darkness was full of a roaring noise. For a second she thought of it as the grinding of just such an earthquake, only infinitely worse: the sound of spacetime being shattered and remade—a memory. Then, through her still-closed lids, she realized there was no more darkness. Boat had diverted what remained of her power into turning on her searchlights, making night into day, and the racket was the chattering of a helicopter coming in to land.

Abruptly she realized who and where she was, and whose the presence at her back had been during her dream. Also she registered that her pain was arriving in rhythmical waves and there was wetness between her legs. Opening her eyes in terror, she found that the cave had been invaded by men and women peeling off coveralls to reveal green sterile clothing. Alongside them marched machines on legs, better than wheels for such rough going. Some of them, fitted with their own lights, carried TV cameras. Humming softly, they settled around her like vultures beside a corpse-to-be, and the people closed on her like ghouls.

Oh, this was *wrong!* Here, now, should be a time of solitude, when the magic and mysterious process of making a new life reached its fulfillment! What business did strangers have to intervene? Or anybody? (She had almost loved someone; she must learn to love her child —children . . .)

She begged for mercy and surcease; they gave her none.

They had dealt with Gene first, in case he interfered with what they planned. Awakened by the row, he had started to his feet and rushed to the cave entrance. A silent machine like a chrome-plated stick figure awaited him. It was impeccably programmed. The back of his head sank into a resilient pad and a band closed around his neck; his arms, his torso, his legs were matched from behind by clasping metal limbs with joints in precisely the right places to let him move provided he did so very slowly. At the least hint of an attempt to break loose, they locked solid.

Also there was the sting of a diadermic on the inside of his left elbow, on feeling which he screamed.

Because at that instant dreadful memories stormed in.

He was cocooned into rigidity and weightless (she also). His face was covered by a mask (like hers). Food and water belonged to his past and maybe future (and hers). Taped to the crook of his elbow (and hers) there was a pipe warranted to deliver sufficient nourishment into his veins (and hers). It was to keep him (her too) alive for an hour before, a week after—and who could say how long between?

Would there be time?

There was nothing to do except report his subjective perceptions. Everything else was taken care of by computers. He was very frightened, and said so once or twice—but they would know that already, because they were monitoring his bodily condition. Minutes ticked away. He could see a clock, but no other instruments—what use would they have been? At least the designers had been thoughtful enough to site a window where he could look out of it, and a couple of times he began to count the stars it made visible. But the stabilization was imperfect, and new ones drifted into view while others vanished, so he kept on losing track.

Around him amazing energies assembled. Eventually his nerves started to sing, as though the fabric of the space he occupied were being warped.

Well, that was true.

He began to feel a sort of separation from himself, his thoughts becoming dreamlike and random. The sensation was not unpleasant, though the frustration he experienced when he tried to describe it was. In fact it became worse than just unpleasant. It became infuriating. He wanted more than anything to flee back into his own past and cancel the decision which had led him to this utter loneliness on a path that others had dared, only to return insane or dead.

As the clock closed on its zero, he found his voice one final time. "I must be out of my mind!" he cried.

And was, for the universe shattered.

Tore apart.

Dissolved.

Ceased.

There were not, never had been, could never be, words to describe the experience.

Except perhaps it felt a bit like being a billion people at once . . . and all of them dead.

Yet he was here: in his body (he sensed the pounding of his heart); breathing without a mask; able to see and hear and feel and doubtless speak, once he could summon up the energy to do so, which had been filched from him by the injection in his elbow. Right now talking didn't seem all that important.

Curious, he gazed around as though he had never seen this place before—and in a sense he hadn't, for not even at midsummer noonday had there been such brilliant light in here. Over the months he and Stacy had brought ashore many of the facilities from Boat, but some were too heavy, some called for power they could not provide, and some she was forbidden to part with by her original programming, so the home they had created was by no means luxurious. Indeed, it now disgusted him, for there was a heap of rubbish by the entrance as foul as a medieval midden (did I pass that every day and disregard it?), and the bed they had shared was—

Best that he could not see it past the clustering people and machines. But it was all being recorded, of course: every last minutest detail . . .

"We couldn't let you go on with your playacting any longer," said a stern voice nearby. Gene turned his head as quickly as the machine that held him in its clutch permitted, and saw that the speaker was a woman with short brown hair, thin enough to be mistaken for a boy, though with betraying lines of age once one looked closely at the skin below her jaw. She went on, "Her waters have broken. She must have been in an incredibly deep sleep, practically a coma. Otherwise the first stage of labor would have roused her, and that must have set in two hours ago . . . Oh, stop looking at me like a stranger! I'm Dr. Catherine Hoy—as you're perfectly aware!"

*Hoy—boy . . .*

"No, you're not," Gene said wearily. "You're Bony, the cabin boy, and you helped to row a boat ashore from that Venetian galley. Where's the captain?"

He tried to turn his head further, but the movement was too hasty for the suspicious machine, and it locked up. Dispirited, he let himself slump against it, whereupon—with due and automatic caution—it relented.

By that time, something more important had claimed his attention. Closing his eyes briefly, he sought words.

"If you say you're called Hoy, and you're a doctor, I guess I have to take your word for it even though I think you're someone else. Doctor or no doctor, though, what I want to know is what you're doing to Stacy. And why!"

"You know why!" came the curt response.

"Simply because she's going to do a perfectly natural thing, and have a baby?"

"Under the most primitive and insanitary conditions!" Hoy flared. "Man, what possessed you to play along so with one another's fantasies? We held back until the last possible minute, but when the birth pangs started—"

He raised his eyes to meet hers, a motion the machine permitted, and for a long moment she was abashed at the intensity of his reply.

"There have been no fantasies, Dr. Hoy. There have been realities."

He was beginning to understand what had happened to him (to them). A sense of intersection filled his mind: yesterday as real as tomorrow and neither any different from today. How to make Hoy recognize the truth whose force had suddenly pervaded his very bones? Suppose he were to say outright, "It's true the universe is solid! So where you sent us must be somewhere else . . . yet we did come back!" Would that plain statement penetrate her world of preconceptions? No, she would not grasp the implications. Could anybody, without having gone where he had been, without treading the long path back through time? It would be like trying to share a dream.

At the same instant, anyhow, Hoy was distracted. A clear faint voice spoke from midair, inquiring how things were progressing, and she snapped a response to the effect: "As well as can be expected!" There followed a number of technical questions, and a request to couple up some item of equipment via a satellite connection to a main computer on a distant continent. This was attended to.

Gene took advantage of the respite to gather his wits. When Hoy turned back to him, he was able to say, "You didn't have to go to all this trouble. The local midwives have been taking turns to stand guard near the cave so they could be called on as soon as labor started . . . Oh, *now* what's wrong?"

She was staring at him with mingled pity and dismay.

"I didn't understand till this very moment how deep your delusions were running," she whispered. "Gene—oh, Gene! How long ago did those midwives promise to stand by?"

"Why, yesterday!" he answered in bewilderment.

"You poor crazy fool! I'm sorry, but that's what you are! This island of Oragalia has been depopulated ever since the water level rose. Your 'yesterday,' as near as we can guess from eavesdropping on you and Stacy while you talked with your imaginary friends, must have been about *three thousand years ago!*"

Had there not been a trace of sympathy in the serious faces which confronted him, at that point Gene might have broken down. Instead, fighting to digest the knowledge that was now invading his mind like floodwaters after a downpour too great for any ordinary channel, he folded his fingers into his palms until he felt the pain of his rough neglected nails, and clung to something Stacy had said when they were talking about—whom? It didn't matter. All that counted was what she had said, about being crazy: "My guess is that it must feel normal."

And he had known and accepted from the beginning that one of the countless risks he was running was insanity.

After a long dead pause punctuated only by mutterings from those attending Stacy, Gene said with such calmness as cost him all his self-control, "We searched Boat from stem to stern. We threw away all the monitors and microphones because we were so desperate for privacy. But you cheated us. You had our home bugged all the time."

"I think normality is creeping back," said Hoy with satisfaction, then caught herself and adopted a gentler tone. "Yes, Gene. We were prepared to respect your wish to be alone. We all agreed—me and Professor Shaw, Professor Yiu and Dr. Ngota, everyone—that we'd kept you far too long in a laboratory situation, and it was time we had a chance to observe your reactions in a setting nearer to everyday life. It was your coldness, you see, the remoteness that you both exhibited. Neither of you could be called insane in any clinical sense. You behaved normally enough; you slept, you got up on time, you bathed and dressed yourselves and turned up for meals and underwent our tests and answered our endless questions, yet gradually we became aware that your attention was elsewhere, and so was hers. You were acting like programmed robots, not like human beings anymore. Something was wrong, and so we let you go, daring to hope you'd make a full recovery.

"Instead, you became more and more lost in a maze of dreams. And then, when Stacy became pregnant . . . Well, without us what would your today have been?"

"Real."

"What!" She blinked at him.

"Real!" Gene repeated. "To me, now, all of this is artificial—hideously so! I want to be beside her, hold her hand, watch while the baby comes, do what a father must and should to help her . . . You won't permit that, though. Will you?"

"She has the best possible care," Hoy countered stiffly. She gestured in the direction of the bed. "Right over there you can see the finest obstetrician we could find, the best anaesthesiologist, a team of top experts flown here at short notice just to help her! And you, of course," she appended hastily.

"I think you're here to kill her," Gene said with terrible directness.

"And I think"—in a soothing tone—"you're overwrought. It would be best if you had a chance to relax."

She reached out with her fingertips and rapped a code on the machine that held him. There was another prick, this time inside his other elbow.

The world vanished instantly—and not just *the* world, but all the worlds. More worlds than there were any means to count.

They had usurped control of Stacy's body, too, disposing her in what official wisdom decreed to be a proper posture. In the no-longer darkness of the cave, she was being kept as still as the convulsions passing through her would permit. She had been intending to let nature take its course. Nature was not to be allowed to. As helpless as when she had been hurled into impossibility, her physical self remained passive while her mind sought ways of—escape? No, continuance. The ancient realities held: birth, nourishment, learning, making, breeding, teaching, dying . . .

Suddenly frightened, she groped with closed eyes for a familiar hand, whispering, "Gene? Gene!"

But what she touched was smooth plastic overlying something solid, which vibrated but did not respond. No one seemed to notice that she'd stirred.

*A snowflake dissolving in the ocean . . .*

"Gene . . ." she murmured in a failing voice, and knew that her lost mind now had no haven to return to.

# Part Eleven

*THE EXHIBIT*
*can walk and talk, can suffer and dream.*
*It keeps asking how and to what purpose*

*THE MONTH*
*is December*

*THE NAME*
*is (in both senses) Gene*

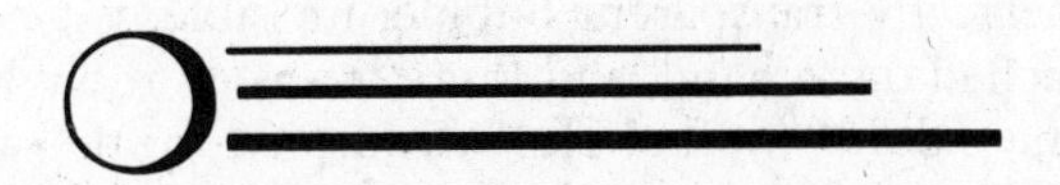

"*I* can't find a way back!"

He was moaning. He could not hear the words, but he recognized them from the shape his tongue and lips imposed on air, and he knew what he meant whether or not anybody else did.

"Gene!"

Not his voice. A firm, commanding one, which he ought to recognize—only something far more important occupied his mind. He said, "There's no way—but there must be!"

"Gene, don't pretend you're talking in your sleep! We know you're awake!"

Oh yes, indeed, he was. His brain was crackling with insight like a thunderhead sparking lightning from peak to peak—against a gray-black ground of misery.

"Gene!"

So why would this intrusive bastard not listen to what he was saying? In sudden rage he reared up and shouted.

"THE UNIVERSE IS SOLID, DAMN YOU—SOLID!"

But as a shout, it was feeble, and his rearing up was frustrated by the fact that he lay on a couch of such resilience, his elbows sank into it, deep, deep.

He had, though, forgotten until now that his eyes were shut.

Opening them, he saw bright scudding grayish clouds. It was high noon—insofar as noon could be high on this, the shortest day of the year. He was no longer in the cave. He was on the afterdeck of a smart modern ship, much larger than Boat and far better equipped, a prime example of the generation of seagoing vessels called into being by the loss of so much land after the thawing of the ice caps. And he was afraid of what might be in store for him.

Did they plan to peel his mind apart like an onion, layer by layer, with a skill born of centuries of practice? It had happened to him before—how long ago? It could at most have been one year, yet it felt far further in the past than the three thousand Hoy had mentioned.

But if they tried that again, all the knowledge he had garnered on his trip beyond the limits of infinity might well be lost forever. He would no longer preserve the difference between himself and them. He had to stop it happening, and he had no faintest notion how to do so.

This bitter conclusion made him take proper stock of his surroundings. It was not an open deck he lay on. He, and those near him, were enclosed by a perfectly transparent bubble: invisible, yet nonetheless a cage. He reached out a hand, and there it was, as though the air had solidified. One side of the bubble was formed by the white flank of the ship's bridge, and the sole door set in that was like the entry to an armor-plated bunker. He wasted no time on looking for cameras and microphones and the hidden sensors that would trap and analyze his very skin secretions. He took it for granted they were there. Once more he was not a human being, but a specimen. All he could do was cling with might and main to his own self . . .

But who was he? What was he, who remembered being the jock who ran away with an heiress—the shipwrecked fisherman who claimed the hand of an island's most marriageable virgin—the slave who swam through stormy seas to liberty and love? Who was the man who had traversed impossibility and come home whole?

He didn't know.

But perhaps (suspicion grew at the edge of consciousness) he knew who was the mistress that had claimed him.

A shiver crawled down his spine, although he was not cold. There was something awe-inspiring in that thought.

"Gene, look at me, will you?" the same voice said.

Remembering that for a while he had not even been able to turn his head, and relishing this petty degree of freedom, he complied, and focused on the man who was leaning over him. The face wasn't right—No, more exactly, the garb wasn't. He wore a peaked cap and a white jersey, and he should have sported a brown velvet slouch hat and a stained doublet . . . The captain of the Venetian galley! Of course! And Hoy equaled boy, and where was Scarface?

This sensation was abominably unpleasant, as though he were a set of badly meshing gears.

"I read recognition in your eyes," the man said softly. Gene summoned concentration and made shift to answer.

"Yes, you're the captain," he answered in a dull tone. "I didn't register your name when you visited us. Why didn't you come straight out and tell us who you were?"

"When was that?" the man countered, glancing sidelong. Hoy appeared next to him. Still no sign of Scarface . . .

"Why, when you brought us all that strange food . . ." But the memory grew dream-elusive as he spoke. "Anyway, this is the wrong ship. You had oarsmen, and your sail was furled for lack of wind. And you talked incredible nonsense!"

"For example?"

"Oh, you tried to tell us . . ." Gene squeezed his eyes shut with effort, but it was useless. Concepts, phrases, images that sprang to mind vanished instantly, lost to him behind as dense a barrier as the one that walled the universe. He found himself saying over and over, "It's solid! You've got to understand me—got to!"

The man raised his eyebrows, once more glancing at his companion Hoy, and now they were at last joined by the one Gene still thought of as Scarface . . . but he differed most from recollection. Clad in a quilted cotton jacket, he was thickset and square-faced, and his cheek was as remembered scarred, but it was pitted with the traces not of a wound but of disease. At any rate, though, he was sallow and his eyes were shaded by the epicanthic fold.

He said, "Make sure he realizes who he's talking to."

"I know only too well," Gene muttered. "You're Professor Yiu—hah! You're yiu! Of course! Sorry about that. Bad joke. It's just that I need to find something funny in the world, or I'll go mad . . . And"—forcing himself into a sitting position despite the reluctance of his too-soft couch, so he could look directly at the captain—"I'm *shaw* about you as well: Benedict Shaw."

"So you finally accepted that," the other murmured. He had a clear and level gaze. He had never actually worn a brown velvet hat. "What else do you recall?"

"Infinitely more than you, if you live to be a million."

"That isn't quite what I wanted to know," Shaw returned patiently. "You recall my name. But do you remember—ah—what post I hold?"

"I held a sharpened one. Used it to dig that bad salty ground."

"We'll come to you in a moment. We're talking about me."

Abruptly further obstinacy seemed fruitless. Gene let himself slump back on the couch.

"You're the chief psychologist of Project Go."

"What's that?"

"It's all to do with ships."

"What kind of ships? Ships like this? Ships like Boat? Look, there she is yonder." He pointed.

Reflexively Gene turned his head. Indeed, she rode at anchor off the western cape of the beach where he and Stacy had—had . . . That, though, was beyond him to define.

She was somewhat battered after nine months at anchor off this rocky shore, but not greatly harmed. Also she was no longer alone. She had been joined by half a score of other vessels.

"I'm waiting for an answer," Shaw prompted gently.

"Oh, damn you . . ." Gene passed a hand across his forehead. "Why do you have to pester me like this?"

"Because you accepted it might be necessary. Now we say it is."

That was logic he could not dispute. He murmured, "If there is a hell, perhaps it consists in living up to all one's promises."

"What?"—from Hoy and Yiu together, while Shaw knit his brows in search of meaning.

"Oh, never mind. Of course I know what sort of ships!" (The stark metal hulls; the scentless stench of artificial air; the vacancy beyond; the rawness of the force they summoned from the sun . . . His body was pouring sweat in torrents.) "Just as I know who I am and Stacy was!"

"Then say it, man! Say it aloud!"

"Ships to exceed the speed of light! And we your sole successful guinea pigs!"

Hoy uttered a yell of delight and flung her arms around both Shaw and Yiu. Shaw, though, pushed her brusquely aside.

"You said: 'who Stacy was'—" he had begun, when a harsh voice interrupted from the air. The sound was directionalized, and Gene could not hear clearly, but the other three instantly lost interest in him and Shaw began to issue a series of brisk orders. A few moments later, there was an indistinct commotion on the beach. Shortly the helicopter's blades blurred and it rose swiftly from the sand and headed back this way.

A premonition clutched Gene's heart. With immense effort he forced himself over the side of the couch and rose, swaying. Nobody made any attempt to stop him. Anyhow, it was too late to do more than he had done already. Maybe three thousand—maybe a million years too late . . .

"The baby!" he exclaimed. "What's wrong with it?"

"Nothing's wrong with the baby," Shaw said curtly. "By the way" —in a more placatory tone—"it's a girl."

"Then what—?

"We don't know! We'll have to wait!"

Deep within himself Gene found some resource of calm, and though he realized it might be due to drugs was grateful for it.

Without such help, he would have gone berserk. Aching, he stared as the helicopter touched down the other side of the invisible barrier. Its door was flung open and Stacy was lifted out on a stretcher.

On seeing her clear, he felt terror no chemicals could disguise.

For her face was covered by an oxygen mask, and even as the stretcher was lowered to the deck a technician scrambled after, striving to keep in position on her naked chest a shiny chromed electrode.

"I did say 'was,' didn't I?" he whispered.

Shaw nodded, and his face turned paper white.

After the stretcher, they unloaded something else from the helicopter: an oblong box with a soft but tough transparent lid, an incubator, with two nurses in attendance and many tubes and instruments attached to it.

"Let me out!" Gene cried. "I must go to her!"

Shaw, having listened to the air again, laid a hand on his arm.

"There's nothing you can do, Gene. I'm desperately sorry. It seems there's nothing anyone can do."

"What?"—not wanting to understand.

"Her heart will not respond. They don't know why."

Gene's hands fell to his sides in a posture of uttermost defeat. Turning away, he muttered, "I do. I said to Hoy: you came to kill her. And you have."

"We came to help her!" Hoy exclaimed.

"Help her? *Help* her? She didn't need your help! She was doing exactly what was right to save herself! If only you'd let *me* tend her—she'd taught me well . . . Oh, you idiots!" Clarity was returning to his thoughts by giant strides as his subconscious found ways to turn insight into words. Had they not drugged him—

No, it would have been too late in either case.

As well as rage, a hint of resignation showed in his voice when he went on.

"Haven't your computers figured it out yet? No? Then what use are they?" He took a pace toward them, and they flinched back against the unseen wall.

"There's Stacy dead, and you wouldn't even let me hold her hand while she was dying, and you don't know why it happened anyhow! I do! She sent you a message by the only means you left her, and you ignored it because you thought you knew it all—didn't you?"

"We never claimed—" Shaw began. Gene cut him short.

"The message that she's sent you is her death *in birth!* She opted to die! Opted to, d'you hear me? Because she knew she could never find her way back to any world that we call real unless she bore our child when it was due—three thousand years in the past! And you, you *fools*, dragged her back to the here and now without a by-your-leave!

"Now you've stranded me on my own, without her, without anybody, loster and lonelier than any refugee that ever was! Oh, I've found *my* way home—she's made me whole by leaving me to spell out a message you lot are too thick to interpret, and I know that because I'm mourning her! I can feel again! I'm no longer just responding like a robot, and I only wish I could hate you as much as you deserve!" Glaring, he clenched his fists.

"I want to hate you for all the reasons in the universe! I don't care how much time, how much effort, how many people you've spent on trying to find a way to reach the stars! You've had your chance, and for all I ought to care you and everybody else might find your own way to hell! You've sent me there, and now you've slammed the door on my escape! Because I dare not hate you—not after the sacrifice she's made for all your sakes! I'd be betraying her!"

Abruptly there were tears streaming down his cheeks. He turned to the side of the ship's bridge and leaned his forehead against its smooth white surface. After a while he began to beat his fists on the painted metal, moaning what sounded like a blend of all the names by which his mistress had been known to him.

This too was recorded by the dutiful machines.

# Part Twelve

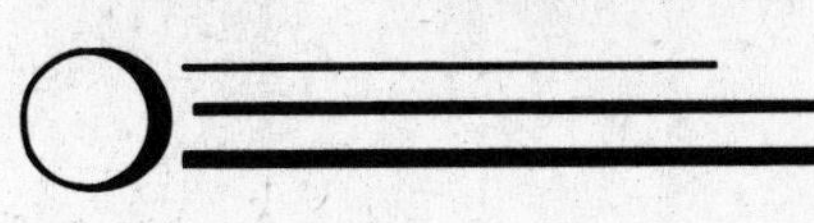

THE EXHIBIT
*is small and weak and ignorant and helpless . . . but alive. It's you, and me, and everyone, as we once were*

THE MONTH
*is any month*

THE NAME
*is its mother's, and your mother's, and mine too*

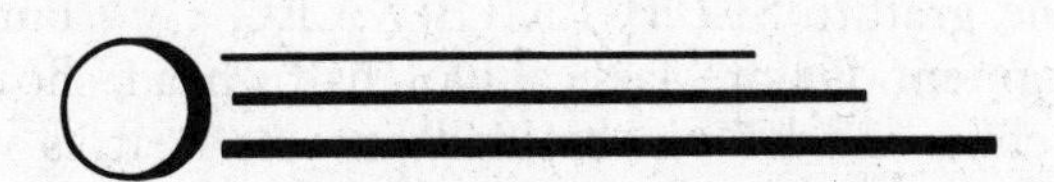

"So here's another child who'll only ever know her real mother."

Gene's words hung heavy on the air. It was warm, but in his heart there was eternal winter.

Shaw responded after a dreadful interval, leaden as the silence of the grave. His face was gray and lined, as though he had aged a lifetime in a single day.

"I wish I could believe you're mouthing nonsense. But I'm terribly afraid you're talking more sense than I can grasp, even if it is wrapped up in riddles."

An hour remained before sunset, but for the sake of the inevitable concealed cameras multiple lamps shed their brightness in the ship's resplendent cabin, where he, Hoy and Yiu sat opposite Gene on deep comfortable couches. At least they were treating him like a human being again, instead of trapping him in a barless cage for computerized interrogation, which was what he had been most afraid of.

Because they were shamed by Stacy's death? Because he had guessed right when they were wrong, even though they believed him to be crazy? Who was to say what was sane when nothing like it had ever happened before?

At least Shaw was making a valiant attempt.

"You have a beautiful daughter," Hoy ventured. She seemed to be very far from understanding. "The obstetrician assures us she's in perfect health."

Their eyes turned to the incubator on its shiny metal trolley. Gene was staring down at the baby's wrinkled features through its transparent hood. He had insisted on placing it where he could see her clearly. The others, at worse angles, saw only patches of reflected light.

He had also insisted on certain objects being brought from the cave where, magpie-fashion, he had accumulated them over the past nine months: a brochure from a last-century travel agency, its colorful photographs smudged by seawater; a handful of empty shell cases from a World War II gun; a Victorian preserving jar, its glass lid chipped and its rubber sealing ring long perished, but its wire closure intact despite corrosion; a weathered icon recovered from the half-drowned church; the hilt of a sword, its blade shortened to a stump; several shards of decorated pottery which he had painstakingly assembled until their common form appeared, hinting at a jar for wine or oil; a broken tile bearing the graffito SEP:IUL:CORN:LEG . . . but the rest was lost; and a fragment of a preclassical idol, half a head, showing one ear, part of the chin, and hair in braided lines as neat as well-plowed furrows. All these were landmarks in what had happened to him and Stacy.

The survivor said eventually, "Have you worked out yet why it had to be her and me, not any of the others?"

The others exchanged glances. Hoy said at length, "We're evaluating various hypotheses."

"You can take your hypotheses and—!" But Gene's reflex fury died before he completed the sentence. Wearily he corrected himself.

"After what I said just now, I hoped you would have. Your minds seem to work so slowly, though . . . Okay, I'll have to do it the long way.

"You weren't responsible for choosing us, I admit. But it should have been you who figured out why Stacy and I proved more resilient than the rest. I know why we were allowed to volunteer, of course. Everything had gone wrong when they used smart people like trained scientists. So maybe it would succeed with someone ignorant, who could be relied on to react instead of reasoning."

"Gene!" Hoy was half out of her seat. "That's scarcely a fair description of either of you!"

"Yeah, it applies better to Shanti, right? I recall we talked about her one night. But you must have all that down in your computer records." He appended a sour grin.

The other three were tense as skyhook wire, aware that now Gene alone might hold the key to the universe, desperate to find out what he could teach them to help in planning future expeditions, but at a loss to know what they could safely say without provoking a renewal of his fugue.

Making a desperate effort, Yiu/Scarface ventured, "If you've figured it out, we'd be glad to hear your views. Can you express them for us?"

*Express . . .*

The word was /pregnant/ with meaning. Gene said reflectively, "Can I convey the truth to you? I doubt it! If you could be so unforgivably stupid as to kill Stacy, you must be too thickheaded to catch on! In fact you are! You didn't hear what I said about my—our—daughter!"

But even after silent consultation of the computers which were monitoring everything that transpired in the cabin, the others continued to exchange baffled glances. Gene lost patience.

"Oh, get me a drink and a bite to eat, and I'll explain . . . Has *she* been fed?" he added, indicating the cot.

"Yes, exactly as if Stacy—" Hoy bit her lip.

"I get it," Gene said with heavy irony. "You've programmed a computer to synthesize colostrum. As though any machine, any creation of our own . . . Never mind. That can wait."

He leaned back and crossed his legs, staring through the portholes toward the silhouette of the island which had almost the shape of the sphinx, poser of the riddle he had unforeseeably learned how to answer. After a while he began to weep again, soundlessly.

Later on, though, setting aside an empty glass and a plate with nothing on it but crumbs, he spoke calmly enough—indeed, in a meditative tone, aware he was putting everything he said on record, aware it would be analyzed and dissected by a thousand strangers. But he was used to that.

"I kept saying: 'The universe is solid.' Did you at least latch on to what I meant by that?"

The others nodded uncertainly. This exceeded the boundary of their own specialisms, but they had perforce been brought in contact with the concept.

Shaw said at last, "I think we did, but we'd rather you explained it to us."

"What's to explain? Even at the lowest level beyond the ordinary quark, every time an event occurs which can have more than a single outcome, all the outcomes do in fact take place. This makes the cosmos solid, in the sense that there is no more room inside it for anything else."

He hesitated, tilting his head to one side as though striving to hear a voice at the limit of audibility, and added in a half-surprised tone, "Hmm! Maybe that accounts for the way I used to claim that thanks to my ancestors my subconscious pictured the universe as a continent which could be trekked across . . . until I realized that Stacy's view was precisely the reverse, and she'd survived at least as well as I had, so one of us had to be wrong. In the upshot, of course, we both were, so—

"Never mind that, though. It's for later, when I can spare time to mourn her properly. Right now what matters is that this explains why, for so long, people were content to accept it was impossible to exceed the speed of light.

"Not that most of us imagined it would ever become necessary to try and do so. Here we were, on this small but comfortable planet, cheerfully abusing her hospitality as though her resources were inexhaustible, fighting wars, squandering our children's patrimony as though she belonged to just one generation, smugly convinced the rest of the universe was much too far away to worry about—except perhaps the sun, and so long as that rose every morning! . . .

"And then—!" Gene uttered a harsh laugh. "You know, I'm beginning to wonder whether something out there decided to teach us better!"

Suddenly afraid he might have disturbed the baby, he leaned toward the cot, but she was sleeping peacefully, and he resumed.

"At all events, that sun we'd taken for granted for so long turned out to be a variable star, didn't it?

"Oh, the experts who educated me and Stacy before our respective trips had worked it all out afterward: how minimal the fluctuation, how long the periodicity, how difficult to detect at a distance of even a few light-years . . . Nonetheless, it was enough to change the world.

"Not just by melting so much ice that the ocean level rose and half the people on the planet died, either as a direct result or because of the wars we fought to claim the remaining land. More importantly, it scared the rich and powerful among us in a way they'd never been scared before.

"Space travel had been a toy for the wealthy countries, hadn't it? They put up their communications satellites, they dreamed of establishing a High Frontier, they spent a little time and money on exploring the Moon, Venus and Mars—but always in the expectation of a payoff, if not in cash then in prestige. Survival was very far from people's minds in those dead days. Oh, some planned against the risk of war, but only a handful thought about keeping human stock alive were some universal catastrophe to overtake the Earth. And then, all of a sudden, our so-trustworthy sun—! Hence desperation; hence meteor mining and crewed trips to the other planets, which served only to confirm they could never be rendered fit for habitation. Hence, in the upshot, Project Go."

Shaw leaned forward. "It's hard for me to say this, but I think I must. Our first volunteers all died or went out of their minds. Would it be true to say that you and Stacy too became what's generally regarded as insane—if less extremely so—but that you had to because there was no alternative?"

Gene looked at him with fresh respect. He said, "Now it's your turn to spell something out. I can tell by their expressions that neither Hoy nor Yiu have caught on yet."

The others confirmed with nods. Dismayed, Shaw leaned back, gazing into nowhere.

"I'll do my best, but how to frame it in words? . . . Ah! There was a question no one thought to ask."

"I hear you," Gene encouraged.

"Well—what becomes of 'I' when it's doing something deemed to be impossible?"

Silence fell, broken finally when Yiu exhaled.

"Oh, yes. *Oh*, yes! But why you two?"

"Because, like her," Gene said patiently, and rested his hand on the incubator that enclosed his daughter, "we only knew one true parent."

"How are you going to call the baby?" Hoy demanded with a flash of insight. "After her mother?"

"I thought about that, since they tell me Anastasia means 'resurrection.' But—no. After *my* mother, and Stacy's."

"But you're an orphan!" Yiu was shaking his head in confusion. "So was she! How will you name the baby, then?"

"After my mother! I just told you! And yours, and everyone's! Now you've remembered about orphans, surely you must be able to figure out why only she and I came back healthy and partway sane. If not, there's little hope for humankind!"

He surveyed them, his expression challenging. Realizing that Yiu, confused, was about to call on the omnipresent aid of computers again, he checked him with a glare.

"Heaven's name, man! Have you so far forgotten how to reason for yourself? Then maybe we should abandon the universe to machines, like Suleyman!"

"You talked about him and all the others, didn't you?" Hoy probed, struck by sudden recollection.

"Yes, of course. Why?"

She put a hand to her forehead. "I almost see it but it keeps eluding me . . . Your mother, and ours, and hers too—Wait a second. You're arguing that you survived *because* you're an orphan, and so is Stacy?"

"Was"—in a tone like the grinding of icebergs.

"Was," she accepted. "Sorry. But is my guess right?"

"I still don't know what it is."

She bit her lip. "All right, I'll do my best . . . Even though so many of the human race had been left parentless after the oceans rose, from the beginning we of Project Go selected people who had known a stable childhood. There must have been an unspoken assumption that they'd be better able to withstand the new experience. But you and Stacy came back in far better shape than they did, even if you did eventually decide to run and hide from us . . . Are you claiming that that was our main mistake?"

"Of course." Gene spoke over his shoulder while pouring himself another drink. "The worst mistake you could have made. Who wants to leave behind, at the probable cost of life or sanity, a parent who's been kind and trustworthy? Not till you scraped the bottom of the barrel—not till you'd met with so many failures that any average person would decline—was Project Go obliged to turn to folk like me and her. We neither of us knew a mother apart from Earth herself."

"Your daughter's name, then?" Shaw demanded.

"Terra."

And, as one, they imagined he'd said *terror*.

But in a sense it would have been the same.

Later:

"You talked constantly of the—the ones who didn't make it," Shaw muttered. "There's a hint of a pattern in our records which I can't make out; none of us can, and it's too subtle for even our best computers. I have a dreadful suspicion that it will turn out to be as obvious as the connection between orphanhood and your survival, once you show us what it is . . . but you'll have to."

"I say again: who wants to leave behind a loving parent? And what motives are there to venture into the unknown?"

"Oh! . . ."—from Shaw in a sort of sigh. "I got the picture. Finally I got it. You reviewed those motives one by one."

"If I'd only realized you didn't understand—" Gene muttered. "But there's no help for that. We still can't turn back time, though I dare believe that some day . . . Ah, but that must take very long to learn. Probably none of the science we've invented yet will show us how. By then, Stacy and I will be forgotten; so will you."

He drained his glass and set it by.

"Yes, we experienced—we didn't plan or map, we simply underwent—the reasons that there are for leaving home. Call on your computers if you don't remember in what order. For me, it's all as clear as yesterday."

*Though yesterday can be three thousand years ago* . . . He felt a pang of dizziness. It passed. He waited for someone else to speak, recalling that he owed a duty to his species.

The air filled with a susurrus of sound not aimed at him. Hoy said, "Well, first you talked of Suleyman."

"Who went in search of certainty," Gene grunted. "It's not allowed—not even to machines."

"Ingrid, then!" Shaw snapped.

"Worship. And gods or goddesses that fail are spurned."

"Cedric was next," Hoy said, frowning. "Was his quest not also for certainty?"

"In some sense, yes, it was. But he sought it from his own convictions. No faith can possibly suffice. It's always undermined by ignorance."

"Oh, this is absurd!" Yiu burst out. "You never met these people, and we did! We recruited them, we trained them, we prepared them as completely as we knew how! What you're saying about them is based on—on guesswork!"

Gene gazed at him stonily. He said, "It stopped being guesswork a long time ago—a thousand years at least. When we started to sense why we were cast adrift in time."

"You mean you were aware—?" Yiu began. Gene cut him short.

"Not until the very end. I said 'sense'! Do you have to turn every last gut feeling into words?"

"Let's finish the list," Shaw suggested placatorily, laying a hand on Yiu's arm. "Shanti?"

"Indolence! A life of ease!"

"We already mentioned her," Hoy said, biting her lip. "But who was next? . . ." She listened to the air. "Oh, of course: Giacomo."

"You talked about him the day we decided to risk visiting you in person," Shaw said. "We were worried about malnutrition. We'd kept Boat well stocked with provisions, but you seemed to be neglecting them in favor of what little you could grow or catch. Some of the food you forced down . . . Hmm! That's a point I'd like to clarify. So many of your—your *episodes* seemed to turn on food."

Gene stared at him in blank bewilderment. At length he said, "But there's no nourishment in space! It is this world that's always fed us: Mother Earth!"

"Yet our source of energy remains the sun!"

"Oh, yes: the Father, as it were, who got us in a womb of primal mud. But do you feel that to be true? Do we absorb raw energy, like plants—or Suleyman's machines?"

For a second Shaw's eyes locked with Gene's; then Hoy said, "I can't feel it, in the sense he means, and I doubt that anybody can. It's a question of intellectual acceptance . . . We were talking about Giacomo, weren't we?"

"Whose motive was perhaps the only noble one," Gene sighed, reaching for his glass.

"Was there not a noble element in all cases?" Yiu countered. "Is not self-sacrifice a noble thing?"

"Sometimes," Gene answered grayly, "it's due to nothing nobler than despair . . . But he was a true explorer, granted. You who knew him told us so. The lust for discovery is relatively pure, compared to some of what we've talked about."

"I . . ." Yiu shrugged and leaned back. "Okay, I accept that. Please go on." Cocking his head, he once more checked the data the computers were supplying. "Hedwig came next."

"Ah, yes. The missionary. That says it all."

"What?"

"Think about it." Gene leaned to confirm that the baby was still asleep. She was, though a discontented scowl was dawning on her face.

"But surely she was driven by a high ideal—"

Yiu broke off in confusion. Hoy and Shaw had laughed.

"This time at least," the former said, "I see what Gene is driving at. To dream of changing the whole universe in accordance with a set of local preconceptions! . . . Oh, it's ridiculous!"

"A missionary," Gene repeated with a solemn nod. "By definition: a person who does without intending it more harm than good."

"The verdict of history," Shaw sighed, deciding to copy him and take another drink. "Ingrid shared some of the same characteristics, of course. Now I come to think of it, I realize where you borrowed her story from."

"I don't get you," Gene said, blinking.

"That makes a change . . . Sri Lanka, if you want to know. Over two thousand years ago there was a king in the island who irrigated vast areas and made them flourish for everything except people. Before he decreed his reservoirs there were no mosquitoes. They came, they bred, and spread malaria. His kingdom died."

Gene uttered a soft chuckle. "Well, that proves what I'd started to suspect: no matter what far world we talked about, it was always Earth —always, because we know no other."

"Missionaries act as though they do," said Hoy in a somber tone. "Go on, Gene. You still haven't told us what you thought about Pedro."

"Poor fellow! With his plain and shameless greed!" Gene seemed to relax for the first time since this interrogation started. "What crueler fate than to set up as a merchant of unprecedented goods, only to find no market for them?"

Thoughtful, Hoy said, "So far you've talked of explorers and missionaries and merchants, but—"

Yiu interrupted, having once more had his memory refreshed with the aid of computers. "I want to hear your view of Naruhiko! He was next!"

"One more addition to the list of motives: conquest."

"But according to the story you and Stacy told—"

"He conquered nothing in the end? Oh, no! He did. He was obliged to."

"What?"

"Himself."

The trolley carrying the incubator was fitted with microphones to pick up any sound the child might make. They relayed a whimper, and Gene was prompt to drop to his knees beside it. But she was only stirring in her sleep, and after a moment he resumed his seat.

"That leaves Olga," Shaw said. "I can't see where she fits into the pattern you're outlining. Was she perhaps an exception to the rule?"

"There are no exceptions,"Gene retorted. "The universe includes every possible event, and events include all our thoughts, because we're in it. I still can't be sure—probably I'll never know—whether I 'thought' in any sense while I was *out there.*"

For a while they were overwhelmed by the totality of his outness. At length Shaw returned to his point.

"But, according to what you and Stacy said to one another, she was searching—"

"For something beyond the universe? Oh, indeed! But she was found insane, remember, when they caught and opened up the ship she'd flown in."

At this reference to the fate of so many pioneers, they all felt a pang of the chill which had pervaded Gene since he was told of Stacy's death, and had long ago eroded the mental armor loaned to him by drugs. None of them had been hurled past the barrier of lightspeed, but they had all flown space during the desperate quest for starflight; they had endured the burden of knowing, awake and asleep, that nothing protected them from death in vacuum save a flimsy metal hull, which any speed-massive particle from otherwhere might breach . . . Shaw said, "You found what she was after. You survived. And then you went—?"

"Back to our mother," Gene replied.

"I do believe I understand at last!"

"More than I do!" grumbled Hoy.

"Or I!"—from Yiu.

"Now listen!" Rounding on his companions, Shaw hammered fist into palm. "The ship they flew in—Stacy first, then Gene—it did exceed the speed of light, correct?"

"And was the first that we recovered in good enough order to be used again," said Hoy. "We all know that! So what?"

"So this! Gene has made it clear that he, his ego, his identity, his 'I,' was—was squeezed out of existence during the trip, and had to find a way home! And likewise Stacy's!" Shaw was almost babbling with the intensity of insight no computer could have offered.

"So far, so good," Gene said drunkenly. He had filled his glass yet again, in search of protection from full awareness of the loss of his beloved . . . yet in a sense she was still with him, and with everyone—Oh, paradox!

Shaw leapt to his feet, pointing to the objects Gene had had brought into the cabin.

"They *had* to run away from us! We interrogated them, didn't we, pestering them over and over for information they didn't yet know how to put into words? Remember their helpless bafflement when they replied to our questions and in their turn asked how come we didn't understand their answers? I thought, like everybody else, that they were mad to flee, because there was no place on Earth or off it where they could escape surveillance, but now I believe they were sane to choose this island for their refuge, because it forms a link with all our roots—a bare and stony nowhere-much, yet full of relics, a counterpart of this our planet, whose history is writ in rock formations!"

"But why?" Yiu demanded.

For a second Shaw glared at him. Gene interrupted, rising to his feet.

"It can't be helped. That's the way it is. Until this generation, all the voyagers who ever set forth—even the crews of the ships we sent to Mars and Venus and the moons of Jupiter—fell into the same plain categories as we were used to, the ones that Stacy and I discussed. Most were explorers eager for new knowledge; some looked for new worlds to conquer; some hoped for profit; some were simply bored or scared by ordinary life.

"But lacking patience as we do, the only way to reach another star, for us, is to take a route outside the universe. It can be done, and I'm the—living—proof . . .

"*Where, though, outside it, is there room for mind?*"

While they sought an answer to the unanswerable question Shaw had posed, Gene indicated each in turn of the relics he had had brought in.

"Because of this"—brochure—"Stacy and I were able to relive a past of luxury and relaxation, when there was no fear of what the sun might do except it gave you sunburn!

"Because of these"—the empty shell cases—"we were reminded of the way so many people fled from war, as refugees! When we found this"—preserving jar—"it made us think about planning for tomorrow, or next winter, or next year. And as for this"—he caught up the icon and held it before his chest like a shield—"it forced us to repopulate an empty island! You came, you saw us then, *and didn't understand!*"

He was panting with the violence of the truth he struggled to impart. Shaw said in a thin voice, "That's true, and I'm ashamed. Above all we failed to understand that the people you were 'meeting' all the time had once been real. I still don't have the faintest notion how, but we checked back over what records concerning this island had survived the Flood, and name after name proved to correspond with what we'd heard over the mikes in your cave: Hamilton, Kreutzer, Osman, Cornax—Greek, German, British, Turkish, Roman . . . There's no way you could have learned from trivial relics like these"—a thump on the table—"who they were and when they came to Oragalia!"

"I could have told you how that came about if you'd left us alone! . . ."

Gene laid the icon down and swallowed hard. "Well, anyhow, you didn't, and your damned machines—! Forget it; it's too late. My lady's dead, and I dare not cry for fear of waking Terra."

The ancient implications of the name made them sit still and pay attention.

"By then we knew what path we had to take for home: no path you choose, but one you let compel you! With a force as irresistible as hunger, our instincts guided us unquestioning along a road we never dared imagine, like a wild animal on the spoor of prey! Resist? As well resist a whirlwind! And all we had for to guide us was this junk! Look at that"—the sword hilt—"and think about the hatred and the madness it implies! Consider the false convictions that informed its wielder, sure of his faith!"

He was trembling worse than ever.

"And yet this madness is true knowledge, nonetheless! We found our way to this"—he touched the fragments of the broken jar—"and started to suspect the basic facts.

"What you prevented us from doing when you charged in with your pigheaded preconceptions and your steel machines . . . *was finishing our journey home.*"

"Are you implying"—this faintly from Hoy—"that we'd done the same, only worse, to the others?"

"Hooray!" Gene crowed—and was instantly concerned that he might have disturbed the baby, but she did not more than fidget at the noise.

"You mean the volunteers that survived might have—have come sane if we'd let them go on being crazy?" Yiu complained. "I don't follow that at all!"

"That's obvious," Gene sighed. "Try following me the rest of the way, though."

He laid his hand on the tile with the Latin inscription. At once Hoy said eagerly, "I get the association with conquest and taking over, but I miss the next bit."

"Good. It had nothing to do with that."

Baffled, she blinked at him, and he stamped his foot with rage.

"Just pay attention to my words! Open your mind and let the truth pour in! We'd finally worked our way to concepts of settlement and occupation—not conquest, but living somewhere else! Is that plain enough, or must I repeat it again, and again, and again?"

Under his glare Hoy shrank back, abashed. The force of his fury and frustration seemed to make the atmosphere crackle, as with invisible lightning.

"Thank *you* at long last! There's one thing left!" He picked up and kissed the broken face of the idol.

"You've got to accept that we came to this planet as though we ourselves were colonists. Okay, we evolved here, but the moment we developed imagination we cut loose from the limits imposed on lesser animals. So we grew lonely—lost in time, as no other creatures on the Earth could be. We did our best to turn the living rock into something we could talk to like another person; we sought chance resemblances in wood and stone, and eventually carved idols. Here is one." He set it down again, and paced the cabin, both fists clenched.

"Oh, I see it so plainly, and I can't convey it! . . . Let me make one last attempt. I'll ask you all to think about *rejection.*"

Shaw tensed. He said, "That's strange! It was a word the others used—all of them—and I just realized I never heard it from you before . . . or Stacy," he added, as though embarrassed at the mention of her name.

"You can't mean 'all,' " Gene corrected in a glacial tone. "Suleyman and Ingrid were recovered dead."

Shaw met his gaze. "We had the tapes," he murmured.

"Yes. Yes, of course. I'm sorry; please go on."

"About rejection? What rejection is there more complete than being forced outside the very universe?"

"Now finally," said Gene, "you've understood."

The sun set on the implications of his words. Eventually Yiu stirred and sighed. "You had already been rejected, though—and Stacy too. At last I see the import of your comment about your daughter. It isn't rational but it's a fact: the only rejection that's comparable is when a parent dies before or at your birth."

"Out there," said Gene, "that doesn't matter any longer. But the earth your mother and the sun your father—they are the ones to whom you must return, the prodigal."

"And beg to be forgiven?" whispered Hoy.

"Yes, indeed. And there remains one question you've not asked. I think you know what it is. I think you are afraid to put it to me."

He waited.

At last Shaw stirred, not looking at him. He said, "It could be this. Who were the people that populated your—your—?"

"Fantasies?" Gene offered wryly.

Shaw shook his head. "I have to accept that travel outside the universe makes nonsense of conventional divisions between what's real and what is not. It'll be years before we digest the implications of what you've told us. I'm asking about—" He had to swallow hard. "I'm asking about the people who seemed real to you in other ages. How could they correspond so perfectly with a past you never had the chance to research, whose traces since the Flood are so scarce and hard to find that none of our archeologists can contradict your view of it? You even invented sailors from the Venetian period to disguise us when we were right there in front of you!"

"I don't know how to answer." Gene frowned, deep furrows developing between his eyes. "I can only"—with a sidelong glance at Yiu—"hazard a guess. This island has been a crossroads of the world. I think they may have been . . . well, forebears."

"Literally?" Hoy stabbed. "And physically?"

He didn't look at her. "Past a certain point there's no way that can matter. All our predecessors are also our ancestors."

"Three thousand years is far too short a time for that!"

"Of course it is." Gene bestowed a skeletal smile on her. "But it's as near, it seems, as natural law permits."

"You mean you couldn't find your way back to a closer time?"

"Ah! You're finally accepting what I say as true!"

She bit her lip, hands writhing in her lap, and said, "You and Stacy were each outside the universe for the equivalent of—"

"Don't guess; calculate. Or get your computers to do it for you. Our voyages were carefully controlled: we flew in the same ship for the same time, though not together, and by then the tolerances were down to fractions of a microsecond. Yet because we've built so fragile a bridge of intellection between the primal state and ships that can traverse the impossible, it took Stacy and me *three thousand years of detour* via the past before we could reconnect with the continuum of human experience. Or would have done, had Stacy been allowed to bear our child."

"Why?" Hoy erupted to her feet. "What's so marvelous about giving birth? Millions of babies are born every year!"

"Because"—he met her gaze levelly—"it's a miracle every time it happens. It's the only way we have to communicate between the past and the future. It lifts us out of time to raise a child that will survive us. And, like it or not, the deepest levels of the subconscious mind accept that as a greater truth than any other."

"But now we can travel faster than light—"

"Another door has opened to the future: yes! Something in us has overcome the limitations of the physical universe, something you and I and all of us possess. Mind? Reason? Intelligence? We have plenty of words for it, but no faintest notion which is aptest. All we can say is that we can do this thing, and when we do it, whatever makes it possible is forced outside all of space and all of time, and has to find a route back to reality for which there are and very likely can be neither maps nor charts. Explaining why may take a million years."

He concluded in a slow, grave tone, each word bearing its full burden of unprecedented meaning. Under the impact she sank back in her seat, her face pale.

"In that case is there any hope? Shall we in our time be able to send colonists to other stars?"

"Oh, very possibly. But I doubt whether those who survive the trip will long remain human in any sense you or I would recognize. After all, they'll have to learn a road back to reality along the worldline of a planet which is not our own. What to do about that, of course, is up to you to figure out, not me. But there's something comforting about it nonetheless—isn't there?"

Unexpectedly, Yiu gave a smile. "It matches the traditions of those teachers who have always said: we are not as bounded as the universe."

"That something in us can exceed it?"

"Yes!"

"Well, I'm a proof of that, I guess. But as to what you or I or any of us can do with the first objective evidence for immortality, I've no idea. Right now—" Gene drained his glass and glanced toward the porthole.

"Right now it's dark. I must bury my dead."

"*What?*" Hoy stood before him, rocking back and forth on her heels. "You just said we are immortal after all, and now you're talking about a burial—!"

"What I went through, Stacy went through too. It hasn't stopped her body being dead, has it? Nor has it changed our nature!"

Of a sudden, she folded her hands and turned away, sobbing. Retaining his composure, he laid his hand consolingly on her shoulder and spoke to her and Shaw both.

"Take care of the child. I'll come back at dawn. Find me a spade and carry Stacy to the beach."

"Oh, Gene, surely—!"

The intervention came from Yiu, whom he silenced with a scowl. "My journey isn't over! One thing remains. I must accept she's past recall, and so must you. With luck, tomorrow I'll be as sane as anyone, more so than most. I've been on a longer journey than any other of my kind, and it must end as every lifetime journey ends: with the acceptance of death, and a new birth. *Do as I say!*"

"But," protested Yiu, "you just said you're the proof of our immortality!"

"As usual, you didn't get my point, but I was thinking of *her,*" countered Gene in a voice as cold as tombstones. He peeled back the cover of the incubator and touched his daughter's cheek, featherlightly. It was too much. She woke up fretting and began to wail. A nurse who had been eavesdropping rushed in and scolded him as she caught the baby up to comfort her.

"Gilgamesh," murmured Shaw.

"What did you say?" Gene rounded on him. "Was it a name? I seem to remember it, but . . ."

The other hoisted himself to his feet. "Yes, the Roman that you fantasized about—or maybe met. He mentioned Gilgamesh and his boon companion Enkidu. It's the oldest story in the world. It tells of the king who lost his best friend when the gods sent a plague against his city, so he set out in search of the herb of immortality. Such was his love for Enkidu that when he found it he would not use it himself. But he fell asleep beside a pool, and it was stolen from him by a water snake. Then, when he came home, he was so changed that at first his own people failed to recognize him.

"But when he died, they wrote his epitaph, and I recall it word for word."

Solemnly, in the manner of one performing a ritual, he closed his eyes and recited: " 'He went on a long journey, was weary, worn-out with labor, and, returning, engraved on a stone the whole story.' "

There was a pause. Even the baby, as though she understood, fell silent in the nurse's arms.

"Give him the spade," said Shaw at last. "It's time he had the chance to be human again."

# Epilogue

*Hoy and Shaw laid Stacy on the beach, wrapped in a shroud—of natural fiber, which would rot. Gene had insisted.*

*He waited in the gathering dark until they went away. Then he whirled his spade at the full stretch of his arm and tossed it up to the headland he had selected for her burial, thinking how much higher would have been his cast before the oceans rose.*

*Gathering her body to him, he struggled up the steep and rocky path. He was not altogether surprised when near the top he sensed a presence at his back. He laid her down at last beside the spot that he had chosen, and looked around.*

*There were so many of them that he could not count. All were a little faint, a little indistinct, yet now and then he caught a detail as the clouds above parted and revealed the moon: there the glinting of a watch's crystal; there a military cap badge; there a rusty iron helm . . .*

*Also there were other signs: a waft of incense, the echo of a chant.*

*But mostly and above all there were silent folk in drab plain clothing, whose very bodies knit the land together into flesh and bone.*

*Not questioning, he plied his spade and dug a pit. He'd chosen well: this was the deepest patch of earth above the rock. His muscles rejoiced in the resistance of it.*

*But they wearied, and when it came time to lay the body in its grave he was glad of the help of those who carried it. He recognized them: Milo Hamilton, and Leutnant Kreutzer; Osman Effendi, and the captain of the galley; the honorable knight, and the shipmaster from Africa; the angry officer who hated emperors, even the old woman who had sat day-long in case her skill was needed, who hobbled up and spoke a charm as earth was tossed to cover Stacy.*

*After that, for a while, he was blinded by tears.*

* * *

*Much later, when dawn was lightening the sky, he found himself among a crowd around a fire, which he had no memory of having lit. They were in solemn mood until the sun pierced the clouds; then they passed wine, making no offer to share it with him. As day broke, they doused and scattered the embers and revealed baked meat—just meat and nothing more. They divided it and gave a piece to all.*

*To all, save him.*

*Then, with looks of infinite pity, each provided for a journey into somewhere else, they took their leave.*

*He sat awhile on a cold flat rock, aching but unable to move, until full daylight overtook him. At last he leveled the earth and made his slow way down the path again, back to the shore.*

*His long, long trip was over. Now he could make clear to those who planned to follow how best they might prepare themselves to take the road around the universe, yet never lose touch with the continuum which was all the life and all the lives of humankind.*

*Waiting on the beach, he found he still knew how to smile.*

# The Crucible of Time

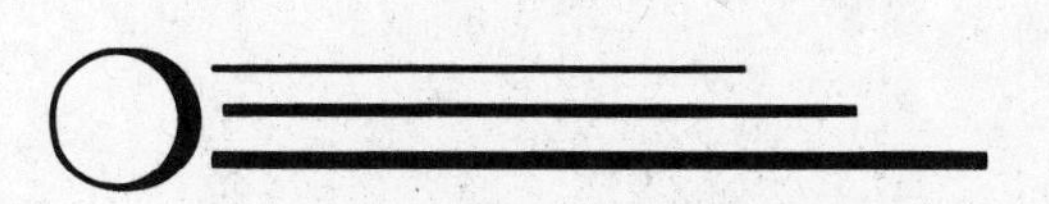

To Christopher Evans
*In memoriam*

# Foreword

It is becoming more and more widely accepted that Ice Ages coincide with the passage of the Solar System through the spiral arms of our galaxy. It therefore occured to me to wonder what would become of a species that evolved intelligence just before their planet's transit of a gas-cloud far denser than the one in Orion which the Earth has recently—in cosmic terms—traversed.

In my attempt to invent its history I have frequently relied on the advice of Mr. Ian Ridpath, whose prompt and generous aid I gratefully acknowledge.

—JKHB

# Prologue

*In the center of the huge rotating artificial globe the folk assembled to await retelling of an age-old story.*

*Before them swam a blur of light. Around them was a waft of pheromones. Then sound began, and images took form.*

*A sun bloomed, with its retinue of planets, moons and comets. One was the budworld. Slowly—yet how much more swiftly than in the real past!—a wild planet curved out of space towards what had once been their race's home.*

*"If only they had known . . . !" somebody murmured.*

*"But they did not!" the instructor stressed. "Remember that, throughout the whole of what you are to watch! You are not here to pity them, but to admire!"*

# Part One

# The Fire is Lit

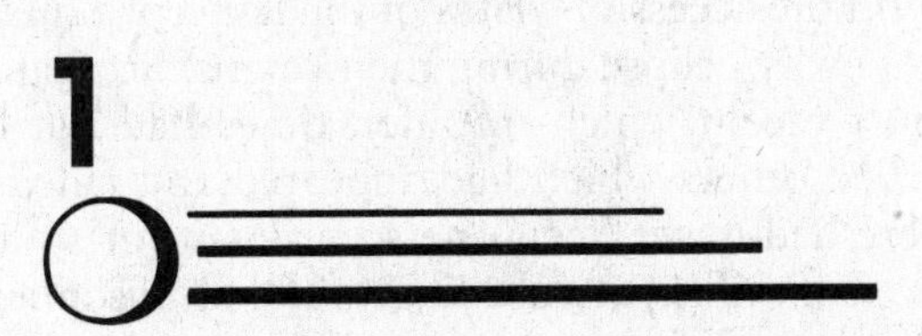

*N*ow the sun was down, the barq was growing tired. The current opposing her was swift, and there was a real risk she might be driven against the rocks that beset the channel and puncture her gas-bladders. After countless attempts to sting her into more vigorous activity, the steersman laid by his goad and grumpily tipped into her maw the last barrelful of the fermented fish and seaweed which served to nourish boat, crew and passengers alike. Waiting for the belch that would signal its digestion, he noticed Jing watching from her saddle of lashed planks, as anxious as though his weather-sense were predicting storms, and laughed.

"You won't be a-dream before we get where we're bound!" he promised in the coarse northern speech which the foreigner had scarcely yet attuned his hearing to.

It was hard to realize there was anywhere worth traveling to in this barren landscape. Most of the time the shore was veiled with rags of fog, because the water was so much warmer than the air. What a place to choose for studying the sky! Even though, with the sun setting so much earlier every day, it was possible to believe in the legend which had lured him hither: a night that lasted almost half a year. Not that there could ever be total darkness; here, as everywhere, the Bridge of

Heaven—what these northerners called the Maker's Sling—curved in its gleaming arc across the welkin. And, near the horizon, less familiar and altogether awe-inspiring, the New Star was framed in its irregular square of utter black like a jewel on a pad of swart-fur.

But neither that celestial mystery, nor the prospect of going hungry, was what preyed most on the mind of Ayi-Huat Jing, court astrologer and envoy plenipotentiary of His Most Puissant Majesty Waw-Yint, Lord of the Five-Score Islands of Ntah. Compelled by his sworn oath, a whole miserable year ago he had set forth in state, riding the finest mount in his master's herd and accompanied by forty prongsmen and ten banners inscribed with his rank and status. His mission was to seek out wise folk beyond the mountains that ringed the Lake of Ntah and inquire of them the meaning of the New Star. His countrymen had long imagined that they understood the reason why the heavens changed—for change they definitely did. He carried with him a fat roll of parchment sheets on which had been copied star-maps depicting the sky on the accession-dates of the last score rulers of Ntah, and on the date of every eclipse during their reigns. Sixteen stars were shown on the most recent which in olden times had not been there, and marks recorded others which had appeared and faded in a matter of days. But there had never been one so brilliant, or so long-lasting, or in so black a patch of sky. According to the philosophers of Ntah, right action was reflected in heaven, and sufficient of it earned a diminution of the darkness. Eventually, they promised, the time would come when the heavens would be as bright by night as by day.

And it had happened, and it had ceased, and everyone was grievously disturbed, for blight and plague had followed what should have been a sign of unprecedented good fortune . . .

Jing's journey had been fruitless so far, but it was not yet doomed to failure. His store of pearlseeds from the Lake was less than half-exhausted, for they grew stranger and more precious as he traveled, exchangeable for more food and longer lodging, and he had clung to his roll of maps even though in all the lands and cities he had visited he had met only one person who appeared to grasp their significance. He had expected students of heaven-lore as dedicated as himself, libraries too—albeit in alien script on unfamiliar materials—because tradition told of merchants from Geys and Yown and Elgwim who had brought amazing horns, hides, seeds and spices along with boastful tales about the riches of their homelands. What he had actually found . . .

Half-starved mud-scrabblers incapable of distinguishing dream from reality, ascribing crop-failure, blight and murrain to supernatural beings, imagining they could protect themselves by sacrificing most of what remained to them—whereupon, of course, weakness and fatigue allowed dreams to invade their minds ever further. Madness, madness! Why did not everybody know that the heavens bodied forth an impersonal record of the world below, neither more nor less? How could anybody, in these modern times, credit a god prepared to launch missiles at random with a view to killing people? The welkin shed messages, not murder!

His whole course since leaving Ntah had been a succession of horrid shocks. Geys, one of the first cities he had planned to visit, stood abandoned and overgrown, for—so he was told—a flaming prong from the sky had struck a nearby hill and everyone had fled in panic. Moreover, of the escorts and banners who had set out with him (any other of the court officers would have had concubines as well, but Jing was obliged by his calling to accept celibacy) most had deserted on finding how squalid was the world beyond the mountains, while not a few had succumbed, as had his mount, to bad food or foul water.

One alone had survived to accompany him into the branchways of the great city Forb, where first he had encountered learned men as he regarded learning. Yet they were parasites, Jing felt, upon their city's past, disdainful of sky-shown truths, able only to expound concerning inscriptions and petty relics which they claimed to be older than anything elsewhere. Jing was reticently doubtful, but it was impolitic to speak his mind, partly because he was unfluent in the speech of that region, partly because its masters exercised very real power which he had no wish to see turned against Ntah, and chiefly because of the nature of that power.

His tallness, and the fact that his companion was taller yet, made him remarkable. The nobility bade him to banquets and festivities as a curiosity. It was a time of dearth, as he had discovered on his way; nonetheless, the fare at such events was lavish. It followed that the lords of Forb must control vast domains—not, however, vast enough to satisfy them, as was apparent from the way they spent all their time maneuvering for advantage over one another, and instructed their interpreters to ply Jing with questions concerning weaponry. They were prepared to descend as far as spreading disease among a rival's crops, than which only the use of wildfire could be baser. Were such monsters to be let loose in the peaceful region of Ntah . . . !

Shuddering, yet determined to pursue his quest, Jing eventually discovered the secret of their dominance. It lay not in their armies, nor their treasuries. It consisted in the deliberate and systematic exploitation of the dreams of those less well-to-do than themselves, a possibility which had never occurred to him, and which the language barrier prevented him from comprehending until a lordling he had disappointed in his hope of brand-new armaments set sacerdotes upon him at his lodgings.

He had frequently seen their like bringing up the tail-end of a noble's retinue, always gaunt in a manner that contrasted greatly with the glistening plumpness of their masters, and initially he had assumed them to be nothing more than servants: scribes, perhaps, or accountants, though it was hard to conceive how such dream-prone starvelings could be relied on.

Acting, however, more like persons of authority than underlings, these visitors interrogated him concerning Ntah. Pleased to meet anyone prepared to discuss what he thought of as serious subjects, Jing answered honestly, hoping to show that the relationship between Ntah and its satrapies, being sustained by trade in information concerning what the heavens portended, was more civilized than rule by force.

Did he not—they responded in shocked tones—acknowledge the example of the Maker of All, who daily surveyed the world with His all-seeing eye, the sun, and nightly dispatched fiery bolts by way of warning that His way must be adhered to on pain of uttermost destruction? Was he not aware that the arc in the sky was the Maker's sling, that the Maker's mantle was what lighted the heavens with the glimmer of marvelous draped colors? Then he was in peril of imminent disaster, and were he still to be in Forb when it overtook him, scores-of-scores of innocent people would be caught up in the catastrophe! He must leave the city at once, or they would execute the Maker's will upon him themselves!

Jing's lifelong faith in the beneficence of the universe had been shaken, but he was not about to enter someone else's fever-dream. He did his best to scorn the warning—until the day when his sole surviving escort, Drakh, was set on by an unknown gang and attacked with weapons such as would never have been permitted in Ntah: prongs steeped in the ichor from a rotting carcass, warranted to poison the slightest cut even though it was not deep enough to let out life.

Now Drakh lay delirious beside him, as for days past, shivering less at the bitter air than the racking of his sickness. He would have been dead but that Jing's treelord—a Shreeban, well accustomed to being shunned by his Forbish neighbors and mocked by their children when he went abroad—had called a doctor, said to breed the best cleanlickers in the city.

And the doctor had saved not only Drakh's life (so far, Jing amended wryly, for the licker was weakening and the sorbers it passed repeatedly over his wound were turning yellow) but also the mission they had been sent on. Forgetful of his other clients, he had sat for days greedily studying Jing's star-maps, mentioning now and then that such-and-such a one of his forebears had claimed to be older than this or that star: heretical information in Forb where the Creation was supposed to have been perfect from the Beginning.

How could such dream-spawned nonsense survive the appearance of the New Star, which for a score of nights had outshone the Bridge of Heaven, and still after four years loomed brighter than anything except the sun and moon?

It might well not, explained the doctor. As people became more prosperous and better fed, so they naturally grew more capable of telling dream from fact. This led them to mock the sacerdotes, whose power had been decreasing from generation to generation despite their deliberate self-privation. Now they were reduced to claiming that the New Star was a delusion due to the forces of evil, which—they said—dwelt in that bleak zone from which the Maker had banned all stars as a reminder of the lightless eternity to which He could condemn transgressors. But there were those who maintained that one supremely righteous person was to be born—now: *must* have been—who could hold up a lamp where the Maker had decreed darkness, and lead folk out of mental enslavement.

Looking at the glowplants that draped the walls of his rented home, Jing prompted him to more revelations. Were there none here in the north who studied star-lore?

The chief of them, the doctor said, had taken refuge with the Count of Thorn. Branded by the sacerdotes as victim of a divine curse, that lord had retreated to an arctic fastness where hot springs bubbled out of frozen ground—clear proof, said the sacerdotes, of his commitment to evil, for in the absence of sunlight water could be heated only by fire, the prerogative of the Maker: hence those who usurped it must be on His adversary's side. Where Thorn had gone, besides, report held that a night might last for half a year, and evil dwelt in darkness, did it not? Yet it was also rumored that those who had followed him were prosperous while everywhere else epidemics were tramping in the pad-marks of famine . . .

"There has been some kind of change," the doctor whispered. "My best remedies have ceased to work, and many babies bud off dead or twisted. Also there is a taint in this year's nuts, and it seems to drive folk mad. If I had more courage I too would go where Thorn has gone . . . Pay me nothing for the care of your man. Promise only to send news of what they have found out in that ice-bound country. It is a place of ancient wisdom which the sacerdotes interdicted, saying it was dreamstuff. I think they were in error in that also."

Now Jing, so weary he too was having trouble telling dream from fact, was come to Castle Thorn at the head of the warm channel. The fog parted. The moon was rising, gibbous in its third quarter, and as usual its dark part sparkled.

If Forb was old, then Castle Thorn was antique. Guarding the entrance to a bowl-shaped valley, it loomed as large as a city in its own right—not that its whole bulk could be seen from the outcrop of rock serving it as a wharf, despite the glowplants which outlined it at a distance, for its defenses were elaborate and far-reaching. On either bank bomas trembled ready to collapse their spiky branches, while masses of clingweed parted only in response to blasting on a high-pitched whistle. Prongsmen came to hitch the barq's mooring-tentacles, accompanied by enormous canifangs.

Just before docking Jing had realized that a range of hills on the horizon was gleaming pure white in the moonshine. He had said, "Snow already?"

And the steersman had grunted, "Always."

So there truly was a place where ice might defy summer. For the first time Jing felt in his inmost tubules how far he was from home.

But there was no time for reflection. A voice was calling to him in city-Forbish: "Hail to the foreigner! I'm told your prongsman is sick. As soon as he's ashore I'll see what I can do for him. I'm Scholar Twig, by the way."

Who was a person of advanced years, his tubby shortness—characteristic of these northerners—aggravated by loss of pressure in his bracing tubules, but his expression alert and manner brisk. Grateful, for Twig was the name the doctor had told him to ask for, Jing returned the greeting.

"How you know I coming?" he demanded.

"Oh, you've made news over half the continent," was the prompt reply. "Sorry we don't have anyone around who speaks Ntahish, but until you showed up most people thought your homeland was just a legend, you know? Say, is it true you have star-maps going back to the Beginning? How soon can I look at them?"

Groping his way through the rush of words, Jing recalled the protocol which attended ambassadors to Ntah.

"Not I must at once pay respect the lord?"

"He's dining in the great hall. You'll meet him in a little. First let me present my colleagues. This is Hedge, this is Bush, this is—"

It was impossible to register so many strangers when he was so fatigued. "But my man-at-arms . . . ?" he ventured.

"Ah, what am I thinking of? Of course, we must get him and you to quarters right away!"

Detailing some junior aides to carry Drakh, Twig led the way at half a trot.

Jing could have wished to move more slowly, because nothing had prepared him for the luxury he discerned all about him. The very stones were warm underpad. The gnarled trunks of the castle were thicker than any he had ever seen, and even at this season they were garlanded with scores of useful secondary plants. Steaming ponds rippled to the presence of fish, while fruit he had not tasted the like of since leaving home dangled from overhanging boughs, and everywhere trailed luminescent vines. Through gaps between the boles, as he ascended branchways in Twig's wake, he caught glimpses of a landscape which reminded him achingly of parts of Ntah. He had thought in terms of a mere clawhold on survival, but the valley must support a considerable population. He saw three villages, each with a score of homes, surrounded by barns and clamps large enough to store food for a year—and that was only on one side of the castle. Amazing! His spirits rose.

And further still when Drakh was laid in a comfortable crotch and a maid brought warm drink. Passing him a huskful, Twig said dryly, "In case you're superstitious about fire, it's untouched by flame. We keep the bags in a hot spring."

Jing's people cared little about fire one way or the other, so he forbore to reply. Whatever its nature, the drink effectively drove away dreams. Meanwhile Twig was inspecting Drakh's licker and saying in disgust, "This should have been changed days ago! Here!"—to the maid—"take it away and bring one of my own at once. They're of the same stock," he added to Jing, "though here we have fewer outlandish poisons they can learn to cope with. Faugh! They do stink, though, don't they, at that stage?"

Now that Jing's perceptions were renewed, he had realized that the very air inside the castle stank—something to do with the hot springs, possibly. Never mind. He posed a key question.

"Drakh will live, yes?"

"I'm not a specialist in foreign sicknesses, you know! But . . . Yes, very probably. I'll send for juice which can be poured between his mandibles. Wouldn't care to offer him solid food in his condition."

Jing nodded sober agreement. Reflex might make him bite off his own limbs.

"Are those your maps?" Twig went on, indicating the rolled parchments. "How I want to examine them! But you must be hungry. Come on, I'll show you to the hall."

There, at its very center, the true antiquity of the castle was revealed. Despite the dense clusters of glowplants which draped the walls, Jing could discern how the ever-swelling boles of its constituent bravetrees had lifted many huge rocks to four or five times his own height. Some of them leaned dangerously inward where the trunks arched together. None of the company, however, seemed to be worrying about what might happen if they tumbled down. Perhaps there were no quakes in this frozen zone; the land might stiffen here, as water did, the year around. Yet it was so warm . . .

He postponed such mysteries in order to take in his surroundings.

The body of the hall was set with carefully tended trencher-stumps, many more than sufficed for the diners, who were three or at most four score in number. Not only were the stumps plumper than any Jing had seen in Forb; they were plentifully garnished with fruit and fungi and strips of meat and fish, while a channel of hollow stems ran past them full of the same liquor Twig had given him. Entrances were at east and west. At the south end a line of peasants waited for their dole: a slice of trencher-wood nipped off by a contemptuous kitchener and a clawful of what had been dismissed by diners at the north. Jing repressed a gasp. Never, even in Ntah, had he seen such lavish hospitality. It was a wonder that the Count's enemies in Forb had not already marched to deprive him of his riches.

"So many peasants isn't usual," murmured Twig.

"I believe well!" Jing exclaimed. "Plainly did I see villages with land enough and many high barns!"

"Except that on the land the trencher-plants are failing," Twig said, still softly. "Take one of these and transplant it outside, and it turns rotten-yellow. But save your questions until you've fed, or you'll spend a dream-haunted night. Come this way."

Jing complied, completing his survey of the hall. In a space at the center, children as yet unable to raise themselves upright were playing with a litter of baby canifangs, whose claws were already sharp. Now and then that led to squalling, whereupon a nursh would run to the defense of its charge, mutely seeking a grin of approval from the fathers who sat to left and right. Each had a female companion, and if the latter were in bud made great show of providing for her, but otherwise merely allowed her to bite off a few scraps.

And at the north end sat the Count himself, flanked by two girls, both pretty in the plump northern manner, but neither budding.

The Count was as unlike what Jing had been led to expect as was his castle. He had been convinced by the doctor that he was to meet a great patron of learning, more concerned with wisdom than material wealth. What he saw was a gross figure so far gone in self-indulgence that he required a sitting-pit, whose only concession to stylish behavior was that instead of biting off his trencherwood he slashed it with a blade the like of which Jing had never seen, made from some dark but shiny and very sharp substance.

"Sit here with my compeers," Twig muttered. "Eat fast. There may not be long to go. He's in a surly mood."

Thinking to make polite conversation, Jing said, "Has two lovely shes, this lord. Is of the children many to him credit?"

The scholar's colleagues, Bush, Hedge and so on—names doubtless adopted, in accordance with local custom, when they took service with the Count—froze in unison. Twig whispered forcefully, "Never speak of that where he might overhear! No matter how many women he takes, there is no outcome and never has been, except . . . See the cripple?"

Previously overlooked, there sat a girl by herself, her expression glum. She leaned to one side as though she had been struck by an assassin's prong. Yet she bore a visible resemblance to the Count, and she was passably handsome by the standards of Ntah where the mere fact of her being a noble's daughter would have assured her of suitors. She was alone, though, as if she were an unmated or visiting male. Had he again misunderstood some local convention?

Twig was continuing between gobbles of food. "She's the reason I'm here—eat, eat for pity's sake because any moment he's going to order up the evening's entertainment which is bound to include *you* and over there"—with a nod towards a trio of emaciated persons whom Jing identified with a sinking feeling as sacerdotes—"are a bunch of charlatans who would dearly have liked to sink claws in you before I did except that I put it about I wasn't expecting you before the last boat of autumn in ten days' time. Anyway, Rainbow—who is much brighter than you'd imagine just looking at her—is his sole offspring. Naturally what he wants is a cure for infertility and an assurance that his line won't die out. So our real work keeps getting interrupted while we invent another specious promise for him."

For someone afraid of being overheard, Twig was speaking remarkably freely. But Jing was confused. "You not try read his future from stars?" he hazarded. "You not think possible?"

"Oh, it may well be! But before we can work out what the sky is telling us, we must first understand what's going on up there. My view, you see, is that fire above and fire below are alike in essence, so that until we comprehend what fire *can* do we shan't know what it *is* doing, and in consequence—Oh-oh. He's stopped eating, which means the rest of us have to do the same. If you haven't had enough to keep you dreamfree I can smuggle something to your quarters later. Right now, though, you're apt to be what's served him next!"

In fact it didn't happen quite so quickly. With a spring like a stabberclaw pouncing out of jungle overgrowth, a girl draped in glitterweed erupted from shadow. She proved to be a juggler, and to the accompaniment of a shrill pipe made full use of the hall's height by tossing little flying creatures into the air and luring them back in graceful swooping curves.

"She came in on the first spring boat," Twig muttered, "and is going away tomorrow—considerably richer! Even though she didn't cure the Count's problem, he must have had a degree of pleasure from her company . . ."

Certainly the performance improved the Count's humor; when it was over he joined in the clacking of applause.

"We have a foreign guest among us!" he roared at last. "Let him make himself known!"

"Do exactly as I do!" Twig instructed. "First you—"

"No!" Jing said with unexpected resolve. "I make like in *my* country to *my* lord!"

And strode forward fully upright, not letting the least hint of pressure leak from his tubules. Arriving in front of the Count, he paid him the Ntahish compliment of overtopping him yet shielding his mandibles.

"I bring greeting from Ntah," he said in his best Forbish. "Too, I bring pearlseeds, finest of sort, each to grow ten score like self. Permit to give as signing gratitude he let share knowledge of scholars here!"

And extended what was in fact his best remaining seed.

For an instant the Count seemed afraid to touch it. Then one of his treasurers, who stood by, darted forward to examine it. He reported that it was indeed first-class.

Finally the Count condescended to take it into his own claw, and a murmur of surprise passed around the company. Jing realized he must have committed another breach of etiquette. But there was no help for that.

"You have no manners, fellow," the Count grunted. "Still, if your knowledge is as valuable as your pearlseed, you may consider yourself welcome. I'll talk with you when Twig has taught you how to address a nobleman!"

He hauled himself to his pads and lumbered off.

"Well, you got away with that," Twig murmured, arriving at Jing's side. "But you've pressurized a lot of enemies. Not one of *them* would dare to stand full height before the Count, and they claim to have authority from the Maker Himself!"

Indeed, the three sacerdotes he had earlier designated charlatans were glowering from the far side of the hall as though they would cheerfully have torn Jing mantle from torso.

# 3

"And here is where we study the stars," said Lady Rainbow.

It had been a long trek to the top of this peak, the northernmost of those girdling the round valley. Their path had followed the river which eventually created the channel used by boats from the south. It had not one source, but many, far underground or beyond the hills, and then it spread out to become a marsh from which issued bubbles of foul-smelling gas. Passage through a bed of sand cleansed it, and thereafter it was partitioned into many small channels to irrigate stands of fungi, useful trees, and pastures on which grazed meatimals and furnimals. Also it filled the castle fish-ponds, and even after such multiple exploitation it was warm enough to keep the channel ice-free save in the dead of winter. The whole area was a marvel and a mystery. It was even said that further north yet there were pools of liquid rock which bubbled like water, but Jing was not prepared to credit that until he saw it with his own eye.

Despite her deformity, Rainbow had set a punishing pace, as though trying to prove something to herself, and Twig had been left far behind on the rocky path. He was in a bad temper anyway, for he had hoped to show off his laboratory first, where he claimed he was making amazing transformations by the use of heat, but Rainbow had insisted on coming here before sunset, and Jing did want to visit the observatory above all else.

However, he was finding it a disappointment. It was a mere depression in the rock. Walbushes had been trained to make a circular windbreak, and their rhizomes formed crude steps enabling one to look over the top for near-horizon observations. A pumptree whose taproot reached down to a stream of hot water grew in the center where on bitter nights one might lean against it for warmth. A few lashed-together poles indicated important lines-of-sight. Apart from that—nothing.

At first Jing just wandered about, praising the splendid view here offered of Castle Thorn and the adjoining settlements. There were more than he had imagined: almost a score. But when Twig finally reached the top, panting, he could contain himself no longer.

"Where your instruments?" he asked in bewilderment.

"Oh, we bring them up as required," was the blank reply. "What do you do—keep them in a chest on the spot?"

Thinking of the timber orrery which had been his pride and joy, twice his own height and moved by a pithed water-worm whose mindless course was daily diverted by dams and sluices so as to keep the painted symbols of the sun, moon and planets in perfect concordance with heaven, Jing was about to say, "We don't bother with instruments small enough to carry!"

But it would have been unmannerly.

Sensing his disquiet, Twig seized on a probable explanation. "I know what you're tempted to say—with all that steam rising from our warm pools, how can anyone see the stars? You just wait until the winter wind from the north spills down this valley! It wipes away mist like a rainstorm washing out tracks in mud! Of course, sometimes it brings snow, but for four-score nights in any regular year we get the most brilliant sight of heaven anyone could wish for, and as for the aurorae . . . !"

Touching Rainbow familiarly, he added, "And you'll be here to watch it all, won't you?"

"You must forgive Twig," she said, instantly regal. "He has known me since childhood and often treats me as though I were still a youngling. But it's true I spend most of my time here during the winter. I have no greater purpose in life than to decipher the message of the stars. I want to know why I'm accursed!"

Embarrassed by her intensity, Jing glanced nervously at her escorting prongsman, without whom she was forbidden to walk abroad, and wished he could utter something reassuring about Twig's abilities. But the words would have rung hollow. He had pored over Jing's starmaps, cursing his failing sight which he blamed on excessive study of the sun—in which Jing sympathized with him, for his own eye was not as keen as it had been—and exclaimed at their detail, particularly because they showed an area of the southern sky which he had never seen. All he had to offer in exchange, though, were a few score parchments bearing scrappy notes about eclipses and planetary orbits, based on the assumption that the world was stationary, which had been superseded in Ntah ten-score years ago, and some uninspiring remarks about the New Star. It was clear that his real interest lay in what he could himself affect, in his laboratory, and his vaunted theory of the fire above was plausibly a scrap from a childhood dream. Jing was unimpressed.

He said eventually, "Lady, where I from is not believed curses anymore. We hold, as sky tend to fill more with star, so perfectness of life increase down here." And damned his clumsiness in this alien speech.

"That's all very well if you admit the heavens change," said Twig bluffly. "But we're beset with idiots who are so attached to their dreams they can go on claiming they don't, when a month of square meals would show them better!"

He meant the sacerdotes, who—as Jing had learned—had been sent to Castle Thorn unwillingly, in the hope of winning the Count back to their "true faith," and were growing desperate at their lack of success even among the peasants, because everyone in this valley was well enough nourished to tell dream from fact. One rumor had it that they were spreading blight on the trencher-plants, but surely no one could descend that far! Although some of the lords of Forb . . .

Disregarding Twig, Rainbow was addressing Jing again. "You say I can't be cursed?"

"Is not curse can come from brightness, only darkness. More exact, is working out pattern—I say right *pattern,* yes?—coming towards ideal, and new thing have different shape. You noble-born, you perhaps a sign of change in world."

"But if change is coming, nobody will prepare to meet it," Twig said, growing suddenly serious. "With the trunks of Forb and other ancient cities rotting around them, people shout ever louder that it can't be happening. They'd rather retreat from reality into the mental mire from which—one supposes—our ancestors must have emerged. You don't think Lady Rainbow is accursed. Well, I don't either, or if she is then it's a funny kind of curse, because I never met a girl with a sharper mind than hers! But most people want everything, including their children, to conform to the standards of the past."

"My father's like that," Rainbow sighed.

"He's a prime example," Twig agreed, careless of the listening prongsman. "He thinks always in terms of tomorrow copying today. But our world—I should say our continent—is constantly in flux; when it's not a drought it's a plague, when it's not a murrain it's a population shift . . . Where you come from, Jing, how does your nation stay stable even though you admit the heavens themselves can change? I want to know the secret of that stability!"

"I want to know what twisted my father!" snapped Rainbow. "Bent outwardly I may be, but he must be deformed within!"

Aware of being caught up in events he had not bargained for, Jing thought to turn Rainbow a compliment. He said, "But is still possible to him descendants, not? Surprise to me lady is not match often with persons of quality, being intelligent and of famous family."

Later, Twig explained that to speak of a noblewoman being paired was something one did not do within hearing of the party concerned. For the time being he merely changed the subject with an over-loud interruption.

"Now come and see what's really interesting about the work we're doing!"

Yet, although she declined to accompany them to the laboratory, the lady herself seemed rather flattered than upset.

* * *

This time their path wound eastward to the place where the hot river broke out of shattered rocks. Alongside it a tunnel led into the core of a low hill, uttering an appalling stench. Yet the heat and humidity reminded Jing's weather-sense of home, and inside there were adequate glowplants and twining creepers to cling to when the going became treacherous. Sighing, he consented to enter.

When he was half choking in the foul air, they emerged into a cavern shaped like a vast frozen bubble, at whose center water gushed up literally boiling. Here Hedge, Bush and the rest were at work, or more exactly directing a group of ill-favored peasants to do their work for them. They paused to greet their visitor, and Twig singled out one husky fellow who sank to half his normal height in the cringing northern fashion.

"This is Keepfire! Tell Master Jing what you think of this home of yours, Keepfire!"

"Oh, it's very good, very safe," the peasant declared. "Warm in the worst winter, and food always grows. Better here than over the hill, sir!"

Jing was prepared to accept that. Anything must be preferable to being turned loose to fend for oneself in the barren waste to the north, where no plants grew and there was a constant risk from icefaws and snowbelongs, which colonized the bodies of their prey to nourish their broodmass. Twig had described the process in revolting detail.

Having surveyed the cavern and made little sense of what he saw, Jing demanded, "What exact you do here?"

"We're testing whatever we can lay claws on, first in hot water, then on rock to protect it from flame, then in flame itself. We make records of the results, and from them we hope to figure out what fire actually can do."

To Jing, fire was something viewed from far off, veiled in smoke and to be avoided, and flame was a conjurer's trick to amuse children on celebration days. More cynically than he had intended—but he was growing weary and dreams were invading his mind again—he said, "You are proving something it does?"

Stung, Twig reached up to a rocky ledge and produced a smooth heavy lump which shone red-brown.

"Seen anything like this before? Or this?"

Another strange object, more massive and yellower.

Realization dawned. "Ah, these are metals, yes? You find in water?" Sometimes in the streams which fed the lake of Ntah placer-nuggets turned up, softer than stone ought to be, which after repeated hammering showed similar coloration.

"Not at all! This is what we get when we burn certain plants and then reheat their ash. Don't you think some of the essence of fire must have remained in these lumps? Look how they gleam! But I should have asked—what do you already know about fire?"

"Is to us not well known. In dry land is danger for plants, homes, people. But in Ntah is air damp same like here. Is down in this cave possible flame?"

His doubt was plain. Twig snorted.

"I thought so! The more I hear, the more I become convinced we must be the only people in the world seriously investigating fire. Either they think it's blasphemous because it's reserved to the heavens, or they're as wrong as you about the way it works. Let a humble peasant show you better. Keepfire, make a flame for the visitor!"

Chuckling, the peasant rushed to a recess in the cavern wall. From it he produced articles which Jing's poor sight failed to make out in the dimness.

"Long before anyone came here from as far south as Forb," Twig said softly, "Keepfire's ancestors were priests of a cult which now has vanished—based on dreams, of course. But they found out some very practical techniques."

"What he do?"

"It's so simple you wouldn't believe it. I didn't when I first came here. He uses dry fungus-spores, and a calamar soaked in fish-oil, and two rocks. Not just ordinary rock, a kind that has some of the fire-essence in it. Watch!"

Something sparkled. A flame leapt up, taller than himself, and Jing jumped back in alarm. He risked tumbling into the hot pool; Twig caught him, uttering a sour laugh.

"Doesn't that impress you?"

"I guess so . . ." Jing was trembling. "But what to do with? Is not same fire and in—*as* in sky! Is under the ground!"

Twig said with authority, "The idea that fire belongs to the sky is false. Using it, we've made—not grown but made—things that were never in the world before."

"Did you make Count's blade?" Jing ventured, prepared to be impressed.

"Oh, no. That's a natural rock you find a lot of around here. But it too must have fire in its essence, or heat at any rate. It seems to be like this stuff." Twig reached to another ledge and brought down a clawful of smooth transparent objects shaped like half a raindrop, most bluish, some greenish, one or two clear. "The peasants' children use these for playthings. They hate me because I take away the best ones for more important use. On a fine day you can catch sunfire with them and set light to a dry calamar or a dead leaf. What better proof could there be of my opinions? Look, here's a particularly clear one!"

To Jing's touch the droplet was relatively cool, so he could not imagine how fire could be trapped within. All of a sudden, however, as he was inspecting it, he noticed something remarkable. At a certain distance he could see his claw through it, only enlarged.

"It make big!" he breathed.

"Oh, that too! But it's no use holding it up to the sky. Every youngling in the valley must have tried that, and me too, I confess. But it won't make the moon or stars any plainer, and as for looking at the sun—well!"

"I can have, please? Not to start fires. Is good for look my star-maps."

Twig started. He said in an altered voice, "Now, why didn't I think of that? But of course I never saw maps like yours before, with such fine detail . . . Sure, take it. We keep finding them all the time. Now we'd best get back to the castle."

He padded away, exuding an aura of annoyance.

This was no astrologer: Jing was satisfied on that point. Maybe when it came to trying this or that in a fire Twig's record-keeping might be accurate, but given he could overlook such an obvious use for a magnifying drop it seemed unlikely. Anyhow, what value could his data have? It was inconceivable that fire in heaven could be identical with fire underground!

So perhaps there were several kinds of fire? And surely there must be *some* way of enlarging the heavens if it could be done at close range . . . ?

Jing sighed heavily. He had to make an immediate decision: whether to remain here in the hope that studying the stars uninterruptedly for longer than he had imagined possible would bring unexpected insights, or leave by the final autumn boat. But the continent was already in the grip of winter; he could scarcely reach home any sooner, if he left now, than if he stayed until spring. And Waw-Yint would certainly not forgive him for abandoning his mission. He was not one to be bought off with such petty marvels as a magnifying drop. True, he was old, and by now might well be dead—

Shocked at his own disloyalty, Jing firmly canceled such thoughts. No, he must remain, and if necessary next year carry on beyond the ocean, riding one of the half-legendary giant barqs of which they spoke in Yown and Forb . . . if they were not compounded of dreams.

Besides, this magnifier . . . It had seized his imagination, an ideal tool for astrologers hampered only by its present imperfection. He had been brought up to believe that perfection inhered in everything, even people; it needed only to be sought out.

Just before entering the castle again, Twig turned to him and said bluffly, "Put what I know about the world below together with what you know about the sky, and we might get somewhere one of these days, right? Shall we try?"

It was a formal invitation not just to collaborate but to make friends. Jing felt obliged to treat it as such, despite his reservations concerning Twig's researches. They locked claws accordingly.

Later, Jing reflected it was as well they concluded their compact at that juncture, for the first person to meet them within the castle reported Drakh's death; the best of Twig's cleanlickers had failed to purify his wound. Grief at being shorn of his last Ntahish companion might have driven him to dreamness and made him reject Twig-friend because of Twig-physician. Yet no blame could attach save to those who had stabbed Drakh a month's journey ago.

When, in compliance with local custom, they consigned Drakh's remains to a pullulating pond surrounding a handsome blazetree, Twig spoke much about loneliness and isolation, and Jing was touched and grateful.

As though the funeral were a significant occasion, the Maker's Sling delivered a cast of long bright streaks across the zenith.

But that was apt to happen any night.

# 4

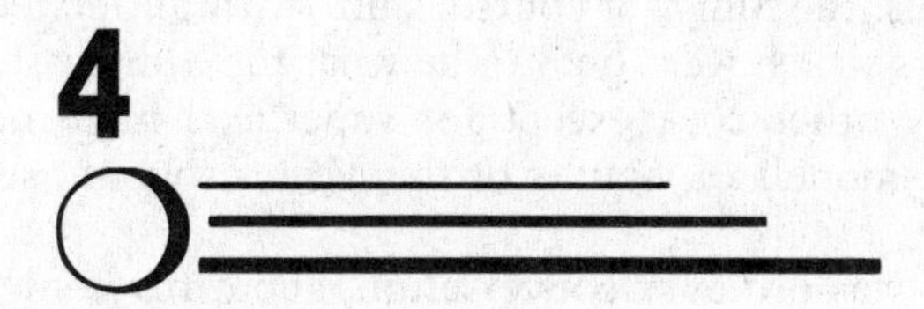

*N*ext day distraught peasants came crying that a snowbelong had killed a child from the furthest-outlying village, and the Count hauled himself out of his sitting-pit and set off to hunt it down with hoverers and canifangs. Twig predicted it might be several days before he returned, and Jing looked forward not only to improving his Forbish but also to cleansing his mind of the nostalgic dreams which since the death of Drakh threatened to overwhelm him.

Taking advantage of his absence, however, the sacerdotes promptly summoned Jing to their chapel, an enclosure within the north wall of the castle which they had been granted because the Count, despite being well fed, was sufficiently at the mercy of his dreams to half believe their dogma.

"You'll have to go, I'm afraid," sighed Twig.

"Here I thought had they no power. How they force me?"

"Hmm! It isn't quite like that. True, the Count's rule is absolute here, and the people, if they have a religion at all, adhere to superstitions even more absurd than the sacerdotes', though some of their knowledge, especially where fire is concerned . . . Excuse me. The point is, the Count has opened up this place to trade with the south, and that means contact with southern believers. Most of the summer there are at least half a score of the faithful here, and the sacerdotes incite them to put pressure on the Count, who's growing senile. What I'm afraid of is that sooner or later he may conclude that they're right after all, and hoping to escape the curse he'll go whining to them for forgiveness, and you can guess what'll become of the rest of us then! At all events they're getting bolder, and if you don't obey their summons you could well find your food poisoned or a prong stuck in your back."

Jing would have dismissed the idea as ridiculous but for what had happened to Drakh. Sensing his dismay, Twig added, "If it's any comfort, though, you should bear in mind that it would be a far greater coup for them to convert you than kill you. They may be a nuisance but they're not likely to be a menace."

At least these sacerdotes were less determined to execute what they held to be the Maker's will than their counterparts at Forb. They greeted him politely as he entered the chapel, which was decorated with makeshift symbols: the Sling, of course, shiny with glitterweed; a pile of the seared rocks which were held to be what the Sling cast, but looked much like any other rock except for superficial melt-marks; some rather repulsive models of victims of the Maker's wrath, struck down from on high.

For a while there was ordinary conversation, about his homeland and his various travels. Jing answered as best he could, wishing he had asked Twig their names, for they had not offered them and direct inquiry might be rude. There were a chief, a middle and a junior; that would have to do.

Finally the chief broached the main subject. He said, "What god is worshiped in your land?"

"Most people not," Jing said. "Is some old and sick folk think of pleasing gods, but to rest of us is imaginary thing. We tell easily dream from fact, same as here."

"You don't believe in a creator at all?" the middle one demanded. "You don't think the world *was* created?"

"Is certain," Jing said. "But very long past. We think"—he groped for words—"world is made as path for us to go on as we choose. Important is to learn from sky whether we take right or wrong way. Creator is watch us, but not for punish, not for want offerings, just for see how done by us. When well done, more star come in sky. Perhaps in farthest future all sky is starry, and all here below walk in light all time."

He hated to give this bald account of the system Ntahish philosophers had evolved over many score-of-score years, but it was the best he could manage.

The junior, who was better-favored than his colleagues, spoke up eagerly. "But the New Star did light the whole of the night sky! For a while it could even be seen by day! Do you think—?"

"There is no New Star!" the chief snapped. "It's an illusion!"

Humbly the junior said, "Sir, I'm aware of that. But with respect it seems our visitor is not. I only wish to learn what explanation his people have—well, invented for it."

Gruffly, the chief granted permission for the question.

"We not have explanation," Jing admitted. "Never saw so much bright star appear in past, not at any rate to stay so long. In Ntah is no great change to explain it. Here why I am sent to ask in foreign lands."

"You actually imagine there have been other new stars?" asked the middle one. "Dreamstuff!"

"Can show you true. I bring copies of old sky-maps to make proof. Is also much difference in time of rise and set from old days. Will explain meaning of maps when want you!"

"Your star-maps," said the chief sacerdote coldly, "are of no interest to us. Any apparent change in the heavens must be due to the working of evil forces passing off dreams as reality. Bring your maps, yes, but so that we can burn them and save other people from your mad ideas!"

That was more than Jing could bear. Rising to his full height in the most disrespectful manner possible, he said, "Is your belief, anyone make use of fire is companion of evil, yes? You just propose that same! I say plain: I better tell dream from true than you! And anyway, is not place of you to order foreigner, guest of Count!"

The middle one scowled a warning, aware his chief had gone too far. After a moment the latter rose, glowering.

"The Count is not yet back! He is a reckless hunter and may well not come back at all! And if he doesn't, then we'll see about *you!*"

He stormed away.

Greatly distressed, the junior sacerdote escorted Jing to the exit, muttering apologies. And, as soon as they were out of hearing, he did the most amazing thing. Leaning confidentially close, he whispered, "Sir, *I* would like to see your sky-maps! Since coming here, I no longer think the heavens never change! I think new stars signal the birth of righteous persons, and the most righteous of all must now be among us!"

Before Jing could recover from his startlement, he was gone.

At first Jing was inclined to hasten straight back to Twig, but a moment's reflection changed his mind. Even in peaceful Ntah there were such things as court intrigues, and while in his profession he had been largely insulated from them, he was well aware of the need to protect himself. Given the Count's absence, might his daughter offer a degree of help, or at least advice? From a passing prongsman he inquired the way to her ladyship's quarters.

They proved to be in a large and comfortable bower on the west side of the castle, where she sat poring over a table of Ntahish mathematical symbols he had prepared for her. He was relieved to find she did not resent interruption; on the contrary, she declared herself delighted, and sent her maids to bring refreshments.

"I'm so pleased you're here!" she exclaimed, speaking as directly as a man. "Here at Castle Thorn, I mean. I'd never say so in Twig's hearing, but I long ago learned all he had to teach me about the sky, and it didn't even include the idea that the sun stands still while we move around it. It makes everything so much simpler when you look at things that way, doesn't it? I look forward to having you as my constant companion at the observatory this winter."

"To me will much pleasure," Jing affirmed. "But if to explain correct meaning I want say, must I very more Forbish learn."

"I'm sure you'll learn quickly, and if you have problems, turn to me. I have little enough to occupy me," she added in a bitter tone.

Thus emboldened, Jing said, "Is of problem I come now. See you . . ." And he summed up his encounter with the sacerdotes.

"You're right to beware of them!" Rainbow asserted. "How can I but hate them for claiming that my birth was the sign of a curse on my father? For him I have small love either, since he sent my mother away, but at least he had the kindness to bring me with him when he left Forb instead of abandoning or even killing me, and he provided for my education by offering Twig a refuge here. Without *him* I think I would have lost myself in dreamness. If only he hadn't more or less quit studying the sky when his eye began to fail . . . Still, he had only himself to blame for looking directly at the sun. He told you, did he, how he saw dark markings on it?"

"I hear of it in Forb, but he not say himself."

"Do you think it's credible? Sometimes when there's thin gray cloud, so the sun doesn't hurt your eye, I've imagined that I too . . . But what do you think? Is it possible for dark to appear out of bright, as bright may out of dark?"

"Is not in the knowledge of my people. Where I lived, is either clear day-sky or thick rain-cloud. Was to me new, see sort of thin cloud you mention."

"Is that so?" She leaned forward, fascinated. "I should ask you about your homeland, shouldn't I, rather than about stars and numbers all the time? Have you been away long? Do you miss it very much? Is it a place of marvels? I suspect it must be, particularly compared to this lonely backwater . . . But quickly, before my maids return: I'll assign you one of my own prongsmen to replace Drakh. I'll say it's because you need someone to practice Forbish with. I'll give you Sturdy. With him at your side you need fear nothing from the sacerdotes."

"Am not sure all to be feared," Jing muttered, and recounted the odd behavior of the junior sacerdote.

"Interesting! That must be Shine you're talking about. I realized long ago he was too sensible to deprive himself of the good fare we can offer, but I'd no idea he'd become so independent-minded. Cultivate him! It could serve us well to have a split in the enemy's ranks."

Jing noted in passing how swiftly she had begun to say "us."

"Tonight in hall sit with me," Rainbow continued. "I'll feed you from my own trencher-stump. That is, unless you're afraid of offending my father's wives. But they have no power; he takes and dismisses them according to his mood, and until one of them buds I remain his sole heir. Now here come my attendants. Let's change the subject. You were telling me about your homeland. The very weather is different there, I think you said. In what way?"

With infinite gratitude Jing slipped into memory, purging the risk of dangerous dreams. He described the sub-tropical climate of Ntah, and then progressed to a general account of the Lake and its environs —the creeper-bridges stranding out from island to island; the Lord's palace at the center, a huge tree sixty-score years old, whose sides were draped with immense waxy blossoms that scented the air for miles around; the western cataract where a broad river plunged over a cliff and kept the Lake from growing stagnant; the delectable flesh of the nut called hoblaq, enclosed in a shell too hard for anyone to break, which people gathered on the hillside and pitched into the river so that the falls would do the work for them and send the shattered kernels drifting across the water for everybody to enjoy; the game animals large and small which haunted the copses, the shallows and the watermeadows; the venomous insects and noxious berries which were obliging enough to advertise themselves by distinctive coloring, so even children might avoid them; and of course his prized observatory, with its orrery and its transits and its levels and its gnomons and its great trumpet-shaped viewing-funnel of dried pliobark, which blanked off all light from below and permitted the eye to adjust completely to its task of registering the stars . . .

"And we think we're advanced!" Rainbow cried. "How could you have brought yourself to leave such a place?"

It was a question Jing was to ask himself countless times during the next few months, particularly after the last boat of autumn had come and gone and the sun had set for the last time in six-score days.

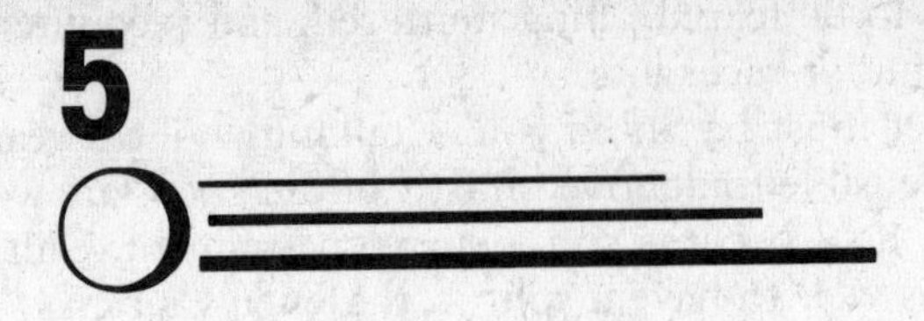

The slopes and branchways of the castle were eerie in the long darkness, although the glowplants drew enough warmth from underground to provide faint luminance right through until spring. They were, Jing thought, like a model of his mind, a pattern matching himself alone as the sky matched the entire world. Some areas were darkly red, like those deep-lying mental strata concerned with fundamental processes such as digestion, where one might venture only in emergency and at the cost of immense concentration; others were pinker and brighter, like the levels where one might issue commands to oneself about sitting or standing, walking or climbing—or fighting; others again tended to be bluish, like the dreams harking back to childhood incomprehension of the world which could so easily overpower a person when weary, sick, frightened, grief-stricken or undernourished, and which sacerdotes and other fools deliberately cultivated because they had never learned to prize dreams less than memory; yet other levels were greenish as memory was; more still gleamed clear yellow like imagination; and just a few, including the great hall itself, shone with the white brightness of reality.

Contrary to what the chief sacerdote had hoped, the Count had a successful hunt, and his prongsmen dragged back enough snowbelong meat to garnish a score of winter meals. But he had fallen into a crevasse and ruptured some of his interior tubules. More bloated than ever, he summoned Jing to attend him under the misapprehension that all foreigners were skilled physicians. Jing, having seen a similar case when an elderly man slipped on the approach to the cataract at Ntah, offered suggestions which appeared to give relief from pain, if nothing more. Impressed, the Count made a vague attempt to engage in debate concerning the patterns in the sky, but after that he seemed to lose interest.

Much the same could be said of Twig. Once he realized that Jing's star-maps were not only in an alien script but based on a sun-centered convention, he gave up. It was not because he shared the sacerdotes' conviction that the sun was only the Maker's Eye and therefore could not be the focus around which the planets revolved; enough observations had been amassed here in the north to indicate to him how far superior the Ntahish system was. No, the problem arose from a wholly unexpected source: Keep-fire.

As the story came back to Jing, the elderly peasant whose ancestors had been a priesthood was angered by the fact that certain substances resisted change in his hottest flames. He therefore set about interrogating the oldest of his kinfolk in search of ways to make them even hotter. Siting a fire at the spot where a crack in the rock, leading to the outside, was aligned with the prevailing wind made the fuel blaze up violently. Winds, though, were unpredictable; how to cause an artificial one? Well, when a barq's bladder burst . . . Suppose one made a giant bladder out of hide? But that wasn't the answer by itself. It needed to be filled, and refilled, and refilled, and . . . How about tethered hoverers?

The problem engaged Twig's total attention. Sighing, Jing left him to get on with it, feeling lonelier than ever.

In absolute contrast, Rainbow was desperate for the information contained in Jing's maps. The regular winter wind had set in, but actual star-study was out of the question; there were constant snow-flurries, and whenever the gale died down the water was warm enough to generate fog. Jing, though, was in no mood to complain. He was taking a long while to adjust to the loss of his last Ntahish companion, and until he had rid his mind of intrusive dreams he was content to tutor Rainbow. He was greatly impressed by her quick wits. She had realized at once how much simpler a sun-centered system made it to keep track of the outer planets, and the inner one which was so rarely visible. Moreover, when she ran across a technical term in Ntahish for which she knew no equivalent, she simply adopted it. Within a few days she was using words nobody else at Castle Thorn would have understood.

Except one . . .

It astonished Jing when the young sacerdote Shine lived up to his promise and shyly came to beg a sight of the star-maps. Instantly fascinated, he set about matching the names they bore with their Forbish equivalents. Soon his colleagues were openly quarreling with him. One evening only the authority of the Count prevented a fight breaking out in the hall.

Quite without intention, Jing thereupon found himself the center of interest throughout the castle. He could go nowhere without some wench accosting him to demand a favorable horoscope for her family, or a prongsman wanting to be told he would be promoted chief-of-guard over his rivals, or peasants seeking a cure for trencher-plant blight—though luckily the latter had been less virulent of late.

As soon as the air cleared, therefore, he and Rainbow went to the observatory as often as possible. All Twig's extravagant claims proved justified. The stars shone down sharp as stabberclaws, from a background so nearly black Jing almost could not believe it. Even the square surrounding the New Star was barely a contrast to the rest. As for the Bridge of Heaven, it gleamed like a treasury of pearlseeds.

A faint suspicion trembled on the edge of his awareness. But it refused to come clear as he strove with chill-stiff claws to prepare for the portion of the sky not seen from Ntah maps and tables as exact as those he had brought from home. Often dreams threatened to engulf his consciousness, and then he had to break off and embrace the warm trunk of the pumptree until he regained his self-possession.

It was a marvelous juncture for observation, though. Time had brought all five outer planets into the same quadrant—an event which might or might not have significance. A year ago he would have insisted that it must; now he was growing skeptical. But there was reddish Swiftyouth, currently in a retrograde phase of the kind which had led Ntahish astrologers to center their system on the sun; there was Steadyman, almost white, lagging behind; there was Stolidchurl, somewhat yellower; there were Stumpalong and Sluggard, both faintly green, the latter markedly less bright . . .

Why were there moving bodies in the sky, and of such different sizes? And why were they so outnumbered by the stars? Shine was eager to explain the teaching he had been brought up to: that each corresponded with a region of the world, and moved faster or slower according to whether the people of that region obeyed the Maker's will. One day they would all rise together at the same time as the sun rose in eclipse, and—

Patiently Jing pointed out the fallacies in his argument. Clacking his mandibles, he went away to think the matter through. Apparently it was news to him that a solar eclipse was not simultaneously observed everywhere, a fact one might account for only by invoking distances beside which Jing's journey from Ntah to Castle Thorn was like a single step. It hurt the mind to think in such terms, as Rainbow wryly put it when he showed her how to calculate the circumference of the world by comparing star-ascensions at places on the same meridian but a known distance apart. He found the remark amusing; it was the first thing that had made him laugh in a long while.

Plants which swelled at noon and shrank at midnight were used in Ntah to keep track of time if the sky was clouded over and the weather-sense dulled. Whenever it snowed, Jing occupied himself by hunting the castle for anything which might exhibit similar behavior. The effect the long night was having on his own weather-sense was disquieting; without sunlight to prompt him back to rationality, he found dreams creeping up on him unawares when he was neither hungry, tired nor upset.

He was engaged in this so-far vain quest when he was hailed by a familiar voice. Turning, he saw Twig, filthy from pads to mandibles with blackish smears.

"*There* you are! I was surprised not to find you in Rainbow's quarters—they tell me you two have grown very close lately!"

For an instant Jing was minded to take offense. But Twig knew nothing of his being compelled to celibacy so long as Waw-Yint lived. And lately he had felt pangs of regret at not having left offspring behind in Ntah. Rainbow and Shine were about half his age; talking to them, he had realized how much happier he would have been had he passed on his knowledge to a son and daughter before setting forth on his travels . . .

Before he could reply, however, Twig had charged on, plainly bursting to impart information. "Take a look at this!" he exclaimed, proffering something in his left claw. Jing complied, hoping it was not something as irrelevant as Twig's last "great discovery": a new kind of metal, grayish and cold, which broke when it was dropped. This one, however, he thought he recognized.

"Ah! You found another magnifying drop. It's especially clear and fine, I must say."

"Not found," Twig announced solemnly. "Made."

"How? Out of what?"

"Sand, would you believe? Yes, the same sand you find beside the hot marsh! Keepfire's flames are getting better and hotter—oh, I know people are complaining about the smell, but that's a small price to pay! —and this time he's excelled himself! And there's more. Look at *this!*"

He produced what he had in his other claw. It was of similar material, equally clear, but twice the size.

"Hold them up together—no, I don't mean *together*, I mean—Oh, like this!" Twig laid claws on Jing in a way the latter would never normally have tolerated, but it was certainly quicker than explaining. "Now look at something through both of them, and move them apart or together until you see it clearly. Got it?"

Jing grew instantly calm. There presented to his eye was an image of Twig, albeit upside-down . . . but larger, and amazingly sharp except around the edges.

Very slowly, he lowered and examined the two pieces of glass. They were not, as he had first assumed, in the regular half-droplet shape; they were like two of the natural kind pressed together, but considerably flatter.

"You made these?" he said slowly.

"Yes, yes!" And then, with a tinge of embarrassment: "Well—Keepfire made them, under Bush's supervision. All I was hoping for was better magnifying drops. I never expected that when you put one behind another you'd get even more enlargement the wrong way up! At first I thought I was in a dream, you know? But you agree it works?"

"Yes—yes, no doubt of it!"

"Right! Let's go and look at stars!"

"It's snowing. That's why I'm here."

"Oh, is it? Oh. Then—"

"Then we'll just have to force ourselves to wait until it blows over. But I promise you, friend Twig, I'm as anxious as you are to inspect the heavens with such amazing aids!"

The moment the weather cleared, he and Twig and Rainbow and Shine—for the secret was so explosive, it had to be shared—along with Sturdy, who hated coming here in the cold and dark, plodded to the observatory, forcing themselves not to make a premature test. Then it turned out that the lenses had misted over, and they had to find something dry enough to wipe them with, and . . .

"Jing first," Twig said. "You're the most knowledgeable."

"But surely you as the discoverer—"

"The credit is more Keepfire's than mine! Besides"—in a near-whisper—"my eye's not keen enough."

"My lady—" Jing began. Rainbow snapped at him.

"Do as Twig says!"

"Very well. Where shall I look first?" He was shaking, not from cold, but because excitement threatened to release wild dreams to haunt his mind like savage canifangs.

"At Steadyman," she said, pointing where the gaps in the cloud were largest. "If there's a reason why some stars are wanderers, it may be they are specially close to us. You've taught me that our own world whirls in space. Maybe that's another world like ours."

It was a good, bright and altogether ideal target. Jing leaned on the walbush stems, which were frozen stiff enough to support him. It took a while to find the proper position for the lenses, and then it took longer still for his sight to adjust to the low light-level—particularly since there were curious faint colored halos everywhere except at the dead center of the field. Eventually, however, he worked out all the variables, so he had a clear view. At last he said:

"Whether it's a world like ours, I cannot say. But I do see two stars where I never saw any before."

"Incredible!" breathed Twig, and Jing let go pressure from his limbs with a painful gasp and passed the lenses on. In a while:

"Oh! Oh, *yes!* But very indistinct! Rainbow, what do you see?"

She disposed herself carefully, leaning all her weight on her crippled side. Having gazed longer than either of them, she said, "Two stars beside the planet. Sharp and clear."

Turning, she sought Stolidchurl, and did the same, and exclaimed. "Not two more stars, but three! At least I think three . . . I—Shine, you look. Your sight is very keen, I know."

His mandibles practically chattering with excitement, the young sacerdote took his turn. "Three!" he reported. "And—and I see a disc! I always thought the planets were just points, like the stars! But I still see *them* as points! And what do you make of the colored blurs these lenses show?"

"Could it be that we're seeing a very faint aurora?" Rainbow ventured. "Jing, what do you think?"

Jing ignored her, his mind racing. If one put such lenses in a viewing funnel—no, not a funnel, better a tube—of pliobark, or whatever was to be had here in the north, and made provision for adjustment to suit different observers . . .

He said soberly, "Twig, this is a very great invention."

"I know, I know!" Twig clapped his claws in delight. "When I turn it on the sun, come spring—"

"You'll burn out what's left of your sight," Rainbow interjected flatly. "Making the sun as much brighter as the stars now appear will blind you. But there must be a way. Apply your genius to the problem, while the rest of us get on with finding unknown stars. Perhaps they hold the key to what's amiss with cripples like me."

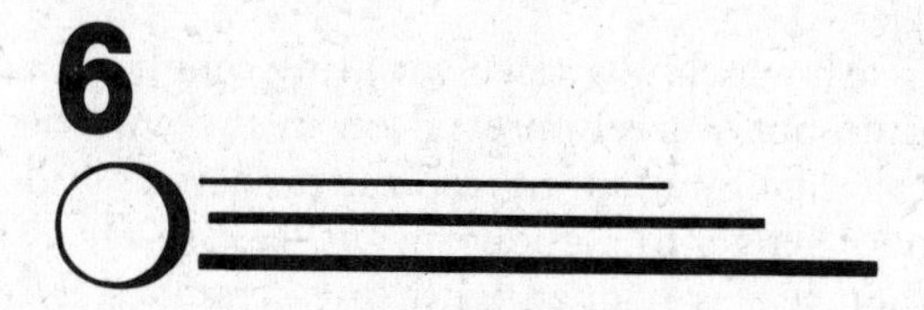

For the rest of the winter all four of them were embarged on a fabulous voyage of discovery. The world receded until they could wander through it unheeding, like a thin mist; all that mattered was their study of the sky. Shine abandoned his duties altogether, and his superiors threatened to kill him, but he put himself under Rainbow's protection and with Sturdy and her other prongsmen ready to spring to his aid they dared not touch him.

Growing frightened because his ruptures would not heal, the Count occasionally sent for them to demand how their work was progressing, but during their eager attempts at explanation his mind tended to stray, and he invariably wound up by raging at them because they cared more for star-lore than medicine. Nobody else in the castle —not even Twig's aides like Hedge and Bush, who refused to venture forth when the wind was bitter enough to build frost-rime on one's mandibles—seemed to care that a revelation was in the making. Twig said it was because the cold weather had sent their minds into hibernation, like the dirq and fosq which were so abundant in the summer and vanished into burrows in the fall.

There was one signal exception: the peasant Keepfire.

Throughout his life he had scarcely seen the stars. It was a tradition in his family that at winter sunset they should retreat to their cavern until spring reawoke the land. Twig, however, was sure it could not always have been so, and because he was so excited by what the lenses were revealing he patiently taught Keepfire how to store warm air under his mantle and persuaded him to the observatory at a time when the air was so clear the brilliance of the heavens was almost hurtful.

Such was Keepfire's amazement on learning that the glass he had melted from sand could show sparks of light where to the naked eye was only blackness, he returned home full of enthusiasm to improve on what he had already done. It being impossible to find fuel for new and hotter fires at this season—and hard enough at any time—he set about collecting every scrap of glass he could, whether natural or resulting from their experiments. For hours on end he sat comparing them, wondering how each differed from the rest. At last, in what the jubilant Twig termed a fit of genius, he thought of a way to shape the ones which were nearly good until they outdid those which were excellent.

Using the skin of a fish which was sown with tiny rough crystalline points, hunted by people but scarcely preyed on in the wild because swallowing it tail-first as it fled was apt to rasp the predator's gullet, he contrived to grind a poor lens into a good one, at least so far as form was concerned. But then it was seamed with fine scratches. How to eliminate them? There was no means other than rubbing on something softer than the glass, until the glass itself shed enough spicules to complete the task. This he set himself to do.

Nightless days leaked away, and Jing and his companions almost forgot about Keepfire, because every time they went to the observatory some new miracle presented itself.

At first Jing had thought it enough that, in the vicinity of the bright outer planets, there should suddenly appear new starlets which—as time passed—clearly proved to be satellites of what Shine had been the first to recognize as actual discs. But then they looked at the Bridge of Heaven, otherwise the Sling, and save at its midline it was no longer a band of uniform light; it was patently a dense mass of individual stars.

And there were so *many* stars! Even when the lenses were directed towards the dark square surrounding the New Star, at least a quarter-score (Shine claimed eight) other points of light appeared. At the zenith, near the horizon, it made no odds: wherever they looked, what had always been lightless zones turned out to be dotted with tiny glowing specks.

The New Star itself resolutely refused to give up any secrets. Even Shine's keen vision, which far surpassed the others', failed to reveal more than a bright spot with a pale blur around it, a cloud lighted as a fire might light its smoke from underneath. Was it a fragment of the Maker's Mantle, the aurora which at unpredictable intervals draped the sky in rich and somber colors? In Jing's view that was unlikely.

Before coming to Castle Thorn he had only heard of aurorae. Now, having witnessed several, he was satisfied they must partake more of the nature of clouds than of stars, for they affected the weather-sense, as stars did not; moreover they did not necessarily move in the same direction as the rest of the sky. Were they then looking down on starfire from above? The image came naturally to folk whose ancestors had been treetop-dwelling predators, but by the same token "up" and "down" meant one thing to them: towards or away from the ground underpad.

Jing and Rainbow debated long about the matter as soon as they realized that the little stars shuttling back and forth beside the planets must in fact be revolving around them, moon-fashion. By that stage Jing's prized star-charts were little more than memoranda; he already knew there was a lifetime's work in filling the gaps the unaided eye had left. The perspectives opened up to him were terrifying. Because if there were any number of different up-and-downs, then not only must the planets be worlds like *the* world, with their own—plural!—moons, but the sun, whose planets circled it like moons, might be circling something greater yet, and . . . and . . . It was dizzying to contemplate!

At least the moon lent them clues. Observations at the full showed that the sparkles visible on the dark part of its disc were only a fraction of what was actually going on. Flash after brilliant flash came and went seemingly at random, lacking even the momentary trace which followed a meteor. And here again Keepfire proved to possess unexpected insight. Shown the moon through his original lenses, he said at once, "It's like when I make a fire!"

And it was. By this time they had all watched his trick of striking rocks together and catching a spark on a tuft of shredded calamar.

Striking . . .

Jing felt he was being not so much struck as battered. It had been hard enough to accept the distances he had been taught about in childhood, necessary to let Sunbride race around the sun, the world stride around it, and the outer planets follow at their own respective speeds. What to make of a cosmos in which scores-of-scores-of-scores-of-scores (but it was pointless to try and count the stars in the Sling) of not just suns but their accompanying planets must be allowed for? If the sacerdotes were right in claiming that their sacred stones had fallen from heaven, and they were so tiny, could those brilliant lights above also be minute? Shine suggested as much, for he desperately wanted not to forsake all his former beliefs; in particular he clung to the notion that the New Star must indicate some great event in the world below. During a late snowstorm, however, Jing set him to making calculations based on the new observations, couched in the Ntahish symbols which were wieldier than what obtained in the north, and the results overwhelmed the poor ex-sacerdote, even though he had been properly fed for moonlongs past and learned to separate dream from fantasy as never before in his young life. They demonstrated beyond doubt that in order to leave room for planetary motions the lights in the sky must be not only far off but enormous. Did not a lantern fade to imperceptibility, no matter how skillfully you bred your gleamers, almost before its bearer was out of hearing? And when one added in an extra fact which Shine himself had drawn to their attention—that Swiftyouth sometimes appeared out of round, as though attempting phases like the moon's—there was precisely *one* explanation which fitted the evidence. The universe must be full of suns, and therefore presumably of planets too faint and far away for even their precious lenses to reveal.

A cosmic hierarchy of fire evolved in Jing's imagination: from the Sling compound of giant stars down to the briefest spark made by clashing rocks. Something pervaded all of them, something luminous, hurtful, transient, imponderable, yet capable of being fixed and leaving traces. Perhaps it penetrated everything! Was it the same force which made treetrunks strong enough to lift gigantic boulders, the same which brought forth blossoms, fruit and nuts? It might be, surely, for fire shone brightly and so did glowplants and glitterweed although they were cold to the touch and in color much like Stumpalong or Sluggard. So was there a connection? Suppose it was a matter of speed; suppose the slowness of plant-growth, and of the outer planets, meant *cool*, and the rapidity of flame meant *hot:* what did that imply about the stars? Remaining visibly the same for countless scores of years, must they not also be cool? Yet did not some of them now and then flare up? What about the bright streaks that nightly laced the firmament—must they not be cool, because manifestly the air was warm only when the sun had long shone on it? Yet Shine declared that those who had come on one of the Maker's slingstones immediately after it landed invariably stated that it was too hot to touch, and indeed the surrounding area was often charred! What fantastic link was there between light and heat?

Vainly Jing sought to convey his thinking to his companions. He was as fluent now in spoken Forbish as Rainbow in the use of Ntahish numbers. She, though, had not yet escaped her original obsession; she had only come around to the view that it was pointless to try and read from the heavens the true reason for her deformity, because if there were so many invisible stars there might be one for everybody, and you could waste a lifetime seeking out your own. Before leaving home, or even as recently as the first time he looked at the sky through lenses, Jing might have considered such an argument valid; since getting over Drakh's death, however, he had experienced preternatural clarity of thought, and ideas which for half his life he had treated as rational had been consigned to memory, reclassified as imaginary or as dreamstuff. Perhaps this was due to the plain but nourishing diet he was eating; perhaps it had something to do with the monotonous environment of the long night, when he was free from the cyclic shock of sunrise and sunset; it didn't matter. What counted was that he could now clearly envisage other worlds. What a plethora of individuals might not inhabit all those planets, seen and unseen! What marvels might lie yonder in the dark, more astonishing to him than Ntah to those who knew only Castle Thorn!

And what daunting celestial oceans of knowledge remained to be traversed, when by happenstance a humble peasant could open people's eyes to the miracles inherent in plain sand!

"We'll learn more of the answers," Twig kept promising in what he intended as a tone of comfort, "when the sun rises again. Darkness makes one's mind dull . . . as the saying goes!"

Yet Jing's was not, nor Shine's. Could this be due to their constant intake of starfire? Could the mind as well be driven by the mysterious force? Was that why Keepfire, shut away in his foul-smelling cavern, believing in nothing and nobody save his traditional lore, was able to choose and pursue a course of action when Jing's mind was foggy with whirling symbols? Hedge and Bush became angrier and angrier with him, and subsided into sulky grumbling, so that no more new results emerged from the laboratory. Yet Keepfire worried on, and polished and pondered and talked to himself and polished some more, and . . .

And on that spring day when the sun's disc cleared the horizon entire for the first time since fall, he came in triumph to Twig and Jing and Rainbow, and unfolded a scrap of the softest icefaw-hide, and revealed a pair of lenses of such impeccable shape that all the results of nature, or of early pourings, faded into insignificance.

Proudly he said, "Do I not bring the gift you wanted most? So I'll ask for what I want. You have shown me stars. They are little fires like the ones I understand. Now I want to see the biggest fire. Show me the sun!"

"But—" Rainbow began, and clipped off the words. Mutely she appealed to her companions, who could envisage as well as she the effect of looking at the sun through nearly perfect lenses.

Twig, however, was oblivious. He breathed, "To see the sun once with these would be enough to sacrifice my sight for!"

"Oh, shut up!" Jing roared. They shrank back as he erupted to his full height, every muscle and tubule in his body at maximum tension. "You're talking like a senile fool, and I speak to you as a sworn friend! Don't you think your eyesight will be useful tomorrow, too? What we need is a way to look at the sun without going blind!" He rounded on Keepfire. "Would you give up all vision for one fleeting glimpse of the sun? You'd rather see it over and over, wouldn't you?"

Alarmed, Keepfire signaled vigorous agreement.

"Very well, then!" Jing relaxed into a more courteous posture, but still tenser than his usual stance among friends. "What do we know of which makes a scene darker without blurring detail? In Ntah old folk sometimes protected their sight on a sunny day"—he used the past tense unconsciously, and later thought of it as a premonition—"by using thin gray shells. But those deformed the image. Well?"

There was a long pause. At last Rainbow said, "You find membranes inside furnimals that are no good for parchment because you can see through to the other side."

Shine clacked his claws. "Yes! And stretching them can make them thinner still, yet they diminish light!"

"They make everything yellower!" Twig objected, and at once caught himself. "Ah, but the thinner, the clearer! So if we put several one behind another, and take away each in turn until the eye hurts . . . Jing, I'm pleased to be your friend! Once again you see to the core of the matter when I spring to premature conclusions."

"If you want to honor someone, honor Keepfire," Jing said, and reached a decision not foreshadowed by intention. Taking the new beautiful lenses one in either claw, he shrank from his overweening posture to the lowest he could contrive without pain, and remained there while he uttered unpremeditated words.

"You know and I know, without putting it to the test, that these will reveal to us yet more amazing private knowledge. It should not be private; it would not be private, had anybody else within this castle shared our interest. But it *is* so, and must not *remain* so. Already we have learned so much, I want to share our findings with Ntah. The dullwits of Forb and every other city I traversed to come here ought to have their eyes opened—no? Even if like your fellow sacerdotes, Shine, they decline to take advantage, do they not deserve to have this knowledge pointed out to them?"

Shine shouted, "Yes—*yes!*"

Thus encouraged, Jing yielded to a half-guilty, half-ecstatic temptation and let his mind be taken over by the dream-level. Imagination was not enough; it was handicapped by rational considerations like distance, delay, expenditure of effort, the obstinacy of other people. But already their new discoveries had made it plain that everyday knowledge was inadequate to analyze the outcome. For once his dream faculty might be wiser than his sober and reflective consciousness.

Suddenly his head was roaring-loud with revelations, as though he had tapped the sap-run of time. He marveled at what he heard himself say—or rather declaim.

"*Oh-hya-na-ut thra-t-ywat insky-y-trt ah-hng-llytr-heethwa ibyong hr-ph-tnwef-r heesh-llytr-kwu-qtr-anni-hyong*—ah, but I tackle poorly this speech of foreigners and wish I could say what is needful in the speech of the folk I grew up among! But I am far away and lonely beyond bearing so now my community is these who welcome me as friends and I speak to them and to the world because I overflow with knowledge born of fire! I have been set alight like dry crops on a distant hill and the scent of smoke from what I know must carry on the wind and warn the world of what's in store when heaven's fire descends to burn the densest wettest jungle and boil the Lake of Ntah! Vast fires surpassing number or belief loom yonder in the dark and we are cast away upon a fragile barq, this little world, and more and more fires loom and every night the dark is pierced with streaks of fire and what it is we do not know but we must master it or it will utterly consume us! We must pledge ourselves to spare the world the doom of ignorance, not keeping any knowledge private that we've found, but spreading it about to last beyond our lifetimes! You three and I must make a vow together, and in token of it take half another's name. The half is *fire!* It leaves a crust of dirty ash but in another season it may turn to life anew and so our world must do although the prong of heaven strike us down! Take the vow, I beg you, I beseech you, and let not our secret knowledge vanish from the minds of those who on this lost and drifting orb hope to make something greater than themselves!"

He was almost screaming with the fury of his visions, for the countless stars were crashing together in a colossal mass of flame, and the world itself was ripe to be their fuel.

Fuel—?

Abruptly he was back to normal consciousness, and wanted to say something quiet and ordinary, though perfused with unexpected insight, but he could not, for Shine was clutching his claw and crying at the top of his voice.

"I know now what the New Star signified! One is come among us who has wisdom we have never guessed! I'll take the extra name and vow my service!"

"I too!" Old Twig was lowering himself, though his agony was plain. "You have united fire above and fire below and we must tell the world your teaching!"

Last, Rainbow, awkwardly, with her lopsided gait, drew close and said, "I vow the same. For what it's worth I'll bind my followers as well."

There was a pause. She looked at him uncertainly and said at long last, "Jing . . . ?"

The tempest of impressions was fading from his mind. He rose, a little shyly, as though embarrassed. She said again, "Jing!" And continued: "What did you see? What did you see?"

But it was useless to try and describe everything that had so briefly stormed into awareness. He said eventually, "If stars are fire, then new stars happen when fresh fuel is fed to them. What fuel is there, barring worlds like ours? If we would rather not be fuel for a star, there's no one who can save us but ourselves . . . I've dreamed. It's made me weary. I must rest."

That evening Rainbow sent for Keepfire to share food publicly with them and cement their compact, which the peasant did nervously yet with obvious glee. This act made Shine a formal enemy of the other sacerdotes; it was, however, scarcely necessary, since he had long disdained the asceticism they relied on to make their dreams vivid. Afterwards Jing found his companions hanging on his every word as though he were indeed the ultimately righteous person harbingered by the New Star. He did his best to dissuade them, but the force of his vision had profoundly affected them, and it was useless. He resigned himself to being adulated. When they pressed him for some new revelation, all he was able to say was what they must already have known: "It will be spring tomorrow."

Further revelations from the sky, though, were delayed. Warm air from the south, drawn in by the constant thermals rising above the valley, met the still-frozen ground beyond the mountains, and fog and cloud veiled the sun. The ice which had temporarily blocked the access channel began to fracture with noises like a gigant snapping trees, and Jing was moderately content to occupy himself by preparing a detailed report of their discoveries for the doctor in Forb, which he planned to send south by the first barq of spring.

It arrived, and like the one which had brought him and Drakh, it carried a sick passenger.

Leaving Rainbow to polish his final draft, Jing went to the wharf to see the barq come in. He was unprepared to hear a voice hail him in Ntahish.

"It is the Honorable Jing? Here am I, Ah-ni Qat!"

Supported by two youthful aides, a boy and a girl, a stooped yet familiar figure limped ashore. Jing said disbelievingly, "The son of my dear friend the Vizier?"

For he remembered Qat as a sprightly youth, and this personage looked so old and moved so slowly . . . and his skin was patched with ugly scars.

"Indeed, indeed! All winter I've struggled across this snowbound continent because at Forb I heard rumors concerning your whereabouts. I'd not have had the endurance to continue but that my father laid on me the duty of seeking you out and telling you: Ntah is no more!"

For an instant Jing stood frozen. Then he said uncertainly, "Young friend, you're sick. You're ruled by dreams."

"Would that I were," Qat whispered. "After your departure plague ran wild among us. Never were such horrors witnessed by a living eye! People died where they stood, their bodies fell into the lake and river until the water grew so foul the very fish were poisoned. Those who survived lost their reason and fled under the lash of horrid dreams. Most went south. I doubt they escaped like me and my companions. Our northern route must have saved us. It seems the plague loves heat."

"Your father—" Jing began.

"Died among the first. So did Lord Waw-Yint. There is no use in speaking of his heir. Ntah is a land of rotting carcasses, and all who used to live there have run away."

Qat's girl companion uttered a groan of misery. Jing said slowly, "We must find you quarters. The Count has treated me kindly, as has his daughter. You will be made welcome."

Surrounded by the high-piled parchments on which he was recording their discoveries, Jing sat blindly staring at the overcast sky. His mind was fuller of despair than ever in his life before; he wanted to renounce consciousness and retreat to dreams, where Ntah would last for all eternity and its glory never fade.

Behind him creepers rustled. A soft familiar voice said, "Is it true about your homeland?"

He did not turn. "Yes, Lady Rainbow. If Qat says so, he speaks the truth. I no longer have a home."

"You have made one here," she said. "By your kindness to me from the beginning, when first you told me I was not after all accursed; when you said you were surprised I had not found mates in spite of my misshapenness; when you opened my sight to a heaven full of so many stars it's absurd for any one of us petty beings to count on reading his or her fate up yonder—Oh, Jing!" Spreading her mantle, she embraced him as he made to rise. "You have caused me to love you, poor twisted creature that I am! Let me prove that you have a home wherever I am and for as long as I may live!"

She hesitated, and added in an altered voice, "That is, if you do not find me totally repulsive."

There was a moment of absolute stillness. Jing looked at her, and saw through her outward form, to the bright keen mind within. And his oath of celibacy was to lost Ntah . . .

They were both very clumsy, but they found it funny, and afterwards he was able to say, in full possession of his rational faculties, "But your father? He cares nothing for our work, and may despise me."

"He is sad and sick and this winter has shown him he too can grow old. He has spoken much about over-close breeding, as one sees with canifangs, and has even mentioned the idea of a grandchild. Inwardly I think I may be normal, and most certainly you and I cannot be cousins to any degree. We shall find out. If not—so be it."

She refolded her mantle about her. Checking suddenly, she said, "Jing, if tomorrow you decide you never want to see me again—if you feel it was only misery which made you desire me—I shan't care, you know. You've given me such a gift as I never hoped for."

"And you," he said fondly, "have given me such courage as an hour ago I thought I'd never enjoy again."

"So you want my ill-starred daughter?" grunted the Count, when with difficulty his attendants had roused him from the mist of dreams in which he now passed most of his time. His ruptured tubules had been unable to heal, owing to his corpulence, and he slumped in his sitting-pit like a half-filled water-bladder. "Well, I always thought you were crazy and now you're proving it. Or have you scried something in the stars to show she's fitter than she looks? Wish you'd do the same for me!"

"I want her," Jing said firmly, "because she possesses a sharp mind, a keen wit and an affectionate nature."

"More than I could say of most of the women I've taken," the Count sighed. "Had I been gifted with a son . . . You want a grand celebration? You want mating-presents?" Suddenly he was suspicious.

"Nothing but your authority, Father, to continue our work together as mates as well as friends," said Rainbow.

"Hah! Work, you call it! Wonderful benefits it's brought us, all your noble gabble about stars the naked eye can't see—and the same goes for your people, Jing! Wiped out by plague, so they tell me! Still, you're of good stock, and maybe cross-breeds are what's been lacking in our lines. I'd rather believe too many cousins mated with cousins to keep control of the best homes and richest land, than that I was cursed by the Maker!"

"You are perfectly correct, sir. We too, after all, are animals."

"Hah! What animal could find more stars in the sky than the sacerdotes say were put there at the Beginning? Oh, take her, and bring me a grandchild if you can. For myself, I'm beyond hope, And—" He hesitated.

"Yes, Father?" Rainbow prompted, taking his claw in hers.

"Dream of me as long as you can after I'm dead. Try not to let the dreams be ugly ones."

* * *

"Look, Jing!" Rainbow exclaimed as they left the Count's presence. "The skies are clearing! In a little we shall see the sun!"

But there were other matters to attend to. Qat was weak, and his servants in scarcely better shape. All of them bore plague-scars. Apparently the illness began with sacs of fluid under the skin, accompanied by fever and delirium. If they burst outward, the patient might survive, at the cost of being marked for life. If they burst inward, the victim died. Applying cleanlickers was useless; none could digest the foul matter exuded by the sores. Neither Jing nor Twig had heard of any disease remotely similar.

"Maybe this was what the New Star heralded!" said Qat in an access of bitterness.

"Were that so," Jing responded stonily, "would not I, the most dedicated seeker of its meaning, have been the first to be struck down?"

Thinking how pleased the sacerdotes would be to hear of such a notion.

By then it was midday, and the sun shone clear, albeit not very bright, being at this season close to the horizon. Rainbow was eager to get to the observatory, and Jing—reluctant though he was to abandon these three who might well be his last surviving compatriots—was on the point of consenting to accompany her, when Keepfire came hurrying with news that settled the matter.

"Sir, Scholar Twig is at the observatory with Shine, and they have shown me yet more marvels! Come at once!"

All else forgotten, they rushed in his wake.

"I was right!" Twig crowed. "I did see dark patches on the sun! Now Shine has seen them too!"

"It's true," Shine averred. He had stretched layers of furnimal membrane across the branches of walbush so that one might look at the sun through them. Even so, long staring with the tubed lenses had made his eyes visibly sore. "And something more, as well!"

"What?" Jing seized the tube.

"Look to right and left of the sun's disc, and you'll notice little sparks! They're very faint, but I definitely saw them. Perhaps they're distant stars, far beyond the sun, which just happen to lie in that direction, but your charts show that some of the brightest stars in that area of sky must lie near the sun right now, and I can't see any of *them!*"

Jing did not need to consult his maps to know what stars were meant. Bracing himself on a stout branch, he aligned the tube. At first his sight, after the low light-levels of winter, would not adjust, and he saw only a blur.

"Too bright? I can add another membrane," Shine proposed.

"No, I'm getting a clearer view now . . ." Jing's ocular muscles were adapting with painful speed. "And—oh, that's incredible!"

What he saw was not a blank white disc. There were three dark spots on it. How could that be?

"Do you see the bright sparks?" Shine demanded.

But his vision was overloaded. He stood back, relinquishing the tube, and for a long while was unable to make out his immediate surroundings.

"I was right, wasn't I?" Twig exclaimed.

"Yes," Jing said soberly. "Yes, friend, you were right."

This too must be added to his report on their discoveries. And, given the delay caused by his grief, it could not possibly be ready for the barq presently in harbor here. At all costs, however, it must be sent by the next one. He said so, and Twig objected. "But if we have to take time to write up our findings—"

Jing cut him short. "Did we not pledge to share what we learn with as many other folk as possible?"

"So we did," Twig admitted humbly.

"Well, then! Let's have a score, a score-of-scores, of keen young eyes like Shine's at work on this! I want a full account of our fantastic news in circulation during the coming summer. Even without the resources of Ntah, there must surely still be people on this continent who will respond and imitate what we are doing—and some of them, with luck, may do it *better!*"

Shine had reclaimed the lenses and was staring through them again. Now he gave a gasp.

"I see half of Sunbride!"

"What?" The others turned to him uncertainly.

"Half!" he repeated obstinately. "Tiny, but perfectly clear—half a disc, like half the moon, and as far from the sun as she ever wanders! Our conclusions must be true! They *must!*"

# 8

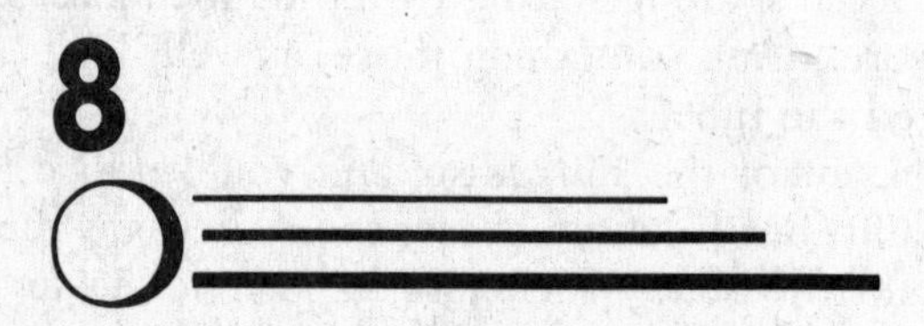

**P**archments in one claw, pearlseed in the other, the steersman of the barq about to depart said, "So you want this delivered to your doctor friend in Forb, do you?"

Something about his tone made Jing react with alarm. He said, "The price is fair, surely! If you doubt the quality of the seed, come and see what a jeweltree the Count sprouted from one I gave him last fall. Even during the winter—"

"So you can still grow jeweltrees, can you? When your trencher-plants rot in the ground!"

It was true; with the return of warm weather, the blight which had affected last year's crop was spreading again, and trencher-plant was their staple diet.

"What does that have to do with—?" Jing began. The steersman cut him short.

"Your doctor had better be cleverer than most! We aren't going as far as Forb this trip. The Maker knows whether anyone will want to go there ever again!"

"What are you saying, man?" Jing advanced, clenching his claws.

"The plain truth! Some filthy plague spawned of the far south is rife in Forb, and a murrain is abroad among the livestock, and the very bravetrees are wilting! We've been here three days—how is it this is the first you've heard?"

"I've . . . uh . . . I've been preoccupied," Jing muttered.

"Dreamlost, more like it!" The steersman returned the parchments with a contemptuous gesture and—more reluctantly—the pearlseed too, adding, "You'll need this to pay for medicine, I've no doubt! If you yourself plan on returning to Forb, which I don't counsel!"

He turned away, shouting orders for his crew to pry loose the barq's tentacles and head down-channel.

"Sure we came by way of Forb," Qat husked. "I told you so. But we aren't sick any more, none of us. Maybe I'm still softer than I should be, but that's a matter of time."

"Yes—yes, of course," Jing muttered comfortingly. He nonetheless cast a worried glance at all three of them: Qat still limp enough to hobble rather than walk, and the boy and girl with their disfiguring scars. Not, according to rumor, that that had prevented their being taken up as curiosities by the younger members of the staff. When even the Count presently approved of outcrossing, and had let his own daughter choose a foreigner for her mate, it was the fashionable thing. Besides, the sacerdotes maintained that no plague could smite those who defied it boldly, so . . .

Their influence was rising again since news of Ntah's downfall. Was this not, they declared, perfect proof of the Maker's vengeance against those who defied His will? In any normal year, such a claim would have been laughed out of conscience; now, though, the blight on the trencherplants meant that many families were facing a hungry summer, and famine went claw-in-claw with madness, even when no plague exacerbated the victims' predicament.

Jing had witnessed, on his way hither from Ntah, how precarious was sanity among his folk—how a single year's crop-failure might entrain surrender to the tempting world of dreams. When he paid full attention to his imagination, he was chilled by the all-too-convincing prospects conjured up. The Count's illness was withdrawing one psychological prop from the minds of the people of the valley; it was certain that when he died some of his old rivals from Forb, or their descendants, would come to squabble over his legacy—that was, naturally, if they weren't caught by the plague already. Hunger and sickness might withdraw the others, and then . . .

Jing trembled at the threat the future held.

Yet his companions declined to worry, even about a means of getting their knowledge spread abroad. If this barq's crew refused to return to Forb, they said, another steersman could be found more susceptible to a handsome payment, more prepared to run risks. It was with some reluctance that they agreed to make extra copies of the parchments Jing had already drafted; Keepfire, of course, could not write, and Twig was constantly on call to administer medicine to the Count. Shine and Rainbow, however, did their best, and by the time the next barq arrived there were six copies of the report at least in summary outline—enough, with luck, for learned folk elsewhere to repeat their studies.

But they, and Jing too, would far rather have continued investigating the dark spots on the sun, and the bright nearby sparks which so far Shine alone had actually seen. Only their sworn pledge, Jing sometimes thought, made them obey his orders. How quickly they were defecting from their brief period of professed admiration!

Could it be because—?

He roused one morning from reverie with a firm and fixed dream-image in his mind, and it was shocking in its import. At once he rushed in search of Twig, and found him coming away from the Count's chamber with a grave expression.

Not waiting for an exchange of greetings, he said in a rush, "Twig, I believe the plague is at work among us!"

Twig gazed soberly at him. He said at length, "How did you know? I thought you said the disease was new to you, and you were unacquainted with its preliminary symptoms."

Jing tensed in horror. He said, "But I guessed it from a dream!"

"Then your weather-sense is far sharper than mine! Did you know the Count attempted to mate with the girl your friend brought here?"

"I'm not surprised, but—No, I didn't know!"

"It was futile, of course, but . . . Well, today he exhibits all the signs Qat said we should watch out for. I'm on my way to check out the other partners she and her brother have engaged with. Have you—? No, forgive me. I'm sure neither you nor Rainbow would consider the idea. But I must ask you a physician's question. Is the Lady Rainbow successfully in bud?"

Jing nodded. "We realized yesterday. Last night we went to the observatory, but there was a bright aurora, so we talked about the future. We're both afraid."

"Internally she's as sound as any woman," Twig assured him. "All the normal pressures are there; only her stance is distorted. But given that the Count, already weakened . . . Your weather-sense informs you of what I mean?"

"Even more. Even worse."

"Very likely." Twig hesitated. "Tell me: how did you decide the plague had got a grip here?"

"Because you in particular—forgive my bluntness—seemed to forget your enthusiasm for my leadership so quickly. A pledge is given with full rationality; dreams erode the recollection of it. I don't speak now of your duty to the Count, of course, but it was never my intention to prevent you serving him. It's a matter of priorities."

"You're right," Twig said after reflection. "In my present mood of calm, I see what you mean. Service to the whole world, which can be performed by spreading our knowledge, is more important than service to an old man whose life I can't prolong with all my skills. We must get those reports away at once, in all possible directions. I'd have realized this truth myself but that—yes, you guessed correctly: I'm being pestered by hideously persuasive dreams such as I haven't known since long before I came to Castle Thorn. And fever due to the onset of the plague would best explain that."

"I think I must believe the same," Jing muttered.

"Oh, no! You of all people! No, you must survive! It would be unbearable to think that the greatest discoverer of our age must be struck down randomly! Far better you should escape to tell the world your tale!"

"But I've kept company with Qat," Jing said stonily. "Out of nostalgia, I've spent half-days at a time talking with him and neglecting my own greater duty. Miraculously I believe Rainbow still to be unaffected. She and the child she buds must go away and take our reports. Might I beg you to attend her before you continue with other matters?"

"Yes! Yes, certainly! But I must warn you that nothing I say or do can alter an established fact. She may already—"

"I know there's a risk. I want to diminish it. We'll buy the steersman of the next barq, give him all my pearlseeds so he can make for the great ocean and find one of the monster barqs that legend says can ply across it to another continent."

"Legend? You want to trust in legends now? Surely you must after all be afflicted!"

"I speak out of imagination rather than dream—though the two sometimes become so intermingled . . . Yes, I think there's no alternative. In one of the visions which haunted me this morning, I saw the bravetrees of Forb rotting from the base wherever a corpse had been deposited. What manner of sickness can attack trees as well as people?"

"A new kind," Twig said slowly.

"As new as the New Star?"

"Ah, but it was only a dream-guess!"

"I think we'll see the same when the first victims die at Castle Thorn."

Clenching his claws, Jing added as he turned away, "I wish with all my might it may just be a dream. But I fear it may well be correct imagining. The blight upon our trencher-plants, at any rate, is real enough."

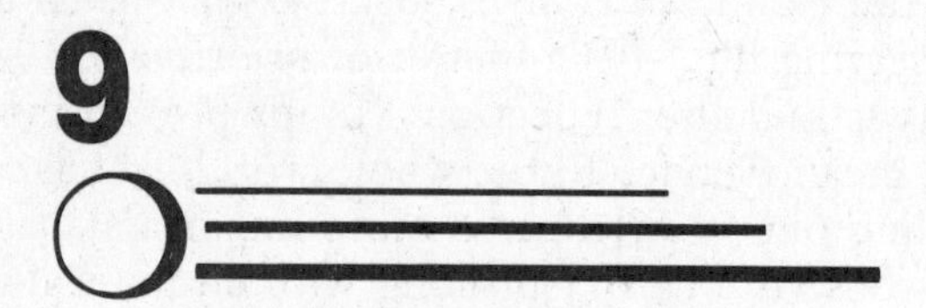

When next they heaved the Count out of his sitting-pit to cleanse and salve him, there were the betraying sacs beneath his skin. And they were readily recognized, for a girl at one of the outlying villages who had partnered the boy from Ntah had died from their inward rupturing that very day.

Instantly the sacerdotes announced that this was the doom pronounced by the Maker against anyone who harbored heretics from foreign lands, and in the grip of the fever which preceded the visible outbreak of sores the peasants forgot what those same sacerdotes had been saying only days earlier about confronting the risk of plague with boldness. Keepfire managed to prevent his family and followers from being deluded; from one of the confusing visions that now beset him, part sane imagination and part lunatic dream, Jing almost extracted a clue concerning life below the massive layers of rock that sheltered Twig's laboratory, but it evaded him at last because he cared more about the survival of his wife and child.

For a little it seemed that Hedge and Bush were certain to escape, which would have dealt a logical blow to the sacerdotes' argument, especially since Twig's sole ulcer had burst outward and his cleanlickers proved able to deal with it. All three had been particularly close with Jing, and it was being claimed that associating with the Ntahans was the key to guilt and the Maker's punishment. But the day came when Bush succumbed, and admitted contact with the Ntahish girl, and a frenzy of hate exploded like one of the geysers that snowbelong-hunters reported far to the north.

"On the way to the observatory they set their canifangs at me," Rainbow said. "Only Sturdy's quickness with his prong prevented me from being badly hurt."

They sat in her bower, high in the castle and well defended, at a time when normally the night would be quiet but for distant icefaw screams and maybe a little music.

They all cast uncertain glances toward Sturdy. Were a trained prongsman to become delirious before he was restrained there could be considerable slaughter, especially when reflex due to killing had already been established in his mind. And killing canifangs was normally no part of an escort's duty.

Still, there were no marks to be seen on him.

"It's essential now for you to get away," Twig said to Rainbow. Her condition was barely perceptible, fortunately, owing to her lop-sidedness. But her attendants could not be trusted to keep such a secret. Let the sacerdotes once get news of it, and they would no longer be confronting angry peasants, but a systematic series of clever attempts to frustrate the budding.

Jing drew a deep breath. "You don't yet know how essential," he said, and spread the right side of his mantle in a manner he would never normally do in anybody's presence except hers . . . but these were intimate friends.

"You too!" Twig blurted as he recognized what Jing was now revealing.

"It would appear," Jing said with all the detachment he could command, "that even those who make a good recovery, like Qat and his companions, still carry the plague with them."

"I'll kill him! I'll *kill* Qat!" Shine screamed, erupting to his full height. "He's going to deprive us of—"

"You will do no such thing," Jing decreed. It was strange, he reflected, how cold he felt, when he knew abstractly that he must be in the grip of fever. Just so long as he could continue to separate dream from reality . . . "You will hew to your oath. You will undertake the protection of Lady Rainbow and her bud and all the parchments on which we have copied details of what we have discovered. You will escort her away from Castle Thorn before the peasants storm it, which will doubtless be the day after they notice its bravetrees rotting where corpses have been consigned to feed the roots." This, with a meaningful glance at Twig. "I have no homeland. I have no future. I have used my life as it befitted me to do. You have sometimes appeared to look on me as a substitute for the imaginary maker who so long ruled your life. I'm not a god. If there is one, He watches us but does not interfere. He speaks to us, perhaps, but if His voice is couched in the language of the stars it's up to us, not Him, to spell out the message . . . Oh, I ramble!"

"Not at all!" cried Shine. "You tell me what I most need to be told!"

"Believe it when I'm gone, and you'll do well," Jing said. Already he could feel the sac he had exposed starting to throb. "Now, take the future in trust. You here—you, Shine; you, Scholar Twig; you Keepfire, who made us the tools to reveal unknown truth; you, my lady, who bear something of me which would otherwise be as hopelessly lost as Ntah itself—*all* of you must listen to my words and cherish what I say as proudly and as fiercely as when we took our oath. And by the way, Shine!"

Humbly the ex-sacerdote looked a question.

"Don't ever speak again of killing. Qat will die young; he was weakened anyhow by his suffering. Or if not, some crazy fool with a mindful of lunatic dreams will dispose of him. But this is neither justice nor vengeance. No, we must speak always and forever of life instead of death; we must fight the foolishness of dreams and concentrate on sanity. We must feed and shelter and educate our people, until the dawns when we know how to conquer sickness and famine, blight and murrain. Then, and only then, shall we be fit to understand the message of the sky. Then, and only then, will the tools Keepfire created for us fall into the proper claws. And yours too, Twig, and mine—the star-charts created by my people . . . my *former* people."

He was briefly silent, and the pause was full of sorrow.

"But let nothing that has been well done go to waste!" he resumed at length. "Not that it can, if it's recorded in the stars . . . but we don't speak that language yet, and maybe it will be a long time before we do. Knowing now how many more stars there are than we believed, we must never be arrogant again! In all humility, going as it were in a mental crouch, we must patiently await the time when we are entitled to stand up to our full height, *and that height shall reach the stars to take them in our grasp like ripened fruit!* I say to you—"

At that moment he felt the sac under his mantle rupture.

Inward.

While they looked at him in wonder, for his peroration had been charged with the same power which persuaded them to join him in their common pledge, he said gently, "I am as good as dead, my friends. Tomorrow I shall surely be insane. I speak to you with the last vestige, the last shred, of what was Ayi-Huat Jing, court astrologer to His Most Puissant Majesty Lord Waw-Yint of Ntah, who set forth upon a journey longer than any of his nation previously, and must now die as my nation died. Dream of me. Make others dream of me. Or all my work will go for naught."

He added silently, "Would I had said that in my own speech. I could have expressed it so much better . . ."

# 10

The day after the Count's death, another of the regular barqs came to the castle wharf. Her steersman was horrified to learn that the plague was here ahead of him, and was in mind to put about at once and risk her starving under him on the return trip. But Twig ceded him all the pearlseeds left in Jing's store—enough to buy the barq and her crew a score of times over—and he was reassured that at least his journey would not be as fruitless as he had feared. The peasants were in the grip of delirium; only the precarious loyalty of Sturdy and the other prongsmen kept them at bay while Rainbow and Shine, in obedience to Jing's order, scrambled on board with the precious parchments.

"But where shall we go?" the steersman cried. "Forb is rotting like a blighted fungus! I saw its bravetrees lean towards the river as though they had been snapped by gigants!"

"Any place the water carries you away from plague!" Twig retorted. "Do they not tell of folk who ply the ocean aboard barqs that make yours look like half-grown pups?"

"We'd have to chance the rapids of the Sheerdrop Range!"

"Then chance them, on a route you never dared before! It's better than the certainty of plague!" Rounding on the prongsmen, Twig ordered them to prod loose the barq's tentacles despite her groans of hunger.

"Won't you come with us?" Rainbow shouted. "Even if—"

"Your father's dead. Your husband told me he would rather you did not watch him follow the same course." Twig descended to the wharf's edge and gently touched her claw. "No, Shine is to take care of you now. I've had my life, as Jing had his. If only we could read the stars more clearly, we might know why. But what you bear with you will instruct the future. You are the wife, my lady, of the greatest man it's been my privilege to know. Create a posterity for him. If the bud fails, then do so anyhow. I cannot; I'm old and weak and I must resign myself to facts."

"If by some miracle—"

"Qat has told us positively there are no miracles with this disease. Only if the sac ruptures to the outside like mine . . . and Jing's did not."

"Couldn't you have *made* it rupture?"

"That too was tried, in Ttah. It always failed."

The steersman was glancing nervously from one to the other of them. He said, "If this woman has the plague-mark on her—"

"No, she does not!" Twig flared. "That's precisely why we want to get her out of here! You have pay for twenty voyages! Go as far as you can, go anywhere you can, and deliver our message to the world. Next time, perhaps, we may know enough about the universe to conquer such a plague! But without the information that you carry, someone else in the far future will have to start all over again! Oh, get under *way*, will you? The castle will be stormed within the day!"

The steersman flogged the barq's tentacles, and they unwillingly let go their grip; she put about and made downchannel. Watching, Keepfire—who had had the chance to travel with Rainbow, but refused because he feared the water more than fire—said, "Do you think, sir, that our work has gone to waste?"

"I sometimes fear it, sometimes think it can't," was Twig's reply. "Sometimes I feel it's like the seed funqi sow on the spring wind, so numerous that a few at least must find a lodging in good ground; sometimes I can imagine it being like a trencher-plant, at risk from unknown kinds of blight predicted or maybe not predicted by the New Star . . . At all events I know one thing. We are to consign the remains of Master Jing to your hot pool, instead of to a pool with fishes in or the roots of a tree."

Startled, Keepfire said, "This is to do more honor to me and my family? Sir, it's already been enough!"

"Not honor," Twig sighed. "He said when he still possessed some trace of rationality that he'd been told how hot pools can break up a dead animal. Did Hedge or Bush mention this, or was it you?"

"I think I did!" said Keepfire with a trace of pride.

"He wants to die more completely than anyone before, dissolved if possible into his finest shreds. He wants to leave a legacy of health and information, and not a rotting body to convey more plague. Come with me. He said he had chosen to die on the departure of his wife, and when we enter his chamber we shall find a corpse for sure."

"But we shall dream of him," said Keepfire, following. "We shall make sure he is dreamed of for all time."

# Part Two

# Fusing and Refusing

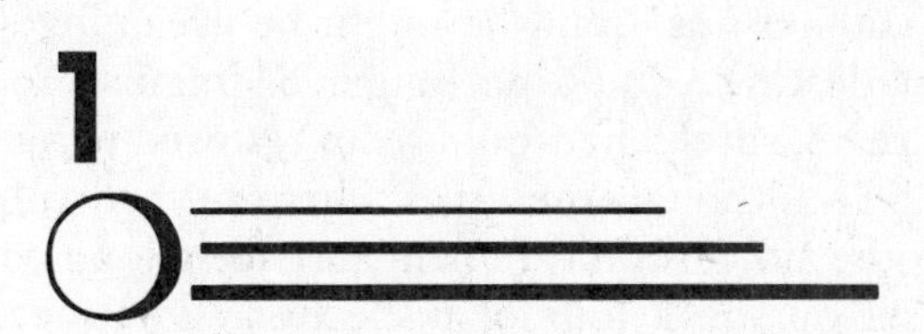

After half a score of days the storm was over. Weathersense and a familiar, reassuring noise lured Skilluck back from the dreamness whither he had been driven by exposure, privation and sheer terror. Slackening his mantle, he relaxed his death-grip on the pole he had clung to while he was reduced to primitive reflexes, concerned only to escape the fury of the elements as his ancestors might have hidden from a predator larger than themselves.

The sound he had recognized was the unmistakable munch-and-slurp of Tempestamer feeding.

Weak exultation filled him. Surely she was the finest briq ever to set forth from Ushere! He had pithed her personally with all the expertise at his command, leaving untouched by his prong nerves which other Wego captains customarily severed. At first his rivals had derided him; then, however, they saw how docile she was, and how fast she grew, and in the end came begging a share of his knowledge, whereupon it was his turn to scoff. Now she had proved herself beyond doubt, for she had defied the worst weather in living memory and—he looked about him—brought her crew to a safe haven, in a bay landlocked among low hills and sunlit under the first cloudless sky he had seen in years.

But where that haven was, the stars alone could tell.

With agony stabbing through his every tubule, he forced himself more or less upright, though it would be long before he regained his usual height, and uttered a silent blessing for his name. Those of his companions who had been called by opposites—Padrag and Crooclaw—had been lost overside on the third day of the storm. But the rest, better omened, were in view, though still unaware: the boy Wellearn, whose first voyage had come so near to being his last, and Sharprong, and Strongrip, and Chaplain Blestar . . . Was the chaplain also alert? His voice could be heard mumbling, "Let each among us find his proper star and there add brightness to the heavens in measure with his merit in the world . . ."

But—no. His prayer was mere reflex. He was still lost between dream and imagination. And in a bad way physically, too; his mantle was bloated and discolored, a sure sign of cresh. The same was true of the others, and Skilluck himself.

For an instant the captain was afraid he might be dreaming after all, that he was so near death he could no longer distinguish reality from fantasy. But in a dream, surely, he would seem restored to health.

His pain was receding, although the areas where he had rubbed against the pole during the storm would remain sore for a long while. He forced himself to set out on a tour of inspection. One piece of essential equipment remained functional: the northfinder, tethered in its cage, responded weakly to his order and uncoiled itself in the correct direction. Also his precious spyglass had been so tightly lashed to a crossbar, all the gales and waves had not dislodged it. That apart, things looked grim. Most of Tempestamer's drink-bladders had burst, the trencherplants had been so drenched with salt water they looked unlikely to recover, the vines had been torn bodily away leaving raw scars on the briq's hide, and—as he already knew—their reserves of fish and pickled weed had been used up.

He sipped a little water from an intact bladder, struggling to make plans. Food must come first, and more water. Were there edible plants on this strange shore? Was there any chance of trapping a game-animal? He needed the spyglass to find out. But his claws felt weak and clumsy, and the rope was swollen with wet; the knots defied him.

A shadow fell across him. He glanced round, expecting Sharprong or Strongrip. But it was young Wellearn who had joined him, hobbling along at barely half his normal height.

"Where are we, Captain?" he croaked.

"No idea, but I'd rather be here than in mid-ocean. Take a drink—but slowly! Don't try and put all your fluid back at one go, or you'll burst a tubule. Then help me untie the spyglass."

Despite the warning, he had to stop Wellearn after several greedy gulps.

"There are three more of us, you know, and only three full bladders!"

Wellearn muttered an apology and turned his attention to the knots. After much difficulty they loosened, and Skilluck unwrapped the hide around the tube.

"Take drink to the others. But be careful. The state they're in, they may not know the difference between you and food. Or themselves, come to that. I guess you never saw anyone with cresh before, hm?"

"Is that what we've got?" Wellearn's eye widened in horror. "I heard about it, of course, but—well, what exactly is it?"

"Who knows? All I can say is, I've seen a lot of it at sea when our trencher-plants got salt-poisoned and our vines were blown away, same as now. Most people think it comes of trying to live off stale pickles. Makes you leak, drives you into dreamness, kills you in the end . . . Oh, curse the weight of this thing!" Skilluck abandoned his attempt to hold up the spyglass normally, and slumped forward in order to rest its end on the ridge of the briq's saddle. "I bet we'll be seeing cresh on land again one of these days, if the winters go on getting longer and harsher and seeds don't sprout and fish don't run . . . But you shouldn't worry too much about yourself. It always hits the biggest and strongest first and worst. Dole out a sip at a time and be specially wary of Blestar—he's delirious."

Carefully filling a gowshell from the drink-bladder in use, Wellearn heard him continue, mainly to himself: "Not a trencher-plant to be seen. Don't recognize a single one of those trees, don't spot a single animal. No sign of a stream unless there's one behind that cape . . ."

The boy shivered, wondering whether his own mantle was as patched with creshmarks as the others', and the captain was speaking only to reassure him. All things considered, though, he felt remarkably well after his ordeal: weak and giddy, of course, so that he wondered how he would fare if he had to leap clear of a cresh-crazed crewman; thirsty in every fiber of his being; and hungry to the point where he wished he could browse off floating weed like Tempestamer. Yet he was still capable of being excited about their arrival in this unknown region, and that was an excellent sign.

So Skilluck must be telling the truth. Sharprong, on the other claw, was almost too ill to swallow, and neither he nor Strongrip had the energy to attack a helper. Ironically, Blestar was worst off of them all, his mantle cobbled with irregular bulges as though it were trying to strain outward through a badly patterned net. He was talking to himself in a garbled blend of half a dozen learned idioms. Wellearn recognized them all; it was his quickness at language that had earned him a place among the crew. Their mission was to trade hides for food-plant seeds in the hope of cross-breeding hybrids which would grow very quickly during the ever-shortening northern summer.

Many briqs this year had scattered on the same quest. If it failed, the Wego might have to move south en masse, and the hope of finding habitable but unpopulated lands was dreadfully slim. So there would be fighting, and the weakened northerners might lose, and that would be the end of a once-great folk. At best they might leave behind a legend, like Forb or Geys or Ntah . . .

Tormented by the sun, Blestar was reflexively opening his mantle as though to roll over and cool his torso by evaporation. Wellearn had never been in such a hot climate before, but he knew enough to resist the same temptation; in their dehydrated state it could be fatal. Anxiously he wondered how he could provide shade for the sick men, and concluded there was no alternative but to untie one of the precious remaining bales of hides. The outer layers were probably spoiled, anyway.

He contrived to rig two or three into an awning; then he distributed the rest of the fresh water and returned to the captain, dismayed to find him slumped in exhaustion.

But he was alert enough to say, "Good thinking, young'un. Give me a little more water, will you? Even holding up the spyglass has worn me out. And I don't see very clearly right now. We'll have to wait until Tempestamer has finished feeding and see if we can make her beach herself."

"Sharprong told me she hated that," Wellearn ventured.

"Oh, she does, and I'd never try it normally, of course. But that's our only hope; we've got to get ashore! Maybe while she's digesting she'll be tractable. Otherwise I'll have to pith another of her command nerves, and if I miss my mark because she bucks and bolts, then the stars alone know how we'll find our way home—Did you give water to the northfinder?"

"I didn't think of that!" Wellearn exclaimed, and hastened to remedy his oversight.

Returning, he looked at the ruptured drink-bladders, wondering whether any were likely to heal. But they were past that, hanging in salt-encrusted rags. In time Tempestamer would grow new ones, but it might be a score of days before they were full enough to tap. There was only one thing to be done.

"I'm going to swim ashore," he announced.

"You *have* got cresh! You'd never make it." Skilluck brushed something aside. A strange kind of winget had settled on him; others, all equally unknown, were exploring the briq, paying special attention to the scars left by the uprooted vines. It was to be hoped they were not in breeding phase, for the last thing Tempestamer needed right now was an infestation of maggors.

It occurred to Wellearn that in these foreign waters there might be creatures as hostile as the northern voraq, but Tempestamer showed no sign of being pestered by any such. He answered boldly, "There's no alternative! If I don't find water I can at least bring tree-sap, or fruit, or—or something."

"Then unlash a pole to help you float," Skilluck sighed. "And take a prong in case a waterbeast attacks you."

After that he seemed to lose interest in reality again.

The water was deliciously cool as Wellearn slid overside, but he was aware how dangerous salt could be to someone with a weakened integument, so he wasted no time in striking out for shore. His mantle moved reluctantly at first, but he pumped away with all his strength, and the distance to land shrank by a third, by half, by three-quarters . . . It was more than he could endure; he had to rest a little, gasping and clinging to the pole. To his horror, he almost at once realized he was being carried seaward again, by some unexpected current or the turn of the tide.

Although fatigue was loosening his grip on reality, he resumed swimming. The sunlight reflected on the ripples hurt his eye, and salty splashes stung it; countless tubules cried pain at being forced to this effort without sufficient fluid in his system; fragments of dream and all-too-vivid imaginings distracted him. He wanted to rest again, relying on the pole, and knew he must not. At last he let it go, and the prong with it, for they were hindering too much.

After what felt like a lifetime, smooth rock slanted up to a little beach, and he crawled the rest of the way as clumsily as a new-budded child. Cursing his bravado, he forced himself across gritty sand that rasped his torso, and collapsed into the shade of bushes unlike any he had ever seen before. Some sort of animal screamed in alarm and branches fluttered as it fled; he could not tell what it was.

In a little, he promised himself, just as soon as he recovered his pressure, he would move on in search of water or a recognizable plant, or risk sampling something at hazard, or . . .

But he did not. After his exertions, cresh had him in its deadly grip, and he departed into a world of dreams compound of memory, so that the solid ground under him seemed to rock and toss like the ocean at the climax of the storm. He did not even have the energy to moan.

From the briq Skilluck saw him fall, and let go the spyglass with a curse, and likewise slumped to his full length. The pitiless sun beat down and, all unheeding, Tempestamer went on gulping weed to cram her monstrous maw.

# 2

He was looking at himself.

Wellearn cried out. He had seen his reflection before, but only in still water, which meant he should be lying down on the bank of a pool. Every sense informed him he was in fact sitting up. Yet his image was confronting him. He was certain it must be confect of dreamness.

Suddenly it swerved aside and vanished. Struggling to accept he was not after all lost in sickness-spawned delirium, he discovered he was now seeing two people taller, slimmer, and with paler mantles than his own folk: a grave elderly man and a most attractive girl.

The former said something Wellearn did not quite grasp, though a tantalizing hint of meaning came across. Then, touching his mandibles with one claw, he said, "Shash!"

Imitating him, the girl said, "Embery!"

Clearly those were their names. Wellearn uttered his own, followed by greetings in his native speech. Meeting no reaction, he switched to others, and as soon as he tried Ancient Forbish Embery exclaimed in amazement.

"Why, you speak what we do!" she said, her accent strange but her words recognizable.

How then could Wellearn have failed to understand before? And now again, as she said something too rapid to follow?

"The language changes," Shash said slowly and clearly. "It has been a score-of-score years since our ancestors settled here. Use only the oldest forms. Wellearn, you comprehend?"

"Very well!"

"Do you remember your voyage hither?"

"The greater part of it." But where was here? Wellearn looked about him, realizing for the first time that he was in a noble house. Never had he seen such magnificent bravetrees—except they weren't exactly bravetrees—or such a marvelous array of secondary plants. Had he been hungry, which to his amazement he was not, he would at once have asked to sample the delicious-looking fruits and funqi which surrounded him. Light slanted through gaps between the boles, which offered glimpses of what looked like a great city. The air was at high pressure and very warm, though not so oppressive as when he swam ashore, and the scents borne on it were absolutely unfamiliar. But one matter must take precedence over the curiosity that filled him.

"My companions! Did you save them too?"

"Oh, yes. They are sicker than you, but we hope to cure them soon."

"But I had cresh . . ." Wellearn hesitated. In his people's knowledge there was no remedy for that affliction. Sometimes it went away of its own accord, no one knew why; more often its victims were permanently crippled.

"No longer. You saw for yourself. Where are the marks?"

"I saw," Wellearn agreed slowly. "But I didn't understand."

"Ah. Embery, show him again."

This time he was able to make out how it happened. She held up a large disc, very shiny, which gave back his reflection. Touching it diffidently, he discerned a peculiar coolness.

"Metal?" he ventured.

"Of course. But your people understand metal and glass, surely? We found a telescope on your briq, as good as our own."

"Captain Skilluck got it in trade," Wellearn muttered. "I can't say where it was made."

"Do you not know and use fire?" Shash demanded in surprise.

"Of course, but in our country there is little fuel and it's too precious to be used for melting rocks. Long ago the weather, they say, was warmer, but now in winter the sea freezes along our coasts, and then it's our only means of staying alive."

"Winter," Embery repeated thoughtfully. "That must be what we read about in the scriptures, the time of great cold which happens once a year and lasts many score days."

*And yearly it grows longer* . . . Wellearn suppressed a pang of envy. What a privilege to live in latitudes where winter never came! He had heard tales about such places from boastful old seafarers, but he had never expected to wind up in one on his maiden voyage.

Yet those same travelers always claimed that they found something grand in the country of their budding, something noble and challenging about its harsh landscape. He must not think of *worse* and *better* until he knew much more.

"May I see my companions?" he requested.

"Certainly, if you're fit enough," Shash answered. "Can you stand?"

Wellearn concentrated on forcing himself upright. He managed it, though he could not regain his normal height. Even had he done so, he would still have been overtopped by these strangers, who must be as tall as mythical Jing—or maybe not quite, for he was said to have been taller than anybody.

"Let me help you," Embery offered, moving to support him. Contact with her was very pleasant. He wondered what the local customs were concerning mating. The Wego themselves welcomed visitors in the hope that outcrossing would bring more and healthier children, for they were barely keeping up their numbers, and he had been told that many foreign peoples felt the same. But it was too soon to think of such matters.

In an adjacent bower Skilluck lay in a crotch made comfortable with masses of reddish purple mosh; he was still not alert but the creshmarks were fading from his mantle. Others beyond held Strongrip, Sharprong, and Blestar, who was visibly the worst affected.

"I've never seen such a severe case," sighed Shash. "One could almost imagine he had weakened himself deliberately."

Wellearn nearly admitted that in fact he had. It was the custom of chaplains, in face of danger, to fast in the hope of being sent a vision from the stars that would save them and their comrades. There was no recorded instance of it happening, but the habit endured.

These people, though, might have no faith in visions, and he did not wish them to mock the strangers who had fallen among them. Instead he voiced a question that was burning in his mind.

"What manner of place is this?"

"A healing-house," Shash replied, and added wonderingly, "Do they not have such in your country?"

"A great house like this, solely for sick people? Oh, no! We're lucky to have enough for those who are well. Sometimes they die, and the occupants must take refuge in caves, or pile up rocks for shelter . . . I'm amazed! When we arrived in the bay, we thought this region was uninhabited!"

"Ah, you were the wrong side of the cape. People rarely visit that bay except for glassmakers needing sand or fisherfolk like the ones who spotted your briq."

"Tempestamer!" Wellearn clenched his claws. "What of her?"

"We have small knowledge of matters of the sea, but we have guarded against her wandering off by fixing strong cables across the mouth of the bay. However, she's so huge . . . Will it be long before she needs to feed again? She's practically cleared the bay of weed."

"I'm afraid you'll have to ask the captain. Usually she only feeds by night as she swims along, but she must have been half-starved after the storm that drove us here."

"Hope then that the captain recovers shortly. "We're doing our utmost for him. Look, here comes curers with more creshban."

Wellearn turned in the indicated direction, but almost literally while Shash was speaking, it grew dark. He gasped. Then festoons of luminous creepers reacted, faster than any gleamers he was used to, coming up to full brightness nearly before his vision adapted to the lower lightlevel, and he saw two husky youths each bearing a round object like an immense nut. There was a sudden pungent smell, which reminded him of a taste that had haunted his long period of dreamness. Also he recalled terrible hunger, and having to be restrained for fear he might attack those who were holding him . . . But that belonged to the past, and in the present Shash was saying, "You must continue the medicine for several days yet. Drink some more now."

Wellearn complied. The nuts were hollow, and contained a bitter liquid of which he managed a few gulps.

"If we could only plant such nut-trees on a briq!" he muttered.

"It's not their natural juice," said the curer who had given him the drink. He spoke without Shash's deliberateness, but by this time Wellearn was adjusting to the local accent. "It's mixed with sap from half a score of plants."

Visions of saving the lives of countless future mariners bloomed and wilted in Wellearn's imagination. He said grumpily, "And I suppose not one of them grows in the north?"

"Later we can show them to you and let you find out," Shash promised. "But now I think you should return to rest."

"I couldn't! I'm too eager to see the marvels of your city, and meet more of its people!"

"In two or three days' time, perhaps. Not right away."

"May I not at least look out at the city, and question someone about it?"

"I'll oblige him, Father," Embery said, and added self-mockingly, "That is, if he can understand me."

"In my young days," Shash sighed, "people your age were wise enough to know when their elders were giving them advice for their own good . . . Oh, very well! But remember, both of you, that the workings of cresh are insidious, and over-excitement is as fast a route as any into dreamness!"

Embery guided Wellearn to the top of the highest tree in the house, which offered a clear view in all directions. The moon was down and the sky was clouding over in a way that upset his weather-sense, but he was too eager to worry about the risk of a lightning-strike. From here the outline of the city was picked out by glowing creepers and funqi, and he was shaken by its huge extent. It even marched over the crest of a hill inland, beyond which faint redness could be seen.

"That's where the fireworkers live," Embery explained. "They make glass and metal—they made the mirror you've seen. The area is sheltered, the wind almost always carries the smoke away from us, and it's easy to find fuel in that direction. They use vast quantities, you know. Some of their furnaces . . . But you have to see them."

Over and over she said the same, when describing the outlying farms, the giant nets which fish-hunters hurled by means of weights and long poles far out to sea from the nearby capes and islands, the work of those who bred mounts and draftimals—"like your briq," she added merrily, "only smaller and going on land!"—those who trained new houses to replace old ones or spread the city on fresh ground, and more and more until Wellearn could scarcely contain himself. How desperately he wanted to explore every nook of—"

"I haven't asked your city's name!" he exclaimed.

"Hearthome."

It was apt. "How many people live here, do you know?" he pursued, thinking perhaps not a great number, if each of five sick strangers could be allotted a separate bower, and then yes a great number, if so many extra houses had been sown.

"Nine score-of-scores, I think, though some say ten."

It was unbelievable. The Wego numbered perhaps a fifth as many. Oh, this *must* be a better land to live in!

"But there are far larger cities inland and all along the coast," Embery said. "Many have a score-of-score-of-scores. None is as rich as Hearthome, though."

"Why is that?"

"Because we are the folk who work hardest at discovering new things. Travelers from a moonlong's journey away come to learn from people like my father, and my uncle who lives yonder"—she pointed in a direction diametrically opposite the furnace-glow—"and devotes his time to studying the stars."

Among Wellearn's people the stars were of little save religious interest. During his entire life at home he had seen a clear sky so seldom he could almost count the total. Before the adoption of the northfinder—a creature which, properly pithed, would always seek out the pole—it was said mariners had been guided by the stars on outward voyages. The return, of course, was never a problem; briqs like Tempestamer could be relied on to retrace their course. Though after such a tremendous storm even she . . .

Dismissing such gloomy thoughts, albeit making a firm resolution to utter thanks, just in case, to the ancestors who—according to the chaplains—must have been watching over him during the voyage, he made shift to repeat a traditional Forbish compliment which Blestar had taught him when he was first apprenticed to the trade of interpreter, and of which mention of the stars reminded him.

"Ah!" he said. "Starbeams must shine on Hearthome even when the sky is cloudy!"

"Why not?" Embery returned. "After all, we are honest followers of Jing."

Wellearn drew back, startled.

"But he was only a legend! Tales about him are compound of dreamstuff!"

"Oh, no!" She sounded scandalized. "True, there is a great dream in his scriptures, but even that is in perfect accord with reality. Have you never studied his teaching?"

At the same moment thunder rolled, but it was not the shock to his weather-sense which made Wellearn's mind reel.

"Your father was right after all about my need for rest," he husked. "Kindly lead me back to my bower."

Where he spent long lonely hours wondering what—after teaching and believing all his life that tales about folk who conjured secrets from the stars were mere superstition—Blestar was going to say when he discovered himself in a land where Jing was real.

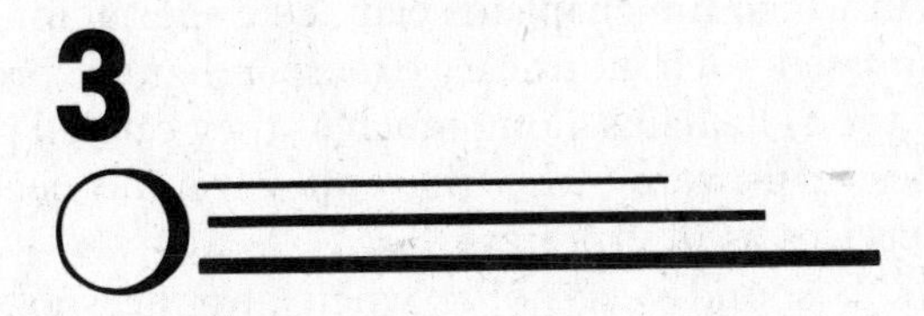

Skilluck's shattered mind crawled back together out of pits of madness and he could see a figure that he recognized. It was Wellearn, addressing him anxiously: "Captain, you're alert again, aren't you?"

Beyond him, unfamiliar plants hanging on what were not exactly bravetrees, immensely tall strangers whose mantles were astonishingly pale . . . They coalesced into a reality, and he was himself and whole and able to reply.

"Tell me where we are, and how Tempestamer is, and how these people treat us."

He was proud of being able to phrase that so soon after regaining normal awareness.

Wellearn complied, but half the time he was almost babbling, plainly having been cozened by the wonders of his first foreign landfall. Skilluck was a mite more cynical; he had spent half his life travelling, and more often than not he had been cheated by the outlanders he tried to deal with. The harsh existence led in northern lands was no school for subtleties of the kind practiced by those who dwelt in southern luxury . . . and it had been obvious, when Tempestamer came to harbor, that she had been driven further than any of the Wego had wandered before, perhaps to the equator itself.

So he merely registered, without reacting to, most of what Wellearn said, until a snatch of it seized his interest.

"—and they have a certain cure for cresh!"

At once Skilluck was totally attentive. Cautiously he said, "It works on everybody, without fail?"

Mantle-crumpled, Wellearn admitted, "Not on all. Blestar, they say, may well not survive. But for me and you, Sharprong and Strongrip, it's proved its worth!"

"Do they understand what we're saying to each other?"

"N-no! And that's something else amazing!" Wellearn blurted. "I have to speak to them in Ancient Forbish!"

Skilluck was unimpressed. His explorations had often brought him to places where relics of that once wide-spread speech survived. Blestar even maintained that many Forbish words had found their way into Wegan, but since they all had to do with fire and stars—things everybody knew about, but in which the chaplains claimed a special interest—sensible people dismissed such notions as mere religious propaganda. Wego seafarers took chaplains along much as they carried pickles: just in case. The best trips were those where they weren't needed.

Of course, their services as interpreters . . .

He forced himself to sound very polite when next he spoke to Wellearn.

"It seems we should behave to our hosts in the friendliest possible fashion. I guess at something we might do for their benefit. How goes it with Tempestamer?"

"That's what I'd just been asked to tell you! She has grazed the bay where we landed clean of weed, and the cables they've strung across its mouth won't hold her much longer, and they fear for their inshore fishing-grounds."

"Let the cables hold but one more day, and I'll put her to sea and feed her such a mawful as will content her for a week. And I'll come back, never fear. A cure for cresh—now that's something worth making a storm-tossed voyage for!"

"There's more," Wellearn said after a pause.

"So tell me about it! Anything we can trade for, I want to hear!"

"I'm not sure it's the sort of thing one can trade," Wellearn said. "But . . . Well, these people have shown me Jing's original scriptures. Or not exactly the originals, which might rot, but accurate copies. And they tell about how the stars are fire and our world will one day go for fuel to make the sun brighter and ourselves with it unless we—"

Skilluck had heard enough. He said as kindly as he could, "Boy, your brush with cresh has affected your perceptions. I counsel you to concentrate on growing up. A little worldly wisdom would do wonders for you."

Wellearn bridled. "Captain, do you know Forbish?"

"I've never taken lessons, if that's what you mean!"

"I have! And the documents I've been shown while you were lying sick have satisfied me that Jing was real!"

Worse and worse . . . Skilluck forced himself to an upright position. He said as emphatically as he could, "Since you oblige me to prove that our people are not all crazy, tell our hosts that I shall at once reclaim command of Tempestamer!"

"But you're not fit!"

"Let me be the judge of that!" Skilluck was struggling to bring his pads under control. "I must—"

But his pressure failed him. He was compelled to slump back to a sitting position, whence he glared at Wellearn as though it were the boy's fault he was so weak.

There was a rapid exchange in Forbish, and Wellearn stated authoritatively, "Shash is the curer-in-chief here. He says you must drink creshban for at least another day before you leave this healing-house."

With a trace of mischief in his tone, he added, "I didn't tell him that was how long you already estimated would be necessary."

At home, mocking his briq-captain in that way would have led to punishment—perhaps lasting punishment, such as having one of his tubules punctured where it would never heal. Since arrival here, though, Wellearn had regretted his oath of fealty, and decided that if all else failed, he could put himself under the protection of the Hearthomers. What did he have to look forward to if he went back to Ushere? More and more hunger, more and more misery! He had never seen cresh on land, as he had told Skilluck, but he had seen old folk lose their minds, reduced to such a state that they scarcely reacted except when they were fed like hoverchicks or barqlings, or when some young'un was brought to them to be mated because a wise'un claimed there was still virtue in that line despite appearances. It had been happening to Wellearn since it became obvious that he was among the lucky bright few, and there were no memories so revolting in his short life as those which reminded him of the foul mindless gropings he had undergone with starvation-crazy ancients. Not one—praise the stars!—of his encounters had so far led to offspring, but if he went home he could certainly be compelled to do the same again, and once the smell and touch took over . . .

He shuddered. And wondered much about the nature of the stars which could dictate so cruel a doom for a person as well intentioned as himself, then pay him back—for it seemed to him to be a reward—with the gentle sweetness of Embery. She had received him twice already, and her father thoroughly approved, for as he said, "We too in this delicious land are plagued by forces we don't understand, and it has been nearly a score of years since one of our family bred true: myself with the lady who gave me Embery and died."

What, on the other claw, they did understand had not yet ceased to astonish him.

Leaving Skilluck's bower, he was overcome by memory.

. . . Behind the inland hills, a valley lined with smoke-blackened rock; heaps of charcoal, even blacker, surrounding cone-shaped furnaces; piles of sand and unknown minerals, green and brown and white and red; sober folk all of whose names ended in -fire, claiming spiritual if not physical descent from Jing's legendary friend who lived underground yet brought the light of heaven forth from a cave—Wellearn knew all the stories, for he had been told them as a child, but later he had been taught to think them fabulous, whereas the Hearthomers took them literally, and by their guidance produced incredible ingots of metal and unbelievable quantities of pure glass. Beyond, a desolation as complete as though a hurricane had laid the vegetation low for a day's walk or more, which was being systematically replanted with oilsap trees that grew quickly and burned hotter than even the best charcoal.

. . . In a fine house overlooking the sea, an elderly couple possessed of tiny miracles in the shape of roundels of glass no larger than a raindrop, but perfectly shaped, through which they showed him the secret structure of plant-stems, funqi, his own skin, immensely magnified, as though a telescope were to look down to the small instead of upward to the large.

. . . In a grove just outside the city, folk who selectively bred meatimals, burrowers, diggets, mounts, draftimals, and a score of creatures he could put no name to, seeking to make them fatter or more docile or in some other way more useful. Their cleanlickers were said to be unique, capable of ridding any wound of its poison within days and making a swift recovery. To take a few of those home to the lands where so often a daring fish-hunter died for his temerity in defying a rasper or a voraq: that would be an achievement! But what to trade for breeding-stock? Did Embery know about northfinders? It seemed not; alas, though, Tempestamer carried only one, which wasn't in brood-phase this year. Besides, they seldom bred true, a problem that plagued the Hearthomer animal-breeders too.

. . . On the highest of the nearby hills, the one Embery had pointed to from the crown of the healing-house, her uncle Chard—older and fatter than his brother—complaining about the difficulty nowadays of studying the stars because the sky was cloudy so much more often than in his youth, and boasting about the knowledge of ice which he had acquired only a few days' journey from Hearthome. There was, apparently, a range of mountains whose peaks were snow-capped even in these latitudes, a fact which dismayed Wellearn, for if the mountains were closer to the sun, how could they be so much colder than the land below? Surrounded by telescopes which made Skilluck's look like a toy, Chard launched into a lengthy lecture concerning reflectivity and absorption, conduction and convection, aurorae and shooting stars and a score of other concepts which Wellearn failed to grasp but which filled him with tantalizing excitement: so much knowledge, so much to be found out!

. . . In a giant tree at the heart of the city, hollowed out deliberately and ornamented with the finest and handsomest secondary plants, a glass container sealed with wax, through which could be glimpsed the original of Jing's scripture. It was uncapped only once in a score of years, so that a fresh copy might be made, but even so it was starting to rot, and next time they planned to make two copies, of which one would be incised on rock instead of perishable wood. In any case, though, by this time the Hearthomers had added many new discoveries to those of Jing and Twig. Everything he was told fascinated Wellearn, and above all he was seized by the tales of the New Star which Chard and Shash and Embery recounted. And, over and over, he pondered the central teaching of Jing's followers: that the stars were fire, and one day the planets would go to feed them, as charcoal was added to a furnace, to make them blaze up anew.

"We do not believe," Embery told him soberly, "that we are here solely to endure until the world falls into a dying sun. We believe it is our duty to escape that fate. Out there are countless worlds; until the end of time, some will remain for us to live on."

"But how can one travel there?" was Wellearn's natural riposte.

"We don't know yet. We mean to find that out."

Everywhere he went Wellearn had a sense of being watched and weighed and scrutinized. Until the captain regained his health, he was the Wego's sole ambassador; he did his best to behave accordingly.

And the day after Skilluck took Tempestamer to sea and brought her back content with what she had engulfed in open water, he found out that his conduct had impressed the citizens. For Shash came to tell the strangers they were invited to a gathering of the general council, to discuss a mutually advantageous proposition.

"What they mean," was Skilluck's cynical comment, "is that they've figured out a way to rob us blind. Well, we have to go along with the deal; we have no choice."

Wellearn bit back his urge to contradict. Time would tell.

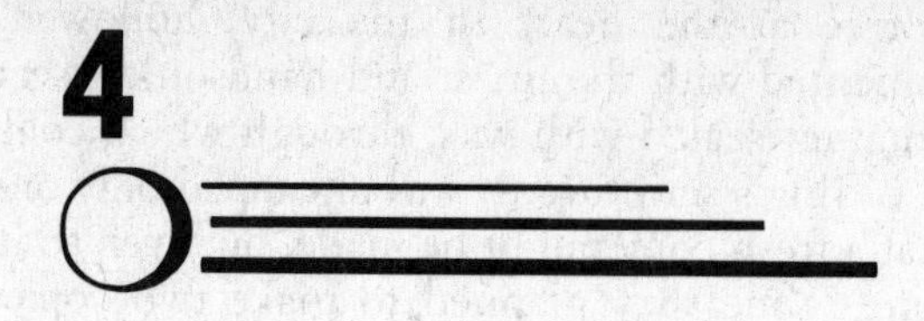

"*I*t grieves us all to learn of the death of our visitor Blestar," Chard said to the assembled council. The foreigners dipped in acknowledgment, although Strongrip and Sharprong were reluctant and only a glare from Skilluck compelled them. Wellearn was still recovering from the shock of having to conduct his first-ever funeral, and in a far-off land at that. But the ceremony had been decent and respectful, even though the Wego tradition of committal to the ocean was unknown here, so Blestar's corpse was fertilizing a stand of white shrubs.

Now it was his duty to interpret some of the most complex statements he had ever heard in any speech. Chard and Shash had given him a rough idea in advance; nonetheless . . . !

Still—he brightened—none of the others spoke Forbish, let alone his modern descendant of it, although he had the distinct impression that Skilluck often understood more than he let on.

At all events, he had the chance to trim the list of the debate. He was determined to do so. He wanted his people and the Hearthomers to be friends; he wanted, in particular, to spend the rest of his own life here . . . not that he would dare risk admitting it. What he hoped was to be appointed resident agent for the Wego, and oversee a regular trade between north and south. So many benefits would flow from that!

But he must concentrate, not rhapsodize. The discussion was likely to be a long one. The Hearthomers took refuge from the hottest part of the day, but the assembly had gathered in late afternoon, and might well continue throughout the succeeding night. He composed his mind and relayed Chard's next remarks.

"We have been told that winters grow colder and longer in your land. Since according to our observations the sun is growing brighter and hotter, we are faced with a paradox."

("What in the world is he on about?" grunted Sharprong. "It doesn't make sense!")

But Wellearn was gripped by Chard's statement and anxiously awaiting what was to follow.

"We know this because we have carefully calibrated the way in which certain substances change after exposure to concentrated sunlight under identical conditions, that's to say, on a completely clear day. Cloudless days, of course, are growing fewer"—and several present glanced anxiously at the sky where yet more thunderheads were brewing—"but we keep up our experiments and we can be nineteen-twentieths sure of our conclusions."

("Is he ever going to come to a point?" was Strongrip's acid reaction.)

"We can only deduce that more solar heat causes more clouds to reflect it and more moisture to fall at the poles as snow, which in turn reflects still more light and heat. At my laboratory the possibility can be demonstrated using a burning-glass and a block of white rock half-covered with soot."

Wellearn had seen that demonstration; he had not wholly understood what he was meant to learn from it, but suddenly a blinding insight dawned on his mind.

("Come on, boy!" Skilluck rasped. "You're falling behind!")

"At a time when mountains here in the equatorial zone can remain snowcapped throughout the year, this is clearly a worrisome situation. Those among us who have never experienced ice and snow may doubt what I say, but I have felt how cold can numb the pads, seen how it affects the plants we here take for granted!"

("Why does he have to go *on* so?" growled Strongrip, but Skilluck silenced him with a glare.)

"We must therefore anticipate a time when mariners from the far north will arrive, not driven hither by a fortunate storm, but because their home has become uninhabitable. Yet this need not be an unmitigated disaster. For if there is one thing we lack, then . . . But I'll leave the rest to Burney."

("I've been told about him!" Wellearn whispered in high excitement. "He's the one-who-answers-questions, their most distinguished administrator! But I never saw him before!")

Burly, yet as tall as his compatriots, Burney expanded to full height as Chard lowered. He uttered a few platitudes about the visitors before picking up Chard's trail.

("I know his sort," Skilluck said contemptuously. "The politer they are, the more you need to brace yourself!")

"What we lack, and in lacking neglect our duty, is access to the oceans!" Burney stated at the top of his resonant voice. "Oh, we've done well by our founders in spreading their teaching across this continent; travel a moonlong overland and you won't find a child of talking age who doesn't grasp at least the rudiments of what Jing bequeathed! But we know there's more to the globe than merely land, don't we? Proof of the fact is that our visitors came to us from a country which can't be reached from here dry-padded!"

("You told them that?" Skilluck snapped at Wellearn. "Oh you threw away a keen prong there!"

("I did nothing of the sort!" Wellearn retorted, stung. "Listen and you'll find out!")

"Suppose, though, we were to combine the knowledge we've garnered with the skills of these strangers," Burney went on. "Suppose the brave seafarers of the Wego could voyage free from fear of cresh; suppose on every trip they carried the knowledge which Jing instructed us to share with everybody everywhere, so that every one of their briqs was equipped not just with a northfinder—I'm sure you've been told of their brilliant development of that creature which can always be relied on to point the same way? Though it does seem," he added with a touch of condescension, "they don't realize that if they really had crossed the equator, as Wellearn appears to imagine, it would reverse itself."

(Amid a ripple of knowing amusement Skilluck fumed, "It doesn't surprise me! After the flattery, the put-down!")

Burney quieted the crowd. "Perhaps that remark was unworthy," he resumed. "At all events, we know these are an adventurous people, who take the utmost care to ensure that when they set out on no matter how risky a voyage they can find their way home by one means or another. Suppose, as I was about to say, they carried not only telescopes useful for sighting a promising landfall, but better ones suitable for studying the sky, and the means to prove to anyone they contacted how right Jing was in what he wrote!"

(Applause . . . but Wellearn had to cede a point to Skilluck when he mused, "So they want to overload our briqs with chaplains worse than Blestar?")

"We therefore offer an exchange!" Burney roared. "I hope Captain Skilluck will accept it! We will share with his folk everything we know—yes, everything!—if the Wego will put their fleet at our disposal every summer for a score of years, to return laden with southern foods and southern seeds and southern tools, after carrying our message to lands as yet unknown! Now this is a grand scheme"—his voice dropped—"and there are countless details to thrash out. But we must first know whether the principle is acceptable."

(Skilluck looked worried. Wellearn whispered, "They do things differently here!"

("That's obvious! *He* never tried to preside at a captains' meeting!")

"I see there are doubts," Burney said after a pause. "Let me add one thing, therefore. Assuming they accept our offer, then—if the winters at Ushere do become intolerable, as we may apparently fear according to what Chard has said—their people can remove hither and settle around the bay where their briq first made landfall. We would welcome them. Are we agreed?"

A roar of enthusiasm went up, and among those who shouted

loudest Wellearn was proud to notice Embery. But Skilluck gave a brusque order.

"Tell him we need time to discuss this idea. Say we will be ready no sooner than tomorrow night!"

Perforce, Wellearn translated, and the assembly dispersed with many sighs.

"It's a trap," said Strongrip for the latest of a score of times. "There must be some snag in it we don't see!"

"I've been everywhere in the city and met many of the most prominent of these people!" Wellearn declared. "They take Jing's teaching seriously—they really do want to spread his knowledge around the globe!"

"That's what frightens me most," grunted Skilluck. "Blestar was bad enough; embriqing with a stranger who has absolute rule over what course I choose is out of the question!"

"That isn't what they have in mind!" Wellearn argued. "These people never travel the oceans—they want to hook on to someone who does, and that could be us!"

"*Budlings!*" Strongrip said, and turned away in disgust.

That was too much for Wellearn. Rising to his maximum height—which, since arriving here, imbibing vast quantities of creshban, and eating the best diet he had ever enjoyed, had noticeably increased—he blasted, "I invoke the judgment of my ancestors in the stars!"

And bared his mandibles, which normally he kept shrouded out of ordinary politeness.

Skilluck said hastily, "Now just a moment, boy—"

"Boy!" Wellearn cut in. "*Boy?* I haven't forgotten my oath of fealty to my captain, but if you can't recognize a man who's just become a man I'll consider it void!"

Following which he opened his claws to full extent, and waited, recklessly exuding combat-stink.

At long last Skilluck said heavily, "It was time, I guess. You're not a young'un anymore. But do you still want to challenge Strongrip?"

"I'd rather we were comrades. But I must. Unless he accepts me for what I am, with all my power of judgment. I did," Wellearn added, "invoke the honor of my ancestors."

There were still creshmarks on Strongrip's mantle, but Wellearn's was clear. Skilluck studied each of them in turn and said finally, "I forbid the challenge. Your ancestors, *young man*, are honored sufficiently by your willingness to utter it. Strongrip, deny what you last said."

He clenched his body into battle posture, mandibles exposed, and concluded, "Or it must be me, not Wellearn, you take on!"

The stench of aggression which had filled the air since Wellearn rose to overtop his opponent provoked reflexes beyond most people's control. Only someone as sober and weather-wise as Skilluck could master his response to it.

Strongrip said gruffly, "He speaks this foreign noise. I admit he knows things I can't."

"Well said, but is he adult, worthy to be our comrade?"

The answer was grumpy and belated, but it came: "I guess so!"

"Then lock claws!"

And evening breeze carried the combat-stink away.

"Captain!" Wellearn whispered as the general council of the Hearthomers reassembled.

"Yes?"

"Did you know I was going to be driven to challenge—"

"Silence, or I'll call you 'boy' again!" But Skilluck was curling with amusement even as he uttered the harsh words. "You haven't finished growing up, you know!"

"I'm doing my best!"

"I noticed. That's why I didn't let Strongrip shred your mantle. He could have, creshmarks or no! So you just bear in mind your talent is for reasoning, not fighting. Leave that sort of thing to us seafarers, because at pith you're a landlubber, aren't you?"

"I—I suppose I am," Wellearn confessed.

"Very well, then. We understand each other. Now translate this. It's exactly what Burney most wants to hear. Begin: 'We can't of course speak for all the briq-captains of the Wego, but we will promote with maximum goodwill the advantages of the agreement you suggest, *provided* that at the end of summer we may take home with us tokens of what benefits may accrue therefrom, such as creshban, better cleanlickers, useful food-seeds, spyglasses and so on. Next spring we'll return with our captains' joint verdict. In the event that it's favorable' —don't look so smug or I'll pray the stars to curse you for being smarter than I thought but not half as smart as you think you are!— 'we shall appoint Wellearn to reside here as our agent and spokesman. Thank you!' "

# 5

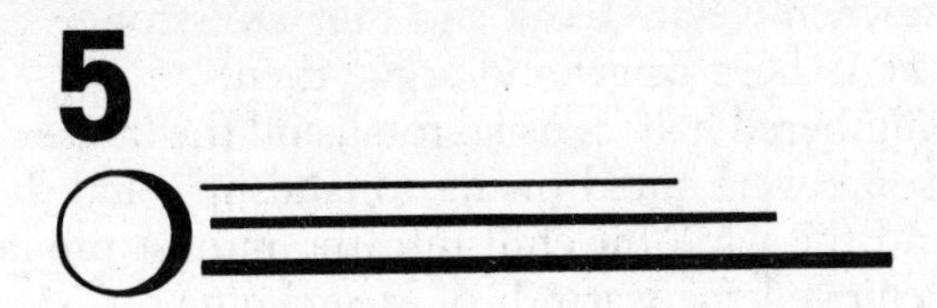

At every summer's end the Wego captains came together for a bragmeet where the wise'uns too old to put to sea might judge whose briq had ventured furthest, who fetched the finest load of fish ashore, who brought the rarest newest goods traded with chance-met strangers. It was the high point not only of their year, but the chaplains' also. For generations the latter's influence had been shrinking, particularly since too many stars fell from the sky for most people to look forward to inhabiting one after death. But when it came to matters of ancient tradition, naturally they were called on to preside.

This meet, though, was different. Now there was no boasting, only mourning. On land things had been bad enough, what with crop-failure, floods and landslips, but at sea they were infinitely worse. Braverrant had not returned albeit her master was Boldare, wily in weatherways. No more had Governature with Gallantrue and Drymantle, nor—next most envied after Tempestamer—Stormock, whose commander had been Cleverule, sole among them to make two-score voyages.

Nor Wavictor, nor Knowater, nor Billowise . . . and even Tempestamer herself had not reported back.

Yet weather-sense warned them: the summer was done. The customary congress must convene.

Frost on every tree, snow on the beach above the tideline, even icefloes—but it was too soon! As Tempestamer closed the last day's gap between her and the waters where she had been broken, uncertainly as though aware something was amiss, Wellearn gazed in horror at the shoreline through drifting mist.

"Captain!" he cried. "Have you ever seen so much ice at this season, or so much fog?"

"Never," answered Skilluck sternly. "maybe what your friends at Hearthome spoke of is coming true."

"I thought—*our* friends . . .?"

"Those who have knowledge sometimes batten on it to gain power," Skilluck said.

"They spoke of partnership, not mastery!"

"What difference, when we are weak and they are strong? Count me the briqs you see at Ushere wharf and argue then!"

Indeed, the fleet numbered half its usual total, and the houses were white with rime and some were tilted owing to landslips, and the sky was dense and gray and the wind bit chill into the inmost tubules of those who lately had enjoyed the warmth of Hearthome.

"What's more, there's nobody to welcome us!" Skilluck blasted, having surveyed the city with his spyglass. "They must have called the bragmeet, giving us up for lost!"

Seizing his goad, he forced Tempestamer to give of her utmost on the final stretch towards her mooring.

Shivering in the branchways, more of the Wego attended the bragmeet than ever in history, and while the wise'uns tried to present the summer's achievements in a flattering light, kept interrupting to ask, "What use is that to us? Can we eat it? Does it help to keep us warm?"

In vain the senior chaplain, by name Knowelkin, strove to maintain formality. The folk mocked the claims of those who had survived the unprecedented summer storms by staying close to home, like Senshower whose Riskall had belied her name by scurrying from inlet to sheltered inlet, like Conqueright who had pledged the reputation of his Catchordes on the chance of garnering vast quantities of fish only to find the schools weren't running where they did. Almost as though they were hungry for news of doom the assembly listened in silence to Toughide and Shrewdesign, who told of icebergs sighted all season long further south than ever known before, fisherfolk driven into midocean clinging to barqs unfit for any but fresh-water work, great trees torn loose by gales and set to drifting with the current, some bearing signs of habitation as though they had formed part of a house, a town or even a city. And when eventually they did make landfall, they reported, they found long tracts of coast abandoned to the dirq and fosq, the icefaw and snowbelong, whose normal range was half-a-score days' journey poleward.

"What we brought home from our voyage," Toughide concluded soberly, "was no better than what we'd have got had we made due north."

The company shifted uneasily, but the chaplains preened. Now the meeting had settled down, they could remind themselves how hunger and anxiety invariably drove folk back to the faith and customs of their ancestors.

But suddenly a roar cut through the soughing of icy wind among the boughs.

"Who *dared* to summon a bragmeet without Skilluck? What misbudded moron told you Tempestamer would not ride out the worst of storms? Let him stand forth who called the meet before I came!"

And the furious captain stomped into the center of the gathering, healthy-tall—taller than any Wego mariner in living memory—followed by Strongrip and Sharprong and someone whom the company had difficulty in recognizing: Wellearn. But a Wellearn transformed, bigger, huskier, and infinitely more self-confident than the callow youth who had set forth in spring.

Knowelkin shrank reflexively at Skilluck's intrusion, all the more because he and his companions were so obviously in good fettle. The captain fixed him with a glare.

"You!" he said accusingly. "*You* took it on yourself to say I must be given up for lost!"

"Not I!" the chaplain babbled, casting around for a way of escape, for combat-stink from Skilluck filled the air and he was weakened by fasting.

"Liar!" hurled Toughide. "You insisted on the meet being held when we captains said to wait a while! You understand the calendar—you know the normal end of summer!"

"But summer this year ended early! Surely a skilled seafarer—"

"We've been in latitudes where there is no winter!" Wellearn shouted.

"That's right!" Skilluck set himself back on his pads, claws poised. "Nor any hunger, either! Look at us! Think we're sick—weak—crazy—dreamlost? See any creshmarks on us? But I see one on you!" Reaching out quicker than Knowelkin could dodge, he nipped the chaplain's mantle and provoked a squeal of pain.

"Thought so," the captain said with satisfaction. "Always the way, isn't it? When things get hard, instead of reasoning and working, you prefer to retreat into dreamness! Strongrip, make him drink a dose of creshban and see sense!"

"Best thing any briq from Ushere ever carried home," the seaman grunted, holding aloft a Hearthomer nutshell. "A certain remedy for cresh!"

That provoked a stir of excitement among the crowd.

"But," Strongrip continued, "do you think we should waste it on this idiot? After all, he's been starving himself like Blestar—deliberately—and Blestar was the only one of us it didn't save!"

"That's a point," said Skilluck ruminatively. "Very well, let them be the ones to go without. It'd be a fit punishment for the way they've insulted us."

"You have a cure for cresh?" Knowelkin whispered, voicing what all present wanted to hear.

"Not we, but allies that we've made in the far south. They've offered us as much as we need—they have plenty!—in return for letting some of their wise'uns travel on our briqs to spread their knowledge. And don't think creshban is the only trick they have under their mantles! *Oh* no! We've brought back marvels which . . . But move over, you! Senior chaplain or not, you're a dreamsick fool and it's your own fault and Wellearn is worth a score like you! *Move,* before I rip your mantle into tatters!"

For an instant it seemed that Knowelkin would defy the captain out of pride; then he humbly crumpled to half normal height and padded aside. Wellearn found himself at a loss. Was he really meant to take over and preside at a bragmeet, youth that he was?

"Well, go on!" Skilluck rasped. "Or I'll start thinking you're as silly as Knowelkin! Speak out!"

"What shall I tell them?"

"Everything! Everything! I never imagined things would come to so grievous a pass this year. Next year maybe, or the year after . . . but it's upon us, and the land is in the claw of ice, and if another summer comes it could be our last chance to move to friendly country. The briqs which survive may already not be enough to shift us all! Hadn't you thought of that?"

Wellearn hadn't, but he pretended, and gave a grave nod of acquiescence as he took over the spot vacated by Knowelkin. After so long among the Hearthomers he felt like a giant compared to his own people . . . as tall as Jing!

And that gave him his opening. Maintaining his maximum height, trying to imitate in Wegan the style and manner of Burney and others who addressed council meetings at Hearthome, he began.

"Teachers like Knowelkin—and even my late mentor Blestar who has gone, let's hope, to make a star shine brighter!—told us to believe there never was a real person called Jing! They've encouraged us to be obedient and small-minded by saying there never was a man who understood the stars and made their nature manifest by transforming dull rock into marvelous new substances! With the evidence of spyglasses and metal blades to contradict it, we chose to accept this nonsense!

"But we have met followers of Jing who actually possess his scriptures, and I've read them and copied extracts for our use! Thanks to what Jing taught, the city of Hearthome is the richest on its continent! By studying Jing's principles the folk there have arrived at creshban and other medicines—they've bred mounts that go on land as our briqs swim the sea" *(thank you, Embery!* he added silently)"—they live in houses which make ours look like hovels—they have such wealth that a bunch of sick seafarers stranded there by accident might each repose in his own bower, recovering with the aid of a cure their own folk might not need in five-score years of which they yet keep stock for chance-come travelers . . ."

Gradually, as he talked, Wellearn let himself be taken over by imagination, sure that in his present state of vitality it would not shade into mere dreamness. He painted a picture of a glorious future to grow from the joint seed of the Hearthomers and the Wego. Some of his audience, he noted with dismay, had ceased to listen the moment he spoke of Jing as a real person; others, however, less parched by cold and shrunken by privation, were clinging with their remaining strength to wisps of hope.

Concentrating on the latter, he concluded with a splendid peroration that sent echoes ringing among the rigid branches and ice-stiffened foliage.

Yet only a few of his hearers clacked their claws, and after a pause Toughide said, "So you're asking us to pile aboard our remaining briqs and set forth now?"

"Of course not!" Skilluck roared. "But next year could see our last and only chance to move to a warm and welcoming land! If you won't hark to the boy—excuse me, Wellearn!—if you won't hark to the *young man*, then trust in me who came home after Knowelkin told you I was dead!"

For a moment Wellearn thought his forcefulness had won the crowd over, but the idea of quitting the land where the Wego had lived since time immemorial was too great to be digested all at once, and the assembly dispersed without reaching a decision. Vastly disappointed, Wellearn slumped to four-fifths height while watching them depart.

"Excellently done," said Skilluck softly at his side.

"I thought I'd failed!" Wellearn countered. "At any rate I don't see them clustering around us to vote Tempestamer the wise'uns' prize for the past summer!"

"Oh—*prizes!*" Skilluck said contemptuously. "To be remembered in a score-of-score years: that's something else. Until I saw how few briqs had made it back to Ushere, all I could think of was how the Hearthomers might cheat us. Now I've felt in my tubules how right they are about the grip of ice. It's time for a heroic gesture, and since someone's got to make one, it might as well be us. If we can get enough of the folk to emigrate next spring, one day they'll talk of us as we do of Jing. I felt this as truth. I couldn't have expressed it. You did. That's why I say you made a great success of it."

"Captain," Wellearn muttered, "I never respected anything so much before as your present honesty. I'm glad to find I guessed right after all, but what you've just said—"

"Save it," Skilluck broke in. "And don't worry about persuading the rest of the folk around to our course. A few score days of cold and hunger will take care of that."

"I wish I could share your optimism," Wellearn sighed. "Yet I greatly fear that some of those who refused to listen did so not because they suspected us of lying, but because misery has already taken them past the reach of reason."

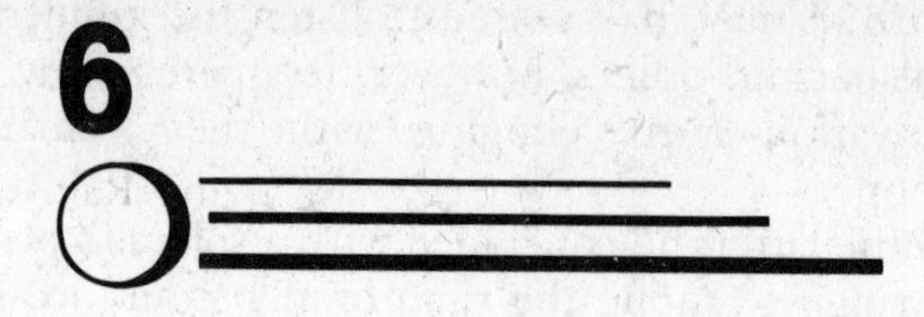

"Uncle," Embery said musingly to Chard, "do you think Wellearn will come back?"

Grousing at the annual need to adjust the mountings of his telescopes because the branches they rested on had swollen in the rainy season, her fat and fussy uncle finally pronounced himself satisfied with the work of his apprentices. Since it was again too cloudy at the zenith for serious star-study, he ordered the instruments to be trained on the skyline.

"Hush, girl," he said absently. "In a little I can show you moon-rise like you never saw it before."

"But *do* you?" Embery persisted.

"With all the joint advantages that will flow from our alliance with his folk, why not?"

"Father says he doesn't think the captain trusted us."

"Just as long as that briq carried them home safely—and who's to say she couldn't if she lived out the awful storm which drove her here?—then you may rely on the powers of persuasion displayed by your young friend to bring more of their fleet here, and, if nothing else, the captain's greed . . . Ah, thank you!"—to the senior apprentice for advising him that the first telescope was properly set. "Now, my dear, come here. Before moon-rise, because this direction is fairly clear, I'd like to show you what they used to call the New Star. Ever since, more than a score-of-score years ago—"

Embery stamped her pad. "Uncle, I'm not some ignorant youngling from the city school, you know!"

He blinked at her. "No need to be offensive, niece! Of course I know you've looked at it before, but I want to share a new discovery with you, and I don't believe you've understood half the implications of what I've tried to teach you."

"I have so!"

"Then tell me how the world can grow cooler even though the sun seems to be getting warmer—and I've worked out why!"

"For the same reason it's better in full sunlight to have a light mantle than a dark one! Reflection!"

But Embery's mood changed even before he could compliment her on a lesson well remembered, and she said, "You think you've worked out why? You never told me *that!* Go on!"

And she cuddled up alongside him much as she used to do when she was barely strong enough to stand upright, so that he had to lift her to the ocular of his telescopes.

Chuckling, Chard said, "That's more like my Baby Rainbow! I used to call you that, you know, until you took offense and said it was ridiculous to use the name of Jing's lady—"

"I still think so!" she interrupted. "Come to the sharp end of the prong!"

"Very well." Chard settled back comfortably. "My line of reasoning goes this way. We have seen, in the place of the so-called New Star, nothing but a cloud of bright gas for many generations. Yet every now and then we have recorded a sort of *wave* passing through it, and comparison of notes made recently with those made just after the first proper telescopes were constructed allows us to hypothesize that the sudden addition of a large amount of new fuel to the fire of a star causes an outburst of colossal proportions, as when one drops a boulder into shallow water. These are splashes!"

"You've told me this before!" Embery complained.

"Ah—but what about the matter that gets splashed?"

She thought about that for a little. Eventually she said, frowning with concentration, "It must spread out, over huge distances. And it must get thinner as it goes."

"Correct! Even so . . . ?"

"Even so, when it reaches another star—Oh!" She stared upright in excitement. "You think a splash from the New Star has got this far?"

"It would explain a lot of things," Chard murmured, looking smugger than an astronomer of his age and distinction had any right to. "Above all, it would explain very well indeed why there are more and more stars falling from heaven—which of course aren't actually stars—at the same time as the sun is growing warmer."

"But this could be terrible!" Embery exclaimed. "Because the matter must have spread out very thin on its way here, so if it's only the first bit that's got to us, then—"

"There may be more to come," Chard confirmed. "And we have no way of telling whether there will be so much that it screens our sunlight, or enough to heat up the sun so that ice will melt again, or as much as we've had already with nothing to follow. Whatever happens, though, the Wego are due for the most appalling trouble. So could we be if the ice melted after forming, all at once. We'd need their help to rescue us if the level of the sea rose. Who knows how much water has already been frozen up? But we keep hearing from the fisherfolk that they have to go further and further every year to cast their nets deep . . . Oh, every way it makes sense to ally ourselves with the Wego! Whether they agree is another matter. I mean, they may be as ignorant of the effects of a polar melting as most of our own folk are of the effects of freezing! When I climbed the Snowcap Range . . ."

Embery sighed. Her uncle was about to launch into one of his self-congratulatory reminiscences. There was no hope of hearing more, as yet, about his new theory, so it would be best to distract him.

"Isn't it time for me to look through the telescope?" she offered.

"Of course! Of course! And I want you particularly to take note of—"

He bustled about, issuing orders to the apprentices, but they were superfluous; all her life, Embery had been accustomed to sighting and using a telescope. She applied her eyes.

And tensed. The tropical night had not yet fallen; the sun, behind a patch of western cloud, still turned the sky to blue. In a few moments it would vanish, but for the time being its rays slanted across the ocean.

"That's not the New Star rising, or the moon either!" she exclaimed.

"Patience, my dear!" said Chard indulgently. "Wait for nightfall. Then, just above the horizon—"

"Not above! *On!*"

"Are you sure?"

"Oh, don't be so silly! Look, *quickly!*"

Sliding aside, she almost dragged him into position behind the eyepiece.

After a long pause he said, "My dear, I owe you an apology."

Upside-down in his field of vision was something like a giant fang, neither white nor blue nor green but a shade between all three.

"I wish them well in the far north," he muttered. "That's all I can say."

"Why?" Embery was almost crying.

"I never saw one before, but I recognize it from the descriptions I've read and heard." Chard glanced at his niece. "I think you must have done the same."

"Yes, but I was so much hoping you would say I'm wrong!" Embery clenched her claws. "Is it—"

"I'm very much afraid it must be. Further south than anybody has ever met one: that's an iceberg."

"You mocked me publicly before the folk!" charged Knowelkin.

A sky full of racing black clouds leaned over Ushere; a bitter gale lashed the wharf, the harbor; snow turning to hail battered land and water like a forestful of spongids uttering their pellets of spawn in an evil season. Behind him ranged the muster of surviving chaplains: those who sacrificed bulk to tallness, who had been infuriated when Skilluck and his companions overtopped them. And all of them were exuding combat-stink of such loathsomeness that even the frigid blast of the wind did not suffice to protect those nearby.

What could protect anybody in the clutch of this terrible winter, when not even seaqs or dugonqs were to be trapped beneath the ice because there were no floes thin enough to stab through, when icefaws and snowbelongs rampaged into the middle of Ushere?

The chaplains said: the stars. But nobody had seen a star in four-score days . . .

Somewhat reduced from the great height they had attained at Hearthome, Skilluck and his comrades confronted them. The crew were at the wharf perforce, for Tempestamer had to be taken to sea once in a while to eat, there being no pickled weed or fish to spare from feeding folk. To the surprise and satisfaction of his captain, Wellearn too had volunteered to turn out, regarding himself now as a full member of the company.

More than one briq was unlikely to live until spring, being already too weak to face open water thanks to the neglect of her captain, but Tempestamer remained fat and energetic, and they meant to ensure she stayed that way.

"Who did the insulting?" Skilluck rumbled, rising to the bait. "Who declared that Tempestamer was too weak to swim through storms? Who said I was too bad a navigator to find a way home?"

"Who said we were crazy to trust to visions sent by the stars?" Knowelkin countered. "Who brought a benefit for all the folk and now is keeping it himself?"

"We're doling out our creshban to those most in need!" roared Sharprong, clenching into fighting posture. "Those who have nothing to offer the folk may mock—like *you!*—and we shan't care!"

"Scores will! Scores-of-scores! You're traitors to the Wego!" Knowelkin shrieked.

Standing a little apart, Wellearn suddenly realized what made the chaplains' stink so harsh: fanaticism. They were so far into the maw of dreamness, reason would not convince them. And already they had deranged Skilluck, normally so self-controlled . . .

"Captain!" he shouted. "They've taken the windward of us! Shift round—*shift round or they will make us mad!*"

Startled, Skilluck shook himself as though emerging on land after a swim. "You're right, by Jing!" he exclaimed. "Sharprong! Strongrip! *Quickly!* Follow Wellearn!"

And with short but menacing strides they marched into the snap of the gale before turning and confronting the chaplains anew.

That put a very different color on the mantle of the situation. The exudate of righteous anger was accessible to those not breathing their own wafts of madness. It made the chaplains think again.

"How fragile is our sanity!" Wellearn whispered, not meaning anyone to hear.

"Once more you're ahead of the rest of us," Skilluck muttered. "But most of them are well and truly dreamlost!"

"Dreamlost?" Wellearn cried, straining to make himself heard against the howling of the wind. "No! They're frightened! And I'll tell you why! It's because if we steer the only sensible course and remove to Hearthome, they'll meet people who can contradict their lies about Jing!"

Skilluck clutched at his mantle. "If you provoke them any more—"

"They outnumber us," Wellearn returned softly. "Surely our best hope is to make them quarrel among themselves?"

Skilluck's eye widened. "Neat!" he approved, and went on at the top of his voice.

"That's right! Now suppose instead of Knowelkin, someone like *you*, Lovirture, or *you*, Grandirection, had been in charge of the bragmeet: you'd not have insulted me, would you? You wouldn't be so afraid of meeting strangers, either, I'm sure!"

"Of course not!" they both exclaimed.

"Nonsense!" Knowelkin roared, turning on them. It very probably was nonsense, but all their tempers were set to snap like saplings in the path of a gigant.

Grandirection, whom Skilluck had picked on because he was visibly near breaking-point, immediately raised his claws and bared his mandibles and began to pad around Knowelkin seeking an opening for attack. In the meantime, several people had emerged from nearby houses and were gazing in wide-eyed astonishment at these chaplains making ready to disgrace their calling.

"Now's our chance," Skilluck whispered. "And—and thank you, Wellearn! Much more of this, and I'll come to think you *are* as smart as you imagine!"

A few moments later, the crew were able to pry Tempestamer's cold-stiff tentacles free of their mooring and goad her towards open water. Such was the violence of the wind, she was already tossing before she quit the harbor-mouth.

"What a disgusting spectacle that was!" shouted Wellearn against the blast.

"There's nothing wrong with them that a mawful of decent food wouldn't cure," Skilluck replied. "If only more of the Hearthomer seeds had taken . . . !"

"How could they," Wellearn sighed, "in a year when even the pumptrees are chill?"

They stood in a grove at the center of Ushere; it had been because of them that the Wego made their original decision to settle here, rather than the harbor, which was like half a score others nearby. Their taproots were known to reach an underwater spring, far below the level where a storm could stir the sea, which brought heat from deep-lying rocks. Carefully pierced and plugged, they furnished a year-round supply of warm fresh water. It was said that in the old days the chaplains denied that heat could come from any source except the sun, holding the stars to be cool because the spirits of the righteous dead departed thither after separating from the unrighteous in the moon—whose phases showed the division taking place—and that it had been the start of their decline when brave divers wearing capsutes under their mantles for a store of air reported that the sea-bed was warmer than the surface at this spot . . . a fact for which they had no explanation.

Accordingly the seeds and spawn from Hearthome, all of secondary and parasitic or symbiotic plants, had been carefully planted in crevices of pumptree bark, not because that was the species most resembling their usual hosts but because they were the only trees likely to remain sap-swollen.

However, the diet didn't suit the strangers; some died off completely, some seemed to be lying dormant, and of those which had sprouted, none yielded the harvest that could be relied on at Hearthome.

Still, any extra nourishment was welcome . . .

Already, though, as the chaplains bore witness, voices were being raised against Skilluck and his crew, blaming them for what was not in their control: bringing the wrong sort of seeds, not insisting on being given more creshban, wasting space on spyglasses and articles of metal instead of food. It would be hard to keep their tempers in face of such taunting. Nonetheless it must be done. No other plan made sense than removal to Hearthome; no briq but Tempestamer could lead the fleet thither. There were no charts for her storm-distorted course.

So she must be fit and lively four-score days from now. Or they were doomed.

## 7

*F*or a while longer the fact that Skilluck and his comrades—surviving on what they had stored during their season of good eating but otherwise, save mentally, in little better shape than anyone else—struggled along the frost-rimed branchways to deliver doses of creshban, together with what scraps of fruit or leaf or funqi-pulp their exotic plantings on the pumptrees yielded, counted heavily in their favor, while the chaplains, who had disgraced themselves by their affray on the wharf, lost countenance.

Then the creshban started to run out, while the number of victims multiplied, and even some who had declared support for the idea of emigration took to accusing Skilluck of lavishing the medicine on himself at others' expense. By that stage it was useless to argue. People were taking leave of rationality and slumping into stupor from which a few at least would never revive.

The sole consolation was that, undernourished and sickly as they were, none of the Wego any longer had the energy for fighting. But that meant, of course, they would have none to prepare for a mass exodus when the weather broke, either.

"Why did we come home?" Wellearn mourned more than once. But Skilluck strictly reprimanded him.

"We had no way of knowing how bad this winter was to be! Nor would we have felt easy in our minds had we abandoned our folk to face it without help!"

"At least we needn't have found out until next summer," Sharprong grumbled.

"By which time our kindred and our young'uns could have been dead! As things are, we stand some slender hope of keeping a clawful of the folk alive."

"Slender . . ." Strongrip muttered, gazing at the drifts which blizzard after day-long blizzard had piled against the bravetrees. Many upper branches and almost all their fronds had frozen so hard the wind could snap them off, and every gust was greeted with their brittle tinkling.

"Next time we take Tempestamer to sea we'll hang a net while she feeds," Skilluck sighed. "Even a load of sour weed could save another briq or two."

"Captain, you can't keep our fleet in being single-clawed!" Strongrip began. Skilluck silenced him with a glare.

"Name me another captain who's fit enough to help?"

There was a dismal pause. At length Wellearn ventured, "Maybe Toughide?"

"One might well try him, sure. Wait on him and ask if he will join us. If he won't, I'll still do what I can to feed his briq, or anyone's!" Skilluck stamped his pad. "How many summers to catch and pith and train the briqs we need to replace Stormock and Billowise and the rest? For all we know, there may not *be* another summer!"

So it was done, and Toughide goaded his weak and weary Watereign forth in Tempestamer's wake the next clear day, and though she was less elegantly pithed, a lucky mawful of fish revived her and he was able to make it back to shore with a mass of weed caught on curved prongs, lacking nets such as Skilluck had preserved.

When it was noised abroad that those briqs too feeble to risk the winter ocean were nonetheless receiving fodder, a few score folk made their way to the wharf and watched the spectacle in silence. It was unprecedented. Never in history had any captain of the Wego acted to aid his rivals; rather, he should frustrate them so they would not win the wise'uns' prize.

It was a new strange thing. The onlookers dispersed and reported it. Next time the weather cleared not two but seven briqs put out: Riskall came, and Catchordes, and Shrewdesign's Neverest, and two more so young their captains had not named them, which seemed barely strong enough to quit the harbor.

Towards these last Tempestamer behaved most strangely, for she slowed her pace instead of exulting in the water, and kept them in her lee as though they were of her own budding. By now Wellearn was informed concerning the manner of pithing and breaking a briq, and therefore he exclaimed in amazement.

"Captain, had I known when I first joined your crew that you'd left Tempestamer with *those* nerves intact . . . !"

He left the rest unsaid. There was no need to explain he meant the nerves governing a briq's response to briqlings. It was generally held to be a recipe for disaster to do as Skulluck had done, for such a briq might fall in with a wild herd and become ungovernable.

Dryly Skilluck made reply, "Most likely my Tempestamer would cut younglings out of the herd without orders and drive them home with her! It's something I've always wanted to try. Is she not huger, even now, than any wild'un?"

It was true. There was no record, not even any legend, of a briq's surpassing her, and she was still growing despite the dreadful winter.

"We'll find a wild herd off the coast near Hearthome," said Skilluck dreamily. "We'll let her pick the young'uns she personally likes. We'll raise such a fleet as will conquer any ocean, any season. Before my time expires, I hope to see the Wego travel round the globe!"

"Captain!" said Strongrip with a sharp reproof. "We have to live until the summer first!"

"Agreed, agreed," the captain sighed, and raised his spyglass to search for weed among the random floes.

They returned with not only weed but plumpfish, for Tempestamer sensed a school of them and patiently circled until they had to approach the surface again where she and her companions could feed and nets haul up what was left. The other captains were loud in admiration, and Skilluck sized his chance to exact a pledge: were spring to be delayed, were the fields to lie under frost a moonlong past usual, they would take aboard whomever of the Wego wished to come and head south, following Tempestamer.

Hearing the vow taken, Wellearn almost collapsed from relief.

"Captain, we're saved!" he whispered.

"Didn't I tell you? A few score days of hunger and cold, and then a mawful of good food . . . But we aren't on course yet. So many of us are too lost in dreamness to work out what's best for our salvation."

For at least a while, though, it seemed Wellearn's prediction was assured of fulfillment. Revived by the gift of fish, half the Wego came to watch the next departure of the fleet—and help carve up the carcass of a briq that had died at her moorings, a tragedy for her captain but valuable food to the folk—and among them were Knowelkin and Grandirection, who had composed their quarrel. They made shift to chant a star-blessing on the departing briqs, and the crowd settled into familiar responses even though a few budlings, too young to have seen a clear sky, were heard to ask fretfully what stars might be.

Two calm days followed, and the nets were quickly filled, suggesting that warm water was working up from the south in earnest of springtime and bringing bounty with it.

But on the fleet's last night before returning home a fiery prong stabbed out of heaven and exploded on a berg, raising a wall of water high enough to swamp the smallest briq. There was a thunderclap, followed by a cascade of ice-chips, but this was not hail and that had not been lightning.

Tempestamer gave forth a cry such as no tame briq had ever been heard to utter, and for hours ran out of control, seeking the lost young'un. Although Skilluck finally mastered her again, and set course for Ushere well before dawn, it was obvious that some captains were regretting their pledge. After all, if despite the chaplains' blessing the sky signaled its enmity, what hope was there of carrying out Skilluck's plan?

"That was an omen!" was his retort. "If we *don't* move south, that's what we can look forward to more of! Wellearn, do the skies hurl such missiles at Hearthome?"

"Not that I was ever told!" Wellearn asserted.

"But you said the stars look down on Hearthome more than us! Maybe we should stay here, cowering under cloud!"

Wellearn was taken aback until he saw what Skilluck was steering towards. Then he roared, "Safe? Did that prong strike from clear air? More likely the stars are warning us to move where we can see them and be seen, instead of hiding from them all the time!"

The force of his logic told to some extent, but what counted most was that their weather-sense had given no warning of that blow from heaven. Had it been a lightning-strike, it would have been preceded by a sense of uncomfortable tightness and uncertainty. As things were, the discomfort had succeeded the impact. The sensation was weirdly disturbing.

Shortly thereafter the chaplains, whose duties included keeping track of the calendar, marked the usual date of spring. Weather-sense contradicted that, too. Traces of a thaw did occur; many beaches were cleared of ice as warm water washed against them. But uplands to the north which ordinarily caught the early sun-heat remained capped with snow, and even in low-lying valleys there were places where the drifts endured. As for the ground where new crops should be planted, it was stiff as stone a moonlong later.

"I hold you to your vow," Skilluck said when that day dawned, and the other captains shuffled their pads noisily. "But for me, would your briqs be even as healthy as they are?"

"Ask the storm-lost," someone muttered.

"They're not here—*we* are!" Skilluck snapped. "So are what's left of the Wego. Must they stay and starve because the bravetrees are frosted and nothing grows on them, because the fields are hard as rock and all seeds die at the sowing?"

"To risk cresh on a crazy course to nowhere?" another cried.

"To suffer cresh right here, when creshban is to be had at Hearthome and Tempestamer can guide us thither?" Wellearn countered.

Of all the various arguments advanced, that struck deepest in his listeners' tubules. Even those who had best planned to cope with the winter were showing creshmarks now, and saw little hope of escape before the sickness claimed their powers of reason.

"We'll follow you," said Toughide finally. "With all the family and friends our briqs can carry. And let those who choose the other way be cast upon the mercy of the stars."

"Then get to work!" Skilluck rose to what was left of his former height, and despite his shrunken mantle still overtopped the rest. "Tomorrow's dawn will see the Ushere fleet at sea, and our landfall will be in a kind and gracious country where we shall be helped by allies—helped by *friends!*"

"Uncle!" Embery cried, rushing up the slope that led to Chard's observatory. "Uncle, great news!"

Worried, absent-minded, owing to old age and the problems of the past few months which had so much interfered with his study of the stars, the old man nonetheless had time to spare for his brother's daughter. He beamed on her indulgently.

"Good news is always welcome! What have you to tell me?"

"Strangers are coming over the northern hills! It must be Wellearn's people at last! Did you not calculate that their spring must have begun by now?"

"Yes, at least a moonlong ago!" Suddenly as enthused as she was, Chard ordered one of his telescopes trained on the high ground to the north, and exercised an old man's privilege by taking first turn at its ocular.

And then he slumped. He said in a voice that struck winter-chill, "My dear, were you not expecting the Wego to arrive by sea?"

"Well, sure! But given how many of them there are, perhaps they had to ferry their folk to the nearest landfall and . . ."

She could hear as she spoke how hollow her words rang.

"This is no question of perhaps," her uncle said. "This is a fact. The fireworkers' district is being attacked. If that's the Wego's doing, neither you nor I want any truck with them!"

**H**eavier-laden than ever before, yet seeming utterly tireless, and with her back sprouting trencher-plants and vines as luxuriant as though this were an ordinary summer voyage, Tempestamer beat steadily southward on the trail which only a briq could follow through the currents of the ocean. Some said it was a question of smell; some, a matter of warmer or colder water; others yet, that briqs could memorize the pattern of the stars though they were invisible by day or cloud-covered at night. After all, maintained these last, a northfinder could be carried anywhere, even in the darkness, and always turn the same unfailing way.

But most were content to accept a mystery and exploit it.

Certainly Tempestamer had learned from last year's storm. Now, if clouds gathered threateningly, she altered course and skirted them without Skilluck needing to use his goad, or when it was unavoidable hove to and showed her companions the way of it, even to locating masses of weed shaken loose by gales from coastal shallows. This gave much food for thought to both Skilluck and Wellearn, who served this trip in guise of chaplain because the passengers they had aboard would not have set forth without one. The former wondered, "Perhaps one shouldn't pith a briq at all. Perhaps there's a way of taming them intact. Could we be partners?"

While Wellearn mused, "The directions she chooses when she meets a storm: they imply something, as though the storm may have a pattern. At Hearthome I must study the globe that Chard offered to explain to me, because watching the sky . . ."

The other captains, though, grew afraid on learning how much of Tempestamer's weather-sense had been left intact. All of them had had the frustrating experience of trying to drive a briq direct for home when bad weather lay across her path, but rations had run so low that only a desperate charge in a straight line would serve the purpose of survival.

So too had Skilluck, as he said, and he preferred to come home late with vines and trencher-plants intact. What then of last year?—countered the others, and he could give no answer, except to say the fortune of the stars must have been shining on him.

Knowing him for a skeptic, they dismissed that and went on worrying.

Still, the weather continued fair. Despite the fact that they had met icebergs further south than even Toughide and Shrewdesign last summer, there had been whole long cloud-free days and nights, and the children had exclaimed in wonder at the marvels thereby revealed, especially the great arc of heaven composed of such a multitude of stars it never dwindled regardless of how many fell away in long bright streaks. Those riding Tempestamer kept begging for a peek through Skilluck's spyglass, and Wellearn amused them with fantasies based on something Embery had said, about the time when folk would travel to not just another continent, but another world.

One, though, acuter than the rest, demanded seriously, "Where do we find the kind of briq that swims thither?"

"If we can't find one," Wellearn answered confidently, "then we'll have to breed one—won't we?"

"She's slowing," Skilluck muttered. "That means landfall, if I'm any judge," Keeping his spyglass trained on the horizon, he swung it from side to side.

And checked.

"Wellearn, did the Hearthomers mention a people around here who consign their dead to the sea?"

Startled, Wellearn said, "That's a custom of seafaring folk like us! They said there were none on this whole coast! That's why when Blestar died we—"

"Oh, I remember," Skilluck interrupted. "But there are bodies floating towards us. Five of them."

It was in Wellearn's mind to ask whether he was mistaking some unfamiliar sea-creature, when his own eye spotted the first of them. No chance of error. Here came five light-mantled people of the Hearthome stock, and none was making the least attempt to swim . . .

"Stop Tempestamer eating them at all costs!" Skilluck roared to Strongrip. "It could be one of them is still alive!"

His guess was right. The last they hauled out of the water, while the passengers gazed in awe and terror, was still able to speak, though salt-perished and on the verge of death. Wellearn's mantle crumpled as he translated.

"We thought they were your people!" the stranger husked. "Even though they came to us by land! We thought maybe you were short of briqs to carry everyone . . ." He reached and choked up salt water.

"Go on!" Skilluck urged, aware how all the other captains were closing their briqs with his to find out what was wrong. Wellearn continued his translation.

"Beyond the mountains, land won't thaw this year! Except along the coasts, snow is still lying and the ground is hard as rock! That's what we found out from a prisoner we took. Never expecting an attack, we met the strangers with courtesy, but they were dreamlost and frantic and wrecked half of Hearthome before we managed to stop them. I never thought to see such slaughter, but they had started to eat us—yes, *eat* us!" A sound between a moan and a laugh. "And some of them were worse! They tried to eat *themselves!*"

"What of Hearthome now?" Wellearn cried, clenching his claws."

"I—we . . ."

The effort was too much. Salt-weakened, one of his lower tubules ruptured, and the victim saved from the sea leaked out his life on Tempestamer's back.

After a long dread pause Skilluck straightened. He said grayly, "We must go on. We can't go back. From what he said it's clear that if Ushere isn't doomed already it will be by next year. We've come south across a fifth of the world, and if even here we find that people have been driven off their lands by cold and hunger . . ."

There was no need to finish the statement. Those around him nodded grave assent.

"But if we can't settle here after all—" Wellearn began.

"Then we'll survive at sea!" Skilluck exploded. "The way the wild briqs do!"

"Not even Tempestamer can bear a load like this indefinitely!" Sharprong objected, indicating the puzzled and frightened passengers. "We've had an easy voyage compared with last year, but if there are going to be more storms—"

"Are there not uninhabited islands with springs of fresh water we can put into when our drink-bladders won't suffice? Aren't there capes and coves to offer shelter? And don't we have more seafaring skill in this fleet than ever was assembled outside Ushere?"

Wellearn shivered despite the warmth of the day. Here was a vision more grandiose than his—indeed, than any save Embery's, which pictured travel through the sky.

But what about the rest? Would they agree?

Strongrip said heavily, "We must at least make landfall, Captain. If our companions don't see with their own eyes what you and I might take on trust, there'll be recriminations."

"Those will follow anyway, the first time we run short of food," said Skilluck. "But you're right. We go ashore with all prongs sharp, if only for the chance to rescue wise'uns who know the secret of creshban. All else from Hearthome may go smash—who's going to light a fire in mid-ocean, let alone carry sand or stone to melt for glass and metal? Burn my Tempestamer's back? Never! Safer to use the stuff of life than the stuff of death! *But I want creshban!*"

Breathing heavily, he turned to Wellearn. "You stay here and keep the passengers soothed. The rest of us—"

"No," said Wellearn firmly. "I'm going ashore, too. If Embery still lives, I want her with me."

"Now you listen to me—" Skilluck began, but Wellearn cut in.

"Here come the other captains! We'd best present a united front."

"Stars curse it, of course! But you can't expect us to load up with every single survivor—"

"Then take her, if I find her, and I'll stay!" Wellearn flared.

"You're being unreasonable—"

"No, Captain. Much more reasonable than you. I've thought this through. If we do take to a nomad life at sea, what are we to do about keeping up our numbers? Already people from Ushere and Hearthome are overbred. We shall have to copy what roving tribes do on land: leave part of our company at the places where we stop in exchange for strangers who want to learn the arts of the sea. It had been in my mind to propose such a policy anyhow, because of a talk I had with Shash. But if we do as you suggest . . ."

Skilluck clattered his mandibles glumly. He said after a pause, "Well, perhaps there will be some among the passengers who want to take their chances on land, even so far from home, rather than carry on at sea. Salt water isn't in the ichor of us all the way it is in yours and mine."

Wellearn wanted to preen. How short a time ago it seemed that Skilluck had called him a landlubber at pith!

Yet he still was, and it required all his self-control to accept that his hopes of settling at Hearthome had been shattered the way the prong from heaven shattered that berg. Maybe after seeing the city in ruins the idea would come real for him. Until then, he must compose himself. Here came Toughide and Shrewdesign to demand what was happening.

"You expect us, in our condition, to plod ashore and win back Hearthome from its invaders?" Toughide snapped.

So much was to be expected. After the long voyage, few of the briqs were as fit and flourishing as Tempestamer.

"Not at all," was Skilluck's wheedling response. "We only expect the combined talents of the Wego to salvage something from the landlubbers, and above all what's going to be most valuable to ourselves: creshban, of course, but also . . ." He paused impressively. "Wouldn't you like spyglasses, all of you, better than this one of mine? The Hearthomers have them by the score! I never admitted it, but I craved one myself! Only they wouldn't part with the one I wanted until we'd concluded our alliance . . . Still, that's water past the prow. But the observatory where the glasses are kept is nearest the ocean and stands the best chance of having been defended! If we can only attain that hill before we're forced to retreat, and hold a bridgehead long enough to gather provisions, we shall retire with the finest treasure any Wegan could imagine!"

Rearing up to his full remaining height, though that strained his voice to shrillness, he brandished his beloved spyglass for all to see.

"If we don't come back with something better for us all, then you may cast lots for who's to have this!"

Uncertain at the prospect of a battle, for the Wego had never been collectively a fighting folk, Shrewdesign said, "We shan't try to retake the city by force?"

"It would be dreamness to attempt it! But what's of use to us, that the invaders would simply smash because they're starved insane—we must take that!"

Unheeded while the debate was raging, the sun had slanted towards the horizon. Suddenly the tropic night closed down, and there were groans from passengers who had not yet adjusted to the speed of its arrival.

During their last day's travel the fleet had broached a latitude further south than any on their course, and it was now for the first time they saw, at the western rim of the world just above the thin red clouds of evening, a great green curving light, edged like a shuddermaker's rasp.

Silence fell as they turned to gaze at it, bar the slop of water against the briqs' sides and the crying of frightened children. The redness faded; the green grew ever brighter.

"What is it?" Skilluck whispered to Wellearn.

"I heard of such things before, and never saw one," was the faint answer. "There are tales about the Blade of Heaven which comes to cut off the lives of the unrighteous—"

"Tales!" Skilluck broke in. "We can do better without those! How about some *facts?*"

"It's said at Hearthome that when a star flares up—"

"Oh, forget it! Leave it to me!" And Skilluck marched towards Tempestamer's prow, where he could be heard on all the prow-together briqs.

"Chaplains! Stand forth! Tell me if that's not the Blade of Heaven!"

A ragged chorus told him, yes it was.

"Tell me further! Is it poised to cut off the lives of the unrighteous? And is it not unrighteous to leave those who offered to ally with us to suffer at the claws of crazy folk?"

The instant he heard any hint of an answer, he roared, "Well, there's our sign, then! Captains, prepare to moor your briqs! Against that cape there's a shelf of slanting rock where one may bring in even so large a briq as Tempestamer and not make her beach herself! And it's exactly below the observatory we're making for!"

# 9

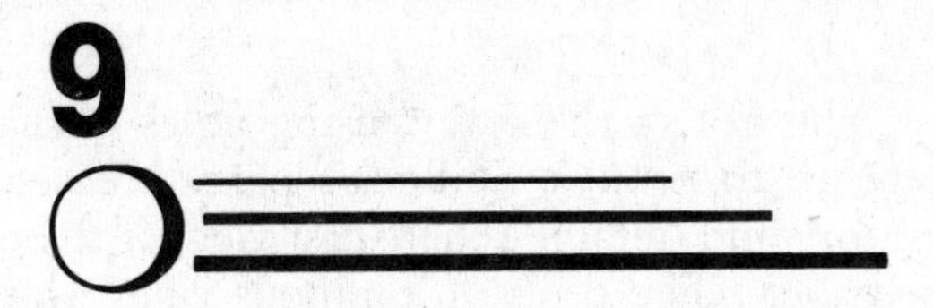

Among the many stories Wellearn had been told when he was a young'un, then taught to disbelieve as he grew up, was a description of what went on in the moon when the righteous and unrighteous were separating. Gradually dividing themselves according to whether they found dark or light more alluring, folk were said to yowl and yammer in imaginary speech; those following star-blessed visions pursued a straight path towards the light, those who doubted kept changing their minds, while only those who had arrived at righteousness by reason were able not to collide with others and be beaten or tripped up and so delayed on their way to the glory of full moon. It was a child's impression of the adult world, perhaps, not stressing what the wicked must have done to deserve the dark.

Skilluck would have been deemed wicked by all the chaplains Wellearn had known, including Blestar, inasmuch as he often mocked and occasionally defied them.

But he was glad to be beside the captain when they went ashore, for what they found was like an actualization of that terrifying childhood story.

No concerted attempt was made to drive off the Wegans who landed; there was neither rationality nor shared insanity to generate resistance. Wild-eyed, stinking, often with their mantles leaking, a horde of starvation-maddened victims ran hither and thither, some sufficiently aware to try and alarm their fellows, many more so distraught that they reacted only to the scent of oozing ichor and under the impression "here's food" began to clap their mandibles excitedly before attacking those who meant to warn them.

It might have been different had the newcomers been exuding combat-stink, but none of them was. They were serious, determined, and—most of all—afraid.

Wellearn was too calm to pretend otherwise. Wherever he glanced, he saw new horrors. One image in particular sank barbs in his memory. There was an elderly man who must have walked, he thought, as far as Tempestamer had swum to get here. For his pads were completely worn away, and he was hobbling along on the underedge of his mantle with vast and painful effort, no taller than a new-budded child, leaving a broad wet trail like a giant sluq . . .

For the first time Wellearn realized: there were some dooms far worse than death.

Beating back those who got in their way, using poles from their briqs' saddles in preference to prongs, Skilluck's party breasted the slope below the observatory and obtained their first view of the entire city. Wellearn repressed a cry. The trails of luminous vines which he had seen in Embery's company were being torn loose and waved madly around until they died, as though the bravetrees of all the houses had suddenly developed palsy. Northward, in the quarter of the fireworkers, there was a vast glare on the underside of a pall of smoke, suggesting that all the stored fuel had been set ablaze at once. And the night breeze carried not just fumes but the sound of screaming.

"Looks to me as if they're even crazier over yonder!" Skilluck muttered. "So who's going to want to quit the briqs and settle *here?* If we can't carry all the sane survivors . . . That's the spyglass-house, is it?"

His answer came in the shape of a well-aimed throwing prong, which missed Strongrip by a claw's-breadth. At once they dropped to the ground, prepared to crawl the rest of the way.

"The defenders are still on guard," Wellearn whispered. "I must let them know who we are!"

"But—"

"I know what I'm doing!" And he began to work his way uphill, soilover-style, using his claws and the edges of his mantle instead of his pads.

Sharpening his hearing to its utmost, he caught faint cries up ahead.

"Looks like a well-organized attack! Stand to!"

Another few moments, and a half-score of prongs flew over him. Somewhere behind was a strangled moan.

Moving as fast as he could, he closed the distance to the side of the observatory: that great complex of bravetrees and countless other plants where he had been shown marvels beyond belief. At every gap between their boles protruded a cruel spike instead of the former telescopes, and from roots to crown prongsmen waited to deliver death like a blow from the sky.

He gathered all his force and shouted, "*Embery!*"

And instantly doubled over, offering the toughest part of his mantle to any missile.

It came—but he felt only a blow, not a stab. The throwing prong skidded away into the undergrowth.

"Someone called my name!" he heard . . . or did he? Had tension allowed him to mistake imagination for reality? Straining perception to the utmost, he waited.

And almost rushed to dreamness with relief. No doubt of what he heard *this* time.

"No, daughter, it isn't possible. The stress has been too much for you—"

"*Embery! Shash! Chard!*"

Wellearn had to straighten out again to deliver his words with maximum force, and for an instant could imagine the prong that was going to lodge in his mantle. But he went on, "The Wego are here! *The Wego are here!* Don't—!"

One of the defenders high in the observatory's treetops heard the warning too late. He had taken aim and let go. Wellearn screamed.

But the prong sank into soft ground . . . so close, he could feel the quivering impact. After a little, he was able to recover himself and return to normal pressure as Shash and Embery and half a score of their friends rushed to meet him.

Shamelessly embracing Embery under his mantle, as though they were about to mate in public—but she was showing his bud, *his* bud!—and anyway nobody would have cared if they had, Wellearn translated the conversation going on softly among the trees of the observatory, trying to make himself believe in his own heroism. That was what they were all calling it, Skilluck too . . . but it wasn't, it was just that he had done what the situation called for, and anyway most so-called heroes turned out to have been temporarily crazy, living a dream instead of reality.

He forced aside the relics of the chaplains' teachings about reliance on visions, and composed himself to concentrate on his duties as interpreter.

"We saw no signs of organization on the way here," the captain was saying. "Does it break down at night, or is it always the same?"

"At the beginning there was some semblance of order among the invaders," Shash said. He was tired but coherent; his older brother Chard was slumped to the point where he looked as though he needed a sitting-pit, and paying scant attention. "They were able to confront us and—well, that was how we lost Burney. We were fit and rational, and thought they would be too. We now believe they must have been the first of their folk to work out what was happening, to decide that they must leave home and take over someone else's territory. And we assume that others fell in behind them when they realized this was their only hope, but by then they were—well—disturbed. And on the way I guess they infected others with their craziness."

"That fits," Skilluck muttered. "Any idea how far north they came from?"

"What few people we've been able to capture and feed up to the stage where they can talk normally—and there aren't many of those—all agree that the cold weather reaches down to the very pith of this continent. If my brother were better he could tell you more. But he's exhausted." Shash spread his claws helplessly. "The further from the sea, it seems, the worse the cold! We know that water retains heat longer than dry land, but even so, this is terrifying! Are we due for frost and snow here in Hearthome? We've never seen such things! One could imagine the whole world turning into a frozen ball!"

"I don't think we have to fear that," Wellearn said, a little surprised at himself. He parted from Embery and leaned forward. "The way Chard explained it to me, warmth at the equator turns water into vapor, so clouds turn into ice at the poles. But if the sun goes on getting warmer—"

"Quite right!" said Chard unexpectedly, and lapsed back into distraction.

"Forget the theories!" Skilluck snapped. "We need to decide on a plan of action! I have one. We should simply—"

"But what about the Blade of Heaven?"—from Toughide.

"Oh, that!" Chard roused himself completely. "We know about such phenomena. When a star—like the famous New Star—explodes, it throws off gobbets which cool down in the interstellar void. If one approaches another sun, it warms up and boils off part of itself. All this follows from the teaching Jing bequeathed."

"Is this going to save our lives?" Skilluck shouted, erupting to full height. "Are you coming with us? Are you prepared to give us what you want to preserve from Hearthome? Make your minds up *now!*"

He was so patently correct, Wellearn found himself upright alongside him.

"Yes! And whatever else you give us, we must have the whole of Jing's scriptures!"

"Creshban!" Skilluck shouted, and the other captains echoed him. "If nothing else, we must have the secret of creshban!"

The wind had shifted; there was something menacing in the air that affected their weather-sense, making tempers raw, and it wasn't just smoke.

After a pause filled only by the noise of the crazy folk smashing and ripping through the city, Shash said heavily, "There's no secret to creshban. We don't know why, but fresh sour juices of new-budded fruits or even newsprouted leaves will do the job so long as they have no animal matter at the roots. Nothing from a briq's back—nothing from a cemetery—only shoots that spring from new bare ground. I'll give you seeds that produce the moist suitable plants, but . . . Well, essentially it's like eating a proper diet at home, instead of wandering across a desert or an ocean and living on stored food."

"That simple?" Skilluck whispered. "If we'd known—"

"If you'd known you'd never have come back," said Chard unexpectedly. *"You said that in Forbish, didn't you?"*

There was a thunderstruck pause, while Wellearn registered the fact that he had not actually translated the last statement, and the rest of the Wego captains were looking blank.

"When you first came here, I thought you were better informed than you pretended," said the fat old astronomer. He squeezed himself upright, and even though the effort slurred his speech he overtopped Skilluck, for his was the taller folk. "Did you wonder on the way home last year why we didn't give you all of everything at once? Did you wonder whether we realized your intention was to cheat us if you could?"

Skilluck cowered back in a way Wellearn had never imagined he would see, not in his wildest fantasies. Chard blasted on.

"But it doesn't matter anymore, does it? You kept your pledge to return, and *you* didn't know you were going to find us in these straits! You've met your honorable obligation, and it remains for us to match the bargain! Take what you can—everything you can, including people!—from this doomed city! Take telescopes and microscopes, take vines and blades and seeds and tools and medicines, and flee at once! Until dawn the attackers will be sluggish, but if you delay past then—! Leave us, the old ones! Leave everything except what your briqs can carry without sinking! And above all, take Jing's scriptures! Wellearn, *here!*" He bowed himself to a dark corner and pulled out a glass jar.

"Take the originals! We salvaged them first of all, of course, and here they are. Now they're yours. Use them as best you can. If you must, leave them where they will freeze. But *don't destroy them!* As for us, of course . . ."

"No! No!" Embery cried, hastening to his side. "I won't leave you, I won't leave father!"

"You'll have to leave me," Chard said gently. "But you'll go, won't you, Shash?"

"They've turned our healing-house into a jungle," the chief curer said. "They've rooted out our medicinal plants. If I stay, the stars alone know what use I could be to our folk."

"Go, then. Me, I'm much too old." Chard settled back comfortably where he had been. "Besides, I'm fat and I'd probably sink even a handsome briq like Tempestamer. Take your leave and let me be. And dream of me kindly, if you will."

Soberly, the visitors prepared to depart. As they were clasping claws with him, he added, "Oh, captain, one more thing, which might be useful to you in your navigation—that is, if you haven't already noticed it. The end of the comet which you call the Blade of Heaven always points directly *away* from the sun. It might amuse you, Wellearn, when you have nothing better to occupy your mind, to devise a theory which will account for that."

"I'll try," Wellearn said doubtfully. "But without the means to conduct experiments—"

"There are always means to conduct experiments. And aren't you part of the greatest experiment of all?"

# 10

*D*uring the hours of darkness some of the briqs' passengers had indeed decided they would rather settle on shore and take their chances. As dawn broke they were heading south, together with several score refugees from Hearthome, in search of a site that would be easier to defend.

Meanwhile Skilluck's party was working out what of their loads—hastily collected in the city—would be least useful, and ruthlessly discarding whatever they did not regard as indispensable. Before the day's heat had fully roused the crazy invaders, the booty had been distributed and so had the two-score Hearthomers who were prepared to risk the ocean.

Skilluck prodded Tempestamer with his goad, and she withdrew her mooring tentacles and made for open water.

"What did uncle mean when he called us an experiment?" Embery asked her father.

"We're mixing like different metals, to see what alloy will result," Shash answered, clinging anxiously to the briq's saddle as they felt the first waves. "It's the start of a new age, whatever the outcome."

"I liked the old one," Wellearn muttered. "And I've been cheated of my share in it."

"Don't think like that!" admonished the old man. "Even the stars can change! And what are we compared to them?"

"We don't yet know," said Embery. "But one day we shall go there and find out."

Overhearing as he issued orders to his crew, Skilluck gave a roar of sardonic laughter.

"Bring me the briq you want to swim to heaven on, and I will personally pith her! Me, with a northfinder I can trust and Tempestamer under me, I'll be content. Now let's go find a herd of wild briqs and start recruiting our new fleet. It's going to be the grandest ever seen!"

But despite the hotness of his words and the bright rays of the morning sun, the wind struck chill from the north.

# Part Three

# The Outpouring

When northern summer ceased, the weight of ice leaned hard on those gnarled rocks which fearful wanderers had named The Guardians of the Pole. Slanting up either side of an underwater shelf that grudgingly permitted the highest tide to wash over it, they resembled prongsmen turned to stone, their mantles drawn aside and weapons clutched in both their claws.

Few were the mariners who braved the channel they defined; fewer still the ones who returned to tell of a colossal valley surrounding a land-locked sea so salty that what ordinarily ought to sink there was buoyed up. It was a foul and poisoned zone, though life endured. Chill and salt conspired to make its growths disgusting in the maw. Desperate commanders who imagined their junqs would nourish themselves off such weed as the water sustained watched in horror how first the drink-bladders burst, then the floats, and finally the major tubules, so they died.

By then, of course, the crews that clung to their haodahs were for the most part much too mad to care.

For a while after the last summer the Salty Sea remained liquid, roiling under hail and gale. At length, however, ice filled the valley and beset the Polar Guardians, shattering the rock they were composed of, and down it sped to gather on the shelf. In a single season boulders and ice were too high-piled for any warmer flow to pass. After that glaciers shed bergs until the isolated sea was covered; then it froze also.

The last foolhardy travelers who let a poorly-pithed briq carry them into such latitudes, thinking that because they had rounded Southmost Cape they were safe from the enmity of the stars, unaware that the briq knew nothing of this ocean dominated by junqs and was lost and panicking, struggled ashore on a desolate beach with the precious secrets it was their task to spread around the world, and sought shelter in a cave which became their tomb.

## 2

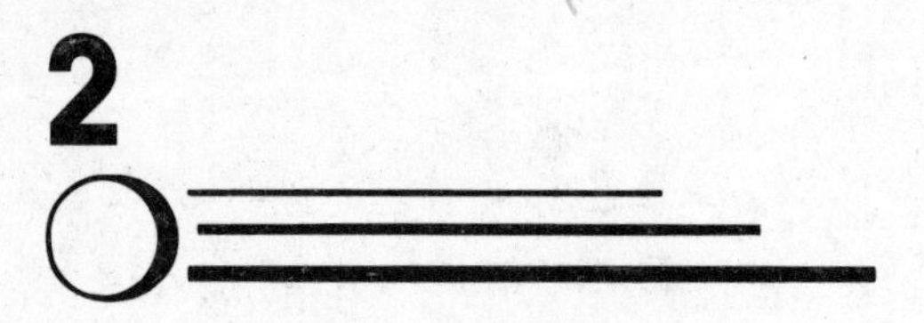

*T*he water was rising, or the land was sinking. Either way the event spelled trouble for the people of Ripar, despite the work of their far-famed inventor Yockerbow.

Some of the inhabitants claimed that their city was the oldest in the world. Others, more cautious, admitted that its records might have been—as it were—revised, because the rotting trunks of sweetwater trees had been found too far out in the lagoon for them to date back to the age of the alleged foundation, when salt tides rolled a long day's walk inland and Ripar River was as yet unfed by its giant tributary, the Gush.

It was thanks to the latter's change of course that the city had flourished. Reason, and relics exposed when mud was being pumped away from the harbor, combined to suggest that originally it had been a mere hamlet, huddled on a narrow flood-plain constricted between dry plateaux. Only when (and this was attested not by legend alone but by recent discoveries) a ball of blazing rock fell out of the sky and blocked the old channel of the Gush was there enough fresh water for dense roots to lock up silt and build a delta, forcing back the sea.

Now a score-of-score-of-scores of people, at the lowest estimate, swarmed along its branchways, got on one another's pith and cursed and sometimes fought and always schemed to secure more than their proper share of the goods attracted to this uniquely sited entrepôt, whether they arrived by junq or were carried by a caravan of droms. The majority cared nothing for the past and little for the future. Their homes grew of their own accord, did they not? There was always sustenance, though it be dull, to be snatched from an overhanging bough or filched from a plot of funqi or—if all else failed and they must endure actual work—dragged up on a line from the lagoon. Fish did not abound as formerly, of course, but even mudbanks supported crupshells and other edible mollusqs.

So they were as content as the folk of any big city.

That was the majority. There were, however, others whose traditional obligation was to view Ripar in the context of the world: not only of the globe, but of the universe which comprehended all time and all space. It was said they possessed arcane knowledge dating back before the Northern Freeze. Always there were half a score of them; always they were presided over by the incumbent Doq; always they were collectively disliked because they levied duty on cargoes passing from sea to land or vice versa, and because they enforced the ancient laws with neither fear nor favor. Were one among their own number to succumb to a plague brought by strangers, for which no cure was known, he would quit the city himself before prongsmen came to expel him; were one of his relatives to enter into an unauthorized mating, he would be prompt to bring the new-budded youngling before a eugenic court to determine its fitness to survive; were it his own home that became infested with teredonts, or boraways, or a putrefying mold, he would be the first to pour the poison at its roots.

And it was among these notable and austere personages—short of their customary total by one, for the doyen Chelp had died a few days earlier—that the inventor Yockerbow was summoned to stand today, beneath the interlaced branches of the Doqal Hall, with water plashing underpad. Acutely conscious of being no more than half as old as anyone else present, he strove to reason out why he had been sent for. Surely it could not be, as his beautiful spouse Arranth insisted, that he was to be invited to replace Chelp! His weather-sense informed him that the idea was ridiculous, for the peers were exuding a distinct aura of incipient panic.

But the fact was in no way reassuring.

He sought some kind of signal from Iddromane, spokesman for those who worked with fire and metal, and the only one of the peers he could claim close acquaintance with, but the old fellow remained stolidly imperturbable.

Yockerbow trembled a little.

Then the period of waiting was over, and the Doq rose to his full height.

"Greetings to my brothers, and to Yockerbow the stranger, who is uninformed concerning the reason for his attendance. All will be made clear in moments.

"Since time immemorial"—catching on, Yockerbow glossed that as meaning, in practice, a few score-of-score years—"the Great Fleet of the Eastern Sea has enjoyed harborage rights at Ripar. It has been a considerable while since those rights were exercised. Today, however, notice has been served that the Fleet is to call here very shortly."

So *that* was it! Making no attempt to maintain a stoical demeanor like the others, Yockerbow clenched his claws. He was schooled in history, and knew that there had been times when a visit by the Fleet was welcome; then the folk boasted how they on land shared ancestors with the People of the Sea, and clamored to trade and intermarry. On the other claw, there had been occasions when the Fleet arrived storm-bedraggled and half-starved, and crazed mariners stole what they could and spoiled the rest, whereupon the folk vowed they could never be called kin to such monsters.

Yockerbow's lifetime had elapsed without a sight of the Fleet; it was working the broadest equatorial waters. Reports from travelers indicated that it had a new commander—land-budded, they said as one—who, having deposed the former admiral, was interesting himself more than any of his predecessors in what the continents could offer.

His name, they said, was Barratong, and his shadow fell across the day-half of the world at every dawn. In Yumbit he had agents who seized the sharp spice remotaw and made it a monopoly for those he favored; in Clophical his prongsmen guarded the giant trees beloved of the spuder, and each autumn they rolled up as many webs as a junq could carry and used them for rope to snare wild junqlings and increase the Fleet; in fabled Grench—yes, he had ventured so far!—he held the sole right to export the fine wax known as cleb.

And he was coming here!

Briefly, alarm drove Yockerbow into imagining an unrealized threat. His lovely Arranth had never made any secret of how, as a youngling, she had dreamed of being traded to the Fleet, of touring the globe as the favorite partner of its admiral. Still, after so many years together . . . He had never, though, quite understood why someone like her, so fascinated by the skies, so able to make the dead past come alive, should want to be a partner in his own mundane toil . . .

"The Fleet's new commander," the Doq was saying in a rasping voice, "has sent word that he wishes to examine the famous novelties of our city: to wit, the pumps which have enabled us to withstand the encroachments of the sea. But that is not the only reason for the presence of a stranger. Immediately on the demise of our late brother Chelp, our brother Iddromane advanced Yockerbow's claim to be his replacement. Without his aid, the boles of this hall might be shriveling under the impact of salt water. Moreover, he is city-born and none has been found to speak a word against him. It would certainly be fitting were he to join us in the ranks of the Jingfired."

But this was incredible! How could Arranth's prediction possibly be right, when the aura of everybody present was so wrong? Besides,

Yockerbow had no ambitions in that direction, whatever plans his spouse might have.

A murmur of conversation had broken out. Enjoining silence with a clatter of his mandibles, the Doq continued.

"There is, however, an alternative opinion. Because it is without precedent we have agreed that Yockerbow shall be present when it is put to the vote. It has been suggested that Barrantong be inducted to make up the minyum. Some say he is of the commonalty. True, but he has attained the counterpart of noble status. It is known that the Great Fleet is increasing so fast because from every continent—let alone the islands—folk are flocking to him like cloud-crawlers at migration-time. His declared intention, we are told, is to make us all citizens of a global community. Those among us who are concerned with the future limitations of Ripar, its dependence not only on what others bring us from inland or abroad but on the natural process of weather and climate, faced with the undeniable rise in sea-level which is now putting us to such shifts, should be the first to applaud! And nowhere in the ancient scriptures is it laid down that our Order must be confined to city-budded persons!"

Chill certainty pervaded Yockerbow. He had been drawn into an argument the rights and wrongs of which the Doq had already decided in his own mind, but which other of the peers had doubts about. Now all were looking at him expectantly. What should he say? Should he risk the disfavor of the Doq? Knowing nothing of the intrigues of the Order, he felt hopeless. Hoping for guidance, he glanced at Iddromane, but—as ever—he was preserving perfect impassivity.

Well, then, he must trust to his own feelings, and even though he was sure Arranth would be angry with him afterwards, he could deal with that problem when it arose.

"Speak freely!" the Doq urged. "In meetings of the Order neither dissimulation nor subterfuge is permitted!"

Thus instructed, Yockerbow had the temerity to rise to his full height.

"Within or without the compass of your Order," he declared, "you can rely on me to serve our city. So if by inducting Barratong you may hope to enlist his support for our welfare in the future, I say do it!"

The resultant exudations, in the close air of the hall, made Yockerbow feel as though he were lost at sea and a storm were bearing down on him. Yet, though there was still no sign from Iddromane, the Doq was regarding him benignly.

"Well said!" he announced. "Iddromane, you deserve credit for proposing to the Order someone who can take the long view! Be it then resolved that during his visit we invite the admiral of the Greet Fleet to join the Jingfired, inasmuch as what he is doing is in accord with our ultimate aims!"

* * *

When the Doq had retired, some of the Order came to clasp claws with Yockerbow and compliment him on his selflessness; others departed wearing scowls. Bewildered, he made shift to answer politely, having only the vaguest notion of what he was supposed to have done right.

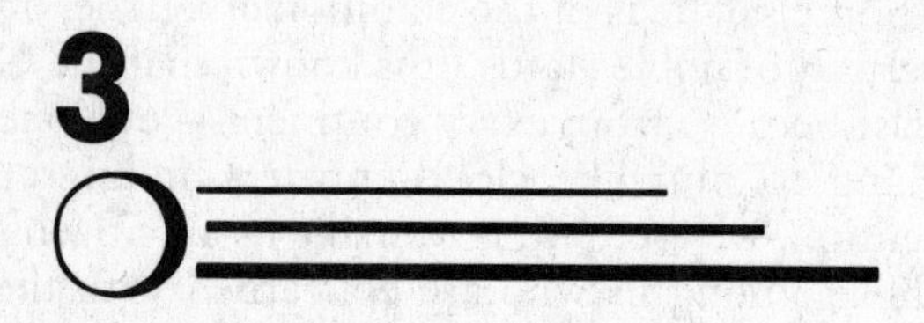

Never had Arranth been in such a rage! It was futile for Yockerbow to try and calm her; all she could say, over and over, was, "You had the chance to join the Order of the Jingfired, *and you turned it down!*"

He countered in his most reasonable tones that he had had no assurance of being elected—that if he had been by a bare majority he would have made himself enemies for life instead of, as it turned out, enjoying the patronage of the Doq—that the administrative duties such rank entailed would have interfered with his work. She refused to listen. She merely repeated facts which he already knew, as though he were some dull-witted youngling who should have been spotted by the eugenic courts.

"The Order is so old, no one can tell when it began! They say it dates back before the Northern Freeze! Its articles have been copied and copied until scarcely anyone can read them—but I'm sure *I* could, if I had the chance, and I'd have had it if you weren't a fool! Or maybe I ought to call you a coward! The path to secret wisdom lay before you, and you turned aside!"

"My dear, what's supposed to be so secret?" he rejoined. "You told me how your cousin Rafflek, who was then attendant on the Doq, reported what he overheard them saying during an induction rite: 'The stars aren't fixed, and sometimes they blaze up!' So much you could be told by any of your friends who study sky-lore!"

"That's not the point!"

"I say it is! All right, some stars aren't stars but only planets, and our world is one of them. All right, other stars may be suns with planets of their own—I see no reason why not! But saying they're inhabited is about as useful as telling me that something's happening in the Antipads, or something happened in the far past! Without means of either communicating with these folk, or visiting them, what good is there in making such a statement?"

"That doesn't mean they don't exist!"

"Well, no, of course it doesn't—"

"And even if we can't communicate with the past, the past can communicate with us, and often does so without intention! Your pumps have sucked up ancient tools in the harbor, and scholars like Chimple and Verayze have worked out how the folk of that distant day employed them! So I'm right and you're wrong!"

As usual, Yockerbow subsided with a sigh, though he still wanted to attack her logic. It was, after all, true that his spouse was highly regarded in intellectual circles, though he did sometimes wonder whether it was because she really displayed such an outstanding knowledge of astronomy and archeology, or whether it was due rather to her slender grace and flawless mantle . . .

No, that was unworthy. But, for the life of him, he could not share her obsession with the unprovable! You didn't need a telescope to discern how the moon's turning, and to some extent the sun's, affected the tides, for instance. But the planets obviously did not; records of water-level had been kept for so long that any such phenomenon must by now be manifest. Therefore the night sky was a mere backdrop of the world's events, and even if there were reasoning beings on other planets, without a way to contact them their existence was irrelevant. Certain authorities claimed there were creatures in the sun, what was more! They argued that the celebrated dark spots on its brilliant surface indicated a cool zone below a layer of white-hot air. And there were dark and light areas on the moon, too, which the same people held to be seas and continents. Given their chance, as Arranth wished, they would have imposed their convictions as dogma on all Ripar!

Perhaps he should wait on the Public Eugenicist and accuse his predecessor of authorizing a mistaken pairing. Things would have been so much simpler had they budded . . .

Yet he could not imagine living alone, and what other spouse could he find who was so stimulating, even though she was infuriating in equal measure?

Finally, to his vast relief, she lost patience, and made for the exit.

"I'm going to Observatory Hill!" she announced. "And while I'm up there, you can think about *this!* I look forward to meeting Barratong! I gather he recognizes merit in a female when he finds it! Maybe I can still fulfill my old ambition, and tour the globe aboard his banner junq!"

And off she flounced.

As the screen of creepers around their bower rustled back into place, Yockerbow comforted himself with the reflection that in the past a night of stargazing had always calmed her mind.

He could not, though, wholly persuade himself that the past was going to be any guide to the future.

But there was work to be done if the admiral was to admire the latest achievement of his beloved city. And he did love Ripar. He could conceive of no more splendid vista than the parallel ranks of giantrees which flanked its access to the ocean, no more colorful sight than the massed bundifloras ringing the lagoon, no sweeter perfume than what drifted up at nightfall from the folilonges as they closed until the dawn.

And he, for all his youth and diffidence, had saved Ripar, thanks to nothing better than sheer curiosity.

At least, that was his own opinion of what he'd done. Others seemed awestruck by what he regarded as obvious, and talked about his brilliance, even his genius. Yet anybody, in his view, might have done the same, given the opportunity. He was not even the first to try and protect Ripar by means of pumps. All along this coast, and far inland, folk made use of syphonids. Their huge and hollow stems could be trained, with patience, so that they might supply a settlement that lacked nothing else with fresh water from a distant lake, albeit there was higher ground between. But in cool weather their action grew sluggish, and sometimes air-locks developed in the stems and the flow failed.

On the coast, cutinates had also long been exploited. These were sessile creatures like immobile junqs that fed above the tide-line by trapping small game in sticky tentacles, yet to digest what they caught required salt water, which they sucked up from inshore shallows and trapped by means of flap-like valves. Fisherfolk would agitate one of them at low tide by offering it a scrap of meat, then gather stranded fish from drying pools as the water was pumped away.

Yockerbow's interest had been attracted to cutinates when he was still a youngling barely able to hold himself upright, by the odd fact that no matter how far inland the creatures might reach (and some attained many score padlongs) they never exceeded a certain height above sea-level, as though some invisible barrier extended over them.

Once, long ago, someone had thought of forcibly connecting a cutinate to a syphonid, so that any air-bubbles which formed in the latter would be driven out by the water-pressure. The project failed; for one thing, the syphonid rotted where it was connected to the cutinate, and for another, the cutinate would only pass water so salty it was useless for either drinking or irrigation.

But the young Yockerbow was excited by the idea of finding practical applications for these abundant creatures. When he discovered that air-locks in syphonids always developed at exactly the same height above water-level as was represented by the limit of the cutinates' spread, he was so astonished that he determined to solve the mystery.

The key came to him when, after a violent storm, he found a cutinate that had been ripped open lengthways, so that its internal tube was no longer watertight. Yet it was far from dead; still having one end in the sea and—fortuitously—the other in a pool left by the heavy rain, it was pulsing regularly in a final reflex spasm.

Yockerbow contrived a blade from a broken flinq with two sharp edges, cut away the longest intact muscles, and carried it home, along with a mugshell full of seawater. To the surprise of his family, he was able to demonstrate that the cutinate's activity depended less on its intrinsic vitality, as the scholars of the city were accustomed to assume, than on the simple relation between salt and fresh water. And then he discovered that, if vegetable material or scraps of meat were steeped in the fresh water, the muscle could actually be made to grow . . .

Lofty and remote, Iddromane came to hear about his work, and sent a messenger to inquire about it, who was sufficiently impressed to suggest that his master invite Yockerbow to wait on him. That was their only private meeting; they had crossed one another's path frequently since, but always at formal events such as season-rites or disposition-meets.

Iddromane's influence, however, was such that when he timidly put forward his idea that detached muscles might do useful work in pumping away flood-water from the city's outermost sea-wall, Yockerbow was overwhelmed with offers of assistance. There were several false starts; at first, for example, he imagined he could overcome the height problem by arranging the muscles to squeeze a succession of ascending bladders with flap-valves in between. That worked after a fashion, but the bladders kept rupturing and synchronization proved impossible. After a year of trial and error—mostly error—he was about ready to give up when one disconsolate day he was wandering along the shore and noticed a long thin log which the retreating tide had stranded so that its heavy root end lay on one side of an outcropping rock and its thin light spike end on the other. The rock was closer to the root than the spoke; as the water withdrew, there came a moment when the log was exactly balanced, and hung with both ends clear of the ground.

Then a mass of wet mud fell away from the roots and the balance was disturbed and the log tilted towards its spike end and shortly rolled off the rock. But Yockerbow had seen enough.

A month later, he had the first pumping-cluster of cutinate muscles at work. Grouped so close together they had to synchronize, they shrank in unison to half their normal length, then relaxed again, exerting a force that five-score strong adults could not outdo. By way of a precisely fulcrumed log, they pulled a plunger sliding inside a dead, dried syphonid, which led to the bottom of a tidal pool. At the top of its travel, the plunger passed a flap-valve lashed to the side of the tube, and water spilled through and ran off back to the ocean.

Much development work followed; in particular, the cords attached to the plunger kept breaking, so that Iddromane had to authorize the dispatch of an agent to bargain for a batch of spuder-web—doubtless thereby arousing the interest of Barratong, for only his factors were entitled to market the webs on this side of the ocean. That problem solved, means had to be found of ensuring that the plunger dropped back to the bottom of its course without jamming halfway; again, that called for an agent to travel abroad in search of cleb, the astonishing wax which, pressed upon from the side, was as rigid as oaq, yet allowed anything to glide over its surface be it as rough as rasperskin.

With a ring of flexible hide around it, the plunger on its web-strand slid back and forth as easily as might be hoped for, and every pulse of the combined muscles could raise the volume of a person in the form of water.

But the purchase of cleb had also been notified to Barratong, and beyond a doubt that must have been what decided him to call here after so long an absence of the Fleet. For now travelers came to gape at the ranked batteries of pumps which, working night and day, protected Ripar from the ravages of the ocean. As often as the tide flooded salt water into the outer lagoon, where it was trapped behind a succession of graded banks, so often did the pumps expel it and allow fresh water back to keep the giantrees in health. A few were wilting, even so, but very few, and the routine difference in water-level was a half-score padlongs.

To Yockerbow's intense annoyance, though, people who ought to have known better—including some members of Iddromane's entourage—expected him to increase this margin indefinitely. To them he spoke as vainly as to Arranth. He said, "I've tried to raise water further than the height represented by the limit of cutinate growth, and it *won't work.*" Not even Arranth believed him; she was more and more rude to him nowadays, and he felt certain it was because he "wouldn't" improve his pumps.

And nobody shared his excitement at the probable implications of his discovery. It seemed to him that the only explanation must be that air was pressing down the water in a pump-tube, so when the weight of water lifted matched the weight of the overlying air, it would rise no further. He had contrived some elegant demonstrations of the theory, using clear glass tubes supplied by one of Iddromane's associates, but not even Arranth would take them seriously. She believed, as everybody did, that air had neither weight nor—what would follow—limitations to its upward extent. Solid substances had much weight; liquids, rather less, because they incorporated more fire; but air's must be negligible, because it filled the universe and neither obstructed nor slowed down the planets. And if the stars were fire, and fire could not burn without air—as was proven by covering good dry fuel, after setting it alight, with something impervious—then there must be air around the stars.

"But just suppose," he argued vainly, "that starfire is different from regular fire—"

"Now you're asking me to believe something much more ridiculous than that the planets are inhabited!" Arranth would crow in triumph, and that was always where the discussion ended, because he had no counter to that.

So, having improved his pumps as far as they would go, he was turning his attention to other matters. He was trying to make a connection between fire and mere heat; he was testing everything known to create warmth, especially rubbing, and he was approaching a theory to explain the brightness of the stones that fell from heaven. It was generally accepted that the glowing streaks which nightly crossed the sky were of the same nature as the lumps of hot rock that were sometimes found at the probable point of impact of one of them. Burning rock? Well, rock could be melted, and if air contained more of the principle of fire the higher one went . . .

It was tolerably logical, that idea. Yet it failed to satisfy Yockerbow, and on the occasions when he had joined Arranth at the observatory on the high hill to the east of Ripar, where there were many good telescopes and files of records extending back nine-score years—it should have been far longer, but a disastrous winter had flooded the pit where earlier records were stored, and they rotted—he always came away disappointed. Some of the astronomers listened to his ideas politely, but in the end they always made it clear that to them he was no more than a lowly artisan, whereas they were refined and erudite scholars.

It was their disrespect which had hardened his view of them, rather than any secure belief that their explanations of the stars were wrong. Essentially, he could not accept the probability of such people being completely right.

And, little by little, he was formulating concepts which he knew made better sense. Suppose he had broached them to the Order of the Jingfired, after insisting on being inducted as Iddromane proposed . . . ?

No, the outcome would have been disastrous. He knew little of the web of intrigue in which the peers held Ripar like a catch of squirmers in a fish-hunter's basket, but he had the clear impression that mastering its complexities must be like trying to weave a net out of live yarworms. Had he uttered his heretical notions in such august company, means would have been found to replace him prematurely. Radicals, revolutionaries, had no place in the deliberations of the Order.

Yockerbow felt caged and frustrated. What he had expected to flow from the acceptance of his pumps, he could not have said.

Certainly, though, it had not been anything like this sense of impotence and bafflement. In a word, he was indescribably disappointed by the reaction of his fellow citizens.

Suddenly he found he was looking forward as keenly as Arranth to the arrival of Barratong. Maybe someone who had traveled half the globe would be more open to new ideas than those who sat here smug behind the defenses he had contrived but paid scant attention to the inventor's other views.

First there was a pale line of phosphorescence on the pre-dawn horizon, so faint only the keenest-eyed could detect it. Then it resolved into individual points of light, each signifying the presence of a junq festooned as lavishly with glowvines as any palace in Ripar. And at last, just as the sun cleared the horizon, the entire Fleet came into sight of land, and the city's breath seemed to stop collectively.

The Fleet was *huge!* Records indicated it had never exceeded four score junqs; now there were seven score, and another score of younglings followed behind, secured with hawsers made of spuder-web until they were safely broken. Each of the adults carried an enormous haodah beset with edible funqi and other useful secondary plants, and each haodah was aswarm with people, from those so old their mantles were shrunken with age down to children who could not yet stand upright, and nonetheless clambered with infinite confidence from pole to creeper to outlying float.

"It looks more like a mobile city than a Fleet!" marveled Yockerbow, and he was not alone.

And the resemblance was magnified a scorefold when, responding to a perfectly drilled system of signals issued by gongs and banners, the junqs closed on the place allotted for their mooring and came to rest, prow against stern, so that one might walk dry-padded from each to the next and finally, by way of the leading junq, to shore.

"That must be Barratong!" Arranth exclaimed, surveying the wondrous spectacle through a borrowed spyglass.

"Where?" Yockerbow demanded. Passing the glass to him, she pointed out a tall, burly fellow at the prow of the lead junq.

"I think not," Yockerbow said after a pause.

"What? Oh, you're always contradicting me!" She stamped her pad.

"He doesn't match the descriptions," was his mild reply. "The person directly behind him does."

"Are you sure? He looks so—so ordinary!"

And it was true. Apart from combining northern shortness with a southerner's pale mantle, he looked in no way exceptional, but he wore crossed baldrics from which depended the ancient symbols of his rank, a spyglass and an old-style steersman's goad, and his companions deferred to him even in their posture.

The Doq and the eight peers were waiting for him, surrounded by their entire retinue, and moved to greet him the moment he climbed down from the junq. After that he was invisible from where Yockerbow and Arranth stood, and the group moved off towards the Doqal Hall where a grand reception had been prepared.

"We should be going with them!" Arranth said accusingly. "If you'd asked Iddromane like I suggested, I'm sure he—"

Yockerbow fixed her with a rock-hard glare.

"No! Am I to wait on him, like a humble underling? Has it not occurred to you, my dear, that *he* is coming to see *me?*"

Her eye widened enormously. After a moment she began to laugh.

"Oh, my clever spouse! Of course you're right! It's much more remarkable like that! It's going to make us famous!"

*As if we weren't already* . . . But it didn't matter. He had made his point, and there was work to do.

It was not long before the mood of excitement generated by the Fleet's arrival started to give way to annoyance. This was not because the visitors were discourteous or rapacious; they traded honestly for what they found on offer, and conducted themselves with tolerable good manners albeit some of them, especially those who hailed from the distant south, had very different customs.

More, it was that they seemed somewhat patronizing about even the best that Ripar had to show, and in this they took after the admiral himself. Blunt, plain-spoken, he refused to be as impressed as the peers expected by anything about the city, including its alleged antiquity, for —as he declared in tones that brooked no denial—his Fleet could trace its origins back to within a score-score years of the inception of the Freeze, when briq-commanders from the west were storm-driven into what was for them a new ocean and found not wild briqs but wild junqs, which none before them had thought to try and tame, yet which proved far superior: more intelligent and more docile, not requiring to be pithed. He even had the audacity to hint that Ripar had probably been a settlement planted by the early seafarers, and that contradicted all the city's legends.

He compounded his offense when, having enjoyed the greatest

honor they could bestow on him and been inducted to the Order of the Jingfired, he made it unmistakably plain that that too was delaying fulfillment of his chief purpose in calling here: inspection of Yockerbow's pumping-system.

The peers seethed. That anyone should find the work of a commoner, a mere artisan, of greater concern than their most ancient rituals . . . !

They yielded perforce, thinking what the Fleet might do were its commander to lose his temper, and sent urgent messages to Yockerbow to meet them on the outer harbor bank.

To the intense annoyance of Yockerbow, but the huge amusement of a crowd of bystanders who had come here to catch a glimpse of the famous admiral, Arranth was rushing up and down in a tizzy of excitement, like a girl waiting to greet her first lover. Not until the procession of the peers and their attendants actually stepped on the high bank did she suddenly realize how unbefitting her behavior was. Speech—fortunately—failed her long enough for Barratong to pace ahead of his companions and confront Yockerbow person-to-person.

"So you're the celebrated inventor, are you?" he said, gazing up at the Riparian who had clean forgotten that, according to normal rules of politeness, he should have reduced his pressure so as not to overtop the distinguished visitor. "I like you on sight. You don't pretend to be what you are not—a stumpy little fellow like myself!" He added in a lower, private tone: "That Doq of yours must be aching in all his tubules by this time! Serves him right!"

At which point, while Yockerbow was still overcome with astonishment, Arranth recovered her self-possession and advanced with all the dazzling charm at her disposal. From somewhere she had obtained thick, fine strands of sparkleweed and draped them about her body in rough imitation of the admiral's baldrics; this, she hoped, would not only be taken as a compliment but maybe start a trend among fashionable circles.

"Admiral, what an honor you've bestowed on us by coming here! I so much crave the chance to talk with you! You know, when I was a girl I used to dream the Fleet might call here so I might beg the chance to make a trip with it and see the stars of the far southern skies for myself—astronomy, you see, is my own particular interest!"

"Then you should talk to Ulgrim, my chief navigator," said Barratong, and deliberately turned his back. "Now, Master Yockerbow, explain your pumps! I came here specially to see them, because—as you can probably imagine—every now and then the Fleet at sea runs into the kind of waves we can't rely on riding, and often our junqs are weighed down by water which we have to bale out with our own claws before they can swim at full speed again. In the wild state, as I'm sure you know, they never experience such swamping, because their flotation bladders always bear them up, so they have no reflexes of their own to cope with such a situation. Still, we've taught them to endure and indeed nourish all sorts of parasitic plants, so maybe we can add something more. Do we go this way?"

He made for the nearest working pump, and Yockerbow hastened to keep pace with him. Nervously he said, "I believe I should congratulate you, shouldn't I?"

"What for, in particular?"

"Were you not just inducted into the Order of the Jingfired?"

"Oh, that!"—with casual contempt. "Sure I was. But I gather its teaching is supposed to be secret, and I can't for the life of me see why. If it's true, then the more people who know about it, the better, and if it isn't, then it's high time it was exposed to ridicule and correction."

The peers who had remained within earshot stiffened in horror at the prospect of this rough intruder revealing their most sacred secrets. Barratong paid no attention. His aroma had the tang of one accustomed to bellowing orders into the mandibles of a gale, and his self-confidence was infectious. Yockerbow found he was able to relax at last.

"Now here you see a pump actually working," he said. "The tide being on the turn, there's relatively little water left beyond this bank. If you want to inspect a dismounted pump, we have one available . . ."

Barratong's ceaseless questioning continued all day and long past sunset, while Arranth hovered sullenly nearby and kept trying to interrupt. At last she managed to make him angry, and he rounded on her.

"If you're so well grounded in star-lore, you can tell me the interval between conjunctions of Swiftyouth and Steadyman!"

"It depends on our world's position in its orbit! The year of Swiftyouth is 940 days, that of Steadyman is 1,900, and our own—as you may perhaps know!—is 550." Clenching her claws, she positively spat the words.

Softening a little, Barratong gave a nod. "Very good! Though I still say Ulgrim is the person you ought to be talking to, not me, a common mariner."

"The most uncommon mariner *I* ever met!" blurted Yockerbow.

Pleased, Barratong gave a low chuckle. "I could honestly match the compliment," he said. "For such a big city, it has precious few people in it worth meeting. I was introduced, though, to some folk called Chimple and Verayze, who do at least base what they say about the history of Ripar on solid evidence."

"We found it for them!" Arranth exclaimed, then amended hastily, "Well, it turned up in the mud the pumps sucked . . ."

"Yes, of course: they told me so." Barratong shook himself and seemed to return to reality from far away. "As it happens, I'm engaged to dine with those two, and it's dark now. You come with me. I find you, as I just said, interesting."

Neglected, insulted, the peers had long ago departed in high dudgeon. There was no one else on the sea-bank except a few dogged onlookers and a couple of Barratong's aides.

"It will be an honor," Yockerbow said solemnly, and could not resist whispering to Arranth as they followed in the admiral's brisk pad-marks, "Isn't this better than being on the outer fringes of some banquet in the Doqal Hall?"

Her answer—and how it carried him back to their time of courting!—was to squeeze his mantle delicately with her claw.

They met with Chimple and Verayze at Iddromane's bower on the south side of the city, where the plashing of waves mingled with music from a flower-decked arbor. It was blessed with the most luscious-scented food-plants Yockerbow had ever encountered, many being carefully nurtured imports. Even the chowtrees had an unfamiliar flavor.

Yet the admiral paid scant attention to the fare his host offered, and at first the latter was inclined to be offended. Yockerbow too began by thinking it was because, after voyaging to so many fabulous countries, Barratong had grown blasé. In a little, though, the truth dawned on him. The signs, once recognized, were unmistakable.

Barratong was in the grip of a vision budded of his vivid imagination, yet founded securely upon fact—a vision of a kind it was given to few to endure without slipping into fatal dreamness. Yockerbow trembled and lost his appetite. Now he understood how Barratong had attained his present eminence.

Musing aloud, the admiral captivated everyone in hearing with words that in themselves were such as anybody might have used, yet summed to an awe-inspiring total greater than the rest of them would dare to utter.

"The ocean rises," he said first. "It follows that the Freeze is ending. If it began, it can just as well end, correct? So what will follow? We've tried to find out. The Fleet has put scouts ashore at bay after cove after inlet and found traces of the higher water-levels of the past. How much of the ocean is locked up in the polar caps we shall discover when the continued warming of the sun releases it. You here at Ripar, despite your wealth and cleverness—despite your pumps!—will have to drag your pads inland and quarrel for possession of high ground with the folk who already live there. You!"—this to Iddromane—"with all your ancient lore, in your famous Order, why did you not speak of this when you inducted me?"

Iddromane's notorious composure strained almost, but not quite, to the bursting point. He answered, "Truth is truth, regardless of when it was established."

"I don't agree. Truth is to be found out by slow degrees, and the world changes in order to instruct us about truth, to save us from assuming that what was so in the past is necessarily bound to be the case tomorrow, too. I'm sure our friends who study relics of the past will support me, won't you?" This with a meaningful glare.

Chimple and Verayze exchanged glances, then indicated polite assent.

"And how say you, Master Inventor?"

Yockerbow hesitated, seeking a way to offend neither Iddromane nor Barratong, and eventually said, "Perhaps there is more than one kind of truth. Perhaps there is the kind we have always known, truth about ourselves and our relations with each other, and then maybe there's the kind which is only gradually revealed to us because we actively seek it out by exploration and experiment."

"Most diplomatically spoken!" said the admiral, and exploded into a roar of laughter. "But what's your view of the origin of the universe? In Grench they hold that once all the stars were gathered right here, in the same world as ourselves, and the advent of unrighteousness caused them to retreat to the furthest heaven in shame at our behavior. In Clophical they say the departure of the stars was a natural and inevitable phenomenon, but that that was the cause of the Northern Freeze, and hence, if the ice is melting again, the stars must be drawing closer once more!"

"If only we could tell one way or the other!" sighed Arranth. "But though it's suspected that the stars move, as well as the planets—if not so visibly—our astronomers have so far failed to demonstrate the fact. Am I not correct, Master Iddromane?"

"Not entirely," was the judicious answer. "Careful observation does indicate that certain stars must be closer to us than others. As the world progresses around the sun, a minute difference in position—relative position, that is, of course—can be detected in a few cases. They are so few, however, that we are unable to decide whether the shift is solely due to a change of perspective, or whether part is motion proper to the stars themselves. The distances involved are so great, you know, Admiral, that if your Fleet could swim through the sky it would take a score-of-score-of-score years to pass the outermost planet Sluggard, and twenty times as long again to reach the star we have established to be nearest."

"Hah! If means were given me, I'd do it! I'd spin a rope of spuder-web and catch the moon, and swarm up it to see what's going on out there! But since we can't, I must be content with my current project. You see, although you may view the rise in water-level as an unmitigated disaster, I say we shall be amply repaid by the recovery of some of our ancient lands. Already at the fringe of melting glaciers we have found frozen seeds, wingets, animal-hides and mandibles, even tools belonging to our remote ancestors. This year I purpose to venture further north than anyone since the Freeze began. It's an ideal time. So far this season we haven't seen a single berg in these latitudes. What's more, there have been many fewer storms than formerly—to my surprise, I might add, because if the sun is heating up I'd expect the air to roil like water meeting hot rock . . . Yockerbow, I detect a hint of wistful envy."

Yockerbow gave an embarrassed shrug. It was true he had been dreaming for a moment, picturing to himself the new lands Barratong described.

"Come with me, then," the admiral said. "The Fleet has the ancient right to select a hostage from among the people of Ripar, exchanged against one of our own as a gage of amity. This time I choose you. And we already know your spouse fancies a sea-voyage; she may come also."

"But—!" Iddromane burst out.

"But what?"

"But he is our most notable inventor!"

"That's exactly why I picked him; he has the sort of open mind which permits him to see what happens, not what one might expect to happen. If you refuse, it will be a breach of our long-standing treaty, and you need not count on us when the time comes—it will, I promise you!—when your folk find you can neither stay here nor flee inland, and require my Fleet to help in your removal to safe high ground! But in any case it will be only for this season, unless Yockerbow decides to opt for a life at sea. It has been known for people to make such a choice . . . Well, Yockerbow?"

There was one sole answer he could give. All his life he had been led to believe that sea-commanders were no more than traders, glorified counterparts of the subtle, greedy folk who thronged the Ripar docks. Barratong, though, was none such. He was a visionary, who shared the passion that drove Yockerbow himself, the lure of speculation, the hunger for proof, the delight to be found in creating something from imagined principles which never was before on land or sea.

How much of this came logically to him, and how much was due to Barratong's odor of dominance, he could not tell. He knew only that his weather-sense predicted storms if he did not accede.

"Arranth and I," he declared boldly, "would count it a privilege to travel with you."

There was a dead pause during which Arranth looked as though she was regretting this fulfillment of her juvenile ambition, but pride forbade her to say so.

"Then there's nothing more to be said," grumbled Iddromane, and signaled his musicians to play louder.

# 5

*Y*ockerbow and Arranth were not the only new recruits to depart with the Fleet. Here, as at every city the junqs had visited since Barratong assumed command, scores of other people —mainly young—had decided that life at home was too dull for them, and they would rather risk the unknown dangers of the sea than endure the predictable monotony of Ripar.

Seventeen of them had survived interrogation by Barratong's deputies, and the peers were not averse to letting them go; the city's population was beginning to strain its resources, so they did not insist on an equal exchange.

Dawn of the fifth day saw the junqs turn outward-bound again—vibrating with hunger by now, yet perfectly drilled. Sedate, majestic, they adopted an echelon formation such that when they came on schools of fish or floating weed there would always be at least a little left even for the younglings that held the rearmost station. Thus impeccably aligned, they beat their way north.

"Is this like what you were expecting?" Yockerbow murmured to Arranth as they clung to the haodah of the banner junq and wondered how long it would be before they could imitate the unfeigned self-confidence of the children who casually disregarded the motion of the waves.

"Not at all!" she moaned. "And I persuaded Iddromane to let me have a first-rate telescope, too, thinking I might make useful observations! How can one study stars from such a fluctuating platform?"

The greatest shock of all, however, was to follow. Who could have guessed that the admiral of the Great Fleet of the Eastern Sea was bored and lonely?

Oh, bored perhaps. After one's sub-commanders had flawlessly executed every maneuver required of them for half a lifetime—after putting in at ports of call on every shore of the world's largest ocean—after dealing with people of different cultures, languages and customs for so long—yes, one would expect him to lose the sharpness of his prong. Yet . . . lonely? When volunteers flocked to join him at every stopover, and even in mid-ocean, as was shortly manifest when the Fleet was accosted by fish-hunters risking their own lives and those of their barqs, only to be turned back to shore disappointed? No, it was incredible!

Nonetheless, it proved to be the case. Yockerbow found out the second dark of the voyage, when chief navigator Ulgrim—amused, apparently, to meet not only a landsider but a female with at least a smidgin of sky-lore—had taken Arranth to the stern for a practical discussion. It was a fine clear night, with little wind, and only a clawful of falling stars. The Great Branch gleamed in all its magnificence, and the Smoke of the New Star was clearly discernible, at least as bright as the glowvines of a city they were passing to the westward. The glowvines on the junqs themselves were shielded, for fear of attracting hawqs or yowls; they were rarely fully exposed, as Yockerbow had been told, except when approaching shore or when the fleet needed to keep in contact during a gale.

And there was Yockerbow, more from courtesy than choice, alone with Barratong at the prow, while the rest of the crew amused themselves with a game that involved casting lots.

"Chance . . ." the admiral mused, making obvious reference to the gamesters. "Well, one can see why people tossed on the ocean by a lifetime of storms may hew to notions such as luck, but—You, Master Inventor! Do you believe your great achievements were the fruit of accident?"

Cautiously, for the "great achievements" were far behind, Barratong having concluded that his pumps could not easily be adapted for use on a junq, Yockerbow answered, "I think luck must be a different phenomenon from chance. I think the world goes about its own business, and those who are ripe to respond do so, much as a fertile plant catches the spores of its kin from a favorable breeze."

"Diplomatic as ever!" said the admiral sourly. "How I wish you'd speak your mind openly! If you only knew how I hunger for someone who might amaze me—startle me by voicing one of my own ideas without being prompted! Better yet, mention something I never dreamed of even when I was half-starved as a youth, plodding from city to city in search of knowledge and instruction!"

"Is that how you began your career?" Yockerbow ventured.

"What else but the quest for knowledge would tempt a sane person away from a comfortable home? What else would persuade a landsider to take to the ocean, except the chance of getting to meet more strangers in a shorter time? Oh, I've sat with scholars in a score of famous cities, listening eagerly to what they purported to teach the world, and after a few years I realized: no one is making new discoveries any more! My sub-commanders long refused to visit Ripar, because last time the Fleet came so far north the junqs were set on by a gulletfish following the drift of the bergs, and two were lost. I acceded for a while, until I heard rumors about the Order of the Jingfired, and even then I held back until reports of your pumps reached me. *I* never expected them to be useful aboard a junq, but it was an excuse to swing the support of other commanders behind me. Then the absence of bergs during our trip this year came to my aid, and now they are agreed that if I've been successful so far the chances are good that I'll continue to be so. Myself, I can't but doubt it. And I have no one I can turn to for sane counsel."

The last words were added in so low a tone that at first Yockerbow was unsure whether to reply. At length he made his mind up.

"Admiral, I recognize you for a visionary. Such folk have always encountered difficulties. In my humble way, I've done the same. But—well, since it wasn't truly news of my inventions which drew you to Ripar, I deduce it was the hope that the Order of the Jingfired possessed data that you lacked."

"Was I to know there would be a vacancy in the Order when I chose to turn up? The decision to head north this year was already taken."

"Then"—boldly—"how did you plan to obtain the Order's secrets?"

There was a long interval during which one of the outlying scouts reported a huge float of qrill, and the entire Fleet altered course fractionally to take advantage of it. When Barratong replied, there were loud squelching noises in the banner junq's maw, and now and then the whole of her body rippled longitudinally and let go a puff of foul-smelling gas.

"Had I not been inducted to the Order," the admiral said at last as though the interruption had not happened, "I did plan to choose Iddromane as my hostage for this voyage, or some other scholar well grounded in the so-called 'secrets' of the Order. I'd have relied on his terror during the first storm we met to make him reveal—"

Pride in his own city made Yockerbow risk breaking in. "It wouldn't have worked!"

"It wouldn't have been worth it," Barratong retorted sourly.

Yockerbow was shaken. "You mean there's nothing worth knowing in what they teach you?"

"I wouldn't say *nothing*," came the judicious answer. "I do accept that, acting as they do to preserve lore garnered in the far past, they have succeeded in assuring the transfer from generation to generation of certain indispensable facts. Of those you meet on the branchways of Ripar, or Grench or Clophical, come to that, or any city, or even as you pass from junq to junq of the Great Fleet, how many folk would you rely on finding whom you could talk to about what really matters—the nature of the universe, the fires of heaven and how they correspond with those down here, the beginning and the end of everything? Hmm? Many would be prepared to debate with you on any such subject, but how few would have solid evidence to back their views!"

"I always thought," Yockerbow admitted, "the Order of the Jingfired did have evidence."

"They claim to have, but when you ask for it, it can't be produced!" Barratong exclaimed. "I'm ready to believe, for instance, that long ago one of the stars in the sky blazed up until it outshone the sun. I can see the cloud of glowing gas they still call its Smoke—it's right there, isn't it? What I want to know, though, is *why* that happened, and why it hasn't happened since! And then there are elderly folk among my own people who say that when they were budded certain stars were not so bright as they are now . . . but who's to define what 'bright' means? Can the members of your Order tell me that? They swear in principle they could—if only they had certain ancient star-maps which were spoiled by a flood! But when I asked for them they hadn't even kept fragments and tatters which I could have shown to Ulgrim!"

He concluded that tirade on a fierce tone, and a second later continued in a much milder voice, as though reminded about Arranth by his reference to his chief navigator.

"They said at Ripar that your buds don't take."

Yockerbow curled his mantle before he could stop himself, and a waft of combat-stink fouled the salty air. Aghast at his bad manners, he was on the point of prostrating himself when he realized that the remark had been made in the matter-of-fact fashion of an equal speaking to an equal. Flattered, he confirmed its truth.

"Nor do mine," said Barratong, staring across the water where the new-risen moon was creating a path of brightness for others to follow—not the Fleet. "Your lady wishes me to join with her, and I shall with pleasure, but don't expect the offspring you can't give her. Were I capable, my line would be among the greatest in history. But the only thing that keeps the Fleet in being—the only thing that helps so many cities to survive around the shores of the eastern ocean—is the fact that a first-time mating between strangers takes more often than not, so your seventeen from Ripar will engender enough progeny to keep us going for quite some while . . . Oh, Yockerbow, I almost look forward to the tumult the great melting will entail! We must stir the folk around more! Little by little, thanks to our habit of choosing *either* sea *or* land, *either* drom *or* junq, *either* this *or* that, we are breeding apart! And the same holds for the inventions made in one place or another! Do you know about the longwayspeakers that they have at Grench? No? I thought not. But think what use you could have made at Ripar of a means to communicate simply by beating on a distended bladder in a patterned code, comprehensible to somebody the other side of a mountain range: they can do that! And they can signal orders at Clophical by using trained and brightly colored wingets which make patterns that are visible from end to end of the valley, but they don't survive being taken out to sea. And the use they could make of your pumps at Gowg . . . ! Do you see what I mean?"

Yockerbow certainly did, but already he was lost in contemplation of the possibilities. He stood silent for a long while, until Barratong roused him with a nudge, pointing to the north.

"Look yonder! What can the Jingfired tell me about that—*hmm?*"

For an instant Yockerbow thought he must be watching a drift of cloudcrawlers on their migration route; some species displayed bright flashes from time to time, and occasionally they synchronized to make bright polychrome bands. But this was much too blue, and too near the horizon, and anyway the season was wrong.

"Tonight the sky is clearer than I ever saw it," said Barratong. "You're looking at the aurora round the pole. I've been told that when one draws close enough it reaches to the apex of the sky. Not that anyone has seen it in all its glory since the Northern Freeze—*but on this trip we shall!* Even my sub-commanders don't know what I have in mind, friend Yockerbow, but on this voyage I mean to break all records for a northern swim, and go where nobody has dared to venture since the ice claimed what was habitable land. I want to witness the rebudding of the continents! Don't you?"

After a few days of steady northward travel, they made the first of many detours. Fog and mist did not deceive the northfinders carried by the Fleet, but this time a violent storm lay across their course. At about the same time the sea became noticeably cooler, as though chilled by melting ice. Paradoxically, however, at the same time it started to teem with a wider range of life-forms than could be found in the waters nearer Ripar, from the tiniest qrill which Barratong scooped up in a shell and showed to Yockerbow through a single-lensed microscope that magnified better than ten-score times, up to giant schools of sharq. The Fleet accorded these a respectfully wide berth also, not because they were a threat themselves, but because they in turn were hunted by the fiercest predator in these waters, the huge and solitary gulletfish whose mindless charge could rupture the tubules of even the largest junq. For amusement, elderly mariners jelled the ichor of the new recruits by regaling them with tales of what it was like to meet a gulletfish in mid-ocean and try to make it charge a barbed prong. It was worst in the dark, they said, when all one had to guide the eye was the ripple of phosphorescence as it rounded to for yet another onslaught.

"How rich in life the planet is!" murmured Yockerbow, and Barratong gave him a sardonic dip.

"Who says only this planet? Some think the stars may be alive, or harbor life, because living creatures are always warmer than their environment! Myself, though, I suspect the reason we don't find such a plethora of fish in tropical waters is that life requires a differential of heat, the way your pumps require a differential of level, and as the water becomes warmer the task of survival grows harder, just as when it grows extremely cold. What about that?"

Yockerbow felt he would never grow accustomed to the way the admiral kept tossing out provocative ideas, even though he was modest about the source of them, and always gave credit to anonymous scholars said to have been met in distant places. By this time, however, Yockerbow was beginning to doubt their existence. Barratong combined his restless genius with a diffidence more proper to a shy young apprentice.

He said after a pause for thought, "It makes sense to invoke a limit at either end of any scale of events. Just as there is no life in solid ice, so there is probably none in the stars. After all, a living creature which is trapped in wildfire dies, and certain persons have conducted experiments wherein a small animal and some burning fuel were closed up together, and the animal died and the fuel did not burn out."

"I've heard of such cruelty," Barratong said musingly. "I personally would not care to witness it, but I'm glad in a sense that someone could bear to . . . Ah, there is so much to know, my friend! And so much that has already been discovered in one place, yet never conveyed to another! But we have spoken of such matters already."

"As we have," rumbled Ulgrim, approaching from the stern with Arranth—somehow shyly—following him. "Admiral, do we plan to put in at any harbors before we reach the polar circle? The lady has convinced me that it would be of interest were I to peek through her big spyglass on stable ground."

Behind his back Arranth gave a moue, as to tell Yockerbow, "See? There are some who respect my learning even if you don't!"

Whether Barratong noticed or not, he gave no sign. He merely chaffed Ulgrim, who was still tall but whose mantle showed the telltale wrinklings of age.

"What youth and good looks may do to reform a character! You never cared to come ashore with me in other climes to hear what the local philosophers had to say, or view their instruments and their experiments! Lady Arranth, I bow to you; whatever else you may be schooled in, you certainly display a vast knowledge of people's nature! But the answer's no!"

Abruptly he extended to his maximum height, a third or more above his usual stature, and even though this brought him barely equal with Yockerbow and Ulgrim, the effect was as shocking as though he had grown taller than mythical Jing. One more element was added to Yockerbow's understanding of this admiral's dominance over his enormous Fleet.

"We go ashore next time on land newly exposed by the retreating ice! We stocked the junqs with food enough to see us through the trip —their drink-bladders are bulging—no blight or mold afflicts the food-plants—and we have medicines for every conceivable ill! For all I know, the landfall we next make may be shrouded under so much cloud you can't see stars—but never mind! We already know how the ice when it melts reveals wonders from far distant in time, so the wonders that are distant in space may take care of themselves for this season! The stars are slow to bloom and fade, but you and I are not. Time enough for your observations next winter, if the Fleet remains in the far north and we are compelled to lie up a while, which I suspect . . . But tell me, though, old companion"—this as he imperceptibly resumed his normal pressure—"what's excited you anew about the stars you've known so well for so long?"

Embarrassed, but putting a bold countenance on matters, Ulgrim said bluffly, "She speaks of stars which I can't see, and yet they're there. More than once since leaving Ripar, when the water was most calm, I've thought I could discern them—an eleventh in the cluster of the Half-Score Wingets, another at the focus of the Welkin City . . . And of such a color, too: a strange deep red! Yet when I look again—!"

"Master Navigator," Yockerbow said, "have you ever seen a bar of metal heated in a fire until it melts?"

"I never had time for such landsiders' tricks!"

"I know: one dare not carry or use fire aboard a junq. Yet fact is fact. The metal starts to glow in the dark red; afterwards it becomes orange, and yellow, and green—which we see clearest—and then shades through blue to white, just like the rainbow. Eventually it can be made to glow like the sun itself. It follows that a hotter or a cooler star . . ."

His words trailed away, for Barratong was scowling.

"I thought you were never inducted to the Order of the Jingfired!" he said in an accusatory tone.

"What does that have to do with it?" Arranth demanded before Yockerbow could reply. "Had I but the means, I'd show you all this with a glass prism!"

"It is as I feared!" Barratong raged, and began to pace back and forth along the poop of the haodah, spinning at every turn so violently one thought he might blister his pads. "Your vaunted Order possesses no truly *secret* knowledge! Do you realize that the heating of a metal bar is the chief symbol of their most private ritual?"

There was a moment of dead silence, save for the slap-and-hush of waves against the junq's broad flank and the *meep-meep* of a flighter and its young which were following the Fleet in hope of scavenging carrion or floating dung.

All of a sudden Yockerbow started to laugh. As soon as he could he recovered his voice and said, "Admiral—excuse me, because this is truly too silly—but you were right the first time, and this time you're wrong. It doesn't matter that someone else knows the inmost secret of the Jingfired ritual. *What counts is that Ulgrim didn't.*"

"I think I see what you mean," said Barratong, and a waft of anger-stink blew away as he mastered himself. "Clarify!"

"How long ago was such a truth discovered, that may prove to be valid even in the case of the stars? Well before the Northern Freeze, we may be sure! What happened following the onset of it? Why, people driven crazy by hunger and despair felled great civilizations which otherwise might well by now have shown us things we regard as impossible—you might, for instance, have your spuder-web to catch the moon! But nobody among the Fleet would dare to undertake the necessary research because a fire literally cannot be lighted on a junq! Hence no metal—no glass—no melted rocks—no anything of the kind which pertains to such realities!"

He was downwind of Barratong as the Fleet bore into a strong northerly breeze. Whether it was because he scented the admiral's enthusiasm, or because the newly exposed lands which the ice had reluctantly let go were emanating signals from those who had once occupied them, he never knew. But in that moment he was as great a visionary as the admiral.

"Yet we *can* bring our knowledge all together!" he declared, and his weather-sense confirmed that he had safely picked a course into imagination, steering well clear of dangerous dreamness. "Knowledge borrowed from past time will guide us to the future we deserve for all the troubles we've endured! There must be suffering—would I knew why! I don't believe the stars decree it, for they're so remote they might as well be cool and stiff like arctic rocks, yet they *can* blaze up, and I don't want to think it's simply because they suck into themselves the vital force from planets like ours where life exists between the limits set by ice and fire!"

"Say it's because of ignorance," offered Ulgrim, and at once looked surprised at his own improbably philosophical suggestion.

"Yes! Yes!"—from Barratong. "Have we not found remains of animals such as none of us had seen or heard of? Have we not then encountered similar beasts in strange new waters? And are we ourselves not different from our ancestors? It follows that if the stars blaze up it must be for a reason we shan't comprehend until we work out why there are creatures—or were—unknown to us on this small planet!"

"We understand each other," Yockerbow said soberly. "I was so afraid when you invited us to come with you . . ."

"Ah, but we're all bound on one quest," Barratong stabbed. "Some of us seek an answer to a single mystery—you, Yockerbow! You wanted to find out why syphonids and cutinates could never pump water above a certain level. On the way to a solution, you saved your city from being washed away. You still don't know all the reasons why the original phenomenon presented, but you have suspicions, don't you? And Arranth has just drawn my dear old partner whom I've trusted in storm and floe-time, trusted under the onslaught of heaven's crashing meteorites—drawn him too by some miracle into the charmed circle where I hoped to lure him long ago" (this with a dip to her) "and for that I thank you, ma'am—"

Yockerbow was half-afraid the admiral had lost track of his own peroration, but he was wrong, for he concluded it magnificently.

"And here we are together on the sole straight course which any of our people ought to choose! All of us a little angry with the universe because it seems to want to mislead us—all of us determined to find an answer to at least one mystery before our time runs out—all of us resigned to the certainty that we shall uncover many other mysteries in the solving of our own! Perhaps the time may come when there are no more questions to be asked; if that is so, that's when the world will end!"

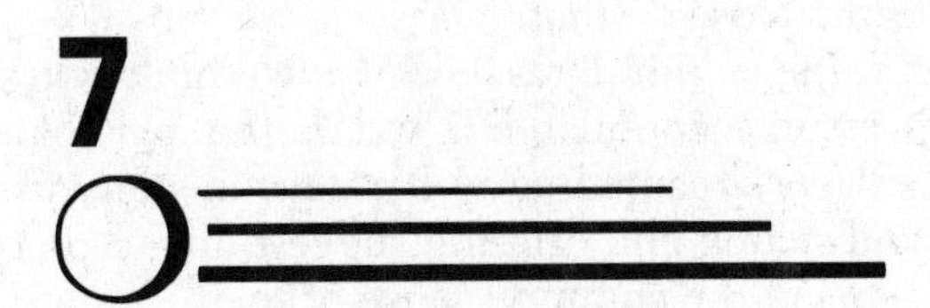

# 7

Cooler it became, and cooler . . . yet not cold. No frostrime formed this season on the rigging of the haodahs, and the junqs themselves responded briskly to the increasing iciness of the water, as though they needed by activity to keep the ichor coursing in their tubules. Awed, those who rode them as they trespassed among bergs and floes under an amazing pale blue sky watched the bare brown land on either side slip by, and marked where it was suddenly not bare, as though the sun had charmed plants out of rock.

"We are approaching the polar circle," Barratong said. "We are the first to come by sea in who can say how long? But we are not the first of all. See how the flighters whirl who brought new life to these mud-flats!"

Watching their graceful swoops, as they glided back and forth and sometimes failed of their prey so they had to whip the water and achieve enough velocity to take off again, Yockerbow said, "How can they eat enough to fly?"

"Sometimes," said Barratong, "they can't, or so I was informed by a fisherman whom we rescued in mid-ocean the summer before last. They breed on high bluffs and launch their offspring into air by laqs at a time when they burst the brood-sac. Those which catch enough wingets and flyspores grow; they soar and mate on the upgusts; then they hunger for what's in the water, and if they're large and fast enough they snatch the surface-breeding fish. If not—well, they can use up what fat they've stored and spring back into air from the crest of a rising wave. But this fish-hunter had many times trapped those which did so, and always found them lean and scant and taint of flesh. It's my view that flighters' natural zone is the air; by contact with either land—except to breed—or sea, they are diminished of their powers. Witness the fact that out of every brood-sac a score or two survive. And is not the same phenomenon apparent in ourselves? Had you and I, and all the other so-called worthy persons, bred at every pairing, would we not by now by laqs and craws have overswarmed the pitiful resources of the Age of Freeze? How many more of the folk could Ripar have supported before either they started to starve off into dreamness or some epidemic sickness rushed through them like a flame in dry brushwood? Hmm?"

Yockerbow, after a second's pause, admitted, "It is in the records of the city that Ripar came close to that."

"As did our Fleet," the admiral rasped. "How think you I—a landsider—was able to assume command? I was better fed than old Grufflank, and that's all! *He* dreamed away his days in nonsense visions! There was I fit and strong and offering suggestions so practical the captains' meet recognized the common sense of them. Yet, given a season's decent diet, any of them might have done the same, and more, for they had sea-experience, while I did not . . ."

He brooded for a moment; then he concluded, "At least I can say this. I'm still in the domain of imagination and not dreamness; my weather-sense assures me of it, and that's the sense that fails us last, even though the eye or the very mantle may be fooled. A sweet taste may deceive you; a fair odor; a sleek touch . . . but weather-sense extends into your very pith and being, and even if you starve it's last to go. Moreover it's what leads us to trust our junqs more than ourselves. At Ripar, do they know the legend of Skilluck?"

Yockerbow looked blank, but to his surprise Arranth, standing by as usual but less bashfully than before, said, "If the name is Skilq, we have the same tale, probably."

"Who swam a wild briq across the western ocean when all others had lost their way, and salvaged something of a now-lost city?" Barratong rounded on her with excitement.

"They say he saved the telescope for us," Arranth concurred. "All younglings at Ripar are told the story."

Having dismissed fables of that sort from his conscious mind because his preceptors so ordered him when he entered into adult phase, Yockerbow was acutely embarrassed. He said, "I too of course heard such stories, but in the absence of evidence—"

"To starfire with your ideas of evidence!" roared Barratong. "For me, it's enough that someone in the Fleet should remember hearing a vague tale! It's because I want to turn the legends of the past into a new reality that we are here! Those which don't stand up to present discoveries may be dismissed as spawn of dreams! But anything I take in claw and hold and *use—!*"

He broke off, panting hard, because he had involuntarily tallened again. Relaxing, he concluded in a milder tone, "Besides if the same tales survive on land as we know among the People of the Sea, there's a double chance of them being based on fact. Do inland folk recount the stories, too? If so, are they just borrowed from contact with mariners?"

The ebb and flow of talk surrounding Barratong was such as Yockerbow had never dreamed of. Once he dared to ask what mix of ancestry had given him rise, and met with a curt—though plainly honest—answer.

"I inquired about that, right up until I found I was a muke, and got no details; there was a famine which affected memory. And after I discovered that my line won't take, there seemed no point in pursuing the matter. I can only suggest and instruct; I cannot breed."

Timidly Yockerbow ventured, "A—a—what did you call yourself?"

"A muke! Take junqs from a northern and a southern herd, and they will mate eagerly enough, and often throw a bunch of first-class younglings. Yet when you try to make the strain continue, it's like me, and you, and—given she's tried me and Ulgrim and a score of others in the Fleet—Arranth as well. We call those mukes, and hope against hope the wild strains will continue to furnish us with the next generation . . ."

With an abrupt shrug of excitement, he added, "Yet there *is* hope! Suppose our heritage has lain under a mantle of impotence as the northern continent lay under ice: the end of the Northern Freeze may signal salvation for us mukes! I couldn't begin to tell you why I foresee this; it may be leaked from dreamness to my mind. Still, the border between dreams and imagination might very well fluctuate just as the boundary between ice and ocean does . . . Oh, time will judge. Now watch the way the land is changing on this coast. Look not just for the flighters that bore back southern seeds when they quested their prey into these waters, because as you know some seeds pass clear through the digestion of a flighter and are nourished by the dung they're dropped in, nor for what they brought when it foliates and blossoms, but for what lay hid till now when the sun came back and released it . . . Ah, but darkness falls. Tomorrow, though—!"

And he was right. He was astonishingly right. Next dawn revealed what he predicted, and Yockerbow decided—though he could not convince Arranth he was correct in saying so—that among Barratong's chief gifts must be the art of assessing whether someone who relayed a story to him told the truth.

For their course came to a dead end in a wide bay whose northern shores were still blocked off by a huge glacier. Some drifts of mist hung about it, but it was a fine morning and a brisk wind disposed of most of them within an hour.

And, either side of the steep bluish mass of ice, life was returning. Not only were the drab gray sand-slopes nearby aweb with creepers and punctuate with burrowers: the air was full of unexpected wingets. The mariners caught as many as they could, for some were known to lay maggors which infested junqs, and brought them to Barratong for examination.

"They're unlike any in the south," he stated. "Even if they are similar, then the colors vary, or the size, or the limb-structure. Is the Fleet still thriving?"

"As ever!" came the enthusiastic report. "We didn't expect to fare so well this far north, but the junqs' maws are crammed and we ourselves enjoy the food we reap from the sea!"

"Then here's our landfall, and our harvest will be knowledge!" cried the admiral. "Report to me whatever you find unusual—"

Something shot past him with a whizzing sound. A moment later, Ulgrim, who stood nearby, cursed and clapped a claw to his upper mantle. Withdrawing it, he displayed a pointed object with a pair of vanes on the after end. Similar noises continued, and complaints resounded from all the nearby junqs.

"What in the world—?" began Yockerbow, but Arranth cut him short.

"Those must be seeds!" she exclaimed. "Did you never play the game we did as younglings—placing seeds like those on a rock and shining sunlight on them through a burning-glass until they flew away?"

Once again Yockerbow found himself at an embarrassing loss. When he was a youngling, he had known nothing of such miracles as lenses, or indeed any form of glass. Attempting to recoup his pressure, he said, "You mean heat bursts them?"

"Burst? Not in the sense a bladder bursts, dear me! They emit some sort of stinking gas from one end, and that makes them leap through the air."

All this time, a horde of the things was descending on them, and Barratong—who else?—was reasoning about the strange phenomenon.

"They must be coming from up there," he said, and pointed to a bluff a little above their own level, where a dark shadow was growing more and more visible as ice melted and water cascaded down the lower rocks. "That's where we'll send explorers first. A sign of life is never to be overlooked."

"And the top of that bluff," said Arranth in high excitement, "would be just right to set up the telescope I brought! That is," she added hastily, "if the dark-time is as clear as this morning, and weather-sense indicates it may be."

Exuding an aura of puzzlement, Barratong said, "I fear you're right."

"Fear?"—from two or three voices simultaneously.

"Our whole voyage has been strange," the admiral said after a brief hesitation. "Too fair weather—no storms to mention—the bergs dissolving as we passed by . . . There is a real change taking place in the world, and it disturbs me. We must seize our chance, though! Overside with you!"

The Fleet having been instructed to make all secure, a small group of crewmen was detailed to follow Ulgrim and find a way to the cliff-top where the telescope might be sited. Meantime Barratong, Yockerbow, and Arranth, who was too impatient to concern herself with preparatory details, set off along a sloping miniature watercourse towards the source of the flying seeds. Its bed was pebbly, and the flow chilled their pads, but they were able to obtain a good grip on the gradient, and shortly they found themselves looking at a shadow behind a veil of ice.

"Now there's a cave!" declaimed the admiral, loudly enough to overcome the rushing of streamlets which was greeting the advent of renewed summer. (Had there been one last year? It seemed unlikely; Yockerbow was prepared to believe that Barratong's weather-sense had picked the very first possible year for folk to return to these latitudes.) "What icefaw or what snowbelong may have laired here! What refuge it may have offered to beasts we exterminated when the Freeze drove them southward! You realize, of course"—lapsing into his most condescending and didactic mode—"that up here there may still be creatures which cannot live off vegetation but devour other animals, as sharqs eat other fish?"

For once the others paid him no attention. They were seeking the source of the flying seeds, and shortly found it: an ice-free patch was exposed to sunlight on the side of the adjacent rock, and a small, tough, low-growing plant was exerting its utmost efforts to reproduce itself, though by this time its main arsenal had been expended and only a few weak flutterings resulted.

Standing back, Arranth began, "I think—"

"Look out!" Yockerbow roared, and dived forward to push her clear of impending disaster.

Whether it was the effect of sunshine, or whether—as they later wondered—the mere vibration of their presence sufficed, the ice-veil before the cave was starting to collapse. A web of cracks appeared; a grinding sound followed . . .

"Down!" roared Barratong, and set the example as great frozen shards fell crunching and slid down the watercourse. They clutched at what they could, including one another, and somehow succeeded in not being carried bodily away.

And got uncertainly to their pads again, for nothing worse emerged from the cave than a most appalling and revolting stench, as of corpses shut up for uncountable years.

It blew away, and they were able once again to venture close, while the low northern sun beamed on them from a clear blue sky. At the cave-mouth things glistened wetly, and a few were instantly identifiable.

"There's a mandible," Barratong muttered, kicking it. "People too were here, you see?"

"Where there were people, I look for what people make!" shouted Arranth, and began to scrabble among the dirt at the opening. And checked, and said something incomprehensible, and rose, clutching a long rigid cylinder such as no creature in the world had generated naturally.

"It's a glass!" she cried. "It's a glass tube! And I hear something rattling inside!"

She made as though to crunch the crackly-dry wax that closed the tube's ends, but Barratong checked her.

"Not here! Whatever's in it must be fragile, for it's certainly very ancient. We'll take it back to the junq and open it with great care in a safe place. Are there any other relics like it?"

Reaching for the mandible, he used it as a scraper, and the others joined him in sifting through the foul mass of putrid matter at the cave entrance. Shortly they were satisfied there was nothing else as durable as the glass tube, and returned on board.

There, quaking with excitement, Arranth broke the wax and removed a stopper made of spongy plant-pith. Tilting the tube, she shook from it a tightly rolled bundle of documents, inscribed on an unfamiliar off-white bark. The moment she unrolled the first of them, she exclaimed at the top of her voice.

"I can't believe it! It's a star-map!"

"Are you certain?" Yockerbow ventured.

"Of course I'm certain!" Studying it feverishly, she went on, "And either it's inaccurate, or . . . No, it can't be! It shows the stars as they were before the Freeze, and straight away I can assure you: some of the constellations aren't the same!"

# 8

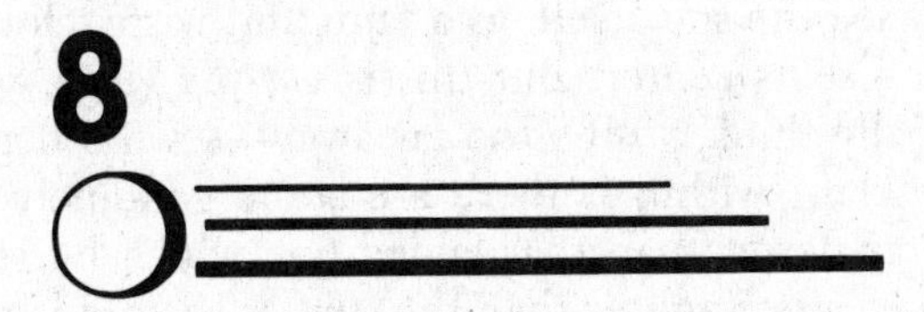

*The past can communicate with us* ' . . .

Echoes of Arranth's repeated argument kept ringing through Yockerbow's mind as he and Barratong, and the senior Fleet sub-commanders, gathered to hear the result of her and Ulgrim's researches. In spite of aurorae and shooting stars they had been pursued through every darktime until now, when their weather-sense warned of an approaching storm and indeed clouds could be seen gathering at the southern horizon. Every junq had been ransacked for writing-materials, and meticulous sketches were piled before Arranth, each adjacent to one of the pre-Freeze maps. Yockerbow shivered when he thought of their tremendous age. Yet they had been perfectly preserved in their airtight container.

Delighted to be the center of attention, Arranth could not resist preening a little, but when Barratong invited her to present her report, she spoke in a clear and businesslike manner.

"With only a single telescope and what crude instruments we could improvise, Ulgrim and I have not been able to make the sort of exact measurements that could be performed at a proper observatory. However, that is paradoxically fortunate. Whoever compiled these ancient maps can have had access to a telescope barely better than our own, if at all, so we have an excellent basis for comparison. In other words, we can be reasonably sure that the stars we see and those depicted on the old maps correspond. Thoughtfully enough, the map-maker indicated which stars were visible to the unaided eye, and which only with the aid of a glass. We have therefore been able to establish the following facts.

"First: the stars do change position—very slowly, but unmistakably—and some have certainly grown brighter.

"Second: there are not just a few but *many* stars now discernible which were not known to the map-maker, and all of them have something most disconcerting in common. They are all deep red, and they all lie in the same general area of the sky. Which leads me to the third point.

"What we have been accustomed to call the Smoke of the New Star can be nothing of the sort. We have traced the site of the New Star, which in the days when these old maps were prepared was still clearly visible, though now it takes a strong glass to detect it. Indeed, one does not so much see the star itself, as a faint and wispy cloud of glowing gas with a dot at its center. But this is *not* the large, widespread cloud we normally think of. It's too far away—several degrees distant. On the other claw, within it there are some genuinely new stars, which must be far newer than that fabled one which burst out without warning and became brighter than the sun, as the old legends claim—though, strangely, no reference is made to heat from it.

"Within the Smoke, as I was saying, we have counted no fewer than ten stars of which there is no sign on the old maps. Moreover, what reference is made to the Smoke is cursory and vague, and no outline is indicated for it, though we can see one fairly clearly. All these ten new stars, what's more, are reddish, even darker than the Smoke, as though they only recently lighted their fires. They are barely bright enough to make the surrounding cloud shine by reflection, and much too far away to account for the ending of the Freeze.

"And even that is not the most astonishing news."

Having helped as best they could with the observations, Yockerbow and Barratong were primed for the final revelation, and glanced covertly around to see what impact it would have on the unforewarned.

Using an image which Barratong himself had supplied, Arranth said, "Imagine the Great Fleet keeping station on a calm sea, and yourselves aboard a solitary junq making haste towards it. Would you not see the nearest of the Fleet diverge to either side as you drew close, while the furthest remained at roughly the same angle?"

Puzzled at being reminded of something that everybody knew, her listeners signified comprehension.

"What disturbs and even frightens me," concluded Arranth, "is that scores of stars whose positions we can check against the old maps appear to have diverged outward from a common center, and that center is located in or near the Smoke. Either we, with the sun and all its planets, are hurtling in that direction, or the Smoke and its associated stars are rushing towards us. It makes no difference which way you look at it; the outcome is the same. And if, as certain astronomers believe, stars begin because they accumulate surrounding matter, be it whole wandering planets or mere dust like what comes to us as meteorites and comets, then there must be incredible quantities of it in any zone where ten new stars have started to burn since these maps were drawn!"

As though to emphasize her words, a meteor brilliant enough to shine through the daytime sky slashed across the zenith, and immediately thereafter Barratong cried, "Get those maps under cover! The storm will be upon us any moment!"

An echo of thunder confirmed his warning, and they scattered, the sub-commanders to their respective junqs, Arranth, Ulgrim, Yockerbow and Barratong to huddle beneath the shelter offered by their own's haodah.

Tucking the precious maps carefully into the tube again, Arranth said, "Do you think they understood?"

"Most of my fellow-navigators," Ulgrim grunted, "have never thought about stars except to figure out what use they are in guiding us, and most of our lives that hasn't been much, you know. The admiral's right: a real change is working in the world. This is more the sort of weather I'd have expected here in the far north, not the clear bright kind we've had since our arrival."

The first assault of rain rattled the canopy of interwoven reeds that formed the haodah's upper deck, and the junq stirred restlessly as the air-pressure changed.

"Will the fine weather return?" asked Arranth.

Her question was mainly addressed to Ulgrim, but before he could answer Barratong cut in.

"It's over-soon to guess, but either way we must get these maps to where they'll be most useful. To begin with, I shall arrange to have them copied with the utmost care. I know who among the Fleet are most skillful at writing and drawing. Of course, I don't know whether we have enough writing-material left. But we'll do what we can, although we have to kill and flay one of the junqlings to make writing-sheets. Beyond that, though, there's the question of what we should do with the originals."

"Why, we take them back to Ripar, obviously!" Arranth burst out.

"It may seem obvious to you; it's not to me. They should go to the finest of modern observatories, and that's not at Ripar. Besides, Ripar is due to be flooded. Not all your spouse's pumps can save it—can they, Yockerbow?"

He made sober reply. "From the bluff where we've installed the telescope, we've seen ice stretching to the skyline. I wouldn't dare to calculate how far the level of the oceans will rise when it melts, but if it's going to be the same as before the Freeze, nothing can save Ripar or any other coastal city."

"Agreed. We should therefore present them to the observatory at Huzertol, inland from Grench and in a zone of clear skies." The admiral spoke in a tone of finality, not expecting to be contradicted.

"Won't do," said Ulgrim instantly.

"What?"

"Won't do," the navigator repeated. "Huzertol may have the best astronomers in the world, the best instruments—it doesn't matter.

That far south, they can scarcely see the Smoke, and some of the other important stars nearby never clear its horizon."

Barratong gave a dry laugh. "You know something, old friend? Next year I think we ought to circumnavigate the globe, if only to impress on your admiral's awareness that we do live on a spherical planet! You're right, of course. We must find a northerly observatory."

"Or found one," said Yockerbow.

"Hmm! Go on!"

"Well, if there isn't any place in the northern hemisphere to outdo Huzertol, there ought to be. Ripar is wealthy, and Ripar is doomed. What better memorial than to create a city dedicated to learning and science on some suitable upland site, to which we could transfer—?"

But Barratong wasn't listening. Of a sudden, he was paying attention to the junq. Her back was rippling in a rhythmic pattern.

"The water's growing warmer," he said positively.

To Yockerbow, that seemed unsurprising, since the heavy rain must be raising its temperature. That, though, seemed not to be what the admiral meant.

A gong-signal boomed across the water. A pattern of banners, rain-limp but comprehensible, appeared at the prow of the junq lying furthest to the eastern side of the bay.

Barratong rose to his normal height as he stepped out from the haodah's protection. He said to Arranth, "Give me the map-tube!"

"What? I—"

"*Give it to me!* Bring cord to make a lashing and a bladder to wrap round it! There's no time to make a new wax seal!"

Ulgrim recognized the scent of authority before the rest of them, and scrambled to comply. While the others stared in astonishment, Barratong folded the tube with its maps inside a skin bag, and tied it tight with all his strength to the thickest of the haodah's multiple crossbars.

"Thus does the legend say Skilluck preserved his spy-glass," he muttered, while the gong-signals multiplied and grew more frantic, and the junqs began to fret and buck. "And for the sake of imitating him, I'm risking the greatest fleet that ever was . . ."

The job was done. He turned back to them, claws clenched.

"*Now*, Ulgrim, give the signal! *Open sea!*"

And the Fleet incontinently turned and fled.

The order came in time, but only just. Wide though the bay-mouth was, the junqs jostled and tossed in their mad retreat, and the first huge slabs of the ice-wall were already sliding down as they escaped and their commanders regained control.

"Scatter!" Barratong yelled, and pounded the banner junq's gong. It could not be heard above the scraping, grinding, splashing noise from astern, and the rushing, pounding, battering racket of the new-budded waves that were smashing floes against the rocks. All of a sudden the world rocked and twisted and great hills of water erupted in their path, and sometimes the junqs ascended them at a giddying angle and came close to capsizing and sometimes they crashed into them prow-foremost so they broke and doused the crews and filled the back-wells, soaking the stored food. There was no need to order scattering; the alternative did not exist.

Out from the bay rushed bergs as keen as new-cut fangs, and the junqs panicked in their attempt to dodge. The haodah lashings creaked and the junqs screamed for pain, and some of the youngest sought to escape their burdens by rolling over, but their flotation bladders obliged them to right themselves, and if any riders were lost they were children and old folk too weak to cling on. Primeval reflexes bound the adults to whatever they could grasp, folding their mantles around to reinforce their claws and pressurizing the edges until they were stiff as stone.

In a moment of lucidity Yockerbow thought: *Just so must Skilq, or Skilluck, or whoever, have endured that legendary storm . . .*

Yet it was not the storm which had caused this. It went on pelting down, but it was trifling. No storm could make the ocean heave and seethe this way! Louder than thunder the noise of shattered ice conveyed the truth.

That warming of the water which Barratong had detected must have presaged the undermining of the high ice-wall. Once it collapsed, whatever was pent up behind it was turned loose, and the Fleet was washed away across the world as randomly as those vaned flying seeds . . .

# 9

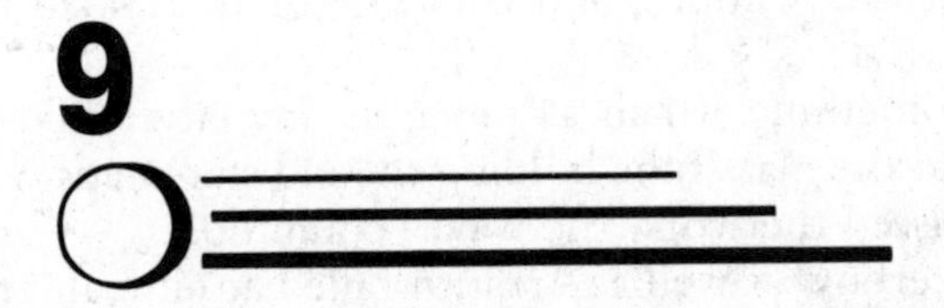

"Has it only been a year?" mourned Arranth, her mantle shrunken by salt and cresh, when next they came to what had been the site of Ripar. There was no more trace of the sea-defenses, no sign of the pumps Yockerbow had been so proud of—only some wilting treetops bending to the water, and a trapped mass of what had been prized personal possessions that washed back and forth, back and forth, in time to the waves. Any corpses must have been devoured long ago, for now a horde of greedy sharqs ruled where the Order of the Jingfired had held sway.

Not all the destruction, of course, had been caused by a simple rise in water-level. Maps and charts explained why Ripar had been worse affected than so many other cities they had visited. Northward, an archipelago had focused the impact of the first gigantic wave, driving it into a single channel where it could no longer spread out relatively harmlessly. Some of the islands had been completely washed away; enough, though, had resisted to ensure that Ripar's fragile protective banks dissolved under the eventual onslaught. Once the city's roots were exposed to the intense saltiness of the warm northern water—warm!—they were doomed.

But the melting was certain to continue, as was betokened by the presence of countless bergs following the same currents as the Fleet, and when—if—all the polar ice returned to the liquid state, the world would be transformed unrecognizably.

They had talked long and long about the future as they strove to recreate the Fleet. Barratong had had the foresight to decree what none of his predecessors had thought necessary: a rendezvous in mid-ocean, near four islands with fresh water and ample vegetation. That was where they had waited out the winter, but one of the islands was shrunk to half its normal size and many of the edible plants were dying . . . as were too many of the reunited junqs. There was a loathsome taint in the air, and every gust of northern gale brought a drift of grittiness that revolted the maw and made the torso itch beneath the mantle. Sometimes the aurora towards the pole was blanked out not by regular clouds but by some kind of dust, not cleanly star-budded dust such as gave rise to meteors—few, come to that, had been seen this year, hidden no doubt by the same ghastly veil—instead, like the much-feared smoke which drifted from the world's rare drylands when a lightning-strike released wildfire, and could blind and choke those trapped downwind.

"But we saved something worth as much as any city," said Barratong, and pointed to the glass tube holding the old star-maps, which had miraculously resisted the worst the waves could do.

Embittered, Yockerbow as well as Arranth railed at him, and to all their complaining he responded imperturbably:

"You will die, and I, and all we can create—why not a city? But if there is one thing that deserves to be immortal, it is knowledge. Perhaps in the far future like my web to catch the moon a means will exist to unite past and present, here and there, abolishing distance and anxiety at a blow. We spoke a while back, though—did we not?—of an observatory, and a city we shall dedicate to science?"

"A while back" had been very nearly a full year, and Yockerbow, overcome with misery and privation, had long ago dismissed his proposal to the realms of fantasy. He was amazed to hear the admiral repeat it seriously.

"It's out of the question after a catastrophe on this scale," he muttered. "And it isn't over yet. It may take scores of years before the water-level stabilizes. If all the polar ice melts, there may be no dry land whatsoever."

"I don't believe it," Barratong responded. "But even if that's so, we shall build continents of floating weed! We'll not go tamely to an accidental doom! And if we can't learn about the stars, we'll learn about ourselves and the life around us!"

He drew himself up stern and tall, and now he did overtop his companions, for their dispirited mood had sorely shrunk them.

"This you must understand at least: *we* are the Jingfired now."

Eventually the implications of his words penetrated the dismal fog in Yockerbow's mind, and he too straightened. He said, "You intend it seriously?"

"Oh, not at once, of course. First we have other duties to attend to. I shall break up the Fleet, and dispatch it to every corner of the world, bearing seed and medicine and knowledge above all. At every port of call my commanders will be instructed to inquire after secure sites where people may remove to, and rescue whoever needs to be conveyed thither. Also they shall diligently search out scientists and scholars, so that when we choose the site for our new city—not this year, not next, perhaps not in our lifetime—our successors will know where to recruit a population for it. Then let them assemble with their books and instruments and do as you, friend Yockerbow, suggested: combine their knowledge so that none be lost."

"Will you be obeyed in this?" husked Arranth.

"Oh, I think pride will serve to persuade the ones I have in mind."

"Pride in independence, because they will be in command of their own Fleets, with the right to take wild junqlings and increase them?" Ulgrim's tone was cynical; for countless generations, it had been a punishable offense to do so.

"In part." Barratong was unperturbed. "More to the prong, however, pride in ancestry—which I, an ex-landsider, cannot boast of. Think, Ulgrim! Think of how the People of the Sea must already be reacting to the news that their forebears chose correctly! We face nothing worse than storms and tidal waves. If an island we're accustomed to put in at vanishes, we find another; if the waters rise and swamp what was dry land, so much the better, for where there were isthmi now we find new channels that will take us into undiscovered seas . . . Oh, we shall be rulers of the western ocean too, and very soon! And will not it make for pride that we give aid to those who boasted of security on land?"

"You think more clearly and more distantly than anyone," said Ulgrim in a sober voice.

"Not I! Not I! But Arranth and her like. You chided me for not reacting to the fact the world is round! She saw the very stars moving apart like local floes!"

He gave a little crazy laugh. "That's why I must break up the greatest fleet that ever was. There aren't enough of us to fight the stars, and after this long melting we'll be fewer still. We need a score of Fleets, a score-of-scores! We have to be so crowded and so crammed together that we can burst outward from the world—become like these!"

From one of his baldrics he produced a tiny object, dry and shriveled.

"Remember these?"

"One of the seeds that pelted us up north," said Yockerbow.

"Correct! Well, if a mindless plant can find a way to spread beyond its isolated patch, why shouldn't we? Did it ever strike you that there must have been a first person who pithed a barq or briq, just as there was certainly a first who tamed a junq? Then, folk were confined to continents or islands, and had to trudge wearily from place to place unless they had a drom—and someone, equally, must have been first to ride a drom!"

Ulgrim and Yockerbow exchanged worried glances. Sometimes nowadays Barratong spoke so strangely . . . Only Arranth seemed totally to understand him, as though he and she, during this dreadful winter, had found a skyward course into the future in their joint imaginations. But how sane was their shared vision, when the world itself was dissolving back into its primeval waters?

"I wish," said Yockerbow, scarcely realizing he had spoken audibly, "I'd never left Ripar. I'd rather have been here to tend my pumps, to learn their limitations and escape to high ground where I might have built them anew and much improved."

"Somebody will," said Arranth with assurance. "Now your task is to wander the world teaching those who need to know how it was done, just as mine is to explain the star-maps that—thanks to Barratong—have been preserved. You never respected the Order of the Jingfired, and you had some justification, I suppose, given that you devised new methods not envisaged by its ancient wisdom. But I always did, even when I was angry at the way intrigue and self-seeking tarnished its ideals. And if Barratong, who at first mocked it, has come around to my point of view—well!"

Acid rose in Yockerbow's maw. He was minded to utter cruel truths, for she had not truly respected the Order, only envied its members, wanted her spouse to be inducted for the glory of it. He meant to tax her with her ridiculous adoption of crossed strands of sparkleweed in imitation of an admiral's baldrics, seeking petty temporary fame by setting a trend.

Yet he could not. This last appalling year had altered her. The first signs had already been apparent when she spoke with such authority of the discoveries she had made with Ulgrim. Now she had grown used to being someone other than her old self. In a way not even she could have foreseen, she had fulfilled her ambition and become the admiral's lady.

Who was this new strange person who confidently claimed to understand the actions of the stars?

Not his spouse. Not anymore . . .

So leave her the luxury of self-deception, that she might the better convince the few who, like her and Barratong, could see beyond the current crisis. For his part, he had information about techniques that would be useful everywhere when folk settled on new lands and needed fresh water drawn from a distance, or irrigation systems, or means to lift a heavy load. Suppose, for instance, there were other creatures than cutinates whose muscles could be isolated and made to grow . . .

All of a sudden he felt as though a great burden had been taken from him. His mind cleared. Without his realizing, his life had been spent in the shadow of those allegedly greater than himself. They were nothing of the sort; they were merely more powerful. And the power they wielded was puny compared to Barratong's, yet the admiral was ultimately humble before the marvels of the boundless universe, which —Arranth said—now threatened them with something no Great Fleet, no member of the Jingfired, no person whatsoever could defy: a cloud of stars and interstellar gas that must be burning at temperatures unmatched by any furnace.

Compared to the cosmos, everyone was equal. Everyone was a bud of this small planet. Either everyone must work together, or in a few score generations there would be no one.

A flock of cloudcrawlers was passing. He looked up, wondering whether in their serial migration might be sought the secret of survival.

But he knew too little. Still, he had about half his life before him; there could well be time to find out what had been discovered or invented on other continents, as well as by the People of the Sea. The most amazing chance could, as he realized, lead to practical results, and whatever chance itself might be, it had already supplied the most important information.

"The past *can* communicate with the future," he said aloud. "And we're the past."

"Yes, of course," said Barratong. "We have to devise gongs and banners in order to signal our successors as the Fleet does. At every port we shall leave copies of the star-maps, ancient and modern; at every port we shall leave ashore folk who, having fled drowned cities, want to start anew on land with foreign knowledge . . . We dare not let blind fortune alter the world without hindrance. We too must play our part in changing it. Ulgrim, call a general meet. Today I purpose to divide the Fleet, and the planet."

# 10

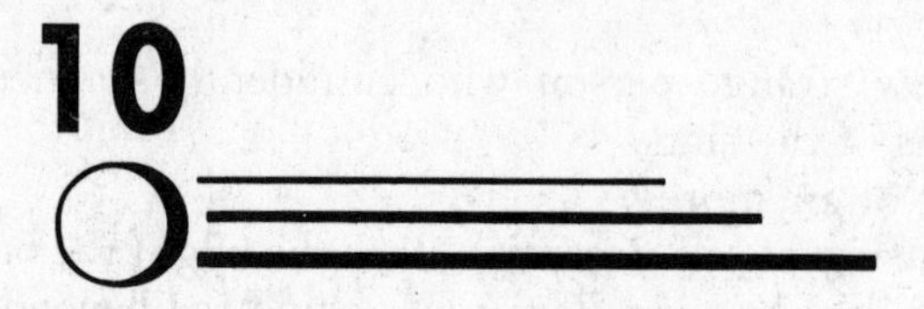

*T*he ice's burden lifted swiftly from the northern lands, and new huge rivers carved their course through what had been dry plains. Gigantic floods drowned forests and the creatures living in them; meantime, the ocean-level marked new records every spring. What had been land-bridges turned to open channels; what had been island-chains were strings of shoals.

But most important of all, the weight of frozen water had held down a necessary, long-impending shift of one continental plate against another. Part of the Great Thaw was due to absorption by the sun of a wisp of interstellar gas which for a brief while had helped to mask its radiation. The local space was temporarily clear now, and extra warmth was piercing the atmosphere because fewer dustmotes were falling from the sky to serve as nuclei around which drops of rain or hailstones might develop, and the long ice-age had inhibited production of natural nuclei due to vegetation or the smoke of wildfire.

Another reason for the Thaw, however, was to be sought in the conversion of kinetic energy to heat. Around the north pole there were geysers and volcanoes testifying to the presence of magma near the crust. Patient, they had waited out the period during which so monstrous a mass of ice lay over them that all their heat could serve to do was make a glacier slide or melt a summer valley for migrating flighters. The continental plates which powered them, however, were on a different and grander scale. No ice could long have resisted their padlong-per-year progress, and the added solar warmth did no more than hasten what was inevitable.

The ice-cap shattered in a laq of seizures, each one casting loose a craw of bergs. Lava leaking from far underground met open water and solidified and then was cast high into the air when water turned to steam. Plume followed eruption followed temblor, and at every stage more water streamed back from the arctic plateau to the ocean.

Somehow the separated Fleets survived, even though their business became, first and foremost, mere survival, and their admiral's vision of immediate salvation was eroded by the giant waves that unpredictably rushed from the north and, later, from the south as well, where there was no such enormous valley as the one which had penned in the Salty Sea to deliver its new water all at once.

Often overloaded, so they were forced to land unwilling riders on half-sunken islands in the hope at least their mountain peaks might rise above the water when the oceans calmed; often driven off course by storms such as nobody had seen in living memory; often picking their cautious way over what had been a land-mass a scant year or two ago, searching for anything which might be useful, be it edible carrion or a batch of tools and instruments which would float; often rescuing survivors from a sunken city most of whom were starved into dreamness already and having to make the harsh decision that they must be again abandoned, for their sanity was poisoned past all hope of cure; often—once the barriers between the eastern and the western oceans had been breached—confronting herds of wild briqs, savage in a way that junqs had never been and panicked by an amazing explosion of gulletfish, so that they had to reinvent on the basis of legend and guesswork the means to pith a briq, with the minor consolation that if the attempt failed there would at least be food for the folk on board, and the major drawback that the taint of their own kind's ichor in the water drove the other briqs frantic with terror; often near despair and redeemed only by messages from another luckier Little Fleet, with an achievement to boast about such as the safe delivery of a group of scholars to an upland refuge . . .

The People of the Sea endured the horrors of the Thaw and by miracles preserved the vision Barratong bequeathed to them.

Meantime, the landsiders moved along the tracks and paths available. Confronted by the rising water, they summoned droms and other mounts and loaded them, and struggled up steep mountainsides, collecting useful seeds and spores. Again and again the caravans were overwhelmed by hunger or sickness caught from murrained water, or trapped on a valley path when floods came rushing down. Desperate, some resorted to the use of fresh-water barqs, only to see them wilt and die when salt afflicted their tubules.

A few, however, found a way to safety, and after cautious negotiation settled on high ground near existing hamlets, being eventually made welcome because they had brought new food-plants and, above all, because they offered the chance of fertile first-time matings to communities whose numbers were diminishing.

Following the caravans, though often having to invent new routes, discontented wandering scholars trudged from town to new town seeking their lost equals, each bearing something of what had been known in a city sunk beneath the waves or lost when a hillside slumped into the sea. Occasionally they borrowed the services of the tramp junqs which, after the dispersal of the Lesser Fleets, traveled in groups of three or four and traded as best they could along inlets of the sea that formerly had been mountain passes or river-valleys. The hegemony of the People of the Sea endured, but the mixing of the landsiders resulted, almost at once, in an explosion of population, for instead of one pairing in several score producing a bud, suddenly five took, or even seven, and wise persons argued about miscegenation, and proper diet, and the influence of privation, and it seemed that most of them must be at least partly correct.

The sea-level stabilized. Those fortunate astronomers who had access to long-term brightness records for the sun admitted cautiously that it looked as though the extra heat due to infalling matter was over. Those who had preserved their presence of mind during the period of violent quakes, devising means to mark and measure the trembling of the land, noted with satisfaction that it shook only now and then, and hilltops seldom broke loose anymore. Such scientists, when they met them, the People of the Sea declared to be Jingfired, and gave them copies of the ancient star-maps. It was a mere token, for the donors scarcely understood what the maps recorded, yet they were seeds of knowledge, after their fashion. The skies cleared, and there was no longer a gritty stench when the wind blew from the north. Daringly, a few started to maintain that an outburst of volcanic dust had protected life on the planet from the worst effects of increased solar radiation . . . but it was at best a guess, lacking evidence.

When the world settled back to an even keel, explorers set forth once more who employed techniques that once had been the private property of jealous cities: means to signal across vast distances, means to preserve knowledge by multiplying it in countless copies; medicines to cure common illnesses, others to master strange rare disorders; tools for tasks that most people had never dreamed of undertaking; seeds so treated they would yield edible fruit simply by being soaked in salty water when required; vegetable parchments that changed color when light shone on them, which placed at the proper distance from a lens would fix an image; juices and saps which served to bind together plant and rock, or glass and metal; vessels not of wood or hide but melted sand, not exactly glass but stiffer, wherein a fire might safely be lighted on the back of a junq without the creature suffering . . .

Tricks and ideas, hints and suggestions, cross-fertilized and bred faster than the population. A means was needed that would match one invention, to be exchanged, against another. After much fierce debate, it was agreed that persons schooled in the desired technique should be the unit, and the surviving Little Fleets should carry them for longer or shorter periods among the folk requesting the new knowledge. By now, however, many of the new cities had their own research groups, not to mention their own miniature Fleets, and the system rapidly broke down.

It made no odds. The time was past when one city might strive for superiority over its neighbors. The impulse was for sharing, because over all of them loomed the threat which they could now read directly from the sky. Even the southmost of the settlements, shielded from all the new stars in the Smoke, accepted it. Beyond a doubt the day would dawn when the folk, in order to survive, must quit their world.

*How*, naturally, none yet knew . . .

As for the banner junq of the Great Fleet of the Eastern Sea, her last recorded trace was when they brought to Yockerbow, old then and shrunken-mantled, a bundle found among jetsam on what had been the slopes of a mountain inland from Clophical, and now was a steep beach beset by trees. His name was inscribed on it three times. The finders located him without trouble; he was famous, because he had become the lord and leader of a scientific community not quite like what he, Barratong and Arranth had envisaged, but near enough. Scholars flocked to him from every land, and new discoveries and new inventions flooded out as water had poured forth when the ice-wall broke and loosed the Salty Sea.

"Here is," he said when he had opened the bundle—with assistance, for his pressure was now weak—"the original glass tube which held the ancient star-maps. I wonder what happened to the maps themselves. Not that it matters; we've found other better copies. What map, though, could show me where to find my lost lady Arranth? What chart could guide me to my old friend Barratong? . . . Oh, take this thing to the museum, will you? I have much work to do, and little time."

# Part Four

# Breaking the Mold

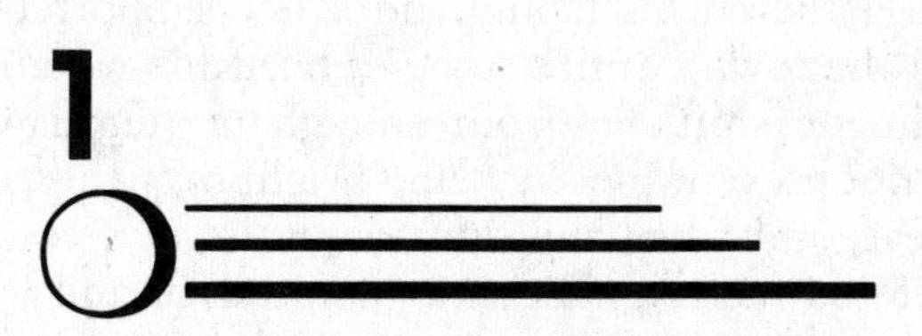

*F*ew communities on the planet were more isolated than the settlement at Neesos, a dark-and-a-bright's swim from the mainland. Once the island had been linked to it by a narrow isthmus passable even at high tide, but the Great Thaw had drowned that along with most of its fertile land, and for scores of years it was visited solely by fisherfolk riding kyqs with their trained gorborangs perched on the saddle-branches like dull red fruit. There were still sandbanks, though, and tradition held that in the past such sand had furnished excellent glass. A certain Agnis eventually made an expedition thither and, finding the tale correct, set about producing magnifiers.

However, he did so at a time when a chillward shift in the weather had led to a revival of religion. Made hungry by the failure of staple crops, the folk were as ever victimized by those who, by starving themselves voluntarily, claimed to obtain visions of a higher reality. In truth, so Agnis charged, what they craved was power over others, and they hoped to gain it by preventing the public from directly consulting the Jingtexts, wherein might be sought solutions to all worldly woes . . . not, naturally, that every humble person might aspire to read the ancient teachings without guidance, for they were couched in archaic symbols, a far cry from the crisp and simple script used for modern messages, and the speech itself had changed almost beyond recognition.

This did not content the relidges, eager as they were to draw down everybody to that mental level where reason was indistinguishable from dreamness. Sight was the first mode of perception to be diminished by famine, as weather-sense was the last, but it was in vain for Agnis to argue that by providing artificial aid he was encouraging the spiritual advancement of the folk. The relidges countered by saying it made them more vulnerable to the rationalist writings now being distributed in countless copies thanks to the invention, by some foreigner beyond the horizon, of a vegetable which could be made to ooze blackish stains on a dry absorbent leaf in exact imitation of any mark inscribed on its rind. Images had long been fixable, at least in one color; soon, it was claimed, means would be found to reproduce them as well.

Despairing, Agnis gathered his family and a few supporters and made for Neesos with the town's entire stock of burnable wood. The cool phase of the climatic shift, far from enough to reinitiate the Northern Freeze, did not prevent the sky being bright over this region for almost half the year, and when the sun was up its rays could be focused. Using his pilfered fuel, Agnis cast a giant mirror and with it melted colossal quantities of sand. This served to fabricate spyglasses of outstanding quality, such as lured not only fisherfolk but even the all-powerful People of the Sea. Shortly his village was better off than the town its inhabitants had quit, since the latter had little left worth trading for.

Sometimes the settlers found relics of the far past in the shallow waters around Neesos, and they too served for trading purposes, mysterious though their nature might be to the modern mind. In consequence, it was into a community more prosperous than its isolation might have suggested that Tenthag—half a score of generations in direct succession from Agnis himself—was budded in the year called Two-red-stars-turn-blue.

But the community was so small that the People of the Sea were rarely able to trade what they most wanted and needed at Neesos: stock with which to cross-breed themselves. They had sampled every genetic line on the island, and every line, in turn, was already spiked with some of the travelers' ichor.

Long-lived, reasonably content, the folk of Neesos were resigned to budding being rare. It was not until three quarter-score of years had slipped away that they began to notice:

*There has been no new bud since Tenthag.*

As soon as they realized he was "special" the folk of Neesos started to pamper the boy, which he found no fun at all, for it meant he was forever being prohibited from doing the things the other young'uns enjoyed. The old'uns said "protected," but it amounted to the same boring thing.

Yet his slightly older companions were contemptuous of his youth, and very shortly there was only one left for him to play with. The rest had gone on to the pretence of being grown-up, although their matings led to no offspring. Tenthag wished achingly that they would, to release him from his confinement in a web of concern.

Still, his father Ninthag was a perennial optimist and, despite the pleas of Sixthon who had budded Tenthag for him and never childed with anybody else, he was happy to turn a blind eye when his son did what in olden times all young'uns were accustomed to—go swimming out of storm-season on the northern coast—along with Fifthorch, who was next-to-youngest.

Here there were beaches sown with rocks defining the trace of what had been Prefs, the port serving crag-beset Thenai in the days before the water-level rose a score of padlongs. Great ocean-going briqs and junqs had unloaded here, revealing marvels brought from half the world away, and sometimes odd bits and pieces that had proved unsalable had been tossed overside before the fleets returned to sea. Young'uns sought for them, trapping as much air as possible beneath their mantles before they dived, in the hope of retrieving artifacts intact. But that had been in the old days. Now only scraps were to be found, at least at any level they could reach.

Nonetheless Fifthorch spent as much time as he was spared from his apprenticeship at the general trade of glassworking, plunging and basking around the northern shore, and perforce Tenthag tagged along. He did not really like Fifthorch, but there was no alternative; he so hated being fussed over and petted by the old'uns.

Eventually, they all assumed, he would fall into the standard pattern of the island's folk, and were its population to die out, someone else would take it over. That was the way it had been since time immemorial, and even though a few stars might turn color, life down here was not expected to alter very much. The age of changes seemed to be long past, bar the occasional shift of weather.

It did sometimes puzzle Tenthag why, if nothing was to change worth mentioning, there should be so many relics of a different past lying just off shore. But when he tried to talk about this to the old'uns they were always busy with something else, and if he voiced his private anxieties to Fifthorch, the latter mocked him, quoting what he had been told by his own father, who despised the Jingtexts.

"The form of now is permanent," he would insist. "If there were changes in the past, it must have been because what passed for people then were only animals. We were set here by the Evolver to use and exploit the lower orders. Now we know how to do it—we have gorborangs to catch fish for us, we have kyqs to ride on when we put to sea, we eat enough to let us tell reality from dreamness, we live a proper life that must not be disturbed! And nothing can, and nothing will, disturb it!"

Thereat, becoming bored, he would propose a diving expedition, and—not wanting to seem ungracious, nor to become bored himself—Tenthag would once more risk the effect of salty water on his tegument.

He relished the experience of plunging through the ocean shallows, as his ancestors must once have plunged through air from branch to branch of forests now lost beneath the waves, but he could never quite rid himself of awareness of what nightly he saw marked out on the sky. Since he quit infancy and was able to erect himself and raise his eye to the zenith, he had been fascinated by those brilliant spots and streaks . . . and started to wonder why his elders never paid them any attention except when there were unusual displays, and seemed almost to welcome the dull season—regardless of its storms—when clouds closed over land and sea alike. Did not the Jingtexts refer to changes which . . . ?

But "change" and "Jingtext" were incompatible, they said, one necessarily contradicting the other. If a scripture spoke of change, it must be taken metaphorically, as parable. The year of his birth, when two stars turned to blue, was dated in the manner of a nickname.

And so it went, with Tenthag defeated at all turns, until the year whenafter the world could never be the same.

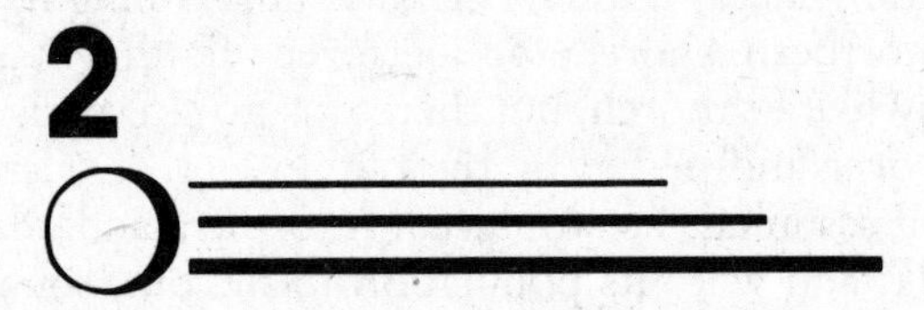

## 2

It wasn't kyqs that year which swam into the bay as soon as the spring hail died away, but junqs and briqs far grander than ever had been seen before at Neesos. Moreover, they arrived without the slightest warning.

Led by Ninthag and his deputy, Thirdusk, the folk assembled on the shore in mingled wonder and apprehension. Even the People of the Sea did not boast such magnificent steeds, so finely caparisoned with secondary life-forms. Who could these strangers be?

Very shortly the explanation spread, and generated universal amazement. Those who had come hither were not any sort of common trader, though prepared to pay for what they took; they hailed from a city far to the south, called Bowock, and they went by a name whose roots were drawn from Ancient Forbish, "archeologists"—which some of the more learned of the folk patronizingly rendered into today's speech for the commonalty, making it "pastudiers."

What they wanted, they declared, was to explore the underwater ruins, and they would offer either food and tools for the privilege, or new kinds of seed and animal-stock, or something abstract known as "credits" which allegedly would give the folk of Neesos privileges in return if ever they were to visit Bowock. Since nobody from here in living memory had voyaged further than the horizon, the latter were turned down at once, but the rest appealed, and a bargain was struck with which the majority of the folk were in agreement. What little wariness remained soon melted when the newcomers exclaimed over the fineness of the local glass and ordered magnifiers, microscopes and new lenses for a strange device used to find relative positions, hence distances otherwise impossible to measure. These they exchanged for the right to deepwater fish caught from their junqs and briqs.

Almost the sole person who continued to grumble about this intrusion was Fifthorch, because the strangers had occupied his favorite area for swimming.

Not wanting to lose his only friend, or what passed for one, Tenthag dutifully agreed with him, even though his pith wasn't in it. He was fascinated by the newcomers, above all because, for people concerned with the past, they had so many new gadgets and inventions at their disposal. They had set up a mainland base, where they were necessarily treating with the folk of the town the Neesans' ancestors had fled from—though time had healed most of the old wounds—and made some sort of connection with it to carry news faster than the swiftest briq could swim. A cable like a single immensely long nerve-strand had been laid along the sea-bed between the two places, and covered over with piles of rock carefully set in place by divers wearing things called air-feeders: ugly, bulging, parasitical organisms bred from a southern species unknown, and unhappy, in these cool northern seas, which somehow kept a person alive underwater. Also they had means to lift even extremely heavy objects, using some substance or creature that contracted with vast force.

Such matters, though, the Bowockers were secretive about. To those who asked for information concerning them they named an impossibly high price. Anyway, there was scant need for such devices here.

Otherwise they were not unfriendly, and came ashore by dark to chat, share food and otherwise socialize; a few of them knew songs and tales, or played instruments, and became tolerably popular. Inevitably, too, there were pairings, but none resulted in a bud, although Tenthag desperately hoped they might. He was tired of being the permanently youngest.

The same problem apparently beset Bowock, though. Now and

then the divers, ashore to recover from the toll exacted by their work, would grow confidential after sampling the powerful local araq, and admit that at home there were too few buds to keep up the population, despite contacts with other cities and the People of the Sea. Some went so far as to wonder aloud what they were doing all this for, if in a few score-of-score years there might be no one left to enjoy the knowledge. But they kept on regardless.

What precisely the knowledge was that they hoped to garner from the broken fragments they brought up, the folk of Neesos could not imagine. Little organic material resisted the erosion of salt water; tides and currents had scattered what did endure, like blades, lenses and the burnt-clay formers used to compel houseplants to grow into the desired shape. Within a couple of months most people stopped wondering, and treated the strangers as a familiar feature of the locality.

Tenthag was almost the only exception.

Nonetheless, the day came when some most exciting discovery was made—to judge by the noisy celebrations the pastudiers spent a whole dark in—and shortly afterwards a single rider arrived mounted on a sea-beast such as nobody had ever sighted in these latitudes before. She was unbelievably swift in the water, casting up a snout-wave that broke in rainbow spray, and nearly as large as the smaller junqs, but with a tiny saddle and virtually no secondary plants. She had an appetite of her own, though, and a huge one. Cast loose to browse in the next bay to where the pastudiers were working, she gulped and chomped and gobbled and gulped again the whole dark long. When they were asked about her, the strangers said she was an unpithed porp, specially bred for high-speed travel.

The idea of a porp, even a tame one, in the local waters was not calculated to appeal to the folk of Neesos. Schools of such creatures were reputed to strip vast areas clear of weed and drive away the sorts of fish the folk depended on. However, the Bowockers promised that she would leave again at dawn, carrying important news. What kind of news, they as usual declined to say.

By now there was a feeling among the folk that they should be entitled to a share in the pastudiers' discoveries, and Fifthorch's parents were among the loudest with complaints, although they personally did nothing to cultivate the visitors' acquaintance and laid all the responsibility on Ninthag and Thirdusk. The night when the porp was feeding, Tenthag grew sufficiently irritated by Fifthorch's automatic repetition of his father's arguments to counter them with some of Ninthag's. The result was a quarrel, and the older boy went storming off.

Alone in the dark, under the bright-sown canopy which was as ever shedding sparkling starlets, Tenthag turned despondently towards the beach. He was so lost in a mix of imagination, memory and dream that he was startled when a female voice addressed him.

"Hello! Come to admire my porp? I understand you people don't tame any sea-creatures but kyqs, right?"

Taken aback, he glanced around and spotted the person who had spoken: a she'un only some half-score years his senior, relaxing in a pit in the sand.

This was the rider who had made so spectacular an entry into the bay? But by comparison with the monstrous beast she rode, she was puny! Even erect, she would be a padlong below him, and he was not fully grown.

"We—uh—we don't know much about them," he forced out as soon as enough pressure returned to his mantle. "Certainly taming porps is a new idea to us."

"Oh, where I come from there's never any shortage of new ideas! Our only problem is finding time to put them all into practice. Are you going anywhere, or would you like to talk awhile? I'm Nemora of the Guild of Couriers, in case you hadn't guessed. And you are—?"

"Tenthag," he answered, feeling his courage grow. "And . . . Well, yes, I'd love to talk to you!"

"Then make yourself comfortable," she invited. "You've eaten, drunk, and so on?"

"Thank you, yes. We feed well here, and all the better"—he thought of the compliment barely in time—"because of the Bowockers who bring us deepwater fish."

"Yes, normally you only work the shallows, I believe. Well, here's something from my homeland which may tempt you even if you're not hungry. Try some yelg; it's standard courier ration, but I have more than enough for this trip because my lovely Scudder is so quick through the water."

What she offered was unfamiliar but delicious, and within moments he felt all temptation to slip into dreamness leave him. He was in full possession of himself.

"I hope I'm not keeping you from your friends," he said.

"Friends? Oh, you mean the archeologists! No, I don't know them. Anyhow, they're too busy to be bothered with a mere courier. They hadn't finished preparing their reports and packaging what they've found, because they figured I wouldn't be here until tomorrow. But, like I said, Scudder is the record-breaking type . . . Oh, there goes a beauty!"

A wide and brilliant streak had crossed the sky, to vanish behind low cloud on the eastern horizon. For a moment it even outshone the Major Cluster, let alone the Arc of Heaven.

"There isn't much to do when you're a courier," she said musingly, "except to watch the weather and the sky. Yet I wouldn't trade my job for anyone's."

"I don't believe I ever heard of the Guild of Couriers before," Tenthag admitted.

"Really?" She turned to him in surprise. "I thought we'd pretty well covered the globe by now—but come to think of it they did warn me I was going to a very isolated area. Well, essentially what we do is keep people in touch with one another over distances that nervograps can't span, and transport bulky items which briq and junq trade would delay or damage. That's why I'm here, of course: they found what they were looking for, and the relics are extremely fragile. But you must know about that."

"I'm afraid they don't talk to us about what they're doing," Tenthag muttered. "Not even to the old'uns, let alone someone of my age."

"Oh, that's absurd! I'll have to mention it when I get home. We couriers have strict instructions from the Order of the Jingfired to maximize trade in information. The Guild was originally founded to spread news of the musculator . . . but I sense you aren't following my meaning."

By now Tenthag was emitting such a pheromone-load of incomprehension he was embarrassed. Nemora, in contrast, exuded perfect self-confidence and, impressed by her tact, he was shortly able to respond.

"The word is new to me," he confessed. "Same as—what was it you said?—nervograp?"

"Hmm! No wonder you still only hunt the shallows! But you must have seen the musculators working here, and you could trade something for a brood-stock. They say you make good glass, and—Oh. Never tell me these 'friends' of mine have bought your entire supply for much less useful goods!"

"I believe," Tenthag answered, quoting what he had heard from Fifthorch, "they've commissioned a whole summer's output."

"For supposedly dedicated students of the past, they're far too mercenary, then. I'll report that, definitely. Well, a musculator is what you get when you breed a particular type of shore-living creature for nothing but strength—not even mobility, nothing else except the power to contract when one end is in fresh water and the other in salt. You feed it a few scraps, you can breed from it in turn, and you use it for—oh—pumping water where it's needed, lifting heavy weights, hauling a load across a mountain gorge where mounts can't go, and things like that. And a nervograp . . . But there's one in operation between here and the mainland, isn't there?"

"A way of signaling?"

"Ah, you know about that, at least. That's much newer than musculators, of course—in fact, so new that we're still stringing them overland between cities, and I think this is the first-ever underwater connection. I hope it's being done in time, that's all. We've got to link up everybody on the planet if we're ever to get away."

There followed a long baffled silence. Reacting to it, Nemora said eventually, "I'm sorry about that. I was just so stunned to realize you had no idea what I'm referring to. Aren't the Jingtexts available on Neesos?"

"Not many people can read them," Tenthag muttered. "I've never been allowed even to study the language of them."

"But this is awful!" She erupted out of her sitting-pit in a single graceful surge, and Tenthag had his first chance to see her entire. He was embarrassed all over again. She was perfectly lovely, and there was no way he could hide the exudate that signaled his reaction. Luckily she took it as a compliment.

"Hold that for a while, young'un!" she commanded. "There are some things more important than pairing, you know! You really haven't been told that our sun and all its planets are being drawn into the Major Cluster, and if we don't escape we shall wind up fueling a celestial fire? My goodness, how old are you?"

He had to answer frankly, though he could have wished to pretend he was older. Lying was pointless with anybody who had a weather-sense as acute as Nemora's . . . and would not someone who piloted a porp singleclawed across great oceans have been selected for precisely that talent?

"I was born in the year called Two-red-stars-turn-blue."

"Then you really ought to be better informed! Why did they turn blue?"

"People here don't pay much attention to the sky," he said defensively.

"That's obvious! Well, the answer is this." Padding up and down, so that her mantle rippled in curves it almost hurt him to watch, she launched into the sort of lecture he had always dreamed of being given by someone older and wiser than himself. "The fixed lights in the sky are suns like ours, but far away. We have records showing that some of them, the nearest, are moving apart; this proves that we're approaching them. I don't mean the ones that move visibly. They're planets like ours, revolving around our sun, and the ones that spill out of the sky are just odd lumps of nothing much which heat up when they fall into our air. But there are too many of them for comfort. We think we're drawing closer to a volume of space where there are so many of these lumps that some must be very big indeed, big as the nubs of comets, and if one of them falls on a city, or even in mid-ocean—! And eventually we think our whole world may be drawn into a sun and go up in another star-turned-blue. The more fuel you put on a fire, the hotter it gets, right? And we don't want to be burned!"

Once more there was a period of silence, but this time it was for reflection. Tenthag felt as though he had been afflicted with acute mental indigestion, but what Nemora had said made excellent sense. Besides, how could someone as ignorant as himself challenge her?

He wanted to ask another million questions, but suddenly one became more urgent than any other. He said faintly, recalling what he had heard about the Bowocker divers, "Just now you told me there were some things more important than pairing. But suppose we don't breed, and there aren't enough people left when we find out how to—what did you say?—escape? In any case, I don't see how we could! First we'd have to learn to fly like cloudcrawlers, and then . . ."

Speech failed him; he sat dumbstruck.

With a deep chuckle she dropped beside him, so close their mantles touched.

"There are people working on means to fly *better* than cloudcrawlers," she murmured. "One of these days I hope to carry the news of somebody's success in that endeavor. But you're perfectly correct. There must be people to enjoy the benefit of what we're doing now. Would you like to pair with me? I guess it may be your first time, and they do say a first time can be fruitful."

When she departed after dawn, she left behind a transformed Tenthag, who knew beyond a doubt what he wanted to make of his life. To the dark with glassworking! He was determined to be like Nemora: a courier.

# 3

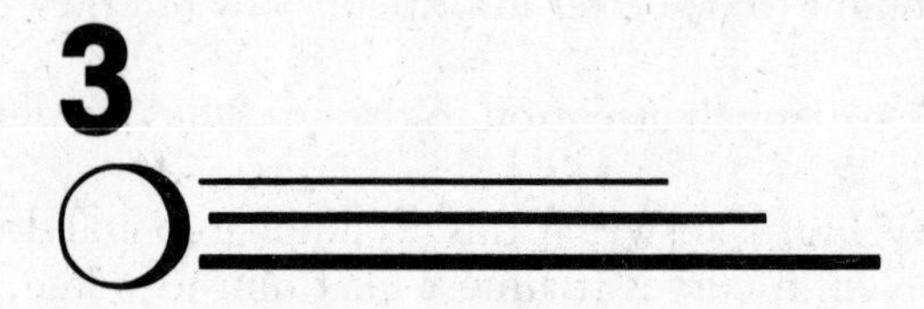

Later Tenthag concluded ruefully that if he'd realized how much he had to learn, he would probably have changed his mind. Life on Neesos had not prepared him for the complexity of the modern world, and particularly not for Bowock with its eleven score-of-scores of people, its houses every one of which was different (for the city itself served as a biological laboratory and experimental farm), and its ferment of novelty and invention.

Despite its multiplying marvels, though, which rendered public notice-slabs essential—announcing everything from goods for trade through new discoveries seeking application to appeals for volunteer assistance—there was a taint in Bowock's air, an exudate of anxiety verging on alarm. It was known that scores-of-scores-of-scores of years remained before the ultimate crisis, and few doubted their species' ability to find a means of escape, were they granted sufficient time.

In principle, they should be. Disease was almost unknown here and in other wealthy lands; crop-blights and murrains were held in check; everyone had food adequate to ensure rational thinking; maggors and wivvils and slugs were controlled by their own natural parasites—oh, the achievements of the Bowockers were astonishing!

But Nemora had not taken his bud, or anyone's. His first frightened question, so long ago, so far away, on the dark beach of Neesos, was one which everybody now was asking. Indeed, it had been Nemora's commendation of his instant insight which had secured him his appointment as a courier-to-be.

Hence his excitement at the challenging future he could look forward to was tempered by the sad gray shadow of a nearer doom. He tried to lose himself in training and caring for the porp assigned to him, modestly named Flapper, but even as he carried out his first solo missions—which should have been the high point of his life so far—he was constantly worrying about the folk he had left behind on Neesos, condemned to grow old and die without a single youngling to follow them.

He felt a little like a traitor.

"It is Neesos that you hail from, isn't it?" said the harsh familiar voice of Dippid, doyen of the couriers.

Tenthag glanced round. He was in the pleasant, cool, green-lit arbor of the porp pens, formed by a maze of root-stalks where the city's trees spanned the estuary of a little river. Porps became docile automatically in fresh water, a fact first observed at Bowock when one of them was driven hither from the open sea for an entirely different purpose, and between voyages they had to be carefully retamed.

Alert at mention of his home, he dared to hope for a moment that he was to be sent back there. Giving Flapper a final caress, he swarmed up the nearest root-stalk to confront Dippid . . . who promptly dashed the notion.

"The stuff that Nemora brought back from the trip when she met you: it seems to have borne fruit. You know about the work that Scholar Gveest is doing?"

Tenthag scoured his pith, and memory answered. "Oh! Not much, I'm afraid—just that he's making some highly promising studies on a lonely island. It's an example of information trade in which has not been maximized," he added, daring.

But it was a stock joke, and Dippid acknowledged it with a gruff chuckle.

"People's hopes must not be inflated prematurely," was his sententious answer. "But . . . Well, we've had a message from him. He believes he's on the verge of a breakthrough. What he needs, though, is someone from Neesos to calibrate his tests against."

"Why? What sort of tests?"

"You know what it was that they recovered from the sea-bed at Prefs?"

"I'm not sure I do. I—ah—always got the impression I was supposed not to inquire. Even Nemora was elusive when I asked about it. So . . ."

Dippid squeezed a sigh. "Yes, you judged correctly. I sometimes wish I didn't know what Gveest is working on, because if he fails, who can succeed? But enough of that." He drew himself up to a formal stance.

"Here's your commission from the Council of the Jingfired, boy. You're to make with all speed for the island Ognorit, and put yourself at Gveest's entire disposal."

"Did you say Ognorit?"

"I did indeed. What of it?"

"But that's south of the equator, isn't it—part of the Lugomannic Archipelago?"

"You've learned your geography well!"—with irony.

"But I've never been into the southern hemisphere before!"

"There's a first time for everything," Dippid snapped, and clacked his mandibles impatiently. "And if what Gveest is doing turns out wrong, it would be a great advantage to have the equatorial gales between us and Ognorit! Don't ask what I mean by that. Just put to sea. You'll find out soon enough."

It was by far the longest voyage Tenthag had undertaken, and he often wished that Flapper were as swift as Scudder. But each brighttime she pursued her steady way, and each dark she fed and gathered strength anew. She might not be particularly quick, but she was trustworthy, and never turned aside, not even when all her instincts tempted her to run off with a school of wild'uns, or follow a sharq's trail of murder across a shoal of erringq, or flee from the suspected presence of a feroq, the traditional enemy of porps. Little by little he was able to relax.

Cronthid went by, and Hegu, and Southmost Cape, and another day saw them entering the Worldround Ocean, that huge sea where currents flowed around the planet uninterrupted by continental masses. Once it had been different; the Great Thaw had altered everything. Tenthag watched the patterns in the sky change as they drove south, and felt in his inmost tubules, for the first time, that he did truly live on a vast globe adrift in space.

He had to apply all his navigational skills to the correction of Flapper's course; her impulse was to follow odor-patterns and temperature-gradients. He was obliged to ply his goad more often than he liked, but she responded, though she grew a trifle sullen.

Stars he had never seen were their guide now. But he had been well taught, and felt relieved to find his instructors' maps reflected in reality.

Islands loomed and faded, but he ignored them save to check his calculations. Then came a major problem: rafts of rotting weed, each alive with its own population of wild creatures, and uttering pestilential swarms of mustiqs. Someone had forgotten to advise him that it was the southern breeding-season . . . though, of course, he should in principle have known. Itching, swollen, worried by the way they clustered on Flapper's mantle, he was overjoyed when he raised a squadron of free junqs belonging to the People of the Sea. They were much less pleased than he by the encounter, for they regarded the Bowocker courier service as having cheated them of their ancestral rights; for scores-of-scores of years it had been their sole prerogative to trade in information, ever since the days of the Greatest Fleet created by Admiral Barratong.

Tenthag, though, was empowered to issue certain credits redeemable at Bowock and its allied cities, and some of them ensured the chance of pairing. Like every other branch of the folk, the People of the Sea were growing frightened at the fewness of their buddings, so he was able to convince them to part with a couple of spuderlets. Within half a day Flapper was protected from prow to tail by a dense and sticky web, and so was he; it made life easier to watch the baffled mustiqs fidget and struggle in their death-throes. Also they were a useful adjunct to his stock of yelg, and rather tasty.

Then came a storm.

It blew and poured and pelted down for a dark and a bright and a dark, and when it cleared Tenthag was more scared than ever he had been in his young life. He had clung to Flapper—who seemed almost to exult in the violence of the waves—and his stores were safe under her saddle and the spuderlets had made themselves a shelter out of their own web-stuff, and all seemed properly in order but for one crucial point:

Where had the tempest driven them?

There were islands low on the horizon when dawn broke. It was self-insulting for a courier to ask the way, but there seemed to be no alternative. He goaded Flapper towards a cluster of small barqs putting to sea under the wan morning sky, their riders trailing lines and nets for fish.

When he hailed them, they said, "Ognorit? Why, it's half a day's swim due south!"

Half a day? The storm had done him favors, then! Even the fabled Scudder—growing old now—could have brought Nemora to this spot no quicker!

He was already preening when his porp rushed into a narrow bay between two rocky headlands, and an old, coarse-mantled figure padded into the shallows to shout at him.

"You'll be the courier from Neesos that I asked for! It's amazing that you're here so soon—though I suppose you actually started from Bowock, didn't you? Welcome, anyway! Come ashore! I'm Scholar Gveest, in case you need a name to tell me apart from all the animals!"

# 4

The meaning of that cryptic statement was brought home to Tenthag as soon as he had set Flapper to browse—a duty he discharged meticulously despite Gveest's obvious impatience.

Then, heading inland in the scholar's pad-marks, he found himself assailed by hordes of wild creatures. Some leapt; some slithered; some sidled; some moved with sucking sounds as they adhered and freed themselves. Gveest was not afraid of them, and therefore Tenthag was not. But what could they possibly be?

Abruptly he caught on. He recognized them, or at any rate the majority; it was just that he had never seen more than one or two of them before in the same place. Whoever heard of six vulps in a group, or nine snaqs, or a good half-score of jenneqs, or such an uncountable gang of glepperts?

His tubules throbbed with astonishment. Whatever Gveest was doing, it had resulted in a most amazing change of these species' usual habits!

And the house he was taken to, on a crest dominating the whole of the island, reflected the same luxuriance. There were trees and food-plants massed together in quantities that would not have shamed Bowock itself, or any rich city in the north. Suddenly reacting to hunger despite his intake of yelg and mustiqs, Tenthag could not help signaling the fact, and Gveest invited him to eat his fill.

"Be careful, though," he warned. "Some of the funqi in particular may be rotten."

Edible food, left to rot? It was incredible! Was Gveest here alone? No, that couldn't be the explanation; here came two, three, five other people whose names he barely registered as he crammed his maw.

Belatedly he realized that his journey had made him sufficiently undernourished to exhibit bad manners, and he quit gobbling in embarrassment, but Gveest and his companions reacted with courteous tolerance.

"You got here with such speed," the scholar said, "we can't

begrudge recuperation time. My colleague Dvish, the archeologist, informed me that the courier who brought away his precious discoveries from Neesos also surprised his party. The efficiency of the Guild remains admirable."

*Though as soon as they learn to string nervograps from continent to continent, and convey images along them . . .*

Tenthag clawed back the thought. It was bitter for him to admit that, in his amazement at the greater world, he had committed his life to what might shortly become an obsolescent relic of the past. But pretense was useless when dealing with a weather-sense as keen as Gveest's; the scholar must be a match for Nemora, for he was going on, "And despite your worries, there will be need for courier-service for a long, long while. Regardless of the principle of maximizing trade in knowledge, some things are too fraught with implications to be turned loose . . . *yet.* That's why you're here."

Confused, Tenthag said, "I expected to bear away news of some great discovery you've made!"

The party surrounding Gveest exchanged glances. At length one of them—a woman, whose name he faintly recalled as Pletrow—said, "It's not what you're to take away that matters right now. It's what you brought!"

"But I brought nothing but myself!"

"Exactly."

After a pause for reflection, Tenthag still found no sense in the remark. Moreover she, or someone, was exuding a hint of patronizingness, which in his still-fatigued condition was intolerable. He rose to full height.

"I am obliged to remind you," he forced out, "that a courier is not obliged to wait around on anyone's convenience. Unless you have data in urgent need of transmission—"

"We sent for you not because you're a courier but because you're from Neesos!" Ill-tempered, Pletrow strove to overtop him, and nearly made it. The air suddenly reeked of combat-stink.

"Calm!" Gveest roared. "Calm, and let me finish!"

Always there was this sense of being on the verge of calamity, and for no sound reason . . . In past times, so it was taught, only male-and-male came into conflict; Pletrow's exudations, though, were as fierce as any Tenthag had encountered. But a timely breeze bore the stench away.

"We had expected," Gveest said in an apologetic tone, "that any courier sent here would be fully briefed about our work."

"Even the chief courier told me he wished he didn't know about it," Tenthag retorted. "So I didn't inquire!"

"Then you'd better make yourself comfortable, for when I explain you'll have a shock. The rest of you, too," Gveest added, and his companions swarmed to nearby branches, leaving a place of honor to Tenthag at the center.

Lapsing into what, by the way he fitted it, must be his own favorite crotch, the scholar looked musingly at the patches of sky showing between the tangled upper stems of his house. The fisherfolk's estimate of half a day's swim had been based on the southern meaning of "day"—one dark plus one bright—and the sun had set about the time Tenthag came ashore. Clouds were gathering, portending another storm, but as yet many stars were to be seen, and some were falling.

"Are you surprised to find so many animals here?"

"Ah . . . At first I was. I wondered how this island could support so many. But now I've seen how much food you have—some of it even going bad—I imagine it's all the result of your research, on plants as well as animals."

"You're quite correct. It seemed essential to improve the food-supply before—" Gveest checked suddenly. "Ah, I should have asked you first: do you know what Dvish recovered from the underwater site at Prefs?"

"The people who dived there wanted too much for the information," Tenthag answered sourly. "And since I joined the Guild the Order of the Jingfired have decreed it a restricted question."

"Hmm! Well, I suppose they have their reasons, but I for one don't accept them, so I'll tell you. During the years prior to the Great Thaw, the people there—presumably having noticed that ice could preserve food for a long time against rotting—became sufficiently starved to imagine that living creatures, including the folk, could also be preserved and, at some future time, perhaps resurrected. Nonsense, of course! But they were so deranged, even after the Thaw began, they went right on trying to find ways of insuring a dead body against decomposition. And one of their late techniques, if it didn't work for a whole body, did work for individual cells. We found a mated pair, sealed so tightly against air and water that we were able to extract—You know what I mean by cells?"

"Why, of course! The little creatures that circulate in our ichor and can be seen under a microscope!"

"Ah, yes—your people make good magnifiers, don't they? Good, that saves another lengthy exposition . . . Excuse me; it's been so long since I talked to anyone not already familiar with our work." Gveest drew himself inward, not upward, into a mode of extreme concentration. Frowning from edge to edge of his mantle, he continued, "But that's only one kind of cell. Our entire tissue is composed of them. And even they are composed of still smaller organisms. And, like everything else, they're subject to change."

This was so opposed to what he had learned as a child, Tenthag found himself holding his pulsation with the effort of paying attention.

"And the same is true of all the creatures on the planet, that we've so far studied. Above all, there was one enormous change, which judging by the fossil record—You know what I mean by fossils?"

There had been few at Neesos, but other couriers had carried examples around the globe, including, now Tenthag thought of it, some from this very island. He nodded.

"Good. As I was about to say: there was one gigantic change, apparently around the time of the outburst of the New Star, which affected all creatures everywhere. We came to Ognorit because it's one of the few peaks of the pre-Thaw continents where many relics of lost animals can be dug up. Better still, some local species endured and adapted. They offer proof that we're descended from primitive life-forms. Marooned on islands like this one, creatures recognizable in basic form on the continents are changing almost as we watch, in order to fill niches in the ecology which were vacated by other species killed off by the Freeze or the Thaw. We mainly haven't changed because, thanks to the People of the Sea, we were protected against the worst effect of those disasters. But even though we don't know how some event far off in the void of space can affect our very bodies, something evidently *did.* There was a brief period when we were multiplying rapidly, owing to the miscegenation which the Thaw engendered. It served to disguise a terrible underlying truth, but now there's no more hope of fooling ourselves. We are afraid—aren't we?—that we may die out."

Hearing it put in such blunt terms, Tenthag could not prevent himself from shrinking.

Rising, starting to pad back and forth like Nemora on that distant beach at Neesos, the scholar continued with a wry twist of his mantle.

"Yet for a species that has the power to reason about a doom written in the stars, it's an unjust fate! Have we not thought—not *dreamed*, but *reasoned*—about surviving even if our planet goes to fuel a star? Have we not contemplated that destiny since the legendary days of Jing and Rainbow? That's what drove me here to work on my theory . . . which, I hope against hope, has proved to be valid."

Calm again, Pletrow said, "You're right, if anybody can be absolutely right in this chaotic universe."

"Thank you for that reassurance. But we must clarify our reason for demanding samples of a Neesan mantle."

"Mine?" Tenthag could achieve no more than a squeak.

"Yes, Master Courier: yours. It is imperative." Gveest turned half-aside, as if ashamed, although his exudates continued to signal arrogant self-confidence. "You are of the only stock on the planet isolated enough to let us make the comparisons necessary if we are to advance our success with lower animals and improve the reproduction of our own kind. We must know exactly what sort of changes have taken place, *because we intend to reverse them.*"

Tenthag sat stunned. It was as grandiose a notion as he had ever dreamed of, and he was hearing it stated in real time, in real life, as cold potential fact.

He husked at last, "I'm not sure, even yet, what it is you want of me!"

"About as much of your mantle as Pletrow could scrape off with one claw . . . Ah, but a final and important question: do you recognize this lady as one of your own species?"

Gveest came to a halt directly confronting Tenthag, and waited.

"Of—of course!"

"But I'm not," said Pletrow, and descended from her branch to stand by Gveest.

"But I could pair with you!" Tenthag exclaimed, beginning to be more afraid than even at the height of the storm on his way hither.

"That's so. But we wouldn't bud."

"How can you be sure? I know mostly it doesn't happen nowadays, and I myself was the last on Neesos, but—Oh, *no!*"

Fragments of what he had learned by chance during his time as a novice courier came together in memory and made terrible sense. He waited, passive, for the truth to be spelled out.

Gveest announced it in a rasping voice.

"Here, and elsewhere around the planet, we have tasted the fossil record. We hunted above all for our common ancestors. We haven't found them. What we have found, and the discovery at Neesos was its final proof, is two separate species which evolved in total symbiosis. You and I, Tenthag, can't reproduce without the mediation of that species which evolved with us and gradually took over the role of bearing our young. We must have been in the closest competition, craws of years ago, equally matched rivals for supremacy. One species, though, opted for acceptance of the other's buds, while mimicking to perfection its behavior—as far as speech, as writing, as intelligence! And we aren't alone in this! Why, for example, does one only tame *female* barqs—briqs—junqs—porps? Those are the malleable, the pliant ones, who adopted the same course as what we call our females, at about the same time in the far past as we were establishing our rule over dry land! We are the highest orders of what some folk are pleased to call 'creation'—though if indeed some divine force called us into existence, I personally would have been glad to give that personage a bit of good advice!"

He was pulsing so hard, Pletrow turned to him in alarm and laid a friendly claw on his back. In a moment he recovered, and spoke normally.

"Well, anyway!" he resumed. "We hypothesize that in the early stages it was approximately an even chance whether implantation of a bud resulted in offspring for the 'male' version, the implanter, or the recipient, whose hormones were provoked into reproductive mode by impregnation and sometimes outdid the invader, thereby budding a female. We know parasitic organisms, especially among jenneqs, which still depend on the host's hormones to activate their buds; sometimes they lie dormant for a score or more of years!

"But at just about the time the New Star is said to have exploded, wherever and whatever it may have been—*I'm* no astronomer, but they say it was somewhere around the Major Cluster—something provoked the 'female' species into yet another round of mimicry. It must have been a valid defense technique at some point in the far past, but extending it has cost them *and us* our reproductive capability. Tenthag, when Pletrow confronted you, were you not shocked at how male her exudates appeared?"

"I was," said Pletrow before Tenthag could answer. "It's the survival of us all that is at stake. New friend!"—she spoke as she advanced on Tenthag, mantle open in the most intimate of all postures—"do help Gveest! Don't turn him down! I cringe before you and invoke your aid!"

Suiting her actions to her speech, she shrank to two-fifths of her normal height, and bent to touch the courier's pads.

"It is other than my familiar duty," Tenthag achieved at last. "But I was instructed to put myself at Gveest's disposal absolutely, so—"

Pletrow uttered a cry of joy, and as she rose scratched the underside of Tenthag's mantle, which by reflex he had opened as to greet her. Before he could even react to the trivial pain, the threatened storm broke over Ognorit, and the house's retracted leaves unfolded, shutting out the sky, so as to channel the precious water to the ditch around its roots. Instantly there was a clamor from the animals outside, for they knew this gift from heaven would result in an explosion of funqi and other food.

"Long ago," said Gveest, during the brief dark before the house's luminants responded, "there must have been a clash between symbiosis and extinction. Our ancestors preferred symbiosis, so we have to accept it. But the natural system was so delicate, so fragile, that even the explosion of a distant star could ruin it. It's up to us to create a better, tougher one. And this gift from you, Tenthag"—he held aloft the scrap of mantle-skin which Pletrow had passed to him—"may provide us with the information that we need. If it does," he concluded dryly, "they'll remember you one day as a savior like Jing!"

"And if it does," Pletrow promised as the luminants grew brighter, "I'll make amends to you for that small theft of your own substance. I want—oh, *how* I want!—to bear a bud!"

She clutched him to her for a moment, and then the company dispersed, leaving Tenthag alone with his mind in tumult.

In its way, Ognorit proved to be a greater wonderland for Tenthag even than Bowock on the day of his arrival there. Never had he seen a place where everything was so single-mindedly dedicated to one common goal. The island was a maze of experimental farms, pens for livestock, streams and rivers dammed to isolate breeding populations of fresh-water fish, salt-water pools above tide-level kept full by musculator pumps . . . and everywhere there were exposed fossils, revealed when thin sheets of compacted clay or slate had been painstakingly separated. He was able to taste for himself how ancestral forms differed from modern ones, though the faint organic traces were evaporating on exposure to the air.

"If only we left behind something more durable than claws and mandibles!" said Pletrow wryly; to compensate for her irascibility she had undertaken to act as his guide, and was proving an agreeable companion. Gveest, once possessed of the tissue-sample he had asked for, had vanished into his laboratory, barely emerging for a bite of food at darkfall. "Suppose," she went on, "we'd had solid shells like mollusqs, or at least supporting frames like gigants! But I suppose the lesson to be learned is that the plastic life-forms do better in a changing environment. Once you develop rigidity you're at risk of extinction."

*But aren't we?* Tenthag suppressed the thought, and merely requested evidence for Gveest's amazing claim about the male and female of the folk actually being separate species.

Much of what Pletrow offered in answer, Tenthag had already partly grasped. Until he went to Bowock, he had been unacquainted with ideas like "symbiosis" and "commensalism"; however, as soon as they were spelled out in terms of, for example, the secondary growths on a junq's back, he instantly recognized how well they matched ordinary observation. And the notion of plasticity was not at all foreign to him. Since childhood he had known about creatures which seemed not to mind what part of them performed what service. If one took care not to dislodge it from the rock where it had settled, one could literally turn a sponqe inside-out, and the inner surface that had been its gut would become a mantle, and vice versa. But he was astonished by a demonstration Pletrow performed for him with a brollican, a mindless drifting creature from the local ocean, avoided by the folk because of the poison stings that trapped the fish it preyed on. To indicate how far back in the evolutionary chain symbiosis must reach, she carefully peeled one of the things apart, dividing it into half a score of entities so unalike one could not have guessed at a connection between them. Then she tossed food into the pool, and within a day each portion had regenerated what it had been deprived of.

"But if you split them up so completely, how is that possible?" demanded Tenthag.

"Because you can't split them up *completely.* Enough cells from each of the components enter the common circulation to preserve a trace of the whole in every segment, but they remain dormant so long as suppressor chemicals are circulating too. When they stop, the cells multiply until they once again reach equilibrium. I'll show you under the microscope."

Sometimes dazed, sometimes dazzled, Tenthag thereupon suffered through a crash course in modern biology. On the way he learned about the invention of musculators and nervograps—a web of the latter, connected to various sensitive plants, reported results from outlying pens and plots and pools—and about the buoyancy of cloud-crawlers, whose gas-distended bladders had furnished the earliest proof that air was not one substance, but a mixture, and about a score of other matters he had previously felt no interest in.

Clacking his mandibles dolefully, he said at last, "And this incredibly complex, interlocking system could be put in danger by something happening out there in the sky?"

"Ridiculous, isn't it?" agreed Pletrow. "Almost enough to drive one back to astrology! But every line we pursue leads us to the same conclusion. Now we think it may have to do with the fact that some kinds of light can burn. You've used burning-glasses?"

"Well, naturally! I grew up with them."

"But do you realize there are kinds of light too wide to see, and also too narrow?"

After proving her point with a small fire and a black filter that allowed no visible light to pass, yet transmitted heat without any direct contact, she introduced him to mutated creatures from the rest of the Lugomannic Archipelago. This was her specialty, and she waxed eloquent over the creatures she kept in pens on the north shore: vulps, snaqs and jenneqs all somehow *wrong*— lopsided, or looking as though one end of an individual did not belong with the other, or missing some external organ, or boasting an excess of them. Tenthag found the sight repulsive, and with difficulty steered her away from the subject, back towards the crisis facing the folk.

If anything, what she told him next was even more disturbing, for she illustrated it with cells cultured from his own mantle, and invited him to compare them with those recovered from Prefs—and then calmly took a sample of her own tegument to complete the argument.

All his life, like virtually everyone in the world, Tenthag had been conditioned against bringing anything sharp towards his own, or anyone's, body. A claw-scratch, such as she had inflicted on him, was nothing, but the risk of having a major tubule punctured, with consequent loss of pressure, was terrifying; it could lead to being permanently crippled. Among glassworkers this was a particularly constant danger. Yet here she was applying a ferociously keen blade to her own side—to judge by the scars already surrounding the area, not for the first time!

Sensing his disquiet, she gave a harsh chuckle.

"They say Jing's Rainbow was deformed, don't they? It can't be *too* disastrous to lose a little pressure . . . but in any case I've had a lot of practice. There we are! Now you can compare one of my cells with one from the female they found at Prefs. You'll notice it's far more like the male's, or, come to that, your own, than it is like hers."

Struggling to interpret the unfamiliar details exposed to him, Tenthag sighed.

"I'm going to have to take your word for it, I'm afraid. I simply don't know what to look for. Can't you tell me, though, what became of our original—uh—females?"

"There never were any," was the prompt response.

"What?"

"Females—that's to say, versions of what we're used to thinking of as females—seem to have occurred very early in the evolutionary process. But prior to their appearance, as is shown by primitive creatures like the brollican, the standard pattern was well established: clusters of simple organisms banded together for mutual advantage and shared a circulation, a chemical bath, which controlled the reproduction of them all. That, though, works only up to a certain level of complexity. If I chopped a claw off you, you couldn't regrow it, could you? And reproduction is only an elaborate version of regrowth. *But*—and here's the main problem—within any single organism there's always decay going on. To renew the stock, without aging, and to *evolve*, calls for some sort of stimulus, some infusion of variety; what, we don't yet know, but we're sure about the principle. We assume it comes from the use of the symbiotic species, whose chemical makeup is much more unlike the donor's than outward appearance would suggest. Or at least it used to be. Now we're back to the change dating from the New Star, and the latest outburst of mimicry, which seems now to be going clear to the cellular level. At all events"—Pletrow briskened, evading the subject that was closest to her pith—"there never were specific females for the folk. Our species evolved together from that stage, craws of years ago, when it became impossible for either of us to continue providing the necessary variant stimuli from our own internal resources. So to say, we'd become so completely efficient as a single organism that we could no longer be peeled apart, and identity had supplanted variety. Probably you males"—with a wry twitch of her mantle—"were essentially parasitic, but you must have been amazingly successful, or you'd never have attracted such a promising species as us females into dependence!"

Controlling himself with extreme effort, Tenthag said, "If Gveest's research is successful, and his techniques can be applied to—to us, what will it involve?"

"Modification of another permanent symbiote that will survive transmission into our own bodies by way of the food we eat, and then restore the original bud-reaction."

For a moment the scope of the plan took the air from Tenthag's mantle. Eventually he husked, "But what about numbers? Gveest himself has said it will be necessary to build up the food-supply—that he had to do it here before trying his methods on vulps and snaqs and so on. Suppose we do suddenly find we can produce buds, if not every time, then twice as often as before, five times, half-a-score times: might we not outstrip our resources?"

"Gveest plans to give us new delicious foods. You've tasted some. But in any case . . ."

She fixed him with so piercing a glare it transfixed him to the inmost tubule, and her voice was like a prong as she concluded:

"Let the future take care of itself! I only know one thing! *I mean to bear a bud before I die!*"

# 6

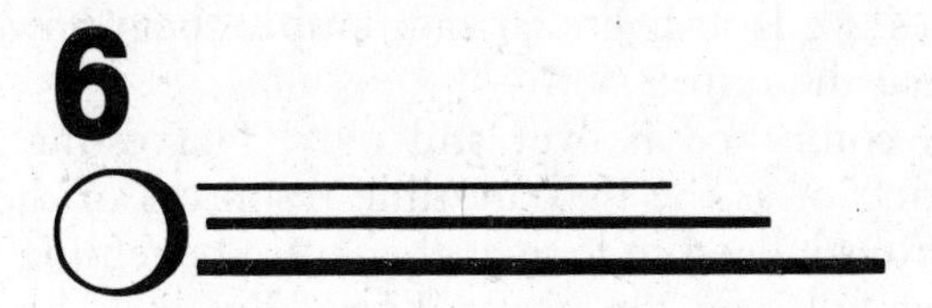

After so long a delay that Tenthag was afraid he might lose control over Flapper, who should either have departed on a new voyage or been retamed in fresh water, Gveest emerged weary but triumphant from his laboratory to announce he had no further need of Tenthag's presence.

"We've successfully established a reproducible strain of your cells," he explained. "That will furnish us with all the data we require. You've performed an invaluable service, Master Courier! Permit us, in return, to re-equip your porp."

"Thank you, but I'm content with the growths that she already bears," was Tenthag's stiff reply. "Besides . . ."

He hesitated, not wanting to be tactless to this elderly scholar who was, after all, an uncontested genius and on the verge of a breakthrough which might benefit the whole planet.

Might . . .

It was pointless, though, trying to elude Gveest's weather-sense. Dryly he said, "You're concerned about the probable success of my work. Pletrow told me. That's why I'm disappointed that you won't let me refit your porp. Now we shall have to signal the People of the Sea and let them spread the first stage of our techniques."

"I—I seem to have misunderstood something," said Tenthag slowly.

"So you do, and I'm surprised." Gveest turned to pad up and down along the stretch of beach where they had met, glancing now and then towards Flapper, fretful at her long confinement in the shallows. "I know as well as anybody that, unless we vastly increase our food resources first, doubling or trebling the rate of budding could lead to dreadful consequences. But we're not the only people who've been working on this problem, you realize. There are outstanding scientists among the People of the Sea, just to begin with, who may be more anxious than we are for personal glorification because their traditional role has been undermined by couriers."

Tenthag clenched his mantle as the implications struck him.

"You want to start by publishing your methods of improving crops," he suggested at length.

"Naturally. But the People of the Sea don't keep farms, do they—save on certain islands that they use as temporary bases when the weather's bad? Besides, we land-livers far outnumber them now."

"Is that true? I had the impression—"

"Oh, yes. We've confirmed it over and over. Harvesting what they're used to thinking of as the inexhaustible resources of the sea, they grew very numerous indeed so long as they were benefiting from the interbreeding that followed the Great Thaw. But little by little their population has dwindled, too. Had it not, would there have been a chance to set up the Couriers' Guild, or a need to do so?"

"I've heard that they no longer recruit as many junqs and briqs as formerly," Tenthag admitted.

"They aren't there. Those are life-forms almost as advanced as we ourselves, and subject to the same world-wide problem. What we must do is publish news of what we now know how to do to mounts and draftimals—because improved transport will be imperative—and also to the creatures which our ancestors once used as food."

He uttered the concluding words softly and with reluctance. Tenthag instantly recognized the logic underlying them, but his inmost being was revolted.

"Are we to go back to the ways of savages?" he cried. "I know folk sometimes do in the grip of famine, but for scores-of-scores of years we've fed well enough from *civilized* resources—"

"You eat fish and wingets, don't you?"

"Well, yes, but they're as mindless as plants! I'd never kill a land-creature for food—or a porp like Flapper!"

"We may well have no choice." Gveest was abruptly stern. "We must decide between extinction—slow, but certain—and an increase in our breeding-rate. If we opt for the latter, we must make provision to save ourselves from famine due to overpopulation. Think, *think!* If twice as many buds appear in the next generation, those raising and catching food will just suffice to keep us all well fed—assuming, as I mentioned, better transportation. But if the figure isn't *twice*, but half-a-score times more . . . what then?"

Tenthag's pulsations seemed to stop completely for a moment. He said in an awed whisper, "You think your work has paid off so completely?"

"Think?"—with a harsh chuckle. "Beyond my wildest dreams! I now see how to grow a bud from *every* pairing!"

"This is because of me?"

"Yes, what we learned from you made all the difference. You haven't seen Pletrow the past few days, have you?"

"Ah—no, I haven't! She said she was busy with some new research, and I'm used to being by myself, so . . ."

"She, who never took a bud before, has taken mine, and it's a female, exactly as my theories predicted. Now will you let us re-equip your porp? I should remind you: you're bound by the couriers' oath to distribute whatever information you are given, and there are folk the world around who could learn just by looking at what we plan to graft on her a means to multiply a score of different food-plants! We want—we *need* to have that information running ahead of any news about transforming animals . . . like us!"

A terrible chill bit deep into Tenthag's vitals, but his voice was quite controlled as he replied.

"It is not, as you point out, my place to act as censor. I'll leave that to the Order of the Jingfired. I'm amazed, though, that you want to send off one courier, not laqs of us! Surely this is something every expert in life-studies ought to hear of right away!"

"All the experts on the planet may not be enough, but if we fail . . . Who'd care, if an unpeopled globe crashed on a star? We must have seen it happen countless times! Maybe the New Star itself was some such event! Come, bring Flapper to the fresh-water pool on the east coast. She will be tamer there, and you can retrain her while the grafts are taking."

And, as Tenthag numbly moved to comply, he ended, "But what I said about certain people being able, just by looking, to judge our achievement where plants are concerned, may also hold good for animals and for ourselves. The news you spread will be enough to bring the People of the Sea hither in a year or two. I hope it won't be sooner. The resources of the ocean are no less limited than those of the land, and I greatly fear what would happen were our nomads, already saddened by the fading of their ancient glory, to seize on my techniques before they understood the repercussions. For the time being, therefore, you will be our sole link to the outer world, and Bowock the sole place where all the facts are known."

"But," Tenthag confessed to the Council of the Jingfired a month later, "all Gveest's wise precautions went for nothing. On my outward voyage, beset by mustiqs, I had traded Bowocker credits for a pair of spuders, as you know. Returning, I was accosted by the same fleet, and it appears that rumors of Gveest's success had already reached them. I was faced with the choice between redeeming Bowocker credits against new knowledge—which, I respectfully remind the councillors, is the ultimate justification for their existence—or attempting to dishonor them, and Bowock, by making my escape. The fleet consisted of about a score of junqs, and a few were young and very fast. Not only would I have been trapped for certain; my action would have brought the credibility of Bowock into disrepute. I maintain I had no alternative but to honor the Bowocker pledge."

He fell silent, and waited trembling for the verdict. It was very quiet here in the Grand West Arbor of Bowock; the plashing of waves underpad, where only a mat of roots separated the assembly from ocean ripples, was louder than the distant sound of the city's business. A few bright-colored wingets darted from bloom to bloom; otherwise there was no visible motion beneath the canopy of leaves.

Until the Master of the Order stirred. He was very old, and spoke in a wheezing tone when he spoke at all. His name was known to everyone—it was Iyosc—but this was the first time Tenthag had set eye on him. For years he had been sedentary, like an adult cutinate, incapable of mustering pressure to move his bulk unaided. Yet, it was said, his intellect was unimpaired. Now was the time for that opinion to be confirmed.

"It would have been better," he said at last, "had the credibility of Bowock gone to rot."

A unison rush of horror emanated from the company. Tenthag could not stop himself from cringing to half normal height.

"But the courier is only a courier," Iyosc went on, "and not to blame. It is we, the Order of the Jingfired, who have failed in our duty. We, who supposedly have the clearest insight of all the folk, equipped with the best information and the most modern methods of communicating it, should have foreseen that a solitary courier crossing the Worldround Ocean might be accosted twice by the same squadron of the People of the Sea. Where is Dippid, chief of the couriers? Stand forth!"

Dippid complied, looking as troubled as Tenthag felt.

"We lay a new task on you," Iyosc husked. "Abandon all your others. News of what can be done, thanks to Gveest's research, with food-plants and—yes!—animals *must* outstrip news of what can now be done to people! I speak with uttermost reluctance; like Barratong, who forged the Greatest Fleet in the years before the Thaw, and created the foundations of the modern world, I have hankered all my life after the chance to plant a bud . . . and always failed. Now it's too late. But the notion of two, three, *five* taking in place of one fills me with terror. Long have I studied the history of the folk; well do I comprehend how, when starvation looms, our vaunted rationality flows away like silt washing out of an estuary, to be lost on the bottom mud! Nothing but our powers of reason will save us when the claws of the universe clamp on our world and crack it like a nut! For the far-distant survival of the species, we should have risked loss of confidence in the credits that we issue. Now we are doomed beyond chance of redemption!"

A murmur of furious disagreement took its rise, and he clacked his mandibles for silence. It fell reluctantly.

"Oh, yes! There are many among you who are young enough to benefit—as you imagine—from Gveest's achievement! But are you creating the farms and fields, the forests and the fish-pens, which will be needed to support the monstrous horde of younglings that must follow? Where would you be right now, if you had to support five times the population of Bowock from its existing area? And don't think you won't! As soon as the word gets abroad that the secret of fertility is known here, won't crowds of frustrated strangers quit the countryside and the service of the sea, and concentrate here to await a miracle? We're none of us so absolutely rational as to have forgone all hope of miracles! Besides, by this time it's beyond doubt that the People of the Sea must have landed on Ognorit and appropriated Gveest's techniques."

"No! No!" Tenthag shouted, but realized even as he closed his mantle that Iyosc had seen deeper than he to the core of the matter.

The Master of the Order bent his bleary old gaze on the young courier.

"Yes, yes!" he responded with gentle mockery. "And I still say you were not to blame. You weren't brought up, any more than I or the rest of us, to react in terms such as the People of the Sea are used to. We tend to think more rigidly; we draw metaphors from rock and glass and metal, all the solid changes in the world that fire can wreak. Theirs is the universe of water, forever in flux, forever fluid. They will not heed the strict conditions we'd apply; they'll rush ahead as on the back of a swift junq, and exclaim with pleasure at the sparkle of her snout-wave. Yet some of them are clever scientists. I'll wager it won't be longer than a year before we learn that they are trading Gveest's discovery to just those poor communities which are least fitted to fill extra maws!"

# 7

And those isolated settlements, naturally, were the ones the couriers must leave to last . . .

Obeying Iyosc's directive, the Guild mustered in force to distribute Gveest's data concerning food-plants and—against their will—animals that had once been used for food. Scores of volunteers were impressed to make more and ever more copies, enclose them in waterproof capsules, bind them to the saddles of the porps. Meantime the nervograps were exploited to their utmost and beyond; the two which stretched furthest overland shriveled and died. Therefore old techniques had to be revived, so messages were sent by drum, or tied to flighters, or to bladders cast loose on the ocean currents.

"It must have been like this during the Thaw," Tenthag said suddenly as he, Nemora, Dippid and other couriers readied their porps for departure. Dippid glanced round.

"How do you mean?"

"For the rising waters, put the People of the Sea."

"*Oh,* yes!" said Nemora with a harsh chuckle, giving Scudder a final tap on her flank before ascending the saddle. "Eating away at our outlying coasts, while we make desperate shift to salvage what we can on the high ground! I've always been in love with open water, but for once I wish I could be a landliver, doing something direct and practical to stem the tide!"

"There's nothing more practical than what we're doing!" Dippid snapped. "No matter how much land you cultivate, no matter how many animals you help to breed, you can't withstand the onslaught singleclawed! We must alert the world, not just a chosen few!"

"Oh, I know that." She sounded suddenly weary as she secured her travel-harness. "But I have this lust for something basic instead of abstract! I want to puddle in the dirt and watch a chowtree grow! I want to see more life come into existence, instead of darting hither and thither like some crazy winget that doesn't even drop maggors!"

Her voice peaked in a cry, and to the end of the porp-pens other people checked and gazed at her.

Tenthag, remembering Pletrow at Ognorit, said soberly, "You mean you want a bud."

"Me?" She shook herself, like one emerging from a swim, and curled her mantle's edge in wry amusement. "No, since you I've grown too accustomed to my solitary life! But what I *would* like is a bud from Scudder. Never was there such a swift yet docile porp, and now she's old, and I must train a new one to replace her . . . Had it not been for this emergency, I'd have asked leave to try and breed her with a wild male. Probably it wouldn't take, but I'd have liked to try, regardless. As things are, however—Oh, never mind my dreams! There's work to do!"

And, shouting farewells, she plied her goad and drove the porp to sea.

Watching her go, Dippid said softly, "That's one problem I hadn't thought of."

"You mean her wanting to raise a youngling of Scudder's as a—what's the word?—surrogate?" Tenthag suggested.

"Exactly. I suspect there may be many cases like hers, as soon as the implications of what the People of the Sea are doing have sunk in."

"But they don't take porps, only briqs and junqs," said Tenthag, missing the point. "So even if they multiply—"

"Of course they don't!" Dippid retorted. "Porps are what we couriers have made our own, of all the creatures on the planet! But even before Gveest's discovery, we were looking forward to our own abolition. Have we not envisaged nervograps across the deepest oceans? Have we not heard of means to transmit images as well as symbols? And are there not scholars as brilliant as Gveest working on the idea of actual flight, with gas-bladders and musculators to carry folk aloft? Oh, I know what you'll say to that—I've heard it often from the youngest couriers! Given that our ancestors were flying creatures, we could adapt to the air! Maybe you could. Not me, not Nemora. Yet it would be something to have passed on certain skills, in navigation, for example . . . But that's not what threatens us now: not simple obsolescence. It's actual disaster, the risk that in two or three generations' time there won't be enough sane folk to make new discoveries, there won't be any news to carry, there won't be any reports to publish, there won't be scholars anymore, but just a pullulating mindless mass, alive enough to breed but not well fed enough to reason and to plan."

"It cannot happen," Tenthag said obstinately.

"Don't you mean: you won't admit it's likely?"

Dippid's self-control had slipped. Meantime, silence had fallen over the whole area of the pens, and everybody was listening to the argument. Abruptly aware of anger-stink, Tenthag strove to prevent his voice from shaking.

"Even though I did let the People of the Sea redeem their credits —and nineteen in every score of us would have done the same!—I still say things won't be that bad. It calls for intelligence and planning to apply Gveest's treatment. Without that, our bud-rate will drop back to what it has been."

"But how long would it take before we could restore our food-supplies? *One* explosion in *one* generation would suffice to set us back a score-of-score of years, at least!" Dippid pulsed violently. "Have you not seen the madness due to famine?"

"No, never," Tenthag admitted.

"If you had, you wouldn't treat what you've done so casually! *I* saw it, when I was no older than you are now. There had been a crop-blight at the Southmost Cape. You know about that dreadful episode?"

"I've heard it mentioned, yes."

"That's not enough! You had to be there. I was among the couriers who brought away samples of infected food-plants for Scholar Vahp to study—the same Vahp who taught Gveest, by the way. And the folk were so desperate, we had to land with an escort of prongers because they didn't want us to take even a leaf, even a stalk, infected or not. They were just aware enough to remember that they needed more food, and they were prepared to fight for it. Yes, fight! Tear gashes in each other's mantles, slash each other's tubules if they could! They say everyone's entitled to one mistake, Tenthag, but it's given to few of us to make an error as immense as yours!"

"But I . . . !"

The attempted rejoinder died away. Turning to mount Flapper, he said humbly, "Only time can judge whether it was as grievous as you claim. Deliver my commission and let me go."

Memory of the hostility that had overwhelmed him haunted Tenthag until he was well under way. Objectively he knew that he was not at fault—Iyosc himself had exonerated him—but that didn't alter the impact he had had on the lives of his companions in the Guild . . . and everybody else.

He delayed long before studying his commission, afraid it might be some sort of punishment. On the contrary: the route assigned him was through familiar waters and to familiar ports, and the tour actually concluded at Neesos. Would the People of the Sea have reached his old home before him? He dared to hope it was unlikely. They would have started by selling the knowledge they stole from Ognorit among the islands of the southern and equatorial zones; perhaps they would not get as far as Neesos this summer. He cheered up.

But his optimism faded as he made his assigned stopovers, delivering to the local savants messages concerning plants and animals. Rumor, if not precise information, had outrun the couriers; wherever he called, the folk were impatient to the point of rudeness, and tossed aside his dispatches.

"We want to bud!" they shouted. "We want Gveest's secret of

fertility! There are five-score fewer of us than this time a score of years ago!"

Or "two-score" or "half a score" . . . but always fewer.

It was in vain to insist that before more buds were brought forth there must be extra food. Even the wisest old'uns were in the grip of passion; they dismissed everything he said with a wave of one casual claw.

"We'll take more from the sea!" was a typical answer, or, "We'll go back to wild plants like our ancestors!"

Sharply he said, "It looks as though you already decided to!"

For everywhere he saw the symptoms of decline: parasitic weeds hanging about the eaves of the houses, blocking the sap-run on which depended edible plants and funqi; mold spoiling swatches of good fruit; clamps and copses abandoned in the surrounding countryside as all the folk converged on ports where the latest news was to be expected. The air was full of a dreadful expectation, and the reek had so permeated everyone, they no longer cared to plan for anything except that miraculous day when they too—even they—would parent buds.

Explanations of the dual-species theory met with mockery. Reasoned arguments about numbers versus resources met with boredom. Here and there a few people still remembered sanity and begged to be taken away on Flapper's back, but the couriers were forbidden to carry passengers, and anyhow it seemed better to leave them where they were in the hope that sense might after all prevail.

At Klong, a month after leaving Bowock, Tenthag first encountered an outburst of religion, and trembled to the core of his pith. So dreamness could take a new grip on the folk even before the actual onset of the population explosion. Mere rumor had sufficed, at least in this one land . . .

He fidgeted with the urge to make for Neesos, but defied it. He must make his own obeisance to reason—his own sacrifice, whatever a sacrifice might be.

By dark especially, while Flapper broke the water into glowing ripples as she fed on drifting weed and occasional fish, he stared achingly at the sky wherever it was clear of cloud and wondered about voyages across space. Were there living creatures in that ocean of oceans? Watching a comet bloom out of a dim and distant blur, it was hard not to make comparison with a plant sprouting under the influence of summer. Marking the dark-by-dark progress of the planets, it was tempting beyond belief to imagine other beings capable of transforming inert matter into something that could feel, and react, and devise and plan and—make mistakes . . .

In ancient times, he had been told, some folk held that when the welkin shed its fleeting streaks it was a means of signaling, which no one here below could understand. With all his pith he wished he could send back a message of his own:

"Help us, strangers! Help us! We're in danger!"

Budded in the year called Two-red-stars-turn-blue, Tenthag sought comfort in the unaltered patterns of the sky, and found none. For they weren't unaltered.

As though to harbinger the shock the folk must bear, the dark before the bright that saw him at his bud-place was lighted by a singular event.

One of those very stars, on the fringe of the Major Cluster, which had gone to blue from red, changed yet again. A hint of yellow touched it. It seemed brighter . . . but a cloud drifted across it, and there was no way of being sure about the outcome before dawn.

## 8

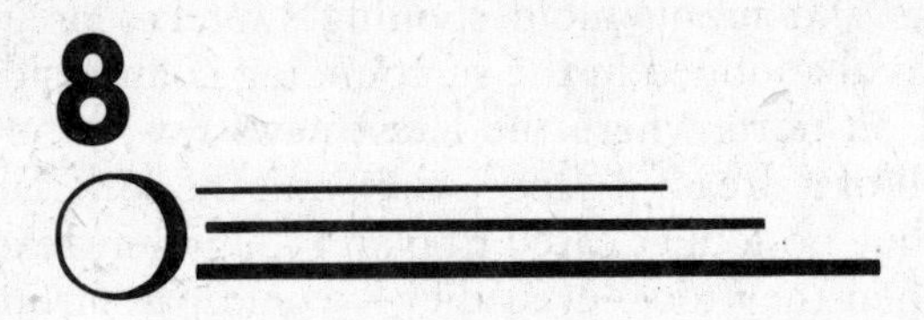

*B*ut where was everybody?

Goading Flapper into the bay that covered the site of Prefs, Tenthag surveyed the vicinity with his telescope. Normally by dawn the fisherfolk would be launching gorborangs, and sand-collectors loading raw material for the glass-furnace. Because it had been so long since he left here, he had been prepared for some changes, but not for this feeling of vacancy which set his weather-sense to full alert.

Leaving the porp to browse, he waded ashore carrying the last of his copies of Gveest's food-data. As soon as he was clear of the water, he shouted with all the force of his mantle.

There was no answer.

Becoming more and more alarmed, he padded along familiar tracks—how often had he come this way with Fifthorch, to swim from the gentle beach and sometimes dive for relics?—noting with dismay how well-tended clusters of food-plants had been let run wild. He came across sleds of the kind used to bring home sand, abandoned by the path; creepers were twining over them in a way that indicated they must have been dumped a moon-long ago, at least. And his forebear's mirror, source of Neesos's prosperity, was pointing at nowhere.

Shortly, breasting a rise, he came in sight of the little town at the center of the island, sheltered in a hollow against the worst of winter weather. Here at last were people, though nothing like as many as he would have expected. Draped on slanting branches, or lying under rocky overhangs for protection against the morning sunlight, they were listening to someone talking in a loud rough voice. Before he drew close enough to make out what was being said, Tenthag had already discerned that they were surrounded by all the goods they could assemble, be it foodstuffs or glassware or seed-stock or objects salvaged from Prefs.

Something prompted him to great caution. Lowering to minimum bearable height, he stole among shadows cast by bushes until he reached a rocky niche where he could look on unobserved. Fortunately the wind prevented anyone from scenting him . . . but the stink it bore to him from the crowd was enough to make him quail. It uttered a whole history of greed and jealousy, and the speaker at the middle of the group was fomenting it.

And the orator was—

Recognizing him, Tenthag was almost snatched by dreamness. It was Fifthorch.

Who was saying, "—so *of course* they want to keep the secret for themselves! It's lucky for us that the People of the Sea aren't under the pads of the Bowockers and their precious Order of the Jingfired! Jing was never real! Jing was a figment to keep young'uns quiet! Well, some of us grew out of childhood tales! I wish we all had! The fact that supposedly adult people right here on Neesos still claimed that the Jingtexts must be truth—until we drove them out as they deserved!—isn't that enough to curdle your maw? It certainly did mine! Be thankful for the People of the Sea, who are coming to our rescue! I'm sure we've brought together enough goods to make them give us the secret of fertility! *They* care about the fact that we've been left without a single new bud since traitor Tenthag ran away! They aren't cold and cynical and cruel like the Bowockers, who weren't content to take our most valuable possessions from beneath the Bay of Prefs, but stole our youngest young'un as well! And what did they leave in exchange? Rubbish! Scraps and oddments any one of us could have got by making a voyage to the mainland! Things you trade for common seed or common glass! Not glass like ours, the finest on the planet! Did they offer musculators and nervograps? Did they give us anything useful? No, they robbed us of what we didn't even realize we owned, and laughed when they went away! Taking our last new-budded youngling with them, what is worse!"

His memory echoing with Nemora's comment about the archeologists who were far too mercenary for her liking, Tenthag found that more than he could endure. Rising to normal height, he padded forward, shouting, and all eyes turned on him with amazement . . . save for Fifthorch's, which was full of hate.

"I never dreamed you'd miss me so much, Fifthorch!" he roared. "Did it not suit you to become the youngest when I left—not stolen, but of my own free will?"

His diet of yelg, in spite of his lonely and inactive life aboard a porp, kept him fit and well pressurized; he was able to overtop

Fifthorch without effort. Taking station higher on the branchway, where he could continue to dominate the other, he filled his mantle with air for the loudest possible shout. These people looked as though they needed to be startled back to reality.

But a shrill voice took the pressure out of him with a single question.

"Are you one of the People of the Sea, who are going to show us how to breed again?"

He turned, seeking the source of the inquiry . . . and was instantly deflated.

"Ninthag!" he blurted, scarcely recognizing the old, bloated, half-blind shape that clung to a slanting bough befouled with tatters of wild orqid—colorful, but unfit for food. "Ninthag, don't you know your own sole bud?"

"Are you pretending to be Tenthag?" the old man wheezed. "I'm not such a fool as to believe you! He went away, long, long ago, stolen by the Bowockers! I see him in visions now, and he's laughing at us—laughing at the poor folk he left behind while he rejoices in the best the world can offer! We stay here, wondering when if ever another bud will come among us, and—Keep away from me!"

Tenthag was scrambling towards him, but on the instant half a score of others rose to block his way. Their exudates took on the taint of combat-stink.

Slowly Tenthag retreated, recognizing what he had encountered at Klong and sundry places since. These folk were starved into dreamness . . . of their own volition.

He said, "Aren't you ashamed to deny your own? Fifthorch knows me—why don't the rest of you?"

"We know what we want to know," said one of them, and there was a rumble of agreement.

"But you can't! You're underfed, you're going crazy! Yet there's food all around you!" Tenthag clenched his claws in impotent rage.

"We have to keep everything we can spare to trade with the People of the Sea," said Ninthag obstinately. "Who knows how much they'll demand for the secret of fertility? We must be sure that there's enough."

"But here I am, who was at Ognorit where the secret was discovered, and I bring data due to Gveest himself—free of charge!"

With that shouted boast Tenthag broke through their apathy. They reared back and gazed at him with pitiable eagerness. Even Fifthorch was taken off guard, and gapped his mandibles.

"Is it truly you?" whispered Ninthag, staring blearily. "Your voice, your scent . . . But it has been so long!" He summoned a last trace of his old authority. "Show what you've brought, then! Not to me, for my sight has failed. Where's Thirdusk?"

"He betrayed us!" shouted Fifthorch. "He fled with the cowards who were prepared to let Neesos die!"

That statement made everything clear to Tenthag. He could picture how it must have been: one faction, the more rational, counseling that life go on as normal, with enough food eaten and enough new crops planted for next year; the other so obsessed with the lack of new buds as to forget the need to provide for them if they happened, ultimately seizing the goods of their rivals and driving them away. It was much like what had happened at his other ports of call. But in his pith he had hoped that his own homeland might be a little different, a little better . . .

He'd been wrong. He knew that even as he proffered the documents he had brought, and a half-score of greedy eyes fixed on them as Fifthorch spread them out.

"There's nothing here to touch the folk!" the latter yelled. "It's all to do with plants and animals!"

"But if there's not enough food—"

"We manage well with half the food we used to gobble! We must save the rest to pay the People of the Sea! You're a coward like Thirdusk! You're a traitor!"

All at once they were pelting him with insults and trampling his precious message underpad. He could do nothing but turn and flee, or they would have torn him torso from mantle in their fury.

Luckily—luckily!—they were too weak to overtake him on his way to the bay where he had left Flapper. By the time he stumbled into the shallows, he also was weakened by his efforts, and his perception was diminished. Had it not been, he would have reacted to what was happening on the skyline before he remounted his porp and turned her seaward.

Only then, though, and much too late, did he realize what was looming towards Neesos.

Here came the visitors the relic of the folk were waiting for: five junqs, four briqs, with bright banners hung on poles to tell the world—

WE HAVE THE SECRET OF FERTILITY! AND IT'S FOR SALE!

He crumpled on Flapper's saddle, utterly dispirited, and offered no resistance when they detached him from his travel-harness, dragged him aboard the commander's briq, and lashed Flapper to her side with yells of triumph.

He was too busy mourning for a world that never was.

The commander of this raggle-taggle fleet still wore ancient symbols of rank on thongs crossed about his body: a spyglass lacking its objective, a briq-goad worn to a stump. Crusty-mantled from bad food and long exposure to the elements, he interrogated Tenthag about Neesos, wanting to know whether any folk were left, or whether they had all fled as from so many other lonely islands.

"They might as well have run away," was Tenthag's bitter answer. "They took leave of their senses long ago. But why ask me? I'm just a visitor, and there they are who can answer for themselves!"

He pointed. Those who had rushed in pursuit of him were milling about on the beach, amazed at the sight of the fleet, and he could almost hear the arguments over who must return to town and collect trade-goods.

"Hah!" said the commander with satisfaction. "Let's go see what they can offer worth the taking! You!"—handing a prong to a nervous she'un—"keep watch over him, hear me?"

And, surrounded by his sub-commanders, headed landward.

More miserable than ever, Tenthag was compelled to look on as the Neesans delivered everything they owned for the visitors' inspection. Meantime, however, a suspicion began to gnaw at the back of his mind. At first he was too despondent to react; by degrees it overcame his depression, and he roused himself enough to survey the close-clustered briqs and junqs.

They still bore their complement of old'uns and she'uns. But not a single one among the latter was in bud . . .

The monstrosity of the deceit these nomads were perpetrating stabbed him to the pith, and he almost made a leap for Flapper. But the she-guard was ready to spike him, and he was in no hurry to become an underwater banquet.

He must match their deception without giving off a betraying odor, therefore. Would anger-stink cover up a lie?

Well, by now experience had made him cynical enough to try . . .

He and the guard were isolated near the briq's after end; the rest of her riders were gathered forward. He said softly, "What's your commander's name?"

She hesitated; then, finding no reason to refuse the information, muttered, "He's called Sprapter."

"And he is a good person to serve under?"

"He does well by us. He's clever. The proof's around you." Her tone was curt, but uneasy, as though she feared a trap.

Tenthag saw nothing special about the accoutrements of the briqs and junqs—indeed, they could have been matched by any kyq from his youth, and the latter would have been set about with useful gorborangs, as well—but now was no time to be patronizing. He said hastily, "And you are . . . ?"

"Veetalya."

"Do you believe it to be part of Sprapter's plan that I must parch to death?"

Taken aback, she said, "You heard his order to me!"

"So I did. It made no mention of my being denied water. Oh, I know the People of the Sea hate us couriers nowadays, but our lives have much in common, and I take it that if Sprapter ordered you to guard me he'll expect to find me fit and well when he returns."

Alongside the briq Flapper was growing restive, as always in salt water. Why had they not turned her loose, or stripped and killed her? Did Sprapter cherish grandiose dreams of adding a porp to his little fleet? Or did he think she might prove useful for trade purposes when they headed south in search of the secret they claimed to possess, but did not? Whatever the reason, it was a stroke of luck. Tenthag said in his most wheedling tones, "Your drink-bladders are bulging, aren't they? And if there's one thing a porp lacks, it's adequate drink. A briq is far superior in that regard. You People of the Sea know ancient tricks that we ought really to have studied, but of course, as you know, we tend to be arrogant. With a few exceptions, like myself for example. But isn't that a fault you too display?"

She was nervously tightening her grip on the prong. With a reflex glance at the drink-bladders, she said, "I don't know what you mean!"

"Oh, it's plain as sunlight! You're not in bud, although your folk possess the secret of fertility, and I can only explain the fact by assuming that you angered Sprapter, and he refused to let you have a bud until you'd made amends for some offense you'd given. Well, if you give me drink, I'll speak up on your behalf when he returns."

By this time, as he had dared to hope, she was thoroughly confused. Providentially, a shout rose from the beach at the same moment. The distance was too great for Tenthag to make out exactly what was being said, but a fair guess suggested that one of the Neesans had complained about all their best possessions being taken, and one of the visitors had demanded what price was too high to pay for fertility.

The same might be asked concerning freedom. Accustomed, like almost everybody else, to imagining that the risk of being stabbed through a major tubule was sufficient to make anyone sit quiet, Sprapter had relied on Veetalya's possession of a good sharp prong a padlong distant to ensure his captive would obey her. But he had seen Pletrow calmly cut her own body with a far keener blade, and heard her casual dismissal of the risk . . .

"Oh, come now!" he said, as Veetalya glanced towards the row on shore, and took a stride that brought him within the range of her prong. "A drink is not too much to—"

And *snap.* At maximum pressure his claws closed on the prong and broke it off, and he was all over her, trusting to his greater weight to force her backward. She wasted her spare pressure on a scream, and that sufficed. He trampled on her as though she were not there and swarmed over the briq's side into Flapper's saddle, which the People of the Sea had not found time to dismount. With claws and mandibles and the stub of the prong he slashed at the bonds restraining her, and before the startled crewfolk at the forward end could get to him, he had weakened them enough for the porp to break the rest with one great heave and surge. Half-swamped in a deluge of water, he clung valiantly and jabbed her back with the prong in lieu of a goad. With all her well-fed force she rushed for open water, leaving his captors to fret and curse and hurl obscenities.

The breeze bore him one furious shout: "Well, a courier's no loss to us, any more than a porp!"

*Wrong*, promised Tenthag silently. *I'm going to cost you more than you can possibly afford!*

After so long a period of forced inaction, Flapper rushed straight for the horizon, and he let her go, glad that his provisions had not been pilfered. He drank a lot and ate a little, restoring his normality while calculating how long it would be before the trading on the beach came to an end. If tradition were anything to go by, it would last until dark, and some kind of celebration would follow. The People of the Sea would not dare risk departure without the regular formalities, or even in their debilitated state the Neesans might suspect the trick that had been played on them. Therefore he should have time to swing around on a long circular course and bring Flapper back to the island just after darkfall, when her return was least likely to be noticed.

Cold anger colored his mind gray. Stark facts like distant mountains marked the boundary of his thinking. He was possessed, for the first time in his life, by lust for vengeance.

As darkness fell, he sought the star which had caught his attention at the fringe of the Major Cluster. There was no mistake. It had turned yellower and brighter. Perhaps someone who had not watched the sky from the lonely vantage of a porp's back in mid-ocean might have overlooked the change, but to Tenthag it was past a doubt.

In ancient times they'd said the stars reflected what went on below. He was too well informed to swallow such deceits. But the image, nonetheless, was powerful, and struck chords in that level of his mind where dreamness ruled.

Perhaps that star was shedding bright new light on what had been dead planets, conjuring the force of life from them. It didn't matter. For him it was a symbol, and a challenge. He must cast light of his own on his own folk . . .

Luminants faintly outlined the island, but there were wide gaps where they had not been properly tended and he was able to steal ashore without being spotted. He left Flapper to fend for herself. If he came back by dawn, she would probably still be here; if not, she would shed her saddle as soon as it rotted, but with luck keep the secondary plants Gveest had bestowed on her, which would be an example to any other of the folk who ran across her later on. Maybe, if she bred in the wild, some of them might cross-take on her bud . . .

Who, though, would help the porps if the Guild of Couriers all met the same doom as Tenthag? In a few years, following the population explosion, they would surely be hunted down for food!

Repressing all such horrible previsions, he crept over the hill-crest on which stood the derelict solar mirror, and found his guesses accurate. Reluctant to leave before sharing refreshment with the local people, the visitors were sitting under arbors of luminants and pretending to be polite. Fifthorch, recognizable by scent and voice, was lavishing on them what food and liquor remained, while others waited in shadow, exuding the stink of greed . . . or was it from the outsiders? At this distance he could not be certain.

But that was irrelevant. Hastening down the old familiar path, he headed for the crowd—and was brought up short, so that he clutched his sole weapon, the broken prong, and spun around with a hiss of terror. He had abruptly caught a waft of death, and there were overtones to it that he recognized.

Beside the path, clearly having collapsed as he moved away from the town, leaking his stale ichor on the ground after a major rupture of a lower tubule . . . Ninthag.

He who had been the town's elder for so long, its guide and counselor: left here to rot unheeded! Had he been stabbed? But a quick tactile check confirmed that he had simply died from stress. Well, that was a relief, of a sort—but still an insult!

Tenthag drew himself together and put on the best imitation he could contrive of his father's appearance. Maintaining it, while imitating an old'un's hobble, he let himself show in the circle of brightness shed by the town-center lights.

It was Sprapter who first noticed him, accepting a shell of araq. He was so startled that he tilted it and cursed as the biting liquid spilled down his torso. Before he could speak, while others were still turning to gaze at him, Tenthag said loudly enough to be heard by everyone, "Have they shown you a female with a bud?"

Fifthorch, offering more araq to another of the People of the Sea, started so violently he almost slumped, and Tenthag, still posing as his father, padded towards him. In a thin voice he repeated, "A female with a bud—have they shown you one?"

"Drive him off!" Sprapter cried, struggling to full height.

"Why?" Tenthag countered. "You have the secret of fertility, or so your banners claim! That means you must have buds and young'uns in your fleet!"

"Of course they have the secret!" Fifthorch shouted, while the hunger-sluggish minds of those around him registered what Tenthag was saying. "They've sold it to us, and on fair terms, what's more!"

"But have they shown a single young'un, or a she'un budding?" Tenthag abandoned his disguise and strode to take station at Sprapter's side, his prong leveled. "I say they haven't even met the southern fleets which raided Ognorit, but stole everything you could offer in the hope that when they do they'll get the secret! Truth, Sprapter—tell the truth! And for every lie I'll let the pressure out of one of your tubules!" He jabbed the commander's torso, just enough.

Terrified, Sprapter babbled, "I swear we would have kept our bargain! We needed to buy the secret and we'd have come back and—"

"You mean you didn't give it to us?" Fifthorch said, belatedly reacting to the commander's reek of guilt and shame.

Without compunction Tenthag slit a minor tubule in the trickster's torso, forcing him to fold over and compress the leak until it sealed.

"I don't know what they clawed off you," he said mildly, "but as I tried to tell you earlier, I was at Ognorit, and learned from Gveest himself what must be done. On the briq where I was captive, I met a she'un who was ripe for budding, and she had no bud. I saw not a single bud or young'un in this fleet that claims to sell the secret! What do you make of that, you fools who left Ninthag to leak away his life on that path yonder? Who'd have the secret merely to sell to others, without using it to benefit themselves?"

A pulsation later he was frightened by the forces he had loosed, for Fifthorch roared with mindless rage and launched himself at Sprapter. Before the two could be separated the commander was as dead as Ninthag, and the air was foul with the stench of drying ichor and loud with screams of pain.

But within moments the seafolk were cowering to the ground, emitting the odor of surrender, and finding themselves about to slash or stab with whatever weapon came to claw, the Neesans recovered enough of their normal awareness to realize what they had done, and be horrified at it. Weak, but calm, they began to mutter among themselves that Tenthag had been right, and they were stupid not to have insisted on being shown a budded she'un before parting with their goods.

Suddenly Tenthag found them all looking to him for guidance, seafolk and Neesans alike . . . except for Fifthorch, who faded into the dark moaning about the need to wash off Sprapter's ichor.

He said after a pause for reflection, "Eat what there is. Give nothing more to the seafolk. You must restore your strength of mind and body both, because you're going to make these liars pay for their deceit. Not only are they going to return what they cheated you out of; they're going to be set to work recovering the plants you've let run wild, ridding the town of mold and orqid, bringing fish from deep water, and laying up great stores of food against the time when the real secret of fertility is brought hither. It won't be long, I'm sure. *But there must be food first!*"

The seafolk whispered among themselves. Eventually one subcommander rose to normal height.

"It's fair judgment," he admitted sullenly. "I'm Loric. I've been chosen as Sprapter's successor. I'll abide by your terms, but I'll ask one thing in return."

"You don't deserve anything," Tenthag snapped. "Feel free to ask, though, as I shall to refuse."

"You do owe me something," Loric insisted. "Sprapter wanted to kill your porp, or at any rate drive her to open water. But I've been in charge of our food-plants for years, and I saw new ones on the porp which gave me ideas. That's why I insisted on her being lashed alongside the briq. I wanted to study and adapt them. They told us that was how you were able to escape, though I must admit none of us expected you to return. It was a brave thing to do, and your countryfolk ought to be proud of you. Instead, they described you as a traitor and a runaway, especially Fifthorch, and in the end they made us believe it, so you took us completely by surprise . . . Don't you owe me something, though, for saving your porp?"

"I guess so," Tenthag admitted gruffly. "Very well. When you leave here, which won't be soon, you'll have grafts of Gveest's new food-plants to help you on your way. But it may take months before there are enough for both Neesos and your fleet, and in spite of being foolish my people are still my people, and they get first call. By that time you'll have learned a lot about food-plants on land, I promise you."

"You're an honest man in spite of being a courier. You won't regret striking this bargain. How do you think I was able to persuade your folk that we did truly have the secret of fertility? Could I have convinced them without considerable understanding of all sorts of life-forms? Oh, I'm not a Gveest; I'm more the practical type. But if there's any connection between his work with plants and lower animals, and what he's discovered that will make us breed, then don't be surprised if I figure out the secret for myself eventually. I'd like to, obviously. It'd save us a trip south, into waters where there are already too many of us for the junqs and briqs available, not so?"

It was impossible not to be won over by this fellow's audacity. Tenthag tried to stop himself quirking into a smile. Loudly he said, "Work, then, if you want to clench the deal! We have two funerals to conduct immediately. Then we must tell the rest of your company the fate in store."

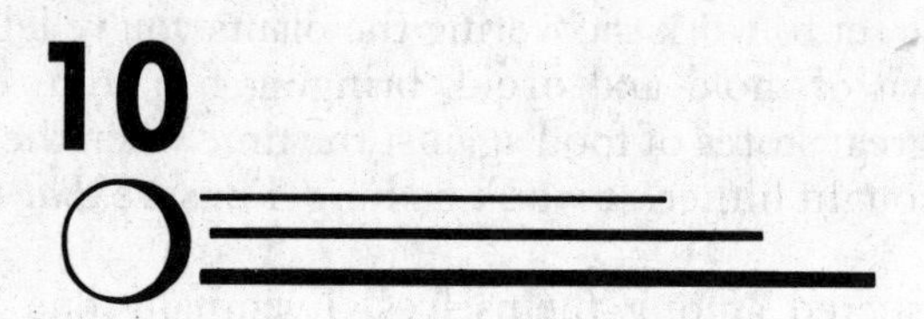

What Tenthag was doing was not in accord with his commission; he should have returned directly to Bowock. But after the hostility he had met on the day of his departure, he was in no hurry. Besides, his actions were consonant with his courier's oath, at least in his opinion. By summer's end there would be at least one fleet—small, admittedly—in possession not of the secret of fertility but of information far more essential, which it could then trade to supplement the couriers' efforts. And the seafolk would need to trade if they did begin to multiply; one bud per she'un would require at least two extra briqs or another junq, complete with food-plants, and this far north there were few young wild'uns nowadays.

He occupied himself not only with supervising the restoration of Neesos's fortunes, but with retaming and exercising Flapper, whom he took to sea almost daily with the fleet on its fishing-trips. Once they had grown resigned to the failure of their intended fraud, the seafolk proved to be friendly enough, and of course they had far more in common with couriers than they were usually prepared to admit. In the end even Veetalya recovered from the shame she felt at having let Tenthag escape, and their relations became very friendly. Loric, too, turned out to be likable, and interested not only in life-study but star-study also. Together they pondered the possible meaning of that star which almost nightly shone yellower, brighter, hotter. Through a good telescope it could be seen to be surrounded by a sort of aura, like drifting smoke.

"That's some of the cold matter massing to block our way to the future," Tenthag explained soberly. "But before we get that far, more of it will doubtless turn into stars, more will be drawn into our own sun, more will tumble out of space and crash into the oceans, raising huge waves, or smash down on land and burn forests to ash . . . Oh, Loric, we are caught in a trap worse than a gigant's claw! On the one side, the risk that there won't be enough of the folk for us to save ourselves; on the other, that there may be far too many!"

"Don't you think we'll make it?" Veetalya asked timidly.

Tenthag shrugged with his entire mantle. "When I see what we can do when we combine our efforts, as here on Neesos, I feel very optimistic. But when I remember how nearly my own people went insane, and how you tried to take advantage . . . Who can say?"

Turning the telescope curiously in all directions, for it was superior to any he had used before, Loric suddenly stiffened.

"Another fleet!" he whispered. "Look! See the glimmer on the water?"

"Where . . . ? Oh, yes! Give me the telescope . . . But those aren't junqs or briqs! They're porps—you can tell by the way they move! And none but couriers use porps, and that must be half the complement the Guild can boast! Quick, to the beach, and signal!"

As he incontinently led the way, hoping no loose rock would betray his steps in the dark, he wondered silently what disaster had brought *this* about.

Within a very short time, as all the folk of the island gathered on the beach, he learned the terrible truth. First to land was Dippid himself, followed by Nemora, and then another score of his friends and colleagues. When they had got over their astonishment at finding Tenthag alive and well, they told their story.

"We thought you must be dead," Dippid rasped. "Many of the couriers have been attacked for not possessing the secret of fertility, by people convinced they did but were holding out for the highest price. It's a rumor started by the Major South Fleet. Iyosc was right; they did raid Ognorit and now they're trading what they're pleased to call 'the right to bud' . . . against everything they can lay their claws on, especially seed and food-plants!"

Tenthag exchanged glances with his companions, who by now included Fifthorch. He said slowly, "What's the situation like at Bowock? Have you been driven away?"

"Yes," was Nemora's simple answer, and she turned aside in grief. Dippid amplified.

"Iyosc was right about that, too. She'uns in bud and their companions, deprived of all their food-stocks by the greed of the People of the Sea, naturally started heading for the cities, not just Bowock, but any place where it looked as though there were still plenty of victuals. Bowock has been the chief magnet, obviously, because of that rumor that we were withholding the secret. And I regret to admit . . ."

He hesitated. Recovering, Nemora said curtly, "Some of the Jingfired betrayed their trust. Either they got hold of Gveest's technique, or they were able to work it out from what was already known.

Anyhow, they applied it to themselves. It was impossible to keep *that* secret. As soon as the news got out . . . Well, you can imagine its effect. We clung on as long as we could, but when we learned that couriers were being hunted down and killed we decided to flee. I remembered coming to Neesos, all those years ago, and as near as we could calculate we believed it must still be well beyond the sweep of the Major Fleet. Besides, the closer we got, the more we heard rumors that the people of lonely islands like this one were abandoning their homes and making for mainland cities, where the bud-right might be theirs all the sooner."

"Some of the folk did leave here," Tenthag muttered, and went on to explain what he had found on his arrival.

"You were very sensible not to return to Bowock," Dippid pronounced at last. "It may not have been what you were supposed to do, but it's turned out for the best."

"Do you have the bud-secret?" Loric demanded suddenly.

There was a pause like the interval between the lightning and the thunder. At last Dippid heaved a sigh.

"Yes. We had to bring something we could trade for food."

"That's liable to draw crowds of crazy folk to Neesos, then!" cried Fifthorch, indicating how much he had learned about the real world since Tenthag's return. "We must think of ways to defend ourselves—"

"We must think of ways to feed ourselves," Tenthag corrected stonily. "Sane, well-nourished folk are always our friends and allies. Only the crazy ones are a threat. And now we have a vast stockpile of precious knowledge; couriers are as well informed as anybody short of the Jingfired themselves, or scientists like Gveest. Is there news of him, by the way?"

Dippid clacked his mandibles. "Report has it that he and Pletrow and the rest are captives with the Major Fleet. But nobody knows for certain. It may just be another rumor put about to encourage folk to pay extortionate prices."

"I hope for his sake he's not," Tenthag said softly. "I got to know him pretty well while I was at Ognorit, and I'm certain he would be horrified to see the dreadful impact his discovery is having. He knew about it, he tried to guard us against it, and through ill-luck I was the one who was obliged to undermine his precautions."

"Iyosc forgave you for that," Nemora said, laying a claw friendly on his mantle-edge. "And what you're doing here is making further amends. What's more, perhaps the star—"

"We've been over that!"—morosely from Dippid. "More likely it's a harbinger of catastrophe, like the old New Star."

"It can't be! It's not at all the same!" Nemora hunched forward. "We know the other one outshone the Major Cluster, to begin with. No, I think this is more likely a stroke of good fortune. Changes like that going on in the sky are just what people will need to keep reminding them of Jingtruths. Things must have been equally bleak when the Northern Freeze began, and again at the time of the Great Thaw—yet here we are, and we have some achievements of our own to boast of!"

"There's no comparison," Dippid maintained. "This time we're breaking the very mold we were cast in by our evolution!"

Tenthag thought of Pletrow's collection of mutated animals, and shuddered as the chief courier went on.

"No, it's going to be a different world. Even during the famine at Southmost Cape I never saw anything as horrible as what's now happening at Bowock. For all we can tell, there's something in the radiation from the stars that drives us crazy now and then, and what can we do to withstand that? Grow a roof over the entire planet?"

"What use would a roof be against what's sure to fall on us one of these days?" said Tenthag wearily, and forced himself to full height. "No, we dare not try and hide from our doom. The universe will not permit it. We must carry on somehow, preserving at least a nucleus of reason . . . There's a tale about the legendary Barratong. When he realized the Thaw was bringing more and more of the planet under his people's sway, he didn't rejoice or boast about it. He accepted the duty which the past had laid upon the present. Do you remember what he said?"

"Of course," said Loric as he also rose. "All we People of the Sea are brought up to regard it as the finest principle of our heritage, though since it led to the foundation of Bowock and the Guild of Couriers—Never mind! This is not a moment for squabbling over what's past and done with. Barratong said, in fact, 'We are the Jingfired now!' "

"It's our turn to say the same," said Tenthag, and padded miserably away towards the first glint of dawn, wondering how much sorrow and insanity the sun must shine on before the folk recovered from the shock of being multiplied.

And if they would.

# Part Five

# Bloom

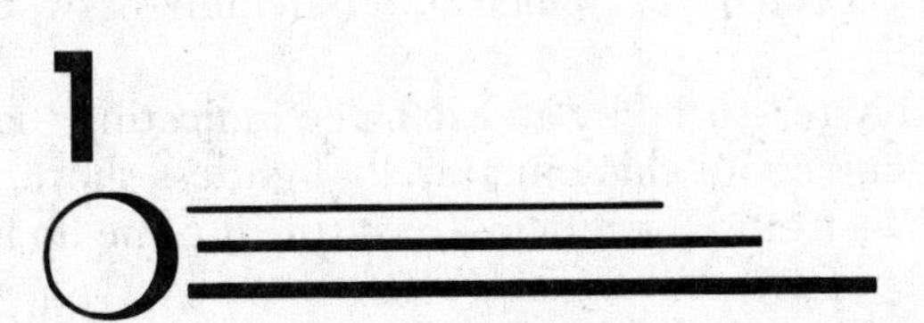

*T*he city of Voosla was allegedly approaching her landfall, but Awb could scarcely credit it. There was too much dark on the horizon.

Wherever there was habitable ground there were people, and even more than food-crops the folk cultivated plants which, after sundown, either glowed of their own accord or gave back the light they had basked in earlier. Troqs who had taken to caves for refuge in desert regions where houses would not grow, squimaqs who eked out their existence around the poles where darkness could last for half a year—they knew that trying to manage without luminants was to risk being driven into dreamness as certainly as by starvation, if not so quickly.

And indeed, throughout the voyage until now, there had always been distant glimmerings: nothing like as bright, of course, as the lights of the city, but discernible with even a crude telescope like Awb's, which he had made himself and was very proud of. Thilling the picturist had ceded him a couple of lenses too worn for fixing perfect images, and fitted into a tube they afforded a view of the strange northern coasts they were paralleling.

However, they also showed, much too plainly for comfort, that blank gap on the edge of an otherwise populous continent. There was something so eerie about it that it made his weather-sense queasy. He found himself longing for the familiar scenery of the tropics which, since his budding, the city had never previously left.

To think that one new moon ago he had been beside himself with excitement at the prospect of this journey to the intended site of the World Observatory . . . !

Swarming along the branchways in search of distraction, he shortly discovered that a crowd had gathered on the lookout platform at the prow, including most of the delegation from the University of Chisp. Their chief, Scholar Drotninch, was conferring with Mayor Axwep.

Awb also found it disturbing to have so many foreigners traveling with them. Voosla was by no means a large city, and he knew all her inhabitants at least by sight. Before this trip he had been used to meeting strangers, if at all, by ones and twos, not scores together. Still, the scientists were polite enough, and some—like Thilling—were positively friendly, so he decided to chance a rebuff and draw close enough to overhear.

And was considerably reassured by an exchange indicating that he was not alone in worrying about this unnaturally lightless shore.

"Amazing, isn't it?"—from Drotninch. "Last time I came up here, this was the brightest spot for padlonglaqs."

To which Axwep: "The city's growing fractious, as though she senses something amiss. Could be a taint in the water; we're well into the estuarial zone. I'd be inclined to hold off until sunrise. It won't mean too much of a delay, and it'll give us a chance to feed and rest the musculators. I can send a pitchen ahead to explain why we aren't landing at once."

Drotninch pondered, and one could almost scent her indecision . . . but, like most landlivers nowadays, she coated her torso with neutralizing perfumes. It had become a mark of good manners, and those—as Awb knew from his few visits to shore—were far from a luxury in the overcrowded conditions of a fixed city. Life at sea, in his view, was superior; if Axwep noted an accumulation of combat-stink she needed only to consult her weather-sense about what course to set and let a fresh breeze calm things down.

Finally the scholar signed agreement, and Axwep issued the necessary orders. The group dispersed, some to tend the musculators, others to prepare the pitchen. Slowly, owing to her colossal bulk, the city ceased to thrash the water. The group of interlinked junqs around which she was built exuded relief, for even in calm weather they disliked being brought near land, perhaps owing to some ancestral fear of being stranded on a beach or dashed against rocks. Not, naturally, that they could do anything against the resistless force of the musculators.

When it was uncaged the pitchen seemed equally unhappy, as though it too were alarmed by the dark shore, but that was fanciful nonsense, since it did not depend on sight—indeed it possessed no eye, and reacted solely to magnetic fields, like the ancient northfinders which had died off during the Northern Freeze. When it was dropped overside with Axwep's message tied to its claws, it set out obediently enough for the place it had been conditioned to regard as home, leaving patches of phosphorescence to mark each of its leaps. Watching it go, Awb reflected what a benefit its kind had proved to be, especially since they had been modified to follow canals and winding inland channels as well as pursuing a direct course across open water. He wished he knew who had been the first to domesticate pitchens, but during the Age of Multiplication people had been much more concerned with staying alive and sane than with keeping records of who invented what.

"That's much better!" said a she'un's voice behind him, and he lowered reflexively as Thilling swarmed down an adjacent branchway with, as ever, her image-fixer at the ready. "Maybe now I'll get the chance to cut a few new lenses! I've lost count of how many got spoiled when a wave disturbed me while I was trimming them, and I do so want to catch everything that happens when we go ashore . . . And what's wrong with you, young'un? You seem worried."

"I never saw a coast so dark before!" Awb blurted.

"Hmm! I did! Once I was sent to cover an epidemic on Blotherotch—went in with a medical team looking for the causative organism, assigned to picture the victims for future reference. Some of the folk there had turned so dreamish, they imagined they could prolong their lives by eating luminants, and they'd absolutely stripped the area. It was ghastly. Still, we got away safely, and now we're all immune against *that* disease. On the other claw . . ."

She hesitated. Greatly daring, he prompted her.

"Oh, I was only going to say: we've discovered cures for so many disorders including infertility, it seems incredible there should be a brand-new one, least of all one that can afflict an entire countryside—people and animals and plants as well!"

"Is that really what we can look forward to finding?"

"You're asking me? I never set pad here, haven't even had a sight of the nervograp messages that got through before the link failed. Phrallet must know more about those than I do; doesn't she tell you anything?"

"As little as possible," Awb muttered. He was always embarrassed when someone mentioned his budder, who flaunted her five bud-scars in a manner most people regarded as indecent and seemed to think that because Axwep only had four she had the better claim to be Voosla's mayor.

"Well, you should pester her more," Thilling said, loading a sensitive sheet into her fixer. As much to herself as him, she added, "I wish I'd had time to graft a new lens on this thing, because I'm sure there's a salt-water blister somewhere, but with dawn so close I'll have to make do . . . Keep your eye skinned, young'un. If what I've been told is reliable, we should be in for a treat. Look yonder, where I'm pointing."

Awb complied, but still all he could make out, even with his telescope, was a vague patch of black-on-blacker. In the south-east the first hint of dawn was coloring the air, not nearly enough as yet to dim the Arc of Heaven, let alone the Major Cluster. There was a bank of dense cloud to the north, veiling any aurora there might be, and that surprised him, for visibility in this region was reputed the best in the hemisphere; why else choose it for the World Observatory?

On the other claw, no place on the planet was immune from what happened next. A streak of yellow light slashed out of the east, and at its tip a fireball exploded, scattering trails of luminance across a quarter of the welkin. Caught by surprise, Thilling uttered a curse.

"That's spoiled my leaf good and proper! Young'un, keep looking, and warn me if I'm apt to miss anything!"

Hastily she threw away the sheet she had been mounting in the fixer, and peeled another from the stack.

By this time Awb was beginning to guess at what she meant. The flash of the meteor had revealed something outlined against the northern clouds. He had had too brief a glimpse to make out details, but there was only one thing it could be: Fangsharp Peak, on top of which the observatory was being grown. Of course, since it was so much higher than the surrounding land, it was bound to catch the sun's rays first. So—

"Quick!" he cried, suddenly aware that all about them the branchways were alive with folk scrambling to seek a vantage point and watch the unique spectacle. Barely in time Thilling leveled her fixer.

The sky grew brighter, though the land and sea remained virtually featureless. The world paused in expectation. And there it came!

On the very crest of the mountain, so high above them that it looked as though a huge and jagged rock were floating in mid-air, a single shaft of sunlight rested.

It was the most awe-inspiring event that Awb had ever seen. Without intention, he found himself counting his own pulsations to find out how long the sight would last: three, four, five, six—

It was over, and the sky was turning daytime blue, and he could see the whole mountain. Its flanks were scarred where the natural vegetation had been stripped away in favor of what would be needed to support the observatory. Guide-cables for construction floaters swooped down to either side. A passenger-carrying floater, five bladders glistening, was descending slowly from the top. Awb had never seen one so close; usually they passed over at pressure-height, mere sparkles to the unaided eye.

Axwep and Drotninch returned to the lookout platform, and waited along with everybody else until full daylight also overspread the shore, revealing a stark, discolored mass of shriveled foliage.

"That's *worse* than what we were warned to expect," muttered Thilling as she stored away her exposed sheets. Awb was about to reply, when—

"Look!" somebody screamed.

On the top of the peak something was moving. No: the top of the peak itself was moving! It was cracking apart, it was shedding chunks of rock, it was tilting, it was sliding and rasping and collapsing and slamming down with horrible slowness in an inexorable paradigm of disaster. The guide-cables snapped, the passenger floater leapt up the air like a frightened pitchen taking off from a wave-top, the new plants on the mountainside vanished in a cloud of dust and boulders, so all at once that Awb could not take everything in.

The avalanche subsided into a monstrous scree, blocking a canal that led from the base of the mountain to the shore along which, presumably, rubble had been carried to create the sheltering mole now visible between the city and the land, the first stage in preparation for a full-scale harbor. All the seafarers stood transfixed with horror as the dawn breeze carried off the dust.

But from the shore, incurious and dull as mere animals, most of them sickly and with their mantles ulcerated, a few natives gazed at the city before dismissing it as incomprehensible and setting off to seek food in the shallows.

What Awb found most appalling, as he strove to hold his telescope steady, was that not a single one among them made for the scene of the catastrophe, to find out whether anybody lay in need of help.

## 2

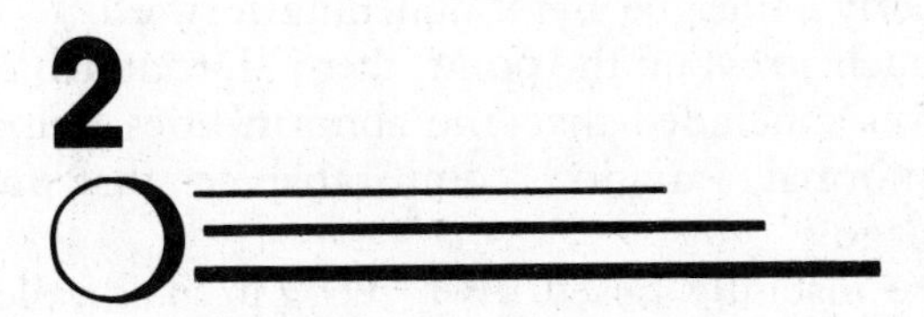

"Of course we know *what* happened," said Lesh, so weary she could scarcely flex her mantle, let alone stand upright. "It's another of the unforeseen disasters that bid fair to wreck our project! Without our noticing, a pumptree shoot invaded a slanting crevice and expanded there, turning the crevice into a crack and the crack into a split. Finally it sprang a leak. Water by itself might not have made the rock slide, but mixed with nice greasy sap—smash! You can see the way it must have gone quite clearly from the air. But what we now have to find out is *why*. Pumptrees simply aren't supposed to act like that!"

She was the resident chief designer for the observatory project. She and a couple of assistants had been all dark on the mountain-top investigating reports of irregular pulsation in the pumptrees. About the time Voosla hove in sight they had concluded the trouble was due to nothing worse than irritation caused by the topsoil they were carrying in the form of slurry, which necessarily contained a trace of sand and gravel. The roots of the toughtrees which would eventually form a foundation for the large telescopes needed more nutriment than they could extract from bare rock, at least if they were to grow to usable size in less than a score of years. Besides, the intention was to keep the peak in more or less its original form, and toughtrees certainly did erode rock, given time.

Down below there was plenty of rich fertile dirt, and it had seemed like a brilliant shortcut to mix it with water and render it liquid enough for pumptrees to transport it upward. This was not entirely a new technique; something similar had been attempted recently in desert-reclamation.

So Lesh and her companions had remounted their floater, to take advantage of the coolness of the gas in its bladders before sunshine increased its buoyancy and obliged them to have it hauled down, and that lucky chance had spared their lives. In fact, as things had turned out, everybody was safely accounted for, except perhaps a few natives, and they were so stupid they could rarely be taught to answer their names. Still, the harm done was severe enough.

"It's set us back years!" Lesh mourned.

"Well, I did warn in my original report, when the site was first surveyed, that there must be something amiss in this area!" That was from Drotninch's elderly colleague Byra, hunching forward.

"You didn't lay much stress on the point, then," Drotninch countered. "As I recall, you concluded that 'the abnormalities found fall within a range of normal variation comparable to that in the Lugomannic Archipelago!' "

Other voices were instantly raised. Awb recognized Phrallet's—trust her to poke a claw in, he thought morosely—but none of the others. It was dark again now, and even though a few luminants had been brought from Voosla it was hard to make out anybody's features, here on the gritty beach beside the unfinished mole.

In any case, he was too worn out to care. So much had happened, he was half-convinced he had wandered into dreamness and would recover to be told he was suffering from fever and delirium. He *wanted* to have imagined what he had witnessed today, the stench of shock and misery exuded by the people working here as they surveyed the ruin of years of effort. At his age he had scarcely begun to conceive ambitions, let alone put them into practice, and he had been stabbed to the pith on realizing how trivial an oversight could cause such a calamity. That vast mound of shattered rock blocking the canal; that dismal garland of carefully tended plants now dangling over the new precipice so high above; those tangled cables which only yesterday had guided massive loads up and down Fangsharp Peak . . .

Too many images, too much emotion. He let his mind wander and made no attempt to follow the discussion.

Then, unexpectedly, he heard Axwep's boom of authority, and reflex snatched his full attention, just as though they were in mid-ocean with a line-squall looming.

"Now that's enough of this wrangling!" the mayor rasped. "I thought we were bringing cool-minded scientists here! I'd like to see a bunch like you put in charge of a city when one of her incorporated junqs turns rogue and has to be shed because you can't kill her without attracting sharqs or feroqs! Fancy trying to keep your musculators working when rogue ichor's leaking through the circulation, *hmm?* If you can't cling to your drifting wits when you're not even in danger of your lives, it's a poor lookout for your project anyhow! So shut up, will you? And that goes for you as well, Phrallet! I don't care how much of the voyage you spent chatting up our guests while I was busy running Voosla—you can't possibly know enough about the problem to discuss it. Even Drotninch hasn't been here for two years, remember."

The direct insult provoked Phrallet to a reeking fury, and she rose to full height in a way that proved she had worked little, if at all, during the bright-time; none of the others present had pressure left to match her. For an instant she imagined she was at an advantage.

Then, suddenly, she realized that those nearest her were all land-livers, perfumed against such a naked show of emotion, and they were shuffling away from her in distaste. With a muttered curse she stormed back to the city, splashing loudly off the end of the mole.

And good riddance, Awb thought. He had long wished that something of the sort might happen. Of course, like everyone else, he would have hoped to love his budder . . . but did she like him? Had she liked any of her offspring? True, it was a custom in every floating city to trade off young'uns to communities where, for some reason, the fertility treatment had not properly taken, or been counteracted in emergency, but she never stopped boasting about what splendid bargains she had struck for her four eldest . . . all of whom were she'uns.

Awb's mantle clenched around him. So were three of Axwep's—and they were still in the city, one studying, two working on the secondary plants. The mayor didn't object to their presence. But Phrallet could all too easily have seen her buds as potential rivals, and that would explain so much, so much!

Oh, if only he had been budded to somebody like Thilling! But the picturist must be sterile; she had no bud-scars at all.

A faint idea hovered at the edge of his awareness, in that dim zone where memory, imagination and reason blurred together. He was far too tired to pursue it, though, and turned his mind back to the discussion. Axwep was presiding over it now, directing its course like a commander of old at the bragmeets recounted in ancient legend.

She was saying: "So when you first came here, and heard about peculiar plants and deformed animals, you found no actual evidence, correct?"

"The nearest reports," Byra confirmed, "were from several padlonglaqs away. The local vegetation displayed some unusual features, but that's often the way with modified Gveestian secondaries, isn't it?"

"What about the natives? I haven't seen much of them, but they strike me as very peculiar indeed!"

Axwep's thrust went home. Byra broke off in confusion. But Drotninch spoke up bluffly.

"It was regarded by the Council of the Jingfired as a great advantage that the folk hereabouts were unlikely to protest at our intrusion!"

There was a murmur of approval from the assembled scientists, growing restive at the mayor's intervention.

"I thought so too," Lesh said suddenly. "But now I don't. Oh, it's very well for you lot to argue in such terms, comfortable at home in Chisp! What do you think it's been like for us, though, surrounded by people we can't even talk to? It's been preying on my pith, I tell you straight, and I don't think I'm the only one."

Seizing her chance, Axwep said, "Can you relate the loss of your luminants to any particular event? Or the failure of your nervograps? After all, when you first arrived everything seemed normal except for the people. What did you do that might have—oh, I don't know!—imported a new infection from beyond the hills, say?"

There was a pause. Lesh said at last, with reluctance, "Well, I have wondered about . . ."

"Go on!"

"Well, we do require a lot of fresh water, you know, and we were running short the winter before last, because it freezes so hard around here, and one of our aerial surveys noted that a stream just the other side of the local watershed was still free of ice. So last spring we tapped it with some quick-growing cutinates, and by the end of the summer we had a good supply. It's lasted through the winter exactly as we planned. But in any case, what could that have to do with the sudden blight we've suffered? We're all trained personnel, and we have the most modern medical knowledge, and—"

"Nobody's told me," Axwep cut in, "but I'll wager that the local folk have long been accustomed to collecting food from beyond the watershed. Correct?"

"Ah . . . Yes, I believe so."

"Because the vegetation there is lusher, or better to eat, or superior in some other way? Or don't you know?"

"I already told you: some of the Gveestian secondaries are unfamiliar, but we're on the edge of a climatic boundary, so I suppose the cold—"

"It's time to stop supposing and start thinking," murmured a soft voice at Awb's side, and Thilling settled close to him. "No need to explain what's going on. I can guess, even though it's taken me until now to get all my images developed. They practically tell the story by themselves . . . Say, wasn't it Phrallet I sensed passing me on the way here? What's with her? She was reeking!"

Awb summed up the reason, and Thilling clacked her mandibles in sympathy.

"It's not going to be much fun for you on Voosla for the foreseeable future, is it?"

That was it. That was the hint he needed to complete the idea which had been so elusive before. Even though life at sea was preferable, life anywhere in company with so foul-tempered a budder . . .

"Do you spend most of your time on land?" Awb whispered.

"No more than I can help. I like to travel, I'm good at what I do and get plenty of commissions. Why?"

"Would you accept me as an apprentice?"

"Hmm! I don't know about that! But"—quickly before he let his mantle slump—"you can help me on shore until Phrallet gets over her present mood. Then we'll see. Fair?"

"I can't thank you enough!"

"Then please me by keeping quiet for a bit. Oh, if there were a bit more light . . . ! But this sort of thing needs to be fixed in sound, really. You should be listening: all these recriminations about who betrayed Lesh and her chums by not exploring the far side of the watershed properly!"

Awb composed himself and did his best to concentrate. But all he could think of was how suddenly the blight must have struck if a mere two years before experienced investigators like Drotninch and Byra had found nothing in this area to worry them.

*F*inally a weak conclusion was reached. After the extent of the damage had been assessed, so a report could be sent back to Chisp, an expedition must cross the watershed and test the plants there for infective organisms, even though none had been found over here.

So much could have been agreed straightaway, in Awb's view, but everybody was so overwrought, making decisions seemed like excessively hard work. He was as affected as anyone else. He felt he ought to be doing something, if only getting better acquainted with the observatory site, but it was still dark, and what could he learn without adequate luminants? Voosla carried seed of a recently developed type that rooted immediately in a shellful of soil and could be carried around draped over a pole, lasting for up to half a score of darks, exactly the kind of thing that was called for in a crisis like this. But nobody had expected a crisis, so none of them had been planted in advance, and even if they were forced now it would be days before they ripened.

In the end he remained inert, pondering a mystery that had often troubled him before.

Why was it that, when the world was generally calm by dark, it was always harder to analyze and act on important memories? Surely the opposite should have been true! Yet it never was. While the sun was down, memories lurked on the edge of consciousness like dormant seeds, only to burst out when there was so much else going on that one would have expected them to be smothered. Oh, they were accessible enough at a time like now . . . but they didn't seem to connect to activity.

Awb had been puzzled about this for a long time, for a reason he suspected people from fixed cities would not appreciate. Incomprehensibly, though, when he mentioned it to people on Voosla—Tyngwap the chief librarian, for example, who had custody of not only the city's history and navigation records, but also data concerning all the shores she had touched—they missed the point of his question too, brushing him aside with some casual reference to the light-level or the local air-pressure.

Which manifestly could have nothing to do with what he was trying to figure out

Even though cities like Voosla were commanded by experienced weather-guessers, storms sometimes broke out unexpectedly across their course, perhaps precipitated by a meteor; nobody could forecast those, but the sparks they shed through the upper air did often seem to provoke foul weather. If such a thing happened in the dire middle of the dark, the people's response was as prompt and efficient as by day, and they were quite well able to put off their usual time for rest and reflection. But they never seemed to need to make it up later! Physical exhaustion due to lack of pressure was one thing; it demanded food and drink and that was enough. Mental exhaustion was something else; it gathered in the lower reaches of the mind, and eventually burst out in altered form. Take Phrallet as an example. What she had done this dark, by intervening in the scientists' debate without knowing the facts, was typical of her excessive need to be active, vocally or otherwise. It didn't render her unattractive to males, but her fellow she'uns didn't like her much, and as for the status accorded to mere males ever since it had been established that originally they had been parasitical on females and used them simply to bear their buds . . . !

Well, only the fact that inbreeding rapidly led to deformity had prevented cities like Voosla, and probably fixed cities as well, from reducing males to simple tokens, like certain lower animals whose symbiosis must go back so far in the history of evolution that even the finest modern techniques could not recover a single independently viable male cell. Luckily—from Awb's point of view—it had early been shown, in the light of Gveest's pioneering work (and he was male and some said had betrayed his kind!), that species lacking the constant chemical renewal due to symbiosis were precisely those most vulnerable to climatic change. Where were the snowbelongs of yesterday, hunted to extinction as soon as the Great Thaw overtook them? Where were the canifangs, pride of the earliest bioscientists—not that they called themselves by any such name in that far past? They had been deliberately made to specialize, and they died out. The list was long: northfinders, hoverers, fosq, dirq, some exploited by folk for their own ends, some simply unable to compete when their range was invaded by a more vigorous rival or even a rash of Gveest's new plants!

Beyond them, too, according to the latest accounts, there had been ancestral creatures without names, which pastudiers labeled using Ancient Forbish, receding to the very dawn of time.

Did they think? Did they reason? Certainly they left no message for the future, which was a mark of the folk; as long ago as the age of legendary Jing, means had been found to warn posterity about the menace looming in the sky. Without such aids, probably the Age of Multiplication would have proved a disaster—

No, not necessarily, Awb corrected himself. Eventually the truth could have been rediscovered. But perhaps there would have been less reason to go in search of it, and by the time it was once more chanced on it might have been too late: the sun might be being drawn inexorably into some new star, up there in the Major Cluster . . . He tipped his eye in search of it, and was astonished to realize that it was nowhere to be seen; the sky was blue, and everybody was dispersing to daylight duties.

What was Thilling apt to think of him if he stayed here mooning? Hastily he scrambled to his pads and set out after her. It was a vast effort to catch up, since his pressure yesterday had been so badly lowered, but he struggled on, reminding himself that all effort was made the more worthwhile by knowing how the ancestors had dedicated their lives to the survival of descendants they could never meet.

The first part of the bright was spent in making a careful record of the damage caused by the landslide, and Awb followed Thilling from place to place carrying bulky light-tight packs of the sensitized sheets she still referred to as "leaves" in memory of a more primitive technology. For the first time he gained a proper impression of the complexity of the work that had gone into creating the site for the observatory. Planning it must have been even harder than, say, founding a new fixed city, what with digging the canal to carry broken rock and make the mole, stringing the floater-cables, supplying food and accommodation for the workers, all of whom had had to be recruited at a distance and were used to a high standard of living. Several times he heard it vainly wished that the natives could have been enlisted, but today, again, they went about their own animal business, apparently incapable even of wondering about this intrusion into their placid world. If any of them had indeed been killed by the landslide, they showed no signs of grief.

Moreover there were mounts and draftimals to provide for, the musculators and cutinates, the floaters themselves constantly in need of the right nourishment to replenish the light gas in their bladders . . . Awb knew perfectly well that when they first joined Voosla the people from Chisp had occasionally had difficulty finding their way around on her numerous levels, but he couldn't help feeling that, if they were accustomed to places like this, they ought to have found so small a city comparatively simple.

When the sun was at its highest—not very high in these latitudes, of course—Lesh gathered her companions on the top of the scree caused by the landslide, and started working out how long it might take to clear away. Already draftimals were dragging musculators towards it, along with grabbers and scoopers.

This spot afforded a splendid prospect of the area including the bay where Voosla was lying, minus her giqs, all of which had been detached and were now spread as far as the horizon. Delighted, Thilling used up her stock of sheets in fixing a view in each direction, returned them to their pack, and asked Awb to take them back to the city and bring replacements. Nervously, because he had no wish to encounter Phrallet, but equally none to disappoint Thilling, he complied.

It took him a long time to regain the shore because the usual branchways were decaying, like so much of the vegetation on this blighted coast, and he had to stay on the ground most of the way. The stink of rotting foliage was all-pervasive, and he wondered how the people working here could bear it.

Coming in sight of the sea again, he discovered that a strange briq had entered the bay. She must have been just around the western headland when he looked before, because she was of a type by no means speedy, the broad northern breed called variously smaq or luqqra much in favor for carrying bulky freight. Voosla had crossed a number of them during the couple of brights prior to landfall.

As she touched the side of the city, Axwep came to greet her commander, and by the time Awb arrived they were deep in conversation.

"There's somebody who can probably tell us," the mayor said, interrupting herself. "Awb! Do you know where Lesh is?"

"When I left, she was on top of the rockpile trying to work out how long it will take to clear," Awb called back.

"Will you be going back there?"

"Yes, I'm on an errand for Thilling."

"Then you can carry a message. Come here. This is Eupril; she's from the quarry down-coast which we passed the dark before last."

Awb remembered that being pointed out to him, at a spot where luminants grew normally. He had never seen a quarry, but he knew about such places where specially developed microorganisms were used to break up rock and concentrate valuable elements to enrich poor soil, or even to extract metals. In ancient times, it was said, the folk had employed fire for similar purposes: however, during the Age of Multiplication fire had fallen out of use except for very special purposes, because most burnable substances were far too valuable for other applications. Most people nowadays were terrified of it. Sometimes, far out at sea, one could smell smoke on the wind, and the Vooslans would mutter sympathy for the poor landlivers whose homes and crops were going up in flames.

"I don't suppose it'll do much good," Eupril said sardonically. She was thickset, with the forceful voice of one used to calling over long distances, rather like Axwep. "I've warned and warned those people that they picked a bad site for this observatory of theirs. We surveyed it when we first came up here, and though there were a lot of useful minerals we decided against prospecting further. We didn't like the look of the natives, nor what we found the other side of the ridge. People who won't listen make my pith ache, you know? Of course, when we saw a chunk had fallen off the mountain, we thought we'd better come and see if they needed help. We have no other way of finding out. Used to have a nervograp link but it went bad on us."

"From the same blight that's spoiling everything else?" Awb suggested.

"Now that's the other reason I'm here," Eupril said. "We have news for Lesh. It's not a blight. It's a poison."

"How can you be sure?" Axwep demanded. "I mean, I know the people here haven't been able to isolate a causative organism yet, but there's a lot of talk about germs you can't see even with the best microscope, that go through the finest filters and can still do damage—"

"We're sure," Eupril cut in. "Who'd know better than a concentration specialist? Matter of fact, we've been worrying about something of the sort ever since they warned us they were going to tap water from beyond the ridge and discharge it here, because there's a current that follows the coast and washes right down to our place. Still, they claimed it was only going to be for a year or two, and a bit of extra fresh water might conceivably have been an advantage, because we use a lot of cutinates and even with our best salt-precipitators they tend to wear out pretty quickly. So we didn't raise as much objection as we should have, what with the delay involved in sending a delegation to Chisp *and* the rigid attitude of the Jingfired. Everybody knows they think they're incapable of making a mistake, hm? Bunch of arrogant knowalls, that lot!"

She shrugged with her entire mantle. "Anyway, nothing much happened last year, so we more or less stopped worrying. This season, though, our concentration-cultures have started to die off, and our cutinates are developing blisters like we never saw before, and just the other day we finally traced the problem. Of course we thought it was disease at first. It's not. It's definitely a poison that's coming to us in solution, in the water, and even diluted as it is when it reaches the quarry it's deadly dangerous. We don't have anything that can resist it. Our toughest precipitators turn black and rot within a month."

Stunned, Awb said, "Mayor, I think this is something Lesh ought to hear personally. I mean, I couldn't possibly repeat such an important message and be sure of getting all the details right."

"That's not the message," said Axwep with gentle irony. "The message I meant was simply a request to get here as quickly as she can. I'm sure you can manage to relay that much!"

"Probably not," said a harsh voice, and Phrallet appeared, swarming along the nearest slanting branchway. "Even if he is of my own budding, I wouldn't trust him to find his way from one side of Voosla to the other!"

Furious, Awb reared back, holding up the pack of image-sheets like a shield. "Thilling trusts me!" he blurted. "She sent me to bring a fresh batch of these for her!"

"Instead of which you're standing about gossiping?"

"But—!"

It was no good. All his life he had found it impossible to get his budder to take him seriously. Clamping his mandibles tight shut, he muttered an apology to Axwep, who seemed mildly amused—a reaction calculated to irritate Phrallet still further—and hastened in the direction of Thilling's bower.

# 4

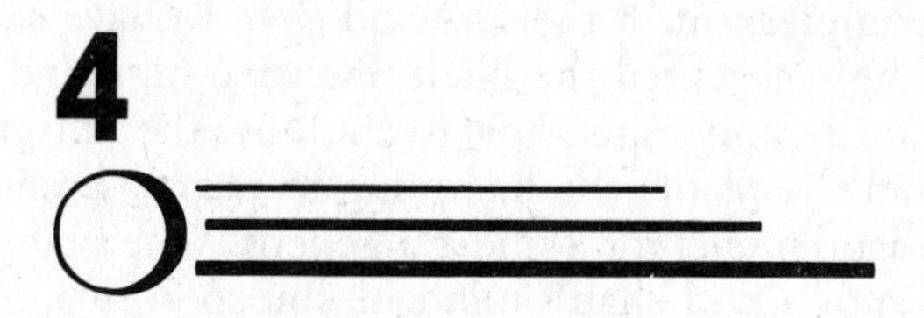

The first thing Axwep asked Lesh when the latter returned to Voosla—annoyed at the interruption even though Awb had done his utmost to explain its reason—was whether water was still being drawn from beyond the ridge; if so, the city should be moved.

"All our cutinates got crushed by the rockfall," was her curt reply. "They're not pumping anything right now, and in fact I'm not sure they'll survive. Now what's all this about, Eupril?"

The concentration expert sighed. "Oh, I know you suspect our people of wanting to drive you away because we have designs on this site for our own purposes, but that's untrue and unfair! I came with proof of the danger you're in. Carry on like you're doing, and those toughtrees you're planting on the peak will turn as rotten as everything else. Then what will become of your telescopes?"

"Proof? Let's see it!" Lesh snapped.

"I'd rather present the evidence in proper order. You're supposed to have a ripe bunch of experts here now, or so Axwep tells me. Maybe some of them will be a bit less—ah—emotionally committed. Let them be the judges."

For a second it seemed that Lesh was going to yield to rage; then, resignedly, she slumped to four-fifths height.

"Very well, I'll send for Drotninch and the rest. But where are we going to get the water we need if we can't take it from across the ridge?" With sudden optimism: "Maybe from the sea! You can let us have some of your salt-precipitators!"

"They're dead or dying," Eupril answered. "We've had to order fresh stock, and it'll be months before we have any to spare."

Thilling, never one to miss important news, had accompanied Lesh back to the city, and stood beside Awb listening keenly. Now, however, she muttered, "This could go on for ages. Come with me. You said you'd like to be my apprentice, so let's see if you can learn to trim a lens while I develop the images I've caught so far."

Excited, he followed her down into the very core of the city, where the junqs fretted and throbbed, dreamlost perhaps in visions of their ancestral freedom. Here a small dark bower had been assigned to the picturist, which she could make entirely light-tight. Judging by the stink of juices and concentrates which blew from it when she finished work, it must be very unpleasant in there. Awb began to have second thoughts. But he willingly accepted the blade she gave him, and paid total attention when she demonstrated how to cut loose the full-grown lenses that bulged from the plants she had hung to nearby branches.

"Here are the measurements for a mid-range lens," she said. "Try this kind first. If you spoil one I shan't mind. If you spoil two, I'll be disappointed. If three—well, I'll probably part you torso from mantle! Understood?"

Awb signed yes.

"Get on with it, then. Go back where there's better light. And take your time. I may not be through with this lot before sundown."

And indeed the sun was touching the horizon when she rejoined him. He had completed two of the lenses, and the second was flawless as near as he could tell, but he waited on her verdict nervously.

"Hmm! Very good!" she pronounced, surprised and pleased. "More than I can say about the one I have on the fixer at the moment. I mean, look at these, will you?"

She flourished a selection of the sheets she had exposed in the morning. Awb examined them. To his untutored eye they appeared satisfactory, and he said so.

"No, look again! Here, here, here!"—each time with a jab of her claw. "There's a blur, there's a smear, there's a streak . . . At first I thought the fixer must be leaking light, but I've checked and doublechecked. I suppose there must be a blister in the lens, but I can't locate it."

Awb ventured, "But then wouldn't the blurs always reappear in the same place? And these don't."

Taken aback, she said, "Give those back to me . . . Hmm! I wonder if it could have to do with the angle of incidence of the light—No, that wouldn't fit either. And most of the early ones, come to think of it, are all right. It's only from about the point where we climbed up the rockfall that I started having trouble. Maybe a wind-blown drop on the lens, but I was careful to shield it . . . Oh, *I* can't figure it out, unless . . ." She fixed him with a stern glare. "You didn't drop the leaf-pack by any chance?"

"No, I promise I didn't!" Awb cried, recoiling in alarm. "And if I had, surely the damage would show on one edge or one corner?"

"Ah . . . Yes, of course it would. I'm sorry." Thilling clattered her mandibles in confusion. "This makes no sense at all, you know. It's as though some trace of light—very bright light—got through the pack-wrap, and . . ."

"A fault in the making," Awb offered.

"I suppose so." All of a sudden she sounded weary. "But I never had trouble with my supplier before. I've been trying not to arrive at that conclusion, because if all the leaf-packs I have with me are faulty, I might as well not have come."

Startled to find himself in the unprecedented situation of having to reassure an adult, Awb said, "Please, you're making too much of this. As far as I could tell, those images were fine until you pointed out the flaws. Nobody is likely to notice what worries you so much, except maybe another picturist."

"I suppose you're right," Thilling sighed. "Let's go and eat something. I've had enough for one bright, or even two."

Because the scientists were still arguing, Axwep had suggested that Lesh and her senior colleagues, along with Eupril and some of her companions, should eat this evening on Voosla, where the food was better than on shore. However, although she made it clear that she could not repeat the invitation regularly, because any floating city was in a delicate balance with its inhabitants and the best efforts of the giqs could never gather as much nourishment as she collected for herself in open water, there were some who instantly accused the mayor of wasting public resources. Wasn't it bad enough to have brought these scores of passengers all this way?—that was their cry, and they took no account of the fact that Voosla had been specially replanted with new high-yielding secondary growths developed at the University of Chisp, which would continue paying her back long after the return voyage.

Prominent among those who complained, of course, was Phrallet. Axwep had finally lost patience with her, and ordered that she be forbidden access to the prime food zone. Tagging along behind Thilling, Awb managed to steal in and join the company, hoping desperately as he nibbled a bit here and a bit there that his budder would not get to hear.

Finding herself next to one of Eupril's fellow quarry-workers, whom she had seen earlier but not spoken with, Thilling said, "What's all this about a poison, then? Why can't it be a disease? Name of Thilling, by the way."

"Name of Hy," said the other. "Well, it's because of the way it acts in living tissue, of course. Ever hear of a disease organism that simply killed the cells around it, without spreading, or reseeding itself at a distant site? Oh, we've carried out all the tests we're equipped for, and we even managed to get our claws on the corpses of some of the natives. They don't seem to care about their dead, just leave 'em to rot. And in every single case we've found necrotic tissue, either in the digestive tract or quite often in the nerve-pith, and if you take the dead center—excuse me!—and triturate it and apply microscopic drops to a suitable test medium, like the partly flayed rind of a cutinate . . . Well, what would you expect to see?"

Thilling frowned with her entire mantle. "A whole series of infection-sites, obviously."

"That's exactly what we thought. Wrong. One and only ever *one* new patch of necrosis. The rest is unaffected."

Chomping solemnly, Thilling pondered that awhile. At last she heaved a sigh.

"It doesn't sound any more like a poison than a disease, in that case, does it? Still, it's not my specialty, so I have to take your word. But I always thought poisons worked by spreading throughout the system."

Awb was glad to hear her say that; it meant his own main question was likely to be answered.

"So they do, for the most part. I've been dealing with poisons much of my life, because you never know, when you feed new ore to a concentration-culture, whether it's going to survive on it. But I never saw the like before: a poison so lethal that a particle too small to see with a microscope can kill cells over and over. It doesn't dissolve, it doesn't disperse, it just sits there and kills cells!"

"Thilling!"

They all turned, to find Drotninch approaching.

"You are coming with us to check out this hot stream tomorrow, aren't you? Yes? Good! We're going to leave at first bright. Lesh is working out how many mounts can be spared. Will you need a whole one for your equipment?"

With a wry twist of her mantle Thilling answered, "Not a whole one. I have a volunteer helper now."

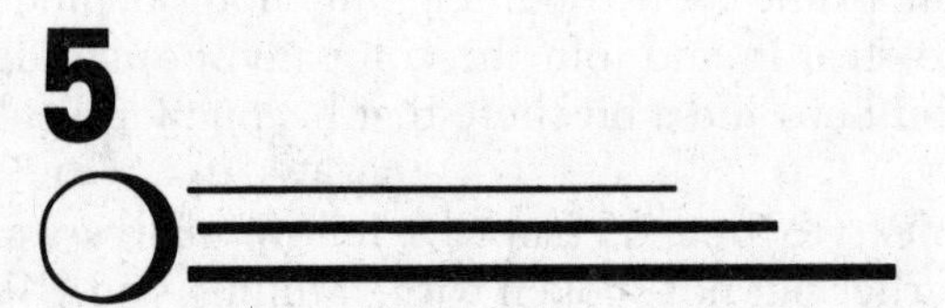

# 5

*S*lowly the expedition wound its way up the narrow trail cut to facilitate laying of the cutinate pipeline. It had remained alarmingly clear of overgrowth, though Lesh said it had not been recut this spring. It was as though the surrounding plants, both Gveestian and natural, had bowed away from it.

The air was comfortably calm, and since the morning of the city's arrival there had been scarcely a cloud in the sky, let alone the threat of a storm. Nonetheless Thilling's weather-sense was reacting queasily. She did her best to convince herself it was because of her unpremeditated decision to accept Awb as an apprentice. Taking on someone from so utterly different a background, and with such an awful budder to hint at how he might turn out in the long term . . . Had it been wise?

Just to complicate matters, Phrallet was a member of the party. Whether out of misplaced ambition, because she fancied she might make a better impression this trip than usually at home on Voosla, our out of jealousy of Awb, or simply out of bad temper because of what Axwep had said to her last dark, she had insisted on coming along. Drotninch, who had gotten to know her slightly during the voyage, was no more in favor than was Thilling; however, Axwep was glad of the chance to be rid of her for a while, and she possessed sufficient charm as regarded strangers for Lesh to say with a shrug, "Why not? We can always do with an extra set of claws, and a volunteer is better than a draftee."

Thilling's view was that she was apt to be more of a nuisance than a help. And she was equally dubious about Awb. She still could not quite rid herself of the suspicion that her images might have been spoiled by his carelessness. Moreover she was moderately certain that his ambition to spend his future in light-tight bowers reeking of chemical was due less to a genuine interest in the work than to the fact that if he became Voosla's first official picturist he would always have an excuse to shut himself away from his budder.

Still, there was little point in speculating. Determinedly she forced her attention back to the country they were traversing, only to find that the view made her more worried than ever.

From the canal which carried waste and usable rock to the new harbor, irrigation ditches had been ichored off for the crops that fed the work-force. So much was normal; so much was sensible economy.

Yet the point in time at which the crops began to fail coincided with the failure of the nervograp links to the outside world, and in turn followed the first use of water from beyond the watershed. How was it that supposedly rational people could have overlooked the connection? They definitely had! Even in the light of what Eupril and Hy reported, Lesh was still obstinately hoping to find that the water-supply had nothing to do with the—the blight, the poison, whatever it might ultimately prove to be.

Now, fixing images of the true extent of the devastation in the morning shadow of Fangsharp Peak, Thilling started to wonder whether those who had been living here for two or three years might not already be affected, already be on the way to matching the miserable mindless natives.

Then she noticed something else even more alarming as the mounts wound in single file up and over the ridge. During the first part of the bright, the beasts had too much sense to browse off the nearby foliage, sere and discolored as it was. About noon, however, when presumably they were starting to thirst, the one carrying among other loads her own equipment did begin to help itself now and again from the nearest branches. But the leaves were wilting, and the rind of the cutinates whose line they were following was patched with suppurating black.

She glanced at Awb, laboring along behind her under the burden of her spare image-fixer and a spare lens-plant, and realized that he too appeared uneasy. But neither Lesh nor Drotninch seemed concerned. Why not?

Well, perhaps she was worrying overmuch. She strove to make herself believe so.

Night fell late in these latitudes, and was short. They crossed the watershed before they lacked enough light to wait for tomorrow's dawn. The chance to rest was welcome; they all needed to accumulate pressure for the next stage of the journey. But Thilling was dismayed anew when she realized that Lesh, who had been responsible for organizing the expedition, expected everybody, and the mounts too, to subsist off the local plants because, as she said, "it would only be for a day or two." This was enough to startle even Drotninch and Byra, and a furious argument broke out in which—predictably—Phrallet was prominent.

True, there were plenty of edible secondary growths of the kind which that far-sighted genius Gveest had modified to provide for the folk during their traumatic population explosion. Possibly, as Lesh was now claiming, the planners of the observatory project had seeded them deliberately to furnish an emergency resource for the workers. More likely they had arrived of their own accord; their spawn was designed to drift on the wind and displace natural rivals when it settled. But those which grew close to the path were so unwholesome both in appearance and in odor . . .

Even though she had no luminants, and as yet only a shred of moon was visible, very close to the horizon, Thilling slipped away to a spot where a few cautious bites convinced her the food was safe, or at least safer. Glancing up on hearing a noise nearby, she was amazed to discover that Awb was here already. Good for him!

But he was tensing as though afraid of being reprimanded, and small wonder, for that was certainly how Phrallet would have reacted. Suddenly full of sympathy for this young'un, Thilling said sharply, "All right, keep your pith from boiling! What made you come this way?"

"I just didn't like the smell of what the mounts were eating," he muttered.

"Nor do I. I think that worn-out old nag they assigned to us is going to rot in her pad-marks before we get where we're going . . . By the way!"

"Yes?"

"I'm sorry I accused you of dropping my leaf-packs. I've been watching you all this bright, and I'm satisfied that you've been taking great care of my gear. I'm also convinced that there's something in what Eupril says about poison. When you're through eating, come and set up my dark-bower. I expect all today's images to be faulty."

"Do you want them, then?" Awb countered in confusion.

"What I mostly want is to do Drotninch and Byra in the eye because I have an eye that they don't. If I'd been here with the original expedition that chose the observatory site—! But never mind that. I sense something's bothering you. Out with it!"

"Are you really going to spend all dark developing your—uh—leaves?"

"And why not?"

"Well, I'd have thought . . ." Awb shifted uncomfortably from pad to pad. "You know—review today into memory, build up pressure for tomorrow . . ." He subsided, more at a loss than ever.

"Oh, there's plenty of time for that while you're waiting for images to develop—"

It was her turn to break off, gazing at him with astonishment in the faint starshine. "Are you trying to tell me you've never been educated in dark-use?"

"I don't know what you mean!"

"Oh, dear!" Seizing a clump of funqi, she settled beside him. "It's no news to me that cities like Voosla are behind the times, but this is incredible."

"Sorry to appear so ignorant," Awb muttered resentfully.

"Oh, I don't mean to be matronizing, I promise. But . . . Look, young'un, I just took it for granted that you must have your own version of dark-use training. I mean, I know the People of the Sea are contemptuous of landlivers who can't move to avoid bad weather or follow the best seasons, and the rest of it, and what's more I know they can turn to in mid-dark and cope with gales and storms, so . . . Well, surely we have to exploit all the time at our disposal if we're to meet the challenge of the future, right? You know what I mean by that, at least?"

"Of course!"

"That's a mercy . . . Oh, I'm starting to sound like Phrallet, and I'm ashamed. She's anti-male, by the rude way she treats you, and I'm not. I admit I'm sterile, and the fertility treatment won't take in me, but that's neither here nor there. Just makes me wonder about those it took in much too well! But I sense you have a whole branchful of questions, so I'll see if I can answer them without being told what they are."

She filled her mantle for a long speech; he heard the hiss.

"Why shan't I mind if my images are faulty? Because I think the faults may teach us something we never knew before. Why am I appalled that you haven't been trained in proper dark-use? Because I don't hail from where you think I do. You believe I'm from Chisp, don't you?"

"I—ah—I did assume . . ."

"Eat your assumptions, then. I was budded in the Lugomannic Archipelago."

"Where Gveest discovered the cure for infertility?" Awb burst out, and was instantly horrified at himself, because she had just mentioned her own sterility. But her only reaction was mild amusement.

"More to the point: where someone you never heard of, called Pletrow, realized after she'd finally had the bud of her own which she longed for that in order to cope with the consequences of Gveest's success there had to be a means of exploiting dark-time, instead of squandering it."

Exuding fascination, Awb hunched forward. "I've always resented that myself! I mean, one never really stops thinking, does one? It's just that by dark it always seems so much harder to make action match intention!"

He added self-excusingly, "I envy you the fact that you're going to spend this dark doing something constructive, you see. I don't know how."

For a long while Thilling remained indecisive. Should she broach her most precious secret to this chance-met stranger? Yet the magnitude of the catastrophe that was set fair to overwhelm the great observatory was daunting, and the need for the information it could supply was so urgent. Could she confront the insights she was burdened with entirely alone?

No: she could not. She needed to confide in someone, and none of the scientists from Chisp was right to share her private anxiety. At least Awb had fought back against the handicap of being Phrallet's bud . . .

She said after a small eternity, "Then I must teach you how to liberate consciousness from concern with digestion. That's the first of the mental exercises Pletrow developed for the Jingfired."

"You mean *you* . . . ?" Awb's pressure failed him.

"Yes, I do mean!" Already she was half regretting her admission. "But if you so much as hint that you're aware of the fact, I'm bound by oath to leak you. Understood?"

Fervently he echoed, "Understood!"

"Very well, then. Now there's one other thing I ought to ask you.

But I'm not going to. If you're the person I think and hope you are, you'll work it out yourself."

"Does it have to do with why Lesh doesn't want to consider any other site for the observatory?"

"Very indirectly I suppose it does. We all hope to bequeath some achievement to the future . . . No, that's not what I want you to say. Think it over. In the meantime, what about setting up my dark-bower for me?"

# 6

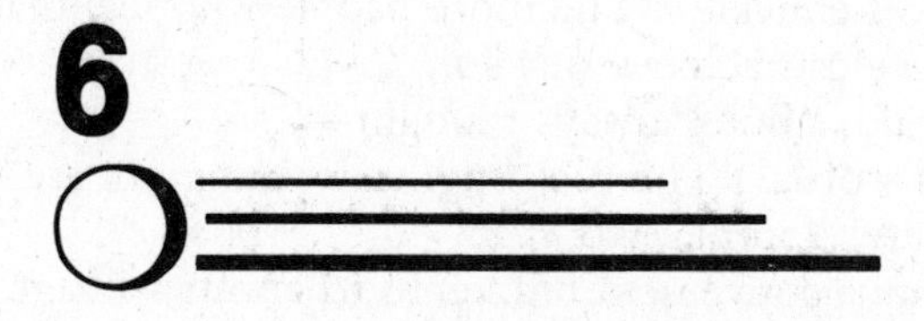

*W*as Thilling truly one of the legendary Jingfired?

That question haunted Awb as the party wended its way down from the crest of the ridge, still following the line chosen for the cutinates, either side of which the trees were stunted and their secondary growths pale and sickly. The stink of decay in the air was worse than where they had started from because it was older, as though even storms could not disperse it. Its impact was unnerving; one heard fewer voices raised to normal pitch, more murmurs of apprehension and more cries from unseen creatures in the overgrowth.

Along the bottom of the valley, where they were bound, ran a watercourse formed by the confluence of three streams half a day's journey to the east. It was the middle one which remained so warm during the worst of winter that it could keep the whole river free of ice. Nobody had explored it to the source, but presumably it must rise where there was hot rock of the sort well known on other continents, that created geysers or pools of bubbling-hot mud.

An earth dam had been built to make an artificial lake for the cutinates to draw from. Now and then they could glimpse the sunlight gleaming on its surface, wherever the vegetation had died back sufficiently.

That was disturbingly often.

Byra announced loudly, "This is far worse than what I recall from my first visit! If things had been this bad then I'd have argued strongly against choosing this site."

"I thought the Jingfired didn't make mistakes like that," was Lesh's snappish response. Close enough behind to overhear the exchange, Awb whispered to Thilling:

"Is *she* one of—?"

"Of course not!"—with contempt. "She's enjoyed giving herself the sort of airs she thinks might suit one of us ever since the first time she was assigned to a foreign survey team. She carries it off well enough to mislead the ignorant, but she's never dared to make the claim outright. One of the reasons I was sent here was to make sure about that. It's all right, though: it's a bit of harmless vanity, no more."

"What do you think about Eupril's attitude towards the Jingfired?" Awb risked.

Thilling gave a soft chuckle. "The more people who feel that way about us, the better we can achieve our aim."

Confused, Awb said, "But I always thought—"

She cut short his words. "The real Jingfired, young'un, are never who you think they are. You have to *know.*"

And she hurried up a convenient branch to fix another image from the treetops.

Awb found himself wishing they didn't have to rely on mounts, for it would have been quicker and more pleasurable to swarm along branchways in the ancient fashion instead of padding along on the ground. Away from the water's edge, and away from these discolored cutinates, the overgrowth mostly smelled normal despite its peculiar tint, so—

His thoughts came to a squeaking halt.

Why weren't there any people in this valley?

Where else on the entire globe was there such lush terrain without a city, a town, even a hamlet?

*This is what the world must have looked like before the Age of Multiplication.*

The thought struck him so forcibly that he uttered it aloud. Some of those within hearing responded as though he had chanced on a profound truth.

But not all. Phrallet was close beside Byra; she had moved in to offer comfort after Lesh made mock of her. Now she turned and said loudly, "Ah, that's my youngest bud making noises again! I wish I'd had another she'un that I could have traded off to benefit Voosla, but who wants a he'un, particularly a useless lazy one like Awb?"

*Clack:* Awb's mandibles rattled as he rose in fury to maximum height, heedless of Thilling's gear which he was carrying. There was no case on record of a budling fighting his budder, but after that—!

Except, amazingly—

(As the pheromones mingled in the taut still air with what the rotting plants exuded, but far fiercer . . .)

*Clackonclackonclackonclack:* and abruptly climaxing—

"SHUT UP!"

It was Drotninch, fuming with chemical proof of the reason why she had been chosen to lead the university team.

"I don't want to hear any more arguments until we get to the lake and have something solid to argue about! In the meantime, save your pressure for moving your pads!"

Phrallet slanted her mantle as though to puff a blast of combat-stink directly at Drotninch, but Lesh, Thilling and even Byra signaled a warning of the consequences. She subsided, still angry, and let the rest of the party go by, falling in right at the end. As Awb sidled past, she glowered with her whole mantle, but said nothing.

He was indescribably relieved.

The sun was just at the zenith when they emerged on a flat bare outcrop of rock overlooking the artificial lake. The water-level was a little below maximum, as could be judged from the mud along the banks, some of which was a curious yellow color. There were automatic spillways to cope with the rise due to a spring thaw: a dense mat of small but coarse-stemmed plants along the top of the dam, designed to float upward and lift their root-masses just enough for the surplus to spill over without letting the dam erode.

At least, there should have been. In fact, the plants were decaying like everything else in the vicinity, and the mud along the banks was actually bare, whereas ordinarily it would have been fledged with shoots sprung from the riverside vegetation.

"Have you noticed," Byra said after a pause, "that you can tell at a glance which of the trees have taproots long enough to reach the river? They're dying off. Look!"

In a dull voice Lesh said, "So they must be sucking up the poison, if that's what it actually is."

"And the state of these cutinates!" Byra went on as she clambered over the edge of the rock and gingerly descended to the waterside. She prodded the nearest, and its rind yielded, soft as rotting funqus. A swarm of startled wingets took to the air, shrilling their complaint at being disturbed. Awb, with the quick reflexes of youth, snatched one as it shot past, and bent his eye to examine it.

"How long since you sent anyone to check out the cutinates?" Drotninch demanded of Lesh.

"As soon as the snow melted," was the muttered reply. "I was assured that everything was in order. At any rate the spillways were working properly, and above the water-level the cutinates looked pretty much all right."

"You didn't haul their ends to the surface and—?" The scholar broke off. "No, I don't imagine you'd have seen the need if they were still pumping normally. Were they?"

"Oh, they've been functioning fine. Though, now that I've seen the state they're in, I'm surprised they haven't burst at a score of places."

"So am I . . . Well, before we disturb anything else we'd better fix some images. Thilling!"

"Just a moment," the picturist called back. "Awb, can I take a look at that winget?"

He surrendered it gladly. "Do you know if it's a regular local species?" he demanded. "I don't recognize it, but then I've never been so far north before."

"I have, and it's not," Thilling answered grimly. "It's deformed. Its body has tried to—well—double, hasn't it? Byra, I think you should see this right away!"

As she hastened toward the biologist, Phrallet drew close to Awb.

"Do anything to get yourself well in with the folk from Chisp, won't you? Eat any sort of dirt they throw at you! I did my best to be friendly, but I'm leaked if I'm going to bother anymore. I never met such a rude, bossy bunch."

Surprised at his own audacity, Awb said, "Maybe they just reflect your own attitude back at you."

"Why, you—!" Phrallet swelled with renewed anger.

"Awb!" The shout was from Thilling. "Bring those leaves we developed last night, will you?"

"Coming!" Awb responded, mightily flattered.

And Phrallet, luckily, did not dare to follow, but remained seething by herself.

Taking the image-pack, Thilling said, "I was just explaining that I don't expect any images I fix here to be of the usual quality. You haven't seen these yet, nor has anyone else, but . . . Well, look at this one, for example, which was taken right next to the cutinates where there was a leak most probably caused when the top fell off Fangsharp Peak. Notice all those blurs and streaks?"

"It's as though the poison can attack your image-fixer too!" Awb exclaimed.

Passing the picture around, Thilling said dryly, "I shan't argue. I reached the same conclusion. I shall of course try fixing more images here, but like I said I don't expect them to be much good."

"But how—?" Drotninch began, and interrupted herself. "Now I'm going against my own orders, aren't I? We'll wait until we have something to discuss. Lesh, if you'd . . ."

Briskly she issued orders to each of the party, pointedly ignoring Phrallet until, conquering her annoyance, the latter advanced to ask if she could help too. She was sent to fetch samples of the dead plants from the top of the dam, while Byra set up a microscope to examine them with, and Awb followed Thilling to the best points of vantage for general images, before descending to the lake for close-ups of the bare mud and ruined cutinates.

Very shortly after there was a cry from Phrallet, in her usual bad-tempered tone.

"That was a foul trick to play on me! You did it deliberately, didn't you?"

The others stared in astonishment as she fled back from the dam without the samples she had been asked to collect.

"What in the world is wrong?" Drotninch demanded.

"It's hot! The top of the dam is *hot!* Oh, my poor pads! And the water isn't just warm, it's *steaming!* Look!"

"Why, so it is! But I promise I hadn't noticed. By dark I would have, but—Well, you didn't notice either, did you?"

The pressure taken out of her by that awkward fact, Phrallet subsided, grumbling. Regretting his earlier rudeness, for she was bound to seek revenge for it eventually, Awb muttered a word of apology to Thilling and himself hurried to the side of the dam. Cautiously he lowered to minimum height and began to probe the area, reporting in a loud voice.

"There must be water seeping around the end of the dam here—the subsoil is marshy. But it's definitely warm, and I don't understand why. All the roots are dead but they're still meshed together. And the top of the dam . . ."

He moved on, half a padlong at a time. "Yes, it's very warm, and very hard, too. Completely dried out, almost as hard as rock." He rapped it with one claw. "And there's this funny yellow mud; it's building up in layers. And—Ow! That *is* hot!" He recoiled in surprise.

"I think you'd better come away," Thilling shouted, and he was just about to comply when there was an unexpected commotion.

The mount that carried Thilling's equipment, which she had dismissed as an old nag, uttered a noise between a grunt and a scream, lost all her pressure, and measured her length on the ground.

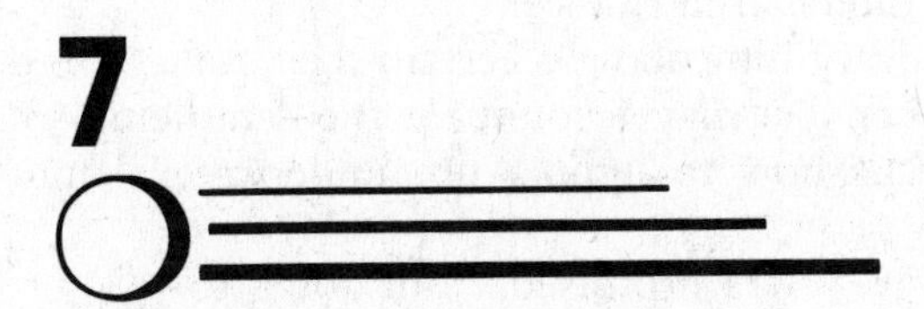

# 7

**T**hat nightfall none of the party had much maw for food. Byra had carried out a cursory examination of the dead mount, and what her microscope revealed exactly matched the description Eupril had given of the way the poison affected cutinates and precipitators at the quarry. The certainty that at least some of it must be at work in their own bodies took away all appetite.

While Thilling occupied herself developing the day's images, not calling on Awb for help, the rest of them lay up on the branches of the nearest healthy trees, as though being clear of the ground could offer them security in the dark, like their remotest ancestors. Of course, if any of the local animals had been as altered as that mutated winget . . . But the Freeze, the Thaw, and the greed of the half-starved folk who had exploded across the world during the Age of Multiplication had combined to exterminate almost all large predators, and turned avoidance of animal food among the folk themselves from a moral choice into a necessity. Even fish nowadays was in short supply, more valuable to nourish cities than their citizens.

Awb thought of having to ingest the flesh of the mount whose stench drifted up to him, and shuddered.

As though the trembling of the branch he clung to had been a signal, Byra said suddenly, "What I don't understand is how there can be burns without fire."

"I thought you Jingfired knew all about everything," came the sour riposte from Phrallet.

"I never said I was Jingfired!" Byra snapped. "If I was, do you think I'd be here? They have too much sense!"

In the startled pause that followed, Awb found time to wonder why she had chosen this of all moments to disclaim the pose she had—according to Thilling—long adopted, and also whether Thilling herself . . . But there was no time to ponder such matters. Perceptibly desperate to avoid moving the observatory to another site, Lesh was saying, "We've got to isolate this stuff! Once we know precisely what it is—"

"Isolate it?" countered Drotninch. "When it can kill any concentration-culture it comes up against? You heard what Eupril said, and the folk at the quarry have only been dealing with a trace of it, diluted over and over."

"Well, there are filters, aren't there?"

"Filters will trap everything above a certain size. In fact I'm beginning to wonder whether that may account for the dam being so hot."

"Next you show us how to light a fire underwater," muttered Phrallet.

"Any moment now," Byra promised, "I'm going to—"

"Byra!" Drotninch said warningly. But it was too dark and their pressure was too low for combat-stink; the keener note of simple fear predominated, and was compelling them gradually towards cooperation, much as it must have bonded their ancestors into forming tribes and eventually communities.

Awb shuddered again, but this time with awe and not disgust. It was amazing to be participating in so ancient an experience. Of course, something similar happened now and then at sea, when a storm assailed the city, but then wind and spray carried off the pheromones, and the decision to work together was dictated by reason.

How much was left of the primitive in modern folk? He must ask

Thilling. If she were truly one of the Jingfired, she would certainly be able to answer such a question.

But the argument was continuing. Sullenly, as though not convinced that the others wanted to hear, Byra was saying, "It was the heat of the water that made me start thinking along these lines. Now I've realized what the tissue-damage in that poor mount reminded me of. I've got a scar where some young fool shone a burning-glass on my mantle when I was a budling. Instead of just comforting me, my budder made me turn even that silly trick to account. She dissected out a tiny scrap of tissue and showed me the way the heat had ruptured the cells. I noticed just the same effect in the mount. Of course, the damage is deep inside, instead of just on the surface."

"But so are the blemishes on Thilling's leaves!" Awb burst out. "They happen right inside a light-tight pack, or inside the fixer!"

Once again there was a pause during which he had time to feel dismayed by his own boldness. Byra ended it by saying, "Phrallet, I can't for the life of me understand why you think your budling is unworthy of you. I'd be proud if one of my young'uns had come up with a point like that."

Set to grow angry again, Phrallet abruptly realized she was being indirectly complimented, and made no answer.

Drotninch, less tactfully, said, "Going back to where we were just now: you can very well have heat without fire, or at least without flame. Using a burning-glass is something else, because we assume the sun to be made of fire fiercer than what we can imitate down here. But if you rub something long and hard enough, it gets warm, and likewise air if you compress it with a bellower. Don't you know about that sort of thing on Voosla, Phrallet?" She sounded genuinely curious.

"You should know better than to ask"—unexpectedly from Lesh. "The People of the Sea did study heat and even flame at one time, using substances that protected their junqs and briqs from feeling the effect. But it was hard to keep a fire alight at sea, and eventually they lost interest because they didn't have any ore to melt, or sand for glass, and they could always trade for what they needed."

"That's right!" Phrallet agreed, and it was plain she was relaxing at long last.

Drotninch rattled her mandibles. "This gives me an idea. Do you think there's enough burnable material around here to start up a—what do they call it?—a furnace?"

"What for?" Byra countered.

"Well, in olden times they used fire to separate metal from ore, didn't they? Even if we can't use a concentration-culture, we might get at this poison using heat."

"Hmm! I'm inclined to doubt it," Byra said. "We don't yet know whether it's a simple substance, for one thing."

"If it weren't, and a very rare one, surely we'd have encountered it before?"

"Maybe we have," Lesh suggested. "Or at any rate its effects. I've never really believed that hot rock—let alone actual volcanoes—can be accounted for by saying that there's a leak from the core of the planet. For one thing the core must be *too* hot; for another, the magma would have to rise for many padlonglaqs, and I can't envisage channels for so much lava remaining open under the enormous pressures we know must exist down there."

"What does this have to do with—?" Drotninch had begun to say, when there was a rustle of foliage and Thilling arrived to join them. Parting the leaves revealed that the new moon was rising, a narrow crescent, just about to disappear again as it crossed the Arc of Heaven.

"I wish we'd had time to force some of those special luminants Voosla brought," said the picturist as she settled in a vacant crotch. "Or that the moon were nearer full, or something. I spend too much of my working life in total darkness to be comfortable by mere starlight. It's not so bad if your maw is full, but . . . Any of you manage to eat anything tonight?"

They all signed negative.

"Me neither. Never mind that, though. What annoys me most is that I can't examine my images properly before dawn. But I'm sure they're going to be full of smears and blurs again, and it isn't my fault. Any explanations?"

Drotninch summarized the discussion so far.

"Awb hit on that idea, did he?" Thilling said with approval. "I agree: he's a credit to his budder, and I'm glad I decided to take him on as my apprentice. Sorry I didn't ask you to help out this time, by the way, young'un, but you realize I have to be score-per-score certain that any flaws in the images are due to me, or some outside force. All right?"

"Yes, of course," Awb answered, trying not to swell with pride, and realizing this was just the kind of attitude he would have expected one of the true Jingfired to display.

"What I'm going to do tomorrow," Thilling resumed, "is a pure gamble, but if I'm right in my guess, then . . . But wait a moment. My new apprentice is pretty quick on the uptake, so let's ask him. Awb, in my position, what would you do?"

Awb's pulsations seemed to come to a complete halt. Here in the dark his mind felt sluggish, and with his maw empty the problem was worse yet. Struggling with all his mental forces, fighting to distinguish what he could rationally justify from what was seeping up from wild imagination or even the utterly logic-free level of dreamness, he reviewed everything he had been told at the observatory site, and what he had seen on the way, and what Thilling had had time to teach him . . .

The silence stretched and stretched. Eventually, reverting to her usual mood, Phrallet said, "Not much use asking him, was it? Now if you'd asked *me*—"

"But I didn't," said the picturist with point. "Well, young'un?"

That insult from his budder had been like dawn breaking inside his mind. Awb said explosively, "Take some of your leaves and just lay them around the dam, see what shows on them without being put in a fixer!"

"Well, well, well!" Thilling said. "You got it! It looks as though that's the only way to detect the effects of the poison short of letting something be killed by it. I like Byra's idea that it's a kind of burning, I like the idea that it may have something to do with hot rocks and volcanoes, and I *don't* like the idea that it's getting to my insides without my being able to sense it. But that's about all we'll be able to do on this trip, isn't it, Drotninch?"

"I'm afraid so," the scholar confirmed. "We'll have to bring safe food not only for ourselves but for the mounts on our next visit, and someone is going to have to travel all the way to the headwaters of the warmest stream, and one way and another I'm not sure we can tackle the job properly before next year. And—Lesh—you know what I'm going to have to say next, don't you?"

"The work we've done at the observatory has gone for nothing," was the bitter answer. "It will have to be sited somewhere else."

She clenched her mantle tight around the branch she lay on, like a mariner preparing for a gale. They left her alone with her thoughts. But it was with deliberate loudness that Drotninch continued, "Still, one all-important purpose has been served. We have found something totally new on our own planet, which we sometimes imagine to have been exhaustively explored. It's well for us to be reminded now and then that the unforeseen can break out under our very pads. If we don't keep that constantly in mind, what's going to become of us when we venture into space?"

Very softly, and for Awb alone, Thilling said, "Spoken like one of the Jingfired . . . ! Think about that, young'un. You still haven't told me what I'm most waiting to hear."

She stretched out and parted the overhanging leaves, and they all gazed up, except for Lesh, at the beautiful and terrifying fires of the Major Cluster, where since time immemorial new stars had, slowly and implacably, crept into view.

"Might as well use my entire stock of leaves on this," Thilling told Awb as dawn broke. "If anything more important turns up during the trip, I shan't want to know . . . We'll time the job by the sun; every score degrees it moves, we bring in one batch of 'em. Leave the bower set up so I can develop them as they come in."

Still baffled by the implied question the picturist expected him to answer, Awb helped her to lay out unexposed sheets by groups of five along the dam. But he found himself far more fascinated by what was happening in and on the lake. It was impossible to see more than a padlong below the surface, but here and there bubbles rose, and drifts of steam puffed up, and peculiar pale blue water-walkers scuttled hither and thither, avoiding the hottest spots but far more active than their cousins on cool rivers. As soon as Thilling let him go, he gathered up a few and offered them to Byra, who was packing every available container with specimens of flora and fauna.

"Where from exactly?" she demanded. "Near the dam? But how far from it?"

Why, she was a worse precisian than Axwep trying to balance Voosla's food-and-people accounts! But Awb preserved a courteous meekness.

"Between four and five padlongs from the thickest part of the yellow mud, where the bubbles rise most often."

"Hmm! That'll do very well! One thing I must give you, young'un: you have a keen eye on you. Yesterday that mutated winget, now this lot . . . What I'd really like to find, though, is a thriving root-mass of the spillway plants. We need some clue to resistance against this poison. Without that I don't know what we'll do."

But could any resistance be found to it among the folk? What if the only possible adjustment they could make in this region was the one adopted by the natives, able to feed and breed but nothing more?

However, Awb kept such thoughts to himself. After all, the scientists did have behind them the resources of one of the planet's greatest centers of knowledge.

It was time to take Thilling the first batch of exposed leaves. When he delivered them, she said, "Drotninch wants you to collect samples of the yellow mud. She's going to load one of the mounts with it. I told her to make sure it's the one furthest from my stuff."

"How did yesterday's images come out?" Awb inquired.

"What makes you think they came out at all?" Thilling countered sourly, but fanned a quarter-score of them for his inspection. All were weirdly streaked and smeared.

"What am I looking at?" Awb whispered.

"Something scarcely any eye has seen before," was the muttered answer. "The telescopes they meant to build on Fangsharp Peak were supposed to gather so much light from such faint sources, no one could possibly sit and register it. So they planned to make them deliver their light to sheets like these, using astrotropes whose growth is controllable to a laqth of a clawide to keep the image steady. Oh, the effort they've wasted on breeding those 'tropes!"

"You sound as though the observatory is never going to be built, not here, not anywhere!" Awb cried.

"Maybe it won't. Because the only time I saw patternless faults like these on an unexposed image-leaf . . ."

She shook her mantle, returning the sheets to their pack. "It makes common-type sense, doesn't it, to grow observatories on mountain-tops? There are four or five such, and I'm an advisor to the one near Chisp. They called me in because even when they're using the finest leaves things go wrong. There are smudges, there are blurs, there are distortions. Often they spoil a whole dark's work, especially when the telescope is aimed at the Major Cluster."

"What causes them?" Awb clenched his claws.

"We think it's tiny particles of matter blasted out from the new stars forming so far away. And they carry with them something of the terrible stellar heat. At any rate, they burn their way into the leaves. But I never imagined that something at the bottom of a valley . . . *Hmm!*"

As though struck by sudden insight, she turned back to the dark-bower, intent on developing the latest sheets.

"Go get Drotninch's mud-samples," she ordered. "But remember to time the next lot of leaves, too."

Awb hastened to comply. At least, down by the dam, he could be sure of avoiding Phrallet, who still seemed to harbour the suspicion that her heat-sore pads were owed to some sinister plot by Drotninch and the other scientists.

But there was something amiss.

He fought the knowledge for a long while, digging up the yellow mud, collecting the rest of the leaves at proper intervals and bringing them to the dark-bower, making himself as useful as he could to everybody.

Then, tiny as a falling star viewed through the wrong end of a spyglass, a spark crossed his eye.

Puzzled, he looked for more, but found only a red trace across his field of vision, rather as though he had gazed too long at something very bright but very narrow, like—

Like what? There was nothing it was like at all.

Simultaneously he became aware of a sensation akin to an itch, except that it wasn't one. It was just as annoying, but he couldn't work out where it was, other than very vaguely. And whoever heard of an itch in red-level pith, anyway? Determinedly he went on with his work, and shortly was rewarded by spotting another mutated water-walker, not blue this time, but pure white.

He dived after it and trapped it in his mandibles, and bore it to Byra in triumph.

Standing by as she inspected it under the microscope, he heard her say irritably, "Stop fidgeting, young'un! You look as though a mustiq got under your mantle . . . Oh, this is even more ridiculous than the last one! I don't see how it can survive, let alone reproduce itself!"

He scarcely noticed the last comment. A mustiq under his mantle? Yes, that was a little like it. He'd been twitching without realizing until he had his attention drawn to it. He was pulsating out of rhythm with himself; instead of the normal ratios between mantle-ripple, gut-shift, breath-drawing, ichor-peristalsis and eye-flick which he was accustomed to, in the perfect proportions of bass, third, fifth, seventh and octave, he was shuddering as though about to burst.

Having his maw empty for so long, for the first time in his life, was proving to be a very odd experience indeed.

Yet if hunger were the sole explanation (and surely he hadn't gone without for long enough?)—

Oh, NO!

*POISONED???*

He peeled apart from himself, much like the brollicans that teachers on Voosla grew excited about when they chanced across a shoal of them so large the city had no time to eat the lot before a few could be salvaged for educational purposes. For scores-of-scores of years they had been providing real-time evidence for symbiosis, the phenomenon that underlay the folk's modern predicament.

*Coevolution* . . . said something from the deep red level of his consciousness, but everyone knew that that level didn't deal in speech, only in hunger and breeding-need and the repair of vital organs.

(But who had told him that was true? Maybe someone would come along to tell him different, like Thilling! Maybe the exercises she had promised him, concerning dark-use, didn't refer only to outside-dark but inside-dark as well . . .)

In the distance, though very close in time, like right now:

"Help!" (It was Byra's voice.) Drotninch, Thilling, Phrallet, anybody! Awb's gone dreamish!"

*Dreamish? Me? Me . . . ?*

But he didn't know who he was any longer. There wasn't a "myself" controlling the physical envelope known as Awb. There was a muddle of memory and imagination, a chaotic slew of information and sensory input, and what trace of identity did remain—thanks to his having been budded on a small but wealthy city, where no one in living memory had gone dreamish through simple hunger—was capable of no more than observation: as it were, "So this is what must have happened to our poor ancestors who multiplied themselves without making provision for proper nourishment! I'm amazed they ever clawed their way back out of the mental swamp they fell in, regardless of Gveest's best efforts, or the Jingfired's!"

Then even that last vestige of himself dissolved, and his pith started to react as though he were his own remotest forebear, assailed by predatory gigants and striking out at random in the faint hope that at least his body might block one monster's maw and choke it to death.

It took three of them to subdue his violent flailing.

Late that dark Thilling lay in a tree-crotch well away from the dam, which her images had convinced her was the chief source of danger, while the scientists wrangled among themselves. Awb had been temporarily quieted; Lesh had dispatched two of her assistants to find fruit and funqi from which nourishing juices could be extracted, at a safe distance from the lake, and herself administered a calmative from the first-aid pack she had brought. It was to be hoped that his youth and slightness of build accounted for his extreme vulnerability to—to whatever had afflicted him. At any rate the rest of them seemed to be in fair shape, with the exception, Thilling reflected cynically, of Phrallet, who was on the verge of hysteria. She kept saying over and over, "We must get out of here! We must go back at once! Who knows what damage is being wrought in our very pith? My pads are still hurting, you know!"

And when she found her companions ignoring that line of argument, she tried cajolement: "If only for the sake of my youngest budling, we must go back! Oh, I know I'm sometimes hard on him, but really I do care for him, and if he dies because of this . . ."

At which the others simply turned their backs in the most insulting fashion possible. So for some while now she had been sulking, which at least allowed the rest of them to debate the core of the problem.

Drotninch was saying, "I'm coming around to the conclusion that we not only have to deal with the poison per se, but also with its effects on living organisms, including disease germs. You know there's a theory that the New Star triggered off the latest round of female mimicry, the one which made so many of us too like males to bud anymore. Given what Thilling has told us about the resemblance between what she finds on her image-sheets and what happens when sheets are exposed at high altitude—"

Lesh cut in. "I've heard that theory, and to me it smacks of the rankest astrological superstition!"

Byra said heavily, "There's only one way of settling the matter. We're going to have to study this poison *in vivo.* Right now, of course, we only have one subject: Awb. But it's beyond a doubt that some at least of the same effect must be working in all of us."

Rousing from her apathy, Phrallet shouted, "What do you want us to do—stay here until we all collapse the way he did? You must be out of your pith! Anyway, I won't let you treat a budling of mine like a laboratory animal!"

Doing her best to disregard the interruption, Byra went on, "We can extrapolate from cutinates to some extent, of course, and I've taken samples from the mount that died, and with luck the rest of them will have been affected—"

"With luck?" Lesh echoed sardonically. "When I need every mount and draftimal I can lay claws on to rescue my expensive equipment from the observatory site? You're not killing any of my beasts for your researches, I'm afraid! In any case, mounts aren't enough like us, are they?"

Sighing, Byra admitted as much. "We'll have to rely on what we can learn by studying Awb, then, and since of course we all hope he'll make a quick recovery, that may not be very much. Still, we can call for volunteers who've been in the area since the project started, and that may help."

"You can get all the specimens you need," Phrallet said. "Why haven't you thought it through? If studying the poison in a living person means saving our lives—I mean Awb's life—you could just kidnap a few of the natives. They're worthless for anything else, aren't they?"

Thilling clenched her mantle in horror. Surely this group of civilized scientists must reject so hideous a notion out of claw? But no! To her infinite dismay she realized they were taking it seriously. Byra said after a pause, "It would certainly be very useful."

And Lesh chimed in: "We have plenty of nets! I'll get my staff on the job the moment we return!"

In that moment Thilling realized that she despised Phrallet more completely than anyone she had ever met or even heard of.

And what would Awb say when he learned that his life had been spared at such revolting cost?

But perhaps he would care no more than his budder.

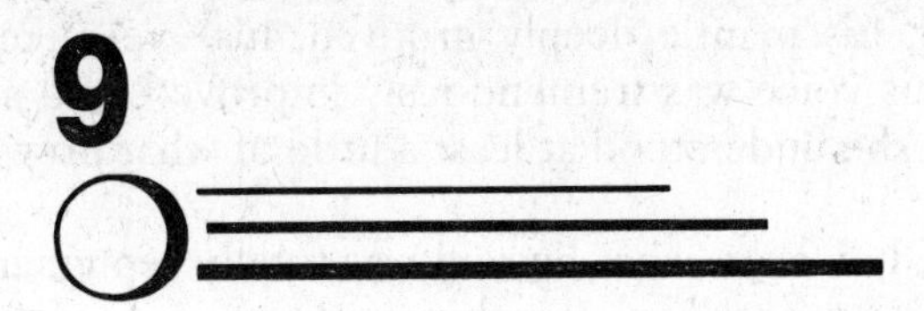

How everything had changed in three-score years! Not least, of course, thanks to the mutated diseases the workers from the abandoned World Observatory had carried away with them. Thilling shivered as she reflected on how vast a mystery those mutations had then seemed, how simple the explanation had proved to be once it was properly attacked . . .

Why was it that so many people declined to pay attention to such matters? Here in the crowded branchways of Voosla—a city transformed and twice enlarged since she last set pad on her—she knew without needing to be told that anyone she accosted at random would be as likely as not to dismiss her scientific knowledge out of claw, as totally irrelevant to their own concerns.

In the distant past, when there had been religions, it must have been similar for a traveler from afar; how had Jing reacted to those who honestly believed that the Arc of Heaven was the Maker's Sling, and shed meteors on the world as a warning of divine retribution? And here she was, under orders to confront a teacher whom his followers regarded as fit to be mentioned alongside Jing himself, even though he encouraged them to despise the greatest discoveries and inventions of his own lifetime.

If only the Jingfired had picked on someone else for this mission . . . But their old acquaintance had tipped the balance: Thilling was forbidden to disobey.

She had no difficulty in locating the venue of Awb's daily meeting, of course. Scores-of-scores of people were making for it, so she simply let herself be carried along.

It was, she must admit, a considerable achievement for a mere male to have got himself regarded as his city's most outstanding bud, granted the use of the handsome open bower at the very center of Voosla which was normally reserved for public debates on matters of policy. She imagined it was seldom so packed for one of those. It was with relief that she noticed, as she made herself comfortable in an inconspicuous crotch, that she was not the only person present with the traces of old age on her mantle, though the vast majority of the attendance consisted of young'uns chattering away like piemaqs.

But they fell silent the instant Awb appeared: plumper than

Thilling remembered, his mantle deeply grooved, his eye—like her own—less keen. Yet his voice was tremendously improved, and at his first utterance she felt she understood at least a little of what drew folk to him.

Persuasive or not, however, what he said was totally repugnant to her. He taught that no "proper" relationship, with one's community, even with one's budder or budlings—let alone the commensality of all living things—could be established without prior comprehension of oneself. Sometimes he urged people to starve in the midst of plenty, like the ancient sacerdotes; sometimes he expounded on ideas drawn from dreamness, as though they warranted equal treatment with rational knowledge; frequently he declared that those who sought means to escape the planet were actually fleeing from true awareness of themselves.

And all this, Thilling thought bitterly, because of the load of guilt he had carried ever since he learned that Phrallet's monstrous scheme to kidnap those mindless northern natives and experiment on their living bodies had saved his life . . . but not her own.

He spoke freely enough about his illness and recovery; what he never mentioned, according to her briefing—nor did he prove the contrary today—was the self-sacrifice of Drotninch and Eupril and Lesh, who had each in her respective way struggled to make sense of the heat arising in that yellow mud, and in less than a generation revolutionized the folk's understanding of matter. Above all, their legacy offered clues to the processes that lit the stars.

Because of them, and their successors, the chemistry of other elements than woodchar was at long last being studied thoroughly. The ancient use of fire had been resuscitated; brilliant young minds had been brought to bear on the questions posed by metal, glass, rock, plain ordinary water! A whole new universe of knowledge had been opened up. And did Awb care? Not by any clue or sign he gave!

Of course he did still hew to his belief that life among the People of the Sea was inherently superior to life on shore. To this fact he modestly attributed his remarkable success in treating deranged landlivers, whose behavior was sometimes dangerously abnormal even though the most delicate analyses revealed nothing amiss in their nerve-pith or ichor. More cynical, Thilling thought of the cleansing ocean breezes that bore away intrusive pheromones. Sea-travel had been regarded as beneficial long before Awb's reputation converted Voosla into the most sought-after of floating cities, in demand to touch at every continent in the course of every year. And she was sure Awb himself must be aware of that fact.

But if she were to mention it to those around her, would they be interested? Would they believe her? Most likely not. Awb and his disciples seemed to be set on creating a generation of young folk who cared as little for the past as for the future. Neither the study of history nor planning for the salvation of the species could attract them. They were assured that they need only study themselves, and all would be well, for ever and ever . . .

The meeting had assembled before sundown. Darkness overtook it while Awb was still answering questions. Suddenly Thilling noticed that something was distracting the crowd, and everyone was glancing upward. Copying their example, she realized why. There was a small yellow comet in the sky, but that was commonplace; what had drawn their gaze was a meteor storm, a horde of bright brief streaks coming by scores at a time.

She thought for a moment about challenging Awb to deny that that was a reminder of the doom the planet faced, another promise of the dense gas-cloud the sun was drifting towards. But she lacked the courage. She remained meekly where she was until he was done, and then—equally meekly—made her way towards him, surrounded by a gaggle of his admirers. Most were young she'uns, doubtless hoping for a bud from so famous a teacher.

In old age her own sterility had become a source of gall to Thilling; she strove not to let it prey on her pith.

There was little chance, though, of actually reaching Awb in this small but dense throng, for everyone was respectfully lowering as they clustered about him, leaving no gaps for passage. Hating to make herself conspicuous, but seeing no alternative, she did the opposite and erected to full height . . . such as it was at her age.

"Awb, it's Thilling! Do you remember me? We used to know each other many years ago!"

There was a startled pause, and all eyes turned on her. A whiff of hostility reached her—how dare this old'un claim acquaintance with the master? But then Awb replied, in a gruffer and lower voice than when addressing the crowd.

"I remember you. Wait until the rest have gone."

And he dismissed them with gentle shooing motions of his mantle. Disappointed but compliant, they wandered off.

When they were alone but for two thick-set individuals who appeared to be his permanent attendants, his age-dimmed eye surveyed her from crest to pad.

"Oh, yes. It is the same Thilling in spite of the time that's passed. Your voice has changed, but so has mine, I imagine . . . Tell me, are you still subject to your delusion about being able to recruit people to the Jingfired?"

*Delusion?*

For an instant Thilling, who had devoted her entire life to the cause she regarded as the greatest in history, wished she might hurl herself bodily at him, shred his mantle with claws and mandibles before his companions could prevent her. But she conquered the impulse, as she had overcome so many before, and a gust of wind dispersed her betraying anger-stink.

With careful effort she said, "Wy do you call it a delusion?"

He stiffened back, again examining her curiously. "Hmm! Persistent, I gather! Well, if you've come for help, I might perhaps—"

"You haven't answered my question. As once, long ago, you failed to answer another."

Missing the allusion, he countered, "Does it really call for an answer? But for the sake of an old friendship, I'll offer one."

*Friendship? Is that what he calls it now? When he begged to be made my apprentice, and ran away as soon as he knew his budder was dead and couldn't plague him anymore?*

But Thilling feigned composure in spite of all.

"How life has treated you, I'm unaware, though I suspect unkindly. For myself, I've forced it to treat me well, with the result that I'm now acquainted with the Councils of the Jingfired in every city on every continent and every ocean. They send embassies to me seeking advice and guidance, they anxiously await the appearance of Voosla on the horizon, they take my words and convert them into action—with what advantages to all, you may observe." A large gesture to indicate the globe. "Not one of those people has ever mentioned you. But don't worry. I've kept your affliction secret for the most part, though I confess I may now and then have referred to it during some of my lectures, purely as an illustrative example, you understand."

Everything came clear to Thilling on the instant. Of course! He had confused her with Byra . . . Her voice level, she said, "I take it you have studied Jinglore, then?"

"To some extent"—in an offclaw tone. "It does furnish a store of poetic metaphors and images, which may help us the better to understand our experience of dreamness. But that's all."

"I regret to say you're wrong. Just as wrong as you are about my so-called 'delusion.' " She moved so close that, had she been a total stranger, the trespass on his private space would have been an insult, and continued before the bodyguards could intervene.

"How would your followers react to the news that you who preach the need for perfect relationships rejoiced at your budder's death, or to being told how you broke your apprentice's pledge? Or to learning how you, who boast of saving the sanity of others, have become so senile as to confuse me with Byra, may she rest in peace? She too was silly enough to assume that city-bosses who call themselves Jingfired actually are so. But they're not. If your memory isn't totally wrecked, if you have any shred of conscience left, you'll recall my telling you when you pleaded to become my apprentice that it's no use trying to guess who the Jingfired actually are. You have to *know.*"

After that she fully expected the bodyguards to close on her and drag her away. But they hesitated; an aura of uncertainty was exuding from their master.

At long last he said, not looking at her, but towards the sky where the rain of meteors had now redoubled, "So it's come to this. A voice has spoken from my past which I can neither challenge nor deny."

Hope leapt up in her pith. For an instant she thought she had already won.

But the hope was dashed when he relaxed with a sigh, and continued: "Such a long-lasting and intractable psychosis is probably beyond even my methods, which normally prove so successful. Still, for old friendship's sake I can at least attempt to show you where you went astray."

He added to the attendants, "Scholar Thilling will be my guest at dinner. Apologize to those who have prior claims on my time, but meeting someone from one's younghood is a rare event. And perhaps good may come of it in the long run."

## 10

If there was one thing Thilling could reluctantly admire about Awb now, it was his skill in keeping up appearances. He closed the gap between them and by embracing her contrived to transfer some of the pheromone-masking perfumes he wore on his torso, leaving the bodyguards confused.

Then he led her along the branchways to a bower where the city's finest foods were lovingly tended by experts who—so he told her—claimed to inherit their knowledge from someone who had studied under Gveest.

But if he expected to impress her by boasting, he was wrong. Nothing could more have firmed her determination than this display of the luxury Awb had attained through corrupting the minds of the younger generation. Had she not needed food to power the argument she foresaw as inescapable, she would have voiced her contempt of his tactics; as it was, she resignedly filled her maw and, confident that even yet he would never have been trained in the Jingfired's techniques of dark-use, waited until he chose to speak again.

Eventually, replete, he let himself slump on his branch and said, "So you thought you could threaten me by raking up my past, did you? That must be because you envy the course my life has taken."

"On the contrary!" she snapped. "Thanks to the images I made on that dam banked with yellow mud, I went on to share in some of the most notable discoveries of this or any age. Have you no faintest notion what marvels lie in the secret pith of matter? Because of my skills, I was close at claw when Eupril first separated the heavy elements which break up of their own accord. I was there when Lesh—"

"It hasn't made amends for being sterile," he cut in.

"Oh, because it was an obsession with Phrallet you think everything can be reduced to whether or not one has budded!" retorted Thilling. "Let me remind you—"

He raised a claw. "If you're going to quote Jinglore at me, be warned that others have tried without effect."

"I have no intention of it. I was about to say that in your attempts to atone for hating Phrallet, you saw no alternative but to outdo Jing and Yockerbow and Tenthag and the other heroes of the past. You're not equipped to."

Awb had had much practice at appearing resignedly wise. Adopting the appropriate expression, he said, "If each age is to surpass its forepadders, then some individual must respond to its unique and particular challenge. In the present epoch . . . Well, you see the truth all around you."

"In other words, you think that your success in turning people inward upon themselves, making them preoccupied with their personal motives and reactions, is the response best fitted to the plight we find ourselves in?"

Awb curled his mantle into a patronizing smile.

"Very interesting," Thilling murmured, resorting to the ultimate line of attack which the Jingfired had prepared for her. "This fits superbly with Yegbrot's studies of the effect of radioactivity on nerve-pith, which demonstrate how even temporary exposure can derange the system."

She refrained from mentioning how much she hated Yegbrot's ruthlessness, which stemmed directly from Phrallet's original proposal. If only Awb had chosen to attack the fact that nowadays psychologists were using experimental subjects deliberately rendered mindless by pithing . . .

In the act of reaching for a fresh and succulent fungus he checked and twisted towards her, glaring. "How dare you accuse me of being insane?"

*A breakthrough!*

"But I didn't. My mission is merely to establish whether your regrettably successful attempt to distract the best of our young'uns from the branchway that alone can lead to the survival of our species is due to perversity or injury. I now conclude the latter. So you're not to blame."

Recovering, he chuckled. "You're a classic case of the type I so often invoke in lectures: a sterile she'un determined to project a surrogate immortality on the rest of us because she can't produce her own buds. Sorry to be so blunt, but there it is. And there are many who would pay handsomely for so accurate a diagnosis from Scholar Awb!"

"Yet you sense my authority, don't you?" she countered. "Despite smearing me with that repulsive muck you wear!"

He clattered his mandibles in amusement. "The more you say, the more you support my theory that people like you at some stage lost the ability to distinguish input due to the real world from what stems out of imagination and hence ultimately dreamness. How I wish I had a way to transcribe this conversation! It would confirm—"

"You'd like a recordimal, you mean."

"Well, out of courtesy I didn't bring one along, but if you'd permit it, certainly I—"

"Do you know who invented the recordimal?"

"No, I don't believe I was ever told," he answered, taking care as usual to protect his ego by not admitting he might have forgotten. "Who?"

"I was at her side during its development. Byra! With whom you won't stop confusing me!"

"That," Awb murmured, "must be because if anyone out of our group at the observatory had devised such a useful tool, I'd have expected it to be you. Sure you aren't being modest?" He settled down with the comfortable air of one who, having turned a neat compliment, was expecting to be paid in kind.

But she reacted otherwise, sure now of her ascendancy.

"Once I hoped you'd find the answer to a question I never put to you. I was hoping you might say of your own accord what I once said, like all the Jingfired—the true Jingfired!—and declare that you wanted to devote your life to ensuring that we can overcome the worst the universe can throw at us. Don't interrupt!"—as he showed signs of doing so. "I know what answer you'd give now, and it's the same you'd have given then, had you been honest enough. In your own words, you're a classic case. Yegbrot could tell me to a fraction of a clawide where particles of stumpium and sluggium have settled in your pith. But the real damage had been done already. Lesh died, Eupril died, Byra died, but to the last they fought to understand why, and to save others from the same fate! Whereas you've given up, for the sake of making over countless scores of young'uns into worshipers of Awb!"

By mustering her resources of contempt-stink, she had finally made an impression on him. He said at length, "But you seem to be claiming that I'm responsible for what Phrallet suggested. At that time, though, I was sick and mindless, remember. And I detest the cost of our recent advances in chemistry and medicine! Of course, I suppose you make out that the benefits outweigh—"

"I do not! What would we have lost if we hadn't kidnapped the natives and experimented on them? Half-a-score years at worst, until we could duplicate isolated cells, create synthetic ichor, grow pith in isolation the way we grow nervograps! But if we'd done that, you'd be dead, wouldn't you? You'd have missed your chance to scorn my friends who've invented intercontinental nervograps and freight-pitchens and recordimals and now are set to outdo floaters by attaining controlled atmospheric flight, a first pad-mark on the road to space! By all *their* work, you're as unimpressed as by a pebble on a pathway!"

Breathing hard, she subsided, wondering whether what she had said had registered, or whether the terrible metal from the accidental stumpium pile at the river-dam had lodged in too many crucial junctions of his nerve-pith.

And also how many of his followers, when they inveighed against fumes and furnaces, were doing so because they had reason on their side rather than because the very metals that experimenters now were working with had deformed their thoughts.

Her own as well . . . ?

The possibility was too fearful to think about. She shut it resolutely away.

Her weather-sense was signaling danger, but she put it down to feedback from the reek of tension she and Awb were generating, about which other clients of the food-bower had started to complain. At their insistence, the roof of leaves was being folded back. Perhaps, Thilling thought, she might exploit the incontrovertible reality of the sky to make Awb see sense . . . but discovered, even as she glanced upward, that that hope too was vain.

Across the welkin slashed a giant ball of light: vast, eye-searing, shedding lesser streaks on its way to—where? The Worldround Ocean, with a little luck, rather than dry land. Yet even there—!

Oh, so much like what the astronomers had predicted from the images she had fixed on sheet after sensitive sheet!

Preserving her pride to the last, she rose while Awb—the poor vainglorious victim of a chance mishap, who had been poisoned in his mind before he was poisoned in his pith, yet whom the future would not forgive for contaminating a later generation with his falsehoods—was still struggling to deny the reality of this event.

"The real world has one resource our minds do not," said Thilling loudly and clearly. "It can always chasten us with a discovery we couldn't plan for, like the exploding atoms which spoiled the leaves you brought me from the dam—remember? Well, now it's curing us of arrogance again. This is a tenet of the Jingfired, Awb: not the shabby shams whom you're so proud to know, who usurp the name in cities round the world, but us, the secret ones, who work and slave and hope and always seem to find a fool like you to block our way—"

She got that far, thanks to her greater skill in dark-use, before the noise arrived: a terrible noise such as must last have been heard when the ice-packs broke up after the Great Thaw, worse than the worst growling of a pack of snowbelongs when they crawled into lonely settlements in search of folk to feed their broodmass.

Already the officers of Voosla were issuing orders: cut loose from shore and who cares if we kill our musculators, get into open water at all costs and stay afloat, signal the giqs and hope to pick them up while we're under way . . .

It was all well and correctly done, and Axwep, had she survived, would have been proud, and even Phrallet—so thought Thilling in the grayness of uncalled-for memory—might have relented in her constant criticism.

But it was too late. Like her errand to Awb, it was far too late.

The meteor outmassed a score of Vooslas. It boiled and smashed the ocean all at once, and raised a giant wall of water round its impact point that nearly but not quite outraced the sound of its arrival. Every coast that fringed the ocean shattered under the rock-hard water-hammer; Voosla herself was carried screaming far inland in a catastrophic shambles of plants and people, which for a crazy instant made Thilling think of what it must be like to fly . . .

"Comet! Comet!" she heard, and moaned, "Fools!" with the last pressure in her body before the blast exploded her.

Speech ended. Thought endured longer, enough for her to think: *Had it not been for Awb . . . No, that's unfair. When we escape to space those like him, poisoned by no fault of their own, must still be a part of us, because who can say what other poisons await us out there . . . ?*

Not Thilling; she dissolved into the dark, while steam and dust and shreds of what had been the folk and all they cherished set off on their stratospheric journey round the globe.

It was to last more than a score of years.

# Part Six

# Hammer and Anvil

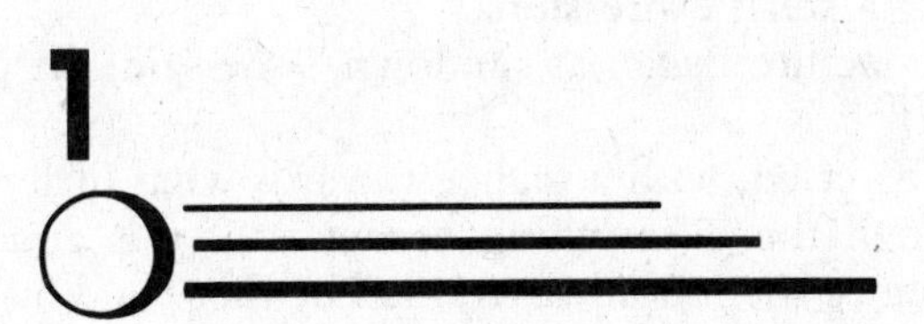

"*Y*our business?" said the house in a tone as frosty as a polar winter. Then followed a dull and reflex hiss as its vocalizing bladders automatically refilled.

At first Chybee was too startled to respond. This magnificent home had overwhelmed her even as she approached: its towering crest, its ramifying branches garlanded with countless luminants, its far-spread webs designed to protect the occupants against wingets and add their minuscule contribution to the pool of organic matter at its roots, cleverly programed to withdraw before a visitor so that they would not be torn—all, all reflected such luxury as far surpassed her youthful experience.

But then her whole trip to and through this incredible city had been a revelation. She had heard about, had seen pictures of, the metropolis of Slah, and met travelers whom business or curiosity had lured hither. Nothing, though, had prepared her for the reality of her first-ever transcontinental flight, or the jobs she had been obliged to undertake to pay her way, constantly terrified that they would make her too late. No description could have matched the sensation of being carried pell-mell amid treetops by the scampering inverted fury of a dolmusq, with its eighteen tentacles snatching at whatever support was offered and its body straining under the weight of two-score passengers. Nor could anyone have conveyed to her the combined impact of the crowds, the noise, and the universal stench compound of pheromones, smoke from the industrial area to the west, and the reek of all the material that must go to rot in order to support the homes and food-plants of this most gigantic of cities. Never in all of history had there been one to match it, neither by land nor by sea—likely, not even in the age of legend.

From the corner of her eye she detected the house's defenses tensing, gathering pressure to snare her if, by failing to respond, she identified herself as a mindless beast. Hastily she forced out, "My name is Chybee! I've come to hear the lecture! Never say I've missed it!"

Modern and talented as the house was, that exceeded its range of responses; she had to wait for a person to answer. Eventually the thorny barrier blocking the entrance drew aside and revealed an elderly woman wearing a stern expression.

"The professor's lecture began at sundown," she said. "It is now halfway to midnight."

"I know!" Chybee cried, with a glance towards what little of the sky was visible through the overarching branches of this and other nearby homes. By chance the moon was framed by those and by a ring of thin cloud; it was just past the new, and its dark part was outlined by sparkles nearly as bright as those which shot continually through the upper air . . . a constant reminder, Chybee thought, of the rightness of her decision.

She went on pleadingly, "But I've come from Hulgrapuk to hear her! It's not my fault I've been delayed!"

"Hulgrapuk?" The woman's attitude softened instantly. "Ah! then you must be one of Professor Wam's students, I suppose. Come in quickly, but be very quiet."

Injunctions to be quiet struck Chybee as rather silly when the hordes of the city made such a terrible droning and buzzing noise, sometimes punctuated by loud clanging and banging from the factories whose fumes made the air so foul, but she counted herself lucky not to have been turned away, and did as she was told.

Wondering who Professor Wam might be.

The woman indicated that she should follow an upward-slanting branchway towards the crest of the house, and there she found at least five-score folk gathered in a roughly globular bower. At its focus, comfortably disposed on large and well-smoothed crotches, were three persons of advancing age whose exudations indicated they were far from happy to be in such proximity. The rest of the attendance consisted of a few males scattered among numerous females, mostly young, who were trying hard not to react to their elders' stench; that was plain from their own emanations.

Recordimals had captured Ugant's voice for her many supporters around the planet. Chybee recognized it the moment she entered, and was so excited to hear her idol in reality that she bumped against a boy not much older than herself as she sought for space to perch.

Instantly: "Chhht!" from half a score of those nearby.

But the boy curled his mantle in a grin as he made room alongside him. Muttering thanks, she settled down and concentrated . . . rather to the boy's disappointment, she gathered, but she was here for one purpose and one purpose only: to hear Ugant's views in her own words.

It was clear that the formal lecture must long be over, for she was engaged in debate, either with those flanking her or with some doubter elsewhere in the bower. She was saying:

". . . our researches prove conclusively that the fall of the civilization which bequeathed to us most of our modern skills—indeed, which unwittingly gave us this very city, changed though it now is out of recognition by those who created it as a sea-going entity!—was due to the impact of a giant meteorite, whose traces we can only indirectly observe because it fell into deep water. Given this indisputable fact, it can only be a matter of time before another and far larger impact wipes us out too. It's all very well to argue that we must prepare to take the folk themselves into space, with whatever is necessary for their survival. I don't doubt that eventually this could be done; we know how to create life-support systems that will sustain us for long periods on the ocean bed, and they too have to be closed. We know, more or less, how to shield ourselves against the radiation we are sure of meeting out there. But I contest the possibility of achieving so grandiose a goal with the resources available. I believe rather that we, as living creatures, owe it to the principle of life itself to ensure that it survives even if we as a species cannot!"

Suddenly there was uproar. Confused, Chybee saw one of Ugant's companions turn her, or possibly his, back insultingly, as though to imply: "What use in arguing with such an idiot?" Meantime a few clear voices cut through the general turmoil; she heard "True! True!" and "Nonsense!" and then, "But the folk of Swiftyouth and Sunbride will hurl more missiles at us to prevent it!"

That was so reminiscent of what she was fleeing from, she shivered. Mistaking her response, the boy beside her said, "She does underestimate us, doesn't she?"

"Uh—who?"

"Ugant, of course!"—in a tone of high surprise. "Going on all the time about how we can't possibly succeed, and so we have to abandon the planets to bacteria! You should have been here sooner. Wam made sludge of her!"

"Wam?"

"On the left, of course! From Hulgrapuk, no less! How many

scores-of-scores of padlonglaqs did she have to travel to be here this dark? That shows her dedication to the cause of truth and reason!"

*I bet she had an easier journey than I did . . .* But Chybee repressed the bitter comment, abruptly aware that she was hungry and that this bower was festooned with some of the finest food-plants she had ever set eye on.

Instead she said humbly, "And whose back is turned?"

"Oh, that's Aglabec. Hasn't dared utter a word since the start, and very right and proper too. But I'm afraid a lot of his supporters are here. I hope you aren't one of them?" He turned, suddenly suspicious.

"I don't think so," Chybee ventured.

"You don't know you aren't? By the arc of heaven, how could anybody not know whether giving up reason in favor of dreamness is right or wrong? Unless they'd already decided in favor of dreamness!"

Aglabec . . . ? The name floated up from memory: it had been cited by her parents. Chybee said firmly, "I'm against dreamness!"

"I'm glad of that!" said the boy caustically. But they were being called on to hush again. Wam was expanding her mantle for a counter-blast.

"There is one point on which Professor Ugant and myself are entirely in agreement! I maintain that her scheme to seed the planets with microorganisms is a poor second-best, because what we must and can do is launch ourselves, or our descendants, and our entire culture into space! But we unite in despising those who spout nonsense about the nature of other planets totally at odds with scientific reality, those who claim that they can make mental voyages to Swiftyouth and Sun-bride and indeed to the planets of other stars! Such people are—"

What carefully honed insult Wam had prepared, her listeners were not fated to find out. A group of about a score of young people, with a leavening of two or three older, outshouted her and simultaneously began to shake the branches. Resonance built up swiftly, and those around cried out as they strove to maintain their grip. The slogans the agitators were bellowing were like the one Chybee had caught a snatch of a few moments earlier, warnings that the folk of other planets were bound to drop more rocks from heaven if any plan to carry "alien" life thither were put into effect. But who could respect them if they were capable of slaughtering fellow beings for their own selfish ends . . . ?

Chybee caught herself. There was no life on Swiftyouth and Sun-bride; there couldn't be. Modern astronomy had proved it. Fatigue and hunger were combining to drive her into dreamness herself . . . plus the shock of realizing that she could never go home again. Had she really gambled the whole of her future life on this one trip to Slah, which her budder had forbidden?

Indeed she had, and the knowledge made her cling as desperately to rationality as to her swaying branch.

She barely heard a new loud voice roaring from the center of the bower, barely registered that Aglabec the leader of the agitators had finally spoken up, and was shouting:

"You're wasting your efforts! You'll never shake this lot loose from their grip on the tree of prejudice! Leave that to the folk of other worlds—they'll act to cure such foolishness in their own good time!"

Disappointed, his reluctant followers ceased making the branches thrash about. But at that point Chybee could hold her peace no longer.

Rising as best she could to full height on her swaying perch, she shouted back, "There aren't any folk on other worlds, and there never will be if you get your way! We can't live there either! Our only sane course is to hope that the seeds of life can be adapted to germinate and evolve elsewhere!"

*What am I saying? Who am I saying it to?*

Mocking laughter mingled with cheers. She slumped back on the branch, folding her mantle tightly around her against the storm of noise, and heard at a great distance how the company dispersed. Several in passing discourteously bumped against her, and she thought one must have been the boy from the adjacent perch. It was a shame to have made him dislike her on no acquaintance, but after what Aglabec had said . . . after what her parents had tried to force down her maw . . . after . . .

She had imagined herself young and strong enough to withstand any challenge the world might offer. The toll taken by her journey, her emotional crisis, her lack of food, maybe the subtle poisons some claimed to have identified in the air of Slah, proved otherwise. Her mind slid downward into chaos.

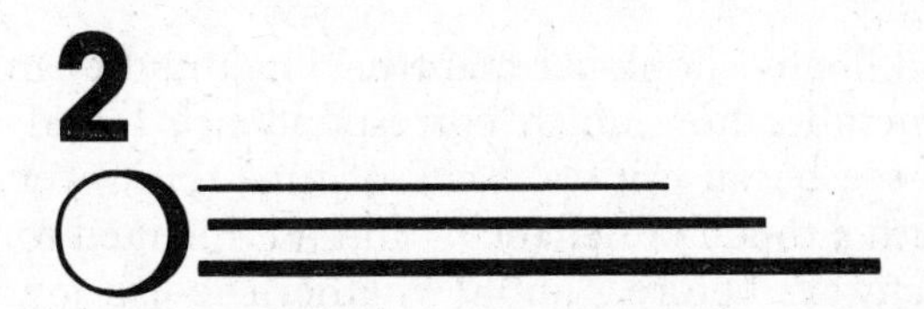

Reacting to the reek of hostility that permeated the bower, Wam snapped, "I knew it was a crazy idea inviting Aglabec to take part in a scientific debate!"

She swarmed down from the crotch she had occupied during the meeting and gazed disconsolately at the departing audience.

"You can't have thought it was that stupid if you came so far to join in!" Ugant retorted, stung.

"Oh, one always hopes . . ." Wam admitted with a sigh. "Besides, the dreamlost are gathering such strength at Hulgrapuk, even among my own students, and I imagined that things might be better here. Apparently I was wrong. What do we have to tell these folk to convince them of the doom hanging over us all?"

"Beg pardon, Professor!" a diffident voice murmured, and old Fraij, Ugant's maestradomi, slithered down to join them. "You mentioned your students just now. The one who spoke up at the end hasn't left with everybody else. I think she's been taken ill."

"Hah! As if we didn't have enough problems already . . . Well, it's up to you to look after your own." Ugant turned aside with a shrug, scanning the available food-plants in search of anything particularly delicious.

From a pouch she wore on a baldric slung about her, Wam produced a spyglass and leveled it at the other remaining occupant of the bower. After a moment she said, "She could be of a Hulgrapuk strain, I suppose, but clasped around her branch like that I can't be sure. At any rate I don't recognize her."

Fraij said uncertainly, "I'm sorry. She said she'd come specially from Hulgrapuk, so naturally I assumed . . ."

"I'm afraid your assumption was wrong," Wam murmured, and joined Ugant in her quest for refreshment, adding, "Whatever I may think of your views, by the way, I find no fault with your hospitality. Many thanks."

But Ugant was snuffing the air, now almost cleansed as the roof-leaves flapped automatically to scour away the remanent pheromones.

"I do recognize her . . . I think. Fraij, do you remember a message from some youngling in that area saying her parents had gone overside into the psychoplanetary fad, and she needed arguments to combat them? About a month ago. Wasn't the trace on that very much like hers?"

Fraij hesitated, and finally shook her mantle. "I'm afraid I can't be sure. You have to remember how much correspondence I deal with that you never get to see because it's a waste of time. However that may be," she added with a touch of defiance, "I'm not inclined to turn her out into the branchways before I know whether she can fend for herself."

"Well, she did sound comparatively sensible . . ." Ugant crammed her maw with succulent funqi and swarmed over to where the girl was lying. Another sample of her odor, and: "Hmm! I was right! Her name's something like Chylee, Chy . . . Chybee! I don't know why you haven't met her, Wam. From her message she seemed like just the sort of person you want for your campaign against the— You know, we need a ruder and catchier nickname for the psychoplanetarists. It might help if we persuaded our students to invent one. Ridicule is a powerful weapon, isn't it?"

By now the girl was stirring, and Wam had no chance to reply. Maw full, she too drew close.

"I think she's hungry," she pronounced. "Fraij—?"

But the maestradomi had already signaled one of her aides, a gang of whom had appeared to clear the bower of what litter the audience had left which the house could not dispose of unaided. It was another point of agreement between those who supported Ugant and those who followed Wam that Aglabec and his sympathizers were disgustingly wasteful . . . to which charge the latter always retorted that what the planet offered it could reabsorb, and in any case the age of psychic escape would dawn long before it was too polluted for life in a physical body to continue. However that might be, some of them had left behind odds and ends of heavy metal and even bonded yellowite, and those could harm the germ-plasm of a house. Had they done it deliberately, or out of laziness? One would wish to believe the latter, but certain rumors now current about their behavior hinted at sabotage. . . .

The girl pried herself loose from the branch, exuding shame from every pore. Fraij gave her a luscious fruit, and she gulped it down greedily; as though it were transfusing energy directly into her tubules—which it should, given that Ugant's home had been designed by some of the finest biologists of modern times—she shifted into a mode of pure embarrassment.

Touched, Ugant settled beside her and uttered words of comfort. And continued as she showed signs of reacting:

"You're not one of Wam's students? No? So why did you come all the way from Hulgrapuk?"

"To hear you! But I had to run away from home to do it."

"Why so?"

"Because my parents are crazy."

"What do you mean by that?"—with a look of alarm aimed at Wam.

"Their names are Whelwet and Yaygomitch. Do you need to know any more?"

On the point of reaching for another clump of funqi, Wam settled back on her branch and uttered a whistle of dismay.

"Even you must have heard of those two, Ugant! Of all the pernicious pith-rotted idiots . . . !"

"But she didn't identify them in her message," Ugant muttered. "Chybee—you are called Chybee, aren't you?"

Excited, she tried to rise, but lacked pressure. "So you did get my note! I was afraid it had been lost! You never answered it, did you?"

Fraij said, "Girl, if you knew how many messages the professor gets every bright—!"

"That will do, Fraij," Ugant interrupted. "Chybee, I promise that if I'd only realized who your family are, I'd . . . Well, I can scarcely say I'd have come running, but I would certainly have told Wam about you."

"But—!" She sank back, at a loss. For the first time it was possible to see how pretty she was, her torso sleek and sturdy, her claws and mandibles as delicate as a flyet's. Her maw still crowded, she went on, "But I always thought you and Professor Wam were enemies! When I heard you were giving a lecture and she had agreed to reply to you, I couldn't really believe it, but I decided I had to be present, because you're both on the other side from my parents. They *are* crazy, aren't they? Please tell me they're crazy! And then explain how you two can be acting like friends right here and now! I mean," she concluded beseechingly, "you don't *smell* like enemies to each other!"

There was a long pause. At last Wam sighed. "How wonderful it is to meet somebody who, for the most naïve of reasons, has arrived at a proper conclusion. I thought the species was extinct. Shall we attempt the real debate we might have had but for your mistake in inviting Aglabec?"

For a moment Ugant seemed on the verge of explosion; then she relaxed and grinned. "I grant I didn't bargain for the presence of his fanatical followers and their trick of trying to shake the audience off the branches. I'm not used to that kind of thing. With respect to your superior experience of it, I'll concur. Who's to speak first?"

All of a sudden the enormous bower became small and intimate. Far above, the roof continued to flutter, though less vigorously because—as Chybee's own weather-sense indicated—rain was on the way, and shortly it might be called on to seal up completely. But, to her amazement and disbelief, here were two globally famous experts in the most crucial of all subjects preparing to rehearse for her alone the arguments she had staked everything to hear.

She wanted to break down, plead to be excused such a burden of knowledge. But was she to waste all the misery she had endured to get here? Pride forbade it. She took another fruit and hoped against hope that it would be enough to sustain her through her unsought ordeal.

Wam was saying, "We don't disagree that it should shortly be possible to launch a vehicle into orbit."

"It could be done in a couple of years," Ugant confirmed, accepting more food from one of Fraij's aides.

"We don't disagree that, given time, we could launch not just *a* vehicle but enough of them to create a self-contained, maneuverable vessel capable of carrying a representative community of the folk with all that's needed to support them for an indefinite period."

"Ah! Now we come to the nub of the problem. Do we have the time you're asking to be given? Already you're talking about committing the entire effort of the planet for at least scores of years, maybe scores-of-scores!" Ugant made a dismissive gesture. "That's why I claim that our optimal course is to use what's within our grasp to launch not interplanetary landing-craft, but containers of specially modified organisms tailored to the conditions we expect to encounter on at least Swiftyouth and Sunbride, and maybe on Steadyman and Stolidchurl, or their satellites, which if all else failed could be carried to their destinations by light-pressure from the sun. If then, later on, we did succeed in launching larger vehicles, we could at least rely on the atmospheres and biospheres of those planets being changed towards our own norm, so—"

"But you can't guarantee that such a second-best project would enlist enough support to—"

"No more can you guarantee that we have as much time as you need for your version! According to the latest reports, there's a real risk of a major meteorite strike within not more than—"

"Stop! Stop!" Chybee shouted, horrified at her temerity but unable to prevent herself. "You don't know what you're talking about, either of you!"

Fraij tried to silence her, but, oddly enough, both Wam and Ugant looked at her with serious attention.

"Let her explain," the former said at length.

Thus challenged, Chybee strove to fill her mantle for a proper answer, but could not. She merely husked, "You keep assuming that everybody else is going to fall in with your ideas, whichever of you wins the argument. It doesn't work that way! The people I've met at my home—my parents themselves—are too crazy to listen! I *know!* Oh, I'm sure it's wonderful to dream of other planets and other civilizations, but I don't believe they exist! Why not? Because of what you and other scientists have taught me! Of course, it's folk like you that my parents call crazy," she appended in an ironical tone. "One thing I am sure of, though, is what I said before. You don't know what you're talking about . . . or at any rate you aren't talking about what most other people are prepared to do!"

There was dead silence for a while. Fraij seemed prepared to pitch Chybee bodily out of the house, and she herself cringed at her audacity. But, at long last, Wam and Ugant curved into identical smiles.

"Out of the mantles of young'uns . . ." Ugant said, invoking a classical quotation. "Wam, I've often felt the same way. Now I have an idea. If she's willing, could we not make good use of someone who has impeccable family connections with a psychoplanetary cult, yet who believes in my views instead of theirs?"

"Whose?"—with a disdainful curl.

"Mine, or yours, or both! You'd rather tolerate my victory than theirs, and I'd rather tolerate yours! Don't argue! For all we know, ours may be the only life-bearing planet in the universe, and it's in danger!"

"I see what you mean," Wam muttered, just as the long-threatened rain began to drum on the roof. "Very well, it's worth a try."

*F*or a good while Chybee paid little or no attention to what was being said. The rushing sound of the rain soothed her as it flowed over the tight-folded leaves of the house and found its way through countless internal and external channels not only to the roots of its bravetrees but also to the elegant little reservoirs disposed here and there to supply its luminants and food-plants . . . and sundry other secondary growths whose purpose she had no inkling of.

Maybe, she thought, if her parents had enjoyed more of this sort of luxury they would not have gone out of their minds. Maybe it was bitterness at the failure of every venture they attempted which had ultimately persuaded them to spurn the real world in favor of vain and empty imaginings. Yet she and her sibs had shared their hardships, and clung nonetheless to the conviction that plans must be made, projects put into effect, to prevent life itself from being wiped out when the sun and its attendant planets entered the vast and threatening Major Cluster.

Then, quite suddenly, normal alertness returned thanks to the food she had eaten, and memory of what Wam and Ugant had proposed came real to her. She could not suppress a faint cry. At once they broke off and glanced at her.

"Of course, if you're unwilling to help . . ." Wam said in a huffy tone.

"But you're drafting a scheme for my life without consulting me!" Chybee countered.

"A very fair comment!" Ugant chuckled. "Forgive us, please. But you must admit that you haven't vouchsafed much about yourself. So far we know your name and your parents', and the fact that you've run away from them. Having got here, have you changed your mind? Are you planning on returning home?"

"I wouldn't dare!"

"Would your parents want it noised abroad that their budling—? One moment: do they have others?"

"Two, older than I am. But they went away long ago. Until very recently I thought of them as having betrayed the family. Now I've done the same myself. And I can't even pity my budder for losing all her offspring. She didn't lose them. She drove them out!"

"So what plans do you have for yourself now?"

"None," Chybee admitted miserably.

"And your parents would *not* want it published that all their young'uns have rejected them and their ideas?"

"I'm sure they'll do their utmost to conceal it!"

"Then it all fits together," Ugant said comfortably. "I can help you, and you can help me. Were you studying at Hulgrapuk?"

"I should have been"—with an angry curl. "But Whelwet wouldn't let me choose the subjects I wanted, archeology and astronomy. She kept saying I must learn something useful, like plant improvement. Of course, what she was really afraid of was that I might find out too much about reality for her to argue against."

Wam moved closer. "I've never met any adult dupes of the psychoplanetary movement, only a clawful of fanatical young'uns. How do you think it's possible for grown-ups to become dreamlost, when famine is a thing of the past?"

Conscious of the flattery implicit in having so distinguished a scientist appeal to her, Chybee mustered all her wits. "Well, many people claim, of course, that it's because some poisons can derange the pith. But I think my parents brought it on themselves. They never let their budlings go hungry; I must say that in their defense. Throughout my childhood, though, they were forever denying themselves a proper diet because of some scheme or other that they wanted to invest in, which was going to be a wild success and enable us to move to a grand house like this one, and then somehow everything went wrong, and . . ." She ended with a shrug of her whole mantle.

"In other words," Wam said soberly, "they were already predisposed to listen when Aglabec started voicing his crazy notions."

"They didn't get them from Aglabec. At least, I don't think they did. Someone called Imblot—"

"She was one of my students!" Ugant exclaimed. "And one of the first to desert me for Aglabec. She—No, I won't bore you with the full story. But I do remember that Aglabec quarreled with her, and she left Slah and . . . Well, presumably she wound up in Hulgrapuk. Wam, have you padded across her?"

"I seem to recognize the name," the latter grunted. "By now, though, there are so many self-styled teachers and dream-leaders competing as to who can spin the most attractive spuder-web of nonsense . . . I guess Whelwet and Yaygomitch have disciples of their own by this time, don't they?"

"Yes!" Chybee clenched her claws. "And it's tubule-bursting to see how decent ordinary people with their whole lives ahead of them are being lured into a dead-end path where they are sure to wind up deliberately starving themselves in search of madder and madder visions! They're renouncing everything—all hope of budding, all chance of a secure existence—because of this dreamlost belief that they can enter into psychic contact with other planets!"

"Would I be right in suggesting," Ugant murmured, "that it was as the result of one particular person falling into this trap that you decided to run away?"

Chybee stared at her in disbelief. At last she said gustily, "I could almost believe that you have psychic powers yourself, Professor. The answer's yes. And I was so shocked by what was happening to him, I just couldn't stand it anymore. So here I am."

"You yourself accept," Ugant mused aloud, almost as though Chybee had not made her last confession, "that the planets are uninhabitable by any form of life as we know it." Raising a claw, she forestalled an interruption from Wam. "Granting that we don't yet know enough about life to say it cannot evolve under any circumstances but our own, at least the chance of other intelligent species existing close at claw is very slim. Correct?"

Wam subsided, and Chybee said uncertainly, "Well, we have discovered that Sunbride must be much too hot, let alone the asteroids that orbit closer to the sun, which are in any case too small to hold an atmosphere. And even Swiftyouth is probably already too cold. Some people think they've detected seasonal changes there, but they might as easily be due to melting icecaps moistening deserts during the summer as to any form of life. And what we know of the larger planets, further out, suggests that they are terribly cold and there are gigantic storms in their immensely deep gas-mantles. Just possibly their satellites might provide a home for life, but the lack of solar radiation makes it so unlikely . . . Oh, Professor! This is absurd! I'm talking as though I were trying to persuade some of my parents' dupes not to commit themselves to dreamness, whereas you know all this much better than I!"

"You have no idea how reassuring it is to find a person like you," Ugant sighed. "If you'd followed formal courses in astronomy, you might just be parroting what your instructors had told you. But you said you haven't. Yet you take the result of our studies seriously. Someone is listening, at least."

"And sometimes I can't help wondering why," muttered Wam. "Dreams of colorful and exotic alien civilizations are obviously more attractive than dull and boring facts. The giant planets which you, like us, believe to be vast balls of chilly gas—are not they among the favorite playgrounds of the psychoplanetarists?"

"Indeed yes!" Chybee shuddered. "They like them particularly because they are so huge. Thus, when two—well—teachers, or dreamleaders, make contrary claims about the nature of their inhabitants, Imblot can reconcile them with one another on the grounds that on such a vast globe there's room for scores, scores-of-scores, of different species and different cultures."

"That may be relatively harmless," Ugant opined. "What frightens me above all is this new yarn that's spreading so rapidly, most likely thanks to a pithstorm on the part of Aglabec himself."

"You mean the idea that our ancestors were on the verge of spaceflight, so alien creatures hurled the Greatest Meteorite at them?" Wam twisted her mantle in pure disgust. "Yes, I'm worried too at the way it's catching on here. Chybee, had you heard of it in Hulgrapuk?"

"It's very popular there," the girl muttered. "Just the sort of notion my parents love to claw hold of!"

"Not only your parents," Ugant said. She turned back to Wam. "I'll tell you what worries me most. I'm starting to suspect that sooner or later projects like yours and mine will be attacked—physically attacked—by people who've completely swallowed this kind of loathsome nonsense and now feel genuinely afraid that if either of us achieves success we can look forward to another hammer-blow from on high."

"But we have to anyway!" Chybee cried.

"Yes indeed!" Wam said. "That's why it's at once so subtle and so dangerous, and also why Ugant proposes to enlist your help. Will you do as she suggests?"

Chybee searched her memory for details of Ugant's plan, and failed to find them. She had been too distracted during the earlier part of the discussion. At length she said, "Perhaps if you could explain a bit more . . . ?"

"It's very simple." Ugant hunched forward. "What we don't understand, what we desperately need to understand, is how to prevent the spread of this—this mental disorder. As you mentioned just now, some folk suspect that modern air-pollution has already rendered a counterattack hopeless. Even our ancestors, according to the few records we've managed to excavate or recover from under the sea, realized that tampering with metals can be dangerous to our sanity—not just radioactive metals, either, like stumpium and sluggium, but any which don't occur naturally in chemically reactive form. If I start using too many technical terms, warn me."

"I understand you fine so far!"

"Oh, I wish there were laqs more like you in Slah, then! But we're trapped by this fundamental paradox: no substance of organic origin can withstand the kind of energy we need to deploy if we're to launch even the most basic vehicle into space. Correct, Wam?"

"I wish I didn't have to agree, but I must," the other scientist grumbled. "Though I won't accept the view that we've been poisoned into insanity. If that's the case, then our opponents can just as well argue that we too have lost our wits. Hmm?"

"Not so long as we benefit from the best available advice concerning our homes and our diet. But few people share our good fortune—Yes, Chybee?"

"I was thinking only a moment ago that if my parents had been as well off as you, then maybe . . ." She broke off in embarrassment, but she had given no offense. Ugant was nodding approval.

"One reason why I feel that trying to go the whole way at once is over-risky! We might harm the very people we're most eager to protect from the consequences of their own folly . . . All right, Wam! I'm not trying to reopen the whole argument! I'm just asking Chybee whether she's willing to act as a spy for us, pretend she's still a dedicated follower of Aglabec and infiltrate the psychoplanetarist movement on our behalf. I won't insist on an immediate answer. Before you return home, I want you to look over my experimental setup. We'll take her along, and leave it to her to judge whether what we're doing justifies our making such a demand."

# 4

In fact, by first bright Chybee had already made up her mind. What alternative lay before her? Even at Hulgrapuk, far smaller than Slah, she had seen too many young people struggling for survival because they had quit the fertile countryside, or life at sea, to seek a more glamorous existence in the urban branchways, ignorant of the fact that in a city every fruit, every funqus, every crotch where one might hope to rest, belonged to somebody else, perhaps with a claim stretching back scores-of-scores of years. Consequently they often fell into the clutches of the psychoplanetarists, who offered them a meager diet (spiked, some claimed, with pith-confusing drugs) in order to recruit yet more worshipful admirers for their fantastic visions. If she could do something to save even a clawful of potential victims—

No: she was too honest to believe the yarn she was spinning herself. There was nothing impersonal or public-spirited about the decision she had reached. It stemmed partly from the fact that she was terrified she might otherwise creep home in a year or two's time, dreamlost from hunger and misery, reduced to just another of what Wam had termed "dupes," and partly from . . . She hesitated to confront her knowledge, but at last she managed it.

She wanted revenge, precisely as Ugant had guessed. She wanted a revenge against all those who had stolen his future from a boy called Isarg.

* * *

Before dawn the rain drifted westward. As soon as the sun broached the horizon, creatures she recognized only by descriptions she had heard appeared to groom and cleanse the occupants of the bower: expensive variants of the cleanlickers used in medicine since ancient times. At first she was reluctant, but they exuded such alluring perfumes that she was soon won over, and readily submitted to their mindless yet enjoyable attentions.

A little later Fraij announced that Ugant's scudder was ready for them, and a storm-pulse afflicted Chybee. On the rare occasions when she had ridden one before, it had been in the wild forest around Hulgrapuk; the idea of traversing Slah in competition with so many dolmusqs, haulimals and—come to that—people, alarmed her.

But Ugant was being unbelievably generous and helpful, and it was such a privilege to be in her and Wam's company. As best she might, she controlled her reaction.

She could not, of course, conceal it entirely; her exudates betrayed her. Ugant, however, was affability itself as the beast swung into the interlocking tree-crowns and headed east, adroitly dodging other traffic without further orders, and her small talk was calmative, at least.

"Is this the first time you've been to Slah? Yes? But perhaps you know the story of how it came about?"

"I'm not sure," Chybee muttered, thinking how many padlongs they were from the ground. Once beyond the city boundary, things might not be so bad; here, though, everything happened so fast!

"As nearly as we can establish, Slah was once a city of the People of the Sea," Ugant expounded in a perfectly relaxed tone. "That may sound ridiculous, given how far it now lies above sea-level, but our researches have confirmed what for countless generations was only a folktale. When the Greatest Meteorite hit, the city Voosla was borne many padlonglaqs from the nearest ocean. Naturally the over-pressure killed its inhabitants.

"But by chance enough salt water was carried up with it to fill that valley you see to our left—yes? All the creatures originally composing the city died off too, but their secondary growths flourished thanks not only to the nutriment offered by the carcasses of the barqs and junqs and whatever that it was assembled from, but also to the availability of the same kind of dissolved salts they had been used to before. By the time the temporary lake drained away or was diluted by rainfall, the plants had adapted themselves and spread to occupy much of the area we're now looking down on. Naturally, when the folk started to recover from the effects of the meteorite, this was one of the places they made for first, to see whether anything useful could be found hereabouts. There must have been several brilliant biologists in the community, because some of the food-plants in particular were unique.

You've probably been enjoying them all your life without realizing they were rediscovered right here."

"The changes weren't just brought about by the plants' new environment," Wam put in. "The radiation flux as the meteorite hit may account for some of them, and sunshine must have been cut off for scores of years by the dust and vapor it threw up. Besides, it's unlikely that there was a single meteorite. The one which moved Slah to its present position was probably the biggest among a full-scale storm. By boiling off part of their mass in the upper air, the others spread metallic poisons clear around the globe. And that could happen again at any time!"

"Ah, we're clearing the edge of the city at last," Ugant exclaimed. "Stop fretting, Chybee! The air will be a lot fresher from here on, space-budded poisons or not!"

And, still apparently convinced that chitchat was all the girl needed to help her relax, she continued pointing out sights of interest as the scudder hurtled onward, no longer having to make do with the random grip afforded by bravetree branches within Slah itself, where the wear and tear of traffic might lead to accidents if a single overloaded vehicle added too great a strain, but racing along a specially planted line of toughtrees that slanted around a range of gentle hills. Below, morning sun gleamed on a stream diverted and partly canalized to make a route for freight-pitchens, mindlessly plodding from loq to loq with their massive burdens. Now and then flashes showed how they were being overtaken by courier-pitchens, but of course most urgent messages were conveyed these days by nervograp or by air. Above, looming as vast and brilliant as the sparse white clouds, passenger-floaters were gathering for a landfall at Slah: some, Chybee knew, must have crossed three oceans since the beginning of their voyage. And how much air had been gulped into their ever-flexing bellowers to drive them over such colossal distances? If mere interference by the folk could bring about such incredible modifications, then . . . !

"Is something wrong?" Ugant said suddenly.

"No—But I mean yes!" she exclaimed. "If plants were changed, and . . . Well, don't they also think that some kinds of animal were exterminated too?"

"It's generally accepted that that's what happened," Ugant confirmed gravely. "Many fossils have been found that scarcely resemble the species we're familiar with."

"So what about ourselves?"

The scudder, relieved at having reached open country, was swinging along with a pulsating rhythm; now and then it had to overtake another vehicle, so the rhythm quickened, and occasionally it had to slow because traffic grew too dense for speed. For a while Wam and Ugant seemed to be absorbed by it. If they were exuding pheromones, the wind of their rapid passage carried them away.

Finally, though, Ugant sighed loudly.

"To quote my colleague and rival: I wish I could disagree, but I can't. We *were* altered by the Greatest Meteorite. We had the most amazing luck, to be candid. Or, putting it another way, our ancestors planned better than they imagined. Would you believe that some of the records we've recovered suggest we were in a fair way to extinction *before* the meteorite?"

"Ugant!"—in a warning tone from Wam. "Galdu hasn't published her findings yet, and they may be adrift."

Chybee was feeling light-pithed by now. Never before had she imagined that her idols, the scientists, could argue as fiercely as any psychoplanetarist maintaining that her, or his, version of life on the moons of Stolidchurl must be more accurate than anybody else's.

She said, "Oh, spin your webs for me! You said I was coming along today to make up my own mind!"

But they both took the remark seriously. Ugant said, "If we can't convince her, who can we hope to convince?"

Wam shrank back, abashed. "You're right. And Galdu's primary evidence, at least, does seem convincing."

"She's a pastudier, remember, working in a field you and I know little about . . . What it comes to, Chybee, is this." Adapting herself to the swaying of the scudder as it rose to pass over the lowest point along the line of hills that up to now they had been paralleling, Ugant drew closer. "None of our biologists can see how we could have escaped dying out ourselves unless some genius of the far past foresaw the need to protect us against just such an event as the fall of the Greatest Meteorite. Almost all the large animals on the planet disappeared because they were—like us—symbiotes. The regular adaptive resource of the 'female' sex among them was to become more male. In the end, naturally, this resulted in a zero bud-rate. But because we'd been somehow altered, the process came to a dead stop in the folk. In you and me, that means."

"Not a complete dead stop," Wam objected. "Another such calamity, and . . . !"

"Now you're arguing for Galdu's most extreme ideas!" crowed Ugant. "A moment ago—Still, that's of no significance right now. What is important is that once again young Chybee here has clawed hold of something most people overlook even when they have access to the evidence. I'm impressed by this girl, you know!"

"Save the compliments," Wam grunted. "Stick to the point she originally set out to make. Yes, Chybee, there was a change in us too, and the only reason we can conceive for it is that some of our ancestors must have arranged it. Compared with that gigantic achievement, what use are our petty undertakings unless they result in the exportation to space of our entire culture?"

"I thought we were going to sink our differences for the time being!" Ugant began.

But Chybee had already burst out, "How? How was it done?"

"We think most of the food-plants we rely on had been modified," came Ugant's sober answer. "We think they had been so far modified that merely by eating them we arrested part of what until then had been our normal evolutionary adaptation. We think—some people think, in deference to Wam's reservations, but I'm an admirer of Galdu—that had it not been for this most important of all inventions, we would have long ago become extinct. If you and I met one of our male ancestors right now, for instance, we couldn't bud together. We'd been used for generations to believing that evolution took place over countless score-score years. Suddenly it turns out that someone, long ago, must have ensured a change in us such that next time a crisis of habitability occurred on this planet—"

"Stop! Stop!" Chybee cried, and a moment later added in an apologetic tone, "You did tell me that if you started to use too many technical terms . . ."

Ugant relaxed with a mantle-wide grin.

"Point well taken," she murmured. "Well, a crisis of habitability is what follows, for instance, a meteorite fall or an ice-age. What, with deference and respect to our forepadders, we are trying to avoid by creating such research projects as the one you can now see yonder."

She gestured with one claw, and Chybee turned her eye as the scudder relaxed into a crotch at journey's end. What met it dismayed and baffled her. Across a broad and level plain flanked by low hills, not familiar plants but objects unlike anything she had encountered before extended nearly to the skyline.

"All this has been created," Ugant said, "because what saved us last time may all too easily not save us twice."

# 5

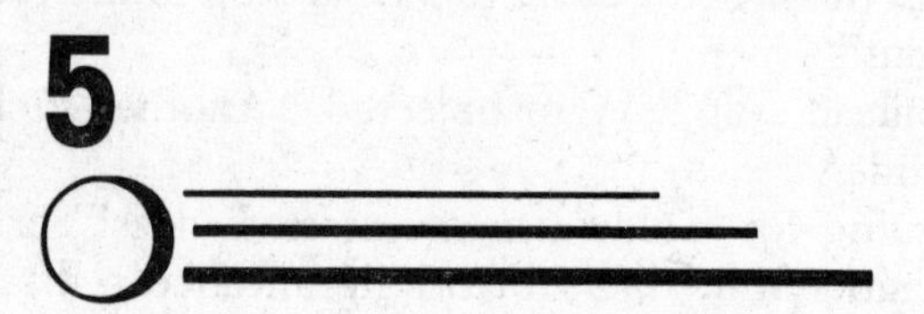

"How much do you know about the dual principles of flight?" Ugant inquired of Chybee as they padded between countless huge and glistening globes, each larger than any unmodified bladder she had ever seen. Because pumplekins were forcing them full of pure wetgas, and there was inevitable leakage—though it was not poisonous—their surroundings were making the girl's weather-sense queasy. Sensing her distress, the professor went on to spell out information most of which in fact she knew.

"The first clues must have come from cloudcrawlers so long ago we have no record of it. Archeological records indicate that we also owe to the study of natural floaters the discovery that air is a mixture of several elements. Of course, it was a long time before the lightest could be separated out by more efficient means than occur in nature. And floaters drift at the mercy of the wind, so it again took a considerable while before we invented bellowers like those over there"—with a jab of one claw towards a bank of tubular creatures slumped in resting posture on a wooden rack. "How did you travel from Hulgrapuk to Slah?"

"I flew," Chybee told her, wide-eyed with wonder.

"So you've seen them in operation, gulping air and tightening so as to compress it to the highest temperature they can endure, and then expelling it rearward. We got to that principle by studying the seeds emitted by certain rock-plants. But of course it's also how we swim, isn't it? And there's even a possibility that our remotest ancestors may have exploited the same technique by squirting air from under their hind mantles. You know we evolved from carnivores that haunted the overgrowth of the primeval forest?"

"My parents don't believe in evolution," Chybee said.

"Ridiculous!" Wam exclaimed. "How can anybody not?"

"According to them, intelligence came into existence everywhere at the same time as the whole universe. On every world but ours, mind-power controls matter directly. That's how Swiftyouth and Sunbride hurled the Greatest Meteorite at us. Our world alone is imperfect. They even try to make out that other planets' satellites don't sparkle or show phases, but are always at the full."

Wam threw up her claws in despair. "Then they *are* insane! Surely even making a model, with a clump of luminants in the middle to represent the sun, would suffice to—"

"Oh, I tried it once!" Chybee interrupted bitterly. "I was punished by being forbidden to set pad outside our home for a whole moonlong!"

"What were you supposed to learn from that?"

"I suppose: not to contradict my budder . . ." Chybee gathered her forces with an effort. "Please go on, Professor Ugant. I'm most interested."

With a doubtful glance at her, as though suspecting sarcasm, Ugant complied.

"What, though, you might well say, does our ability to fly through the air have to do with flying into vacant space? After all, we know that even the largest and lightest floaters we can construct, with the most powerful bellowers we can breed to drive them, can never exceed a certain altitude. So we must resort to something totally new. And there it is."

Again following her gesture, Ugant saw a long straight row of unfamiliar trees, boughs carefully warped so as to create a continuous series of rings from which hung worn but shiny metal plates and scores of nervograp tendrils.

"Ah!" Wam said. "I've seen pictures of that. Isn't it where you test your drivers?"

"Correct. And the storage bladders beyond are the ones we had to devise specially to contain their fuel. What can you show to match them?"

Wam shrugged. "As yet, we've concentrated less on this aspect of the task than on what we regard as all-important: eventual survival of the folk in space."

"But what's the good of solving that problem," Ugant snapped, "if you don't possess a means to send them there?"

"With you working on one half of the job, and me on the other . . ." Wam countered disprongingly, and Ugant had to smile as they moved on towards the curiously distorted trees. Hereabouts there was a stench of burning, not like ordinary fire, but as though something Chybee had never encountered had given off heat worse than focused sunlight. Under the warped trees there was no mosh such as had cushioned their pads since leaving the scudder; indeed, the very texture of the soil changed, becoming hard—becoming *crisp*.

"You're in luck," Ugant said suddenly, gazing along the tree-line to its further end and pointing out a signal made by someone waving a cluster of leaves. "There's a test due very shortly. Come on, and I'll introduce you to Hyge, our technical director."

Excitedly Chybee hastened after her companions. They led her past a house laced about with nervograps, which challenged them in a far harsher tone than Ugant's home, but the professor calmed it with a single word. Some distance beyond, a score of young people were at work under the direction of a tall woman who proved to be Hyge herself, putting finishing touches to a gleaming cylinder in a branch-sprung cradle. It contained more mass of metal than Chybee had ever seen; she touched it timidly to convince herself that it was real.

In a few brief words Ugant summed up the purpose of their visit, and Hyge dipped respectfully to Wam.

"This is an honor, Professor! I've followed your research for years. Ugant and I don't always see eye to eye, but we do share a great admiration for your pioneering experiments in spatial life-support. How are you getting on with your attempt to create a vacuum?"

"Fine!" was Wam's prompt answer. "But unless and until we resolve our other differences, I don't foresee that we shall work together. Suppose you continue with your test? It may impress me so much that . . . Well, you never know."

Smiling, Hyge called her assistants back to the house, while Ugant whispered explanations to Chybee.

"To drive a vehicle those last score padlonglaqs out of the atmosphere, there's only one available technique. If there isn't any air to gulp and squirt out, then you have to take along your own gas. We borrowed the idea from certain sea-creatures which come up to the surface, fill their bladders with air, and then rely on diving to compress it to the point where it's useful. When they let it go, it enables them to pounce on their prey almost as our forebudders must have done."

"I don't like to be reminded that our ancestors ate other animals," Chybee confessed.

"How interesting! I wonder whether that may account for some of the reaction people like your parents display when confronted by the brutal necessity of recycling during a spaceflight . . . But we can discuss that later. Right now you need to understand that what Hyge has set up for testing is a driver full of two of the most reactive chemicals we've ever discovered. When they're mixed, they combust and force out a mass of hot gas. This propels the cylinder forward at enormous speed. Our idea is to lift such a cylinder—with a payload of adapted spores and seeds—to the greatest altitude a floater can achieve. Then, by using the special star-seekers we've developed, we can orient it along the desired flight-path, and from there it will easily reach orbital height and velocity."

"But scaling it up to carry what we'll need for actual survival out there is—" Wam began.

"Out of the question!" Ugant conceded in a triumphant tone. "Now will you agree that our best course is to—?"

Hyge cut in. "Scaling up is just a matter of resources. Save your disputes until after we find out whether our new budling works! Don't look at the jet! Slack down to tornado status! Keep your mandibles and vents wide open! The overpressure from this one will be *fierce!*"

And, after checking that the cylinder's course was clear of obstructions and that all the stations from which reports were to be made were functional, she slid back a plank of stiffbark in the control house's floor and imposed her full weight on something Chybee could not clearly see but which she guessed to be a modified form of mishle, one of the rare secondary growths known as flashplants which, after the passage of a thunderstorm, could kill animal prey by discharging a violent spark, and would then let down tendrils to digest the carcass.

Instantly there was a terrible roaring noise. The cylinder uttered a prong of dazzling flame—"Look that way!" Ugant shouted, and when Chybee proved too fascinated to respond, swung her bodily around and made her gaze along the tree-row—and sped forward on a course that carried it exactly through the center of the wood rings, clearing the metal plates by less than a clawide.

Almost as soon as it had begun, the test was over bar the echoes it evoked from the hills, and a rousing cheer rang out. But it was barely loud enough to overcome the deafness they were all suffering. Chybee, who had not prepared herself for pressure as great as Hyge had warned of, felt as though she had been beaten from crest to pads.

"Oh, I'm glad we were here to witness that," said Ugant softly. "Wam, aren't you impressed?"

"She should be," Hyge put in caustically, checking the recordimals connected to the incoming nervograps. "That's the first time our guidimals have kept the cylinder level through every last one of the rings. And if we can repeat that, we'll have no problem aiming straight up!"

"Are you all right, Chybee?" Ugant demanded as she recovered from her fit of euphoria.

"I—uh . . ." But pretense was useless. "I wasn't ready for such a shock. I was still full of questions. Like: what are the metal plates for?"

"Oh, those," Hyge murmured. "Well, you see, not even the most sensitive of our detectors can respond to signals emitted by the cylinder as it rushes past faster than sound. If you were standing right near the arrival point, you'd be hit by a sonic blast, a wave of air compressed until it's practically solid. Even this far away it can be painful, can't it? So we had to find a method of translating the impact into something our normal instruments can read. What we do is compress metal plates against shielded nervograp inputs, compensating for the natural elasticity of the trees, which we developed from a species known to be highly gale-resistant—"

She broke off. Chybee had slumped against Ugant.

"Does she need help?" Hyge demanded. "I can send an aide to fetch—"

At the same time making it clear by her exudates that this would be an unwarrantable interference with her immediate preoccupations.

"No need to worry," Ugant said softly, comforting the girl with touch after gentle touch of her claws. "She's a bit distraught, that's all. Wam and I are at fault; on the way here we should have explained more clearly what we were going to show her."

"Yes, I'm all right," Chybee whispered, forcing herself back to an upright posture, though lower than normal. "I just decided that all your efforts mustn't go to waste. So I'm willing and eager to do what Ugant wants."

"What's that?" Hyge inquired with a twist of curiosity as her assistants started to arrive with the first of the nonremote readings.

"You'll find out," Ugant promised. "And with luck it may make the future safe for sanity. If it does, of course—well, then, the name of Chybee will be famous!"

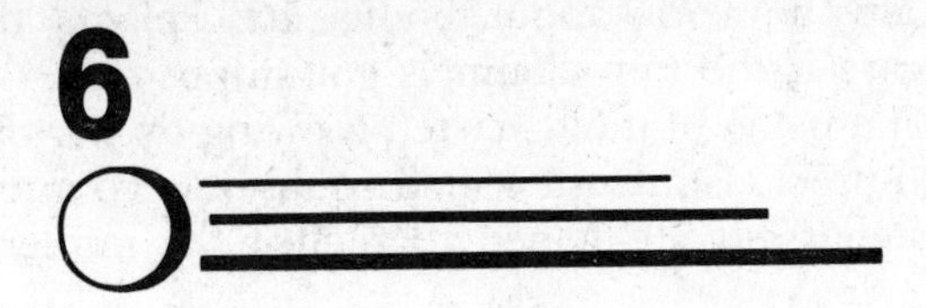

Here, houses and food-plants alike were neglected and ill-doing, surviving as best they could on what garbage was thrown to rot at their roots. Many rain-channels were blocked and nobody had bothered to clear them, allowing precious growths to die off. Even a heavy storm might not suffice to wash away all the stoppages; several were sprouting weeds whose interlocking tendrils would hold against any but the most violent onslaught of water. There were scores of people in sight, most of them young, but with few exceptions they were thin and slack, and their mantles were patched with old or the scars of disease.

Chybee almost cried out in dismay. She had thought things bad enough at Hulgrapuk, but in that far smaller city there was no district which had been so completely taken over by the psychoplanetarists. How could anybody bear to live here, let alone come sight-seeing as that well-fed couple yonder were obviously doing?

She caught a snatch of their conversation. "It's a different lifestyle," the woman was saying. "Simpler, nearer to nature, independent of things like nervograps and scudders and luxury imports. You have to admire the underlying principle."

Preening a little as he noticed Chybee looking at him, the man retorted, "If living the simple life means you have to put up with all sorts of loathsome diseases, I'd rather settle for the modern way."

"Come now, you must admit that it's a devastatingly attractive notion . . ."

Still arguing, they drifted on along the branchways.

But the woman was right. There was something subtly alluring about this run-down quarter of Slah, and the reason for it was all around them. The air was permeated with the pheromones of people experiencing utter certainty. A single breath was enough to convey the message. Here, the aroma indicated, one might find refuge from constant warnings about how any dark or bright might bring just such another meteorite as had carried an ocean-going city far inland to create the foundations of modern Slah. (How deep underpad were those foundations now? Some of the oldest houses' roots were alleged to stretch for padlonglaqs, though of course not directly downward . . .)

And, inevitably, the path to that sense of security lay through hunger. Why should anyone worry about tending food-plants, then? Why should anyone care if the rain-channels got stopped up? Why should anyone object if a patch of mold started growing on her or his mantle? It all liberated precious dreams which could be recounted to innumerably eager listeners. It all helped to reduce the intolerable burden of reality.

Moreover, there was an extra benefit to be gained from moving to this squalid district. It was the lowest-lying part of Slah, sheltered by thickly vegetated hills, and the prevailing wind rarely did more than stir the pool of air it trapped. Little by little, the pheromone density was building up to the point where feedback could set in. Some time soon now its inhabitants might conceivably cease to argue about the content of their visions. No longer would there be endless disputes about the shape and language of the folk in Stumpalong. Gradually the chemical signals they were receiving would unify their mental patterns. And then: mass collective insanity . . .

It had never happened in living memory, but it was theoretically possible. Archeological records indicated that certain now-vanished epidemic diseases had had a similar effect in the far past, possibly accounting for the collapse of once-great cities. All this and more had been explained to Chybee by Ugant and her friends after Wam's return to Hulgrapuk: Glig the biologist, Galdu the pastudier, Airm the city councillor . . . the last, the most pitiable, because she was worn out from trying to persuade her colleagues that the psychoplanetarist quarter represented a real danger to the rest of the citizens.

What a topsy-turvy universe Chybee's prong-of-the-moment decision had brought her into, where she could pity a major public figure in the world's greatest metropolis! Yet how could she not react so when she listened to what Airm had to complain about?

"They always think it's other people's budlings who wind up in that slum!" she had explained over and over. "Well, I grant that's been the case up till now. Young'uns from prosperous and comfortable homes are relatively immune. What are they going to do, though, if this threatened mass hysteria actually sets in? The likeliest effect will be to make all the victims decide they have to drive the rest of us around to their way of thinking, correct? And how could they achieve that goal? By spoiling other people's food! By cutting off nutrients and water from their homes, by fouling cargoes at the docks, even by spreading drugs which suppress normal appetite! Worse yet, they could poison our haulimals, and how could we feed everybody without them? If Slah attempted to support its citizens off its internal resources, we'd all be dreamlost within a moonlong! What are we going to *do?*"

Hearing that, the full magnitude of what she was committed to came home to Chybee. A few brights ago, all she had thought of was escape from her crazy parents. Now, because of who her parents were, she was embarquing on a course that might mean the difference between collapse and survival for the planet's most populous city. She could scarcely credit how completely, as a result of Ugant's unpremeditated suggestion, people were coming to rely on her.

Was she equal to the task? She greatly feared she was not; nothing had prepared her for such immense responsibility. True, she had chided her budder again and again for continuing to treat her like a budling when she believed she was grown-up enough to think for herself. What a world of difference there was, though, between the ambition and the reality!

But the reality was the buried ruin of Voosla, deep beneath the branchways scudders swarmed along. The reality was the corpses of its inhabitants that had rotted to fertilize evolving plants. The reality was that modern Slah could be overrun by scores-of-scores of madfolk. The reality was that unless Ugant and Hyge and Wam saw their efforts crested with success life itself might be abolished by the mindless workings of celestial chance.

She had not so far found words to explain what had overcome her while watching Hyge's driver being demonstrated. In her most secret pith, though, she had already started to compare it with what her parents, and their psychoplanetarist friends, called "stardazzle"—a moment of total conviction after which one could never be the same.

At its simplest, she had abruptly decided that so much effort and ingenuity, dedicated to so worthwhile a goal, must not be allowed to go to waste because of a bunch of dreamlost fools.

Hidden under her mantle was a bunch of leaves which, so Glig had assured her, would protect her against the insidious effect of the local pheromones. She slipped one into her mandibles as she reviewed her immediate task. They wanted her to ingratiate herself with the psychoplanetarists; she was to establish what food they ate and what if any drugs they used, and bring away samples not just of those but, if possible, mantle-scrapings or other cells from their very bodies.

Ugant had been blunt. She had said, "If necessary accept a bud from one of them! Embryonic cells are among the most sensitive of all. Glig can rid you of it later without even a scar, if that worries you"—glancing down at the two bud-marks on her own torso. "But that would help us beyond measure in determining how close we are to disaster."

Chybee hoped against hope it wouldn't come to that . . .

Well, she had stood here gazing about long enough. Now she must act. Presumably she ought to start by getting into conversation with somebody. But who? Most of those nearby were clearly lost in worlds of their own. Over there, for example: a girl about her own age, very slowly stripping the twigs off a dying branch and putting them one by one into her mandibles. She looked as though, once having settled to her task, she might never rise again.

And to her left: a boy trying to twist his eye around far enough to inspect his mantle which, as Chybee could see—but he couldn't—was patched with slimy green and must be hurting dreadfully.

She knew, though, what kind of answer she would get were she to offer help. She had seen similar cases at home. Her parents even admired young'uns like that, claiming that they were making progress along the path that led to mind being freed from matter, so that it could exert total power instead of merely moving a perishable carcass. She had often angered them by asking why, if that were so, they themselves didn't go out and rub up against the foulest and most disease-blotched folk they could find.

She tried not to remember that by now Isarg might all too easily have wound up in a similar plight.

So she left the boy to his endless futile attempts to view his own back, and moved along the branchway. The pheromones grew stronger with every padlong.

Abruptly she grew aware that people were staring at her. It wasn't surprising. At Ugant's she had enjoyed the best diet of her life, and she was tall and plump—too much so, in fact, to suit the role she was supposed to adopt. Who could believe she was a dedicated psycho-planetarist when she was in this condition?

She clung desperately to her recollection of how well favored Aglabec had appeared at Ugant's house. More than once, thinking back over his appearance, she had wondered whether he was sharing his followers' privations. If not, did that imply that he was crazy for some other reason? Was he spreading his lies for personal power and gain? If only one of the scientists she had met at Ugant's had broached the subject . . . But none had, and she was too timid to suggest the idea herself.

Suddenly she wanted to flee. It was too late. Three young'uns—two girls and a boy—detached themselves from the group who had been looking at her with vast curiosity and approached in such a way as to cut off her retreat. She summoned all her self-control.

"Hello! My name's Chybee and I'm from Hulgrapuk. Maybe you heard tell of my parents Whelwet and Yaygomitch? They sent me here to dig into a report they picked up off the wind, about how it was the folk of Swiftyouth and Sunbride that threw the Greatest Meteorite at us. I can trade information about life on Sluggard's moons for fuller details."

She curled her mantle into an ingratiating posture and waited for their response.

It came in the form of excitement. One of the girls said, "I didn't know Sluggard had any moons!"

"Sure it does!" the boy countered. "Much too small to see, but there they are! Five, right?"—to Chybee.

Ugant and her friends had briefed Chybee carefully. "Only four. What they thought was a fifth turned out to be last year's red comet on its way to us."

"I made contact with the folk on that comet!" the other girl declared.

*How can anyone be so crazy as to believe that comets are inhabited?* But Chybee kept such thoughts to herself as far as her exudants allowed; at least the all-pervading pheromones masked most of them.

"Well, if your budder is Whelwet," the first girl said, "I know who'll want to talk to you. Come with us. We're on our way to a meet with Aglabec himself!"

*Oh, NO!*

But there was no gainsaying them; they fell in on either side like an escort and swept her along.

# 7

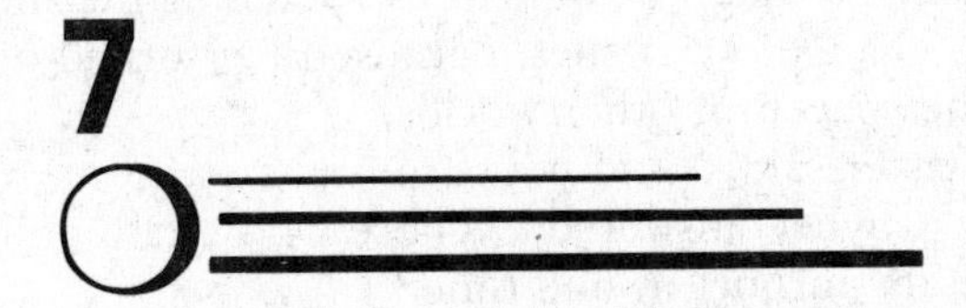

At least the leaves Glig had provided were working. Chybee had no idea what they were, but the scientists of Slah had many secrets. Not only did they protect against the terrifying pheromones surrounding her; they seemed also to mask her own exudations. And that too was terrifying, in a way. It was a popular pastime for younglings at Hulgrapuk and elsewhere to reenact stories from the legendary past, but only the very young could so far submerge themselves in a false identity as to make each other and their audience believe in the rôles they were playing. As soon as they started to secrete adult odors, the illusion waned.

But suppose adults too could fake such a transformation. Suppose, for instance, Aglabec had figured out a way . . . ?

She wanted not to think about him, for fear of betraying her imposture, but her companions kept chattering on with mad enthusiasm, saying how he must be the greatest male teacher since Awb. Privately, Chybee did not believe Awb had ever existed. She had often been punished by her parents for saying so. If she were to voice a similar opinion right now, though, she could surely look forward to something worse than the penalties meted out to a budling. What if Aglabec were to recognize her from the meeting at Ugant's? She could only reassure herself that there had been too many people present for anybody to single out one person's trace, and try and believe that he would have refused on principle to register what she said.

Struggling to divert the conversation along another path, she demanded what the trio's names were. The replies added to her dismay.

"I'm Witnessunbride," stated the first girl.

"And I, Cometaster!" declared the other.

While the boy said, as though it were the most natural thing in the world, "Startoucher!" He added with curiosity, "Do Chybee and Whelwet and Yaygomitch have arcane meanings? At Slah we discard our old names after entering the knowledge state."

But before Chybee could reply, Witnessunbride rounded on him. "And your new one is ridiculous! I could cite five-score of us who know more about what goes on under other stars than you do! Don't take him seriously, Chybee! But how and why did you choose your new name?"

Chybee was briefly at a loss. Then inspiration struck. She said with contempt she did not need to feign, "Some of us, including me and my parents, felt no call to change our names, because they turned out to have significance in the speech of other worlds."

Impressed, Cometaster said, "And yours means . . . ?"

With stiff dignity, Chybee answered, "Those who attain enlightenment will recognize its purport in due time."

The other three exchanged glances.

"Aglabec is going to be very interested in you," said Witnessunbride. "He's the only other person I ever heard say anything like that. *And* the only other person so advanced he can contact other planets without needing to fast. That is, assuming you got your knowledge about Sluggard direct. Did you? Or were you just told it by your budder or someone?"

Chybee was so taken aback by the audacity of Aglabec's excuse for being in better fettle than his disciples, she could not think of a suitable answer. Luckily they mistook her silence for wounded pride.

"Hurry up!" Startoucher said. "It's nearly sunset!"

And, hastening towards the fringe of this decrepit quarter, he explained how it was that he and his friends were going to meet Aglabec in person.

"Every full moon, unless he's traveling to spread his knowledge, he returns to us, going from home to home to visit his oldest and most loyal followers. Sometimes, when he's due to leave for a long trip, sick people choose to liberate their minds in his presence, for fear of never seeing him again. Isn't that marvelous?"

To liberate—? Oh. Chybee hoped against hope that Glig's leaves would mask the signs of her nausea. Hastily she said, "How did you earn your name?"

"Witnessunbride is jealous of it," Startoucher said with a pout of his mantle. "But I'm fully entitled! Aglabec told me so—he said there are going to be a lot more cases like mine, people who start getting knowledge from other stars instead of just our local planets. Well, I mean I must have done! None of what I see and hear matches with what other people get from Sunbride, or Swiftyouth, or Stolidchurl, or *anywhere!* Unless, of course—"

He broke off, while Chybee wondered how anyone could be deluded by so transparently silly an explanation. But it was politic to seem interested. She said, "Unless what?"

"I was going to say: unless it comes from somewhere like the moons of Sluggard. But if that were so, then Aglabec would have told me, wouldn't he?"

Much relieved, he hurried on in advance of the group, announcing that they were almost at their destination and it looked as though Aglabec must already have arrived, since nobody was outside watching out for him.

Oh, why could these people not have been on their way to a meeting where she could melt into the crowd? Inside a house, how could she disguise her true detestation of Aglabec? How could she keep up the pretense that she and her parents were still on good terms?

She would simply have to try.

The house was a little better cared for than most in the area. In its main bower Aglabec rested in a curved crotch, surrounded by fervent admirers. He acknowledged the late arrivals with a courteous dip; if his gaze rested longer on Chybee than the others, that could be ascribed to her being a stranger and much better nourished than the rest . . . except himself.

"As I was about to say before you came in," he stated in resonant tones, "it always does my pith good to learn how many more people are coming around to the view that we must not and *dare* not allow scientists to persist in their crazy attempts to launch artificial moons and even space-going cities. They are, of course, impervious to reason; it's futile to warn them that they risk forcing our planetary neighbors to act against us in self-defense. I know! I've tried, and I haven't yet given up, but it's a weary task . . . Scientists they call themselves!"—with vast contempt. "Yet they don't appear to realize how dangerous it would be to convey life from one planet to another. Some of them are actually plotting to do precisely that: to export bacteria and other organisms to Swiftyouth and Sunbride, to *infect* them, to *contaminate* them! How would they like it if the prong were in the other claw? Luckily for us, all the planetfolk we've contacted so far seem to be cognizant of the risks. They would never dream of doing such a thing, would they?"

Able to relax a little now that it was plain that Aglabec did not after all remember her, Chybee joined in the murmur of agreement which greeted his declaration. Witnessunbride, to her surprise, did not, and Aglabec inquired why.

"You did once say," the girl ventured, "that next time we try to fly into space we can look forward to being stopped not by another gigantic meteorite but perhaps something subtler, like a plague."

"Ah, I'm glad that registered. My compliments on your excellent recollection. Yes, I did say that. Moreover a number of our comrades have reinforced me, have they not? There is, however, a great moral difference between seeding organisms into space merely to conduct a blind and futile experiment, and doing so with infinite reluctance in order to prevent invasion from another world. What point is there, anyhow, in traveling through space? It would be absurdly dangerous; it would be terribly slow, and living in such confinement—even assuming we can survive in the absence of gravity, which has not been proved—would be a strain on anybody's sanity. What purpose would it serve to deliver a briqload of lunatics to another world? In any case, those of us who have discovered how to make mental voyages have chosen the path that avoids all such perils. If not instantaneously, then at speeds which exceed that of light itself, we can find ourselves on virtually any planet, any moon, we choose, to be greeted by the inhabitants as honored guests, because we understand and accept the reasons why we must not make a physical journey. If the discipline we have to endure in order to achieve our goal is harsh, so be it. Once we have been stardazzled, the need for it dies away, and we can enjoy the best not of 'both' worlds but of as many as we like! I emphasize that because I notice among us a stranger who seems unwilling to enter upon the pathway of privation."

All eyes turned on Chybee, who mustered maximum self-control. She was saved from immediate speech, though, by Startoucher.

"She's already been 'dazzled! She can tell us about life on Sluggard's moons! I never met anyone who's been in contact with those folk before—except you, of course," he added deferentially. "And she came all the way from Hulgrapuk specially to find out about how it was Sunbride and Swiftyouth that hurled the Greatest Meteorite at us."

"Hulgrapuk," Aglabec repeated, his voice and attitude abruptly chill. "Now, that is a city I have little truck with. To my vast regret, the traitor Imblot, whom some of you may remember, who rebelled against me on the grounds that I was a 'mere male,' has established a certain following there. It would not in the least surprise me if by now she had persuaded a clawful of ignorant dupes that there is no need to fast, or cultivate the welcome assistance of a moldy mantle, in order to attain the knowledge state. But, as you know very well, it is granted only to a dedicated few to learn that mind is all and matter is nothing. It is dependence on the material world which blinds us to this central truth. Our luxury homes, our modern transport and communications, our telescopes and our recordimals and everything we prize in the ordinary way—those are the very obstacles that stand between us and enlightenment. If they did not, why, then there would be enough mental force in this very bower to put a stop to what the so-called scientists are doing!"

He hunched forward. "Who are you, girl? By what right do you claim to have been stardazzled?"

Terrified, Chybee could do nothing but concentrate on masking her reactions. With a puzzled glance at her, Cometaster said, "Her name is Chybee and her parents are Whelwet and Yaygomitch. At least that's what she told us."

"You're a long way from enlightenment, then, you three, despite having dared to take new names!" Aglabec quit the crotch he had been resting in and erupted to full height. "I hereby decree you shall renounce them! Revert to what you were called before! It will be a fit punishment for your indescribable stupidity!"

Cringing in dismay, the trio huddled together as though their dream-leader's wrath were a physical storm.

"But—but what have we done that's so bad?" whimpered Startoucher-that-was.

"You brought among us, right here into *my* presence, a follower and a budling of followers of Imblot! You took her story at mantle value, didn't you? You forgot that I have many enemies, who will stop at nothing to ruin my work!" Aglabec checked suddenly, leaning towards the petrified Chybee.

"I thought so," he said at last. "I've seen you before, haven't I? You were at Ugant's, at the pointless so-called debate she organized. Very well! Since you've chosen to come here, we shall find out why before we let you go. It may take some time, but we'll pry the truth out of you whether you like it or not!"

# 8

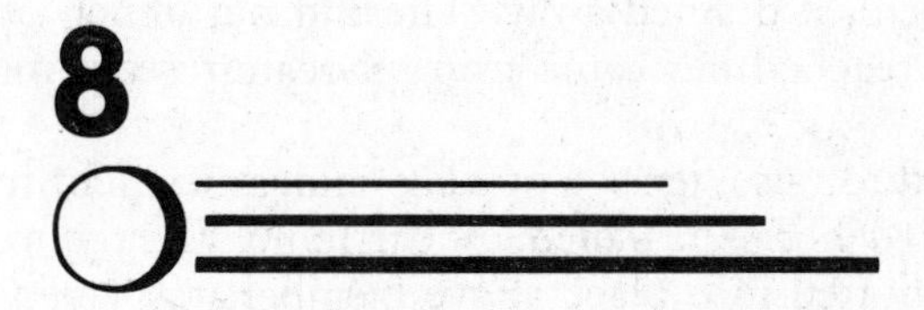

**B**eing in so much better health, Chybee might have fought free of any two, or even three, of Aglabec's adorers. But, as he himself watched with a cynical air, everyone else in the bower either seized hold of her or moved to block the only way of escape. A tight grasp muffled her intended cry for help . . . though, in this quarter of Slah, who would have paid attention, let alone come to her rescue?

Half-stifled, wholly terrified, she felt herself being enclosed in some kind of lightproof bag that shut the world away. Still she resisted, but within moments she discovered that it was also airtight, and she must breathe her own exudations. Just enough power of reason remained to warn her that if she went on struggling she would lose consciousness at once, and the sole service she could do herself was to try and work out what her captors intended. She let her body go limp, hoarding the sourgas in her tubules.

"What shall we do with her?" demanded a voice much like ex-Startoucher's; perhaps it was his, and he was eager to curry new favor with his dream-leader.

"There's a place I know," replied Aglabec curtly. "Just follow me."

And Chybee was hoisted up unkindly by three or four bearers and carried bodily away.

If only odors as well as sounds could have penetrated the bag! Then she might have stood some chance of working out where she was being taken. As it was, she had to rely on fragmentary clues: there, the moan of an overloaded draftimal; there, the chant of someone selling rhygote spice; there again, the boastful chatter of a gang of young'uns . . .

But so much might have identified any part of any large city, and the strain of concentration was too great. Despairing, at the last possible moment she surrendered her grip on awareness, wondering whether she would die.

"Water!" someone shouted, and doused her with it. She opened her maw, but not soon enough. By the time she had registered that she was still alive, reflex had dropped her to the floor, gasping for any drop that might remain. But she lay on an irregular mesh of tree-roots with wide gaps between them; it drained away. There was a stench of ancient rot. What light reached her came from phosphorescent molds, not decent luminants.

Moaning, she tried to raise her eye quickly enough to identify the person who had soaked her. She failed. A barrier of tightly woven branches was being knotted into place above her. A harsh laugh was followed by slithering as her tormentor departed.

But at least she wasn't dead.

Summoning all her remaining energy, Chybee felt for any spongy-soft areas that might have absorbed a little of the water. She found two or three, and though the taint nauseated her, she contrived to squeeze out enough to relieve the dryness of her maw.

By degrees she recovered enough to take stock of her predicament. The roots she was trapped among were so tough there was no hope of clawing or gnawing through them. The sole opening was blocked. Her weather-sense informed her that she was far below the bower where she had encountered Aglabec. There was one and only one explanation which fitted. He had ordered her brought to the deep foundations of Slah, where nobody had lived for scores-of-scores of years. Above her there must be layer upon layer of dead and living houses, totaling such a mass that it amazed her to find this gap had survived without collapsing.

With bitter amusement she realized how fitting his choice had been. Did he not wish to lure everyone into the pit of the dead past, instead of letting the folk expand towards the future?

And those he could not dupe, he would imprison . . .

Was she close to the outcrop of rock which must account for the existence of this tiny open volume, little wider than she herself was long? She hunted about her for a probe—a twig, anything—and met only slimy decay and tough unbreakable stems.

At that point she realized she was wasting energy. What she needed more than all else was something to eat. Because otherwise . . .

Oh, it was clear as sunlight. They were going to starve her. When she was as dreamlost as Isarg, they would lay siege to her mind with fawning talk. In the end she would accept passively whatever Aglabec chose to say, until she betrayed Ugant and Hyge and Wam, until—

No! It must not happen! Feverishly she scoured her prison, tasting the foulest patches of rot in the hope that some trace of nourishment might inhere in them . . . and at last slumped into the least uncomfortable corner, having found not a whit of anything less than utterly disgusting. Somehow she had lost even Glig's protective leaves. She could only hope they hadn't been noticed and identified.

Well, if all else failed, she could gulp down some poisonous mess and cheat Aglabec that way. But she was determined not to let him overcome her hatred of him and all he stood for. She would fight back as long as she could.

And surely, long before she was driven to such straits, Ugant would have started to worry and sent out searchers!

Compacting her body to conserve warmth, for there was a dank chill draught here, redolent of loathsome decay, she set about giving herself instructions for resistance, even though already a hint of anger colored her thoughts when she remembered Ugant so prosperous in her fine home, so ready to enlist a stranger in her cause . . .

The only way she had to measure time was by the changing air-pressure of successive dawns and sunsets, for as it turned out the person who had been assigned to pour water over her—the absolute minimum needed to keep her alive—was also instructed to do so at random intervals. Sometimes the chilly shower occurred four times in a single day; then a whole one might pass without it, and she was almost reduced to begging as she watched, in the wan glow of the molds, how her mantle was shrinking from thirst. Enough of her pride remained thus far to protect her against that humiliation. But she could discern how hunger was taking its toll. At first she had kept careful count of darks and brights; then after a while she was alarmed to realize she no longer knew precisely how long she had been shut up. Her trust in Ugant gave way first to doubt, then to sullen resentment. The pangs of anger multiplied, until it came to seem that the scientist, not Aglabec, was her true captor, because as yet she had not succeeded in locating this secret prison.

Then voices began to whisper to her.

At first she was aware that what she heard formed part of Aglabec's plot. Out of sight behind the mesh of roots must be two or three of his disciples, under orders to confuse her by telling fantastic tales about life in Swiftyouth and Sunbride, Steadyman and Stolidchurl and Sluggard and their multiple moons unknown before the telescope. She called to them, demanding food, and they refused to answer, but kept on with their whispering.

For a while she argued, reciting what astronomers had worked out from the planets' spectra concerning conditions there, inquiring why anyone should believe Aglabec rather than Ugant and her colleagues. At last, when she was so weak she could scarcely raise herself to half normal height, she received an answer.

Someone said, and it could have been Startoucher: "You and all those like you want to deny life. But we affirm it. We share the fiery joy of existence near the sun. We enjoy the frozen beauty of the giant worlds. We know what it means to be weighed down by gravity a score-score-fold, and not to care, because we borrow bodies suited to it. From searing heat to bitter cold, we transcend the dull plain world of every day, and eventually we shall perceive the universe. When our task is done, no one will care if this petty planet is destroyed."

"The destiny of bodies is to rot," said another voice. "The destiny of mind is glorious!"

"I'm losing mine!" whimpered Chybee against her will. The confession was greeted with a chuckle, then with silence.

But it didn't last. After she had made one last futile search for something she might eat, new whispering began. This time she could not convince herself there was anybody talking to her. There was only one voice, and it was inside her very pith, and it was her own, so how could she deny what it said? It told her that life must exist everywhere, in an infinite range of guises, and that only a fool could imagine that this was its sole and unique haven. It told her she was guilty of despair, when she needed only to look within her and seek the truth. It echoed and repeated what her parents told their followers, what they had learned from Imblot . . . but she was a traitor, wasn't she? She'd dismissed Aglabec as a "mere male" although Aglabec was powerful, *all*-powerful, exercised the right of life and death over this person Chybee . . .

Occasionally she stirred as though touched by a sharp prong. Then the suspicion did cross her mind that some of her thoughts were being imposed from outside. But she lacked the energy to claw hold of the idea. Likewise, she sometimes experienced the shock of realizing that she was beginning to digest her own tissue, and that her mantle was patched with molds like those afflicting her cage of roots, as though the tiny organisms had decided she too was fit to putrefy. But she shut such notions out of thinking, obsessed with yearning for the beautiful visions of life on other worlds which she had been promised. Where were they? Why could she only perceive this horrible, this revolting dungeon?

Because . . . Ah, but bliss, but miracle! Something sweet and delicious had been poured into her mandibles, restoring her strength. She strove to thank whoever had aided her at last, and could only whimper, but at least the sound was recognizable.

"Ugant . . . ?"

"Ah, so it was Ugant who reduced you to this plight!"

A booming voice, a waft of pheromones redolent of well-being and authority. Timidly she agreed.

"She sent you to spy on us, was that it?"

"Yes, yes! More food, more food!"

"Of course you shall have more! I'm appalled to find you in such a state because of what Ugant did! Help her out, quickly!"

Suddenly she was surrounded by familiar figures: Aglabec, ex-Cometaster, ex-Startoucher. She curled her limp mantle into a sketch for gratitude as they half led, half carried her upward, pausing now and then to offer more of the delicious liquor which had so revived her.

At last they reached the open air, under a clear sky sown with stars. Weakly she raised a claw to indicate Stumpalong.

"I see the folk up yonder!" she declared. She did not, but she knew it was what her saviors expected.

There was a puff of excitement from the young people. Aglabec canceled it with a quick gesture.

"You believe at last?" he challenged Chybee.

"How could I not, after all the visions that have come to me?"

"Are you obliged to Ugant for them?"—in a stern commanding tone.

"Ugant? What I've been through, all my suffering, was due to her! You saved me, though! You saved me!"

"Then," said Aglabec with enormous satisfaction, "you must tell us what Ugant is planning, and all the ways in which we can forestall her frightful plot."

But Aglabec did not begin his interrogation at once, as though afraid that Chybee's obedience might still be colored by excessive eagerness to please. He had her taken to the home of one of his followers, a certain Olgo. It was neither large nor well kept, but in comparison with the place where she had been incarcerated it was paradise. There she babbled of indebtedness while her sore mantle was tended and food and drink were meted out to her, enough to restore part of her lost bulk, but far from all.

This, though, was only half the treatment he had decided on. Much more important was the fact that by dark and by bright other of his disciples came to visit, and greeted her as one saved for the cause of truth, and sat by her telling wondrous stories about their mental voyages to the planets. Dimly she remembered there was a reason not to believe such yarns, but she was afraid to claw hold of it; she knew, though nobody had said so, that if she expressed the slightest doubt she would be returned to captivity.

Besides, the pheromones inciting to credulity were denser than ever, not only within the house but throughout the psychoplanetarist quarter. Docile under the impact of them, she listened passively as she heard about the vigorous inhabitants of Sunbride, reveling in the brilliance of the solar glare, absorbing and transmuting it until by willpower alone they could sculpture mountain ranges to amuse themselves . . . or hurl a giant rock on any reckless race that tried to bridge the spatial void.

Others told her of the ancient culture on Swiftyouth, so far advanced that bodies were scarcely necessary to them anymore. There, she learned, budding and death had long been obsolete; perfected minds could don and doff a physical envelope at whim.

Yet more marvels were recounted to her, concerning the giant planets each of which was itself a conscious being, the end-product of craws of years of evolution, so perfectly and so precariously adapted that a single seed from any other world might destroy them, and thus waste the fruit of an age-long study of the universe. (Dimly Chybee realized that this contradicted what she had been told at Hulgrapuk, but that of course was due to Imblot's heresy.) To such colossal beings even the inhabitants of their own moons were dangerous; therefore the latter had been taught, by channels of mental communication, to rest content with their own little spheres. Awed, yet determined to fulfill their several destinies, they had set about contacting intelligences more like themselves, using techniques the giant worlds had pioneered, with success in every case bar one: this world whose moon was dead.

"Our world!" Chybee whispered, and they praised her for her flawless understanding.

"Perhaps, in the very long ago," someone said, "our moon too was an abode of life. But arrogant fools down here must have sent a vessel thither. What else can account for it being barren, when none other of the solar family is so except the asteroids, which orbit too close to the sun?"

"Not even they, in one sense," someone else objected. "We know of life existing in hot gas-glouds, don't we? I think some of them make use of the asteroids, for purposes we dare not dream of!"

All the listeners murmured, "Very likely!"

And one of them added with a sigh, "What miracles must be taking place in the Major Cluster! What would I not give to eavesdrop on the feelings of a new-budded star!"

"Oh, yes!" whispered Chybee. "Oh, *yes!*"

They turned to her, their exudations sympathetic and inviting. Thus encouraged, she went on, "And to think that what Ugant and Hyge are planning could despoil it all!"

"Would you not work with us to stop them?" demanded her hostess, Olgo.

"Of course! I want to! It's my duty!"

A wave of satisfaction-odor rose from the company, and one who was near the entrance slipped away, shortly to return with Aglabec in high excitement.

"At last!" he said as he accepted the place of honor at the center of the bower. "I've been making inquiries about the situation at Hulgrapuk. It seems that the traitor Imblot has ensnared many folk there who should be wiser than a youngling like yourself. Yet you came hither, did you not, in search of truth?"

"I did!" Chybee confirmed excitedly.

"Well, you were guided to where I was, even though you failed to understand the reason. Now you've been shown the error of your ways, are you resolved to make amends?"

"With all my pith! I never dreamed what harm would stem from what Ugant and Hyge are doing!"

"And what exactly does that amount to?"

So she described what she had seen at the test site—the metal tube with its prong of fire, the huge floaters designed to lift it to the limits of the atmosphere, the instruments which reported on its behavior even when it was traveling faster than sound. At each new revelation the company uttered fresh gusts of horror, until by the end Chybee was dreadfully ashamed of her own words.

"You said they're close to success?" Aglabec demanded at last.

"Very close indeed!"

"That breeds with what I've been hearing recently." The dream-leader pleated his mantle into a frown. "We must move against them before it's too late. Chybee, have you been in contact with Ugant or any of her associates since—well, since our meeting before last?"

There was a reason for his awkward turn of phrase; she was aware of the fact, but the reason itself eluded her. She uttered a vehement denial, and Olgo confirmed that at no time had she been away from the supervision of someone utterly trustworthy.

"Very well, then," Aglabec decided. "We must rely on you for a delicate mission. Presumably Ugant will be expecting you to make a report. You are to go back to the test site, but this time on our behalf, to lull the suspicions of those who work there. To make assurance doubly sure, I'll send you with a companion, supposedly someone you've converted to the scientists' views. Creez, I offer you a chance to redeem yourself!"

And Creez was he who had braggartly been known as Startoucher . . . and who voiced a question Chybee meant to.

"But how can we possibly conceal our true opinions?"

"I will give you a—a medicine," Aglabec said after a fractional hesitation. "It will suffice for a short time."

That too should have been significant, Chybee thought. Once again, though, the notion was elusive.

"Now pass the news," said Aglabec, rising. "At dawn tomorrow we shall strike a blow against the scientists such as it will take them a laq of years to recover from! By then, I trust, no one will any longer pay attention to their foolishness! You, Creez and Chybee, come with me, and receive your full instructions."

All the next dark the word spread among the psychoplanetarists, and the pool of pheromones in their quarter of Slah became tinged with violent excitement. Around dawn they started to emerge from their homes and move towards the test site, not in a concerted mass but in small groups, so as not to alert the authorities. The morning breeze today was very light, and few outsiders caught wind of what was happening.

Aglabec was not with them. He had declared that he was too well known and too easily recognizable.

Chybee and Creez, fortified with the "medicine" which disguised pheromones, went in advance of the others. They were to announce an urgent report for Ugant or Hyge, which would require everyone working at the site to be called together. For so long the psychoplanetarists had merely talked instead of acting, Aglabec was convinced this simple stratagem would suffice to postpone any warning of the actual attack. And the nature of the latter was the plainest possible. The huge bladders being filled to raise the rocket contained fiercely inflammable gas; let but one firebrand fall among them, and the site would be a desert.

"Though of course," Aglabec had declared, "we only want them to yield to our threats, and—like you, Chybee—acknowledge that the popular will is against them."

With a nervous chuckle Creez had said, "I'm glad of that!"

And now he and Chybee were cresting the range of hills separating the city from the site, formerly a bank of the salt lake where Voosla had taken root. On the way she had repeatedly described for him what he must expect to see. But the moment she had a clear view from the top of the rise she stopped dead, trembling.

"What's wrong?" Creez demanded.

"It's changed," she quavered, looking hither and yon in search of something familiar. Where was the row of distorted trees along which Hyge's pride and joy had become a shining streak to the accompaniment of sudden thunder? Where was the monstrous cylinder itself, built of such a deal of costly metal, with its clever means of guidance warranted to thrive in outer space? Where was the control-house, which surely should have been visible from here?

Nothing of what she remembered was to be seen, save a mass of gigantic bladders swelling like live things in the day's new warmth, rising at the midpoint of the valley into a slowly writhing column tethered by ropes and nets.

"It looks as though they're actually going to try a shot into space!" Chybee whispered, striving to concentrate on her errand. The clean morning air was stirring buried memories, and they were discomforting.

"Then we have to hurry!"

"Yes—yes, of course! But where is everybody?"

"We must go and look," Creez declared, and urged her down the slope.

A moment later they were in the weirdest environment she had ever imagined, under a roof of colossal swollen globes that looked massive enough to crush them, yet swayed at every slightest touch of the breeze, straining at their leashes and lending the light an eerie, fearful quality, now brighter, now darker, according to the way it was reflected from each bladder to its neighbor.

"It's like being underwater!" Creez muttered.

"My weather-sense disagrees," Chybee answered curtly, fighting to maintain her self-control. "Listen! Don't I sense somebody?"

"Over there! Something's agitating the bladders!"

And, moments later, they came upon a work-team wielding nets and choppers, harvesting more and ever more full bladders to be added to the soaring column. One of them had incautiously collected so many, she risked being hoisted off her pads by a puff of wind.

Keeping up her pretense with all her might, Chybee hailed them. "Is Ugant here, or Hyge? We have an urgent message!"

Resigning half her anti-burden to a colleague, the one who had so nearly soared into the sky looked her over.

"I remember you!" she said suddenly. "Weren't you here with Ugant a moonlong past?"

All that time ago? Chybee struggled more valiantly than ever to remember her promise to Aglabec.

"Is she here now? I have to talk to her!"

"Well, of course! Didn't you know? Today's the day for the trial launch—that is, if we turn out to have enough floaters for a really high lift, which is what we're working out right now. We got our first consignment of modified spores of the kind which ought to reproduce on Swiftyouth, and the line-up of the planets is ideal for them to be carried there by light-pressure! Of course, we can't be certain things will all go off okay, but we're doing our utmost. Only there have been some nasty rumors going around, about crazy psychoplanetarists who'd like to wreck the shot."

"That's exactly what I've come to warn you about!" Chybee exclaimed, seizing her opening. "I've been among them for—well, ever since I last saw Ugant! Call everybody together, please, right away! I have important news!"

"Say, I recall Ugant mentioning that you'd agreed to go undercover for us," said another of the work-team. "But what about him?" —gesturing at Creez.

"It's thanks to him that I know what I do!" Chybee improvised frantically. Something was wrong. Something was changing her mind against her will. She was still thinner and lower than when she set off on Ugant's mission, but with regained well-being those buried memories were growing stronger . . . particularly now that she was clear of psychoplanetarist pheromones.

"Hurry!" she moaned. "Hurry, *please!*"

But they wouldn't. They didn't. With maddening slowness they debated what to do, and at last agreed to guide her and Creez to the control-house, whence messages could be sent faster by nervograp.

She was going to be too late after all, Chybee thought despairingly as she plodded after them under the canopy of translucent globes. Oh, to think that so much effort, so many hopes and ambitions must go to waste because—

*Because Aglabec knows how to disguise the pheromones which otherwise would betray his true convictions.*

Enlightenment overcame her. Suddenly she realized what was meant by being stardazzled.

She looked about her with a clear eye. They had reached the

entrance platform of the control-house, whence Ugant was emerging with cries of excitement. Chybee ignored her. From here she could plainly see the way the bladders were humped, netful by netful, in a carefully planned spiral. Without being told she deduced that the first batch due for release must be that over there; then those; then those—and lastly those through which could now and then be glimpsed the shining metal of Hyge's cylinder.

And on the hills which she and Creez had lately crossed: Aglabec's disciples, surging this way like a sullen flood. They were passing flame from each to the next under a smear of smoke, igniting firebrands turn and turn about, seeking a vantage point from which to hurl them.

"But Aglabec promised—!" Creez exclaimed. Chybee cut him short.

"He lied! He's always lied to all his followers! He has a means to hide his lying, and he gave some to us for this mission! Ugant, forgive me, but they starved and tortured me until I couldn't help myself!"

Taken aback, the scientist said, "Starved? Tortured? Oh, it can't be true! I knew they were crazy, but surely even they—"

"No time!" Chybee shouted as Hyge too emerged from the control-house. "Everybody slack down to tornado status! *I mean now!*"

This drill was known to all the personnel from their test-firings. A single glance at the threat posed by the psychoplanetarists and their multiplying firebrands caused them to respond as though by mindless reflex, dragging Creez inside with them.

But, seizing one of the work-team's choppers, Chybee flung herself over the side of the platform and rushed back the way she had come.

Without realizing until she had an overview of the complete spiral, she had noticed how the bladders were lashed to pumplekins by clusters, each connected by only a single bond for the sake of lightness, and if she could sever just one of those ropes, one that was all-important, there was a thin, faint, tenuous chance that when Aglabec's crazed disciples began to fling their torches, then . . .

But which one? Where? She had imagined she fully understood the layout, yet she came to an abrupt halt, baffled and terrified. Had she wandered off course in her panic? All these groups of bladders looked alike, and all the ropes that tethered them—

A chance gust parted the dense globes and showed her the horde of attackers moving down the slope with grim determination, poising to toss their firebrands, heedless of any hurt that might come to them. Well, she had long craved vengeance on behalf of her friend Isarg; how could she do less than match their foolhardiness?

With sudden frantic energy she began to slash at every restraining rope in reach, and cluster after cluster of the bladders hurtled upward as though desperate to join the clouds.

To the psychoplanetarists perhaps it seemed that their prey was about to escape. At any rate, instead of padding purposefully onward they broke into a rush, and some of those at the rear, craving futile glory, threw their brands so that they landed among the others in the front ranks. A reek of fury greeted the burns they inflicted, and many of the foremost spun around, yelling with pain. Later, Chybee found herself able to believe that that fortunate accident must have saved her life. At the moment, however, she had no time to reason, but frenziedly went on cutting rope after rope after rope . . .

Abruptly she realized the sky above was clear, but the attackers had recovered from their setback, and were once more advancing on the remaining floaters.

Flinging aside her chopper, she fled towards the control-house, her mind failing again as she exhausted her ultimate resources. Suddenly there was a dull roaring noise, and a brilliant flare, and heat ravaged her mantle and dreadful overpressure strained her tubules.

She slumped forward to seek what shelter was offered by a dip in the ground, welcoming her agony.

For one who had been a double traitor, it felt like just and proper punishment.

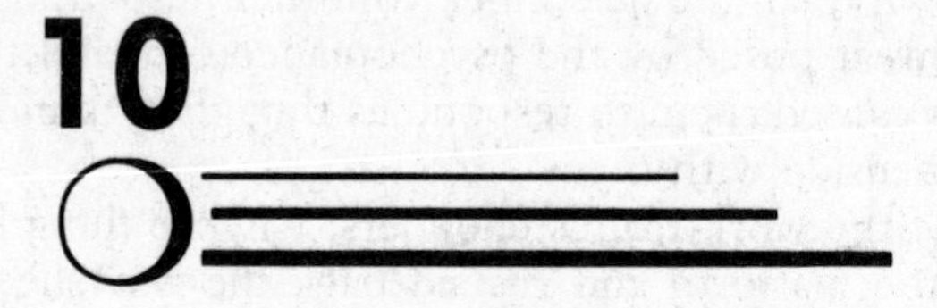

## 10

Piece by painful piece Chybee reconstructed her knowledge of the world. While being carried to a healing-house she heard a voice say, "She cut loose just enough of the bladders to create a fire-break. Naturally it's a setback, but it'll only mean a couple of moonlongs' extra work."

Later, while her burns were being tended: "A lot of the poor fools inhaled flame, or leaked to death because their tubules ruptured, or ulcerations on their mantles burst. But of course the updraft swept away the mutual reinforcement of their pheromones. Once they realized what a state they'd been reduced to, the survivors scattered, begging for help. Apparently they're ashamed of what they tried to do. It doesn't square with the perfect morality of these imaginary other worlds of theirs. So there's hope for them yet—or a good proportion, at any rate."

Chybee wanted to ask about their dream-leader, but for a long time she lacked the necessary energy to squeeze air past the edge of her mantle. By the time she could talk again, she found she was in the presence of distinguished well-wishers: Ugant, Wam, Glig, Airm, Hyge . . .

"What about Aglabec?" she husked. As one, they exuded anger and disappointment. At length Ugant replied.

"He's found a score of witnesses to certify that you came to him pleading for enlightenment, and that what he subjected you to was no more than the normal course of instruction all his disciples willingly undergo."

"It's a lie!" Chybee burst out, struggling to raise herself from the mosh-padded crotch she rested in.

"Sure it is," Glig the biologist said soothingly. "So are all the fables he's spun to entrap his dupes. But he defeated himself after a fashion. The 'medicine' he provided to disguise your exudates when you returned to the test site has been known to us for scores of years; it's based on the juice of the plant whose leaves I gave you. His version, though, doesn't only suppress one's own pheromones and protect against the effect of others'. It eventually breaks down the barrier between imagination and direct perception. No one can survive long after that stage sets in, and he's been using the stuff for years. Very probably he was already insane when he called out his followers to attack the test site—"

"He must have been," Airm put in. "Even though the shot was almost ready, his disciples weren't. If he'd waited a little longer, their madness might have been contagious!"

She ended with a shrug of relief.

"Insane or not, he mustn't be allowed to get away with what he did!" Chybee cried.

"Somehow I don't believe he will," said Wam with a mysterious air. "And I've come back specially from Hulgrapuk to witness the event that ought to prove his downfall."

"It's expected to occur not next dark, but the dark after that," Ugant said, rising. "By then you should be well enough to leave here. I'll send my scudder to collect you at sundown and bring you to my place. I rather think you're going to enjoy the show we have for you."

Turning to leave, she added, "By the way, you do know how grateful we all are, don't you?"

"And not just us," Airm confirmed. "The whole of Slah is in your debt, for giving us an excuse to clear out the pestilential lair of the psychoplanetarists. We've been flushing it with clean air for days now, and by the time we're done there won't be a trace of that alluring stench."

"But if Aglabec is still free—" Chybee said, confused.

"It isn't going to make the slightest difference."

At the crest of Ugant's home was an open bower where a good-quality telescope was mounted. Thither, on a balmy night under a sky clear but for stars and the normal complement of meteors, they conveyed Chybee, weak, perhaps scarred for life, but in possession of her wits again.

Not until they had plied her with the finest food and liquor that the house could boast did they consent to turn to the subject preying on her pith: the promised doom of Aglabec.

With infuriating leisureliness, after consulting a time-pulser hung beside the telescope, Ugant finally invited her to take her place at its ocular and stare at Swiftyouth.

"That's where we're going to send our spores," she said. "Before the end of summer, certainly, we shall have grown enough floaters, we shall have retested our starseeker, we shall have enlarged and improved our driver. Once beyond the atmosphere, at a precisely calculated moment, the raw heat of the sun will expand and eventually explode a carefully aligned container, so that it will broadcast spores into the path Swiftyouth will follow as it reaches perihelion . . . Why, you're shaking! What in the world for?"

"I don't know!" came the helpless answer. "But . . . Well, just suppose we're wrong after all. Just suppose not all of what Aglabec teaches is complete invention! Do we have the right to put at risk creatures on another world?"

There was a pause. At length Ugant said grayly, "If there are any life-forms on Swiftyouth—and I admit that, without voyaging there, we can never be certain—then they are due for suffering worse than any we have been through. Be patient. Watch."

Not knowing precisely why, Chybee obeyed, and waited. And then, just as she was about to abandon the telescope with a cry of annoyance . . .

That tiny reddish disc changed to white, and shone out more brilliantly than half the stars.

"Congratulate your colleagues at the Hulgrapuk Observatory, Wam," said Ugant dryly. "They were most precise in their calculations."

"But what are you showing me?" demanded Chybee.

"The kind of proof we needed to destroy Aglabec," the scientist replied composedly. "We maintain a constant watch for massive bodies drifting into the system. Recently we spotted one larger than any on record, or more precisely a whole cluster of them, perhaps the nucleus of a giant comet which was stripped of its gas when passing by a hot white star, then whipped into the void again. At first we were afraid they might collide with us, but luckily . . . Well, you're seeing what saved us: the attraction of an outer planet. So how exactly is Aglabec going to account for the collision of Swiftyouth with not one meteorite but maybe half a score of them, each greater than the one that washed Voosla and half an ocean high into the hills?"

At that very moment the whitened disc of Swiftyouth redoubled in brilliance. Chybee drew back from the ocular and tried to laugh at the prospect of Aglabec's discomfiture.

But she could not, any more than she could explain why to her concerned companions. She only knew she was in mourning of a sudden, for all the marvelous and lovely beings on—or in—the other planets, whom she had known so briefly and who now, even to imagination, were lost for evermore.

# Part Seven

# Well and Fitly Shaped

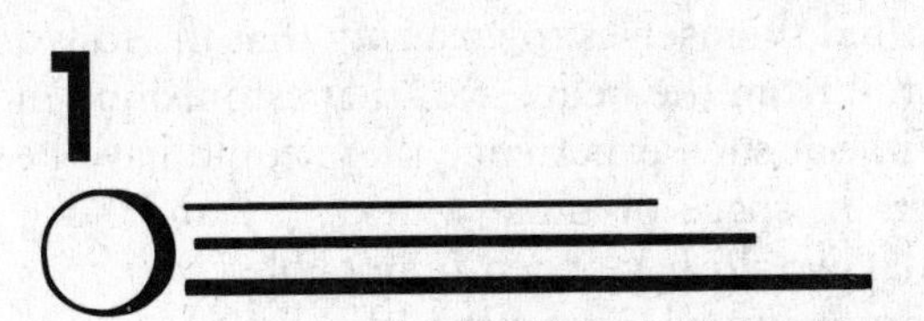

# 1

*E*ven before the sun had broached the dawn horizon, warm breezes wafted over the launching site and made the laqs of gas-globes swell. The mission controllers revised their estimates of available lift to record levels, and congratulated one another on the accuracy of their weather-sense. All was set fair for the first piloted flight beyond the atmosphere, the first attempt to link a group of orbiting ecosystems into what might become a colony, a settlement, and finally a vehicle, a junq to sail the interstellar sea. Compared to this climactic venture, all that had gone before was trivial. The seeding of the moon, the fact that the spectra of Swiftyouth and Sunbride kept changing in amazing fashion since those planets had been sprayed with spores intended to assure the continuance of life after its home world met disaster—those were experiments whose results might well not become known until after the race responsible was extinct. Here, on the other claw, was an undertaking designed to ensure that its extermination was postponed.

Now, just so long as their chosen pilot didn't let them down . . .

Karg was elated. He felt the eyes of history upon him. Soon his name would join the roster of the famous; it would be coupled with those of Gveest, Yockerbow, even Jing—

*Stop! Danger!* He was over the safe limit of euphoria, and took action to correct it. He had been adjusting to his life-supports since sundown. Years of experience underwater had accustomed him to similar systems; moonlongs of practice had prepared him for this particular version. Nonetheless it had taken a fair while before he persuaded it to eliminate from the cylinder's sealed atmosphere all trace of the pheromones that beset the launch site, redolent of doubt about himself, and he must have overcompensated.

Yet there were excellent reasons for choosing a male to venture into orbit first. Had it not been long accepted that legendary Gveest's revision of the folk's genetic heritage lacked certain safeguards, currently being supplied with all possible expedition? Was it not past a doubt that radiation or even minor stress might trigger the masculinizing effect again? Which of the mission controllers would risk such a doom falling on their own buds—?

Unfair! Unfair! They were the latest in line of those who for generations had dedicated themselves to ensuring that the folk of Slah should benefit to the full from the bequest of that astonishing pioneer of genetic control. Without such experience there could have been no hauqs, no life-supports in space or underwater . . . and Karg's epoch-making flight today would have been impossible.

Even so, there were many who resented it!

He struggled to dismiss such thoughts, and failed. What was one to make of people who knew their world might be destroyed without warning, yet scoffed at any attempt to seek refuge in space, called it foolish to obey the dictates of evolution, held that the only moral good consisted in multiplying the folk as much as possible? Oh, they were glad that the astronomers kept constant watch, for the whole world knew they had been right about the comet-head that crashed on Swiftyouth, and nobody in Karg's lifetime had tried to revive the sick and crazy teaching about "planet people" which their forebudders had swallowed—and been poisoned by. On the other claw, if Swiftyouth's gravity had been inadequate, or if it had been elsewhere in its orbit, then the folk of today might be struggling back from the swamps again.

But the past was dead, regardless of how vividly it might survive in one's imagination, and he was due for a ground check. He tensed his right foremantle, his left side being reserved for on-hauq maintenance. The hauq herself was a very refined version, maybe excessively so; she now and then responded to casual pheromones and did her mindless best to please her pilot without asking permission . . .

Well, so did scudders sometimes. Nobody could expect a trailblazing flight like this to be a simple task.

His pressure on the farspeaker stimulated its pith and woke it to signal mode on the correct wavelength. Its response was prompt.

Would it perform as well in space? No good saying others like it had done so; never before had a living person been carried into orbit . . .

"Karg? You register?"

"Clearly! How long until lift-off?"

"Full gas-globe expansion predicted imminently. Final confirmation of system status! Body cushioning?"

Karg reviewed every point at which his mantle and torso were braced by the conformable shape of the far tougher hauq, and announced, "Fine!"

"Propulsion mass and musculator pumps?"

There were no complaints from the docile creatures responsible for his maneuvers in orbit. He said so.

"Respiration?"

"Sourgas level normal."

"Pheromone absorption?"

Traces of his own exudations were still, he feared, leaking back to him before the purifiers could cancel them. But he had endured worse underwater, and it seemed like a trifling matter to complain about.

"Seems satisfactory so far."

The distant voice—he assumed it must belong to Yull, second-in-command at the launch site, but there was a degree of unreality about any communication by audio alone—took on a doubtful note. "Only 'so far'?"

He turned it with a joke. "How far have I got?"

However, there was no amusement in the response. "You realize we can't abort after you leave the ground?"

"Of course I do! Next is remote readings, correct?"

"Ah . . . Yes: we report normal signals. Mutual?"

"Confirm."

"Any unusual textures or odors that might indicate potential navigation or orientation errors?"

"None."

"Unusual coloration of any life-supports?"

"None." Though it was hard to judge under these luminants, selected not so much because they were known to perform well in low pressure and zero gravity as because they tolerated their own wastes in a closed environment.

"We copy automatic reports confirming subjective assessment. All set for release. Clasp your branch!"

There was of course no branch. Yull was trying to sound sociable. Karg couched his answer in equally light tones.

"The next signal you receive will be from our outside broadcast unit. A very long way outside!"

"It's a big universe," came the dry response. "Very well; as of the mark, you're on your own. Ready?"—to someone else. "Confirm! And *mark!*"

"Now I'm just a passenger," said Karg, and waited for the sky to let him through.

To make this voyage possible scores-of-scores-of-scores of folk at Slah and in its hinterland had gone without for generations . . . though never without food, for the effects of starvation, voluntary or not, were much too horrible. Rather, they had resigned themselves and their budlings to less than their share of the wonders of the modern world: houses that thought, scudders and floaters, falqonmail that flew from continent to continent where pitchens had only skimmed, communications that no longer called for nervograps, recordimals offering faithful transcriptions of the greatest thinkers and entertainers, newsimals and scentimals and haulimals, and the rest.

It was the tradition of their ancestors, and they were proud to keep it up.

Elsewhere the pattern had been otherwise. But that was the greatest source of conflict in the world today.

Nothing at all, however, could have prevented the citizens from gathering to marvel at the outcome of their self-denial. As a result of their efforts, gas-globes sprawled not just across the valley whence the launch took place, but over hill and dale and out to artificial islands in the nearest bay, wherever pumplekins might root to fill them with wetgas so light it bore up them, and their tethers, and a burden eloquent of eventual salvation.

Thanks to their hard work, too, Karg was promised survival and return. It had been their forebudders who devised means to break out into the vacuum of space; then they had found themselves short of essential raw materials. Ashamed to cheat their ignorant cousins on Glewm, the southern continent, out of what they did not so far know the worth of, they had resorted to their ancestors' domain, reinventing means to keep mind and pith together in mid-ocean, to locate themselves beneath dense cloud a season's trip from home, and ultimately to visit the sea-bed and supervise the work their creatures were undertaking there on their behalf. All the live tools they had bred to aid them in this venture had been exploited by the scientists who now were offering up Karg as a challenge to the stars.

The moon sparkled whether full or new. Comets were common; one had devastated Swiftyouth. Other rocks from out of nowhere had struck Stolidchurl and Steadyman, their impact sometimes bright enough to see without a telescope. Pure chance so far had saved the folk from another such disaster as created Slah.

All this they fervently believed. Whereas the inhabitants of other lands, not beneficiaries of what had been learned by digging Slah's foundations, reserved the right to doubt, and—almost as though they still accepted crazy Aglabec's ideas—acted as if their planet could endure forever.

That, though, the universe did not permit. The folk of Slah bore the fact in mind as they waited for Karg to take leave of this petty orb.

First on the smooth mirror of the water they cut loose the initial score of bladders. Up they went! A five-score bunch came next, and hoisted far into the clear blue autumn morning. Each batch was larger than the one before, and as the mass of them gathered it seemed that land and sea were uttering messages of hope about the future. Across the beach, across the nearer hills, then across the valley of the launch site, the sequence flowed without a flaw. This was the hugest skein of gas-globes ever lofted, almost a padlonglaq in total height.

At last they stirred the metal cylinder that held not only Karg but the drivers which would blast him beyond the atmosphere, along with creatures designed to keep him alive and in touch, navigate him to his rendezvous, assist his work and bring him back a moonlong hence.

But most of his voyage the watchers would not witness. No one was sure as yet what continent the vessel would be over when its drivers fired. As for its time and place of landing . . .

Oh, but it was a privilege to be present at the launch and see the countless bladders soaring up! (Countless? But they were counted, and farspeakers reported on the state of every single one of them during their brief lives. At a certain height they must explode, and leave the cylinder to fall, and orient, and rise again on jets of vivid fire.)

Through transparent ports Karg watched the world descend, much too busy to be frightened, never omitting to react to what his fellow creatures told him as they drifted towards the moon. It was changing color almost by the day as the life-forms sown there adapted to naked space and fearful radiation. *And what they have done,* he thought, *the folk will do . . . Albeit we may change, we shall endure!*

In a while he was looking down at clouds over Prutaj, that other continent he had never set pad on, where it was held that the hard work of Slah was misconceived, where present gratification was prized more than the future survival of the species.

And then the meteor struck.

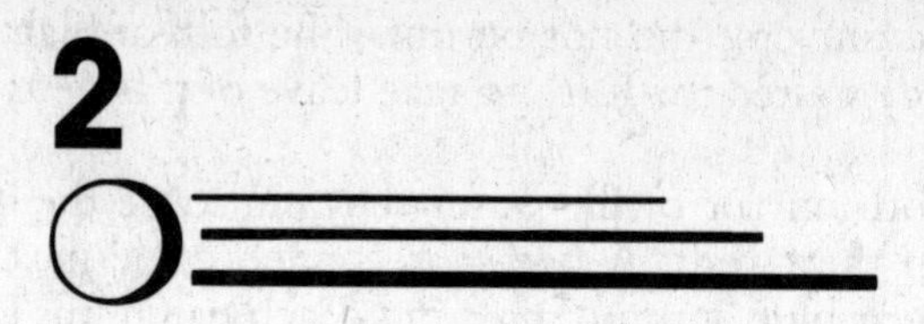

*B*efore the impact of the Greatest Meteorite, when folk debated concerning centers of learning and research, one was acknowledged to stand eye and mandibles above the rest. But Chisp was gone, save for what pastudiers could retrieve from the mudslides which had buried it.

Now there was argument. Some held for Slah, as hewing truest to the principles of the past. Some still named Hulgrapuk, and certainly that city, though in decline, did not lack for dedicated scholars. When it came to innovation, though, there was no contest. Out of Fregwil on Prutaj flowed invention following insight following theory, and almost every theory was audacious, so that students from around the globe came begging for a chance to sit by the pads of those who had made its name world-famous.

And once each lustrum it was not just students who converged on it, but sightseers, merchants, news-collectors . . . for that was when the newest and latest was published to the admiring world. The tradition dated back five-score years. Much interest had then been aroused by the identification of solium in the atmosphere: so rare an element, it had previously been detected only in the spectrum of the sun. An intercontinental meeting of astronomers and chemists being convoked, it was overwhelmed by eager layfolk anxious to find out what benefit such a discovery might bring.

Yet most pronounced themselves disappointed. This news was of small significance to them in their daily lives. What the public mainly liked was something they could marvel at. What the scientists wanted was to attract the best and brightest of the next generation into research. Accordingly, every quarter-score of years since then the staid professors—and some not so staid—had mobilized to mount a spectacle for strangers. Indulgently they said, "We are all as budlings when we confront the mysteries of the universe, and a touch of juvenile wonderment can do no harm!"

Those who made a handsome living out of converting their experiments into practical devices agreed without reserve. And those who were obliged by their knowledge to accept that this touchy, fractious, immature species was unlikely to attain adulthood because the whole planetary system was orbiting into the fires of the Major Cluster—

they resigned themselves to compliance on the grounds that there was nothing better to be done.

This time the Fregwil Festival of Science was nicknamed "The Sparkshow," because it was devoted to sparkforce, that amazing fluid known to permeate stormclouds and nerve-pith alike, which held out promise of an infinity of new advances over and above the miracles it had already performed. And the name on everybody's mantle-rim was Quelf.

Sometimes when voyaging abroad citizens of Prutaj were tactless enough to boast about their superior way of life at home. On being challenged to offer evidence, as often as not they invoked Fregwil as a perfect symbol of the ideals to which Prutaj was dedicated. Its university, along with the healing-house from which it had originally sprung, dominated the city from its only high peak, and looked down on the local administrative complex, thereby exemplifying the preference Prutaj gave to knowledge over power; besides, it was surrounded by huge public parks where the folk might bring their young to enjoy the sight, the smell, the sound, even the touch and taste, of plants and animals that otherwise might long ago have disappeared from this continent at once so wealthy and so well controlled. (Which met, as often as not, with the retort: "So what? We have that stuff underpad anyhow!" And it was hard to tell whether they were jealous of Prutaj's progress, or despiteful of it.)

Sometimes, though, foreigners came to see for themselves, and departed duly abashed . . .

Exactly that was happening today. The parks were crammed with sparkforce exhibits which had attracted visitors from half the world, including a delegation from Slah: new ways of carrying messages, new means to control the growth of perfect primary and secondary plants, new and better styles in housing, feeding, moving, curing . . . Some objected, saying all they found was change for the sake of change. More stood awestricken, particularly those making a first visit to Fregwil. Now and then mongers of overseas news tried to distract the crowds with reports about Karg's spaceflight, but they were generally ignored. Almost everybody took it for granted that the most important and successful research in the world was happening right here at Fregwil. If ever it did become necessary to quit the planet, then it would be Fregwil scientists who found the way.

And the most amazing demonstration was to come by dark.

There was a little ceremony first. Quelf took station on an artificial mound to be invested with the baldric of the Jingfired, a simple garland of phosphorescent leaves such as anyone might gather in a private garden. This provoked hilarity among the onlookers, shaming to her and her nominee Albumarak, and quickly reproved by Doyenne

Greetch, who reminded those in range of the loudeners of the antiquity of this custom. But who in this generation, without visiting Glewm, or maybe the hinterland of Slah, could understand how differently their ancestors had lived? Albumarak, for one, enjoyed the symbolism of the ritual, devoid though it might be of historical authenticity.

At any rate she strove to. It was the least she could offer in return for Quelf's generosity in nominating her at so early an age as a candidate in her eventual turn for the status of becoming Jingfired. Whole families had gambled their possessions, and even the future of their offspring, on the chance of "being nominated."

And it had overtaken her although her parents scorned her. She was rebellious, so they called her stupid . . .

Quelf disagreed. This prestigious neurophysicist had chanced across one of a quarter-score of recordimals which Albumarak had turned loose (she could not afford more, but she had modified them to ensure that they went about stinking good and loud!) to publicize a disagreement with her teachers. Quelf cared little for the argument—she said later it was clever but trivial—but she admired the neatness of the programing, and decided to enroll Albumarak among her students.

So here she was, doing her best not to seem bored even though the ceremony was going on for an awfully long time.

Eventually her attention was distracted by the shrill cry of yet another newsmonger announcing the launch of a piloted spaceship, and she found herself shuddering. At Fregwil the received opinion about such undertakings was the converse of the view the late Professor Wam had imposed at Hulgrapuk. Here it was dogmatically asserted that all preparations to meet a future catastrophe were pointless. No means existed to turn aside such another celestial missile as the Greatest Meteorite. However, if the next one were no larger, then at least some people would survive, conscious of the fact that there was nothing they could have done to fend off the disaster. If it were far bigger, nobody would be left to recriminate. As for lesser meteorites, thousands were falling every day, and patently no precautions could be taken against those because they were far too numerous. The folk of Prutaj were smugly proud of their acceptance of such arguments, and flattered themselves that they were being realistic.

As for escaping into space, out there either radiation or the lack of gravity was sure to kill any creature more advanced than a lowly plant, while dreams of substituting for the latter by spinning a huge hollow globe were countered with calculations showing how much it would cost in time, effort and materials to construct even the smallest suitable vessel. The figures were daunting; most layfolk accepted them without question. Besides, there was one additional consideration which weighed more with Albumarak than all the rest: how, demanded the psychologists at Fregwil, could anybody contemplate fleeing into space and abandoning the rest of the species to their fate? Recollection of their callousness would drive the survivors insane . . . or, if it did not, then they would have forfeited their right to be called civilized.

Albumarak concurred entirely. She could not imagine anyone being so cold-ichored. And yet—and yet, at the very least, this pilot must be brave . . .

Abruptly she realized that the ceremony was over, and it was time for the demonstration which everybody was awaiting. Hastily, for she had a minor part to play in it, she made her way to Quelf's side. By now it was full dark, and a layer of low cloud hid the moon and stars and the ceaseless sparkling of meteors. Moreover the nearby luminants were being masked, to render the spectacle yet more impressive. The crowd, which had been chattering and moving restlessly, quieted as Doyenne Greetch introduced Quelf over booming loudeners.

After a few formalities, the neurophysicist launched into the burden of her brief address.

"All of us must be familiar with nervograps, whose origin predated the Greatest Meteorite. Many of us now benefit, too, from sparkforce links, which carry that all-pervading fluid from pullstone generators like the ones you can see yonder"—her left claw extended, and the crowd's eyes turned as one—"or the more familiar flashplants, which many people now have in their homes. And we've learned that there is a certain loss of sparkforce in transmission. In some cases we can turn that loss to our advantage; anyone who has raised tropical fruit in midwinter thanks to sparkforce heaters knows what I mean by that! But in most cases this has been a serious drawback. And the same holds for communications; over a long circuit, messages can be garbled by system noise, and to ensure accuracy we have to install repeaters, not invariably reliable.

"That age is over, thanks to the hard work and ingenuity of our research team! We can now transmit both simple sparkforce, and messages as well, with negligible loss!"

Some of the onlookers had heard rumors of this breakthrough; others, though, to whom it was a complete surprise, uttered shouts of gleeful admiration. Quelf preened a little before continuing.

"On the slope behind me there's a tower. Perhaps some of you have been wondering what it is. Well, it's a device for generating artificial lightning. It's safely shielded, of course. But we now propose to activate it, using a sparkforce flow that will traverse a circuit more than five score-of-scores of padlonglaqs in length, using only those few generators you can see right over there. Are we ready?"

"Just a moment!" someone shouted back. "We're not quite up to working pressure."

"Well, then, that gives me time to emphasize what's most remarkable about the circuit we've constructed," Quelf went on. "Not only is it the longest ever laid; part of it runs underwater, part through desert, part through ice and snow within the polar circle! Nonetheless, it functions just as though it were entirely in country like this park. We all look forward to the benefits this discovery must entail!"

"I could name some people who aren't exactly overjoyed," muttered Presthin, who stood close enough to Albumarak for her to hear. She was the goadster of the giant snowrither that had laid the arctic portion of the circuit. Many of her ancestors had been members of the Guild of Couriers in the days before nervograps and farspeakers, and she regarded modern vehicles, even snowrithers, as a poor substitute for the porps her forebudders had pithed and ridden. She was blunt and crotchety, but Albumarak had taken a great liking to her.

Right now, however, she had no time to reply, for the ready signal had been given, and Quelf was saying, "It gives me much pleasure to invite the youngest participant in our researches to close the circuit! Come on, Albumarak!"

To a ripple of applause she advanced shyly up the mound. Quelf ceded her place at the loudeners, and she managed to say, "This is indeed a great honor. Thank you, Quelf and all my colleagues . . . oh, yes, and if you look directly at the flash you may be dazzled. You have been warned!"

She stepped forward on to the flashplant tendril through which this end of the circuit was completed. At once the park was lit as bright as day. A clap of local thunder rolled, and a puff of sparkforce stink—due to a triple molecule of sourgas—assailed the watchers.

After an awed pause, there came a storm of cheers. Quelf let it continue a few moments, then called for quiet.

"But that's only part of the demonstration we have for you!" she declared. "In addition to the power circuit, we also have a message link, and in a moment you'll get the chance to inspect it for yourselves, and even to send a signal over it, if you have someone at its far end you'd like to get in touch with. The far end, in fact, is half this continent away, at Drupit! And from Drupit, on receipt of a go signal, one of the people who worked on the northernmost stretch of the message link will tell us the very latest news, without repeaters! Watch for it on the display behind me. Are we ready? Yes? Albumarak!"

Again she closed the circuit, this time using a smaller and finer linkup. There was a pause. It lasted so long, a few people voiced the fear that something had gone wrong.

Something had, but not at Fregwil nor at Drupit.

At long last the display began to show the expected symbols, and some of the onlookers recited them aloud:

"METEORITE BRINGS DOWN PILOTED SPACECRAFT—BELIEVED CRASHED IN CENTRAL UPLANDS—RESCUE SEARCH UNDER WAY!"

Before the last word had come clear, someone giggled, and within moments the crowd was caught up in gusts of mocking merriment.

Even Quelf surrendered her dignity for long enough to utter a few sympathetic chuckles.

"You're not laughing," Presthin murmured to Albumarak.

"Nor are you," she answered just as softly.

"No. I've been in the uplands at this season. It's bad for the health. And if nothing else, that flier must be brave. Foolhardy and misguided, maybe. Nonetheless—!"

"I know exactly what you mean. But I don't suppose there's anything that we can do."

"No. Not until he's spotted, anyway. At least they've stopped laughing; now they're cheering again. Quelf's beckoning. You'd better go and pretend you're as pleased as she is, hadn't you?"

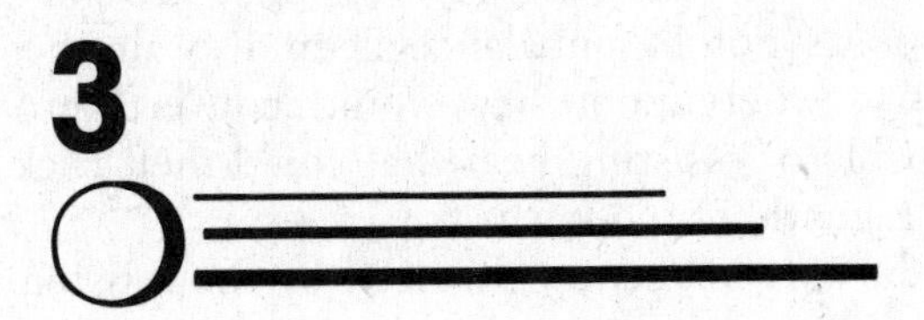

# 3

The meteorite might well not have massed more than one of Karg's own pads or claws, but the fury of its passage smashed air into blazing plasma. Its shock-wave ripped half the gas-globes asunder, twisted and buffeted the cylinder worse than a storm at sea, punished Karg even through its tough protective walls with a hammerslam of ultrasonic boom. Gasping, he wished indeed he had a branch to cling to, for the conviction that overcame his mind was primitive and brutal: *I'm going to die!*

Spinning, he grew dizzy, and it was a long while before an all-important fact began to register. He was *only* spinning. The cylinder was not tumbling end over end. So a good many of the gas-globes must be intact, though he had no way of telling how many; the monitors which should have been automatically issuing reports to him, as well as to mission control and its outstations scattered across one continent and three oceans, were uttering nonsense.

Was he too low to activate the musculator pumps intended for maneuvering in space? They incorporated a reflex designed to correct just such an axial rotation, but if the external pressure were too high . . . Giddiness was making it hard to think. He decided to try, and trust to luck.

And the system answered: reluctantly, yet as designed.

The cylinder steadied. But beneath the hauq on which he lay were bladders containing many score times his body-mass of reactive chemicals. If they sprang a leak, his fate would be written on the sky in patterns vaster and brighter than any meteor-streak. After establishing that all fuel-pressures were in the normal range, he relaxed a fraction, then almost relapsed into panic as he realized he could not tell whether he was floating or falling. Sealed in the cylinder, he was deprived of normal weather-sense, and the viewports were blinded by dense cloud. Suppose he was entering a storm! He could envisage much too clearly what a lightning-strike might do to the remaining gas-globes.

If only there were some way of jettisoning his explosive fuel . . . ! The giant storage bladders were programed to empty themselves, more or less according to the density of air in which the driver fired, and then when safe in vacuum expel whatever of their contents might remain. After that, they were to fold tight along the axis of the cylinder, so as not to unbalance it, and await the high temperature of reentry, whereupon they would convert into vast scoops and planes capable of resisting heat that could melt rock, and bring the cylinder to a gentle touchdown.

But this was not the sort of reentry foreseen by the mission controllers.

Karg's air had begun to stink of his own terror. Frantically he forced the purifiers into emergency mode, squandering capacity supposed to last a moonlong in the interests of preserving his sanity. Then the clouds parted, and he saw what lay below.

He hung about two padlonglaqs above a valley full of early snow, patched here and there with rocky crags but not a hint of vegetation. It was his first view of such a landscape, for he had spent all his life in coastal regions where winter was short and mild, but he knew he must be coming down in the desolate highlands of Prutaj.

Was there any hope that the wind might bear him clear of this continent where the achievements of Slah were regarded with contempt? Noting how rapidly the bitter frost of fall cut his lift, he concluded not, and chill struck his pith, as cruel as though he were not insulated from the outer air.

Striving to reassure himself, he said aloud, "The folk of Prutaj aren't savages! Even in their remotest towns people must have heard about my flight, officials may be willing to help me get back home—"

A horrifying lurch. More of the bladders had burst, or maybe a securing rope had given way. A vast blank snowslope filled the groundward port. He could not help but close his eye.

The cylinder had been swinging pendulum-fashion beneath the remaining gas-globes. Loss of the topmost batch dropped it swiftly towards a blade-keen ridge of still-bare rock, against whose lee a deep soft drift had piled. A chance gust caught it; swerving, it missed the ridge, but touched the snow. Drag sufficed to outdo the wind, and it crunched through the overlying glaze of ice. Absorbed, accepted, it sank in, and the last gas-globes burst with soft reports.

But the driver-fuel did not explode.

In a little while Karg was able to believe that it was too cold to be a threat any longer. That, though, was not the end of the danger he was in. His hauq, and the other creatures which shared the cylinder, had been as carefully adapted to outer space as its actual structure. They were supposed to absorb heat—not too much, but precisely enough—from the naked sun, store it, and survive on it while orbiting through the planet's shadow. As soon as the mandibles of the ice closed on them they began to fail. That portion of the hauq's bulk which kept the exit sealed shrank away, and the sheer cold that entered made him cringe.

Also, but for the sighing of the wind and creaks from the chilling cylinder, there was total silence.

He sought in vain for any hint of folk-smell. Even a waft of smoke would have been welcome, for he knew that in lands like these some people managed to survive by using fire—another wasteful Prutaj habit. He detected none. Moreover, now that the pressure inside and out had equalized, he had normal weather-sense again, and it warned of storms.

He wanted to flee—flee anywhere—but he was aware how foolish it would be to venture across unknown territory rendered trackless by the snow. No, he must stay here. If all else failed, he could eat not only his intended rations but some of the on-hauq secondary plants. He might well last two moonlongs before being rescued . . . at least, so he was able to pretend for a while.

By dawn the overcast had blown away, and the next bright was clear and sunny. But though he searched the sky avidly for a floater or soarer that might catch sight of his crashed spacecraft, he saw none, and the air remained intensely cold. Shortly before sunset the clouds returned, and this time they heralded another fall of snow.

As Karg retreated for shelter inside the cylinder, he found he could no longer avoid thinking about the risk of freezing to death before he starved.

Next bright he was already too stiff to venture out. Little by little he began to curse himself, and the mission controllers, and his empty dreams of being one day remembered alongside Gveest and Jing.

Then dreams of another kind claimed him, and he let go his claw-grip on reality.

For the latest of too many times Albumarak muttered, "Why couldn't he have crashed where a floater could get to him?"

Perched forward of her in the snowrither's haodah, empty but for the two of them, some hastily grafted warm-plants, and a stack of emergency supplies, Presthin retorted, "We don't even know he's where we're heading for! Slah could be wrong about the point where the meteor hit—our wind-speed estimates might be off—someone may have calculated the resultant position wrongly anyhow . . . Not *that* way, you misconceived misbudded miscegenate!"

She was navigating through a blizzard by dead reckoning, and had to ply her goad with vigor to keep their steed on course. Like all the folk's transport, snowrithers had been forcibly evolved, from a strain naturally adapted to polar climate and terrain, but the original species had only spread into its ecological niche during the comparatively recent Northern Freeze, and despite expert pithing this beast, like its ancestors, would have preferred to follow a spoor promising food at the end of its journey.

"Now I've got a question," Presthin went on, peering through the forward window, on which snow was settling faster than the warm-plants could melt it. "And it's a bit more sensible than yours. I want to hear why you volunteered to come with me! No guff about your 'moral duty,' please! *I* think you're here for the same reason I am. You want to see one of these famous space-cylinders, and there aren't apt to be any of them grown on our side of the world!"

"That has nothing to do with it! Anyway, they aren't grown! They're—well—cast, or forged, or something," Albumarak concluded lamely.

"Hah! Well, it's not because you're so fond of my company, that's for sure. Then it must be because you want to get out of Quelf's claw-clutch for a while."

"That's part of it"—reluctantly.

"Only part? Then what can the rest be?"

Albumarak remained silent, controlling her exudations. How could she explain, even to unconventional Presthin, the impulse that had overcome her after she heard the crowd at Fregwil greet the failure of Karg's mission with scornful jeers? Suddenly she had realized: she didn't believe that a person willing to risk his or her own life in hope of ensuring the survival of the species could truly be as nasty as her teachers claimed. So she wanted to meet one, well away from Quelf and all her colleagues.

Of course, if she admitted as much, and they didn't find him, or if when they did he were already dead, as was all too likely, Presthin's coarse sense of humor might induce her to treat the matter as a joke. Albumarak had never liked being laughed at; mockery had been one of her parents' chief weapons against their budlings.

Nonetheless she was bracing herself to disclose her real motive, when Presthin almost unperched her by jerking the snowrither to a convulsive halt.

Why? The blizzard had not grown fiercer; on the contrary, they had topped a rise and suddenly emerged under a clear evening sky.

"Look!" the goadster shouted. "They steered us to the right place after all!"

Across the next valley, on a hillside whose highest and steepest slope, still snow-free bar a thin white powdering, caught the last faint gleam of daylight: the multicolored rags and tatters of burst gas-globes.

"Just in time," Presthin muttered. "By dark we could have missed it!"

Inside the cylinder the luminants were frosted and everything was foul with drying ichor. At first they thought their mission had been futile anyway, for they could find no sign of Karg. Presthin cursed him for being such a fool as to wander away from his craft. And then they realized he had only grown crazy enough to slash open the body of his hauq and burrow into it for warmth. It was long dead, and so within at best another day would he have been.

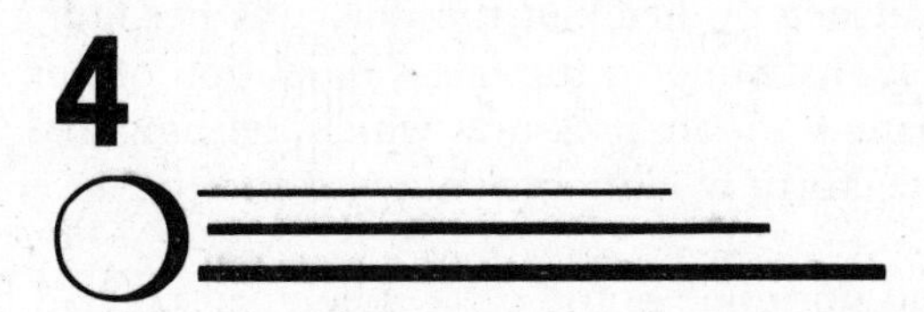

*E*ver since Karg's arrival at Fregwil the university's healing-house had been besieged by sensation-seekers. Over and over it had been explained that the pilot would for long be too weak to leave his bower, and even when he recovered only scientists and high officials might apply to meet him. The crowds swelled and dwindled; nonetheless, as though merely looking at the place where he lay gave them some obscure satisfaction, their number never fell below ten score. Some of those who stood vainly waiting were local; most, however, were visitors to the Festival of Science, which lasted a moonlong and was not yet over.

Now and then Quelf graciously consented to be interviewed by foreign news-collectors, and took station in the nearby park behind a bank of efficient loudeners. The questions were almost always the same, but the neurophysicist's answers were delivered with no less enthusiasm each time. She was positively basking in this welter of publicity, though of course she maintained that her sole ambition was to promote the fame and well-being of Prutaj in general and Fregwil in particular.

Certainly she missed no opportunity of boasting about her city and its skills. For example, to someone making the obvious inquiry about Karg's physical health, she would describe how frost had ruptured many of his tubules and he might lose his right pad, and then continue: "Luckily, as you know, we now have a loss-free sparkforce lead all the way to Drupit, so when one of our ultramodern snowrithers brought him there, a local physician was able to apply penetrative heating to the affected tissues. Now we're attempting to regenerate his damaged nerve-pith, too."

Whereupon someone would invariably ask, "Has he regained full normal consciousness?"

"No, I'm afraid he's still dreamlost, though there are signs of lucidity. When he does recover, by the way, the first thing we shall want to know is whether he still feels the way he used to about the respective merits of what they do at Slah with their resources, and what we do with ours this side of the ocean. I think his views may well have changed since his unreliable toy fell out of the sky!"

Cue for sycophantic laughter . . .

As Quelf's nominee for Jingfired status, Albumarak was bound to dance permanent attendance on her, but the duty was becoming less and less bearable. Today, listening to the latest repetition of her stale gibes, feeling the change in air-pressure which harbingered bad weather, she wished the storm would break at once and put an end to the interview.

If only Presthin had not gone home . . . The goadster had been persuaded to accompany her and Karg to Fregwil, and spent a couple of grumpy days being introduced to city officials and other notables. Suddenly, however, she announced she'd had her mawful of this, and returned to her usual work with the snowrither, surveying the trade-routes which kept the highland towns supplied in winter and making sure that they were passable.

In the pleasant warmth of Fregwil, Albumarak found it almost impossible to recapture in memory the bitter chill of the valley where Karg had crashed. How could anybody want to be there, rather than here? There was, she realized glumly, an awful lot she didn't yet understand about people. Worst of all, she had not yet had a chance to fulfill the purpose which had induced her to join Presthin's rescue mission. All the time she had been in company with Karg, he had been unconscious or dreamlost, and since he had been brought here she had not been allowed to see him. Nobody was, apart from Quelf, a few of her associates, and the regular medical staff.

Wind rustled the nearby trees; the air-pressure shifted again, very rapidly, and people on the fringe of the crowd began to move away in search of shelter. With a few hollow-sounding apologies Quelf brought her public appearance to an end just as the first heavy drops pounded down.

"Do you need me any more right now?" Albumarak ventured.

"Hm? Oh—no, not until first bright tomorrow. Come to think of it, you could do with some time off. You don't seem to have recovered properly from the strain of bringing Karg back. Actually meeting someone who's prepared to abandon the rest of us to our fate is a considerable shock, isn't it?"

Albumarak recognized another of Quelf's stock insults, which the curtailment of today's interview had prevented her from using. But she judged it safest to say nothing.

"Yes, get along with you! Go have some fun with young'uns of your own age. Enjoy your dark!"

And the famous neurophysicist was gone, trailing a retinue of colleagues and admirers.

Dully Albumarak turned downslope, making for a branchway that would take her into the lower city, but with no special destination in mind. She had few friends. Some of her fellow students cultivated her acquaintance, but she knew it was because of her association with Quelf, not for her own sake, so she avoided them as much as possible. Now and then, and particularly since her return from the highlands, she found herself wishing for the old days when she could afford to do outrageous things in order to annoy her family. But she had not yet decided to risk trying that again, for Quelf would never be so tolerant . . . How strange to think of her parents as tolerant, when a year ago she would have sworn they were cruel and repressive!

She was aware of a sort of revolution going on within her. Attitudes she had taken for granted since budlinghood were changing without her willing it. It was like having to endure a private earthquake. She had been dazzled by the idea that one day she too could be Jingfired; she was growing into the habit of behaving herself appropriately. But now she was constantly wondering: do I really want it after all?

"Excuse me!"

A voice addressed her in an unfamiliar accent. She turned to see a she'un not much older than herself.

"Yes?"—more curtly than she intended.

"Aren't you Albumarak, who helped to rescue Karg?"

It was pointless to deny the fact. Any number of strangers recognized her nowadays.

"My name is Omber. I'm from the space-site at Slah."

Albumarak's interest quickened. She knew that a delegation of scientists had arrived a few days ago, to take their pilot home and negotiate for recovery of his cylinder. But this was the first time she had met one of them.

"Ah! I suppose you've been to visit Karg, then."

"They won't let us!" was the astonishing response.

"What?"

"Literally! Not even Yull—she's my chief, second-in-command of the entire project and the senior member of our group—not even she has been allowed to see him yet. Do you have any idea why?"

"This is the first I've heard about it!" Albumarak declared.

"Really?" Omber was taken aback. "Oh . . . Oh, well, then I won't trouble you any further. But I did rather assume—"

With rising excitement Albumarak interrupted. "No, I assure you! I'm horrified! What possible reason can they have to stop Karg's friends from visiting him, even if he isn't well enough to talk yet?"

"I'm not exactly a friend of his," Omber said. "I only met him once or twice during his training. If it were just a matter of myself, I wouldn't be surprised. But Yull . . . ! How is he, really? I suppose you've seen him recently?"

"They won't let me see him either," Albumarak answered grimly. "They didn't let Presthin, come to that."

"Presthin—? Oh, yes: the goadster! You mean not even she . . . ? This is ridiculous! Excuse me; one doesn't mean to be impolite to one's host city, but it is, isn't it?"

"It's incredible!"

"You don't suppose . . . No, I oughtn't even to say it."

"Go ahead," Albumarak urged.

Omber filled her mantle. "You don't suppose he's being submitted to some sort of experimental treatment, and it's going wrong? We can't find out! Not many people here care to talk to us, and the people from our permanent trade mission say it's always the same for them, too."

"You make me ashamed for my own city!"

"That's very kind and very reassuring." Abruptly Omber sagged, revealing that she was dreadfully tired. "Excuse me, but I haven't had a proper rest since we boarded the floater. Yull sent me up here to have one more go at persuading the staff to admit us, while she went to see some official or other about recovering the cylinder. Not that there's much hope of our getting it back before the spring, apparently. They're making excuses about the danger from its unexpended fuel, and nobody understands that the colder it is, the safer. I mean, I work with it every day of my life, back home, and we haven't had any accidents with it, not ever, not even once. By the spring, though, venting it could really be hazardous. Still, with a bit of luck Yull will manage to make them listen."

There was a pause. Except for the hardiest, most of the crowd surrounding the healing-house had dispersed or sought shelter. Abruptly Albumarak realized that she had kept Omber standing in the pouring rain, and hastily urged her to the nearest bower.

"Do you think your colleagues will believe that even I haven't been allowed to see Karg?" she demanded.

Omber gave a curl of faint amusement. "I believe you entirely.

And nothing in this weird city is likely to surprise me after that. Yes, I think they will."

"But just in case they don't . . ." Albumarak's mind was racing. "Would you like me to tell them personally?"

"Why—why, that's too much to ask! But it would be wonderful! That is, if you can spare the time?"

"I have nothing much to do," Albumarak muttered, thinking how accurate that was not only of the present moment but of her entire life. Quelf's idea of encouraging her students' research was to let them watch what she herself was doing and then take over the repetitive drudgery involved . . . and blame them for anything that afterwards went wrong. "Where is your delegation lodged?"

"In a spare house near our trade mission, which they had to wake up specially for us. It's a bit primitive, since it hasn't been occupied for several moonlongs, but if you're sure you wouldn't mind . . . ?"

"It will be a pleasure," Albumarak declared. "Let's go!"

# 5

Nobody paid attention to the creature which Yull, Omber and Albumarak turned loose as they entered the healing-house at first bright next day. It looked like a commonplace scrapsaq—on the large side, perhaps, but one expected that in a public institution. Its kind were conditioned to go about disposing of spent luminants, spuder-webs full of dead wingets and the like, attracted to one or several kinds of rubbish by their respective odors. Having gathered as much as they could cope with, they then carried their loads to the rotting pits, and were rewarded with food before setting off again.

This one, however, was a trifle out of the ordinary.

Having seen it safely on its way, Albumarak turned to her companions.

"Follow me!" she urged. "Quelf is always in the neurophysics lab at this time of the morning."

With Yull exuding the pheromones appropriate to a high official, and Omber playing the role of her nominee as Albumarak had taught her, they arrived at the laboratory unchallenged, along a high branchway either side of which the boughs were festooned with labeled experimental circuitry. Pithed ichormals lay sluggish with up to a score of tendrils grafted on their fat bodies; paired piqs and doqs stirred uneasily as each tried to accept signals from the other; long strands of isolated nerve-pith, some healthy and glistening, some dry and peeling, were attached to plants in an attempt to find better repeaters for nervograp links, for despite Quelf's optimism it would be long before loss-free communication circuits became universal.

"I don't like this place," Omber muttered.

"That's because you're more used to working with raw chemicals than living things," Yull returned, equally softly. "But we exploit them too, remember."

"Yes. Yes, of course. I'm sorry."

Nonetheless she kept glancing unhappily from side to side.

One of Albumarak's fellow students, engaged in the usual drudgery of recording data from the various experiments, caught sight of her and called out. "Hey! You're late! Quelf is fuming like a volcano!"

"I'm on my way to make her erupt," was the composed reply.

And Albumarak led her companions into the laboratory itself, where the neurophysicist was holding forth to a group of distinguished visitors, probably foreign merchants anxious to acquire and exploit some of Fregwil's newest inventions. That was an unexpected bonus!

Albumarak padded boldly towards her, not lowering as she normally would in her professor's presence. Abruptly registering this departure from ordinary practice, Quelf broke off with an apology to her guests and glared at her.

"Where've you been? When I wished you a good dark I—"

"I want to see Karg," Albumarak interrupted.

"What? You know perfectly well that's out of the question! Have you spent your dark taking drugs?"

"Not only I," said Albumarak as though she had not spoken, "but my companions. Allow me to present Scholar Yull, head of the Slah delegation, and her assistant Omber."

"Who are both," murmured Yull in a quiet tone, "*extremely* anxious to see our old friend."

She was a tall and commanding person in her late middle years. Albumarak clenched her claws, trying to conceal her glee. The moment she had set eye on Yull, last evening, she had suspected that she could dominate Quelf—and here was proof. She had an air of calm authority that made the other's arrogance look like mere bluster.

Taken totally aback, and hideously embarrassed that it should have happened in the presence of strangers, rather than only her students whom she could always overawe, Quelf reinforced her previous statement.

"Out of the question! He's still far too ill! Now show these people out and resume your duties!"

"If Karg is still so ill after being so long in your care," Yull said silkily, "that indicates there must be something wrong with your medical techniques."

"They are the best in the world! He was half-frozen! It was a miracle he didn't lose both pads instead of one!"

"I see. How is regrowth progressing?"

"What?"

"I said how is regrowth progressing?"—in the same soft tone but taking a step towards Quelf. "In such a case we would grow him a replacement, which would lack sensation but restore normal motor function. Has this not been done?"

"We—uh, that is, it's not customary . . ."

"Well, it's not important; it will be better for him to have the job done at home anyway, since your methods appear to be suspect." Yull was ostensibly unaware of the grievous insult she was offering, but Quelf's exudations ascended rapidly towards the anger-stink level. She went on, "At least, however, we must insist on verifying that he is not at risk from secondary infection."

"He's in our finest bower, guarded by a score of winget-killers, with filter-webs at every opening!"

"In that case, judging by his medical record, he should have recovered from a slight attack of frostbite long ago. Did the crash cause worse injuries than you've admitted?"

Albumarak was trying not to dance up and down with joy.

But Quelf gathered her forces for an equally crushing rebuttal.

"What you regard as good health may perhaps not correspond with what we of Prutaj take for granted," she said, having recovered most of her poise. "Indeed, perhaps we have made a mistake in trying to bring him up to that level. But you must not prevent it happening, if it can be done."

Yull turned her eye slowly on all those present, while drawing herself up to full height. She overtopped Quelf by eye and mandibles; moreover her mantle was sleek and beautifully patterned for her age. Only the youngest students' could match it. The distinguished visitors, and Quelf too, betrayed the puffiness due to overindulgence, and here and there a fat-sac peeked out under a mantle's edge, yellowish and sickly.

"I like your boss!" Albumarak whispered to Omber.

"She's a terror when you cross her," came the answer. "But this kind of thing she's *very* good at."

There was no need for Yull to spell out the implication of her scornful survey; many of the visitors fidgeted and tried to pull themselves into better shape. Only Quelf attempted to counter it.

"Well, if you prefer to go about half-starved, forever on the verge of becoming dreamlost, that's your lookout!"

"You're implying that I'm in that condition now?" Yull's manner suddenly turned dangerous.

"You? I wouldn't know about you for certain, but it seems pretty obvious that only people who were good and dreamlost would think of trying to send someone out into space!"

Yull turned away. "There seems little point in pursuing this conversation," she said to Omber. "Show them what you're carrying and let's find out the truth."

"Ah! The truth is that your costly toy fell out of the sky!" Quelf declared in triumph, using a phrase she had grown fond of. "You can't deny that, so you refuse to—"

But nobody was paying attention to her. All eyes were on Omber, who had produced from a bag she was carrying something which all present recognized by its unique odor: a farspeaker, smaller, yet patently more powerful, than they had ever seen before.

"This," said Yull didactically, "is one of the miniature farspeakers we developed to communicate with our spaceship when in orbit. We brought a few of them with us so as to keep in touch with the authorities at Slah."

She pinched the creature with a gentle claw. Its colors altered slightly and it gave off an aroma of contentment.

"Albumarak programed a scrapsaq carrying another of these to seek out Karg. By now it should have reached the place where you're imprisoning him. When I—"

"Imprisoning? You have no right to say that!" Quelf shrieked.

"Let's find out whether I do or not," said Yull imperturbably, and activated the farspeaker to maximum volume. At once a voice rang out, impersonal, repetitive: the sound of a recordimal.

"—is better than life at Slah. Having seen for myself, I honestly think life at Fregwil is better than life at Slah. Having seen for myself, I honestly think—"

"They're trying to condition him!" Albumarak burst out.

Silencing the farspeaker, Yull nodded gravely. "I can come to no other conclusion. Having had this gift from the sky drop into their claws, seeing the chance of a propaganda victory over us whom they regard as their rivals, Quelf and her colleagues set out to force poor Karg into such a state of permanent dreamness that when they eventually decided to let him appear in public again he would renounce his former allegiance. Luckily, as is evidenced by the fact that after so long they are still having to force one simple sentence into his memory, this is so transparent an untruth that even in his weakened state he continues to reject their dishonest overtures."

"Untruth?" bellowed Quelf. "What's untrue is what you are saying!"

"Really?" Yull turned an icy gaze on her. "How, then, about the statement 'having seen for myself'? What of Fregwil have you permitted Karg to see? The inside of a healing-house bower, correct?"

"That's exactly what I was thinking!" One of the visitors thrust forward. "I'm Yaxon, merchant from Heybrol! I came here to buy nervograp specifications—never mind that—and I know a conditioning program when I hear one! But I thought they'd been made illegal!"

She was echoed by an angry mumble from the others.

"In *civilized* cities," Yull murmured, "yes, they have!"

Having closed on Quelf, the company now drew back, as though from something emitting a noxious stench. The professor uttered a faint whimper, looking about her for support. None was forthcoming; even her students regarded her with sudden loathing.

"Albumarak," Yull said, returning the farspeaker to Omber's bag, "show us the way to Karg's bower."

They all went, exuding such a reek of fury that no one dared gainsay them. There they found him, comfortable enough to be sure in a luxurious crotch padded with the best of mosh, with a nursh in attendance to change the cleanlickers on his frostbitten pad, and with plenty to eat and drink . . . but dazed, and totally unable to escape the message repeated and repeated by recordimals either side of him. When one grew fatigued the other took over automatically; the programing was impeccable, and—as Albumarak abruptly realized with a renewed access of horror—that meant it had almost certainly been prepared by Quelf in person.

She rushed forward, snatched up both of them, and hurled them out of the bower, careless of the fact that their passage slashed great gaps in the protective spuder-webs which filtered incoming air of not only wingets but microorganisms.

"And now," said Yull with satisfaction, after checking Karg and finding him in good physical condition, at least, "we can arrange for this poor fellow to regain his normal senses. I understand that Quelf is only a research professor here. Who is the actual director? I require to speak with her *at once!*"

Her voice rang out like thunder, and one might have sworn that it altered the air-pressure like an actual storm.

The frightened nursh quavered, "I'll go find her!"

"Does she know about this?" Yull demanded.

"N-no! I'm sure she doesn't! We have at least eight-score folk in here at any given time, so she—"

"Then she's unfit to occupy her post, and I shall tell her so the moment she arrives! Fetch her, and fetch her *now!*"

# 6

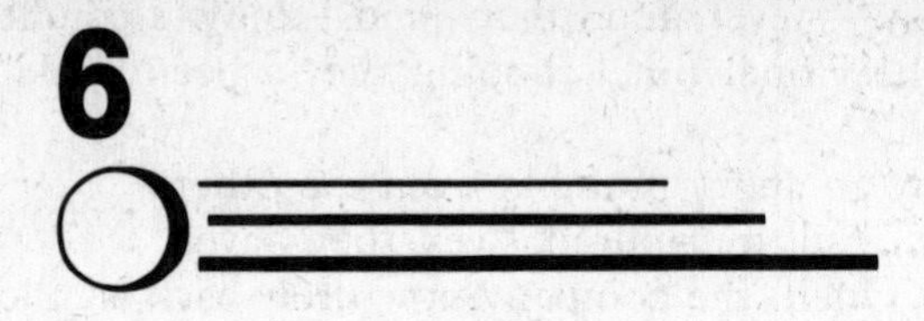

"What's going to happen to Quelf?" Omber asked.

Recriminations had continued all day, and would doubtless resume next bright, but by nightfall everyone was tired of arguing and moreover hungry. The city officials had agreed to arrange for immediate recovery of the space-cylinder, and promised to announce in the morning what other compensation they would offer for Karg's mistreatment. The Slah delegation regarded that as acceptable.

As to Quelf, she had fled the healing-house in unbearable humiliation. Her last message as she mounted her scudder and made for home had been relayed to Albumarak: "Tell that misbudded traitor not to expect any more help from me!"

So there went her future, wiped away by a single well-intentioned decision . . . but how could she possibly have acted otherwise and lived with herself afterwards? Wearily she summoned the energy to answer Omber as they and Yull left the university precincts under a blustery autumn sky.

"Oh—nothing much, probably. She's just been made one of the Jingfired, you know, and they're virtually untouchable. Also she's far too brilliant a researcher for the authorities to risk her moving elsewhere, to Hulgrapuk, for example. On top of that, her sentiments are shared by just about all the teachers here. They really do regard people from other continents as basically inferior to themselves."

"Is the incidence of metal poisoning exceptionally high at Fregwil, then?" Yull murmured, provoking her companions to a cynical chuckle.

And she continued, "I feel a celebration is in order, now that Karg is being properly cared for at last." They had been assured he would be well enough to leave his bower within two or three days. "Let's dine at the best restaurant we can find, and afterwards make a tour of this Festival of Science; I gather it finishes tonight. Albumarak, you'll be my guest, of course. And perhaps you can advise us what we might ask by way of compensation if the proposals made to us tomorrow are inadequate. That is, unless you have a prior engagement?"

"No—no, I don't! I accept with pleasure!" Albumarak had difficulty concealing her delight. Already she had been favorably impressed by the unaffected way these people treated her: naturally, casually, as though she were one of themselves. Rather than seeking a reward for her assistance, she felt she ought to be performing further services for them, if only to salve the good reputation of her city, so disgracefully mildewed by Quelf.

"Then where shall we eat? For choice, suggest an establishment patronized by members of the Jingfired. I feel an unworthy desire to snub their mandibles."

Quelf had invited Albumarak to dine with her the day she decided to cite her as her nominee. The idea of taking her new friends to the same place appealed greatly.

"I know just the one!" she declared. "And there's a dolmusq bound in the right direction over there!"

After the meal—which was excellent—they swarmed the short distance to the park where the Sparkshow was coming to its end. Though the weather was turning wintry, a number of special events had been mounted to mark its final night, and throngs of folk were vastly amused at being charged with so much sparkforce that they shed miniature aurorae from claw-tips and mandibles, yet felt no ill effects.

But Yull and Omber dismissed such shows as trivial, and paid far more attention to experiments with a practical application: gradient separation of similar organic molecules, for instance, and the use of rotating pullstones to prove that the fields they generated were intimately related to sparkforce, though as yet nobody had satisfactorily explained how. Someone had even bred back what was held to be a counterpart of the long-extinct northfinder, and claimed that its ability always to turn towards the pole must have been due to metallic particles in its pith—a challenge to those who believed that reactive metal in a living nervous system invariably led to its breakdown.

At last they came to what had proved the most popular and impressive item in the Festival: the creation of artificial lightning by means of a charge sent along a loss-free circuit. Despite having been fired a score of times every dark for a moonlong, it was still operating perfectly, as was the message-link over which news of Karg's crash had come to Fregwil, although the display on which the information appeared had had to be replaced twice.

Here Yull and Omber lingered longer than at all the other demonstrations put together, insisting on watching two of the artificial lightning-flashes and sending an unimportant message—"Greetings to Drupit from citizens of Slah!"—over the communication link. For the first time Albumarak felt excluded from their company as they discussed what they had seen in low and private tones.

But eventually they turned back to her, curling their mantles in broad grins.

"Did you work on this remarkable discovery?" Yull asked.

"Ah . . . Well, yes, as a matter of fact I did. Quelf has the habit of delegating the details to her students, and—"

"You understand the principle?"

"I'm not sure anybody does, really, but I certainly know how the circuits are grown. Why?"

Yull began to pad meditatively downslope, and the others fell in alongside her.

"Quelf was right in one thing she said to us today," she went on after a lengthy pause. "Our 'costly toy' did fall out of the sky. What served us well when we were only launching spores and spawn and automatic systems designed to fend for themselves in orbit has turned out to be much too risky when it comes to a piloted mission. For a long time we've been seeking an alternative to wet-gas-bladders as a means of lofting spacecraft. We even went so far as to consider using giant drivers directly from ground level, or rather from a mountain-top. But the life-support and guidance systems would burst under the requisite acceleration. As for what would happen to the crew—!

"Have you, though, padded across standing-spark-force repulsion?"

"Of course," Albumarak replied, staring. "But it's a mere laboratory curiosity, with about the power of one of those seeds young'uns put under a burning-glass to watch them leap as their internal gas heats up."

"You do that here too?" Yull countered with a smile. "I guess budlings are pretty much the same everywhere, aren't they? But, as I was just saying to Omber, if one could grow sufficient of these new loss-free circuits . . . Do you see what I'm getting at?"

Albumarak was momentarily aghast. She said, "But if you mean you want to use that method to launch spacecraft, you'd need laqs and craws of them!"

"I think we're less daunted by projects on such a scale than you are; the skein of gas-globes that lofted Karg was already more than a padlonglaq in height. And we don't waste our resources on private luxury the way you do on Prutaj. Excuse me, but it is the case, you know."

"It's often seemed to me," said Albumarak meditatively, "that most of what we produce is designed to keep us from thinking about the ultimate threat that hangs over us all."

"You're very different from most of your own folk, aren't you?" Omber ventured. Albumarak turned to her.

"If Quelf is to be taken as typical—and I'm afraid she is—then I'm proud of the fact!"

"You'd be quite at home in Slah, then," Yull said lightly. "But before we wander off down that particular branchway: do you think we might reasonably, in compensation for what's been done to Karg, ask how to grow a loss-free sparkforce circuit?"

Albumarak pondered for a long moment. Eventually, clenching her claws, she said with barely suppressed glee, "Yes! Yes, that's exactly what you should ask for!"

*And if they refuse to part with it—well, then, I'll go to Slah with you and bring the knowledge in my memory!*

She did not speak it aloud, but the moment she reached her decision, she felt somehow that it was far more right than waiting for her turn to be made Jingfired.

On the morrow Yull and the rest of the Slah delegation were bidden to attend a Full Court of Council, held in a huge and handsome bower in the most ancient quarter of the city. Albumarak tagged along, though on arrival she was quite ignored. It pleased her to see her "superiors" in such a plight; the atmosphere was stiff with the reek of embarrassment, and the welcome offered to the visitors, though correct, was a hollow one.

Sullen, Quelf had been obliged to put in an appearance, and perched with a few of her closest colleagues on one side of the bower. At the center was Ingolfine, old, excessively fat, but the senior of the living Jingfired, to whom all others must defer when matters of high policy were debated.

"Were there not once Jingfired at Slah?" Albumarak asked Omber in a whisper.

"Oh yes! Indeed, they still exist. But ours are mostly scientists who do not make their rank the excuse for show and pomp. They regard it as the greatest possible honor to be elected, and they are charged never to boast about it. Yull may be one; I'd rather lose a claw than ask her."

The more she learned about the way of life at Slah, the more Albumarak approved of it.

And then Ingolfine wheezed a command for silence, and they composed themselves to listen to what she had to say.

"It has been concluded by the members of our Council that a grave—ah—*error of judgment* has occurred in the case of the foreigner Karg, inasmuch as although—and let me emphasize this—he has been afforded the best of medical care, excessive enthusiasm for the merits of life at Fregwil led respected Quelf to overpad the boundary of normal courtesy towards one who was sick and far from home."

Quelf looked as though she would like to disappear.

"Honor obliges us therefore to make restitution. We propose to endow a studentship tenable by a young person from Slah for up to a quarter-score of years, to be devoted to any subject taught at our university."

And she waited for Yull's response to what she clearly regarded as a generous offer.

It followed promptly. "We would be dreamlost and foolish to

commit any of our young people to the claws and mandibles of so-called teachers who regard us as an inferior folk!"

The insult provoked a furious outcry. When Ingolfine quelled it, she demanded, "Then what do you ask for?"

"The secret of loss-free circuitry, so we can put it to better use than what you're sure to waste it on!"

This time the hubbub was reinforced by combat-stink. "Out of the question!" Ingolfine declared after consulting her advisers.

"Very well, then," Yull said composedly. "We have an alternative demand. Regardless of the medical care given him, which we have certain reservations about, it is an undeniable fact that Karg was maltreated here. We will settle for taking one of your citizens home with us, not against her or his will, in order to demonstrate to the world how much better we at Slah can make a foreigner welcome."

Ingolfine and the other officials relaxed. If the Slah delegation were content to achieve a mere propaganda coup . . . More private discussion followed, and finally Ingolfine announced, "To that we see no objection."

"You state that publicly, as a matter of principle?"

Again, hurried consultation. Then, defiantly, "Yes!"

"Very well. We choose Albumarak."

There was a horrified hush. Quelf broke it, rising to full height and shrieking, "But she's my best student!"

"Was!" shouted Albumarak, marveling at how clearly Yull had read her secret intentions. "After what you did to Karg, nobody will respect you again so long as you live!"

# 7

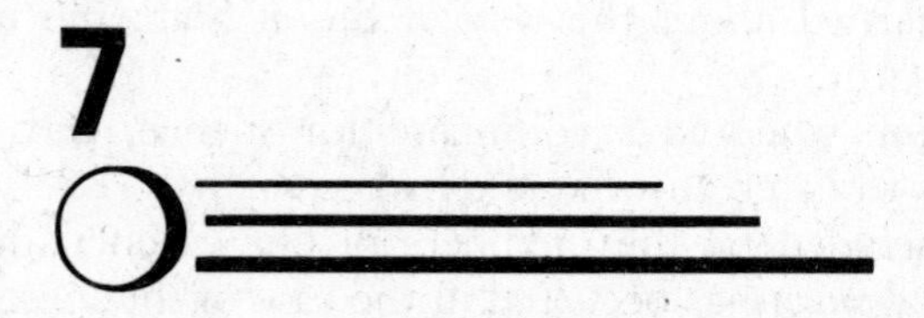

During the dark that preceded her departure, Albumarak perched alone in one of the shabby neglected bowers of the house where the Slah delegation had been obliged to take up lodging. Her mind was reeling under the impact of the hatred she was having to endure. Even in her fits of bitterest loathing for the "high-pressure citizens" of her bud-place she had never imagined that they, in full awareness of what had been done to Karg, would regard her as the traitor and not Quelf. It showed that they too would have wanted the foreigner to be cheated into turning his mantle, heedless of how much he suffered in the process, in order to delude those who were striving to escape the truth.

Soft slithering at the entrance aroused her. The bower's luminants were withering and dim, and the night was cloudy; neither moonshine nor the glimmer of stars and comets lent their light. Not waiting to sense the newcomer's aroma, she said in a dull tone, "Who's there?"

"It's Karg. Do you mind if I join you?"

"Why—why, certainly you may!" She had met him earlier; he was still weak, but had insisted on remaining at Fregwil until arrangements for recovering his cylinder were complete. Thinking he might need assistance, she moved towards him, but he waved her aside with one claw.

"I may not be able to walk properly right now, but I can swarm along a branch all right . . . There." He settled in the crotch next to hers, where they could look out at the city through gaps between the bravetree trunks.

"I suspect I owe you my sanity as well as my life," he said after a while.

Embarrassed, she shifted on her perch. "It was Presthin who actually rescued you. I just went along for the ride. And it was Yull who suggested how we could eavesdrop on what Quelf was doing to you."

"But you programed the scrapsaq, didn't you? She told me it was an amazing job, given the time available."

"Well, we had to keep the snowrither's haodah sealed all the way to Drupit, so I had plenty of time to get to know your aroma. Mimicking it well enough to condition a scrapsaq wasn't hard."

She found herself feeling a little uncomfortable in the presence of this person who had risked and suffered so much in a cause which, a moonlong ago, she had been accustomed to dismissing as worthless.

Sensing her mood, Karg inquired, "Are you having second thoughts about going to Slah?"

"No, quite the reverse!"—with a harsh laugh. "I'm looking forward to it. I never thought my folk could be so brutal!"

After a pause, Karg said, "I've been talking to Yull about your people. She said . . . I don't know if I ought to repeat this. It's indecent to talk that way about another folk."

"Say anything you like and I'll say worse!"

"Very well. But there isn't really another folk, is there? We are all one. We're budded, and we die, and in between we make the most of what's offered to us, and afterwards whatever it was that made us *us* returns to whence it came. Maybe next time it will animate creatures under another sun, so different from ourselves that when what used to make up you and me comes back we won't recognize each other. But of course there can't be any way of knowing."

Albumarak was not in the habit of debating the mystery of awareness; the academics of Fregwil had long ago decreed that certain problems were inherently insoluble and should be left to take care of themselves. She said hastily, "You were about to quote Yull, weren't you?"

"All right, since you insist. She holds that your folk must be less than civilized because you take no thought for the future, and won't invest effort to promote the survival of our species but only for your own immediate enjoyment. She says this is proved by the way you waste so much of your resources on entertainment and distraction. You don't have enough left over to make sure either that your food-plants are healthy or that the air you breathe has been purged of poisonous metals. If you did, you'd be working to ensure that even though we as individuals can't escape into space our budlings or their budlings may. She's so convinced of this, she's going to insist on all of us being purified from crest to pad when we get home. And she swears that's why the people of Fregwil went crazy enough to want the futile victory of conditioning me by force!"

He ended on a defiant note, as though expecting Albumarak to contradict.

And only a short while ago she would have done so. But her journey with Presthin, brief though it was, had given her the shadow of an insight into what Karg must have braced himself for when he volunteered to fly into space. To her the snowbound wastes of the highlands were alien enough; how much more, then, the boundless desert between the stars!

Hesitantly she asked, "Did it do any lasting harm? The conditioning, I mean?"

He gave a dry chuckle. "Probably not very much, vulnerable though I was. I had to learn to cling hard to reality a long time ago. I used to supervise an underwater quarry, you know, in an environment nearly as harsh and lonely as outer space."

"I didn't know! In fact, I know almost nothing about you, do I? This is the first time we've met properly."

He stretched himself; his injuries were tightening as they healed, causing discomfort. "Well, that was why they picked me—that, and the fact that I was much smaller than the other candidates, so they could loft a bit of extra reaction mass for free-fall maneuvering. Do you understand how my craft works, or rather, was supposed to work?"

"I think so. The gas-globes were to carry it above most of the atmosphere, and then the drivers were to blast you into orbit, and then you'd fire them again to—"

"Not quite. Out in space I was to use regular musculator pumps to expel a heavy inert liquid that we've developed. The fuel used for the drivers becomes unstable under free-space radiation. We lost two or three of our early cylinders that way, before we figured out what the problem was. Or rather, I should say 'they,' not 'we,' because that happened long before I joined the team."

Karg heaved a deep sigh. "I was looking forward to it, I really was! And now I've lost my chance forever."

"Surely not! After your pad has grown back"—Albumarak could still not mention that promise without a hint of awe in her voice, for it bespoke medical techniques far surpassing those boasted of at Fregwil —"they won't want to waste someone with your special talents and training."

"Oh, I gather Yull impressed everybody mightily with her reference to regrowth, but the process is actually still in the experimental stage, and in any case you don't get the feeling back. And every square clawide of my body was pressed into service to control the hauq, and the purifiers, and the maneuvering pumps, and the farspeakers and the rest. No, I had my chance, and a meteorite stole it once for all."

"So what will you do now—go back to underwater work?"

"I could, I suppose; it isn't so demanding . . . But I'd rather not. I think I'll stay on at the space-site. I gather Yull told you that we're going to have to abandon our existing plans and try another course."

"Yes, but . . ." Albumarak clacked her mandibles dolefully. "You said your regrowth techniques are still at the experimental stage. The same is true of our loss-free circuits. They still take ages to grow—we'd been working on the one which we demonstrated at the Sparkshow ever since the last Festival of Science—and they haven't yet been proved under field conditions. For all we can tell, they may be vulnerable to disease, funqi, wild beasts, parasitic plants . . ."

"Yes, it seems more than a padlong from demonstration of a pilot version to what Yull is talking about. Even so, a fresh eye cast on the principle . . . What *is* it?"

"The principle? Well . . . Well, how much do you know about sparkforce?"

Karg shrugged; she felt the branches stir. "Take it for granted that I know a little about a lot of things."

"Yes, you'd have to, wouldn't you?" Embarrassed again, Albumarak went on hastily. "What she seems to have in mind isn't even at the experimental level yet. It's a mere oddment, a curiosity. It depends on using sparkforce charges to repel each other."

"I thought that must be it, but if you did put such a huge charge on one of our cylinders, then . . . Hmm! Wait a moment; I think I see how it might be done. If there were some way to alternate the kinds of repulsion—Ach! I'm taking an infusion to control my pain, and my mind is still too foggy for constructive reasoning. But I'll remember to mention my idea to Yull in the morning."

He shifted in the crotch, turning his eye on her. "Did you get enough to eat this sundown?"

"As much as I wanted."

"If you didn't eat properly, you may find your mind is as sluggish as mine when you arrive in Slah. It can take quite a long time to adjust to local dark and bright after traveling to a different continent at today's speeds—Oh, hark at me! I hadn't set pad on a foreign continent myself before my crash. I'm not the person to lecture you. But I thought it was worth mentioning."

"How would you have coped in space, then? There isn't a dark-bright cycle up there!"

"In the orbit I was supposed to follow, there would have been, but six or seven times as fast as a regular day. I didn't expect any trouble, though. Deep underwater you have no dark-bright cycle at all, and I lived through that."

"What exactly were you to do out there?"

Karg stretched again, and a hint of agony discolored his pheromones, but it lasted only a moment.

"Bring together two of our automatic orbital cylinders and connect their ecosystems, then work inside them for a while, making sure everything was going as well as the farspeakers indicate. We do seem to have beaten one major problem: we've developed plants that purge themselves of deleterious mutations due to radiation. Some of them have been through four or five score generations without losing their identity, and should still be fit to eat. But of course there may be changes too tiny for our monitors to locate and report on. How I wish we could get to the moon and back! We need samples of the vegetation up there in the worst way!"

Listening to him in the gloom of the ill-tended bower, Albumarak found herself wondering what Presthin had been like when she was younger and less cynical; much like Karg, she suspected . . . She decided once for all that she had been right to throw in her lot with these people. If they succeeded with their plan to survive in space, they would not be driven mad by the fate of their fellow creatures, any more than Karg by Quelf's mistreatment. But they were no less civilized for that. Yull's contempt for the folk of Prutaj was justified. Worse than primitive, they were insane . . . if sanity consisted in doing the most the universe allowed, and she knew no better definition.

In a tremulous tone she said, "I admire you very much, Karg. I'd invite you to pair with me, but I shouldn't be in bud during my first few moonlongs at Slah, should I?"

"Quite right," was the answer. "And in any case I'm still too weak, though I look forward to the time when it will be possible. And—ah—you say you admire me. But all my life I've been trained under the finest tutors to do unusual and extraordinary work. You've had a truly awful teacher, and yet for me at least you've performed not just one miracle, but two. Thank you again."

And he swarmed away, leaving her delighted with the world.

# 8

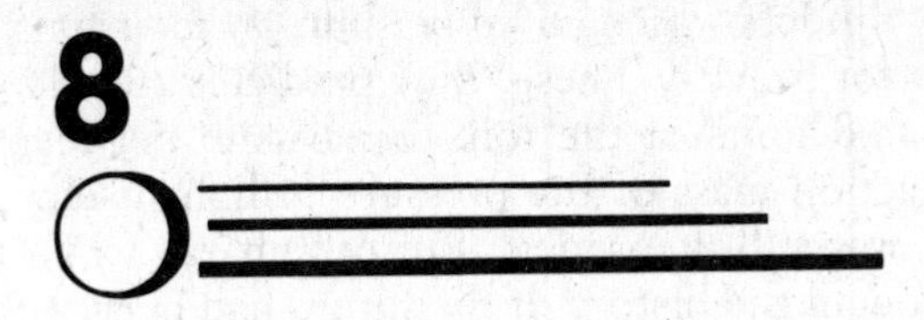

For the first few days, what fascinated Albumarak about her new home was less its modern aspect—its space-site, its laboratories which in many ways were more impressive than those at Fregwil, perhaps because the staff were under less pressure to be forever producing novelties—than its sheer antiquity. She had been vaguely aware that Slah enshrined the last remaining traces of the only ocean-going city to have outlasted the heyday of the People of the Sea, but it was very different to hold in her own claws the mandible of a long-extinct fish, found among the roots of its most ancient trees, or nibble a fragment of funqus and know the species had last been modified by Gveest in person.

As she had expected, the pace of life here was calmer, yet she detected few signs of discontent or boredom. More people were occupied with old-fashioned tasks—such as disposing of dead luminants—which at Fregwil were deputed to creatures programed for them, but there was a greater sense of being in touch with the natural world, which Albumarak found refreshing, and the citizens, most of whom had naturally heard about her, seemed never to lack time to offer advice or assistance.

By stages she began to grasp the full sweep of the plan these people had conceived for the salvation of their afterbuds, and its grandeur overawed her. They referred casually to the astronomers' estimate that it might take ten thousand years for the sun to orbit through the Major Cluster; they accepted without question that its dense gas—from which stars could be observed condensing—would raise the solar temperature to the point where the planet became uninhabitable; they were resigned to the high probability that there would be a stellar collision, and if that did not eventuate, then so much random matter was bound to fall from the sky that it would come to the same thing in the end; and all this was equally well known at Fregwil.

But instead of closing their minds to the catastrophe, these people were prepared to plan against it. They spoke confidently of vehicles carrying scores-of-scores of folk, along with everything needed to support them, which could be moved away from the sun as it heated up, maneuvering as necessary to remain within its biosphere, while adapted plants freed raw materials from the outer planets and their moons. Then, later, they envisaged breaking up the smaller orbs and converting them into cylinders which could be spun on their long axis to provide a substitute for gravity. These, they predicted, would permit at least some isolated units of the folk to navigate between the nascent stars, using reaction mass or the pressure of light itself.

All this, of course, was still theoretical. But Albumarak was astonished to learn in what detail the history of the future had been worked out here. She wondered whether she was worthy to contribute to it.

Inevitably, the bright arrived when she was summoned to the neurophysical laboratory attached to the space-site, well beyond the city limits. Omber appeared to guide her. There she was welcomed by a tubby, somewhat irascible personage called Scholar Theng, who lost no time in getting down to business.

"Well, young'un," she boomed, "it seems we have to reconsider our ideas. Yull tells me loss-free circuits are the answer. She brought me a sample—Don't look so surprised! Turned out a good many of your citizens didn't care for what Quelf did to Karg, and gifted her with a piece of one, enough to culture a few cells from."

"You didn't tell me!" Albumarak cried. "I'd have been here long ago if I'd realized you weren't going to have to start from scratch! I've wasted time trying to reconstruct from memory everything I know about designing the things!"

"So that's what you've been doing, is it?" Theng growled. "I had the impression you were just sight-seeing . . . Well, come and look at what we've got so far."

If it was true that she had started with "a few cells" she had made remarkable progress. Already a web of thin brownish tendrils stretched back and forth over a patch of heavily fertilized ground under a transparent membrane that gathered winter sunwarmth and protected them from storms.

"But this is wonderful!" Albumarak declared.

"Oh, we can grow them all right, and they seem to perform as advertised. Question is, can we make them do what Yull wants? You're an expert on sparkforce, they tell me. What do you think?"

The likelihood of putting Yull's proposal into effect seemed suddenly much greater. Albumarak filled her mantle.

"Omber, it is the case, isn't it, that one would still have to loft drivers and their fuel, even if one did build a—a launcher capable of replacing gas-globes?"

They had occasionally discussed the matter; she knew the answer would be yes before it came. And went on, "So the next step must be to grow a miniature test version of your cylinders and see whether"—*thank you, Karg!*—"we can put sufficient charge on it."

"We can't," Theng retorted briskly. "We already went over that with our chief chemist Ewblet. It would destabilize the fuel. Want to see the simulation records?"

Albumarak was minded to clack her mandibles in dismay, but controlled herself and, so far as she could, her exudations. She said in a tone as sharp as Theng's, "Then let Ewblet find a way of preventing it! My business is loss-free sparkforce circuitry, and I'd like to get on with it!"

Theng looked at her for a long moment. At last she said, "Well spoken. What do you expect to need?"

It was like being on a different planet. Colleagues much older than herself consulted her without being patronizing; others of her own age reported to her the problems they had encountered, described their proposed solutions, and asked for her opinion; in turn, when she swam into a snag they were prompt to offer information and advice. She had already grasped the overall pattern of what the folk here were committed to, but now she was given insight into its minutiae . . . and the multiplicity of details was frightening. So too, in a sense, was the dedication she discovered. She almost came to believe that there was no one in the whole of Slah, bar a clawful of budlings, who lacked a part to play in converting their vision into reality.

Space-launches using gas-globes were continuing despite the winter storms, along with work on every other aspect of the scheme. The orbits of some of the space-cylinders were decaying; it was essential to send up more reaction mass, using automatic control systems, so they could be forced further out. Everybody, not just Karg, wanted to learn what was happening to the vegetation on the moon; one of the younger scientists proposed crashing a cylinder there which would survive sufficiently intact to gather samples and then emit two or three others much smaller than itself, propelled by a simple explosion on to a course that would bring them to rendezvous with a collector in local orbit, and then recovering the collector in the way designed for Karg. Simulations showed it might well succeed, and the job was promptly put in claw.

Eventually Albumarak said despairingly to her new friends, "I don't know how you stand the pressure!"

But they answered confidently, "We enjoy it! After all, is there a better cause we could be working for?"

And then, to their amazement, they realized she had never learned the means to make the most of dark-time, devised long before the Greatest Meteorite, which depended on freeing consciousness from attending to the process of digestion. With only the mildest of reproaches concerning Fregwil's standards of education, they instructed her in the technique, and after that she no longer wondered how they crammed so much into a single day.

As Karg had predicted, casting a fresh eye on the loss-free circuits led to rapid improvement. Winter was milder here than at Fregwil, but that alone did not account for the speed with which the tendrils grew, nor for the flawless way each and every one checked out. Quelf's team had been resigned to losing two or three in every score; here, when one slacked in its growth, the cause was sought and found and in a few days' time it was back to schedule.

Albumarak detected something of the same phenomenon in herself. She was eating an unfamiliar diet, but her mind had never been so active. She mentioned as much to Theng once, when the latter was in a particularly good mood, and was told: "A few generations ago, the air at Slah was always filthy thanks to the metal-working sites nearby. That was at the time of Aglabec and his disciples—heard of them? I thought you would have! Rival cities like Hulgrapuk and Fregwil made the most of it, to disparage us! But we retained our wits well enough to realize it was no use sending crazy people into space, so we put that right, and now there's not a city on the planet where you breathe purer air or drink cleaner water or eat a more nourishing diet. We're allegedly possessed of intelligence; we judged it right to apply our conclusions to ourselves as well as our environment. And it's paid off, hasn't it?"

Indeed it had . . .

At one stage Albumarak came near despair, when a simulation proved that nothing like enough sparkforce could be generated to drive even the smallest of the Slah cylinders to the heights achieved by gas-globes. There were no pullstones worth mentioning on this continent; the world's only large deposit was on Prutaj. Suddenly someone she had never heard of reported that by adding this and this to the diet of a flashplant, and modifying it in such a way, its output could be multiplied until it matched the best pullstone generator. Someone else suggested means of deriving current from the wind; another, from compression using the beating of ocean waves; another, from conversion of sunshine . . .

Yull was in the habit of visiting the laboratory now and then, sometimes with Karg or Omber, more often alone. One day in spring she arrived with a grave expression, and asked Theng, in Albumarak's hearing, what progress had been made.

"Good!" Theng declared gruffly. "Ewblet has stabilized the fuel at last, we have enough sparkforce and nearly enough loss-free circuitry to loft a driver to where it can be fired into orbit, and the eastern side of Spikemount slopes at pretty well an ideal angle to build the launcher. We expect to be at status go by fall."

"You're going to have to do better than that," Yull told her soberly.

Sensing disaster, Albumarak drew close.

"Take a look at these," Yull invited, proffering a pack of images. They were regular astronomical pictures of the kind produced at any major observatory, and they showed a patch of night sky in the vicinity of the Major Cluster. Theng glanced at them and passed them to Albumarak.

"You'll have to explain what's so special about them!"

"This is!" Yull tapped one tiny dot with a delicate claw. "Look again. They were taken on successive nights."

"It's not on this one," Albumarak muttered. "But it's on this one, only fainter, and—no, not on this one, but on this one as well, and brighter if anything . . . Oh, no!"

"I think," Yull murmured, "you've caught on. For nearly a moonlong past, something has been appearing and vanishing in that area of the sky. We have here a score of images that show it and a quarter-score that don't. What is it?"

Albumarak's mind raced. "Something spinning! It's rough on one side and smooth on the other, so it only catches the sun at certain angles!"

"Exactly what our most eminent astronomers suspect," Yull said, reclaiming the pictures. "In addition, though, they can show that it's very far out, beyond Sluggard."

"Then it must be huge!"

"Yes. As big as the moon. And what little of its orbit has been analyzed suggests it may be going to intersect with ours in at most a score of years. Even if it misses us, it will certainly crash into the sun."

# 9

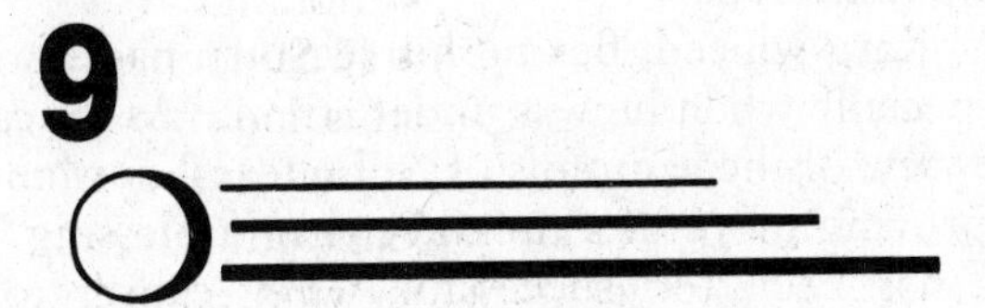

Albumarak felt unbelievably old as she strove to judge the relative merits of a score of rival projects competing for time on the world's only full-scale sparkforce launcher.

Yull's inspiration had been justified over and over. Cylinders had been flung skyward first to where half the mass of the air was below, then four-fifths, then nine-tenths, the magic altitude from which the drivers could reach escape velocity. Now it glowed vivid blue ten times every moonlong, summer and winter alike, and the air for padlonglaqs reeked of sparkforce stink, and the night sky was crowded with artificial stars, one of which loomed brighter than the moon at full: an orbital colony-to-be.

But should she recommend to Theng that their precious future charges be expended on yet more automatic linkup systems, in the hope of making that "moon" habitable by more people than the schedule called for, or should priority be given to this new scheme to win time by crashing on the wild planetoid a load of rockeater spawn modified to digest it into dust? Now it was crossing the orbit of Stolidchurl, so even if all went perfectly the encounter could not occur earlier than when it reached the distance of Steadyman . . .

Life at Slah had grown hard over the past five years.

But there were others it had treated worse. She didn't look up at the visitor who entered her bower in the control-house. A familiar aroma preceded him, tinged with mingled rage and weariness. As soon as she could, she uttered a greeting, and was horrified to see, as he slumped into a crotch, how limp Karg's posture had become.

"I heard how you were received at Hulgrapuk," she said.

"No worse than last time," he sighed. "Same old story! 'There's no means of avoiding the impact of this greater-than-greatest meteorite, so . . . !' But I do have some good news. I bet you won't guess where it's from."

"Fregwil," she offered, intending a joke.

"Correct. Quelf's coming here."

Reflexively she rose to full height. "Incredible! Why?"

"Officially they're talking about a fact-finding mission. Our local informants say different. There's likely to be a revolution at Fregwil if the city officials don't start actively helping our project."

Albumarak slowly subsided. "There are some kinds of aid we'd be better off without," she muttered.

"Don't I know it!" Karg winced, flexing his regrown pad; it continued to give pain, especially when he was under stress. "As we came in to land, I had a fine view of the campfuls of 'volunteers' outside the city. I gather they're proving more of a nuisance than a blessing."

"Our propaganda has been too successful. They expect to be lofted into orbit right away. When they find out their role only involves making sure there are enough raw materials, enough food, enough of everything that has to be at a given place at a given time, they turn nasty on us."

"Figures. But they're leaving Hulgrapuk in droves, you know. And the exodus from Fregwil is scaring Quelf and the rest of her coterie. Their young people are simply moving out, flying here if they can, or taking passage on any old barq or junq that might carry them to Slah. I saw the port at Fregwil. I think a lot of them may get drowned."

After a pause Albumarak said, "I've been asked if I'd like to go to orbit one of these days."

"Grab the chance! I still dream of how wonderful it would have been if I—"

"But everything is still theory! We're investing this colossal effort, and we still haven't sent anybody into space, let alone proved that folk can survive up there!"

Rigid as a rock but for the flexing of his mantle as he spoke, Karg said, "I'd have proved it. I didn't insist on waiting until your huge new complex had been spun up to a rate that will mimic gravity. My chance was stolen from me!"

"Everybody knows that!"

"Everyone except you seems to have forgotten!"

And he erected and stormed out.

For a moment Albumarak thought of rushing after him, to offer consolation. She abandoned the idea. She had come to know him intimately since arriving at Slah, and when a mood like this overcame him there was small point in arguing. Besides, she had more urgent matters on her mind.

Calmly she activated the nervograp that connected her with Theng's bower, and dictated to a recordimal: "Data at claw indicate that we cannot modify rockeater spores in sufficient quantities to demolish the wild planetoid prior to estimated encounter time." She hesitated, then went on, "It is my opinion that far more effort should be directed towards ensuring that the conditions we are establishing for survival in orbit *are actually survivable up to and including reproduction of the species!* Because otherwise we're done for . . . aren't we?"

But the prospect of making an alliance with Fregwil was too good to miss. If the resources of Prutaj were put at Slah's disposal, within a decade most of what the space-planners hoped for could be brought about. Fevered discussions ensued, in which Albumarak resolutely declined to take part, ostensibly on the grounds that she had been away from home too long, in fact because she still hated Quelf's pith.

Obviously, a special demonstration had to be laid on to coincide with Quelf's visit, and in a fit of the same kind of exasperation which had plagued her youth Albumarak suggested they might as well loft her into orbit. Both Theng and Yull vetoed that at once; they maintained she had too many useful skills to let her risk her life. Yet she garnered the impression that someone, at least, had taken her seriously.

She forced herself to continue her normal daily duties, wondering constantly whether she had been wrong to advise against the rockeater project, whether someone had miscalculated the wild planetoid's orbital velocity, whether . . .

Her mind remained incessantly in turmoil. Talking to Omber, talking to Karg now that he was back from the latest of his trips around the world to recruit support—nothing helped, until the dark when Karg said acutely, "You would flee into space, wouldn't you, if it meant escaping Quelf and the memory of shame you brought here?"

That made her laugh at herself, and she said as she embraced him fondly, "Had it not been for the wild planetoid, we would have paired by now. I'd like your bud!"

"I know!" A shadow fell across his words. "You were correct to say we don't know whether we can survive as well as our creatures do in space. I wouldn't curse a budling with deformity—yet evolution must compel it, no?"

"Our distant ancestors . . ."

"Exactly. They were very different from ourselves."

She pondered that.

The floater from Prutaj that brought in Quelf and her party was larger and clawsomer than any other at Slah's touchdown-ground. Albumarak had begged to be excused from the official welcome party, but she was unable to resist joining the crowd which gathered to witness this unprecedented visit. Polite applause greeted Quelf's appearance—from those who had somehow missed hearing about what she had done to Karg, she thought sourly. But when she recognized the second person who descended from the floater, she could control herself no longer.

"Presthin!" she shouted, and rushed towards her.

"That same," came the dry response. "I felt it was high time I said hello to Karg. We never met properly, remember?"

"I must introduce you at once! If he's here, that is. I haven't seen him, but then he has small reason to love Quelf." Albumarak glanced around, but was abruptly reminded that there were formalities to get through; Quelf was fixing her with the same withering glare she had learned to know so well when she was still a lowly student at Fregwil.

"Later!" she whispered as Yull and Theng led Quelf towards the waiting loudeners . . . exactly at the moment when a chorus of execration thundered forth from half the crowd.

Of course! Who more likely to turn up today than those who had quit Fregwil in fury at its rulers' indolence?

Suddenly there was chaos. Albumarak clenched her claws as the speeches of welcome were drowned out. But Presthin only said, "Sometimes I wonder whether this species we belong to can be worth preserving . . ."

Eventually order was restored, and Yull and Theng were able to utter a few generalizations about the value of cooperation between Slah and Fregwil. Then Quelf launched into a carefully planned address, praising the astronomers who had located the wild planetoid and the efforts of those who for so long had been reaching out towards the stars.

"Hypocrite!" Albumarak muttered.

"Oh, no. She means precisely what she says," countered Presthin. "It's finally penetrated her pith that if there is another giant meteorite strike in a few years' time, she won't be more immune than anybody else. Just listen to the conclusion of her speech. She's been rehearsing it on the way here."

Albumarak composed herself. Quelf was saying, "—and if you

prove you can actually keep the folk alive in space, as you have for so long been promising, then you may rely on our supplying both materiel . . . and personnel!"

"She's as bad as the volunteers in the camps!" Albumarak cried. "She expects us to send *her* into orbit!"

"It might be a good way of getting rid of her," said Presthin caustically.

The crowd erupted again, and this time individual shouts were discernible: "About time! What were you saying five years ago? Couldn't you have led instead of following? What were you made Jingfired for?"

Reeking with anger, Quelf bent towards Yull. Albumarak barely caught what she said; it sounded like, "This rowdy reception is no advertisement for your city!"

Turning ever so slightly, just enough for the loudeners to pick up her words, Yull countered, "Normally, at Slah, we don't waste time on this sort of ceremonial. We have urgent work to do. Apparently you've not acquired that habit."

Quelf towered, exuding combat-stink. But Yull's point had registered with the crowd and delighted everyone else within hearing, not just the Fregwil expatriates. A burst of hilarity allowed Theng to claim the loudeners.

"I'm sure you're all anxious," she stated with heavy irony, "to hear more of what our guest has to say. Regrettably"—a well-timed pause —"we've arranged a demonstration of precisely the kind she wishes to see, and it's overdue, so . . . A scudder is waiting, Scholar Quelf. Do come this way!"

# 10

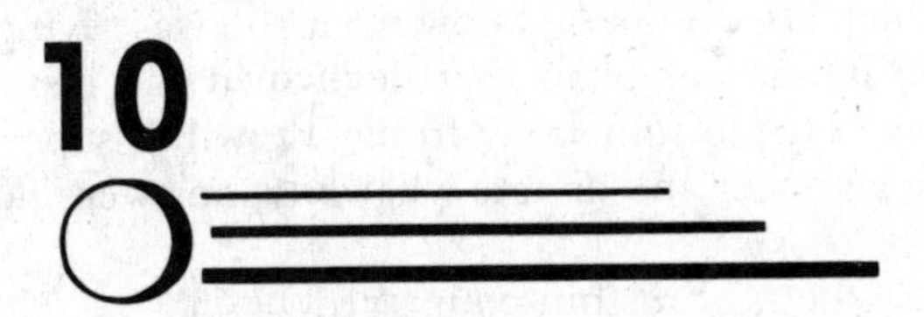

*A*lbumarak was unable to avoid being caught up in the exodus towards the space-site, though she and Presthin did at least manage to mount the scudder behind Quelf's.

"Still no sign of Karg?" the goadster inquired.

"No, but . . . Well, I haven't seen him around much lately, anyhow. Not since the news of Quelf's visit broke."

"Can't say I blame him," Presthin grunted. Surveying the scenery, she went on, "So this is the city you prefer to your own. What's life like here, that it attracts you so?"

"I used to wonder what attracted you to the highlands. I found my own equivalent at Slah. Life is much harder and we enjoy many fewer luxuries. But there's a sense of purpose in the air, a feeling that we're all working towards the best possible goal. Also our leaders aren't so . . . I don't quite know how to define it. Maybe I should just say that nobody like Quelf could wield such influence at Slah."

"All by itself that explains why you like the place," Presthin said dryly. Craning for a better view, she added, "And that must be your space-launcher, right?"

In a dead straight line at the circle/$2^3$ angle, the giant tube sloped sunsetward up the mountain they were passing. At its base a cylinder was being readied for launch. Presthin gazed at it long and hard.

"I've seen images," she said at last, "but the reality is something else. How long is it now?"

"Ten padlonglaqs. We just extended it. But it's been launching cylinders successfully since it was only half that length."

"And you're going to dispatch another specially for us. What sort?"

"I don't know," Albumarak muttered.

"I thought you were among the top scientists here now!"

"Yes, but—well, frankly, Presthin, I didn't want anything to do with making Quelf welcome. I said as much, and they respected my wishes."

Their scudder checked and dropped off the branchway just behind the one carrying Quelf. Yull, compelling herself to be polite, ushered the Fregwil delegation towards the control-house. Contriving to fall back a little, Theng muttered to Albumarak, "No wonder you dislike your old teacher so much! She must be the vainest and most self-important person on the planet! Do you know what she was saying on the way here? Because it was her team that developed the loss-free circuit, we ought to have invited somebody from Fregwil to supervise the construction of the launcher and dictate what missions were flown with it!"

"We're not all like Quelf," Presthin countered.

"Ah . . . No, of course." Theng exuded embarrassment. "I spoke out of turn. I'm sorry. Well, we'd better go inside, or we shall miss the launch-gap."

"Is Karg around? Presthin would like to say hello."

Theng's expression changed to one of utter surprise. She started to say something, but it was drowned out by the racket of a klaxon-plant, warning everybody on the site to prepare for launch. The acceleration imparted to a space-cylinder was relatively gentle now, and created less overpressure than a driver test, but there was still a sonic boom to brace oneself against.

"Inside!" Theng directed, and they hastened to obey.

By now so many launches had occurred, they were reduced to a matter of routine, but this one was made different by Quelf and her companions, who were wandering around demanding the function of this, that and the other device, and on being told declaring that they would have organized things otherwise. Yull withstood the temptation as long as possible, but at last erupted in ill-disguised annoyance.

"Permit me to remind our *distinguished* visitors that from this site we have achieved four-score successful orbital missions employing gas-globes, and twice that number using the sparkforce launcher! I submit this as evidence for the correctness of our approach!"

Albumarak could guess the nature of Quelf's retort before it was uttered. She was right.

"And you still haven't proved that the folk can survive in space. Have you?"

Her tone was harsh, yet unmistakably her exudations contradicted it. She wanted to be told there was an escape from this endangered planet; she simply didn't want anybody but herself to be the one who gained the credit for making it possible.

Her posture eloquent of disdain, Yull snapped her claw against a farspeaker hanging from a nearby branch. At once a voice rang out.

"On-hauq status is *go!* I've been ready for ages—how much longer do you plan to keep me waiting?"

*Karg!*

Albumarak padded half a step towards Yull, but Theng caught her by the mantle's edge.

"Did you really not know?" she demanded.

"I haven't seen him for nearly a moonlong!"

But there was no time to say anything else. Yull was turning to the visitors again.

"I am about to give the launch command. You will oblige us by remaining still and saying nothing as from—*now!*"

First the long straight tube began to hum. Apart from its size, in appearance this launcher was not so different from the ranks of rings which once had served to guide under test the primitive drivers known to Chybee, three generations ago. But it operated on a very different principle. Both the amount of sparkforce it could withstand and the subtlety of its controls bore witness to the unstinting effort of its creators, who had condensed fivescore years' worth of development into less than five.

After the humming came the glow. No matter how perfect the insulation of the circuits, there was always a trace of energy that leaked out as light, because matter was matter and would be so until the universe's end. Ideally it should have been enclosed by vacuum, but the best that could be done was to create a low-pressure zone within the tube. The necessary pumping made a low and grumbling noise.

The cylinder, at this point, began to stir. The charge upon it was enough to counteract its weight.

Inevitably, all communication ceased.

"Why did you let him?" Albumarak whispered to Yull.

"It was a promise," she replied elliptically.

"But he's a cripple!"

"Yes . . ." Yull was scanning the remotes; they were as normal as for any launch. "You never paired, did you?"

"We've always wanted to, but after hearing about the wild planetoid we both agreed it was too risky to start budding. But what does that have to do with—? Oh! *No!*"

"I think you worked it out. He'd never have told you, or anyone, but of course he couldn't keep it from the doctors who treated him after his return. He thinks the reason he can't pair anymore wasn't due to frostbite, but to something done to him at Fregwil, maybe under Quelf's instructions. Those who regard other folk as their inferiors— No time for more! Slack down! You visitors, copy us! There's going to be a very loud noise!"

Those with experience set a prompt example, dropping to the ground as though prong-stabbed. From the corner of her eye Albumarak saw how reluctantly Quelf complied, and hoped she would fail to relax completely. If so, she would be taught a lesson by pain.

A lesson that she clearly well deserved.

The air was full of a familiar grinding noise, like the sound of pebbles on a headland fidgeting under the impact of the tide. This was always the most fearful moment. The launcher, if it failed, would do so now, when the charge on both the cylinder and the tube was at its peak.

No one was watching. No one could watch. All must be reported through sensors and monitors, at which Albumarak stared achingly. All normal—all normal—GO!

She struggled to remember that Karg had lived underwater, that he had survived frostbite, that he had resisted conditioning, that he had retained enough self-control not to become embittered at losing his chance of pairing, and indeed had lived half his life in the hope of just this opportunity. But then the sonic boom made the control-house rock, and he was gone.

When the echoes died away there was another noise: Quelf moaning. It was, as Albumarak had half expected, beneath her dignity to slump on the ground like everybody else. She had no doubt ruptured some unimportant tubule, which would heal. The rest of the company seemed to have reached the same conclusion, for no one was paying attention to her.

"How long do we have to wait before we hear from him?" Presthin asked.

"Oh, quite a while." Yull curled her mantle in a cryptic grin. "But then it won't just be us; it will be everyone who hears from him. Let's go outside. There's very little cloud. We should be able to see his drivers fire."

Leaving Quelf to worry about herself, they quit the control-house. A number of portable telescopes had been provided; Presthin appropriated one at once.

She said what she had said before: "On Prutaj, you know, we aren't all as bad as Quelf!"

"Working with Albumarak has taught me that much," Yull replied. "And you'd agree, wouldn't you, Theng?"

"Of course!" was the bluff and prompt reply. "Our only problem is apt to be with the ones who ran away from Fregwil—because they've never learned the meaning of an honest day's work, and we have to support them until they do!"

"Things are going to change back home," said Presthin, her eye to the ocular. "Of course, as you know, I'm not from Fregwil myself, but I can state that for too long the self-indulgence of that city has offended the ordinary folk on Prutaj. It's been fun having the goodies they produced, but how many of them are directed at ensuring the survival of the folk? Since news of the wild planetoid broke there's been a radical shift of attitudes. I like the young'uns at Fregwil now, and I used to loathe them! By the way, tell me something, Scholar Yull."

"If I can."

"Do you honestly believe we can survive in space?"

"There it goes!"

A unison cry greeted fire blooming at the zenith. Karg's cylinder had reached altitude and was spearing into space. For a while no one could think of anything else but that slowly fading gleam.

When it had been masked by drifting cloud, Yull said, "Yes."

"What?" By then Presthin had forgotten her question.

"I said yes! We're very sure we can survive! It's as though evolution designed us for precisely the role we hope to play out there. Do you know much about biology?"

Unconsciously Presthin echoed what Karg had said to Albumarak: "I know a little about a lot of things!"

"Well, then, you doubtless know that there were once creatures on this planet that had rigid bodies. They supported their weight by using substances so stiff that they became brittle, like a dead tree, and had constantly to be renewed. Imagine what would happen to a species like that if they tried to survive without gravity! They'd become amorphous—they'd wither like spent luminants! But we . . ."

She spoke with swelling pride.

"*We* depend for our survival on nothing more than the tone of our musculature and our tubules! We can live underwater, where effectively one has no weight, and sometimes folk have returned after years without noticeable damage to their health. Karg was chosen for precisely that reason! In the imagery of the Mysteries of the Jingfired, which always have to do with forging metal, we are 'well and fitly shaped'!"

Karg's voice echoed from the control-house. Yull signaled for it to be relayed by loudeners, and instantly they knew he was exultant.

"Listen to me, you down there—listen to me! My name is Karg, and I'm in space, and I feel wonderful! I'm free at last! I'm not trapped on a lump of mud that may be smashed at any moment by gods playing at target-practice! I'm *free!*"

Suddenly grave, Yull was about to suggest that the level of euphoria be reduced, when Karg calmed of his own accord.

"But I'm not out here purely for the pleasure of it. I have a mission to perform. I'm to be the first inhabitant of another planet—a world we devised at Slah, which is just coming over my horizon, so I'm activating the maneuvering pumps—just a moment . . . Done. If you're watching with telescopes, you'll be able to see my cylinder match orbits with the artificial world. And from there, using its farspeakers, I'm going to tell everybody the good news. You and I won't survive our system's passage through the Major Cluster. But we'd be long dead anyhow, remember! What I'm here to prove is that the species can!"

His voice rose in a jubilant crescendo as Albumarak and Presthin clutched each other, not knowing whether to laugh or sob.

"We can escape! We can survive! *We shall!*"

# Epilogue

*"And, of course, we did," said the preceptor.*

*Afterwards there was a long pause. Inevitably one of the youngest budlings broke it by demanding, loudly enough to be heard: "What became of the wild planetoid, then?"*

*"Wait!"*

*The center of the globe, where the marvels of modern technology had recreated Jing and Chybee, Yockerbow and Aglabec, all the characters famous and infamous from the long story of their species, swirled and blurred and resumed its original configuration.*

*Now, though, everything was in closer focus. The budworld was emphasized, the sun and planets far away. Then, from the threshold of infinity, the wild planetoid rushed in. For one pith-freezing moment, which even those who had witnessed the spectacle a score of times found fearful, it seemed as though they were about to crash!*

*A shift of perspective: they were back on the budworld. Its oceans were rising to the wild planet's tug, beating the shores and swamping the cities. The air wrought havoc with fantastic gales. Closeups revealed the naked panic of those who were caught up and burst to death.*

*The youngest of the budlings screamed in terror.*

*"Our species could have been destroyed," said the preceptor as the view shifted again. This time it could be seen how the wild planetoid swung past, disturbing the orbit of the moon, but sweeping by towards the belt of asteroids that ringed the sun.*

*"We think, but because it was hidden from our forebudders we'll never know, that it collided with an asteroid behind the sun. At all events, it did not reappear. But it had done harm enough. Had not the joint resources of both Slah and Fregwil been applied to launching vessels into space, it is beyond a*

*doubt that by this time we'd be extinct. The show is over. Ponder the lessons that it teaches—all your lives!"*

*And suddenly the feigned imagery that had filled the center of the globe was replaced by the reality of what surrounded their fragile home. Beautiful, yet terrible, there loomed the Major Cluster, from which they were being borne away by the pressure of light from its exploding stars; there too was the Arc of Heaven which their forebudders had imagined to be the weapon of a god; there was the sun that had shone on the budworld, fading to the petty status of just another star . . .*

*And far beyond lay the safe dark deeps that they were steering for, where they were certain of energy, and the means to feed themselves and grow more drifting globes, choosing what they wanted from the resources of the galaxy.*

*"Yes?" said the preceptor to another young'un, knowing what question was invariably put.*

*"Scholar, do you think there's anybody else out there?"*

*"There's bound to be!"—with total confidence. "And when we meet them, we shall be able to stand proud on what we've done!"*

## About the Author

John Brunner was born in England in 1934 and educated at Cheltenham College. He sold his first novel in 1951 and has been publishing steadily since then. His books have won him international acclaim from both mainstream and genre audiences. His most famous novel, the classic *Stand on Zanzibar*, won the Hugo Award for Best Novel in 1969, the British Science Fiction Award, and the Prix Apollo in France. Mr. Brunner lives in Somerset, England.